P9-DNE-245

AT THE EDGE OF SPACE

BROTHERS OF EARTH

HUNTER OF WORLDS

C.J. CHERRYH

DAW BOOKS, INC.

DONALD A. WOLLHEIM, FOUNDER

375 Hudson Street, New York, NY 10014

ELIZABETH R. WOLLHEIM

SHEILA E. GILBERT

PUBLISHERS

www.dawbooks.com

The Hanan Rebellion

Someday far, far in the future, in the 4000s, a segment of humanity fairly well splits itself off from the rest of human space and takes armed exception to intervention in their territories.

Out of this era come two stories set on the very fringes of human exploration, in Hanan space. Don't worry that in one of them humanity seems to be on the decline . . . we're widespread by then, and this is a local issue. Science fiction is a literature of optimism, and we're a hardy breed . . . as witness the people caught up in these two tales.

Brothers of Earth was, right along with *Gate of Ivrel* (see: *The Morgaine Saga*), my first novel. *Hunter of Worlds* was right along with these two, very early. Some have asked me where the influence for the culture might lie—and I'll surprise no few critics who think they know by saying really it's closer to Roman than anything you'll see on television.

Hunter of Worlds involves perception and language and what's truly alien—which might look just like us, being real competitors and instinctually different. The language freights the mental differences. If you don't catch a word at first, look at the situation in which it's used. You may find yourself thinking in a predatory way.

—C.J. Cherryh, Spokane, 2003

BROTHERS OF EARTH

1

Endymion died soundlessly, a man-made star that glowed and quickly winked out of existence.

Kurt Morgan watched her until there was no more left to see, eyes fixed to the aft scanners of the capsule. When it was over, he cut to forward view and set his mind on survival.

There had been eighty men and women on *Endymion,* seventy-nine of them now reduced to dust and vapor, one with the ship and indistinguishable from its remains. Two minutes to sunward was another cloud that had been the enemy, another hundred individuals, the elements that had been life from a score of worlds borne still on collision course, destroyer and destroyed.

No report of the encounter would go back to Central. There was no means to carry it. The Hanan planet of origin, Aeolus, was no more than a cinder now, light-years distant; and *Endymion* in pursuing the Hanan enemy had given no reference data to Command. They had jumped on their own, encountered, won and perished at once; the survival capsule had no starflight capability.

A nameless star and six uncharted worlds lay under the capsule's scan. The second was the most likely to support life.

It grew larger in his scanners over the course of seven days, a blue world wreathed in swirling cloud and patched with the brown of land. It had a large, solitary moon. In all particulars it read as an Earth-class planet, one the Alliance would have sacrificed a hundred ships to win—which they had already won if they could have known it.

The feared Hanan retaliation did not materialize. There were no ships to threaten him. The world filled the scanners now. Kurt vacillated between euphoric hope and hopeless fear—hope because he had planned to die and it looked as if he might not; and fear, because it suddenly dawned on him that he was truly alone. The idea of a possible enemy had kept him company until now. But *Endymion* had run off the edge of the charts before she perished. If the Hanan were not here, then there were no other human beings this far from Sol Center.

That was loneliness.

Absolute.

The wedge-shaped capsule came in hard, overheated and struggling for life, plates shrieking as they parted their joinings. Pressure exploded against Kurt's senses, gray and red and dark.

He hung sideways, the straps preventing him from slipping into the storage bay. He spent some little time working free, feverish with anxiety. When he had done so he opened the hatch, reckless of tests: he had no other options.

Breathable. For a time after he had exited the ship he simply stood and looked about him, from horizon to horizon of rolling wooded hills. Never in all his planetfalls had he seen the like of it, pure and unspoiled and but for the stench of burning, scented with abundant life.

He stood there laughing into the sun with the tears running down his face, and shut his eyes and let the clean wind dry his face and the coolness of the air relieve the stifling warmth that clung to him.

The land began to descend perceptibly after the forests: a long hill, a rocky bow of land, a brief expanse of beach on an unlimited expanse of sea. The sun was low in the sky before he had found a way down from the high rocks to that sandy shore.

And there he dropped his gear on the dry sand and gazed out entranced, over a sea bluer than he had ever seen, and greener than the hills, colors divided according to the depth. Isles lay against the horizon. The sand was white and littered with the refuse of the sea, bits of wood and weed, and shells of delicate pinks and yellows, in spiked and volute shapes.

Delighted as a child, he bent and dipped his hands into the

water that lapped at his boots, tasted the salt of it and spat a little, for he had known what a sea ought to be, but he had never
touched one or smelled the salt wind and the wrack on the
beach. He picked up a stick of driftwood and hurled it far out,
watched it carried back to him. Something within him settled
into place, finding all the home-tales of his star-wandering folk
true and real, even if it was in such a place as this, that man had
never touched.

He waded at the edge a while, barefoot, careful of stepping
on something poisonous, and used a stick to prod at things that
lived there. But the daylight began to fade, so he could no
longer see things clearly, and the wind became cold; then he
began to reckon with the coming night, and gathered a great
supply of driftwood and made a fire.

It was the dark that was terrible, lonely as the space between
stars. He had seen birds that day, too high to distinguish; he had
seen the shells of mollusks and nudged at things that scuttled off
into deeper water; and several times he had startled small creatures from the high grass and sent them bounding off, quickly
invisible in the brush and weeds. Nothing yet had threatened
him, and no cries disturbed the night. But his mind invented images from a score of worlds. He started at every sound. The
water lapped and sucked at the shore, and small scavenger crus-
taceans sidled about beyond the circle of firelight, seeking food.

At last he rose up and put a great deal of wood on the fire,
then curled up as closely as he could before he abandoned himself to sleep.

Pebbles grated. Sand crunched. Kurt lifted his head and
strained his eyes in the dying glare of the fire. Beyond it a dark
dragon head rode the waters, rocking with the motion of the sea.

He scrambled for his gun, was hurled flat by sinuous bodies
that hit his back, man-sized and agile. He spat sand and rolled
and twisted, but a blow exploded across the side of his head,
heavy with darkness. He went down again, fading, aware of the
bite of cords, of being dragged through water. He choked in the
brine and went out altogether.

He was soaking wet, facedown on a heaving wooden surface.
He sprang up, and was tripped and thrown by a chain that linked

his ankles together around a wooden pillar; when he twisted over to look up, he could make out a web of ropes and lines against the night sky, a dragon head against the moon. It was a wooden ship, with a mast for a single sail.

Men's voices called out and oars splashed down, sweeping in unison; the motion of the ship changed, steadied,—and with a rustle and snap of canvas the great square sail billowed out overhead, men hauling to sheet it home. Kurt stared up in awe as the swelling canvas blotted out the sky and the deck acquired a different feel as the wind sped the ship on her way.

A man crowded him. Kurt scrambled up awkwardly, the chain keeping his feet apart around the mast. Others were close to him. He saw in the dim light the same structure repeated in every curious face; wide cheeks, flat noses, well-formed, with flaring nostrils; the eyes large and dark, brows wide and heavy, slightly tilted on a plane with the high cheekbones—the faces of wise children, set in a permanent look of arrogant curiosity; but the bodies were those of men, tall and slim and muscular.

They did not touch him. They looked. And finally one spoke to them with authority and they dispersed. Kurt sank down again, sick and trembling, not alone with the chill of the wind. One returned, and gave him a warm cloak for his comfort, and he clutched that about him and doubled up. He did not sleep.

No one troubled him until the first light brought color to things. Then a man set a bowl and cup beside him on the boards, and Kurt took the warm food gratefully, and drank the hot, sweetened tea.

In the growing daylight he found the men of the ship not un-pleasant to look upon. They were brown- to golden-skinned, with black hair. They moved about the tight confines of the ship with amiable efficiency, and their laughter was frequent and not unkind among themselves. Kurt soon began to know some of them,—the one who had brought him the food, the gruff elder man who relayed the orders of a narrow-eyed young officer; and he thought the name of the boy who scurried around on every-one's errands must be Pan, for that was the word others shouted when they wanted him.

They were cleanly, proud folk, and they kept their ship well ordered; human or not, they were a better crew than some lots of *homo sapiens* he had managed.

Fed and beginning to be warmed by the daylight, Kurt had only begun to achieve a certain calm in his situation, when the young officer approached him and had the chain removed. Kurt rose carefully, avoiding any appearance of hostility, and the man nodded toward the low cabin aft.

He let himself be directed below, where the officer opened a door for him and gestured him through.

Another young man was seated at a low writing table, on a chair so low he must cross his ankles on the floor. He spoke and Kurt's escort left him and closed the door after; then he gestured, offering Kurt to sit too. There was no chair, only the woven reed mat on which he stood. With ill grace Kurt settled cross-legged on the mat.

"I am captain of this ship," said the man, and Kurt's heart froze within him, for the language was Hanan. "I am Kta t'Elas u Nym. The person who brought you in is my second, Bel t'Osanef." The accent was heavy, the forms archaic; as *Endymion*'s communications officer, Kurt knew enough to make sense of it, although he could not identify the dialect.

"What is your name, please?" asked Kta.

"Kurt. Kurt Morgan. What *are* you?" he asked quickly, before Kta could lead the questions where he would. "What do you want?"

"I am nemet," said Kta, who sat with hands folded in his lap,—he had a habit of glancing down when beginning to speak. His eyes met Kurt's only on the emphasis of questions. "Did you want that we find you? Was the fire a signal asking help?"

Kurt remembered, and cursed himself.

"No," he said.

"Tamurlin are human like you. You camp in their land like a man in his own house,—careless."

"I know nothing of that." Hope surged wildly in him. Kta's command of human speech found explanation—a Hanan base onworld, but something in the way Kta spoke the word *Tamurlin* did not indicate friendship between that base and the nemet.

"Where are your friends?" Kta asked, and took him by surprise.

"Dead,—dead. I came alone."

"From what place?"

Kurt feared to answer and did not know how to lie, but Kta shrugged, and from a decanter on the table beside his desk he poured drink into two tiny porcelain cups.

Kurt was not anxious to drink, for he did not trust the sudden hospitality; but Kta sipped at his delicately and Kurt followed his example. It was thin and fruity-tasting, and settled in the head like fire.

"It is *telise*," said Kta. "I offer to you tea, but *telise* is more warming."

"Thank you," said Kurt. "Would you mind telling me where we're going?" But Kta only lifted his small cup slightly as if to say they would talk when they were finished; and Kta took his patient time finishing.

"Where are we going?" Kurt repeated the instant Kta set his cup aside. The nemet's short brows contracted slightly.

"My port. But you mean—what is there for you in my port? We nemet are civilized. "You are civilized too, not like the Tamurlin. I see this. Please do not have fear. But I ask: why came you?"

"My ship—was destroyed. I found safety on that shore."

"From the sky, this ship. I am aware of such things. We have all seen human things."

"Do you fight the Tamurlin?"

"Always. It is an old war, this. They came,—long ago. We drove them from their machines and they became like beasts."

"Long ago."

"Three hundreds of years."

Kurt kept his joy from his face. "I assure you," he said, "I didn't come here to harm anyone."

"Then we will not harm you," said Kta.

"Am I free, then?"

"In day, yes. But at night—I am sorry. My men need secure rest. Please accept this necessity."

"I don't blame you," said Kurt. "I understand."

"*Hei yth*," said Kta, and joined his fingertips together before him in what seemed a gesture of gratitude. "It makes me to think well of you, Kurt Morgan."

And with that, Kta turned him out on the deck at liberty. No one offered him unpleasantness, even when his ignorance put him in the way of busy men. Someone would then gesture for him to move—they never touched him—or politely call to him: "*Umanu, o-eh,*" which he thought was his species and a request to move. And after a part of the day had passed and he decided to imitate the crew's manner of bows and courteous downcast looks, his status improved, for he received bows in return, and was called "*umanu-ifhan*" in a tone of respect.

But at night the young officer Bel t'Osanef came and indicated he must take his place again at the mast. The seaman who performed Bel's order was most gentle in applying the chain, and came back afterward to provide him a blanket and a large mug of hot tea. It was ludicrous. Kurt found the courage to laugh, and the nemet seemed also to understand the humor of the situation, and grinned and said, "*Tosa, umanu-ifhan,*" in a tone which seemed kindly meant.

His hands left free, he sipped his tea at leisure and finally stretched out at such an angle that he did not think anyone would trip over him in the dark. His mind was much easier this night, though he shuddered to think what might have become of him if not for the nemet. If Kta's Tamurlin were indeed fallen Hanan, then he had had an escape close enough to last a lifetime.

He would accept any conditions of the nemet rather than fall to the Hanan: and if Kta spoke the truth and the Hanan were powerless and declined to barbarism, then he was free. There was no more war. For the first time in his imagination, there was no more war.

Only one doubt still gnawed at the edges of his mind: the question of why a modern Hanan starship had run from the destroyed world of Aeolus to this world of fallen humans.

He did not want to think on that. He did not want to believe Kta had lied, or that the gentleness of these people hid deception. There was another explanation. His hopes, his reason for living insisted upon it.

In the next two days he walked the deck and scanned the whole of the ship for some sign of Hanan technology, and concluded that there was none. She was wooden from stem to stern, hand-hewn, completely reliant on wind and oars for her propulsion.

The skills by which these men managed their complex vessel intrigued him. Bel t'Osanef could explain nothing, knowing only a handful of human words. But when Kta was on deck, Kurt questioned him earnestly; when the nemet captain seemed finally to accept that his interest was unfeigned, he tried to explain, often groping for words for objects long-vanished from human language. They developed between them their own patois of Hanan-Nechai, Nechai being Kta's own language.

And Kta asked about human things, which Kurt could not always answer in terms Kta could understand. Sometimes Kta looked puzzled at human science and sometimes shocked, until at last Kurt began to perceive the disturbance his explanations caused. Then he decided he had explained enough. The nemet was earthbound; he did not truly conceive of things extraterrestrial, and it troubled his religion. Kurt wanted least of all for the nemet to develop some apprehension of his origins.

A third day passed in such discussions, and at the dawn of the fourth, Kta summoned Kurt to his side as he stood on the deck. He had the look of a man with something definite on his mind. Kurt approached him soberly and gave a little bow of deference.

"Kurt," said Kta, "between us is trust, yes?"

"Yes," Kurt agreed, and wondered uneasily where this was tending.

"Today we go into port. I don't want shame for you, bringing you with chains. But if I bring you in free, if then you do hurt to innocent people, then I have responsibility for this. What must I do, Kurt Morgan?"

"I didn't come here to hurt anyone. And what about your people? How will they treat me? Tell me that before I agree to anything."

Kta opened his hands, a gesture of entreaty. "You think I lie to you these things?"

"How could I know? I know nothing but what you tell me. So tell me in plain words that I can trust you."

"I am of Elas," Kta said, frowning, as if that were accustomed to be word enough; but when Kurt continued to stare at him:

"Kurt, I swear this beneath the light of heaven, and this is a holy word. It is truth."

"All right," said Kurt. "Then I will do what you tell me and I won't cause trouble. Only what is the place where we're going?"

"Nephane."

"Is that a city?"

Kta frowned thoughtfully. "Yes, it is a city, the city of the east. It rules from Tamur-mouth to the Yvorst Ome, the sea of ice."

"Is there a city of the west?"

The frown deepened. "Yes," he said. "Indresul." Then he turned and walked away, leaving Kurt to wonder what he had done to trouble the nemet.

By midday they were within sight of port. A long bay receded into the shoreline, and at the back of it was a great upthrust of rock. At the base of this crag and on its gently rising side were buildings and walls, hazy with distance, all the way to the crest.

"*Bel-ifhan,*" Kurt hailed Kta's lieutenant, and the narrow-eyed officer stopped and bowed, although he had been going elsewhere in apparent haste. "*Bel-ifhan, taen Nephane?*"

"*Lus,*" Bel agreed and pointed to the promontory. "*Taen Afen, sthages Methine.*"

Kurt looked at the crag Bel called Afen, and did not understand.

"*Methi,*" said Bel, and when he still did not understand, the young officer shrugged helplessly. "*Ktas unnehta,*" he said. "*Ktas, uleh?*"

He left. They were going in. Somewhere aft, Bel shouted an order and men ran to their stations to bring in the sail, hauling it up to the yard. The long oars were run out and they dipped together, sweeping the ship toward the now visible dock at the foot of the cliffs, where a shoreside settlement nestled against the walls.

"Kurt."

Kurt glanced from his view of the bay to the face of Kta, who had joined him at the bow.

"Bel says you have question."

"I'm sorry. I tried to talk to him. I didn't mean he should bother you. It wasn't that important."

The nemet turned one hand outward, a shrug. "Is no difficulty. Bel manages. I am not necessary. —What think you of Nephane?"

"Beautiful," Kurt said, and it was. "Those buildings at the top—Afen, Bel called it."

"Fortress. The Fortress of Nephane."

"A fortress against what enemy? Humans?"

Again a little crease of a frown appeared between Kta's wide-set eyes. "You surprise me. You are not Tamurlin. Your ship destroyed, your friends—dead, you say. But what want you among us?"

"I know nothing. I'm lost. I've trusted you. And if I can't trust your given word, then I don't know anything."

"I don't lie, Kurt Morgan. But you try hard not to answer my question. Why do you come to us?"

A crowd was on the docks, gaily colored clothing a kaleidoscope in the sunlight. The oars rumbled inboard as the ship glided in, making conversation impossible for the moment. Pan was poised near them with the mooring cable, ready to cast it to the men at the dock.

"Why," asked Kurt, "do you think I should know my way in this world?"

"The others, they knew."

"The . . . others?"

"The *new* humans. The—"

Kta's voice trailed off, for Kurt backed from him. The nemet suddenly looked frightened, opened his hands in appeal to him. "Kurt," he protested, "wait. —No. We take—"

Kurt caught him by surprise, drove his fist to the nemet's jaw and vaulted the rail, even as the ship shuddered against the dock.

He hit the water and water went up his nose at the impact, and again when something hit him, the gliding hull of the ship itself.

Then he made himself quit fighting and drifted, wrapped in the darkening green of the sea, a swift and friendly dark. It was

hard to move against the weight of the water. In another moment
vision and sense went out together.

He was strangling. He gasped for air and coughed over the
water mingling with it in his throat. On a second try he drew a
breath and heaved it up again, along with the water in his stomach, twisting onto the stones over on his belly while his insides
came apart. When he could breathe again, someone picked him
up and wiped his face, cradling his head off the stone.

He was lying on the dock, the center of a great crowd of
nemet. Kta held him and implored him in words he could not
understand, while Bel and Val leaned over Kta's shoulder. Kta
and both the other men were dripping wet, and he knew that
they must have gone in after him.

"Kta," he tried to protest, but his raw throat gave out only a
voiceless whisper.

"You could not swim," Kta accused him. "You almost die.
You wish this? You try to kill yourself?"

"You lied," Kurt whispered, trying to shout.

"No," Kta insisted fervently. But by his troubled frown he
seemed at last to understand. "I didn't think you are enemy
to us."

"Help me," Kurt implored him, but Kta turned his face aside
slightly in that gesture that meant refusal, then glanced a mute
signal to Val. With the big seaman's help, he eased him onto a
litter improvised out of planks, though Kurt tried to protest.

He was in shock, chilled and shivering so he could hardly
keep from doubling up. Somewhere after that, Kta left him and
strangers took charge.

The journey up the cobbled street of Nephane was a nightmare, faces crowding close to look at him, the jolting of the litter redoubling his sickness. They passed through massive gates
and into the Afen, the Fortress, into triangle-arched halls and
dim live-flame lighting, through doorways and into a window-
less cell.

Here he would have been content to live or die alone, but
they roused him and stripped the wet clothing off him, and laid
him in a proper bed, wrapped in blankets.

There was a stillness that lasted for hours after the illness had passed. He was aware of someone standing outside the door; someone who never left through all the long hours.

At last—he thought it must be well into another day—the guards brought him clothing and helped him dress. From the skin outward the clothing was strange to him, and he resented it, losing what dignity he had left at their hands. Over it all went the *pel,* a long-sleeved tunic that lapped across to close in front, held by a wide belt. He was not even permitted to lace his own sandals, but the guards impatiently took over and, having finished, allowed him a tiny cup of *telise,* which they evidently thought sovereign for all bodily ills.

Then, as he had dreaded, they hailed him with them into the A-shaped halls of the upper Afen. He gave them no trouble. He needed no more enemies than he had in Nephane.

2

A large hall was on the third level. Its walls were of the same irregular stone as the outer hall, but the floor had carpets and the walls were hung with tapestries. The guards sent him beyond this point alone, toward the next door.

The room beyond the threshold was of his own world, metal and synthetics, white light. The furnishings were crystal and black, the walls were silver. Only the cabinet at his left and the door at his back did not belong: they were carved wood, convoluted dragon figures and fishes.

The door closed softly, sealing him in.

Machinery purred and he glanced leftward. A woman in nemet dress had joined him. Her gown was gold, high-collared, floor-length. Her hair was amber, curling gently. She was human.

Hanan.

She treated him with more respect than the nemet, keeping her distance. She would know his mind, as he knew hers; he made no move against her, would make none until he was sure of the odds.

"Good day, Mr. Morgan—Lieutenant Morgan." She had a disk in her fingers, letting it slide on its chain. Suddenly he missed it. "Kurt Liam Morgan. Pylan, I read it."

"Would you mind returning it?" It was his identity tag. He had worn it since the day of his birth, and it was unnerving to have it in her hands, as if a bit of his life dangled there. She considered a moment, then tossed it. He caught it.

"We have one name," she said, which was common knowledge.

"I'm Djan. My number—you would forget. Where are your crewmates, Kurt Morgan?"

"Dead. I've told the truth from the beginning. There were no other survivors."

"Really."

"I am alone," he insisted, frightened, for he knew the lengths to which they could go trying to obtain information he did not have. "Our ship was destroyed in combat. The life-capsule from Communications was the only one that cleared on either side, yours or ours."

"How did you come here?"

"Random search."

Her lips quivered. Her eyes fixed on his with cold fury. "You did not happen here. Again."

"We met one of your ships," he said, and his mouth was suddenly dry; he began to surmise how she knew it was a lie, and that they would have all the truth before they were done. It was easier to yield it, hoping against expectation that these Aeolids would dispose of him without revenge.

"Aeolus was your world, wasn't it?"

"Details," she said. Her face was white, but the control of her voice was unfaltering. He had respect for her. The Hanan were cold, but it took more than coldness to receive such news with calm. He knew. Pylos also was a dead world. He remembered Aeolus hanging in space, the glare of fires spotting its angry surface. Even an enemy had to feel something for that, the death of a world.

"Two Alliance ISTs penetrated the Aeolid zone with thirty riders. We were with that force. One of your deepships jumped into the system after the attack, jumped out again immediately when they realized the situation there. We were nearest, saw them, locked to track—it brought us here. We—fought. You monitored that, didn't you? You know there were no other survivors."

"Keep going."

"That's all there is. We finished each other. We suffered the first hit and my station capsuled then. That's all I know. I had no part in the combat. I looked for other capsules. There were none. You *know* there were no others."

An object was concealed in her hand. He caught a glimpse of it as her hand moved by her many-folded skirts. He saw her fingers close, then relax. He almost took the chance against her then, but she was Hanan and trained from infancy: her reflexes would be instant, and there was the chance the weapon was set to stun. That possibility was more deterrent than any quick oblivion.

"I know," she said, "that there are no other ships, that at least." Her tone was low and mocking. "Welcome to my world, Kurt Morgan. We seem to be humanity's orphans in this limb of nowhere,—there being only the Tamurlin for company otherwise, and they're not really human any longer."

"You're alone?"

"Mr. Morgan. If something happens to me at your hands, I've given the nemet orders to turn you out naked as the day you were born on the shore of the Tamur. The other humans in this world will know how to deal with you in a way humans understand."

"I don't threaten you." Hope turned him shameless. "Give me the chance to leave. You'll never see me again."

"Unless you're the forerunner of others."

"There are no others," he insisted.

"What security do you give me for that promise?"

"We were alone. We came alone. There was no way we could have been traced. There were no ships near enough and we jumped blind, without coordinates."

"Well," she said, and even appeared to accept what he said, "well, it will be a long wait then. Aeolus colonized this world three hundred years ago. But the war—the war— Records were scrambled, the supply ship was lost somehow. We discovered this world in archives centuries old on Aeolus and came to reclaim it. But you seem to have intervened in a very permanent way on Aeolus. Our ship is gone: it could only have been the one you claim to have destroyed; your ship is gone—you claim you could not be traced; Aeolus and its records are cinders. Exploration in this limb ceased, a hundred years ago. What do you suppose the odds are on someone chancing across us?"

"There there is no war. Let me leave."

"If I did," she said, "you might die out there: the world has its dangers. Or you might come back. You might come back, and I could never be sure when you would do that. I would have to fear you for the rest of my life. I would have no more peace here."

"I would not come back."

"Yes, you would. You would. It's been six months—since my crew died here. After only that long, my own face begins to look strange to me in a mirror; I begin to fear mirrors. But I look. I could want another human face to look at,—after a certain number of years. So would you."

She had not raised the weapon he was now sure she had. She did not want to use it. Hope turned his hands damp, sent the sweat running down his sides. She knew the only safe course for her. She was mad if she did not take it. Yet she hesitated, her face greatly distressed.

"Kta t'Elas came," she said, "and begged for your freedom. I told him you were not to be trusted."

"I swear to you, I have no ambitions,—only to stay alive, I would go to him—I would accept any conditions, any terms you set."

She moved her hands together, clasping the weapon casually in her slim fingers. "Suppose I listened to you."

"There would be no trouble."

"I hope you remember that, when you grow more comfortable. Remember that you came here with nothing, with nothing—not even the clothes on your back; and that you begged *any* terms I would give you." She gazed at him soberly for a moment, unmoving. "I am out of my mind. But I reserve the right to collect on this debt someday, in whatever manner and for however long I decide. You are here on tolerance. And I will try you. I am sending you to Kta t'Elas, putting you in his charge for two weeks. Then I will call you back, and we will review the situation."

He understood it for a dismissal, weak-kneed with relief and now beset with new doubts. Alone, presented with an enemy, she did a thing entirely unreasonable: it was not the way he had known the Hanan, and he began to fear some subtlety, a snare laid for someone.

Or perhaps loneliness had its power even on the Hanan, destructive even of the desire to survive. And that thought was no less disquieting in itself.

3

To judge by the size of the house and its nearness to the Afen, Kta was an important man. From the street the house of Elas was a featureless cube of stone with its deeply recessed A-shaped doorway fronting directly on the walk. It was two stories high, and sprawled far back against the rock on which Nephane sat.

The guards who escorted him rang a bell that hung before the door, and in a few moments the door was opened by a white-haired and balding nemet in black.

There was a rapid exchange of words, in which Kurt caught frequently the names of Kta and Djan-methi. It ended with the old man bowing, hands to lips, and accepting Kurt within the house, and the guards bowing themselves off the step. The old man softly closed the double doors and dropped the bar.

"Hef," the old man identified himself with a gesture. "Come."

Hanging lamps of bronze lit their way into the depths of the house, down a dim hall that branched Y-formed past a triangular arch. Stairs at left and right led to a balcony and other rooms, but they took the right-hand branch of the Y upon the main floor. On the left the wall gave way into that same central hall which appeared through the arch at the joining of the Y. On the right was a closed door. Hef struck it with his fingers.

Kta answered the knock, his dark eyes astonished. He gave full attention to Hef's rapid words, which sobered him greatly; then he opened the door widely and bade Kurt come in.

Kurt entered uncertainly, disoriented equally by exhaustion and by the alien geometry of the place. This time Kta offered him the honor of a chair, still lower than Kurt found natural. The carpets underfoot were rich with designs of geometric form and the furniture was fantastically carved, even the bed surrounded with embroidered hangings.

Kta settled opposite him and leaned back. He wore only a kilt and sandals in the privacy of his own chambers. He was a powerfully built man, golden skin glistening like the statue of some ancient god brought to life; and there was about him the power of wealth that had not been apparent on the ship. Kurt suddenly found himself awed of the man, and suddenly realized that "friend" was perhaps not the proper word between a wealthy nemet captain and a human refugee who had landed destitute on his doorstep.

Perhaps, he thought uneasily, "guest" was hardly the proper word either.

"Kurt-ifhan," said Kta, "the Methi has put you in my hands."

"I am grateful," he answered, "that you came and spoke for me."

"It was necessary. For honor's sake, Elas has been opened to you. Understand: if you do wrong, punishment falls on me. If you escape, my freedom is owed. I say this so you will know. Do as you choose."

"You took a responsibility like that," Kurt objected, "without knowing anything about me."

"I made an oath," said Kta. "I didn't know then that the oath is an error. I made an oath of safety for you. For the honor of Elas I have asked the Methi for you. It is necessary."

"Her people and mine have been at war for more than two thousand years. You're taking a bigger risk than you know. I don't want to bring trouble on you."

"I am your host fourteen days," said Kta. "I thank you that you speak plainly; but a man who comes to the hearthfire of Elas is never a stranger at our door again. Bring peace with you and be welcome. Honor our customs and Elas will share with you."

"I am your guest," said Kurt. "I will do whatever you ask of me."

Kta joined his fingertips together and inclined his head. Then he rose and struck a gong that hung beside his door, bringing forth a deep, soft note which caressed the mind like a whisper.

"I call my family to the *rhmei*—the heart—of Elas. Please."
He touched fingers to lips and bowed. "This is courtesy, bowing. *Ei,* I know humans touch to show friendliness. You must not. This is insult, especially to women. There is blood for insulting the women of a house. Lower your eyes before strangers. Extend no hand close to a man. This way you cannot give offense."

Kurt nodded, but he grew afraid, afraid of the nemet themselves, of finding some dark side to their gentle, cultured nature—or of being despised for a savage. That would be worst of all.

He followed Kta into the great room which was framed by the branching of the entry hall. It was columned, of polished black marble. Its walls and floors reflected the fire that burned in a bronze tripod bowl at the apex of the triangular hall.

At the base wall were two wooden chairs, and there sat a woman in the left-hand one, her feet on a white fleece, as other fleeces scattered about her feet like clouds. In the right-hand chair sat an elder man, and a girl sat curled upon one of the fleece rugs. Hef stood by the fire, with a young woman at his side.

Kta knelt on the rug nearest the lady's feet, and from that place spoke earnestly and rapidly, while Kurt stood uncomfortably by and knew that he was the subject. His heart beat faster as the man rose up and cast a forbidding look at him.

"Kurt-ifhan," said Kta, springing anxiously to his feet, "I bring you before my honored father, Nym t'Elas u Lhai, and my mother the lady Ptas t'Lei e Met sh'Nym."

Kurt bowed very low indeed, and Kta's parents responded with some softening of their manner toward him. The young woman by Nym's feet also rose up and bowed.

"My sister Aimu," said Kta. "And you must also meet Hef and his daughter Mim, who honor Elas with their service. *Ita, Hef-nechan s'Mim-lechan, imimen. Hau.*"

The two came forward and bowed deeply. Kurt responded, not knowing if he should bow to servants, but he matched his obeisance to theirs.

"Hef," said Kta, "is the Friend of Elas. His family serves us now three hundred years. Mim-lechan speaks human language. She will help you."

Mim cast a look up at him. She was small, narrow-waisted, both stiffly proper and distractingly feminine in the close-fitting, many-buttoned bodice. Her eyes were large and dark, before a quick flash downward and the bowing of her head concealed them.

It was a look of hate, a thing of violence, that she sent him.

He stared, stricken by it, until he remembered and showed her courtesy by glancing down.

"I am much honored," said Mim coldly, like a recital, "being help to the guest of my lord Kta. My honored father and I are anxious for your comfort."

The guest quarters were upstairs, above what Mim explained shortly were Nym's rooms,—with the implication that Nym expected silence of him. It was a splendid apartment, in every detail as fine as Kta's own, with a separate, brightly tiled bath, a wood-stove for heating water, bronze vessels for the bath and a tea set. There was a round tub in the bath for bathing, and a great stack of white linens, scented with herbs.

The bed in the main triangular room was a great feather-stuffed affair spread with fine crisp sheets and the softest furs, beneath a sunny window of cloudy, bubbled glass. Kurt looked on the bed with longing, for his legs shook and his eyes burned with fatigue, and there was not a muscle in his body which did not ache; but Mim busily pattered back and forth with stacks of linens and clothing, and then cruelly insisted on stripping the bed and remaking it, turning and plumping the big brown mattress. Then, when he was sure she must have finished, she set about dusting everything.

Kurt was near to falling asleep in the corner chair when Kta arrived in the midst of the confusion. The nemet surveyed everything that had been done and then said something to Hef, who attended him.

The old servant looked distressed, then bowed and removed a small bronze lamp from a triangular niche in the west wall, handling it with the greatest care.

"It is religion," Kta explained, though Kurt had not ventured to ask. "Please don't touch such things—also the *phusmeha,* the bowl of the fire in the *rhmei.* Your presence is a disturbance. I ask your respect in this matter."

"Is it because I am a stranger," Kurt asked, already nettled by Mim's petty persecutions, "or because I'm human?"

"You are without beginning on this earth. I asked the *phusa* taken out not because I don't wish Elas to protect you, but because I don't want you to make trouble by offending against the Ancestors of Elas. I have asked my father in this matter. The eyes of Elas are closed in this one room. I think it is best. Let it not offend."

Kurt bowed, satisfied by Kta's evident distress.

"Do you honor your ancestors?" Kta asked.

"I don't understand," said Kurt, and Kta assumed a distressed look as if his fears had only been confirmed.

"Nevertheless," said Kta, "I try. Perhaps the Ancestors of Elas will accept prayers in the name of your most distant house. Are your parents still living?"

"I have no kin at all," said Kurt, and the nemet murmured a word that sounded regretful.

"Then," said Kta, "I ask please your whole name, the name of your house and of your father and your mother."

Kurt gave them, to have peace, and the nemet stumbled much over the long alien names, determined to pronounce them accurately. Kta was horrified at first to believe his parents shared a common house name, and Kurt angrily, almost tearfully, explained human customs of marriage, for he was exhausted and this interrogation was prolonging his misery.

"I shall explain to the Ancestors," said Kta. "Don't be afraid. Elas is a house patient with strangers and strangers' ways."

Kurt bowed his head, not to have any further argument. He was tolerated for the sake of Kta, a matter of Kta's honor.

He was cold when Kta and Mim left him alone, and crawled between the cold sheets, unable to stop shivering.

He was one of a kind, save for Djan, who hated him.

And among nemet, he was not even hated. He was inconvenient.

*   *   *

Food arrived late that evening, brought by Hef; Kurt dragged his aching limbs out of bed and fully dressed, which would not have been his inclination, but he was determined to do nothing to lessen his esteem in the eyes of the nemet.

Then Kta arrived to share dinner with him in his room.

"It is custom to take dinner in the *rhmei,* all Elas together," Kta explained, "but I teach you, here. I don't want you to offend against my family. You learn manners first."

Kurt had borne with much. "I have manners of my own," he cried, "and I'm sorry if I contaminate your house. Send me back to the Afen, to Djan—it's not too late for that." And he turned his back on the food and on Kta, and walked over to stand looking out the dark window. It dawned on him that sending him to Elas had been Djan's subtle cruelty; she expected him back, broken in pride.

"I meant no insult," Kta protested.

Kurt looked back at him, met the dark, foreign eyes with more directness than Kta had ever allowed him. The nemet's face was utterly stricken.

"Kurt-ifhan," said Kta, "I didn't wish to cause you shame. I wish to help you,—not putting you on display in the eyes of my father and my mother. It is your dignity I protect."

Kurt bowed his head and came back, not gladly. Djan was in his mind, that he would not run to her for shelter, giving up what he had abjectly begged of her. And perhaps too she had meant to teach the house of Elas its place, estimating it would beg relief of the burden it had asked. He submitted. There were worse shames than sitting on the floor like a child and letting Kta mold his unskilled fingers around the strange tableware.

He quickly knew why Kta had not permitted him to go downstairs. He could scarcely feed himself and, starving as he was, he had to resist the impulse to snatch up food in disregard of the unfamiliar utensils. Drink with the left hand only, eat with the right, reach with the left, never the right. The bowl was lifted almost to the lips, but it must never touch. From the almost bowlless spoon and thin skewer he kept dropping bites. The knife must be used only left-handed.

Kta was cautiously tactful after his outburst, but grew less so as Kurt recovered his sense of humor. They talked, between instructions and accidents, and afterward, over a cup of tea. Sometimes Kta asked him of human customs, but he approached any difference between them with the attitude that while other opinions and manners were possible, they were not so under the roof of Elas.

"If you were among humans," Kurt dared ask him finally, "what would you do?"

Kta looked as if the idea horrified him, but covered it with a downward glance. "I don't know. I know only Tamurlin."

"Did not—" he had tried for a long time to work toward this question,—"did not Djan-methi come with others?"

The frightened look persisted. "Yes. Most left. Djan-methi killed the others."

He quickly changed the subject and looked as if he wished he had not been so free of that answer, though he had given it straightly and with deliberation.

They talked of lesser things, well into the night, over many cups of tea and sometimes of *telise,* until from the rest of Elas there was no sound of people stirring and they must lower their voices. The light was exceedingly dim, the air heavy with the scent of oil from the lamps. The *telise* made it close and warm. The late hour clothed things in unreality.

Kurt learned things, almost all simply family gossip, for Djan and Elas were all in Nephane that they both knew, and Kta, momentarily so free with the truth, seemed to have remembered that there was danger in it. They spoke instead of Elas.

Nym had the authority in the household as the lord of Elas; Kta had almost none, although he was over thirty (he hardly looked it) and commanded a warship. Kta would be under Nym's authority as long as Nym lived; the eldest male was lord in the house. If Kta married, he must bring his bride to live under his father's roof. The girl would become part of Elas, obedient to Kta's father and mother as if she were born to the house. So Aimu was soon to depart, betrothed to Kta's lieutenant Bel t'Osanef. They had been friends since childhood, Kta and Bel and Aimu.

Kta owned nothing. Nym controlled the family wealth, and would decide how and whom and when his two children must marry, since marriage determined inheritances. Property passed from father to eldest son undivided, and the eldest then assumed a father's responsibility for all lesser brothers and cousins and unmarried women in the house. A patriarch like Nym always had his rooms to the right of the entry, a custom, Kta explained, derived from more warlike times, when a man slept at the threshold to defend his home from attack. Grown sons occupied the ground floor for the same reason. This room that Kurt now held as a guest had been Kta's when he was a boy.

And the matriarch, in this case Kta's mother Ptas, although it had been the paternal grandmother until quite recently, had her rooms behind the base wall of the *rhmei*. She was the guardian of most religious matters of the house. She tended the holy fire of the *phusmeha*, supervised the household and was second in authority to the patriarch.

Of obeisance and respect, Kta explained, there were complex degrees. It was gross disrespect for a grown son to come before his mother without going to his knees, but when he was a boy this difference was not paid. The reverse was true with a son and his father: a boy knelt to his father until his coming-of-age, then met him with the slight bow of almost-equals if he were eldest, necessary obeisances deepening as one went down the ranks of second son, third son, and so on. A daughter, however, was treated as a beloved guest, a visitor the house would one day lose to a husband; she gave her parents only the obeisance of second-son's rank, and showed her brothers the same modest formality she must use with strangers.

But of Hef and Mim, who served Elas, was required only the obeisance of equals, although it was their habit to show more than that on formal occasions.

"And what of me?" Kurt asked, dreading to ask. "What must I do?"

Kta frowned. "You are guest, mine; you must be equal with me. But," he added nervously, "it is proper in a man to show greater respect than necessary sometimes. It does not hurt your dignity; sometimes it makes it greater. Be most polite to all. Don't—make Elas ashamed. People will watch you—thinking they will see a *Tamuru* in nemet dress. You must prove this is not so."

"Kta," Kurt asked, "—am I a man—to the nemet?"

Kta pressed his lips together and looked as if he earnestly wished that question had gone unasked.

"I am not, then," Kurt concluded, and was robbed even of anger by the distress on Kta's face.

"I have not decided," Kta said. "Some—would say no. It is a religious question. I must think. —But I have a liking for you, Kurt, even if you *are* human."

"You have been very good to me."

There was silence between them. In the sleeping house there was no sound at all. Kta looked at him with a directness and a pity that disquieted him.

"You are afraid of us," Kta observed.

"Did Djan make you my keeper only because you asked, or because she trusts you in some special way—to watch me?"

Kta's head lifted slightly. "Elas is loyal to the Methi. But you are guest."

"Are nemet who speak human language so common? You are very fluent, Kta. Mim is. Your—readiness to accept a human into your house—is that not different from the feelings of other nemet?"

"I interpreted for the *umani* when they first came to Nephane. Before that, I learned of Mim, and Mim learned because she was prisoner of the Tamurlin. What evil do you suspect? What is the quarrel between you and Djan-methi?"

"We are of different nations, an old, old war. Don't get involved, Kta, if you did only get into this for my sake. If I threaten the peace of your house—or your safety—tell me. I'll go back. I mean that."

"This is impossible," said Kta. "No. Elas has never dismissed a guest."

"Elas has never entertained a human."

"No," Kta conceded. "But the Ancestors when they lived were reckless men. This is the character of Elas. The Ancestors guide us to such choice, and Nephane and the Methi cannot be much surprised at us."

The nemet's lives were uniformly tranquil. Kurt endured a little more than four days of the silent dim halls and the hushed voices and the endless bowing and refraining from untouchable objects and untouchable persons before he began to feel his sanity slipping.

On that day he went upstairs and locked the door, despite Kta's pleas to explain his behavior. He shed a few tears, fiercely and in the privacy of his room, and curtained the window so he did not have to look out upon the alien world. He sat in the dark until the night came, then he slipped quietly downstairs and sat in the empty *rhmei,* trying to make his peace with the house.

Mim came. She stood and watched him silently, hands twisting nervously before her.

At last she pattered on soft feet over to the chairs and gathered up one of the fleeces, and brought it to the place where he sat on the cold stone. She laid it down beside him, and chanced to meet his eyes as she straightened. Hers questioned, greatly troubled, even frightened.

He accepted the offered truce between them, edged onto the welcome softness of the fleece.

She bowed very deeply, then slipped out again, extinguishing the lights one by one as she left, save only the *phusmeba,* that burned the night long.

Kta also came out to him, but only looked as if to see that he was well. Then he went away, and left the door of his room open the night long.

Kurt rose up in the morning and paused in Kta's doorway to give him an apology. The nemet was awake and arose in some concern, but Kurt did not find words adequate to explain his behavior. He only bowed in respect to the nemet, and Kta to him, and he went up to his own room to prepare for the decency of breakfast with the family.

Gentle Kta. Soft-spoken, seldom angry, he stood above six feet in height and was physically imposing; but it was uncertain whether Kta had ever laid aside his dignity to use force on anyone. It was an increasing source of amazement to Kurt that this intensely proud man had vaulted a ship's rail in view of all Nephane to rescue a drowning human, or sat on the dock and helped him amid his retching illness. Nothing seemed to ruffle Kta for long. He met frustration by retiring to meditate on the problem until he had restored himself to what he called *yhia,* or balance, a philosophy evidently adequate even in dealing with humans.

Kta also played the *aos,* a small harp of metal strings, and sang with a not unpleasant voice, which was the particular pleasure of lady Ptas upon the quiet evenings,—sometimes light, quick songs that brought laughter to the *rhmei,*—sometimes very long ones that were interrupted with cups of *telise* to give Kta's voice a rest,—songs to which all the house listened in sober silence, plaintive and haunting melodies of anharmonic notes.

"What do you sing about?" Kurt asked him afterward. They sat in Kta's room, sharing a late cup of tea. It was their habit to sit and talk late into the night. It was almost their last. The two weeks were almost spent. Tonight he wanted very much to know the nemet, not at all sure that he would have a further chance. It had been beautiful in the *rhmei,* the notes of the *aos,* the sober dignity of Nym, the rapt face of lady Ptas, Aimu and Mim with their sewing, Hef sitting to one side and listening, his old eyes dreaming.

The stillness of Elas had seeped into his bones this night, a timeless and now fleeting time which made all the world quiet. He had striven against it. Tonight, he listened.

"The song would mean nothing to you," Kta said. "I can't sing it in human words."

"Try," said Kurt.

The nemet shrugged, gave a pained smile, gathered up the *aos* and ran his fingers over the sensitive strings, calling forth the same melody. For a moment he seemed lost, but the melody grew, rebuilt itself in all its complexity.

"It is our beginning," said Kta, and spoke softly, not looking at Kurt, his fingers moving on the strings like a whisper of wind, as if that was necessary for his thoughts.

There was water. From the sea came the nine spirits of the elements, and greatest were Ygr the earthly and Ib the celestial. From Ygr and Ib came a thousand years of begettings and chaos and wars of elements, until Las who was light and Mur who was darkness, persuaded their brother-gods Phan the sun and Thael the earth to part.

So formed the first order. But Thael loved Phan's sister Ti, and took her. Phan in his anger killed Thael, and of Thael's ribs was the earth. Ti bore dead Thael a son, Aem.

Ten times a thousand years came and passed away.
Aem came to his age, and Ti saw her son was fair.
They sinned the great sin. Of this sin came Yr,
Yr, earth-snake, mother of all beasts.
The council of gods in heaven made Aem and Ti to die,
and dying, they brought forth children, man and woman.

"I have never tried to think it in human terms," said Kta, frowning. "It is very hard."

But with a gesture Kurt urged him, and Kta touched the strings again, trying, greatly frustrated.

"The first beings that were mortal were Nem and Panet, man and woman, twins. They sinned the great sin too. The council of gods rejected them for immortality because of it, and made their lives short. Phan especially hated them, and he mated with Yr the snake, and brought beasts and terrible things into the world to hunt man.

The Phan's sister Qas defied his anger,
stole fire, rained down lightning on the earth.
Men took fire and killed Yr's beasts, built cities.
Ten times a thousand years came and passed away.
Men grew many and kings grew proud,
sons of men and Yr the earth-snake,
sons of men and inim that ride the winds.
Men worshiped these half-men, the godkings.
Men did them honor, built them cities.
Men forgot the first gods,
and men's works were foul.

"Then a prophecy came," said Kta, "and Phan chose Isoi, a mortal woman, and gave her a half-god son: Qavur, who carried the weapons of Phan to destroy the world by burning. Qavur destroyed the godkings, but Isoi his mother begged him not to kill the rest of man, and he didn't. Then Phan with his sword of plague came down and destroyed all men, but when he came to

Isoi she ran to her hearthfire and sat down beside it, so that she claimed the gods' protection. Her tears made Phan pity her. He gave her another son, Isem, who was husband of Nae the seagoddess and father of all men that sail on the sea. But Phan took Qavur to be immortal; he is the star that shines in morning, the messenger of the sun.

"But to keep Nae's children from doing wrong, Phan gave Qavur the *yhia* to take to men. All law comes from it. From it we know our place in the universe. Anything higher is gods' law; but that is beyond the words of the song. The song is the *Ind*. It is sacred to us. My father taught it to me, and the seven verses of it that are only for Elas. So it has come to us in each generation."

"You said once," said Kurt, "that you didn't know whether I was man or not. Have you decided yet?"

Kta thoughtfully laid aside the *aos*, stilled its strings. "Perhaps," said Kta, "some of the children of Nem escaped the plague; but you are not nemet. Perhaps instead you are descended of Yr, and you were set out among the stars on some world of Thael's kindred. From what I have heard among humans, the earth seems to have had many brothers. But I don't think you think so."

"I said nothing."

"Your look did not agree."

"I wouldn't distress you," said Kurt, "by saying I consider you human."

The nemet's lips opened instantly, his eyes mirroring shock. Then he looked as if he suspected Kurt of some levity, and again, as if he feared he were serious. Slowly his expression took on a certain thoughtfulness, and he made a gesture of rejection.

"Please," said Kta, "don't say that freely."

Kurt bowed his head then in respect to Kta, for the nemet truly looked frightened.

"I have spoken to the Guardians of Elas for you," said Kta. "You are a disturbance here, but I do not feel that you are unwelcome with our Ancestors."

*   *   *

Kurt dressed carefully upon the last morning. He would have worn the clothes in which he had come, but Mim had taken those away, unworthy, she had said, of the guest of Elas. Instead he had an array of fine clothing he thought must be Kta's, and on this morning he chose the warmest and most durable, for he did not know what the day might bring him, and the night winds were chill. So it was cold in the rooms of the Afen, and he feared he would not leave it once he entered.

Elas again began to seem distant to him, and the sterile modernity of the center of the Afen increasingly crowded upon his thoughts, the remembrance that, whatever had happened in Elas, his business was with Djan and not with the nemet.

He had chosen his option at the beginning of the two weeks, in the form of a small dragon-hilted blade from among Kta's papers, where it had been gathering dust and would not be missed.

He drew it now from its hiding place and considered it, apt either for Djan or for himself.

And fatally traceable to the house of Elas.

It did not go within his clothing, as he had always meant to carry it. Instead he laid it aside on the dressing table. It would go back to Kta. The nemet would be angry at the theft, but it would make amends, all the same.

Kurt finished dressing, fastening the *ctan,* the outer cloak, upon his shoulder, and chose a bronze pin with which to do it, for his debts to Elas were enough, he would not use the ones of silver and gold which he had been provided.

A light tapping came at the door, Mim's knock.

"Come in," he bade her, and she quietly did so. Linens were changed daily throughout the house. She carried fresh ones, for bed and for bath, and she bowed to him before she set them down to begin her work. Of late there was no longer hate in Mim's look: he understood that she had had cause, having been prisoner of the Tamurlin; but she had ceased her war with him of her own accord, and in consideration of that he always tried especially to please Mim.

"At least," he observed, "you will have less washing in the house hereafter."

She did not appreciate the poor humor. She looked at him, then lowered her eyes and turned around to tend her business.

And froze, with her back to him, facing the dresser. Hesitantly she reached for the knife, snatched at it and faced about again as if uncertain that he would not pounce on her. Her dark eyes were large with terror; her attitude was that of one determined to resist if he attempted to take it from her.

"Lord Kta did not give you this," she said.

"No," he said, "but you may give it back to him."

She clasped it in both hands and continued to stare at him. "If you bring a weapon into the Afen you kill us, Kurt-ifhan. All Elas would die."

"I have given it back," he said. "I am not armed, Mim. That is the truth."

She slipped it into the belt beneath her overskirt, through one of the four slits that exposed the filmy *pelan* from waist to toe, patted it flat. She was so small a woman: she had a tiny waist, a slender neck accentuated by the way she wore her hair in many tiny braids coiled and clustered above the ears. So little a creature, so soft-spoken, and yet he was continually in awe of Mim, feeling her disapproval of him in every line of her stiff little back.

For once, as in the *rhmei* that night, there was something like distress, even tenderness in the way she looked at him.

"Kta wishes you come back to Elas," she said.

"I doubt I will be allowed to," he said.

"Then why would the Methi send you here?"

"I don't know. Perhaps to satisfy Kta for a time. Perhaps so I'll find the Afen the worse by comparison."

"Kta will not let harm come to you."

"Kta had better stay out of it. Tell him so, Mim. He could make the Methi his enemy that way. He had better forget it."

He was afraid. He had lived with that nagging fear from the beginning, and now that Mim touched nerves, he found it difficult to speak with the calm that the nemet called dignity. The unsteadiness of his voice made him greatly ashamed.

And Mim's eyes inexplicably filled with tears—fierce little Mim, unhuman Mim, that he could have thought interestingly female to Kurt but for her alien face. He did not know if any other being would ever care enough to cry over him, and suddenly leaving Elas was unbearable.

He took her slim golden hands in his, knew at once he should not have, for she was nemet and she shivered at the very touch of him. But she looked up at him and did not show offense. Her hands pressed his very gently in return.

"Kurt-ifhan," she said, "I will tell lord Kta what you say, because it is good advice. But I don't think he will listen to me. Elas will speak for you. I am sure of it. The Methi has listened before to Elas. She knows that we speak with the power of the Families. Please go to breakfast. I have made you late. I am sorry."

He nodded and started to the door, looked back again. "Mim," he said, because he wanted her to look up. He wanted her face to think of, as he wanted everything in Elas fixed in his mind. But then he was embarrassed, for he could think of nothing to say.

"Thank you," he murmured, and quickly left.

4

All the way to Afen, Kurt had balanced his chances of rounding on his three nemet guards and making good his escape. The streets of Nephane were twisting and torturous, and if he could remain free until dark, he thought, he might possibly find a way out into the fields and forests.

But Nym himself had given him into the hands of the guards and evidently charged them to treat him well, for they showed him the greatest courtesy. Elas continued to support him, and for the sake of Elas, he dared not do what his own instincts screamed to do: to run,—to kill if need be.

They passed into the cold halls of the Afen itself and it was too late. The stairs led them up to the third level, that of the Methi.

Djan waited for him alone in the modern hall, wearing the modest *chatem* and *pelan* of a nemet lady, her auburn hair braided at the crown of her head, laced with gold.

She dismissed the guards, then turned to him. It was strange, as she had foretold,—to see a human face after so long among the nemet. He began to understand what it had been for her, alone, slipping gradually from human reality into nemet. He noticed things about human faces he had never seen before, how curiously level the planes of the face, how pale her eyes, how metal-bright her hair. The war, the enmity between them—even these seemed for the moment welcome, part of a familiar frame of reference. Elas faded in this place of metal and synthetics.

He fought it back into focus.

"Welcome back," she bade him, and sank into the nearest

chair, gestured him welcome to the other. "Elas wants you," she advised him then. "I am impressed."

"And I," he said, "would like to go back to Elas."

"I did not promise that," she said. "But your presence there has not proved particularly troublesome." She rose again abruptly, went to the cabinet against the near wall, opened it. "Care for a drink, Mr. Morgan?"

"Anything," he said, "thank you."

She poured them each a little glass and brought one to him. It was *telise.* She sat down again, leaned back and sipped at her own. "Let me make a few points clear to you," she said. "First: this is my city; I intend it should remain so. Second: this is a nemet city, and that will remain so too. Our species has had its chance. It's finished. We've done it. Pylos, my world Aeolus—both cinders. It's insane. I spend these last months waiting to die for not following orders, wondering what would become of the nemet when the probe ship returned with the authority and the firepower to deal with me. So I don't mourn them much. I—regret Aeolus. But your intervention was timely, for the nemet. That does not mean," she added, "that I have overwhelming gratitude to you."

"It does not make sense," he said, "that we two should carry on the war here. There's nothing either of us has to win."

"Is it required," she asked, "that a war make sense? Consider ours: we've been at it two thousand years. Probably everything your side and mine says about its beginning is a lie. That hardly matters. There's only the *now,* and the war feeds on its own casualties. And we approach our natural limits. We started out destroying ships in one little system, now we destroy worlds. Worlds. We leave dead space behind us. We count casualties by zones. We Hanan—we never were as numerous or as prolific as you; we can't produce soldiers fast enough to replace the dead. Embryonics, lab-born soldiers, engineered officers, engineered followers—our last hope. And you killed it. I will tell you, my friend, something I would be willing to wager your Alliance never told you: you just stepped up the war by what you did at Aeolus. I think you made a great miscalculation."

"Meaning what?"

"Aeolus was the center, the great center of the embryonics

projects. Billions died in its laboratories. The workers, the facilities, the records—irreplaceable. You have hurt us too much. The
Hanan will cease to restrict targets altogether now. The final insanity, that is what I fear you have loosed on humanity. I do
much fear. And we richly deserve it, the whole human race."

"I don't think," he said, for she disturbed his peace of mind,
"that you enjoy isolation half as much as you pretend."

"I am Aeolid," she said. "Think about it."

It took a moment. Then the realization set in, and revulsion,
gut-deep: of all things Hanan that he loathed, the labs were the
most hateful.

Djan smiled. "Oh, I'm human, of human cells. And superior—I
would have been destroyed otherwise; efficiently engineered—for
intelligence, and trained to serve the state. My intelligence then
advised me that I was being used, and I disliked that. So I found
my moment and turned on the state." She finished the drink and
set it aside. "But you wouldn't like separation from humanity.
Good. That may keep you from trying to cut my throat."

"Am I free to leave, then?"

"Not so easily, not so easily. I had considered perhaps giving
you quarters in the Afen. There are rooms upstairs, only accessible from here. In such isolation you could do no possible harm.
Instinct—something—says that would be the best way to dispose of you."

"Please," he said, rationally, shamelessly, for he had long
since made up his mind that he had nothing to gain in Nephane
by antagonizing Djan. "If Elas will have me, let me go back
there."

"In a few days I will consider that. I only want you to know
your alternatives."

"And what until then?"

"You're going to learn the nemet language. I have things all
ready for you."

"No," he said instantly. "No. I don't need any mechanical
helps."

"I am a medic, among other things. I've never known the
teaching apparatus abused without it doing permanent damage.
No. Ruining the mind of the only other human accessible would

be a waste. I shall merely allow you access to the apparatus and you may choose your own rate."

"Then why do you insist?"

"Because your objection creates an unnecessary problem for you, which I insist be solved. I am giving you a chance to live outside. So I make it a fair chance, an honest chance; I wish you success. I no longer serve the purposes of the Hanan; I refuse to be programmed into a course of action I do not choose. And likewise, if it becomes clear to me that you are becoming a nuisance to me, don't think you can plead ignorance and evade the consequences. I am removing your excuses, you see. And if I must, I will call you in or kill you. Don't doubt it for a moment."

"It is," he said, "a fairer attitude than I would have expected of you. I would be easier in my mind if I understood you."

"All my motives are selfish," she said. "At least in the sense that all I do serves my own purposes. If I once perceive you are working against those purposes, you are done. If I perceive that you are compatible with them, you will find no difficulty. I think that is as clear as I can make it, Mr. Morgan."

5

Kta was not in the *rhmei* as Kurt had expected him to be when he reached the safety of Elas. Hef was, and Mim. Mim scurried upstairs ahead of him to open the window and air the room, and she spun about again when she had done so, her dark eyes shining.

"We are so happy," she said, in human speech. The machine's reflex pained him, punishing understanding.

It was all Mim had time to say, for there was Kta's step upon the landing, and Mim bowed and slipped out as Kta came in.

"Much crying in our house these days," said Kta, casting a look after Mim's retreat down the stairs. Then he looked at Kurt, smiled a little. "But no more. *Ei* Kurt, sit, sit, please. You look like a man three days drowned."

Kurt ran his hand through his hair and fell into a chair. His limbs were shaking. His hands were white. "Speak Nechai," he said. "It's easier."

Kta blinked, looked him over. "How is this?" he asked, and there was unwelcome suspicion in his voice.

"Trust me," Kurt said hoarsely. "The Methi has machines that can do this. I would not lie to you."

"You are pale," said Kta. "You are shaking. Are you hurt?"

"Tired," he said. "Kta,—thank you, thank you for taking me back."

Kta bowed a little. "Even my honored father came and spoke for you, and never in all the years of our house has Elas done such a thing. But you are of Elas. We are glad to receive you."

"Thank you."

He rose and attempted a bow. He had to catch at the table to avoid losing his balance. He made it to the bed and sprawled. His memory ceased before he had stopped moving.

Something tugged at his ankle. He thought he had fallen into the sea and something was pulling him down. But he could not summon the strength to move.

Then the ankle came free and cold air hit his foot. He opened his eyes on Mim, who began to remove the other sandal. He was lying on his own bed, fully clothed, and cold. Outside the window it was night. His legs were like ice, his arms likewise.

Mim's dark eyes looked up, realized that he was awake. "Kta takes bad care for you," she said, "leaving you so. You have not moved. You sleep like the dead."

"Speak Nechai," he asked of her. "I have been taught."

Her look was briefly startled. Then she accepted human strangeness with a little bow, wiped her hands on her *chatem* and dragged at the bedding to cover him, pulling the bedclothes from beneath him, half-asleep as he was.

"I am sorry," she said. "I tried not to wake you, but the night was cold and my lord Kta had left the window open and the light burning."

He sighed deeply and reached for her hand as it drew the coverlet across him. "Mim,—"

"Please." She evaded his hand, slipped the pin from his shoulder and hauled the tangled *ctan* from beneath him, jerked the catch of his wide belt free, then drew the covers up to his chin.

"You will sleep easier now," she said.

He reached for her hand again, preventing her going. "Mim, what time is it?"

"Late,—late." She pulled, but he did not let her go, and she glanced down, her lashes dark against her bronze cheeks. "Please, please let me go, lord Kurt."

"I asked Djan, asked her to send you word—so you would not worry."

"Word came. We did not know how to understand it. It was only that you were safe. Only that." She pulled again. "Please."

Her lips trembled, and eyes were terrified, and when he let

her hand go she spun around and fled to the door. She hardly paused to close it, her slippered feet pattering away down the stairs at breakneck speed.

If he had had the strength he would have risen and gone after her, for he had not meant to hurt Mim on the very night of his return. He lay awake and was angry, at nemet custom and at himself, but his head hurt abominably and made him dizzy. He sank into the soft down and slipped away. There was tomorrow. Mim would have gone to bed too, and he would scandalize the house by trying to speak to her tonight.

The morning began with tea, but there was no Mim, cheerily bustling in with morning linens and disarranging things. She did appear in the *rhmei* to serve, but she kept her eyes down when she poured for him.

"Mim," he whispered at her, and she spilled a few drops, which burned, and moved quickly to pour for Kta. She spilled even his, at which the dignified nemet shook his burned hand and looked up wonderingly at the girl, but said nothing.

There had been the usual round of formalities, and Kurt had bowed deeply before Nym and Ptas and Aimu, and thanked the lord of Elas in his own language for his intercession with Djan.

"You speak very well," Nym observed by way of acknowledging him; and Kurt realized he should have explained through Kta. An elder nemet cherished his dignity, and Kurt saw that he must have mightily offended lord Nym with his human sense of the dramatic.

"Sir," said Kurt, "you honor me. By machines I do this. I speak slowly yet and not well, but I do recognize what is said to me. When I have listened a few days, I will be a better speaker. Forgive me if I have offended you. I was so tired yesterday I had no sense left to explain where I have been or why."

The honorable Nym considered, and then the faintest of smiles touched his face, growing to an expression of positive amusement. He touched his laced fingers to his breast and inclined his head, apology for laughter.

"Welcome a second time to Elas, friend of my son. You bring gladness with you. There are smiles on faces this morning, and there were few the days we were in fear for you. Just when we thought we had comprehended humans, here are more wonders,—and what a relief to be able to talk without waiting for translations!"

So they were settled together, the ritual of tea begun. Lady Ptas sat enthroned in their center, a comfortable woman. Somehow when Kurt thought of Elas, Ptas always came first to mind,—a gentle and dignified lady with graying hair, the very heart of the family, which among nemet a mother was: Nym's lady, source of life and love, protectress of his ancestral religion. Into a wife's hands a man committed his hearth, and into a daughter-in-law's hands—his hope of a continuing eternity. Kurt began to understand why fathers chose their sons' mates; and considering the affection that was evident between Nym and Ptas, he could no longer think such marriages were loveless. It was right, it was proper, and he sat cross-legged upon a fleece rug, equal to Kta, a son of the house, drinking the strong sweetened tea and feeling that he had come home indeed.

And after tea lady Ptas rose and bowed formally before the hearthfire, lifting her palms to it. Everyone stood in respect, and her sweet voice called upon the Guardians.

"Ancestors of Elas, upon this shore and the other of the Dividing Sea, look kindly upon us. Kurt t'Morgan has come back to us. Peace be between the guest of our home and the Guardians of Elas. Peace be among us."

Kurt was greatly touched, and bowed deeply to lady Ptas when she was done.

"Lady Ptas," he said, "I honor you very much." He would have said—like a son, but he would not inflict that doubtful compliment on the nemet lady.

She smiled at him with the affection she gave her children; and from that moment, Ptas had his heart.

"Kurt," said Kta when they were alone in the hall after breakfast, "my father bids you stay as long as it pleases you. This he asked me to tell you. He would not burden you with giving answer on the instant, but he would have you know this."

"He is very kind," said Kurt. "You have never owed me all of the things you have done for me. Your oath never bound you this far."

"Those who share the hearth of Elas," said Kta, "have been

few, but we never forget them. We call this guest-friendship. It binds your house and mine for all time. It can never be broken."

He spent the days much in Kta's company within Elas, talking, resting, enjoying the sun in the inner court of the house where there was a small garden.

One thing remained to trouble him: Mim was usually absent. She no longer came to his rooms when he was there. No matter how he varied his schedule, she would not come; he only found his bed changed about when he would return after some absence. When he hovered about the places where she usually worked, she was simply not to be found.

"She is at market," Hef informed him on a morning that he finally gathered his courage to ask.

"She has not been much about lately," Kurt observed.

Hef shrugged. "No, lord Kurt. She has not."

And the old man looked at him strangely, as if Kurt's anxiety had undermined the peace of his morning too.

He became the more determined. When he heard the front door close at noon, he sprang up to run downstairs but he had only a glimpse of her hurrying by the opposite hall into the ladies' quarters behind the *rhmei*. That was Ptas' territory, and no man but Nym could set foot there.

He walked disconsolately back to the garden and sat in the sun, staring at nothing in particular and tracing idle patterns in the pale dust.

He had hurt her. Mim had not told the matter to anyone, he was sure, for if she had he had no doubt he would have had Kta to deal with.

He wished desperately that he could ask someone how to apologize to her, but it was not something he could ask of Kta, or of Hef; and certainly he dared ask no one else.

She served at dinner that night, as at every meal, and still avoided his eyes. He dared not say anything to her. Kta was sitting beside him.

Late that night he set himself in the hall and doggedly waited, far past the hour when the family was decently in bed, for the *chan* of Elas had as her last duties to set out things for breakfast tea and to extinguish the hall lights as she retired to bed.

She saw him there, blocking her way to her rooms. For a moment he feared she would cry out; her hand flew to her lips. But she stood her ground, still looking poised to run.

"Mim. Please. I want to talk with you."

"I do not want to talk with you. Let me pass."

"Please."

"Do not touch me. Let me pass. Do you want to wake all the house?"

"Do that, if you like. But I will not let you go until you talk with me."

Her eyes widened slightly. "Kta will not permit this."

"There are no windows on the garden and we cannot be heard there. Come outside, Mim. I swear I want only to talk."

She considered, her lovely face looking so frightened he hurt for her; but she yielded and walked ahead of him to the garden. The world's moon cast dim shadows here. She stopped where the light was brightest, clasping her arms against the chill of the night.

"Mim," he said, "I did not mean to frighten you that night. I meant no harm by it."

"I should never have been there alone. It was my fault.—Please, lord Kurt, do not look at me that way. Let me go."

"Because I am not nemet,—you felt free to come in and out of my room and not be ashamed with me. Was that it, Mim?"

"No." Her teeth chattered so she could hardly talk, and the cold was not enough for that. He slipped the pin off his *ctan,* but she would not take it from him, flinching from the offered garment.

"Why can I not talk to you?" he asked. "How does a man ever talk to a nemet woman? I refrain from this, I refrain from that, I must not touch, must not look, must not think. How am I to—?"

"Please."

"How am I to talk with you?"

"Lord Kurt, I have made you think I am a loose woman. I am *chan* to this house; I cannot dishonor it. Please let me go inside."

A thought came to him. "Are you *his?* Are you Kta's?"

"No," she said.

Against her preference he took the *ctan* and draped it about her shoulders. She hugged it to her. He was near enough to have touched her. He did not, nor did she move back; he did not take that for invitation. He thought that whatever he did, she would not protest or raise the house. It would be trouble between her lord Kta and his guest, and he understood enough of nemet dignity to know that Mim would choose silence. She would yield, hating him.

He had no argument against that.

In sad defeat, he bowed a formal courtesy to her and turned away.

"Lord Kurt," she whispered after him, distress in her voice.

He paused, looking back.

"My lord,—you do not understand."

"I understand," he said, "that I am human. I have offended you. I am sorry."

"Nemet do not—" She broke off in great embarrassment, opened her hands, pleading. "My lord, seek a wife. My lord Nym will advise you. You have connections with the Methi and with Elas. You could marry,—easily you could marry, if Nym approached the right house—"

"And if it was you I wanted?"

She stood there, without words, until he came back to her and reached for her. Then she prevented him with her slim hands on his. "Please," she said. "I have done wrong with you already."

He ignored the protest of her hands and took her face between his palms ever so gently, fearing at each moment she would tear from him in horror. She did not. He bent and touched his lips to hers, delicately, almost chastely, for he thought the human custom might disgust or frighten her.

Her smooth hands still rested on his arms. The moon glistened on tears in her eyes when he drew back from her. "Lord," she said, "I honor you. I would do what you wish, but it would shame Kta and it would shame my father and I cannot."

"What can you?" He found his own breathing difficult. "Mim, what if some day I did decide to talk with your father? Is that the way things are done?"

"To marry?"

"Some day it might seem a good thing to do."

She shivered in his hands. Tears spilled freely down her cheeks.

"Mim, will you give me yes or no? Is a human hard for you

to look at? If you had rather not say, then just say 'let me be' and I will do my best after this not to bother you."

"Lord Kurt, you do not know me."

"Are you determined I will never know you?"

"You do not understand. I am not the daughter of Hef. If you ask him for me he must tell you, and then you will not want me."

"It is nothing to me whose daughter you are."

"My lord,—Elas knows. Elas knows. But you must listen to me now, listen. You know about the Tamurlin. I was taken when I was thirteen. For three years I was slave to them. Hef only calls me his daughter, and all Nephane thinks I am of this country. But I am not, Kurt. I am Indras, of Indresul. And they would kill me if they knew. Elas has kept this to itself. But you—you cannot bear such a trouble. People must not look at you and think Tamurlin: it would hurt you in this city; and when they see me, that is what they must think."

"Do you believe," he asked, "that what they think matters with me? I am human. They can see that."

"Do you not understand, my lord? I have been property of every man in that village. Kta must tell you this if you ask Hef for me. I am not honorable. No one would marry Mim h'Elas. Do not shame yourself and Kta by making Kta say this to you."

"After he had said it," said Kurt, "would he give his consent?"

"Honorable women would marry you. Sufaki have no fear of humans as Indras do. Perhaps even a daughter of some merchant would marry you. I am only *chan,* and before that I was nothing at all."

"If I were to ask," he said, "would you refuse?"

"No. I would not refuse." Her small face took on a look of pained bewilderment. "Kurt-ifhan, surely you will think better of this in the morning."

"I am going to talk to Hef," he said. "Go inside, Mim. And give me back my cloak. It would not do for you to wear it inside."

"My lord, think a day before you do this."

"I will give it tomorrow," he said, "for thinking it over. And you do the same. And if you have not come to me by tomorrow evening and asked me and said clearly that you do not want me, then I will talk to Hef."

*   *   *

It was, he had time to think that night and the next morning, hardly reasonable. He wanted Mim. He had had no knowledge of her to say that he loved her, or that she loved him.

He wanted her. She had set her terms and there was no living under the same roof with Mim without wanting her.

He could apply reason to the matter, until he looked into her face at breakfast as she poured the tea, or as she passed him in the hall and looked at him with a dreadful anxiety.

Have you thought better of it? the look seemed to say. *Was it, after all, only for the night?*

Then the feeling was back with him, the surety that, should he lose Mim by saying nothing, he would have lost something irreplaceable.

In the end, he found himself that evening gathering his courage before the door of Hef, who served Elas, and standing awkwardly inside the door when the old man admitted him.

"Hef," he said, "may I talk to you about Mim?"

"My lord?" asked the old man, bowing.

"What if I wanted to marry her? What should I do?"

The old nemet looked quite overcome then, and bowed several times, looking up at him with a distraught expression. "Lord Kurt, she is only *chan.*"

"Do I not speak to you? Are you the one who says yes or no?"

"Let my lord not be offended. I must ask Mim."

"Mim agrees," said Kurt. Then he thought that it was not his place to have asked Mim, and that he shamed her and embarrassed Hef; but Hef regarded him with patience and even a certain kindliness.

"But I must ask Mim," said Hef. "That is the way of it. And then I must speak to Kta-ifhan, and to Nym and lady Ptas."

"Does the whole house have to give consent?" Kurt let forth, without pausing to think.

"Yes, my lord. I shall speak to the family, and to Mim. It is proper that I speak to Mim."

"I am honored," Kurt murmured the polite phrase; and he went upstairs to his own quarters to gather his nerves.

He felt much relieved that it was over. Hef would consent. He was sure what Mim would answer her father, and that would satisfy Hef.

He was preparing for bed when Kta came up the stairs and asked admittance. The nemet had a troubled look and Kurt knew by sure instinct what had brought him. He would almost have begged Kta to go away, but he was under Kta's roof and he did not have that right.

"You have talked with Hef," Kurt said, to make it easier for him.

"Let me in, my friend."

Kurt backed from the door, offering Kta a chair. It would have been proper to offer tea also. He would have had to summon Mim for that. He would not do it.

"Kurt," said Kta, "please, sit down also. I must speak to you—I must beg your kindness to hear me."

"You might find it more comfortable simply to tell me what is in your mind from the beginning," Kurt said, taking the other chair. "Yes or no, are you going to interfere?"

"I am concerned for Mim. It is not as simple as you may hope. Will you hear me? If your anger forbids,—then we will go down and drink tea and wait for a better mind, but I am bound to say these things."

"Mim told me—about most that I imagine you have come to say. And it makes no difference. I know about the Tamurlin and I know where she came from."

Kta let his breath go, a long hiss of a sigh. "Well, that is something at least. You know that she is Indras?"

"None of that possibly concerns me. Nemet politics have nothing to do with me."

"You choose ignorance. That is always a dangerous choice, Kurt. Being of the Indras race or being Sufaki is a matter of great difference among nemet, and you are among nemet."

"The only difference I have ever noticed is being human among nemet," he said, controlling his temper with a great effort. "I would bring disgrace on you. Is that what you care for, and not whether Mim would be happy?"

"Mim's happiness is a matter of great concern to us," Kta insisted. "And we know you would not mean to hurt her, but human ways—"

"Then you see no difference between me and the Tamurlin."

"Please. Please. You do not imagine. They are not like you.

That is not what I meant. The Tamurlin—they are foul and they are shameless. They wear hides and roar and mouth like beasts when they fight. They have no more modesty than beasts in their dealing with women. They mate as they please, without seeking privacy. They restrain themselves from nothing. A strong chief may have twenty or more women, while weaker men have none. They change mates by the outcome of combat. I speak of human women. Slaves like Mim belong to any and all who want them. And when I found her—"

"I do not want to hear this."

"Kurt,—listen. Listen. I shall not offend you. But when we attacked the Tamurlin to stop their raids—we killed all we could reach. We were about to set torch to the place when I heard a sound like a child crying. I found Mim in the corner of a hut. She wore a scrap of hide, as filthy as the rest of them; for an instant I could not even tell she was nemet. She was thin, and carried terrible marks on her body. When I tried to carry her, she attacked me—not womanlike, but with a knife and her teeth and her knees, whatever she could bring to bear. So she was accustomed to fight for her place among them. I had to strike her senseless to bring her to the ship, and then she kept trying to jump into the sea until we were out of sight of land. Then she hid down in the rowing pits and would not come out except when the men were at the oars. When we fed her she would snatch and run, and she would not speak more than a few syllables at a time save of human language."

"I cannot believe that," said Kurt quietly. "How long ago was that?"

"Four years. Four years she has been in Elas. I brought her home and gave her to my lady mother and sister, and Hef's wife Liu, who was living then. But she had not been among us many days before Aimu saw her standing before the hearthfire with hands lifted, as Sufaki do not do. Aimu was younger then and not so wise; she exclaimed aloud that Mim must be Indras.

"Mim ran. I caught her in the streets, to the wonder of all Nephane and our great disgrace. And I carried her by force back to Elas. Then, alone with us, she began to speak, with the accent of Indresul. This was the reason of her silence before. But we of Elas are Indras too, like all the Great Families on the hill, descended of colonists of Indresul who came to this shore a thousand years ago, and while we are now enemies of Indresul, we are one religion and Mim was only a child. So Elas has kept her secret, and people outside know her only as Hef's adopted Sufaki daughter, a country child of mixed blood rescued from the Tamurlin. She does not speak as Sufaki, but people believe we taught her speech; she does not look Sufaki, but that is not unusual in the coastal villages, where seamen have—*ei*, well, she passes for Sufaki. The scandal of her running through the streets is long forgotten. She is an honor and an ornament to this house now. But to have her in public attention again—would be difficult. No man would marry Mim; forgive me, but it is truth and she knows it. Such a marriage would cause gossip favorable to neither of you."

Instinct told him Kta was speaking earnest good sense. He put it by. "I would take care of her," he insisted. "I would try, Kta."

Kta glanced down in embarrassment, then lifted his eyes again. "She is nemet. Understand me. *She* is nemet. She has been hurt and greatly shamed. Human customs are—forgive me: I shall speak shamelessly. I do not know how humans behave with their mates. Djan-methi is—free—in this regard. We are not. I beg you think of Mim. We do not cast away our women. Marriage is unbreakable."

"I had expected so."

Kta sat back a little. "Kurt—there could be no children. I have never heard of it happening, and Tamurlin have mated with nemet women."

"If there were," said Kurt, though what Kta had said distressed him greatly, "I could love them. I would want them. But if not, then I would be happy with Mim."

"But could others love them?" Kta wondered. "It would be difficult for them, Kurt."

It hurt. Some things Kta said amused him and some no little irritated him, but this was simply a fact of Kta's world, and it hurt bitterly. For an instant Kurt forgot that the nemet thing to do was to lower his eyes and so keep his hurt private. He looked full at the nemet, and it was Kta who flinched and had to look up again.

"Would they," Kurt said, cruel to the embarrassed nemet, "would children like that be such monsters, Kta?"

"I," said Kta hesitantly, "*I* could love a child of my friend." And the inward shudder was too evident.

"Even," Kurt finished, "if it looked too much like my friend?"

"I beg your forgiveness," Kta said hoarsely. "I fear for you and for Mim."

"Is that all?"

"I do not understand."

"Do you want her?"

"My friend," said Kta, "I do not love Mim, but Mim is dear to me, and I am responsible for her as my honored father is. He is too old to take Mim; but when I married, I should have been obliged to take Mim for a concubine, for she is *chan* and unmarried—and I would not have been sorry for that, for she is a most beloved friend, and I would have been glad to give her children to continue Hef's name. When you ask her of Hef, you see,— that is a terrible thing. Hef is childless. Mim is his adopted daughter, but we had agreed her children would remain in Elas to carry on his name and give his soul life when he dies. Mim must bear sons, and you cannot give them to her. You are asking for Hef's eternity and that of all his ancestors. Hef's family has been good and faithful to Elas. What shall I do, my friend? How shall I resolve this?"

Kurt shook his head helplessly, unsure whether Kta thought there could be an answer, or whether this was not some slow and painful way of telling him no.

"I do not know," Kurt said, "whether I can stay in Elas without marrying Mim. I want her very much, Kta. I do not think that will change tomorrow or for the rest of my life."

"There is," Kta offered cautiously, "an old custom—that if the *lechan*'s husband dies and the house of the *chan* is threatened with extinction, then the duty is with the lord of the house nearest her age. Sometimes this is done even with the *lechan*'s husband living, if there are no children after such a time."

Kurt did not know whether his face went very pale or flushed, only that he could not for the moment move or look left or right, was trapped staring into the nemet's pitying eyes. Then he recovered the grace to glance down. "I could even," he echoed, "love a child of my friend."

Kta flinched. "Perhaps," said Kta, "it would be different with you and Mim. I see how much your heart goes toward her, and I will plead your case with Hef and give him my own pledge in this matter. And if Hef is won, then it will be easier to win my lord father and lady mother. Also I will talk to Mim about this custom we call *iquun*."

"I will do that," Kurt said.

"No," said Kta gently. "It would be very difficult for her to hear such words from you. Believe me that I am right. I have known Mim long enough that I could speak with her of this. From her own betrothed it would be most painful. And perhaps we can give the matter a few years before we have concern for it. Our friend Hef is not terribly old. If his health fails or if years have passed without children, then will be the time to invoke *iquun*. I should in that case treat the honor of you and of Hef and of Mim with the greatest respect."

"You are my friend," said Kurt. "I know that you are Mim's. If she is willing, let it be that way."

"Then," said Kta, "I will go and speak to Hef."

The betrothal was a necessarily quiet affair, confirmed three days later at evening. Hef formally asked permission of lord Nym to give his daughter to the guest of Elas, and Kta formally relinquished his claim to the person of Mim before the necessary two witnesses, friends of the family; Han t'Osanef u Mur, father of Bel; and old Ulmar t'Ilev ul Imetan, with all their attendant kin.

"Mim-lechan," said Nym, "is this marriage your wish?"

"Yes, my lord."

"And in the absence of your kinsmen, Kurt t'Morgan, I ask you to answer in your own name: do you accept this contract as binding, understanding that when you have sworn you must follow this ceremony with marriage or show cause before these families present? Do you accept under this knowledge, our friend Kurt t'Morgan?"

"I accept."

"There is," said Nym quietly, "the clause of *iquun* in this contract. The principals are of course Mim and Kurt, and thou, my son Kta, and Hef, to preserve the name of Hef. Three years are given in this agreement before *iquun* is invoked. Is this acceptable to all concerned?"

One by one they bowed their heads.

Two parchments lay on the table, and to them in turn first Nym and then t'Osanef and t'Ilev pressed their seals in wax.

Then lady Ptas pressed her forefinger in damp wax and so sealed both. Then she took one of the *phusmeha,* and with a bit of salt slipped it into the flames.

She uplifted her palms to the fire, intoning a prayer so old that Kurt could not understand all the words, but it asked blessing on the marriage.

"The betrothal is sealed," said Nym. "Kurt Liam t'Morgan ul Edward, look upon Mim h'Elas e Hef, your bride."

He did so, although he could not, must not touch her, not during all the long days of waiting for the ceremony. Mim's face shone with happiness.

They were at opposite sides of the room. It was the custom. The nemet made a game of tormenting young men and women at betrothals, and knew well enough his frustration. The male guests, especially Bel and Kta, drew Kurt off in one direction, while Aimu and Ptas and the ladies likewise captured Mim, with much laughter as they hurried her off.

The bell at the front door rang, faintly jingling, untimely. Hef slipped out to answer it, duty and the normal courtesy of Elas taking precedence over convenience even at such a time as this.

The teasing ceased. The nemet laughed much among themselves, among friends, but there were visitors at the door, and the guests and the members of Elas both became sober.

Voices intruded—Hef,—Hef, who was the soul of courtesy, arguing; and the heavy tread of outsiders entering the hall, the hollow ring of a staff on polished stone, the voices of strangers raised in altercation.

There was silence in the *rhmei*. Mim, large-eyed, clung to Ptas' arm. Nym went to meet the strangers in the hall, Kurt and Kta and the guests behind him.

They were the Methi's men, grim-faced, in the odd-striped robes that some of the townsmen wore, hair plaited in a single braid down the back. They had the narrowness of eye that showed in some of the folk of Nephane, like Bel, like Bel's father Han t'Osanef.

The Methi's guards did not take that final step into the *rhmei,* where burned the hearthfire. Nym physically barred their way, and Nym, though silver-haired and a senior member of the Upei, the council of Nephane, was a big man and broad-shouldered. Whether through reverence for the place or fear of him, they came no further.

"This is Elas," said Nym. "Consider again, gentlemen, where you are. I did not bid you here, and I did not hear the *chan* of Elas give you leave either."

"The Methi's orders," said the eldest of the four. "We came to fetch the human. This betrothal is not permitted."

"Then you are too late," said Nym. "If the Methi wished to intervene, it was her right, but now the betrothal is sealed."

That set them aback. "Still," said their leader, "we must bring him back to the Afen."

"Elas will permit him to go back," said Nym, "if he chooses."

"He will go with us," said the man.

Han t'Osanef stepped up beside Nym and bent a terrible frown on the Methi's guardsmen. "T'Senife, I ask you come tonight to the house of Osanef. I would ask it, t'Senife—and the rest of you young men. Bring your fathers. We will talk."

The men had a different manner for t'Osanef: resentful, but paying respect.

"We have duties," said the man called t'Senife, "which keep us at the Afen. We have no time for that. But we will say to our fathers that t'Osanef spoke with us at the house of Elas."

"Then go back to the Afen," said t'Osanef. "*I* ask it. You offend Elas."

"We have our duty," said t'Senife, "and we must have the human."

"I will go," said Kurt, coming forward. He had the feeling that there was much more than himself at issue, he intruded fearfully into the hate that prickled in the air. Kta put out a hand, forbidding him.

"The guest of Elas," said Nym in a terrible voice, "will walk from the door of Elas if he chooses, and the Methi herself has no power to cause this hall to be invaded. Wait at our doorstep.—And you, friend Kurt, do not go against your will. The law forbids."

"We will wait outside," said t'Senife, at t'Osanef's hard look. But they did not bow as they left.

"My friend," Han t'Osanef exclaimed to Nym, "I blush for these young men."

"They are," said Nym in a shaking voice, "*young* men. Elas also will speak with their Fathers. Do not go, Kurt t'Morgan. You are not compelled to go."

"I think," said Kurt, "that eventually I would have no choice. I would do better to go speak with Djan-methi, if it is possible." But it was in his mind that reason with her was not likely. He looked at Mim, who stood frightened and silent by the side of Ptas. He could not touch her. Even at such a time he knew they would not understand. "I will be back as soon as I can," he said to her.

But to Kta, at the door of Elas before he went out to put himself into the hands of the Methi's guards:

"Take care of Mim. And I do not want her or your father or any of Elas to come to the Afen. I do not want her involved and I am afraid for you all."

"You do not have to go," Kta insisted.

"Eventually," Kurt repeated, "I would have to. You have taught me there is grace in recognizing necessity. Take care of her." And with Kta, that he knew so well, he put out his hand instinctively to touch, and refrained.

It was Kta who gripped his hand, an uncertain, awkward gesture, not at all nemet. "You have friends and kinsmen now. Remember it."

6

"There is no need of that," Kurt cried, shaking off the guards' hands as they persisted in hurrying him through the gates of the Afen. No matter how quickly he walked, they had to push him or lay hands on him, so that people in the streets stopped and stared, most unnemetlike, most embarrassing for Elas. It was to spite Nym that they did it, he was sure, and rather than make a public scene-worse, he had taken the abuse until they entered the Afen court, beyond witnesses.

There was a long walk between the iron outer gate and the wooden main door of the Afen, for that space Kurt argued with them, then found them fanning out to prevent him from the very door toward which they were tending.

He knew the game. They wanted him to resist. He had done so. Now they had the excuse they wanted, and they began to close up on him.

He ran the only way still open, to the end of the courtyard, where it came up against the high peak of the lock on which the Afen sat, a facing wall of gray basalt. It was beyond the witness of anyone on the walk between the wall-gate and the door.

They herded him. He knew it and was willing to go as long as there was room to retreat, intending to pay double at least on one of them when they finally closed in on him. T'Senife, who had insulted Nym, that was the one he favored killing, a slit-eyed fellow with a look of inborn arrogance.

But to kill him would endanger Elas; he dared not, and knew how it must end. He risked other's lives, even fighting them.

A small gate was set in the wall near the rock. He bolted for it, surprising them, desperately flinging back the iron bar.

A vast courtyard lay beyond it, a courtyard paved in polished marble, with a single building closing it off, high-columned, a white cube with three triangular pylons arching over its long steps.

He ran, saw the safety of the familiar wall-street to his left, leading to the main street of Nephane, back to the witness of passersby.

But for the sake of Elas he dared not take the matter into public. He knew Nym and Kta, knew they would involve themselves, to their hurt and without the power to help him.

He ran instead across the white court, his sandaled feet and those of his pursuers echoing loudly on the deserted stones. The wall-street was the only way in. The precinct was a cul-de-sac, backed by the temple, flanked on one side by a high wall and on the other by the living rock.

His pursuers put on a sudden burst of speed. He did likewise, thinking suddenly that they did not want him to reach this place, a religious place, a sanctuary.

He sprang for the polished steps, raced up them, slipping and stumbling in his haste and exhaustion.

Fire roared inside, an enormous bowl of flame leaping within, a heat that filled the room and flooded even the outer air, a *phus-meha* so large the blaze made the room glow gold, whose sound was like a furnace.

He stopped without any thought in his mind but terror, blasted by the heat on his face and drowned in the sound of it. It was a *rhmei,* and he knew its sanctity.

His pursuers had stopped, a scant few strides behind him on the steps. He looked back. T'Senife beckoned him.

"Come down," said t'Senife. "We were told to bring you to the Methi. If you will not come down, it will be the worse for you. Come down."

Kurt believed him. It was a place of powers to which human touch was defilement,—no sanctuary, none for a human,—no kindly Ptas to open the *rhmei* to him and make him welcome.

He came down to them, and they took him by the arms and

led him down and across the courtyard to the open gate of the Afen compound, barring it again behind them.

Then they forced him up against the wall and had their revenge, expertly, without leaving a visible mark on him.

It was not likely that he would complain, both for the personal shame of it and because he and his friends were always in their reach: especially Kta,—who would count it a matter of honor to avenge his friend, even on the Methi's guard.

Kurt straightened himself as much as he could at the moment and t'Senife straightened his *ctan,* which had come awry, and took his arm again.

They brought him up a side entrance of the Afen, by stairs he had not used before. Then they passed into familiar halls near the center of the building.

Another of their kind met them, a stripe-robed and braided young man, handsome as Bel, but with sullen, hateful eyes. To him these men showed great deference. Shan t'Tefur, they called him.

They discussed the betrothal, and how they had been too late.

"Then the Methi should have that news," concluded t'Tefur, and his narrow eyes shifted toward a room with a solid door. "It is empty. Hold him there until I have carried her that news."

They did so. Kurt sat on a hard chair by the barred slit of a window and so avoided the looks that pierced his back, giving them no excuse to repeat their treatment of him.

At last t'Tefur came back to say that the Methi would see him.

She would see him alone. T'Tefur protested with a violently angry look, but Djan stared back at him in such a way that t'Tefur bowed finally and left the room.

Then she turned that same angry look on Kurt.

"Entering the temple precincts was a mistake," she said. "If you had entered the temple itself I don't know if I could have saved you."

"I had that idea," he said.

"Who told you that you had the freedom to make contracts in Nephane—marrying that nemet?"

"I wasn't told I didn't. Nor was Elas told, or they wouldn't have allowed it. They are loyal to you. And they were not treated well, Djan."

"Not the least among the problems you've created for me, this disrespect of Elas." She walked over to the far side of the room, put back a panel that revealed a terrace walled with glass. It was night. They had a view of all the sea. She gazed out, leaving him watching her back, and she stayed that way for a long time. He thought he was the subject of her thoughts, he and Elas.

At last she turned and faced him. "Well," she said, "for Elas' inconvenience, I'm sorry. I shall send them word that you're safe. You haven't had dinner yet, have you?"

Appetite was the furthest thing from his mind. His stomach was both empty and racked with pain, and with an outright fear that her sudden shift in manner did nothing to ease. "You," he said, "frightened the wits out of my fiancée, made me a spectacle in the streets of Nephane, and all I particularly care about is—"

"I think," said Djan in a tone of finality, "that we had better save the talk. *I* am going to have dinner. If you want to argue the point, Shan can find you some secure room where you can think matters over. But you will leave the Afen—*if* you leave the Afen—when I please to send you out."

And she called a girl named Pai, who recieved her orders with a deep bow.

"She," said Djan when the girl had gone, "is *chan* to the Afen. I inherited her, it seems. She is very loyal and very silent, both virtues. Her family served the last Methi, a hundred years ago. Before that, Pai's family was still *chan* to methis, even before the human occupation and during it. There is nothing in Nephane that does not have roots, except the two of us. Forget your temper, my friend. I lost mine. I rarely do that. I am sorry."

"Then we will have out whatever you want to say and I will go back to Elas."

"I would think so," she agreed quietly, ignoring his anger. "Come out here. Sit down. I am too tired to stand up to argue with you."

He came, shrugging off his apprehensions. The terrace was dark. She left it so, and sat on the window ledge, watching the sea far below. It was indeed a spectacular view of Nephane, its lights winding down the crag below, the high dark rock a shadow against the moon. The moonlit surface of the sea was cut by the wake of a single ship heading out.

"If I were sensible," said Djan as he joined her and sat down on the ledge facing her, "if I were at all sensible I'd have you taken out and dropped about halfway. Unfortunately I decided against it. I wonder still what you would do in my place."

He had wondered that himself. "I would think of the same things that have occurred to you," he said.

"And reach the same answer?"

"I think so," he admitted. "I don't blame you."

She smiled, ironic amusement. "Then maybe we will have a brighter future than other humans who have held Nephane. —They built this section of the Afen, you know. That's why there is no *rhmei,* no heart to the place. It's unique in that respect—the fortress without a heart, the building without a soul. Did Kta tell you what became of them?"

"Nemet drove them out, I know that."

"Humans ruled Nephane about twenty years. But they involved themselves with the nemet. The mistress of the base commander was of the great Indras family—of Irain. Humans were very cruel to the nemet, and they enjoyed humiliating the Great Families by that. But one night she let her brothers in and the whole of Nephane rose in rebellion against the humans on the night of a great celebration, when most of the humans were drunk on *telise.* So they lost their machines and fled south and became the Tamurlin in a generation or so—like animals. Only Pai's ancestor On t'Erefe defended the humans in the Afen, being *chan* and obliged to defend his human lord. The human Methi and On died together, out there in the hall. The other humans who died were killed in the courtyard, and those who were caught were brought back there and killed.

"Myself, I have read the records that went before their fall. The supply ship failed them, never came back—probably after reporting to Aeolus; it was destroyed on its return trip, another war casualty, unnoticed. The years passed, and they had made the nemet here hate them. They had threatened them with the imminent return of the ship for twenty years and the threat was wearing thin. So they fell. But when we arrived, the nemet thought the threat had come true and that they were all to die.

For all my crewmates cared, we might have destroyed Nephane to secure the base. I would not permit it. And when I had freed the nemet from the immediate threat of my companions, they made me Methi. Some say I am sent by Fate; they think the same of you. For an Indras, nothing ever happens without logical purpose. Their universe is entirely rational. I admire that in them. There is a great deal in these people that was worth the cost. And I think you agree with me. You're evidently settled very comfortably into Elas."

"They are my friends," he said.

Djan leaned back, leaned on the sill and looked out over her shoulder. The ship was nearly to the breakwater. "This is a world of little haste and much deliberation. Can you imagine two ships like that headed for each other in battle? Our ships come in faster than the mind can think, from zero vision to alongside, attack and vanish. But those vessels with their sails and oars—by the time they came within range of each other— there would be abundant time for thought. There is a dreadful deliberateness about the nemet. They maneuver so slowly, but they do hold a course once they've taken it."

"You're not talking about ships."

"Do you know what lies across the sea?"

His heart leaped; he thought of Mim, and his first terrible thought was that Djan knew. But he let nothing of that reach his face. "Indresul," he said. "A city that is hostile to Nephane."

"Your friends of Elas are Indras. Did you know?"

"I had heard so, yes."

"So are most of the Great Families of Nephane. The Indras established this as a colony once, when they conquered the inland fortress of Chteftikan and began to build this fortress with Sufaki slaves taken in that war. Indresul has no love of the Nephanite Indras, but she has never forgotten that through them she has a claim on this city. She wants it. I am walking a narrow line, Kurt Morgan, and your Indras friends in Elas and your own meddling in nemet affairs are an embarrassment to me at a time when I can least afford embarrassment. I need quiet in this city. I will do what is necessary to secure that."

"I've done nothing," he said, "except inside Elas."

"Unfortunately," said Djan, "Elas does nothing without consequence in Nephane. That is the misfortune of wealth and power. —That ship out there—is bound for Indresul. The Methi of Indresul has eluded my every attempt to talk. You cannot imagine how they despise Sufaki and humans. Well, at last they are going to send an ambassador,—one Mor t'Uset ul Orm, a councilor who has high status in Indresul. He will come at the return of that ship. And this betrothal of yours, publicized in the market today, had better not come to the attention of t'Uset when he arrives."

"I have no desire to be noticed by anyone," he said.

The glance she gave him was ice. But at that moment Pailechan and another girl pattered into the hall cat-footed and brought tea and *telise* and a light supper, setting it on the low table by the ledge.

Djan dismissed them both, although strict formality dictated someone serve. The *chani* bowed themselves out.

"Join me," she said, "in tea or *telise,* if nothing else."

His appetite had returned somewhat. He picked at the food and then found himself hungry. He ate fully enough for his share, and demurred when she poured him *telise,* but she set the cup beside him. She carried the dishes out herself, returned and settled upon the ledge beside him. The ship had long since cleared the harbor, leaving its surface to the wind and the moon.

"It is late," he said. "I would like to go back to Elas."

"This nemet girl. What is her name?"

All at once the meal lay like lead at his stomach.

"What is her name?"

"Mim," he said, and reached for the *telise,* swallowed some of its vaporous fire.

"Did you compromise the girl? Is that the reason for this sudden marriage?"

The cup froze in his hand. He looked at her, and all at once he knew she had meant it just as he had heard it, and flushed with heat, not the *telise.*

"I am in love with her."

Djan's cool eyes rested on him, estimating. "The nemet are a beautiful people. They have a certain attraction. And I suppose nemet women have a certain—flattering appeal to a man of our kind. They always let their men be right."

"It will not trouble you," he said.

"I am sure it will not." She let the implied threat hang in the air a moment and then shrugged lightly. "I have nothing personal against the child. I don't expect I'll ever have to consider the problem. I trust your good sense for that. Marry her. Occasionally you will find, as I do, that nemet thoughts and looks and manners—and nemet prejudices—are too much for you. That fact moved me, I admit it, or you would be keeping company with the Tamurlin—or the fishes. I had rather think we were companions,—human and reasonably civilized. This person Mim, she is only *chan;* she does at least provide a certain respectability if you are careful. I suppose it is not such a bad choice, so I do not think this marriage will be such an inconvenience to me. And I think you understand me, Kurt."

The cup shook in his hand. He put it aside, lest his fingers crush the fragile crystal.

"You are gambling your neck, Djan. I won't be pushed."

"I do not push," she said, "more than will make me understood. And I think we understand each other plainly."

7

The gray light of dawn was over Nephane, spreading through a mist that overlay all but the upper walls of the Afen. The cobbled street running down from the Afen gate was wet, and the few people who had business on the streets at that hour went muffled in cloaks.

Kurt stepped up to the front door of Elas, tried the handle in the quickly dashed hope that it would be unlocked, then knocked softly, not wanting to wake the whole house.

More quickly than he had expected, soft footsteps approached the door inside, hesitated. He stood squarely before the door to be surveyed from the peephole.

The bar flew back, the door was snatched inward, and Mim was there in her nightrobe. With a sob of relief she flung herself into his arms and hugged him tightly.

"Hush," he said, "it's all right; it's all right, Mim."

They were framed in the doorway. He brought her inside and closed and barred the heavy door. Mim stood wiping at her eyes with her wide sleeve.

"Is the house awake?" he whispered.

"Everyone finally went to bed. I came out again and waited in the *rhmei*. I hoped—I hoped you would come back. Are you all right, my lord?"

"I am well enough." He took her in his arm and walked with her to the warmth of the *rhmei*. There in the light her large eyes stared up at him and her hands pressed his, gentle as the touch of wind.

"You are shaking," she said. "Is it the cold?"

"It's cold and I'm tired." It was hard to slip back into Nechai after hours of human language. His accent crept out again.

"What did she want?"

"She asked me some questions. They held me all night—Mim, I just want to go upstairs and get some sleep. Don't worry. I am well, Mim."

"My lord," she said in a tear-choked voice, "before the *phus-meha* it is a great wrong to lie. Forgive me, but I know that you are lying."

"Leave me alone, Mim, please."

"It was not about the questions. If it was, look at me plainly and say that it was so."

He tried, and could not. Mim's dark eyes flooded with sadness.

"I am sorry," was all that he could say.

Her hands tightened on his. That terrible dark-eyed look would not let him go. "Do you wish to break the contract, or do you wish to keep it?"

"Do you?"

"If it is your wish."

With his chilled hand he smoothed the hair from her cheek and wiped at a streak of tears. "I do not love her," he said; and then, tribute to the honesty Mim herself used: "But I know how she feels, Mim. Sometimes I feel that way too. Sometimes all Elas is strange to me and I want to be human just for a little time. It is like that with her."

"She might give you children and you would be lord over all Nephane."

He crushed her against him, the faint perfume of *aluel* leaves about her clothing, a freshness about her skin, and remembered the synthetics-and-alcohol scent of Djan, human and, for the moment, pleasing. There was kindness in Djan; it made her dangerous, for it threatened her pride.

It threatened Elas.

"If it were in Djan's nature to marry, which it is not, I would still feel no differently, Mim. But I cannot say that this will be the last time I go to the Afen. If you cannot bear that, then tell me so now."

"I would be concubine and not first wife, if it was your wish."

"No," he said, realizing how she had heard it. "No, the only reason I would ever put you aside would be to protect you."

She leaned up on tiptoe and took his face between her two silken hands, kissed him with great tenderness. Then she drew back, hands still uplifted, as if unsure how he would react. She looked frightened.

"My lord husband," she said, which she was entitled to call him, being betrothed. The words had a strange sound between them. And she took liberties with him which he understood no honorable nemet lady would take with her betrothed, even in being alone with him. But she put all her manners aside to please him,—perhaps, he feared, to fight for him in her own desperate fashion.

He pressed her to him tightly and set her back again. "Mim, please. Go before someone wakes and sees you. I have to talk to Kta."

"Will you tell him what has happened?"

"I intend to."

"Please do not bring violence into this house."

"Go on, Mim."

She gave him an agonized look, but she did as he asked her.

He did not knock at Kta's door. There had already been too much noise in the sleeping house. Instead he opened it and slipped inside, crossed the floor and parted the curtain that screened the sleeping area before he spoke Kta's name.

The nemet came awake with a start and an oath, looked at Kurt with dazed eyes, then rolled out of bed and wrapped a kilt around himself. "Gods," he said, "you look deathly, friend. What happened? Are you all right? Is there some—?"

"I've just been put to explaining a situation to Mim," Kurt said, and found his limbs shaking under him, the delayed reaction to all that he had been through. "Kta, I need advice."

Kta showed him a chair. "Sit down, my friend. Compose your heart and I will help you if you can make me understand. Shall I find you something to drink?"

Kurt sat down and bowed his head, locked his fingers behind his neck until he made himself remember the calm that belonged in Elas. The scent of incense, the dim light of the *phusa,* the sense of stillness, all this comforted him, and the panic left him though the fear did not.

"I am all right," he said. "No, do not bother about the drink."

"You only now came in?" Kta asked him, for the morning showed through the window.

Kurt nodded, looked him in the eyes, and Kta let the breath hiss slowly between his teeth.

"A personal matter?" Kta asked with admirable delicacy.

"The whole of Elas seemed to have read matters better than I did when I went up to the Afen. Was it that obvious? Does the whole of Nephane know by now, or is there any privacy in this city?"

"Mim knew, at least. Kurt, Kurt, light of heaven, there was no need to guess. When the Methi's men came back to assure us of your safety, it was clear enough, coupled with the Methi's reaction to the betrothal. My friend, do not be ashamed. We always knew that your life would be bound to that of the Methi. Nephane has taken it for granted from the day you came. It was the betrothal to Mim that shocked everyone—I am speaking plainly. I think the truth has its moment, even if it is bitter. Yes, the whole of Nephane knows, and is by no means surprised."

Kurt swore, a raw and human oath, and gazed off at the window, unable to look at the nemet.

"Have you," said Kta, "love for the Methi?"

"No," he said harshly.

"You chose to go," Kta reminded him, "when Elas would have fought for you."

"Elas has no place in this."

"We have no honor if we let you protect us in this way. But it is not clear to us what your wishes are in this matter. Do you wish us to intervene?"

"I do not wish it," he answered.

"Is this the wish of your heart? Or do you still think to shield us? You owe us the plain truth, Kurt. Tell us yes or no and we will believe your word and do as you wish."

"I do not love the Methi," he said in a still voice, "but I do not want Elas involved between us."

"That tells me nothing."

"I expect," he said, finding it difficult to meet Kta's dark-eyed and gentle sympathy, "that it will not be the last time. I owe her, Kta. If my behavior offends the honor of Elas or of Mim, tell me. I have no wish to bring misery on this house, and least of all on Mim. Tell me what to do."

"Life," said Kta, "is a powerful urge. You protest you hate the Methi, and perhaps she hates you, but the urge to survive and perpetuate your kind—may be a sense of honor above every other honor. Mim has spoken to me of this."

He felt a deep sickness, thinking of that. At the moment he himself did not even wish to survive.

"Mim honors you," said Kta, "very much. If your heart toward her changed, still,—you are bound, my friend. I feared this; and Mim foreknew it. I beg you do not think of breaking this vow with Mim; it would dishonor her. *Ai,* my friend, my friend, we are a people that does not believe in sudden marriage, yet for once we were led by the heart, we were moved by the desire to make you and Mim happy. Now I hope that we have not been cruel instead. You cannot undo what you have done with Mim."

"I would not," Kurt said. "I would not change that."

"Then," said Kta, "all is well."

"I have to live in this city," said Kurt, "and how will people see this and how will it be for Mim?"

Kta shrugged. "This is the Methi's problem. It is common for a man to have obligations to more than one woman. One cannot, of course, have the Methi of Nephane for a common concubine. But it is for the woman's house to see to the proprieties and to obtain respectability. An honorable woman does so, as we have done for Mim. If a woman will not, or her family will not, matters are on her head, not yours. Though," he added, "a Methi can do rather well as he or she pleases, and this has been a common difficulty with Methis, particularly with human ones,—and the late Tehal-methi of Indresul was notorious. Djan-Methi is efficient. She is a good Methi. The people have bread and peace, and as long as that lasts, you can only obtain honor by your association with her. I am only concerned that your feelings may turn again to human things, and Mim be only of a strange people that for a time entertained you."

"No."

"I beg your forgiveness if this would never happen."

"It would never happen."

"I have offended my friend," said Kta. "I know you have grown nemet, and this part of you I trust; but forgive me: I do not know how to understand the other."

"I would do anything to protect Mim—or Elas."

"Then," said Kta in great earnestness, "think as nemet, not as human. Do nothing without your family. Keep nothing from your family. The Families are sacred. Even the Methi is powerless to do you harm when you stand with us and we with you."

"Then you do not know Djan."

"There is the law, Kurt. So long as you have not taken arms against her or directly defied her, the law binds her. She must go through the Upei, and a dispute—forgive me—with her lover— is hardly the kind of matter she could lay before the Upei."

"She could simply assign you and *Tavi* to sail to the end of the known world. She has alternatives, Kta."

"If the Methi chooses a quarrel with Elas," said Kta, "she will have chosen unwisely. Elas was here before the Methi came, and before the first human set foot on this soil. We know our city and our people, our voice is heard in councils on both sides of the Dividing Sea. When Elas speaks in the Upei, the Great Families listen; and now of all times the Methi dares not have the Great Families at odds with her. Her position is not as secure as it seems, which she knows full well, my friend."

8

The ship from Indresul came into port late on the day scheduled, a bireme with a red sail—the international emblem, Kta explained as he stood with Kurt on the dock, of a ship claiming immunity from attack. It would be blasphemy against the gods either to attack a ship bearing that color or to claim immunity without just cause.

The Nephanite crowds were ominously silent as the ambassador left his ship and came ashore. Characteristic of the nemet, there was no wild outburst of hatred, but people took just long enough moving back to clear a path for the ambassador's escort to carry the point that he was not welcome in Nephane.

Mor t'Uset ul Orm, white-haired and grim of face, made his way on foot up the hill to the height of the Afen and paid no heed to the soft curses that followed at his back.

"The house of Uset," said Kta as he and Kurt made their way uphill in the crowd, "that house on this side of the Dividing Sea, will not stir out of doors this day. They will not go into the Upei for very shame."

"Shame before Mor t'Uset or before the people of Nephane?"

"Both. It is a terrible thing when a house is divided. The Guardians of Uset on both sides of the sea are in conflict. *Ei, ei,* fighting the Tamurlin is joyless enough; it is worse that two races have warred against each other over this land; but when one thinks of war against one's own family, where gods and Ancestors are shared, whose hearth once burned with a common flame,—*ai,* heaven keep us from such a day."

"I do not think Djan will take this city to war. She knows too well where it leads."

"Neither side wants it," said Kta, "and the Indras-descended of Nephane want it least of all. Our quarrel with—"

Kta fell silent as they came to the place where the street narrowed to pass the gate in the lower defense wall. A man reaching the gate from the opposite direction was staring at them—tall, powerful, wearing the braid and striped robe that was not uncommon in the lower town and among the Methi's guard.

All at once Kurt knew him. Shan t'Tefur. Hate seemed in permanent residence in t'Tefur's narrow eyes. For a moment Kurt's heart pounded and his muscles tensed, for t'Tefur had stopped in the gate and seemed about to bar their way.

Kta jostled against Kurt, purposefully, clamped his arm in a hard grip unseen beneath the fold of the *ctan* and edged him through the gate, making it clear he should not stop.

"That man," said Kurt, resisting the urge to look back, for Kta's grip remained hard, warning him. "That man is from the Afen."

"Keep moving," Kta said.

They did not stop until they reached the high street, that area near the Afen which belonged to the mansions of the Families, great, rambling things, among which Elas was one of the most prominent. Here Kta seemed easier, and slowed his pace as they headed toward the door of Elas.

"That man," Kurt said then, "came where I was being held in the Afen. He brought me into the Methi's rooms. His name is t'Tefur."

"I know his name."

"He seems to have a dislike for humans."

"Hardly," said Kta. "It is a personal dislike. He has no fondness for either of us. He is Sufaki."

"I noticed—the braid, the robes,—that is not the dress of the Methi's guard, then?"

"No. It is Sufak."

"Osanef—Osanef is Sufaki. Han t'Osanef and Bel do not wear—"

"No. Osanef is Sufaki, but the *jafikn,* that long hair braided in the back, that is an ancient custom: the warrior's braid. No one has done it since the Conquest. It was forbidden the Sufaki then. But in recent years the rebel spirits have revived the custom— and the Robes of Color, which distinguish their houses. There are three Sufak houses of the ancient aristocracy surviving, and t'Tefur is of one. He is a dangerous man. His name is Shan t'Te-fur u Tlekef, or as he prefers to be known—Tlekefu Shan Tefur. He is Elas' bitter enemy, and he is yours, not alone for the sake of Elas."

"Because I'm human? But I understood Sufaki had no particular hate for—" And it dawned on him, with a sudden heat of the face.

"Yes," said Kta, "he has been the Methi's lover for many months."

"What—does your custom say he and I should do about it?"

"Sufak custom says he may try to make you fight him. And you must not. Absolutely you must not."

"Kta, I may be helpless in most things nemet, but if he wants to press a fight, that is something I can understand. Do you mean a fight, or do you mean a fight to the death? I am not that anxious to kill him over her, but neither am I going to be—"

"Listen. Hear what I am saying to you. You must avoid a fight with him. I do not question your courage or your ability. I am asking this for the sake of Elas. Shan t'Tefur is dangerous."

"Do you expect me to allow myself to be killed? Is he dangerous in that sense, or how?"

"He is a power among the Sufaki. He sought more power, which the Methi could give him. You have made him lose honor and you have threatened his position of leadership. You are resident with Elas, and we are of the Indras-descended. Until now, the Methi has inclined toward the Sufaki, ever since she dispensed with me as an interpreter. She has been surrounded by Sufaki, chosen friends of Shan t'Tefur, and has drawn much of her power from them, so much so that the Great Families are uneasy. But of a sudden Shan t'Tefur finds his footing unsteady."

They walked in silence for a moment. Increasingly bitter and embarrassed thoughts reared up. Kurt glanced at the nemet. "You pulled me from the harbor. You saved my life. You gave me everything I have—by Djan's leave. You went to her and asked for me, and if not for that—I would be—I would certainly not be walking the streets free. So do not misunderstand what I ask you. But you said that from the time I arrived in Nephane, people knew that I would become involved with the Methi. Was I pushed toward that, Kta? Was I aimed at her,—an Indras weapon—against Shan t'Tefur?"

And to his distress, Kta did not answer at once.

"Is it the truth, then?" Kurt asked.

"Kurt, you have married within my house."

"Is it true?" he insisted.

"I do not know how a human hears things," Kta protested. "Or whether you attribute to me motives no nemet would have, or fail to think what would be obvious to a nemet. Gods, Kurt—"

"Answer me."

"When I first saw you—I thought—He is the Methi's kind. Is that not most obvious? Is there offense in that? And I thought: He ought to be treated kindly, since he is a gentle being, and since one day he may be more than he seems now. And then an unworthy thought came to me: It would be profitable to your house, Kta t'Elas. And there is offense in that. At the time you were only human to me; and to a nemet, that does not oblige one to deal morally. I do offend you. I cause you pain. But that is the way it was. I think differently now. I am ashamed."

"So Elas took me in,—to use."

"No," said Kta quickly. "We would never have opened—"

His words died as Kurt kept staring at him. "Go ahead," said Kurt. "Or do I already understand?"

Kta met his eyes directly, contrition in a nemet. "Elas is holy to us. I owe you a truth. We would never have opened our doors to you—to anyone—Very well, I will say it: it is unthinkable that I would have exposed my hearth to human influence, whatever the advantage is promised with the Methi. Our hospitality is sacred, and not for sale for any favor. But I made a mistake—in my anxiousness to win your favor, I gave you my word; and the word of Elas is sacred too. So I accepted you. My friend, let our friendship survive this truth: when the other Families reproached Elas for taking a human into its *rhmei,* we argued simply that it was better for a human to be within an Indras house than that you be sent to the Sufaki instead, for the influence of the Sufaki is already dangerously powerful. And I think another consideration influenced Djan-methi in hearing me: that your life would have been in constant danger in a Sufak house, because of the honor of Shan t'Tefur,—although I dared not say it in words. So she sent you to Elas. I think she feared t'Tefur's reaction even if you remained in the Afen."

"I understand," said Kurt, because it seemed proper to say something. The words hurt. He did not trust himself to say much.

"Elas loves and honors you," said Kta, and when Kurt still failed to answer him he looked down, and with what appeared much thought, he cautiously extended his hand to take his arm, touching like Mim, with feather-softness. It was an unnatural gesture for the nemet; it was one studied, copied, offered now on the public street as an act of desperation.

Kurt stopped perforce, set his jaw against the tears which threatened.

"Avoid t'Tefur," Kta pleaded. "If the housefriend of Elas kills the heir of Tefur,—or if he kills you—killing will not stop there. He will provoke you if he can. Be wise. Do not let him do this."

"I understand. I have told you that."

Kta glanced down, gave the sketch of a bow. The hand dropped. They walked on, near to Elas.

"Have I a soul?" Kurt asked him suddenly, and looked at him.

The nemet's face was shocked, frightened.

"Have I a soul?" Kurt asked again.

"Yes," said Kta, which seemed difficult for him to say.

It was, Kurt thought, an admission which had already cost Kta some of his peace of mind.

The Upei, the council, met that day in the Afen and adjourned, as by law it must, as the sun set, to convene again at dawn.

Nym returned to the house at dusk, greeted lady Ptas and Hef at the door. When he came into the *rhmei* where the light was, the senator looked exhausted, utterly drained. Aimu hastened to bring water for washing, while Ptas prepared the tea.

There was no discussion of business during the meal. Such matters as Nym had on his mind were reserved for the rounds of tea that followed. Instead Nym asked politely after Mim's preparation for her wedding, and for Aimu's, for both were spending their days sewing, planning, discussing the coming weddings, keeping the house astir with their happy excitement and sometimes tears, and Aimu glanced down prettily and said that she had almost completed her own trousseau and that they were working together on Mim's things, for, Aimu thought, their beloved human was not likely to choose the long formal engagement such as she had had with Bel.

"I met our friend the elder t'Osanef," said Nym in answer to that, "and it is not unlikely, little Aimu, that we will advance the date of your own wedding."

"*Ei*," murmured Aimu, her dark eyes suddenly wide. "How far, honored Father?"

"Perhaps within a month."

"Beloved husband," exclaimed Ptas in dismay, "such haste?"

"There speaks a mother," Nym said tenderly. "Aimu, child, do you and Mim go fetch another pot of tea. And then go to your sewing. There is business afoot hereafter."

"Shall I—?" asked Kurt, offering by gesture to depart.

"No, no, our guest. Please sit with us. This business concerns the house, and you are soon to be one of us."

The tea was brought and served with all formality. Then Mim and Aimu withdrew, leaving the men of the house and Ptas. Nym took a slow sip of tea and looked at his wife.

"You had a question, Ptas?"

"Who asked the date advanced? Osanef? Or was it you?"

"Ptas, I fear we are going to war." And in the stillness that awful word made in the room he continued very softly: "If we wish this marriage I think we must hurry it on with all decent speed; a wedding between Sufaki and Indras may serve to heal the division between the Families and the sons of the east; that is still our hope. But it must be soon."

The lady of Elas wept quiet tears and blotted them with the edge of her scarf. "What will they do? It is not right, Nym, it is not right that they should have to bear such a weight on themselves."

"What would you? Break the engagement? That is impossible. For us to ask that—no. No. And if the marriage is to be, then there must be haste. With war threatening,—Bel would surely wish to leave a son to safeguard the name of Osanef. He is the last of his name. As you are, Kta, my son. I am above sixty years of age, and today it has occurred to me that I am not immortal. You should have laid a grandson at my feet years ago."

"Yes, sir," said Kta quietly.

"You cannot mourn the dead forever; and I wish you would make some choice for yourself, so that I would know how to please you. If there is any young woman of the Families who has touched your heart—"

Kta shrugged, looking at the floor.

"Perhaps," his father suggested gently, "the daughters of Rasim or of Irain . . ."

"Tai t'Isulan,—" said Kta.

"A lovely child," said Ptas, "and she will be a fine lady."

Again Kta shrugged. "A child, indeed. But I do at least know her, and I think I would not be unpleasing to her."

"She is—what?—seventeen?" asked Nym, and when Kta agreed: "Isulan is a fine religious house. I will think on it and perhaps I will talk with Ban t'Isulan, if in several days you still think the same. —My son, I am sorry to bring this matter upon you so suddenly, but you are my only son, and these are sudden times. Ptas, pour some *telise*."

She did so. The first few sips were drunk in silence. This was proper. Then Nym sighed softly.

"Home is very sweet, wife. May we abide as we are tonight."

"May it be so," reverently echoed Ptas, and Kta did the same.

"The matter in council," said Ptas then. "What was decided?"

Nym frowned and stared at nothing in particular. "T'Uset is not here to bring peace, only more demands of the Methi Ylith. Djan-methi was not in the Upei today; it did not seem wise. And I suspect—" His eyes wandered to Kurt, estimating; and Kurt's face went hot. Suddenly he gathered himself to leave, but Nym forbade that with a move of his hand, and he settled again, bowing low and not meeting Nym's eyes.

"Our words could offend you," said Nym. "I pray not."

"I have learned," said Kurt, "how little welcome my people have made for themselves among you."

"Friend of my son," said Nym gently, "your wise and peaceful attitude is an ornament to this house. I will not affront you by repeating t'Uset's words. Reason with him proved impossible: the Indras of the mother city hate humans, and they will not negotiate with Djan-methi. And that is not the end of our troubles." His eyes sought Ptas. "T'Tefur created bitter discussion, even before t'Uset was seated, demanding we not permit him to be present during the Invocation."

"Light of heaven," murmured Ptas. "In t'Uset's hearing?"

"He was at the door."

"We met the younger t'Tefur today," said Kta. "There were no words, but his manner was deliberate and provocative, aimed at Kurt."

"Is it so?" said Nym, concerned, and with a glance at Kurt: "Do not fall into his hands. Do not place yourself where you can become a cause, our friend."

"I am warned," said Kurt.

"Today," said Nym, "there was a curse spoken between the house of Tefur and the house of Elas, before the Upei, and we must all be on our guard. T'Tefur blasphemed, shouting down the Invocation, and I answered him as his behavior deserved. He calls it treason, that when we pray we still call on the name of Indresul the shining. This he said in t'Uset's hearing."

"And for the likes of this," said lady Ptas, "we must endure to be cursed from the hearthfire of Elas-in-Indresul, and have our name pronounced annually in infamy at the Shrine of Man."

"Mother," said Kta, bowing low, "not all Sufaki feel so. Bel would not feel this way. He would not."

"T'Tefur's number is growing," said Ptas, "that he dares to stand in the Upei and say such a thing."

Kurt looked from one to the other in bewilderment. It was Nym who undertook to explain to him. "We are Indras. A thousand years ago Nai-methi of Indresul launched colonies toward the Isles, south of this shore, then laid the foundations of Nephane as a fortress to guard the coast from Sufaki pirates. He destroyed Chteftikan, the capital of the Sufaki kingdom, and Indras colonists administered the new provinces from this citadel. For most of time we ruled the Sufaki. But the coming of humans cut our ties to Indresul, and when we came out of those dark years, we wiped out all the cruel laws that kept the Sufaki subject, accepted them into the Upei. For t'Tefur, that is not enough. There is great bitterness there."

"It is religion," said Ptas. "Sufaki have many gods, and believe in magic and worship demons. Not all. Bel's house is better educated. But Indras will not set foot in the precincts of the temple, the so-named Oracle of Phan. And it would be dangerous in these times even to be there in the wall-street after dark. We pray at our own hearths and invoke the Ancestors we have in common with the houses across the Dividing Sea. We do them no harm—we inflict nothing on them, but they resent this."

"But," said Kurt, "you do not agree with Indresul."

"It is impossible," said Nym. "We are of Nephane. We have lived among Sufaki; we have dealt with humans. We cannot unlearn the things we know for truth. We will fight if we must, against Indresul. The Sufaki seem not to believe that, but it is so."

"No," said Kurt, and with such passion that the nemet were hushed. "No. Do not go to war."

"It is excellent advice," said Nym after a moment. "But we may be helpless to guide our own affairs. When a man finds his affairs without resolution, his existence out of time with heaven and his very being a disturbance to the *yhia,* then he must choose to die for the sake of order. He does well if he does so without violence. In the eyes of heaven even nations are finally answerable to such logic, and even nations may sometimes be compelled to suicide. They have their methods,—being many minds and not one, they cannot proceed toward their fate with the dignity a single man can manage, but proceed they do."

"*Ei,* honored Father," said Kta, "I beg you not to say such things."

"Like Bel, do you believe in omens? I do not,—not, at least, that words, ill-thought or otherwise, have power over the future. The future already exists, in our hearts already, stored up and waiting to unfold when we reach our time and place. Our own nature is our fate. You are young, Kta. You deserve better than my age has given you."

There was silence in the *rhmei*. Suddenly Kurt bowed himself a degree lower, requesting, and Nym looked at him.

"You have a Methi," said Kurt, "who is not willing to fight a war. Please. Trust me to go speak to her, as another human."

There was a stir of uneasiness. Kta opened his mouth as if he would protest, but Nym consented.

"Go," he said, nothing more.

Kurt rose and adjusted his *ctan,* pinning it securely. He bowed to them collectively and turned to leave. Someone hurried after; he thought it was Hef, whose duty it was to tend the door. It was Kta who overtook him in the outer hall.

"Be careful," Kta said. And when he opened the outer door into the dark: "Kurt, I will walk to the Afen with you."

"No," said Kurt. "Then you would have to wait there, and you would be obvious at this hour. Let us not make this more obvious than need be."

But there was, once the door was closed and he was on the street in the dark, an uneasy feeling about the night. It was quieter than usual. A man muffled in striped robes stood in the shadows of the house opposite. Kurt turned and walked quickly uphill.

Djan put her back to the window that overlooked the sea and leaned back against the ledge, a metallic form against the dark beyond the glass. Tonight she dressed as human, in a dark blue form-fitting synthetic that shimmered like powdered glass along the lines of her figure. It was a thing she would not dare wear among the modest nemet.

"The Indras ambassador sails tomorrow," she said. "Confound it, couldn't you have waited? I'm trying to keep humanity out of his sight and hearing as much as possible, and you have to be walking up and down the halls—He's staying on the floor just below. If one of his staff had come out—"

"This isn't a social call."

Djan expelled her breath slowly, nodded him toward a seat near her. "Elas and the business in the Upei. I heard. What did they send you to say?"

"They didn't send me. But if you have any means of controlling the situation, you'd better exert it,—fast."

Her cool green eyes measured him, centered soberly on his. "You're scared. What Elas said must have been considerable."

"Stop putting words in my mouth. There's going to be nothing left but Indresul to pick up the pieces if this goes on. There was some kind of balance here, Djan. There was stability. You blew it to—"

"Nym's words?"

"No. Listen to me."

"There was a balance of power, yes," Djan said. "A balance tilted in favor of the Indras and against the Sufaki. I have done nothing but use impartiality. The Indras are not used to that."

"Impartiality. Do you maintain that with Shan t'Tefur?"

Her head went back. Her eyes narrowed slightly, but then she grinned. She had a beautiful smile, even when there was no humor in it. "Ah," she said. "I should have told you. Now your feelings are ruffled."

"I'm sure I don't care," he said, started to add something more cutting still, and then regretted even what he had said. He had, after a fashion, cared; perhaps she had feelings for him also. There was anger in her eyes, but she did not let it fly.

"Shan," she said, "is a friend. His family were lords of this land once. He thinks he can bend me to his ambitions, which are probably considerable, and he is slowly learning he can't. He is angry about your presence, which is an anger that will heal. I believe him about as much as I believe you when your own interests are at stake. I weigh all that either of you says, and try to analyze where the bias lies."

"Being yourself perfect, of course."

"In this government there does not have to be a Methi. Methis serve when it is useful to have one—In times of crisis, to bind civil and military authority into one swiftly-moving whole. My reason for being is somewhat different. I am Methi precisely because I am neither Sufaki nor Indras. Yes, the Sufaki support me. If I stepped down, the Indras would immediately appoint an Indras Methi. The Upei is Indras: nobility is the qualification for membership, and there are only three noble houses of the Sufaki surviving. The others were massacred a thousand years ago. Now Elas is marrying a daughter into one—so Osanef too becomes a limb of the Families. The Upei makes the laws: and the Assembly may be Sufaki, but all they can do is vote yea or nay on what the Upei deigns to hand them. The Assembly hasn't rallied to veto anything since the day of its creation. So what else do the Sufaki have but the Methi? Oppose the Families by veto in the Assembly? Hardly likely, when the living of the Sufaki depend on big shipping companies like Irain and Ilev and Elas. A little frustration burst out today. It was regrettable. But if it makes the Families realize the seriousness of the situation, then perhaps it was well done."

"It was not well done," Kurt said. "Not when it was done, nor where it was done, nor against what it was done. The ambassador witnessed it. Did your informants tell you that detail? Djan, your selective blindness is going to make chaos out of this city. Listen to the Families. Call in their Fathers. Listen to them as you listen to Shan t'Tefur."

"Ah, so it does rankle."

He stood up. She resented his speaking to her. It had been on the edge of every word. It was in his mind to walk out, but that would let her forget everything he had said. Necessity overcame his pride. "Djan. I have nothing against you. In spite of—because of—what we did one night, I have a certain regard for you. I had some hope you might at least listen to me, for the sake of all concerned."

"I will look into it," she said. "I will do what I can." And when he turned to go: "I hear little from you. Are you happy in Elas?"

He looked back, surprised by the gentleness of her asking. "I am happy," he said.

She smiled. "In some measure I do envy you."

"The same choices are open to you."

"No," she said. "Not by nemet law. Think of me and think of your little Mim, and you will know what I mean. I am Methi. I do as I please. Otherwise this world would put bonds on me that I couldn't live with. It would make your life miserable if you had to accept such terms as this world would offer me. I refuse."

"I understand," he said. "I wish you well, Djan."

She let the smile grow sad, and stared out at the lights of Nephane a moment, ignoring him.

"I am fond of few people," she said. "In your peculiar way you have gotten into my affections,—more than Shan, more than most who have their reason for using me. Get out of here, back to Elas, discreetly. Go on."

9

The wedding Mim chose was a small and private one. The guests and witnesses were scarcely more numerous than what the law required. Of Osanef, there was Han t'Osanef u Mur, his wife Ia t'Nefak, and Bel. Of the house of Ilev there was Ulmar t'Ilev ul Imetan and his wife Tian t'Elas e Ben, cousin to Nym, and their son Cam and their new daughter-in-law, Yanu t'Pas. They were all people Mim knew well, and Osanef and Ilev, Kurt suspected, were among a very few nemet houses that could be found reconciled to the marriage on religious grounds.

If even these had scruples about the question, they had the grace still to smile and to love Mim and to treat her chosen husband with great courtesy.

The ceremony was in the *rhmei,* where Kurt first knelt before old Hef and swore that the first two sons of the union, if any, would be given the name h'Elas as *chani* to the house, so that Hef's line could continue.

And Kta swore also to the custom of *iquun,* by which Kta would see to the begetting of the promised heirs, if necessary.

Then Nym rose and with palms toward the light of the *phus-meha* invoked the guardian spirits of the Ancestors of Elas. The sun outside was only beginning to set. It was impossible to conduct a marriage-rite after Phan had left the land.

"Mim," said Nym, taking her hand, "called Mim-lechan h'Elas e Hef, you are *chan* to this house no longer, but become as a daughter of this house, well-beloved, Mim h'Elas e Hef. Are you willing to yield your first two sons to Hef, your foster-father?"

"Yes, my lord of Elas."

"Are you consenting to all the terms of the marriage contract?"

"Yes, my lord of Elas."

"Are you willing now, daughter to Elas, to bind yourself by these final and irrevocable vows?"

"Yes, my lord of Elas."

"And you, Kurt Liam t'Morgan u Patrick Edward, are you willing to bind yourself by these final and irrevocable vows, to take this free woman Mim h'Elas e Hef for your true and first wife, loving her before all others, commiting your honor into her hands and your strength and fortune to her protection?"

"Yes, my lord."

"Hef h'Elas," said Nym, "the blessing of this house and its Guardians upon this union."

The old man came forward, and it was Hef who completed the ceremony, giving Mim's hand into Kurt's and naming for each the final vows they made. Then, according to custom, Ptas lit a torch from the great *phusmeha* and gave it into Kurt's hands, and he into Mim's.

"In purity I have given," Kurt recited the ancient formula in High Nechai, "in reverence preserve, Mim h'Elas e Hef shu-Kurt, well-beloved, my wife."

"In purity I have received," she said softly, "in reverence I will keep myself to thee to the death, Kurt Liam t'Morgan u Patrick Edward, my lord, my husband."

And with Mim beside him, and to the ritual weeping of the ladies and the congratulations of the men, Kurt left the *rhmei.* Mim carried the light, walking behind him up the stairs to the door of his room that now was hers.

He entered, and watched as she used the torch to light the triangular bronze lamp, the *phusa,* which had been replaced in its niche, and he heard her sigh softly with relief, for the omen would have been terrible if the light had not taken. The lamp of Phan burned with steady light, and she then extinguished the torch with a prayer and knelt down before the lamp as Kurt closed the door, knelt down and lifted her hands before it.

"My Ancestors, I, Mim t'Nethim e Sel shu-Kurt, called by these my beloved friends Mim h'Elas, I, Mim, beg your forgiveness for marrying under a name not my own, and swear now by my own name to honor the vows I made under another. My Ancestors, behold this man, my husband Kurt t'Morgan, and whatever distant spirits are his, be at peace with them for my sake. Peace, I pray my Fathers, and let peace be with Elas on both sides of the Dividing Sea. *Ei*, let thoughts of war be put aside between our two lands. May love be in this house and upon us both forever. May the terrible Guardians of Nethim hear me and receive the vow I make. And may the great Guardians of Elas receive me kindly as you have ever done, for we are of this house now, and within your keeping."

She lowered her hands, finishing her prayer, and offered her right hand to Kurt, who drew her up.

"Mim t'Nethim," he said. "Then I had never heard your real name."

Her large eyes lifted to him. "Nethim has no house in Nephane, but in Indresul we are ancestral enemies to Elas. I have not burdened Kta with knowing my true name. He asked me, and I would not answer, so surely he suspects that I am of a hostile house; but if there is any harm in my silence, it is upon me only. And I have spoken your name before the Guardians of Nethim many times, and I have not felt that they are distressed at you, my lord Kurt."

He had started to take her in his arms, but hesitated now, held his hands a little apart from her, suddenly fearing Mim and her strangeness. Her gown was beautiful and had cost days of work which he had watched; he did not know how to undo it, or if this was expected of him. And Mim herself was as complex and unknowable, wrapped in customs for which Kta's instructions had not prepared him.

He remembered the frightened child that Kta had found among the Tamurlin, and feared that she would suddenly see him as human and loathe him, without the robes and the graces that made him—outwardly—nemet.

"Mim," he said. "I would never see any harm come to you."

"It is a strange thing to say, my lord."

"I am afraid for you," he said suddenly. "Mim, I do love you."

She smiled a little, then laughed, down-glancing. He treasured the gentle laugh: it was Mim at her prettiest. And she slipped her hands about his waist and hugged him tightly, her strong slim arms dispelling the fear that she would break.

"Kurt," she said, "Kta is a dear man, most honored of me. I know that you and he have spoken of me. Is this not so?"

"Yes," he said.

"Kta has spoken to me too: he fears for me. I honor his concern. It is for both of us. But I trust your heart where I do not know your ways; I know if ever you hurt me, it would be much against your will." She slipped her warm hands to him. "Let us have tea, my husband, a first warming of our hearth."

That was much against his will, but it pleased her. She lit the small room-stove, which also heated, and boiled water and made them tea, which they enjoyed sitting on the bed together.

He had little to say but much on his mind; neither did Mim, but she looked often at him.

"Is it not enough tea?" he asked finally, with the same patient courtesy he always used in Elas, which Kta had taught his unwilling spirit. But this time there was great earnestness in the question, which brought a sly smile from Mim.

"What is your custom now?" she asked of him.

"What is yours?" he asked.

"I do not know," she admitted, down-glancing and seeming distressed. Then for the first time he realized, and felt pained for his thoughtlessness: she had never been with a man of her own kind,—nor with any man of decency.

"Put up the teacups," he said, "and come here, Mim."

The light of morning came through the window and Kurt stirred in his sleep, his hand finding the smoothness of Mim beside him, and he opened his eyes and looked at her. Her eyes were closed, her lashes dark and heavy on her golden cheek, her full lips relaxed in dreams. A little scar marred her temple, as others not so slight marked her back and hips, and that anyone could have abused Mim was a thought he could not bear.

He moved, leaned on his arm across her and touched his lips to hers, smoothed aside the dark and shining veil of hair that flowed across her and across the pillows, and she stirred, responding sweetly to his morning kiss.

"Mim," he said, "good morning."

Her arms went around his neck. She pulled herself up and kissed him back. Then she blinked back tears, which he made haste to wipe away.

"Mim?" he questioned her, much troubled; but she smiled at him and even laughed.

"Dear Kurt," she said, holding his face between her hands. And then, breaking for the side of the bed, she began to wriggle free. "*Ei, ei,* my lord, I must hurry,—you must hurry—the sun is up. The guests will be waiting."

"Guests?" he echoed, dismayed. "Mim—"

But she was already slipping into her dressing gown, then pattering away into the bath. He heard her putting wood into the stove.

"It is custom," she said, putting her head back through the doorway of the bath. "They come back at dawn to breakfast with us.—Oh please, Kurt, please, hurry to be ready. They will be downstairs already, and if we are much past dawning, they will laugh."

It was the custom, Kurt resolved to himself, and nerved himself to face the chill air and the cold stone floor, when he had planned a far warmer and more pleasant morning.

He joined Mim in the bath and she washed his back for him, making clouds of comfortable steam with the warm water, laughing and not at all caring that the water soaked her dressing gown.

She was content with him.

At times the warmth in her eyes or the lingering touch of her fingers said she was more than content.

The hardest thing that faced them was to go down the stairs into the *rhmei,* at which Mim actually trembled. Kurt took her arm and would have brought her down with his support, but the idea shocked her. She shook free of him and walked like a proper nemet lady, independently behind him down the stairs.

The guests and family met them at the foot of the steps and brought them into the *rhmei* with much laughter and with ribald jokes that Kurt would not have believed possible from the modest nemet. He was almost angry, but when Mim laughed he knew that it was proper, and forgave them.

After the round of greetings, Aimu came and served the morning tea, hot and sweet, and the elders sat in chairs while the younger people—Kurt and Mim included, and Hef, who was *chan,*—sat upon rugs on the floor and drank their tea and listened to the elders talk. Kta played one haunting song for them on the *aos,* without words, but just for listening and for being still.

Mim would be honored in the house and exempt from duties for the next few days, after which time she would again take her share with Ptas and Aimu; she sat now and accepted the attentions and the compliments and the good wishes,—Mim, who had never expected to be more than a minor concubine to the lord of Elas, accepted with private vows and scant legitimacy—now she was the center of everything.

It was her hour.

Kurt begrudged her none of it, even the nemet humor. He looked down at her and saw her face alight with pride and happiness—and love, which she would have given with lesser vows had he insisted; and he smiled back and pressed her hand, which the others kindly did not elect to make joke of at that moment.

10

Ten days passed before the outside world intruded again into the house of Elas.

It came in the person of Bel t'Osanef u Han, who arrived, escorted by Mim, in the garden at the rear of the house, where Kta was instructing Kurt in the art of the *ypan,* the narrow curved longsword that was the Indras' favorite weapon and chief sport.

Kurt saw Bel come into the garden and turned his blade and held it in both hands to signal halt. Kta checked himself in midstrike, and turned his head to see the reason of the pause. Then with the elaborate ritual that governed the friendly use of these edged weapons, Kta touched his left hand to his sword and bowed, which Kurt returned. The nemet believed such ritual was necessary to maintain balance of soul between friends who contended in sport, and distrusted the blades. In the houses of the Families resided the *ypai-sulim,* the Great Weapons which had been dedicated in awful ceremony to the house Guardians and bathed in blood. These were never drawn unless a man had determined to kill or to die, and could not be sheathed again until they had taken a life. Even these light foils must be handled carefully, lest the ever-watchful house spirits mistake someone's intent and cause blood to be drawn.

And once it had been death to the Sufaki to touch these lesser weapons, or even to look at the *ypai-sulim* where they hung at rest, so that fencing was an art the Sufaki had never employed: they were skilled with the spear and the bow—distance-weapons.

Bel waited at a respectful distance until the weapons were

safely sheathed and laid aside, and then came forward and bowed.

"My lords," said Mim, "shall I bring tea?"

"Do so, Mim, please," said Kta. "Bel, my soon-to-be brother—"

"Kta," said Bel. "My business is somewhat urgent."

"Sit then," said Kta, puzzled. There were several stone benches about the garden. They took those nearest.

Then Aimu came from the house. She bowed modestly to her brother. "Bel," she said then, "you come into Elas without at least sending me greetings? What is the matter?"

"Kta," said Bel, "permission for your sister to sit with us."

"Granted," said Kta, a murmured formality, as thoughtless as "thank you." Aimu sank down on the seat near them. There were no further words. Tea had been asked; Bel's mood was distraught. There was no discussion proper until it had come, and it was not long. Mim brought it on a tray, a full service with extra cups.

Aimu rose up and helped her serve, and then both ladies settled on the same bench while the first several sips that courtesy demanded were drunk in silence and with appreciation.

"My friend Bel," said Kta, when ritual was satisfied, "is it unhappiness or anger or need that has brought you to this house?"

"May the spirits of our houses be at peace," said Bel. "I am here now because I trust you above all others save those born in Osanef. I am afraid there is going to be bloodshed in Nephane."

"T'Tefur," exclaimed Aimu with great bitterness.

"I beg you, Aimu, hear me to the end before you stop me."

"We listen," said Kta, "but, Bel, I suddenly fear this is a matter best discussed between our fathers."

"Our fathers' concern must be with Tlekef; Shan t'Tefur is beneath their notice—but he is the dangerous one, much more than Tlekef. Shan and I—we were friends. You know that. And you must realize how hard it is for me to come now to an Indras house and say what I am going to say. I am trusting you with my life."

"Bel," said Aimu in distress, "Elas will defend you."

"She is right," said Kta, "but Kurt—may not wish to hear this."

Kurt gathered himself to leave: it was Bel's willingness to have him stay that Kta questioned; he had been long enough in Elas to understand nemet subtleties. It was expected of Bel to demur.

"He must stay," said Bel, with more feeling than courtesy demanded. "He is involved."

Kurt settled down again, but Bel remained silent a time thereafter, staring fixedly at his own hands.

"Kta," he said finally, "I must speak now as Sufaki. There was a time, you know, when we ruled this land from the rock of Nephane to the Tamur and inland to the heart of Chteftikan and east to the Gray Sea. Nothing can ever bring back those days; we realize that. You have taken from us our land, our gods, our language, our customs,—you accept us as brothers only when we look like you and talk like you, and you despise us for savages when we are different. —It is true, Kta: look at me. Here am I, born a prince of the Osanef, and I cut my hair and wear Indras robes and speak with the clear round tones of Indresul, like a good civilized man, and I am accepted. Shan is braver. He does what many of us would do if we did not find life so comfortable on your terms. But Elas taught him a lesson I did not learn."

"He left us in anger. I have not forgotten the day. But you stayed."

"I was eleven; Shan was twelve. At that time we thought it a great thing—to be friends to an Indras, to be asked beneath the roof of one of the Great Families, to mingle with the Indras. I had come many times; but this day I brought Shan with me, and Ian t'Ilev chanced to be your guest also that day. Ian made it clear enough that he thought our manners quaint. Shan left on the instant; you prevented me, and persuaded me to stay, for we were closer friends, and longer friends. And from that day Shan t'Tefur and I had in more than that sense gone our separate ways. I could not call him back. The next day when I met him I tried to convince him to go back to you and speak with you,—but he would not. He struck me in the face and cursed me from him, and said that Osanef was fit for nothing but to be servant to the Indras—he said it in cruder words—and that he would not. He has not ceased to despise me."

"It was not well done," said Kta. "I had bitter words with Ian over the matter, until he came to a better understanding of courtesy, and my father went to Ilev's father. I assure you it was done. I did not tell you so; there never seemed a moment apt for it."

"Kta,—if I had been Indras, would you have found a moment apt for it?"

Kta gave back a little, his face sobered and troubled. "Bel, if you were Indras, your father would have come to Elas in anger and I would have been dealt with by mine—most harshly. I did not think it mattered, since your customs are different. But times are changing. You will become marriage-kin to Elas. Can you doubt that you would have justice from us?"

"I do not question your friendship," he said, and looked at Aimu. "Times change, when a Sufaki can marry an Indras, where once Sufaki were not admitted to an Indras *rhmei* where they could meet the daughters of a Family. But there are still limitations, friend Kta. We try to be businessmen and we are constantly outmaneuvered and outbid by the combines of wealthy Indras houses; information passes from hearth to hearth along lines of communication we do not share. When we go to sea, we sail under Indras captains, as I do for you, my friend,— because we have not the wealth to maintain warships as a rule,—seldom ever merchantmen. A man like Shan, that makes himself different, who wears the *jafikn,* who wears the Robes of Color, who keeps his accent—you ridicule him with secret smiles, for what was once unquestioned honor to a man of our people. There is so little left to us of what we were. Do you know, Kta, after all these years,—that I am not really Sufaki? Is that a surprise to you? You have ruined us so completely that you do not even know our real name. The people of this coast are Sufaki, the ancient name of this province when we ruled it, but the house of Osanef and the house of Tefur are Chteftik, from the old capital. And my name, despite the way I have corrupted it to please Indras tongues, is not Bel t'Osanef u Han. It is Hanu Balaket Osanef, and nine hundred years ago we rivaled the Insu dynasty for power in Chteftikan. A thousand years ago, when you were struggling colonists, we were kings, and no man would dare approach us on his feet. Now I change my name to show I am civilized, and bear with you when your cultured accent mispronounces it. Kta, Kta, I am not bitter with you. I tell you these things so that you will understand, because I know that Elas is one Indras house who might listen. You Indras are not trusted. There is talk of some secret accommodation you may have made with your kinsmen of Indresul,—talk that all your vowing war is empty, that you only do this like fisherman at a market, to increase the price in your bargain with Indresul."

"Now hold up on that point," Kta broke in, and for the first time anger flashed in his eyes. "Since you have felt moved to honesty with me,—which I respect,—hear me, and I will return it. If Indresul attacks, we will fight. It has always been a fault in Sufaki reasoning that you assume Indresul loves us like its lost children; quite the contrary. We are yearly cursed in Indresul, by the very families you think we share. We share Ancestors up to a thousand years ago, but beyond that point we are two hearths, and two opposed sets of Ancestors, and we are Nephanite. By the very hearth-loyalty you fear so much, Nephanite, and by the light of heaven I swear to you there is no such conspiracy among the Families. We took your land, yes, and there were cruel laws, yes, but that is in the past, Bel. Would you have us abandon our ways and become Sufaki? We would die first. But I do not think we impose our ways on you. We do not force you to adopt our dress or to honor our customs save when you are under our roof. You yourselves give most honor to those who seem Indras. You hate each other too much to unite for trade as our great houses do. Shan t'Tefur himself admits that when he pleads with you to make companies and rival us for trade. By all means. It would improve the lot of your poor, who are a charge on us."

"And why, Kta? You assume that we can rise to your level. But have you ever thought that we might not want to be like you?"

"Do you have another answer? Some urge it, like Shan,—to destroy all that is Indras. Will that solve matters?"

"No. We will never know what we might have been; our nation is gone, merged with yours. But I doubt we would like your ways, even if things were upside down and we were ruling you."

"Bel," exclaimed Aimu, "you cannot think these things: you are upset. Your mind will change."

"No, it has never been different. I have always known it is an Indras world, and that my sons and my sons' sons will grow more and more Indras, until they will not understand the mind of the likes of me. I love you, Aimu, and I do not repent my choice, but perhaps now you do. I do not think your well-bred Indras friends would think you disgraced if you broke our engagement. Most would be rather relieved you had come to your senses, I think."

Kta's back stiffened. "Have a care, Bel. My sister has not deserved your spite. Anything you may care to say or do with me—that is one matter; but you go too far when you speak that way to her."

"I beg pardon," Bel murmured, and glanced at Aimu. "We were friends before we were betrothed, Aimu; I think you know how to understand me, and I fear you may come to regret me and our agreement. A Sufaki house will be a strange enough place for you; I would not see you hurt."

"I hold by our agreement," said Aimu. Her face was pale, her breathing quick. "Kta, take no offense with him."

Kta lowered his eyes, made a sign of unwilling apology, then glanced up. "What do you want of me, Bel?"

"Your influence. Speak to your Indras friends; make them understand."

"Understand what? That they must cease to be Indras and imitate Sufaki ways? This is not the way the world is ordered, Bel. And as for violence, if it comes, it will not come from the Indras—that is not our way and it never has been. Persuasion is something you must use on your people."

"You have created a Shan Tefur," said Bel, "and he finds many others like him. Now we who have been friends of the Indras do not know what to do." Bel was trembling. He clasped his hands, elbows on his knees. "There is no more peace, Kta. But let no Indras answer violence with violence, or there will be blood flowing in the streets come the month of Nermotai and the holy days. —Your pardon, my friends." He rose, shaking out his robes. "I know the way out of Elas. You do not have to lead me. Do what you will with what I have told you."

"Bel," said Aimu, "Elas will not put you off for the sake of Shan t'Tefur's threats."

"But Osanef has to fear those threats. Do not expect me to be seen here again in the near future. I do not cease to regard you as my friends. I have faith in your honor and your good judgment, Kta. Do not fail my hopes."

"Let me go with him to the door," said Aimu, though what she asked violated all custom and modesty, "Kta, please."

"Go with him," said Kta. "Bel, my brother, we will do what we can. Be careful for yourself."

11

Nephane was well named the city of mists. They rolled in and lasted for days as the weather grew warmer, making the cobbled streets slick with moisture. Ships crept carefully into harbor, the lonely sound of their bells occasionally drifting up the height of Nephane through the still air. Voices distantly called out in the streets, muted.

Kurt looked back, anxious, wondering if the sudden hush of footsteps that had been with him ever since the door of Elas meant an end of pursuit.

A shadow appeared near him. He stumbled off the edge of the unseen curb and caught his balance, fronted by several others who appeared, cloaked and anonymous, out of the grayness. He backed up and halted, warned by a scrape of leather on stone: others were behind him. His belly tightened, muscles braced.

One moved closer. The whole circle narrowed. He ducked, darted between two of them and ran. Soft laughter pursued him, nothing more. He did not stop running.

The Afen gate materialized out of the fog. He pushed the heavy gate inward. He had composed himself by the time he reached the main door. The guards stayed inside on this inclement day, and only looked up from their game, letting him pass,—alert enough, but, Sufaki-wise, careless of formalities. He shrugged the *ctan* back to its conventional position under his right arm and mounted the stairs. Here the guards came smartly to attention: Djan's alien sense of discipline: and they for once made to protest his entry.

He pushed past and opened the door, and one of them then

hurried into the room and back into the private section of the apartments, presumably to announce his presence.

He had time enough to pace the floor, returning several times to the great window in the neighboring room. Fog-bound as the city was, he could scarcely make out anything but Haichema-tleke, Maiden Rock, the crag that rose over the harbor, against whose shoulder the Afen and the Great Families' houses were built. Gray and ghostly in a world of pallid white, it seemed the cloud-city's anchor to solid earth.

A door hissed upon the other room and he walked back. Djan was with him. She wore a silver-green suit, thin, body-clinging stuff. Her coppery hair was loose, silken and full of static. She had a morning look about her, satiated and full of sleep.

"It's near noon," he said.

"Ah," she murmured, and looked beyond him to the window. "So we're bound in again. Cursed fog. I hate it. —Like some breakfast?"

"No."

Djan shrugged and from utensils in the carved wood cabinet prepared tea, instantly heated. She offered him a cup: he accepted, nemet-schooled. It gave one something to do with the hands.

"I suppose," she said when they were seated, "that you didn't come here in this weather and wake me out of a sound sleep to wish me good morning."

"I almost didn't make it here; which is the situation I came to talk to you about. The neighborhood of Elas isn't safe even by day. There are Sufaki hanging about, who have no business there."

"The quarantine ordinances were repealed, you know. I can't forbid their being there."

"Are they your men? I'd be relieved if I thought they were. That is,—if yours and Shan t'Tefur's aren't one and the same, and I trust that isn't the case. For a long time it's been at night; since the first of Nermotai, it's been even by day."

"Have they hurt anyone?"

"Not yet. People in the neighborhood stay off the streets. Children don't go out. It's an ugly atmosphere, I don't know whether it's aimed at me in particular or Elas in general, but it's a matter of time before something happens."

"You haven't done anything to provoke this?"

"No. I assure you I haven't. But this is the third day of it. I finally decided to chance it. Are you going to do anything?"

"I'll have my people check it out, and if there's cause I'll have the people removed."

"Well, don't send Shan t'Tefur on the job."

"I said I would see to it. Don't ask favors and then turn sharp with me."

"I beg your pardon. But that's exactly what I'm afraid you'll do,—trust things to him."

"I am not blind, my friend. But you're not the only one with complaints. Shan's life has been threatened. I hear it from both sides."

"By whom?"

"I don't choose to give my sources. But you know the Indras houses and you know the hard-line conservatives. Make your own guess."

"The Indras are not a violent people. If they said it, it was more in the sense of a sober promise than a threat, and that in consideration of the actions he's been urging. You'll have riots in the streets if Shan t'Tefur has his way."

"I doubt it. See, I'm being perfectly honest with you: a bit of trust. Shan uses that apparent recklessness as a tactic; but he is an intelligent man, and his enemies would do well to reckon with that."

"And is he responsible for the late hours you've been keeping?"

Her eyes flashed suddenly, amused. "This morning, you mean?"

"Either you're naive or think he is. That is a dangerous man, Djan."

The humor died out of her eyes. "Well, you're one to talk about the dangers of involvement with the nemet."

"You're facing the danger of a foreign war and you need the goodwill of the Indras Families; but you keep company with a man who talks of killing Indras and burning the fleet."

"Words. If the Indras are concerned, good. I didn't create this situation: I walked into it as it is. I'm trying to hold this city together. There will be no war if it stays together. And it will stay together if the Indras come to their senses and give the Sufaki justice."

"They might, if Shan t'Tefur were out of it. Send him on a long voyage somewhere. If he stays in Nephane and kills someone, which is likely, sooner or later, then you're going to have to apply the law to him without mercy. And that will put you in a difficult position, won't it?"

"Kurt." She put down the cup. "Do you want fighting in this city? Then let's just start dealing like that with both sides, one ultimatum to Shan to get out, one to Nym, to be fair—and there won't be a stone standing in Nephane when the smoke clears."

"Try closing your bedroom to Shan t'Tefur," he said, "for a start. Your credibility among the Families is in rags as long as you're Shan t'Tefur's mistress."

It hurt her. He had thought it could not, and suddenly he perceived she was less armored than he had believed.

"You've given your advice," she said. "Go back to Elas."

"Djan—"

"Out."

"Djan, you talk about the sanctity of local culture, the balance of powers, but you seem to think you can pick and choose the rules you like. In some measure I don't blame Shan t'Tefur. You'll be the death of him before you're done, playing on his ambitions and his pride and then refusing to abide by the customs he knows. You know what you're doing to him? You know what it is to a man of the nemet that you take for a lover and then play politics with him?"

"I told him fairly that he had no claim on me. He chose."

"Do you think a nemet is really capable of believing that? And do you think that he believes now he had no just claim on the Methi's loyalty, whatever he does in your name? He'll push you someday to the point where you have to choose. He's not going to let you have your own way with him forever."

"He knows how things are."

"Then ask yourself why he comes running when you call him to your bed, and if you discover it's not your considerable personal attractions, don't say I didn't warn you. A nemet doesn't take that kind of treatment, not without some compelling reason. If this is your method of controlling the Sufaki, you've picked the wrong man."

"Nevertheless"—her voice acquired a tremor that she tried to suppress—"my mistakes are my choice."

"Will that undo someone's dying?"

"My choice," she insisted, with such intensity that it gave him pause.

"You're not in love with him?" It was question, and plea at once. "You're too sensible for that, Djan. You said yourself this world doesn't give you that choice. You'd kill him or he'd be the death of you sooner or later."

She shrugged, and the old cynical bitterness that he trusted was back. "I was conceived to serve the state. Doing so is an unbreakable habit. Other people—like you, my friend,—normal people—serve themselves. Relationships like serving self, serving—others—are outside my experience. I thought I was selfish, but I begin to see there are other dimensions to that word. I find personal relations tedious, these games of me and thee. I enjoy companionship. I—love you. I love Shan. That is not the same as: I love Nephane. This city is mine; it is *mine*. Spare me your appeals to personal affection. I would destroy either of you if I were clearly convinced it was necessary to the survival of this city. Remember that."

"I am sorry for you," he said.

"Get out."

Tears gathered to her eyes, belying everything she had said. She struggled for dignity, lost; the tears spilled free, her lips trembling into sobs. She clenched her jaw, turned her face and gestured for him to go.

"I am sorry," he said, this time with compassion, at which she shook her head and kept her back to him until the spasm had passed.

He took her arms, trying to comfort her, and felt guilty because of Mim; but he felt guilty because of Djan too, and feared that she would not forgive him for witnessing this. She had been here longer, a good deal longer than he. He well knew the nightmare, waking in the night, finding that reality had turned to dreams and the dream itself was as real as the stranger beside him, looking into a face that was not human, perceiving ugliness where a moment before had been beauty.

"I am tired," she said, leaning against him. Her hair smelled of these exotic on this world, lab-born, like Djan—perfumes like home, from a thousand star-scattered worlds the nemet had never dreamed of. "Kurt, I work, I study, I try. I am tired to death."

"I would help you," he said, "if you would let me."

"You have loyalties elsewhere," she said finally. "I wish I'd never sent you to Elas, to learn to be nemet, to belong to them. You want things for your cause, he wants things for his. I know all that, and occasionally I want to forget it. It's a human weakness. Am I not allowed just one? You came here asking favors. I knew you would, sooner or later."

"I would never ask you deceitfully, to do you harm. I owe you, as I owe Elas."

She pushed back from him. "And I hate you most when you do that. Your concern is touching, but I don't trust it."

"Nephane is killing you."

"I can manage."

"Probably you can," he said. "But I would help you."

"Ah, as Shan helps me. But you don't like it when it's the opposition, do you? Blast you, I gave you leave to marry and you've done it, you've made your choice, however tempting it was to—"

She did not finish. He suddenly found reason for uneasiness in that omission. Djan was not one to let words fly carelessly.

"When I came here," he said, "whenever I come, I try to leave my relations with Elas at the door. You've never tried to make me go against them; and I do not use you, Djan."

"Your little Mim," said Djan. "What is she like? Typical nemet?"

"Not typical."

"Elas is using you," she said. "Whether you know it or not, that is so. I could still stop that. I could simply have you given quarters here in the Afen. No arrest decree has Upei review. *That* power of a Methi is absolute."

She actually considered it. He went cold inside, realizing that she could and would do it, and knew suddenly that she meant this for petty revenge, taking his peace of mind in retaliation for her humiliation of a moment ago. Pride was important to her.

"Do you want me to ask you not to do that?" he asked.

"No," she said. "If I decide to do that, I will do it, and if I do not, I will not. What you ask has nothing to do with it. But I would advise you and Elas to remain quiet."

12

The fog did not go out. It held the city the next morning, the faint sound of warning bells drifting up from the harbor. Kurt opened his eyes on the grayness outside the window, then looked toward the foot of the bed where Mim sat combing her long hair, black and silken and falling to her waist when unbound. She looked back at him and smiled, her alien and wonderfully lovely eyes soft with warmth.

"Good morning, my lord."

"Good morning," he murmured.

"The mist is still with us," she said. "Hear the harbor bells?"

"How long can this last?"

"Sometimes many days when the seasons are turning,—especially in the spring." She flicked several strands of hair apart and began with quick fingers to plait them into a thin braid. Then she would sweep most of her hair up to the crown of her head, fasten it with pins and combs, an intricate and fascinating ritual daily performed and nightly undone. He liked watching her. In a matter of moments she began the next braid.

"We say," Mim commented, "that the mist is a cloak of the *imiine,* the sky-sprite Nue, when she comes to visit earth and walk among men. She searches for her beloved, that she lost long ago in the days when godkings ruled. He was a mortal man who offended one of the godkings, a son of Yr whose name was Knyha;—and, poor man, he was slain by Knyha, and his body scattered over all the shore of Nephane so that Nue would not know what had become of him. She still searches and walks the land and the sea and haunts the rivers, especially in the springtime."

"Do you truly think that?" Kurt asked, not sarcastically: one could not be that with Mim. He was prepared to mark it down to be remembered with all his heart if she wished him to.

Mim smiled. "I do not, not truly. But it is a beautiful story, is it not, my lord? There are truths and there are truths, my lord Kta would say, and there is Truth itself, the *yhia*,—and since mortals cannot always reason all the way to Truth, we find little truths that are right enough on our own level. But you are very wise about things. I think you really might know what makes the mist come. Is it a cloud that sits down upon the sea, or is it born in some other way?"

"I think," said Kurt, "that I like Nue best. It sounds better than water vapor."

"You think I am silly and you cannot make me understand."

"Would it make you wiser if you knew where fog comes from?"

"I wish that I could talk to you about all the things that matter to you."

He frowned, realizing that she was in earnest. "You matter. This place, this world matters to me, Mim."

"I know so very little."

"What do you want to know?"

"Everything."

"Well, you owe me breakfast first."

Mim flashed a smile, put in the last combs and finished her hair with a pat. She slipped on the *chatem,* the overdress with the four-paneled split skirt which fitted over the gossamer drapery of the *pelan,* the underdress. The *chatem,* high-collared and long-sleeved, tight and restraining in the bodice,—rose and beige brocade, over a rose *pelan.* There were many buttons up either wrist and up the bodice to the collar. She patiently began the series of buttons.

"I will have tea ready by the time you can be downstairs," she said. "I think Aimu will have been—"

There was a deep hollow boom over the city, and Kurt glanced toward the window with an involuntary oath. It was the sighing note of a distant gong.

"*Ai,*" said Mim. "*Intaem-Inta.* That is the great temple. It is the beginning of Cadmisan."

The gong moaned forth again through the fog-stilled air, measured, four times more. Then it was still, the last echoes dying.

"It is the fourth of Nermotai," said Mim, "the first of the Sufak holy days. The temple will sound the *Inta* every morning and every evening for the next seven days, and the Sufaki will make prayers and invoke the *Intain,* the spirits of their gods."

"What is done there?" Kurt asked.

"It is the old religion which was here before the Families. I am not really sure what is done, and I do not care to know. I have heard that they even invoke the names of godkings in Phan's own temple; but we do not go there, ever. There were old gods in Chteftikan, old and evil gods from the First Days, and once a year the Sufaki call their names and pay them honor, to appease their anger at losing this land to Phan. These are beings we Indras do not name."

"Bel said," Kurt recalled, "that there could be trouble during the holy days."

Mim frowned. "Kurt, I would that you take special care for your safety, and do not come and go at night during this time."

It hit hard. Mim surely spoke without reference to the Methi, at least without bitterness: if Mim accused, he knew well that Mim would say so plainly. "I do not plan to come and go at night," he said. "Last night—"

"It is always dangerous," she said with perfect dignity, before he would finish, "to walk abroad at night during Cadmisan. The Sufak gods are earth-spirits, Yr-bred and monstrous. There is wild behavior and much drunkenness."

"I will take your advice," he said.

She came and touched her fingers to his lips and to his brow, but she took her hand from him when he reached for it, smiling. It was a game they played.

"I must be downstairs attending my duties," she said. "Dear my husband, you will make me a reputation for a licentious woman in the household if you keep making us late for breakfast. —No!— dear my lord, I shall see you downstairs at morning tea."

"Where do you think you are going?"

Mim paused in the dimly lit entry hall, her hands for a moment suspending the veil over her head as she turned. Then she settled it carefully over her hair and tossed the end over her shoulder.

"To market, my husband."

"Alone?"

She smiled and shrugged. "Unless you wish to fast this evening. I am buying a few things for dinner. Look you, the fog has cleared, the sun is bright, and those men who were hanging about across the street have been gone since yesterday."

"You are not going alone."

"Kurt, Kurt, for Bel's doom-saying? Dear light of heaven, there are children playing outside, do you not hear? And should I fear to walk my own street in bright afternoon? After dark is one thing, but I think you take our warnings much too seriously."

"I have my reasons, Mim."

She looked up at him in most labored patience. "And shall we starve? Or will you and my lord Kta march me to market with drawn weapons?"

"No, but I will walk you there and back again." He opened the door for her, and Mim went out and waited for him, her basket on her arm, most obviously embarrassed.

Kurt nervously scanned the street, the recesses where of nights t'Tefur's men were wont to linger. They were indeed gone. Indras children played at tag. There was no threat—no presence of the Methi's guards either, but Djan never did move obviously: he had no difficulty returning to Elas late, probably, he thought with relief, she had taken measures.

"Are you sure," he asked Mim, "that the market will be open on a holiday?"

She looked up at him curiously as they started off together. "Of course, and busy. I put off going, you see, these several days with the fog and the trouble on the streets, and I am sorry to cause you this trouble, Kurt, but we really are running out of things and there could be the fog again tomorrow, so it is really better to go today. I have some sense, after all."

"You know I could quite easily walk down there and buy what you need for supper, and you would not need to go at all."

"*Ai,* but Cadmisan is such a grand time in the market, with all the country people coming in, and the artists, and the

musicians—besides," she added, when his face remained unhappy, "dear husband, you would not know what you were buying or what to pay. I do not think you have ever handled our
coin. And the other women would laugh at me and wonder what
kind of wife I am to make my husband do my work, or else they
would think I am such a loose woman that my husband would
not trust me out of his sight."

"They can mind their own business," he said, disregarding
her attempt at levity; and her small face took on a determined
look.

"If you go alone," she said, "the fact is that folk will guess
Elas is afraid, and this will lend courage to the enemies of Elas."

He understood her reasoning, though it comforted him not at
all. He watched carefully as their downhill walk began to take
them out of the small section of aristocratic houses surrounding
the Afen and the temple complex. But here in the Sufaki section
of town, people were going about business as usual. There were
some men in the Robes of Color, but they walked together in casual fashion and gave them not a passing glance.

"You see," said Mim, "I would have been quite safe."

"I wish I was that confident."

"Look you, Kurt, I know these people. There is lady Yafes,
and that little boy is Edu t'Rachik u Gyon—the Rachik house is
very large. They have so many children it is a joke in Nephane.
The old man on the curb is t'Pamchen. He fancies himself a
scholar. He says he is reviving the old Sufak writing and that he
can read the ancient stones. His brother is a priest, but he does
not approve of the old man. There is no harm in these people.
They are my neighbors. You let t'Tefur's little band of pirates
trouble you too much. T'Tefur would be delighted to know he
upset you. That is the only victory he dares to seek as long as
you give him no opportunity to challenge you."

"I suppose," Kurt said, unconvinced.

The street approached the lower town by a series of low steps
down a winding course to the defense wall and the gate. Thereafter the road went among the poorer houses, the markets, the
harborside. Several ships were in port, two broad-beamed merchant vessels and three sleek galleys, warships with oars run in
or stripped from their locks, yards without sails, the sounds of

carpentry coming loudly from their decks, one showing bright new wood on her hull.

Ships were being prepared against the eventuality of war. *Tavi,* Kta's ship, had been there; she had had her refitting and had been withdrawn to the outer harbor, a little bay on the other side of Haichema-tleke. That reminder of international unease, the steady hammering and sawing, underlay all the gaiety of the crowds that thronged the market.

"That is a ship of Ilev, is it not?" Kurt asked, pointing to the merchantman nearest, for he saw what appeared to be the white bird that was emblematic of that house as the figurehead.

"Yes," said Mim. "But the one beside it I do not recognize. Some houses exist only in the Isles. Lord Kta knows them all, even the houses of Indresul's many colonies. A captain must know these things. But of course they do not come to Nephane. This one must be a trader that rarely comes, perhaps from the north, near the Yvorst Ome, where the seas are ice."

The crowd was elbow-to-elbow among the booths. They lost sight of the harbor, and nearly of each other. Kurt seized Mim's arm, which she protested with a shocked look: even husband and wife did not touch publicly.

"Stay with me," he said, but he let her go. "Do not leave my sight."

Mim walked the maze of aisles a little in front of him, occasionally pausing to admire some gimcrack display of the tinsmiths, intrigued by the little fish of jointed scales that wiggled when the wind hit their fins.

"We did not come for this," Kurt said irritably. "Come, what would you do with such a thing?"

Mim sighed, a little piqued, and led him to that quarter of the market where the farmers were, countrymen with produce and cheeses and birds to sell, fishermen with the take from their nets, butchers with their booths decorated with whole carcasses hanging from hooks.

Mim deplored the poor quality of the fish that day, disappointed in her plans—selected from a vegetable seller some curious yellow corkscrews called *lat,* and some speckled orange ones called *gillybai.* She knew the vegetable seller's wife, who congratulated her on her recent marriage, marveled embarrassingly over Kurt—she seemed to shudder slightly, but showed brave politeness—then became involved in a long story about a mutual acquaintance's daughter's child.

It was woman's talk. Kurt stood to one side, forgotten, and then, sure that Mim was safe among people she knew and not willing to seem utterly the tyrant,—withdrew a little. He looked at some of the other tables in the next booth, somewhat interested in the alien variety of the fish and the produce—some of which, he reflected with unease, he had undoubtedly eaten without knowing its uncooked appearance. Much of the seafood was not in the least appealing to Terran senses.

From the harbor there came the steady sound of hammering, reechoing off the walls in insane counterpoint to the noise of the many colored crowds.

Someone jostled him. He looked up into the unsmiling face of a Sufaki in Robes of Color. The man said nothing. Kurt made a slight bow of apology, unanswered, and turned about to go after Mim.

Another man blocked his way. Kurt tried to step around him. The Sufaki moved in front of him with sullen threat in his narrow eyes. Another appeared to his left, crowding him back to the right.

He moved suddenly, trying to slip past them. They cut him off from Mim. He could not see her any longer. The noisy crowds surged between. He dared not start something with Mim near, where she could be hurt.

They forced him continually in one direction, toward a gap between the booths where they jammed up against a warehouse. He saw the alley and broke for it.

Others met him at the turning ahead, pursuit hot behind. He had expected it and hit the opposition without hesitation. He avoided a knife and kicked its owner, who screamed in agony,— struck another in the face and a third in the groin before those behind overhauled him.

A blow landed between his shoulders and against his head, half blinding him. He fell under a weight of struggling bodies, pinned while more than one of them wrenched his arms back and tied his wrists.

He had broken one man's arm. He saw that with satisfaction as they hauled him to his feet and tried to aid their own injured.

Then they seized him by either arm and hurried him deeper into the alley.

The backways of Nephane were a maze of alien geometry, odd-shaped buildings jammed incredibly into the S-curve of the main street, fronting outward in decent order while their rear portions formed a labyrinthine tangle of narrow alleyways and contiguous walls. Kurt quickly lost track of the way they had come.

They reached the back door of a warehouse, thrust Kurt inside and entered the dark with him, closing the door so that all the light was from the little door aperture.

Kurt scrambled to escape into the shadows, sure now that he would be found some time later with his throat cut and no proof who his murderers had been.

They seized him before he could run more than a few steps, hurried him to the dusty floor and slipped a cord about his ankle. Finally, despite his kicking and heaving, they succeeded in lashing both his ankles together. Then they forced his jaws apart and thrust a choking wad of cloth into his mouth, tying it in place with a violence that cut his face.

"Get a light," one said.

The door opened before that was done. Their comrades had joined them, bringing the man with the broken arm. When the light was lit they attended to the setting of the arm, with screams they tried to muffle.

Kurt wriggled over against some bales of canvas, nerves raw to every outcry from the injured man. They would repay him for that, he was sure, before they disposed of him.

It was the human thing to do. In this respect he hoped they were different.

Hours passed. The injured man slept, after a drink they had given him. Kurt occupied himself with trying to work the knots loose. They were not fully within his reach. He tried instead to stretch the cords. His fingers swelled and passed the point of pain. The ache spread up his arms. His feet were numb. Breathing was an effort.

At least they did not touch him. They played at *bho,* a game of lots, and sat in the light, an unreal tableau suspended in the growing blackness. The light picked out only the edges of bales and crates.

From the distance of the hill came the deep tones of the *Intaem-Inta.* The gamers stopped, reverent of it, continued.

Outside Kurt heard the faint scuff of sandaled feet on stone. His hopes rose. He thought of Kta, searching for him.

Instead there came a bold rap on the door. The men admitted the newcomers, one in Indras dress, the others in Robes of Color; they wore daggers in their belts.

One was a man who had watched outside Elas.

"We will see to him now," the Indras-dressed one said, a small man with eyes so narrow he could only be Sufaki. "Put him on his feet."

Two men hauled Kurt up, cut the cords that bound his ankles. He could not stand without them holding him. They shook him and struck him to make him try, but when it was evident that he truly could not stand, they took him each by an arm and pulled him along with them in great haste, out into the mist and the dark, along the confusing turns of the alleys.

They tended constantly downhill, and Kurt was increasingly sure of their destination: the bay's dark waters would conceal his body with no evidence to accuse the Sufaki of his murder, no one to hear how he had vanished—no one but Mim, who might well be able to identify them.

That was the thought which most tormented him. Elas should have been turning Nephane upside down by now, if only Mim had reached them. But there was no indication of a search.

They turned a corner, cutting off the light from the lantern-carrier in front of them, which moved like a witchlight in the mist. The other two men were half carrying him. Though he had feeling in his feet again, he made it no easier for them.

They made haste to overtake the man with the lantern, and cursed him for his haste. At the same time they jerked cruelly on Kurt's arms, trying to force him to carry his own weight.

And suddenly he shouldered left, where steps led down into a doorway, toppling one of his guards with a startled cry. With the other one he pivoted, unable to free himself, held by the front of his robe and one arm.

Kurt jerked. Cloth tore. He hurled all his weight into a kick at the lantern-bearer.

The man sprawled, oil spilling, live flame springing up. The burned man screamed, snatching at his clothing, trying to strip it off. His friend's grip loosened, knife flashing in the glare. He rammed it for Kurt's belly.

Kurt spun, received the edge across his ribs instead, tore free, kneed the man as the burning man's flames reached something else flammable in the debris of the alley.

He was free. He pivoted and ran, in the mist and the dark that now was scented with the stench of burned flesh and fiber.

It was several turns of the alleys later when he first dared stop, and leaned against the wall close to fainting for want of air, for the gag obstructed his breathing.

At last, as quietly as possible, he knelt against the back steps of a warehouse, contorted his body so that he could use his fingers to search the debris in the corner. There was broken pottery in the heap: he found a shard keen-edged enough, leaned against the step with his heart pounding from exertion and his ears straining to hear despite the blood that roared in his head.

It took a long time to make any cut in the tight cords. At last a strand parted, and another, and he was able to unwind the rest. With deadened hands he rubbed the binding from the gag and spit the choking cloth from his mouth, able to breathe a welcome gasp of the chill foggy air.

Now he could move, and in the concealment of the night and the fog he had a chance. His way lay uphill—he had no choice in that. The gate would be the logical place for his enemies to lay their ambush. It was the only way through the defense wall that ringed the upper town.

When he reached the wall, he was greatly relieved. It was not difficult to find a place where illicit debris had piled up against the ancient fortification. Sheds and buildings proliferated here, crowding into narrow gaps between the permitted buildings and the former defense of the high town. He scrambled by the roofs of three of them up to the crest and found the situation unhappily tidier on the other side. He walked the wall, dreading the jump; and in a place where the erosion of centuries had lessened the height perhaps five feet, he lowered himself over the edge and dropped a dizzying distance to the ground on the high town side.

The jolt did not knock him entirely unconscious, but it dazed him and left him scarcely able to crawl the little distance into the shadows. It was a time before he had recovered sufficiently to try to walk again, at times losing clear realization of how he had reached a particular place.

He reached the main street. It was deserted. Kurt took to it only as often as he must, finally broke into a run as he saw the door of Osanef. He darted into the friendly shadow of its porch.

No one answered. Light came through the fog indistinctly on the upper hill, a suffused glow from the temple or the Afen. He remembered the festival, and decided even Indras-influenced Osanef might be at the temple.

He took to the street running now, two blocks from Elas and trusting to speed, not daring even the other Indras houses. They had no love of humans; Kta had warned him so.

He was in the final sprint for Elas' door before he realized Elas might be watched, would logically be watched unless the Methi's guards were about. It was too late to stop. He reached its triangular arch and pounded furiously on the door, not even daring to look over his shoulder.

"Who is there?" Hef's voice asked faintly.

"Kurt. Let me in. Let me in, Hef."

The bolt shot back, the door opened, and Kurt slipped inside and leaned against the closed door, gasping for breath in the sudden warmth and light of Elas.

"Mim," said Hef. "Lord Kurt, what has happened? Where is Mim?"

"Not—not here?"

"No. We thought at least—whatever had happened—you were together."

Kurt caught his breath with a choking swallow of air and pushed himself square on his feet. "Call Kta."

"He is out with Ian t'Ilev and Val t'Ran, searching for you both. *Ai,* my lord, what can we do? I will call Nym—"

"Tell Nym—tell Nym I have gone to get the Methi's help. Give me a weapon,—anything—"

"I cannot, my lord, I cannot. My orders forbid—"

Kurt swore and jerked the door open again, ran for the street and the Afen gate.

When he reached the Afen wall, the great gates were closed and the wall-street that led to the temple compound was crowded with Sufaki—drunken, most of them. Kurt leaned on the bars and shouted for the guards to hear him and open them, but his voice was lost in the noise of the crowds, with all Sufak Nephane gathered into that square down the street and spilling over into the wall-street. Some, drunker than the rest, began also to shake at the bars of the gates to try to raise the guards. If there were any on duty to hear, they ignored the uproar.

Kurt caught his breath, exhausted, far from help of Kta or Djan. Then he remembered the other gate, the sally port in the far end of the wall where it touched Haichema-tleke, and opened onto the temple square. That would be the one for them to guard, that nearest the temple. They might hear him there, and open.

He raced along the wall, jostling Sufaki in his exhausted weaving and stumbling. A few drunk ones laughed and caught at his clothing. Others cursed him, trying to bar his way.

A cry began to go up, resentment for his presence. *Jafikn*-wearing Sufaki barred his path, turned him. Someone struck him from the side, nearly throwing him to the pavement.

He ran, but they would not let him escape the square, blocking his way out,—t'Tefur's men, armed with blades.

Authority, he thought, sensible authority would not let this happen. He broke to one side, racing for the temple steps, sending shrieking women and cursing men crowding out of his way.

Hands reached to stop him. He tore past them almost all the way to the very top of the long temple steps before enough of them seized him to hold him.

"Elas' doing!" a hysterical voice shrieked from below. "Kill the human!"

Kurt struggled around to see who had shouted, looked down on a sea of alien faces in the torchlight and the haze of thin mist.

"Where is Shan t'Tefur?" Kurt screamed back at them. "Where has he taken my wife?"

The babble of voices almost hushed for a moment: the nemet held their women in great esteem. Kurt drew a great gasp of air and shouted across the gathering. "Shan t'Tefur! If you are here, come out and face me. Where is my wife? What have you done with her?"

There was a moment of shocked silence and then a rising murmur like thunder as an aged priest came from the upper steps through the men gathered there. He cleared the way with the emblem of his office, a vine-wreathed staff. The staff extended till it was almost touching Kurt, and the priest spat some unintelligible words at him.

There was utter silence now, drunken laughter coming distantly from the wall-street. In this gathering no one so much as stirred. Even Kurt was struck to silence,—the staff extended a degree further and with unreasoning loathing he shrank from it, not wanting to be touched by this mouthing priest with his drunken gods of earth. They held him, and the rough wood of the staff's tip trembled against his cheek.

"Blasphemer," said the priest, "sent by Elas to profane the rites. Liar. Cursed from the earth you will be, by the old gods, the ancient gods, the life-giving sons of Thael. Son of Yr to Phan united, Aem-descended, to the gods of ancient Chteftik,— cursed!"

"A curse on the lot of you," Kurt shouted in his face, "if you have any part in t'Tefur's plot! My wife Mim never harmed any of you, never harmed anyone. Where is she? You people,—you! that were in the market today—that walked away—Are you all in this? What did they do with her? Where did they take her?— Is she alive? By your own gods you can tell me that at least. Is she alive?"

"No one knows anything of the woman, human," said the aged priest. "And you were ill-advised to come here with your drunken ravings. Who would harm Mim h'Elas, a daughter of Sufak herself? You come here and profane the mysteries— taught no reverence in Elas, it is clear. Cursed be you, human, and if you do not leave now, we will wash the pollution of your feet from these stones with your blood. —Let him go, let go the human, and give him the chance to leave."

They released him, and Kurt swayed on the steps above the crowd, scanning the faces for one that was familiar. Of Osanef, of any friend, there was no sign. He looked back at the priest.

"She is lost in the city, hurt or dead," Kurt pleaded. "You are a religious man. —Do something!"

For a moment pity or conscience almost touched the stern old face. The cracked lips quavered on some answer. There was a hush over the crowd.

"It is Indras' doing!" a male voice shouted. "Elas is looking for some offense against the Sufaki—and now they try to create one! The human is Elas' creature!"

Kurt whirled about, saw a familiar face for the first time.

"He is one of them!" Kurt shouted. "That is one of the men who was in the market when my wife was taken. They tried to kill me and they have my wife—"

"Liar," shouted another man. "Ver has been at the temple since the ringing of the *Inta*. I saw him myself. The human is trying to accuse an innocent man."

"Kill him!" someone else shouted, and others throughout the crowd took up the cry, surging forward, young men, wearing the Robes of Color. T'Tefur's men.

"No," cried the old priest, pounding his staff for attention. "No, take him out of here, take him far from the temple precincts."

Kurt backed away as men swarmed about him, nearly crushed in the press, jerked bodily off his feet, limbs strained as they passed him off the steps and down into the crowd.

He fought, gasping for breath and trying to free hands or even a foot to defend himself as he was borne across the courtyard toward the wall-street.

And the gate was open, and men of the Methi's guard were there, dimly outlined in the mist and the flaring torches, but about them was the flash of metal, and bronze helmets glittered under the murky firelight, ominous and warlike.

"Give him to us," said their leader.

"Traitors," cried one to the young men.

"Give him to us," the officer repeated. It was t'Senife.

In anger they flung Kurt at the guardsmen, threw him sprawling on the stones, and the guards in their haste were no more gentle, snatching him up again, half dragging him through the sally port into the Afen grounds.

Hysterical outcries came from the crowd as they closed the door, barring the multitude outside. Something heavy struck the door, a barrage of missiles like the patter of hail for a moment. The shrieking rose and died away.

The Methi's guard gathered him up, hauling his bruised arms, pulling him along with them until they were sure that he would walk as rapidly as they.

They took him by the back stairs and up.

13

"Sit down," Djan snapped.

Kurt let himself into the nearest chair, although Djan continued to stand. She looked over his head toward the guards who waited.

"Are things under control?"

"They would not enter the Afen grounds."

"Wake the day guard. Double watch on every post, especially the sally port. T'Lised, bring h'Elas here."

Kurt glanced up. "Mim—"

"Yes, Mim." Djan dismissed the guard with a wave of her hand and swept her silk and brocade skirts aside to take a chair. No flicker of sympathy touched her face as Kurt lifted a shaking hand to wipe his face and tried to collect his shattered nerves.

"Is she all right?" he asked.

"She will mend. Nym reported you missing when you failed to return; my men found her wandering the dock. I couldn't get sense out of her; she kept demanding to go to Elas, until I finally got through to her the fact that you were missing too. Then Kta came here saying you'd come back to Elas and then left again to find me; he was able to pass the gate in company with some of my men or I doubt he'd have made it through, given the mood of the people out there. So I sent Kta home again under guard and told him to wait there,—and I hope he did. After the riot you created in the temple square, finding you was simple."

Kurt bowed his head, glad enough to know Mim was safe, too tired to argue.

"Do you even remotely realize what trouble you caused? My men are in danger of being killed out there because of you."

"I'm sorry."

"What happened to you?"

"T'Tefur's men hauled me out of the market, held me in some warehouse until dark and took me out—I suppose to dispose of me in the harbor. I escaped. I—may have killed one or two of them."

Djan swore under her breath. "What else?"

"Those who were taking me from the temple, if your men recognized them—one was in the market. T'Tefur's men. One was a man I told you used to watch Elas—"

"Shall I call Shan here? If you repeat those things to his face—"

"I'll kill him."

"You will do nothing of the sort," Djan shouted, suddenly at the end of her patience. "You caused me trouble enough, you and your precious little native wife. I know well enough your stubbornness, but I promise you this: if you cause me any more trouble, I'll hold you and all Elas directly responsible."

"What am I supposed to do, wait for the next time? Is my wife going to have to go into hiding for fear of them and I not be able to do anything or lay a hand on the men I know are responsible?"

"You chose to live here, you begged me for the privilege, and you chose all the problems of living in a nemet house and having a nemet wife. Now enjoy it."

"I'm asking you to do something."

"And I'm telling you I've had enough problems from you. You're becoming a liability to me."

The door opened cautiously and Mim entered the room, stood transfixed as Kurt rose to his feet. Her face dissolved in tears and for a moment she did not move. Then she cast herself to her knees and fell upon her face before Djan.

Kurt went to her and drew her into his arms, smoothing her disordered hair, and she turned her face against him and wept. Her dress was torn open, buttons ripped to the waist, the *pelan* soiled with mud from the streets and with blood.

"You'd better do something," Kurt said, looking across at Djan. "Because if I meet any of them after this I'll kill them."

"If you doubt I'll do what I said, you're mistaken."

"What kind of place is this when this can happen to her? What do I owe your law when this can happen and they can get away with it?"

"H'Elas," said Djan, ignoring him, "have you remembered who did this to you?"

"Please," said Mim, "do not shame my husband."

"Your husband has eyes to see what happened to you. He is threatening to take matters into his own hands, which will be unfortunate for Elas if he does, and for him too. So you had better find it convenient to remember, h'Elas."

"Methi,—I—only remember what I told you. They kept me wrapped in—in someone's cloak, I think, and I could hardly breathe. I saw no faces—and I remember—I remember being moved, and I tried to escape, but they—hit me—they—"

"Let be," Kurt said, holding her. "Let be, Djan."

"How long have you lived in Nephane, h'Elas?"

"F-four years, Methi."

"And never heard those voices, never saw a face you knew, even at the beginning?"

"No, Methi. Perhaps—perhaps they were from the country."

"Where were you held?"

"I do not know, Methi. I cannot remember clearly. It was dark,—a building, dark,—and I could not see. I do not know."

"They were t'Tefur's men," said Kurt. "Let her alone."

"There are more radical men than Shan t'Tefur, those who aim at creating complete havoc here—and you just gave them all the ammunition they need, killing two of them, defiling the temple."

"Let them come out into the open and accuse me. I don't think they're the kind. Or if they try me again,—"

"I've warned you, Kurt, in as plain words as I can use. Do *nothing*."

"I'll do what's necessary to protect my wife."

"Don't try me. Don't think your life or hers means more to me than this city."

"Next time," said Kurt, holding Mim tightly to his side, "I'm going to be armed. If you don't intend to afford me the protection of the law, then I'll take care of the matter, public or private, fair or foul."

"My lord," pleaded Mim, "please, please, do not quarrel with her."

"You'd better listen to her," said Djan. "Women have survived the like for thousands of years. She will. Honor's cold comfort for being dead, as the practicalities of the Tamur surely taught—"

"She understands!" Kurt cried, hugging Mim to him, and Djan silenced herself quickly. Mim trembled. Her hands were cold in his.

"You have leave to go, h'Elas," said Djan.

"I'll see her home," said Kurt.

"*You're* going nowhere tonight," Djan said, and shouted in Nechai for the guard, who appeared almost instantly, expecting orders.

"I'll take her home," Kurt repeated, "and I'll come back if you insist on it."

"No," said Djan. "I made a mistake ever putting you in Elas, and I warned you. As of this moment you're staying in the Afen, and it's going to take more than Kta's persuasions to change my mind on that. You've created a division in this city that words won't settle, and my patience is over, Kurt.—T'Udein, see h'Elas home."

"You'll have to use more than an order to keep me here," said Kurt.

Mim put her hand on his arm and looked up at him. "Please, no, no, I will go home. I am so very tired. I hurt, my lord. Please let me go home, and do not quarrel with the Methi for my sake. She is right: it is not safe for you or for Elas. It will never be safe for you. I do not want you to have any grief for my sake."

Kurt bent and touched his lips to her brow. "I'm coming home tonight, Mim. She only thinks otherwise. Go with t'Udein, then, and tell your father to keep that door locked."

"Yes, my lord Kurt," she said softly, her hands slipping from his. "Do not be concerned for me. Do not be concerned."

She bowed once to the Methi, but Djan snapped her fingers when she would have made the full obeisance, dismissing her.

Kurt waited until the door was securely closed, then fixed his eyes on Djan, trembling so with rage he did not trust himself.

"If you ever use words like that to my wife again—"

"She has more sense than you do. *She* would not have a war fought over her offended pride."

"You held her without so much as a word to Elas—"

"I sent word back when Kta came, and if you had stayed where you belonged, the matter would have been quietly and efficiently settled. Now I have to think of other matters besides your convenience and your feelings."

"Saving t'Tefur, you mean."

"Saving this city from the bloodbath you nearly started tonight. My men had rocks thrown at them—at a Methi's guards! If they'll do that, they'll cut throats next."

"Ask your guards who those men were. Or are you afraid they'll tell you?"

"There are a lot of charges flying in the wind tonight, none of them substantiated."

"I'll substantiate them—before the Upei."

"Oh, no, you won't. You bring up that charge in the Upei and there are things about many people,—your little ex-slave wife included—that are going to be brought up too, dragged through public hearing under oath. When you start invoking the law, friend, the law keeps moving until the whole truth is out, and a case like that right now would tear Nephane apart. I won't stand for it. Your wife would suffer most of all, and I think she has come to understand that very clearly."

"You threatened her with that?"

"I explained things to her. I did not threaten. Those fellows won't admit to your charges, no, they'll have counterclaims that won't be pretty to hear. Mim's honor and Mim's history will be in question, and the fact that she went from the Tamurlin to a human marriage won't be to her credit or that of Elas. And believe me, I'd throw her or you to the Sufaki if it had to be done, so don't push me any further."

"T'Tefur's city isn't worth saving."

"Where do you think you're going?"

He had started for the door. He stopped and faced her. "I'm going to Elas, to my wife. When I'm sure she's all right, I'll come back and we can settle matters. But unless you want more people hurt or killed, you'd better give me an escort to get there."

She stared at him. He had never seen her angrier; but perhaps she could read on his face what he felt at the moment. Her expression grew calmer, guarded.

"Until morning," she said. "Make your peace there. My men will get you safely to Elas, but I am not sending them through the streets with you twice in one night, dragging you past the Sufaki like a lure to violence. So stay there till morning. And if you cause me more trouble tonight, Kurt, so help me you'll regret it."

Kurt pushed open the heavy door of Elas, taking it out of Hef's hands, closed it quickly upon the Methi's guards, then turned to Hef.

"Mim," said Kurt. "She is here, she is safe?"

Hef bowed. "Yes, my lord,—not a few moments ago she came in, also with the Methi's guard. I beg my lord, what—"

Kurt ignored his questions, hurried past him to the *rhmei* and found it empty, left it and raced upstairs to their room. There was no light there but the *phusa.* That light drew his eyes as he opened the door, and before it knelt Mim. He let his breath go in a long sigh of relief, slid to his knees and took her by the shoulders.

Her head fell back against him, her lips parted in shock, her face filmed with perspiration. Then he saw her hands at her heart and the dark wet stain on them.

"No," he cried, a shriek, and caught her as she slid aside, her hands slipping from the hilt of the dragon blade that was deep in her breast. She was not dead; the outrage of the metal in her flesh still moved with her shallow breathing, and he could not nerve himself to touch it. He pressed his lips to her cheek and heard the gentle intake of her breath. Her brows knit in pain and relaxed. Her eyes held a curious, childlike wonder.

"*Ei,* my lord," he heard her breathe.

And the breath passed softly from her lips and the light from her eyes. Mim was a weight, suddenly heavy, and he gave a strangled sob and held her against him, folded tightly into his arms.

Quick footsteps pounded up the stairs, and he knew it was Kta. The nemet stopped in the doorway, and Kurt turned his tear-stained face toward him.

"*Ai,* light of heaven," Kta whispered.

Kurt let Mim very gently to the floor, closed her eyes and carefully drew forth the blade. He knew it then for the one he had once stolen and Mim had taken back. He held the thing in his hand like a living enemy, his whole arm trembling.

"Kurt!" Kta exclaimed, rushing to him. "Kurt, no! Give it to me. Give it to me."

Kurt staggered to his feet with the blade still in his hand, and Kta's hazy form wavered before him, hand outstretched in pleading. His eyes cleared. He looked down at Mim.

"Kurt, please, I beg you."

Kurt clenched his fingers once more on the hilt. "I have business," he said, "at the Afen."

"Then you must kill me to pass," said Kta, "because you will kill Elas if you attack the Methi, and I will not let you go."

Kta's family: Kurt saw the love and the fear in the nemet's eyes and could not blame him. Kta would try to stop him; he believed it, and he looked down at the blade, deprived of revenge, lacking the courage or the will or whatever impulse Mim had had to drive it to her heart.

"Kurt." Kta took his hand and pried the blade from his fingers. Nym was in the shadows behind him,—Nym, and Aimu and Hef—Hef weeping, unobtrusive even in his grief. Things were suspended in unreality.

"Come," Kta was saying gently, "come away."

"Don't touch her."

"We will take her down to the *rhmei,*" said Kta. "Come, my friend, come."

Kurt shook his head, recovering himself a little. "I will carry her," he said. "She is my wife, Kta."

Kta let him go then, and Kurt knelt down and gathered up Mim's yielding form into his arms. She did not feel right any longer. It was not like Mim—loose, like a broken doll.

Silently the family gathered in the *rhmei:* Ptas and Nym,

Aimu and Kta and Hef, and Kurt laid down his burden at Ptas' feet. Ptas wept for her, and folded Mim's hands upon her breast. There was nothing heard in the *rhmei* but the sound of weeping, of the women and of Hef. Kurt could not shed more tears. When he looked into the face of Nym he met a grim and terrible anger.

"Who brought her to this?" asked Nym, so that Kurt trembled under the weight of his own guilt.

"I could not protect her," Kurt said. "I could not help her." He looked down at her, drew a shaken breath. "The Methi drove her to this."

Nym looked at him sorrowfully, then turned and walked to the light of the hearthfire. For a moment the lord of Elas stood with head bowed and then looked up, lifted his arms before the holy fire, a dark and powerful shadow before its golden light.

"Our Ancestors," he prayed, "receive this soul, not born of our kindred; spirits of our Ancestors, receive her, Mim h'Elas. Take her gently among you, one with us, as birth-sharing, loving, beloved. Peace was upon her heart, this child of Elas, daughter of Minas, of Indras, of the far-shining city."

"Spirits of Elas," prayed Kta, holding his hands also toward the fire, "our Ancestors, wake and behold us. Guardians of Elas, see us, this wrong done against us; swift to vengeance, our Ancestors, wake and behold us."

Kurt looked on, lost, unable even to mourn for her as they mourned, alien even in the moment of her dying. And he watched as Ptas took from Kta's hands the dragon blade. She bent over Mim with that, and this was beyond bearing. Kurt cried out, but Ptas severed only a lock of Mim's dark hair and cast it into the blaze of the holy fire.

Aimu sobbed audibly. Kurt could take no more. He turned suddenly and fled the hall, out into the entryway.

"It is done." Kta knelt where he found him, crouched in the corner of the entry against the door. He set his hand on Kurt's shoulder. "It is over now. We will put her to rest. Will you wish to be present?"

Kurt shuddered and turned his face toward the wall. "I can't," he said, lapsing into his native tongue. "I can't. I loved her, Kta. I can't go."

"Then we will care for her, my friend. We will care for her."

"I *loved* her," he insisted, and felt the pressure of Kta's fingers on his shoulder.

"Is there—some rite you would wish? Surely—surely our Ancestors would find no wrong in that."

"What could she have to do with my people?" Kurt swallowed painfully and shook his head. "Do it the way she would understand."

Kta arose and started to leave, then knelt again. "My friend,—come to my room first. I will give you something that will make you sleep."

"No," he said. "Leave me alone. Leave me."

"I am afraid for you."

"Take care of her. Do that for me."

Kta hesitated, then rose again and withdrew on silent feet.

Kurt sat listening for a moment. The family left the *rhmei* by the left-hand hall, their steps dying away into the far places of the house. Kurt rose then and opened the door quietly, shutting it quietly behind him in such a way that the inner bar fell into place.

The streets were deserted, as they had been since the Methi's guards had taken their places at the wall-street. He walked not toward the Afen, but downward, toward the harbor.

14

Daylight was finally beginning to break through the mists, lightening everything to gray, and there was the first stirring of wind that would disperse the fog.

Kurt skirted the outermost defense wall of Nephane, the rocking, skeletal outlines of ships ghostly in the gray dawn. No one watched this end of the harbor, where the ancient walls curved against Haichema-tleke's downslope, where the hill finally reached the water, where the walls towered sixty feet or more into the mist.

Here the city ended and the countryside began. A dirt track ran south, rutted with the wheels of hand-pulled carts, mired, thanks to the recent rains. Kurt ran beside the road and left it, heading across country.

He could not think clearly yet where he was bound. Elas was closed to him. If he set eyes on Djan or t'Tefur now he would kill them, with ruin to Elas. He ran, hoping only that it was t'Tefur who would pursue him, out beyond witnesses and law.

It would not bring back Mim. Mim was buried by now, cold in the earth. He could not imagine it, could not accept it, but it was true.

He was weary of tears. He ran, pushing himself to the point of collapse, until that pain was more than the pain for Mim, and exhaustion tumbled him into the wet grass all but senseless.

When he began to think again, his mind was curiously clear. He realized for the first time that he was bleeding from an open wound—had been all night, since the assassin's blade had passed his ribs. It began to hurt. He found it not deep, but as long as his hand. He had no means to bandage it. The bleeding was not something he would die of. His bruises were more painful: his cord-cut wrists and ankles hurt to bend. He was almost relieved to feel these things, to exchange these miseries for the deep one of Mim's loss, which had no limit. He put Mim away in his mind, rose up and began to walk again, steps weaving at first, steadier as he chose his direction.

He wanted nothing to do with the villages. He avoided the dirt track that sometimes crossed his way. As the day wore on and the warmth increased he walked more surely, choosing his southerly course by the sun.

Sometimes he crossed cultivated fields, where the crops were only now sprouting, and the earliest trees were in bloom and not yet fruited. Root-crops like *stas* were stored away in the safety of barns, not to be had in the fields.

By twilight he was feeling faint with hunger, for he had not eaten—he reckoned back to breakfast a day ago. He did not know the land, dared not try the wild plants. He knew then that he must think of stealing or starve to death, and he was sorry for that, because the country folk were generally both decent and poor.

The bitter thought occurred to him that among the innocent of this world his presence had brought nothing but grief. It was only his enemies that he could never harm.

Mim stayed with him. He could not so much as look at the stars overhead without hearing the names she gave them: Ysime the pole star, mother of the north wind; blue Lineth, the star that heralded the spring, sister of Phan. His grief had settled into a quieter misery, one with everything.

In the dark, there came to his nostrils the scent of woodsmoke, borne on the northwest wind.

He turned toward it, smelled other things as he drew nearer, animal scents and the delicious aroma of cooking. He crept silently, carefully toward the fold of hills that concealed the place.

There was no house, but a campfire tended by two men and a youth, country folk, keepers of flocks, *cachiren*. He heard the soft calling of their wool-bearing animals from somewhere beyond a brush barricade on the other side of the fire.

A snarled warning cut the night. The shaggy *tilof* that guarded the *cachin* lifted its head, his hackles rising, alerting the *cachiren*, they who scrambled up, weapons in hand, and the beast raced for the intruder.

Kurt fled, seeking a pile of rock that had tumbled from the hillside, and tried to find a place of refuge. The beast's teeth seized his ankle, tore as he jerked free and scrambled higher.

"Come down!" shouted the youth, spear poised for throwing. "Come down from there."

"Hold the creature off," Kurt shouted back. "I will gladly come down if you will only call him off."

Two of them kept spears aimed at him, while the youth went higher and dragged the snarling and spitting guard-beast down again by his shaggy ruff.

Kurt clambered down gingerly and spoke to them gently and courteously, for they prodded him with their spears, forcing him in the direction of the firelight, and he feared what they would do when they saw his human face.

When he reached the light he kept his head down, and knelt by the fireside and sat back on his heels in an at-home posture. The keen point of a spearblade touched beneath his shoulder. The other two men circled to the front to look him over.

"Human," one exclaimed, and point the point pressed deeper and made him wince.

"Where are the rest of you?" the white-haired elder asked.

"I am not Tamurlin," said Kurt, "and I am alone. I beg you, I need food. I am of the Methi's people."

"He is lying," said the boy behind him.

"He might be," said the elder, "but he talks manlike."

"You do not need to give me hospitality," said Kurt, for the sharing of bread and fire created a religious bond forever unless otherwise agreed upon from the beginning. "But I do ask you for food and drink. It is the second day since I have eaten."

"Where did you come from?" asked the elder.

"From Nephane."

"He is lying," the boy insisted. "The Methi killed the others."

"Unless one escaped."

"Or more than one," said the elder.

"May the light of Phan fall gently on thee," Kurt said, the

common blessing. "I swear I have not lied to you, and I am no enemy."

"It is, at least, no Tamurlin," said the second man. "Are you house-friend to the Methi, stranger?"

"To Elas," said Kurt.

"To Elas," echoed the elder in amazement. "To the sons of storm,—a human for a house-friend? This is hard to believe. The Indras-descended are too proud for that."

"If you honor the name of Elas," said Kurt, "or of Osanef, which is our friend,—give me something to eat. I am about to faint from hunger."

The elder considered again and finally extended an arm in invitation to the meal they had left cooking beside their fire. "Not in hospitality, stranger, since we do not know you, but there is food and drink. We are poor men. Take sparingly, but be free of it, if you are as hungry as you say. May the light of Phan fall upon thee in blessing or in curse according to what you deserve."

Kurt moved carefully, for the spear was surely still at his back. He knelt down by the rock where the food was warming and took one of the three meal cakes, breaking off half; and a little crumb of the soft cheese that lay on a greasy leather wrap beside them. But he used the fine manners of Elas, not daring to do otherwise with their critical eyes on him and the spear ready.

When he was done he rose up and bowed his thanks. "I will go my way now," he said.

"No, stranger," said the second man. "I think you ought to stay with us and go to our village in the morning. In this district we see few travelers from Nephane, and I think you would be safer with us. Someone might take you for Tamurlin and put a spear through you before he realized his mistake. That would be sad for both of you."

"I have business elsewhere," said Kurt, playing out the farce with the rules they set and bowing politely. "And I thank you for your concern, but I will go on now."

The elder man brought his spear crosswise in both hands. "I think my son is right. You have run from somewhere, that much is certain, and I am not sure that you are house-friend to Elas.

No, it is more likely the Methi simply missed killing you with the others, and we well know in the country what humans are."

"If I do come from Djan-methi, you will not win her thanks by delaying me on my mission."

"What, does the Methi send out her servants without provisions?"

"I had an accident," he said. "My mission is urgent; I had no time to go back. I counted on the hospitality of the country folk to help me on my way."

"Stranger, you are not only a liar, you are a bad liar. We will take you to our village and see what the Afen has to say about you."

Kurt ran, plunged in a wild vault over the brush barricade and in among the startled *cachin,* creating panic as their woolly bodies scattered and herded first to the rocks and then back toward the barricade, breaking it down in their mad rush to escape. The *tilof's* sharp cries resounded in the rocks. The beast and the men had work enough at the moment.

Kurt climbed, fingers and sandaled toes seeking purchase in the crevices of the rocks, sending stones cascading down the hillside. He cleared the crest, found a level, brushy ground and ran, desperate, trusting pursuit would be at least delayed.

But word would go back to Nephane and to Djan, and she would be sure now the way he had fled. Ships could outrace him down the coast.

If he did not reach his own abandoned ship and secure the means to live, he was finished in this land. Djan would have guessed it already, and now she could lay her ambush with assurance.

If she knew the precise location of his ship, he could not hope to avoid it.

The sun rose over the same grassy rangeland that had surrounded him for the last several days, dry grass and wind and dust.

Kurt leaned on his staff, a twisted branch from which he had stripped the twigs, and looked toward the south. There was not a sign of the ship. Nothing. Another day of walking, of the tormenting heat and the infection's throbbing fever in his wound.

He started moving again, relying on the staff, every step a jarring and constant pain, his mouth so dry that swallowing hurt.

Sometimes he rested, and thought of lying down and ceasing to struggle against the thirst; sometimes he would do that, but eventually misery and the habit of life would bring him to his feet and set him walking.

Phan was a terrible presence in these lands, wrathfully blinding in the day, deserting the land at night to a biting cold. Kurt rubbed blistered skin from his nose, his hands. His bare legs and especially his knees were swollen with sunburn, tiny blisters which many times formed and burst, making a crack-line that oozed and bled.

The thirst was beyond bearing as the sun reached its zenith. There was no water, had been none since the small stream the day before—or the day before that. Time blurred since he had entered this land. He began to wonder if he had already missed the ship, bypassing it over one of the gently rolling hills. That would be irony: to live by the skills of pinpointing a ship from one star to another and to die by missing a point over a hill.

He turned west finally, toward the sea, thinking that he could not fail at least to find that, hoping that the lower country would have fresh water. The changing of the seasons had confused him. He remembered green around the ship, green in winter. Had it been so far south? The sailing—he could not remember how many days it had taken.

By afternoon he ceased to care what direction he was moving in and knew that he was killing himself, and did not care. He started down a hillside, too tired to take the safer slope, and slipped on the dusty grass. He slid, opening the lacerations on his hands and knees, grass and stone stripping sunburned skin and blisters from his exposed flesh as he rolled down the slope.

The pain grew less finally, or he adjusted to it, he knew not which. He found himself walking and did not remember getting to his feet. It was not important any more, the ship, the sea, life or death. He moved and so lived, and therefore moved.

The sun dipped horizonward into dusk, a beacon that lit the sky with red, and Kurt locked onto it, a reference point, a guidance star in this void of grass. It led him downcountry, where there were trees and the land looked more familiar.

Night fell, and he stood on the broad shoulder of a hill, leaning on his staff, fearing if he sat down now he would not have the strength in his burn-swollen legs to get up again. He started the long descent toward the dark of the woods.

A light gleamed off across the wide valley, a light like a campfire. Kurt paused, rubbed his eyes to be sure it was there. It was a pinpoint like a very faint star, that flickered, but stayed discernible in all that distance and desolation.

He headed for it, driven now by feverish hope, nerved to kill if need be to obtain food and water.

It gleamed nearer, just when he feared he had lost it in his descent. He saw it through the brush. Men's voices—nemet voices—were audible, soft, quiet in conversation.

Then silence. Brush moved. The fire continued to gleam. He hesitated, feeling momentary panic, a sense of being stalked in turn.

Brush crashed near him and strong arm took him from behind about the throat, bent him back. He fell, pulled down by two mean, weighted with a knee on his right arm, another hand pinning his left. A knife whispered from its sheath and rested across his throat.

The man on his left checked the other hand on his wrist. Kurt ceased to struggle, trying only to breathe.

"It is t'Morgan," said a whisper. Gentle hands searched his belt for weapons, found nothing, tugged his arms free of those who held him and drew him up, those who had been lately threatening him handling him carefully, lifting him to his feet, aiding him to stand.

"Are you alone?" one asked of him.

"Yes," Kurt tried to say. They almost had to carry him, bringing him into the circle of firelight. Other nemet joined them from the shadows.

Kta was among them. Kurt saw his face among the others and felt his sanity had left him. He tried to go toward him, shaking free of the others.

He fell. When he managed to get his arms beneath him and tried again to sit up, Kta was beside him. The nemet washed his burning face from a waterskin, offered it to his lips and took it away before he could make himself sick with it.

"How did you come here?" Kurt found his own voice unrecognizable.

"Looking for you," said Kta. "I thought you might understand a beacon fire, which drew me once to you. And you did see it, thank the gods. I planned to reach your ship and wait for you there, but I have not been able to find it. But gods, no one walks cross-country. You are mad."

"It was a hard walk," Kurt agreed. Kta smoothed his filthy hair aside, woman-tender, his fingers careful of burned skin, pouring water to cool his face.

"Your skin," said Kta, "is cooked. Merciful spirits of heaven, look at you."

Kurt rubbed at the stubble that protected his lower face, aware how bestial he must be in the eyes of the nemet, for the nemet had very little facial hair, very little elsewhere. He struggled to sit, and bending his legs made it feel like the sunburned skin of his knees would split. "Food," he pleaded, and someone gave him a bit of cheese. He could not eat much of it, but he washed it down with a welcome swallow of *telise* from Kta's flask.

Then it was as if the strength that was left poured out of him. He lay down again and the nemet made him as comfortable as they could with their cloaks, washed the ugly wound across his ribs with water and then—which made him cry aloud—with fiery *telise.*

"Forgive me, forgive me," Kta murmured through the haze of his delirium. "My poor friend, it is done, it will mend."

He slept then, conscious of nothing.

The camp began to stir again toward dawn, and Kurt wakened as one of the men added wood to the fire. Kta was already sitting up, watching him anxiously.

Kurt groaned and sat up, dragging himself to a cross-legged posture despite his knees. "A drink, please, Kta."

Kta nodded to the boy Pan, who hastened to bring Kurt a waterskin and *stas,* which had been baked last night. It was cold, but with salt it went very well, washed down with *telise.* He ate it to the last, but dared not force the second one offered on his shrunken stomach.

"Are you feeling better?" asked Kta.

"I am all right," he said. "You should not have come after me."

And then a second, terrible thought hit him: "Or did Djan send you to bring me back?"

Kta's face went thin-lipped, a killing anger that turned Kurt cold. "No," he said. "I am outlawed. The Methi has killed my father and mother."

"No." Kurt shook his head furiously, as if that could unsay the truth of it. "Oh, no, Kta." But it was true. The nemet's face was calm and terrible. "*I* caused it," Kurt said. "*I* caused it."

"She killed them," said Kta, "as she killed Mim. We know Mim's tale from Djan-methi's own lips, spoken to my father. My people will not live without honor, and so my parents died. My father confronted the Methi in the Upei for Mim's death and for the Methi's other crimes—and she cast him from the Upei, which was her right. My father and my mother chose death, which was their right. And Hef with them. He would not let them go unattended into the shadows."

"Aimu?" Kurt asked, dreading to know.

"I gave her to Bel as his wife. What else could I do, what other hope for her? Elas is no more in Nephane. Its fire is extinguished. I am in exile. I will not serve the Methi any longer, but I live to honor my father and my mother and Hef and Mim. They are my charges now. I am all that is left, now that Aimu can no longer invoke the Guardians of Elas."

Kta's lips trembled. Kurt ached for him no less than for his family, for it was unbecoming for a man of the Indras to shed tears. It would shame him terribly to break.

"If," said Kurt, "you want to discharge your debt to me you have discharged it. I can live in this green land if you only give me weapons and food and water. Kta, I would not blame you if you never wanted to look at me again; I would not blame you if you killed me."

"I came for you," said Kta. "You are also of Elas, though you cannot continue our rites or perpetuate our blood. When the Methi struck at you, she struck at us. We are of one house, you and I. Until one or the other of us is dead, we are left hand and right. You have no leave to go your way. I do not give it."

He spoke as lord of Elas, which was his right now. The bond

Mim had forged reasserted itself. Kurt bowed his head in respect.

"Where shall we go now?" Kurt asked. "And what shall we do?"

"We go north," said Kta. "Light of heaven, I knew at once where you must go, and I am sure the Methi does; but it would have been more convenient if you had brought your ship to earth in the far north. The Ome Sin is a closed bottle in which the Methi's ships can hunt us at their pleasure. If we cannot escape its neck and reach the northern seas, you and I are done, my friend, and all these brave friends who have come with me."

"Is Bel here?" Kurt asked, for about him he saw many familiar faces, but he feared greatly for t'Osanef and Aimu if they had elected to stay in Nephane. T'Tefur might carry revenge even to them.

"No," said Kta. "Bel is Sufaki, and his father needs him desperately just now. For all of us that have come, there is no way back, not as long as Djan rules. But she has no heir, and being human—there is no dynasty. We are prepared to wait."

Kurt hoped silently that he had not given her one. That would be the ultimate bitterness, to ruin these good men by that, when he had brought them all to this pass.

"Break camp," said Kta. "We start—"

Something hissed and struck against flesh, and all the camp exploded into chaos.

"Kta!" a man cried warning, and went down with a feathered shaft in his throat. About them in the dawn-dim clearing poured a horde of howling creatures that Kurt knew for his own kind. One of the nemet pitched to the ground almost at his feet with his face a bloody smear, and in the next moment a crushing blow across the back brought Kurt down across him.

Rough hands jerked him up, and his shock-dazed eyes looked at a bearded human face. The man seemed no less surprised, stayed the blow of his ax, then bellowed an order to his men.

The killing stopped, the noise faded.

The human put out his bloody hand and touched Kurt's face, his hair-shrouded eyes dull and mused with confusion. "What band?" he asked.

"I came by ship," Kurt answered him. "By starship."

The Tamurlin's blue eyes clouded, and with a snarl he took the front of Kurt's nemet garb and ripped it off his shoulder, as though the nemet dress gave the lie to his claim. But then there was a cry of awe from the humans gathered around. One took his sun-browned arm and held it up against Kurt's pale shoulder and turned to his comrades, seeking their opinion.

"A man from shelters," he cried, "a ship-dweller."

"He came in the ship," another shouted, "in the ship, the ship."

They all shouted the ship, the ship, over and over again, and danced around and flashed their weapons. Kurt looked around at the carnage they had made in the clearing, his heart pounding with dread at seeing one and another man he knew lying there. He prayed Kta had escaped: some had dived for the brush.

He had not. Kta lay on his face by the fire, unconscious—his breathing was visible.

"Kill the others," said the leader of the Tamurlin. "We keep the human."

"*No!*" Kurt cried, and jerked ineffectually to free his arms. His mind snatched at the first argument he could find. "One of them is a nemet lord. He can bring you something of value."

"Point him out."

"There," Kurt said, jerking his head to show him. "Nearest the fire."

"Let's take all the live ones," said another of the Tamurlin, with a look in his eyes that boded no good for the nemet. "Let's deal with them tonight at the camp—"

"*Ya!*" howled the others, agreeing, and the chief snarled a reluctant order, for it had not been his idea. He took command of the situation with a sweep of his arm. "Pick them all up, all the live ones, and bring them. We'll see if this man really is from the ship. If he isn't, we'll find out what he really is."

The others shouted agreement and turned their attention to the fallen nemet, Kta first. Him they shook and slapped until he began to fight them again, and then they twisted his hands behind him and tied him.

Two other nemet they found not seriously hurt and treated in similar fashion. A third man they made walk a few paces, but he could not do so, for his leg was pierced with a shaft. One of them kicked his good leg from under him and smashed his skull with an ax.

Kurt twisted away, chanced to look on Kta's face, and the look in the nemet's eyes was terrible. Two more of his men they killed in the same way, and at each fall of the ax Kta winced, but his gaze remained fixed. By his look they could as well have killed him.

15

The ship rested as Kurt remembered it, tilted, the port still open. About it now were camped a hundred of the Tamurlin, hide-clothed and mostly naked, their huts of grass and sticks and hides encircling the shining alloy landing struts.

They came running to see the prizes their party had brought, these savage men and women and few starveling children. They shouted obscene threats at the nemet, but shied away, murmuring together when they realized Kurt was human. One of the young men advanced cautiously—though Kurt's hands were tied—and others ventured after him. One pushed at Kurt, then hit him across the face, but the chief snatched him back, protective of his property.

"What band is he from?" one of them asked.

"Not from us," said the chief. "None of ours."

"He is human," several of the others argued the obvious.

The chief took Kurt by the collar and pulled, taking his *pel* down to the waist, pushed him forward into their midst. "He's not ours, whatever he is. Not of the tribes."

Their reaction was near to panic, babbling excitement. They put out their filthy hands, comparing themselves with him, for their hides were sun-browned and creased with premature wrinkles from weather and wind, with dirt and grease ground into the crevices. They prodded at Kurt with leathery fingers, pulled at his clothing, ran their hands over his skin and howled with amusement when he cursed and kicked at them.

It was a game, with them running in to touch him and out again when he tried to defend himself; but when he tired of it and let them, that spoiled it and angered them. They hit, and this time it was in earnest. One of them in a fit of offended arrogance pushed him down and kicked him repeatedly in the side, and the lot of them roared with laughter at that, even more so when a little boy darted in and did the same. Kurt twisted onto his knees and tried to rise, and the chief seized him by the arm and hauled him up.

"Where from?" the chief asked.

"Offworld," said Kurt from bloodied lips. He saw the ship beyond the chief's shoulder, a sanctuary out of his own time that he could not reach. He burned with shame for their treatment of him, and for the nemet's eyes on these his brothers, these shaggy, mindless, onetime lords of the earth. "That ship brought me here."

"The Ship," the others took it up. "The holy Ship! The Starship!"

"This is *not* the Ship," the chief shouted them down and pointed at it, his hand trembling with passion. "The curse-sign on it—this man is not what the Articles say."

The Alliance emblem. Kurt had forgotten the sunburst emblem of the Alliance that was blazoned on the ship. They were Hanan. He followed the chief's pointing finger, wondering with a sickness at the pit of his stomach how much of the war these savages recalled.

"A starman!" one of the young men shouted defiantly. "A starman! The Ship is coming!"

And the others took up the howl with wild-eyed fervor, the same ones who had lately thrown him in the dust.

"The Ship, ya, the Ship, the Ship, the machines and the armies!"

"They are coming!"

"Indresul Indresul! The waiting is over!"

The chief backhanded Kurt to the ground, kicked him to show his contempt, and there was a cry of resentment from the people. A youth ran in—for what purpose was never known. The chief dropped the boy with a single blow of his fist and rounded on the leaders of the dissent.

"And I am still captain here," he roared, "and I know the Articles and the Writings, and who will come and argue them with me?"

One of the men looked as if he might, but when the captain came closer to him, he ducked his head and sidled off. The rebellion died into sullen resentment.

"You've seen the sign," said the captain. "Maybe the Ship is near. But this little thing isn't what the Writings predict." He looked down at Kurt with threat in his eyes. "Where are the machines, the Ship as large as a mountain, the armies from the star-worlds that will take us to Indresul?"

"Not far away," said Kurt, setting his face to lie, which was never a skill of his. "I was sent out from Aeolus to find you. Is this how you welcome me? That will be the last you ever see of Ships if you kill me."

The captain was taken aback by that answer.

"Mother Aeolus," cried one of the men, though he called it Elus, "the great Mother. He has seen the Great Mother of All Men."

The captain looked at Kurt from under one brow, hating, just the least part uncertain. "Then," he said, "what did she say to you?"

The lie closed in on him, complex beyond his own understanding. Aeolus—homeworld—confounded with the nemet's Mother Isoi, Mother of Men: nemet religion and human hopes confused into reverence for a promised Ship. "She lost you," he said, gathering himself to his feet. They personified her: he hoped he understood that aright. "Her messenger was lost on the way hundreds of years ago, and she was angry, blaming you. But she has decided to send again, and now the Ship is coming, if my report to her is good."

"How can her messenger wear the mark of Phan?" the captain asked. "You are a liar."

The sunburst emblem of the ship. Kurt resisted the impulse to lose his dignity by looking where the captain pointed. "I am not a liar," said Kurt. "And if you don't listen to me, you'll never see her."

"You come from Phan," the captain snarled, "from Phan, to lie to us and turn us over to the nemet."

"I am human. Are you blind?"

"You camped with the earthpeople. You were no prisoner in that camp."

Kurt straightened his shoulders and looked the man in the

eyes, lying with great offense in his tone. "We thought you men were supposed to have these nemet under control. That's what you were left here to do, after all, and you've had three hundred years to do that. So I had no real fear of the nemet and they were able to surprise me some time ago and take my weapons. It took me this long to escape from Nephane and come south. They hunted me down, with orders to bring me back to Nephane alive, so naturally they did me no harm in that camp, but that doesn't mean the relationship was friendly. I don't particularly like the nemet, but I'd advise you to save these three alive. When my captain comes down here, as he will, he's going to want to question a few of the nemet, and these will do very well for that purpose."

The captain bit his lip and gnawed his mustache. He looked at the three nemet with burning hatred and spit out an obscenity that had not much changed in several hundred years. "We kill them."

"No," Kurt said. "There's need of them live and healthy."

"Three nemet?" the captain snarled. "One. One we keep. You choose which one."

"All three," Kurt insisted, though the captain brandished his ax. It took all his self-possession not to flinch as the weapon made a pass at him.

Then the captain whirled the weapon in a glittering arc at the nemet, purposely defying him. The humans murmured, eyes glittering like the metal itself. The ax passed within an inch of Kta and of the next man.

"Choose!" the captain cried. "You choose, starman. One nemet. We take the other two."

The howling began to be a moan. One of the little boys shrieked in glee and ran in, striking all three nemet with a stick.

"Which one?" the captain asked again.

Kurt kept his sickness from his face, saw Kta look at him, saw the nemet's eyes sending a desperate and angry message to him, which he ignored, looking at the captain.

"The one on the left," Kurt said. "That one. Their leader."

One of the two nemet died before nightfall. The execution was in the center of camp, and there was no way Kurt could avoid watching from beginning to end, for the captain's narrow eyes were on him more than on the nemet, watching his least re-action. Kurt kept his own eyes unfocused as much as possible, and his arms folded, so that his trembling was not evident.

The nemet was a brave man, and his last reasoned act was a glance at Kta—not desperate, but seeking approval of him. Kta was standing, hands bound: the lord of Elas gave the man a steadfast look, as if he had given him an order on the deck of their own ship; and the nemet died with what dignity the Tamurlin afforded him. They made a butchery of it, and the Tamurlin howled with excitement until the man no longer re-acted to any torment. Then they finished him with an ax. As the blade came down, Kta's self-control came near to breaking. He wept, his face as impassive as ever, and the Tamurlin pointed at him and laughed.

After that the captain ordered Kurt taken to his own shelter. There he questioned him, threatening him with not quite the conviction to make good the threats, accusing him over and over of lying. The captain was a shrewd man. At times there would come a light of cunning into his hair-shrouded eyes, and he doggedly refused to be led off on a tangent. Constantly he dragged the questioning back to the essential points, quoting from the versified Articles and the Writings of the Founders to argue against Kurt's claims.

His name was Renols, or something which closely resembled that common Hanan name, and he was the only educated man in the camp. His power was his knowledge, and the moment Renols ceased to believe, or ceased to fear, then Renols could dispose of Kurt with lies of his own. The captain was a pragma-tist, capable of it; Kurt was well certain he was capable of it.

The tent reeked of fire, of sweat, of the curious pungent leaf the Tamurlin chewed. One of his women lay in the corner against the wall, taking the leaves one by one. Her eyes had a fevered look. Sometimes the captain reached for one of the slim gray leaves and chewed at it half-heartedly. It perfumed the breath. Sweat began to bead on his temples. He grew calmer.

He offered the bowl of leaves to Kurt, insisting. At last Kurt took one, judiciously tucked it in his cheek, whole and un-bruised. Even so, it burned his mouth and spread a numbness that began to frighten him.

If he became drunk with it, he could say something he would not say: his capacity for the drug might be far less than Renols'.

"When," asked Renols, "will the Ship come?"

"I told you. There's machinery in my own ship. Let me in there and I can call my captain."

Renols chewed and stared at him with his thick brows contracted. A dangerous look smoldered in his eyes. But he took another leaf and held out the bowl to Kurt a second time. His hands were stubby-fingered, the nails broken, the knuckles ridged with cut-scars.

Kurt took a second leaf and carefully eased that to the same place as the first.

The calculating look remained in Renols' eyes. "What sort of man is he, this captain?"

The understanding began to come through. If a ship came, if Mother Aeolus did send it and all points of his prisoner's tale proved true, then Renols would be faced with someone of greater authority than himself. He would perhaps become a little man. Renols must dread the Ship; it was in his own, selfish interests that there not be one.

But it was also remotely possible that his prisoner would be an important man in the near future, so Renols must fear him. Kurt reckoned that too, and reckoned uneasily that familiarity might well overcome Renols' fear, when Aeolus' messenger turned out to be only mortal.

"My captain," said Kurt, embroidering the tale, "is named Ason, and Aeolus has given him all the weapons that you need. He will give them to you and show you their use before he returns to Aeolus to report."

The answer evidently pleased Renols more than Renols had expected. He grunted, half a laugh, as if he took pleasure in the anticipation.

Then he gave orders to one of the sallow-faced women who sat nearby. She laid the child she had been nursing in the lap of the nearest woman, who slept in the after-effects of the leaf, and went out and brought them food. She offered first to Renols, then to Kurt.

Kurt took the greasy joint in his fingers and hesitated, suddenly fearing the Tamurlin might not be above cannibalism. He looked it over, relieved to find no comparison between this joint and human or nemet anatomy. Starvation and Renols' suspicious stare overcame his other scruples and he ate the unidentified meat, careful with each bite not to swallow the leaves tucked in his cheek. The meat, despite the strong medicinal taste of the leaves, had a musty, mildewed flavor that almost made him retch. He held his breath and tried not to taste it, and wiped his hands on the earthen floor when he was done.

The captain offered him a second piece, and stopped in the act.

From outside there came a disturbance. Laughter. Someone shrieked in pain.

Renols put down the platter of meat and went out to speak with the man at the entry to the shelter.

"You swore," said Kurt when he came back.

"We're keeping yours," said Renols. "The other one is ours."

The confusion outside grew louder. Renols looked torn between annoyance at the interruption and desire to see what was passing outside. Abruptly he called in the man at the entry, tersely bidding him take Kurt to confinement.

The commotion sank away into silence. Kurt listened, teeth clamped tight against the heaving of his stomach. He had spit out the leaves there in the darkness of the shelter where they had left him, hands tied around one of the two support posts. He twisted until he could dig with his fingers in the hard dirt floor and bury the rejected leaves.

There was a bitter taste in his mouth now. His vision blurred, his pulse raced, his heart crashed against his ribs. He began to be hazy-minded, and slept a time.

Footsteps in the dust outside aroused him. Shadows entered the moonlight-striped shelter, pulling a loose-limbed body with them. It was Kta. They tied the semiconscious nemet to the other post and left him.

After a time Kta lifted his head and leaned it back against the post. He did not speak or look at Kurt, only stared off into the dark, his face and body oddly patterned with moonlight through the woven-work.

"Kta," said Kurt finally. "Are you all right?"

Kta made no reply.

"Kta," Kurt pleaded, reading anger in the set of the nemet's jaw.

"Is it to you," Kta's hoarse voice replied, "is it to you that I owe my life? Do I understand that correctly? Or do I believe instead the tale you tell to the *umani?*"

"I am doing all I can."

"What is it you want from me?"

"I am trying to save our lives," Kurt said. "I am trying to get you out of here. You know me, Kta. Can you take seriously any of the things I have told them?"

There was a long silence. "Please," said Kta in a broken voice, "please spare me your help from now on."

"Listen to me. There are weapons in the ship if I can convince them to let me in there. If I can fire its engines I can burn this nest out."

"I will forgive you," said Kta, "when you do that."

"Are you," Kurt asked after a moment, "much hurt?"

"I am alive," Kta answered. "Does that not satisfy you?— Shall I tell you what they did to the boy, honored friend?"

"I could not stop it,—Kta, look at me. Listen. Is there any hope at all from *Tavi?* If we could get free, could we find our way there?"

There was no answer.

"Kta,—where is your ship anchored?"

"Why? So you can buy our lives with that too?"

"Do you think I mean to tell—"

"They are your kind, human. It would be possible to survive,—if you could buy your life. I will not give you *Tavi.*"

Against such bitterness there was no answer. Kurt swallowed at the resentment and the hurt that rose in his throat; he held his peace after that. He wanted no more truth from Kta.

The silence wore on, two-sided. At last it was Kta who turned his head. "What are you fighting for?" he asked.

"I thought you had drawn your conclusion."

"I am asking. What are you trying to do?"

"To save your life. And mine."

"What use is that to either of us under these terms?"

Kurt twisted toward him. "What use is it to give in to them? Is it sense to let them kill you and do nothing to help yourself?"

"Stop protecting me. I am better dead."

"Like *they* died? Like that?"

"Show me," said Kta, his voice shaking, "show me what you can do against these creatures. Put a weapon in my hands or even get my hands free and I will die well enough. But what dignity is there in living like this? Give me a reason. Tell me something I could have told the men they killed, why I have to live, when I should have died before them."

"Kta, tell me, is there any possible chance of reaching *Tavi?*"

"The coast is leagues away. They would overtake us. This ship of yours. Is it true what you said, that you could burn them out?"

"Everyone would die,—you too, Kta."

"You know how much that means to me. Light of heaven, what manner of world is yours? Why did you have to interfere?"

"I did the best I knew to do."

"You were wrong," said Kta.

Kurt turned away and let the nemet alone, as he so evidently wanted to be. Kta had reason enough to hate humanity. Almost all he had ever loved was dead at the hands of humans, his home lost, his hearth dead, now even the few friends he had left slaughtered before his eyes. His parents,—Hef,—Mim,—himself. Elas was dying. To this had human friendship brought the lord of Elas, and most of it was his own friend's doing.

In time, Kta seemed to sleep, his head sunk on his breast, his breathing heavy.

A shadow crept across the slatting outside, a ripple of darkness that bent at the door, crept inside the shelter. Kurt woke, moved, began a cry of warning. The shadow plummeted, holding him, clamping a rough, calloused hand over his mouth.

The movement wakened Kta, who jerked, and a knife flashed in the dim light as the intruder drove for Kta's throat.

Kurt twisted, kicked furiously and threw the would-be assassin tumbling. He righted himself, and a feral human face stared at both of them, panting, the knife still clenched for use.

The human advanced the knife, demonstrating it to them, ready. "Quiet," he hissed. "Stay quiet."

Kurt shivered, reaction to the near-slaughter of Kta. The

nemet was unharmed, breathing hard, his eyes also fixed on the wild-haired human.

"What do you want?" Kurt whispered.

The human crept close to him, tested the cords on his wrists. "I'm Garet," said the man. "Listen. I will help you."

"Help me?" Kurt echoed, still shuddering, for he thought the man might be mad. The leaf-smell was about him. Feverish hands sought his shoulders. The man leaned close to whisper yet more softly.

"You can't trust Renols, he hates the thought of the Ship. He'll find a way to kill you. He isn't sure yet, but he'll find a way. I could get you into your ship tonight. I could do that."

"Cut me free," Kurt replied, snatching at any chance.

"I *could* do that."

"What do you want, then?"

"You'll have the weapons in the little ship. You can kill Renols then. *I* will help you. *I* will be second and I will go on helping you."

"You want to be captain?"

"You can make me that, if I help you."

"It's a deal," said Kurt, and held his breath while the man made a final consideration. He dared not ask Kta's freedom too. He dared not turn on Garet and take the knife. The slim chance there was in the situation kept him from risking it; in silence, once inside the ship, he could handle Garet and stand off Renols.

The knife haggled at the cords, parting the tough fiber and sending the blood excruciatingly back to his hands. He rose up carefully, for Garet held the knife ready against him if he moved suddenly.

Then Garet's eyes swept toward Kta. He bent toward him, blade extended.

Kurt caught his arm, fronted instantly by Garet's bewildered suspicion, and for a moment fear robbed Kurt of any sense to explain.

"He is mine," Kurt said.

"We can catch a lot of nemet," said Garet. "What's this one to you?"

"I know him," said Kurt. "And I can get cooperation out of

him. He's not about to cry out, because he knows he'd die; he knows I'm his only chance of staying alive, so eventually he'll tell me all I ask of him."

Kta looked up at both of them, well able to understand. Whether it was consummate acting or fear of Garet or fear of human treachery, he looked frightened. He was among aliens. Perhaps it even occurred to him that he could have been long deceived.

Garet glowered, but he thrust the knife into his belt and led the way out into the tangle of huts outside.

"Sentries?" Kurt breathed into his ear.

Garet shook his head, drew him further through the village, up to the landing struts, the extended ladder. A sentry did stand there. Garet poised to throw, knife balanced between his fingertips. He drew back—

—the hiss and *chunk!* of an arrow toppled him, clawing at the ground. The sentry crouched and whirled, and men poured out of the dark. Kurt went down under a triple assault, struggling and kicking as they hauled him where they would take him, up to the ladder.

Renols was there, ax in hand. He prodded Kurt in the belly with it. His ugly face contorted further in a snarl of anger.

"Why?" he asked.

"He came," said Kurt, "threatened to kill me if I didn't come at once. Then he told me you were planning to kill me. I didn't know what to believe. But this one had a knife, so I kept quiet."

"Sentries are dead," another man reported. "Six men are dead, throats cut. One of our scouts hasn't come back either."

"Garet's brothers," Renols said, and looked at the men who surrounded him. "His folk's doing. Find his women and his brats. Give them to the dead men's families, whatever they like."

"Captain," said that man, biting his lip nervously. "Captain, the Garets are a big family. Their kin is in the Red band too. If they get to them with some story—"

"Get them," said Renols. "Now."

The men separated. Those who held Kurt remained. Renols looked up at the entry to the ship, thought silently, then nodded to his men, who brought Kurt away as they walked through the camp. They were quiet. Not a sound came from the encampment. Kurt walked obediently enough, although the men made it harder for him out of spite.

They came to the hut from which he had escaped. Renols stooped and looked inside, where Kta was still tied.

He straightened again. "The nemet is still alive," he said. Then he looked at Kurt from under one brow. "Why didn't Garet kill him?"

Kurt shrugged. "Garet hit him. I guess he was in a hurry."

Renols' scowl deepened. "That isn't like Garet."

"How should I know? Maybe Garet thought he might fail tonight and didn't want a dead nemet for proof of his visit."

Renols thought that over. "So. How did he know you wouldn't raise an alarm?"

"He didn't. But it makes sense I'd keep quiet. How am I to know whose story to believe?"

Renols snorted. "Put him inside. We'll catch one of the Garets alive and then we'll see about it."

The human left. Kurt tested the strength of the new cords, which were unnecessarily tight and rapidly numbed his hands—a petty measure of their irritation with him. He sighed and leaned his head back against the post, ignoring Kta's staring at him.

There was no chance to discuss matters. Kta seemed to sense it, for he said nothing. Someone stood not far from the hut, visible through the matting.

Quite probably, Kurt thought, the nemet had added things up for himself. Whether he had then reached the right conclusion was another matter.

Eventually first light began to bring a little detail to the hut. Kta finally slept. Kurt did not.

Then a stir was made in the camp, men running in the direction of Renols' hut. Distant voices were discussing something urgently. The commotion spread, until people were stirring about in some alarm.

And Renols' lieutenants came to fetch them both, handling them both harshly as they hurried them toward Renols' shelter.

"We found Garet's brothers," Renols said, confronting Kurt.

Kurt stared at him, neither comforted nor alarmed by that news. "Garet's brothers are nothing to me."

"We found them dead. All of them. Throats cut. There were tracks of nemet—sandal-wearing."

Kurt glanced at Kta, not needing to feign shock.

"Two of our searchers haven't come back," said Renols. "You say this one is a chief among the nemet. A lord. Probably they're his. Ask him."

"You understood," Kurt said in Nechai. "Say something."

Kta set his jaw. "If you think to buy time by giving them anything from me, you are mistaken."

"He has nothing to say," said Kurt to Renols.

Renols did not look surprised. "He will find something to say," he promised. "Astin, get a guard doubled out there. No women to go out of camp today. Raf, bring the nemet to the main circle."

It would be possible, Kurt realized with a cold sickness at the heart, it would be possible to play out the game to the end. Kta would not betray him any more than he would betray the men of *Tavi*. To let Kta die might buy him the hour or so needed to hope for rescue. Possibly Kta would not even blame him. It was always hard to know what Kta would consider a reasonable action.

He followed along after those who took Kta—Kta with his spine stiff and every line of him braced to resist, but making not a sound. Kurt himself went docilely, his eyes scanning the hostile crowd that gathered in ominous silence.

He let it continue to the very circle, where the sand was still dark-spotted with the blood of the night before. He feared he would not have the courage to commit so senseless an act, giving up both their lives. But when they tried to put Kta to the ground, he scarcely thought. He tore loose, hit one man, stooped, jerked the ax from his startled hand and swung it toward those who held Kta.

The nemet reacted with amazing agility, swung one man into the path of the ax, kneed the other, snatched a dagger and applied it with the blinding speed he could use with the *ypan*. The men clutched spurting wounds and went down howling and writhing.

"Archers!" Renols bellowed. There was a great clear space

about the area. Kurt and Kta stood back to back, men crowding each other to get out of the way. Renols was closest.

Kurt charged him, ax swinging. Renols went down with his side open, rolling in the dust. Other men scrambled out of the way as he kept swinging. Kta stayed with him. Their area changed. People fled from them screaming.

"Shoot them!" someone else shrieked.

Then all chaos broke loose, a hoarse cry from the rear of the crowd. Some of the Tamurlin turned screaming in panic, their cries swiftly drowned in the sounds of battle in the center of the crowd.

Kta jerked at Kurt's arm and pointed—both of them for the moment stunned by the appearance of nemet among the Tamurlin, the flash of bright-edged swords in the sunlight. No Tamurlin offered them fight anymore: the humans were trying more to escape than to fight, and soon there were only nemet around them. The humans had vanished into the brush.

Now with Kurt behind him, Kta stood in the clear, with dagger in hand and the dead at his feet, and the nemet band raised a cheer.

"Lord Kta!" they cried over and over. "Lord Kta!" And they came to him, bloody swords in hand, and knelt down in the dust before their almost-naked and much-battered lord. Kta held out his hand to them, dropping the blade, and turned palm upward to heaven, to the cleansing light of the sun.

"*Ei,* my friends," he said, "my friends, well done."

Val t'Ran, the officer next in command after Bel t'Osanef, rose from his knees and looked as if he would gladly have embraced Kta, if such impulses belonged to nemet. Tears shone in his eyes. "I thank heaven we were in time, Kta-ifhan, and I would have reckoned we could not be."

"It was you who killed the humans outside the camp, was it not?"

"Aye, my lord, and we feared they had spoiled our ambush. We thought we might have been discovered by that. We were very careful stalking the camp, after that."

"It was well done," said Kta again, with great feeling, and held out his hand to the boy Pan, who had come with the rescuers. "Pan, it was you who brought them?"

"Yes, sir," said the youth. "I had to run, sir, I had to. I hated to leave you. Tas and I—we thought we could do more by getting to the ship—but he died of his wound on the way."

Kta swallowed heavily. "I am sorry, Pan. May the Guardians of your house receive him kindly. —Let us go. Let us be out of this foul place."

Kurt saw them prepare to move out, looked down at what weight was clenched in his numb hand, saw the ax and his arm bloodstained to the shoulder. He let it fall, suddenly shaking in every limb. He stumbled aside from all of them, bent over in the lee of a hut and was sick for some few minutes until everything had emptied out of his belly—drugs, Tamurlin food. But the sights that stayed in his mind were something over which he had no such power. He took dust and rubbed at the blood until his skin stung with the sandy dirt and the spots were gone. In a deserted hut he found a gourd of water and drank and washed his face. The place stank of leaf. He stumbled out again into the sunlight.

"Lord Kurt," said one of the seamen, astonished to find him. "Kta-ifhan is frantic. Come. Hurry. Come, please."

The nemet looked strange to him, alien, the language jarring on his ears. Human dead lay around. The nemet were leaving. He felt no urge to go among them.

"Sir."

Fire roared near him; a wave of heat brought him to alertness. They were setting fire to the village. He stared about him like a man waking from a dream.

He had pulled a trigger, pressed a button and killed, remotely, instantly. He had helped to fire a world, though his post was noncombat. They had been minute, statistical targets.

Renols' astonished look hung before him. It had been Mim's.

He lay in the dust, with its taste in his mouth and his lips cut and his cheek bruised. He did not remember falling. Gentle alien hands lifted him, turned him, smoothed his face.

"He is fevered," Pan's clear voice said out of the blaze of the sun. "The burns, sir—the sun, the long walk—"

"Help him," said Kta's voice. "Carry him if you must. We must get clear of this place. There are other tribes."

The journey was a haze of brown and green, of sometime

drafts of skin-stale water. At times he walked, hardly knowing anything but to follow the man in front of him. Toward the last, as their way began to descend to the sea and the day cooled, he began to take note of his surroundings again. Losing the contents of his stomach a second time, beside the trail, made him weak, but he was free of the nausea and his head was clearer afterwards. He drank *telise,* the kindly seaman who offered it bidding him keep the flask; it only occurred to him later that using something a sick human had used would be repugnant to the man. It did not matter; he was touched that the man had given it up for his sake.

He shook off their offered help thereafter. He had his legs again, though they shook under him, and he was self-possessed enough to remember his ship and the equipment they had abandoned; he had been too dazed and the nemet, the nemet with their distrust of machines, had abandoned everything.

"We have to go back," he told Kta, trying to reason with him.

"No," said the nemet. "No. No more lives of my men. We are already racing the chance that other tribes may be alerted by now."

It was the end of the matter.

And toward evening, with the coast before them and *Tavi* lying off-shore, most welcome of sights—there came a seaman racing up across the sand, stumbling and hard-breathing.

He saw Kta and his eyes widened, and he sketched a staggering bow before his lord and gasped out his message.

"Methi's ship," he said, "upcoast. Lookout saw them from the point there. They are searching every inlet on this shore— almost—almost we would have had to pull away—but without enough rowers. Thank heaven you made it, sir."

"Let us hurry," said Kta, and they began to plunge down the sandy slope to the beach itself.

"My lord," hissed the seaman. "I think the ship is *Edrif.* The sail is green."

"*Edrif.*" Kta gazed toward the point with fury in every line of him. "Yeknis take them!—Kurt, t'Tefur's *Edrif,* do you hear?"

"I hear," Kurt echoed. The longing for revenge churned inside him, when a few moments before he would never have looked to fight again. He shivered in the cold sea wind, wrapped his borrowed *ctan* about him and followed Kta downslope as fast as his trembling legs would take him.

"We have not crew enough to take him now," Kta muttered beneath his breath. "Would that I did! We would send that son of Yr's abominations down to Kalyt's green halls—amusement for Kalyt's scaly daughters. Light of heaven! If I had the whole of us this moment,—"

He did not, and fell silent with a grimness that had the pain of tears behind it. Kurt heard the nemet's voice shake, and feared for him before the witness of the men.

16

Tavi's dark blue sail billowed out and filled with the night wind, and Val t'Ran called out a hoarse order to the rowers to hold oars. The rhythm of wood and water cadenced to a halt, forty oars poised level over the water. Then with a direction from Val they came inboard with a single grate of wood, locked into place by the sweating rowers who rested at the benches.

Somewhere *Edrif* still prowled the coast, but the Sufaki vessel had the disadvantage of having to seek, and the lower coast was rough, with many inlets that were possible for *Tavi*, a sleek, shallow-drafted longship—while *Edrif*, greater in oarage, must keep to slightly deeper waters.

Now *Tavi* caught the wind, with the water sloughing rapidly under her hull. On her starboard side rose a great jagged spire against the night sky, sea-worn rock, warning of other rocks in the black waters. The waves lapped audibly at the crag, but they skimmed past and skirted one on the left by a similarly scant margin.

These were waters Kta knew. The crew stayed at the benches, ready but unfrightened by the closeness of the channel they ran.

"Get below," Kta told Kurt. "You have been on your feet too long. I do not want to have to pull you a second time out of the sea. Get back from the rail."

"Are we clear now?"

"There is a straight course through these rocks and the wind is bearing us well down the center of it. Heaven favors us. Here, you are getting the spray where you are standing. Lun, take this man below before he perishes."

The cabin was warm and close, and there was light, well-shielded from outside view. The old seaman guided him to the cot and bade him lie down. The heaving of the ship disoriented him in a way the sea had never done before. He fell into the cot, rousing himself only when Lun propped him up to set a mug of soup to his lips. He could not even manage it without shaking. Lun held it patiently, and the warmth of the soup filled his belly and spread to his limbs, pouring strength into him.

He bade Lun prop his shoulders with blankets and give him a second cup. He was able to sit then partially erect, his hands cradling the steaming mug. He did not particularly want to drink it; it was the warmth he cherished, and the knowledge that it was there. He was careful not to fall asleep and spill it. From time to time he sipped at it. Lun sat nodding in the corner.

The door opened with a gust of cold wind and Kta came in, shook the salt water from his cloak and gave it to Lun.

"Soup here, sir," said Lun, prepared and gave him a cup of it, and Kta thanked him and sank down on the cot on the opposite side of the little cabin. Lun departed and closed the door quietly.

Kurt stared for a long time at the wall, without the will left to face another round with Kta. At last Kta moved enough to drink, and let go his breath in a soft sigh of weariness.

"Are you all right?" Kta asked him finally. He put gentleness in his question, which had been long absent from his voice.

"I am all right."

"The night is in our favor. I think we can clear this shore before *Edrif* realizes it."

"Do we still go north?"

"Yes. And with t'Tefur no doubt hard behind us."

"Is there any chance we could take him?"

"We have ten benches empty and no reliefs. Or do you expect me to kill the rest of my men?"

Kurt flinched, a lowering of his eyes. He could not face an accounting now. He did not want the fight. He stared off elsewhere and took a sip of the soup to cover it.

"I did not mean that against you," Kta said. "Kurt, these men left everything for my sake, left families and hearths with no hope of returning. They came to me in the night and begged me—begged me—to let them take me from Nephane, or I would have ended my life that night in spite of my father's wishes. Now I have left twelve of them dead on this shore. —I am responsible for them, Kurt. My men are dead and I am alive. Of all of them, *I* survived."

"I saved *each* of them," Kurt protested, "as long as I could. I did what I knew to do, Kta."

Kta drank the rest of the soup as if he tasted nothing at all and set the cup aside. Then he sat quietly, his jaw knotted with muscle and his lips quivering. It passed.

"My poor friend," said Kta at last. "I know. I know. There was a time I was not sure. I am sorry. Go to sleep."

"Upon that?"

"What would you that I say?"

"I wish I knew," Kurt said, and set his cup aside and laid his head on the blankets again. The warmth had settled into his bones now, and the aches began, the fever of burned skin, the fatigue of ravaged nerves.

"*Yhia* eludes me," Kta said then. "Kurt, there must be reasons. I should have died; but they—who were in no danger of dying—they died. My hearth is dead and I should have died with it; but they—that is my anger, Kurt. I do not know why."

From a human Kurt would have dismissed it as nonsensical; but from Kta, it was no little thing—not to know. It struck at everything the nemet believed. He looked at Kta, greatly pitying him.

"You went among humans," said Kurt. "We are a chaotic people."

"No," said Kta. "The whole of creation is patterned. We live in patterns. And I do not like the pattern I see now."

"What is that?"

"Death upon death, dying upon dead. None of us are safe save the dead. But what will become of us—is still in front of us."

"You are too tired. Do your thinking in the morning, Kta. Things will seem better then."

"What, and in the morning will they all be alive again? Will Indresul make peace with my nation and Elas be unharmed in Nephane? No. Tomorrow the same things will be true."

"So may better things. Go to bed, Kta."

Kta rose up suddenly, went and lit the prayer-light of the small bronze *phusa* that sat in its wood-and-bronze niche. The light of Phan illuminated the corner with its golden radiance and Kta knelt, sat on his heels and lifted his open palms.

In a low voice he began the invocation of his Ancestors, and soon his voice faded and he rested with his hands in his lap. Just now it was an ability Kurt envied the religious nemet—like Kta, like Mim, no longer to feel physical pain. The mind utterly concentrated first upon the focus of the light and then beyond, reaching for what no man ever truly attained, but reaching.

The stillness that had been in Elas came over the little cabin. There was the groaning of the timbers, the rush of water past the hull, the rocking of the sea. The quiet seeped inward. Kurt found it possible at last to close his eyes.

He had slept some little time. He stirred, waking from some forgotten dream, and saw the prayer-light flickering on the last of its oil.

Kta still sat as he had before.

A chill struck him. He thought of Mim, dead before the *phusa,* and Kta's state of mind, and he sprang from bed. Kta's face and half-naked body glistened with sweat, though it was not even warm in the room. His eyes were closed, his hands loose in his lap, though every muscle in his body looked rigid.

"Kta," Kurt called. Interruption of meditation was no trifling matter to a nemet, but he seized Kta's shoulders nonetheless.

Kta shuddered and drew an audible breath.

"Kta. Are you all right?"

Kta let the breath go. His eyes opened. "Yes," he murmured thickly, tried to move and failed. "Help me up, Kurt."

Kurt drew him up, steadied him on his deadened legs. After a moment the nemet ran a hand through his sweat-damp hair and straightened his shoulders.

He did not speak further, only stumbled to his cot and fell in, eyes closed, as relaxed as a sleeping child. Kurt stood there staring down at him in some concern, and at last concluded that he was all right. He pulled a blanket over Kta, put out the main light, but left the prayer-light to flicker out on its remaining oil. If it must be extinguished there were prayers which had to be

said, he knew them from hearing Mim say them; but it would be
hypocrisy to speak them and offensive to Kta to omit them.

He sought the refuge of his own bed and lay staring at the
nemet's face in the almost-dark, remembering the invocation
Kta had made of the Guardians of Elas, those mysterious and
now angry spirits that protected the house. He did not believe in
them, and yet felt a heaviness in the air when they had been invoked, and he wondered with what Kta's consciousness or subconscious had been in contact.

He remembered the oracular computers of Alliance central
command which analyzed, predicted, made policy,—prophesied;
and he wondered if those machines and the nemet did not perceive some reason beyond rationality, if the machines men had
built functioned because the nemet were right, because there
was a pattern and the nemet came close to knowing it.

He looked at Kta's face, peaceful and composed, and felt an
irrational terror of him and his outraged Ancestors, as if whatever watched Elas was still alive and still powerful, beyond the
power of men to control.

But Kta slept with the face of innocence.

Kurt braced himself as Lun heaved a bucket of seawater over
him—cold, stinging with salt in his wounds, but a comfort to the
soul. He was clean again, shaved, civilized. The man handed
him a blanket and Kurt wrapped in it gratefully, not minding its
rough texture next to his abused skin. Kta, leaning with his back
against the rail, gave him a pitying look, his own bronze skin
able to absorb Phan's burning rays without apparent harm, even
the bruises he had suffered at the hands of the Tamurlin muted
by his dusky complexion, his straight black hair drying in the
wind to fall into its customary order, while Kurt's—lighter, sun-
bleached now, was entirely unruly. Kta looked godlike and
serenely undamaged, renewed by the morning's light, like a
snake newly molted.

"It looks terribly sensitive," Kta said, grimacing at the sunburn that bled at Kurt's knees and wrists and ankles. "Oil would
help."

"I will try some in a little while," Kurt said. He took his
clothing and dressed, an offense to his fevered skin: he went

clad this day only in the *ctan*. When there were no women present it was enough.

"How long will it take us to reach the Isles?" Kurt asked of Kta, for Kta had given that as their first destination.

Kta shrugged. "Another day, granted the favor of heaven and the ladies of the winds. There are dangers in these waters besides *Edrif*; Indresul has a colony to the west—Sidur Mel; with a fleet based there,—a danger I do not care to wake. And even in the Isles, the great colony of Smethisan is dominated by the house of Lur, trade-rivals of Elas, and I would not trust them. But the Isle of Acturi is ruled by house-friends: I hope for port there."

The canvas snapped overhead and Kta cast a look up at the sail, waved a signal back to Val. *Tavi*'s crew hurried into action.

"The gray ladies," said Kta, meaning the sky-sprites, "may not favor us for long. Sailors should speak respectfully of heaven and never take it for granted."

"A change in the weather?"

"For the worse." Kta wore a worried look, indicated a faint grayness at the very edge of the northern sky. "I had hoped to reach the Isles before that. Spring winds are uncertain, and that one blows right off the ice of the Yvorst Ome. We may feel the edge of it before the day is done."

By midmorning *Tavi*'s sail filled and hung slack by turns, Kta's ethereal ladies turning fickle. By noon the ship had taken on a queasy motion, almost without wind to stir her sail. Canvas snapped. Val bellowed orders to the deck crew, while Kta stood near the bow and looked balefully at the advancing bank of cloud.

"You had better find heavier clothing," said Kta. "When the wind shifts, you will feel it in your bones."

The clouds took on an ominous look now that they were closer. They came like a veil over the heavens, black-bottomed.

"It will drive us back," Kurt observed.

"We will gain what distance we can and fight to hold our position. You are not experienced in this; you have seen no storms such as the spring winds bring. You ought not to be on deck when it hits."

By afternoon the northwest sky was utterly black, showing

flashes of lightning out of it, and the wind was picking up in little puffs, uncertain at first, from this quarter and that.

Kta looked at it and swore with feeling. "I think," he said,
"that the demons of old Chteftikan sent it down on us for spite.
Sufak is to leeward, with its hidden rocks. The only comfort is
that Shan t'Tefur is nearer them, and if we go aground, he will
have gone before us. —*Hya*, you, man! Tkel! Take another hitch
in that! Wish you to climb after it in the storm? I shall send you
up after it."

Tkel grinned, waved his understanding and caught quickly at
the line to which he was clinging, for *Tavi* was suddenly beginning to experience heavy seas.

"Kurt," said Kta, "be careful. This deck will be awash soon,
and a wave could carry you overboard."

"How do your men keep their footing?"

"They do not move without need. You are no seaman, my
friend. I wish you would go below. I would not have you enter-
taining Kalyt's green-eyed daughters tonight. I know not what
their feelings may be about humans."

Kurt knew the legend. Drowned sailors were held in the do-
main of Kalyt the sea father until proper rites could release their
souls from bondage to the lustful seasprites and send them to
their ancestral hearths.

He took Kta's warning, but it was advice, not order, and he
was not willing to go below. He walked off aft and suddenly a
great swell made him lose his balance. He caught at the mast in
time to save himself from pitching headlong into the rowers' pit.
He refused to look back at Kta, humiliated enough. He found his
balance again and walked carefully toward the low prominence
of the cabin, taking refuge against its wall.

Tavi was soon hard-put to maintain her course against the
seas. Her bow rose on the swells and her deck pitched alarm-
ingly as she rode them down. Overhead the sky turned to premature twilight, and the wind carried the scent of rain.

Then a great gust of wind scoured the sea and hit the ship.
The spray kicked up, the bow awash as water broke over the
ship's bronze-shod ram. Kurt wiped the stinging water from his
eyes as sea and sky tilted insanely. He kept a tight grip on the
safety line. *Tavi* became a fragile wooden shell shrunk to minia-

ture proportions against the waves that this morning had run so
smoothly under her bow.

Wood and rigging groaned as if the vessel was straining to
hold together, and a torrent of water nearly swept Kurt off his
feet. Rain and salt water mixed in a ceaseless, blinding mist. In
the shadowy sky lightning flashed and thunder boomed directly
after, and Kurt flinched against the cabin wall, constantly expecting the ship not to surface after the next pitch downward
or the breaking of spray across her deck. Thunder ripped
overhead—lightning seemed close enough to take the very mast.
His heart was in his throat already; at every crash of thunder he
simply shut his eyes and expected to die. He had ridden out
combat a dozen times. The fury of this little landbound sea was
more awesome. He clung, half drowned, and shivered in the
howling wind, and Kta's green-eyed seasprites seemed real and
malevolently threatening, the depths yawning open and deadly,
alternated with the sky beyond the rail. He could almost hear
them singing in the wind.

It was a measureless time before the rain ceased, but at last
the clouds broke and the winds abated. To starboard through the
haze of rain land appeared, the land they so much wanted to
leave behind, a dim gray line, the stark cliffs and headlands of
Sufak. Kta turned the helm over to Tkel and stood looking
toward the east, wiping the rain from his face. The water
streamed from his hair.

"How much have we lost?" Kurt asked.

Kta shrugged. "Considerable. Considerable. We must fight
contrary winds, at least for the present. Spring is a constant
struggle between southwind and north, and eventually south
must win. It is a question of time and heaven's good favor."

"Heaven's good favor would have prevented that storm," said
Kurt. Cold limbs and exhaustion made him more acid than he
was lately wont to be with Kta, but Kta was well-armored this
day: he merely shrugged off the human cynicism.

"How are we to know? Maybe we were going toward trouble
and the wind blew us back to safety. Maybe the storm had nothing to do with us. A man should not be too conceited."

Kurt gave him a peculiar look, and caught his balance as the
sea's ebbing violence lifted *Tavi*'s bow and lowered it again. It

pleased him, even so, to find Kta straight-facedly laughing at him: so it had been in Elas, on evenings when they talked together, making light of their serious differences. It was good to know they could still do that.

"*Hya!*" Val cried, "My lord Kta! Ship astern!"

There was, amid the gray haze, a tiny object that was not a part of the sea or the shore. Kta swore.

"They cannot help but overhaul us, my lord!"

"That much is sure," said Kta, and then lifted his voice to the crew. "Men, if that is *Edrif* astern, we have a fight coming. Arm yourselves and check your gear; we may not have time later. Kurt, my friend,—" Kta turned and faced him, "When they close, as I fear they will, keep away from exposed areas. The Sufaki are quite accurate bowmen. If we are rammed, jump and try to find a bit of wood to cling to. Use sword or ax, whatever you wish, but I do not plan to be boarding or boarded if I can prevent it. Badly as we both want Shan t'Tefur, we dare not risk it."

The intervening space closed slowly. Nearer view confirmed the ship as *Edrif,* a sixty-oared longship, and *Tavi,* though of newer and swifter design, had ten of her fifty benches vacant. At the moment only twenty oars were working.

"*Ei,*" said Kta to the men in the rowers' pits on either side of him—the other twenty also seated and ready, six of the deck crew taking vacant posts to bring *Tavi*'s oarage closer to normal strength. "*Ei,* now, keep the pace, you rowers, as you are, and listen to me. *Edrif* is stalking us, and we will have to begin to move. Let none of us make a mistake or hesitate; we have no margin and no relief. Skill must save us, skill and discipline and experience; no Sufak ship can match us in that—Now, now, run out the rest of the oars. Hold, you other men, hold!"

The cadence halted briefly, *Tavi*'s twenty working oars poised creaking and dripping until the other twenty-six were run out and ready. Kta gave the count himself, a moderate pace. *Edrif* gained steadily, her sixty oars beating the sea. Figures were now discernible on her deck.

Kurt made a quick descent to seize a blade from a rack in the companionway, and on second thought exchanged it for a short-handled ax, such as was properly designed for freeing shattered rigging, not for combat. He did not estimate that his lessons with Kta had made him a fencer equal to a nemet who had handled the *ypan* all his life, and he did not trust that all Sufaki shunned the *ypan* in favor of the bow and the knife.

He delayed long enough to dress too, to slip on a *pel* beneath the *ctan* and belt it, for the wind was bitter, and the prospect of entering a fight all but naked did not appeal to him.

When he had returned to the deck, even after so brief a time, *Edrif* had closed the gap further, so that her green dragon figurehead was clear to be seen above the water that boiled about her metal-shod ram. A stripe-robed officer stood at her bow, shouting back orders, but the wind carried his voice away.

"Prepare to turn full about," Kta shouted to his own crew. "Quick turn, starboard bank—stand by—Turn! Hard about,—*hard!*"

Tavi changed course with speed that made her timbers groan, oars and helm bringing her about three-quarters to the wind, and Kta was already shouting an order to Pan.

The dark blue sail with the lightning emblem of Elas billowed down from the yard and filled, deck crew hauling to sheet it home. *Tavi* came alive in the water, suddenly bearing down on *Edrif* with the driving power of the wind and her forty-six oars.

Frenzied activity erupted on the other deck. *Edrif* began to turn, full broadside for a moment, continuing until she was nearly stern on. Her dark green sail spread, but she could not turn with graceful *Tavi*'s speed, and her crew hesitated, taken by surprise. *Tavi* had the wind in her own sail, stealing it from theirs.

"Portside oars!" Kta roared over the thunder of the rowing. "Stand by to ship oars portside!—*Hya,* Val!"

"Aye!" Val shouted back. "Understood, my lord!"

A shout of panic went up from *Edrif* as *Tavi* closed, and Kta shouted to the portside bank as they headed for collision. *Tavi*'s two banks lifted from the water, and with frantic haste the men portside shipped oars while the starboard rowers held their poised level.

With the final force of wind and gathered speed, *Tavi* brushed the side of *Edrif,* the Sufak vessel's starboard oars splintering as shouts of pain and panic came from her pits. Sufaki rowers deserted their benches and scrambled for very life, their officers cursing at them in vain.

"Take in sail!" Kta shouted, and *Tavi*'s blue sail began to come in. Quickly she lost the force of the wind and glided under momentum.

"Helm!" Kta shouted. "Starboard oars—in water—and *pull!*"

Tavi was already beginning to turn about under her helm, and the one-sided bite of her oars took her hard about again, timbers groaning. There was a crack like a shot and a scream: one of the long sweeps had snapped under the strain and tumbled a man bleeding into the next bench—the next man leaned to let him fall, but kept the pace, and one of the deck crew ran to aid him, dragging him from the pit. Arrows hissed across the deck—Sufaki archers.

"Portside oars!" Kta shouted, as those men, well-drilled, had already run out their oars to be ready. "All hold! In water—and pull!"

Forty-five oars hit the water together, muscles rippled across glistening backs—stroke—and stroke—and stroke, and *Edrif* astern and helpless with half her oarage hanging in ruin and her deck littered with splinter-wounded men. The arrows fell short now, impotent. The breathing of *Tavi*'s men was in unison and loud, like the ship drawing wind, as if all the crew and the ship they sailed had become one living entity as she drove herself northward, widening the distance.

"First shift," Kta shouted. "Up oars!"

With a single clash of wood the oars came up and held level, dipping and rising slightly with the give of the sea and the oarsmen's panting bodies.

"Ship oars and secure. Second shift,—hold for new pace. Take your beat—Now—two—three—"

They accepted the more leisurely pace, and Kta let go a great sigh and looked down at his men. The first shift still leaned over the wooden shafts, heaving with the effort to breathe. Some coughed rackingly, striving with clumsy hands to pull their discarded cloaks up over their drenched shoulders.

"Well done, my friends," said Kta. "It was very well done."

Lun and several others lifted a hand and signaled a wordless salute, without breath to speak.

"*Hya,* Pan,—you men. It was as fine a job as I have seen. — Get coverings for all those men in the pits. A sip of water too. Kurt, help there, will you?"

Kurt moved, glad at last to find himself useful, and took a pitcher of water to the side of the pit. Two of the men were overcome with exhaustion and had to be lifted out and laid on the deck beside the man whose splintered oar had gashed his belly. It proved an ugly wound, but the belly cavity was not pierced. The man was vowing he would be fit for duty in a day, but Kta ordered otherwise.

Edrif was far astern now, a mere speck, not attempting to follow them. Val gave the helm to Pan and walked forward to join Kta and Kurt.

"The hull took it well," Val reported. "Chal just came up from checking it. But *Edrif* will be a while mending."

"Shan t'Tefur has a mighty hate for us," said Kta, "not lessened by this humiliation. As soon as they can bind up their wounds and fit new oars, they will follow."

"It was bloody chaos on her deck," said Val with satisfaction. "I had a clear view of it. Shan t'Tefur has reason to chase us, but those Sufaki seamen may decide they have had enough. They ought to know we could have sunk them if we had wished."

"The thought may occur to them, but I doubt it will win us their gratitude. We will win as much time as we can." He scanned the pits. "I have not pulled an oar in several years, but it will do me no harm. And you, friend Kurt, you are due gentler care after what you have endured, but we need you."

Kurt shrugged cheerfully enough. "I will learn."

"Go bandage your hands," said Kta. "You have little whole skin left. You are due to lose what remains."

17

The clouds had gone by morning and Phan shed his light over a dead calm sea. *Tavi* rolled with a lazy motion, all but dead in the water, her crew lying over the deck where they could find space, wrapped in their cloaks.

Kurt walked to the stern, rubbing his eyes to keep awake. His companion on watch, Pan, stood at the helm. The youth's eyes were closed. He swayed on his feet.

"Pan," said Kurt gently, and Pan came awake with a jerk, his face flushing with consternation.

"Forgive me, Kurt-ifhan."

"I saw you nod," Kurt said, "only an instant ago. Go lie down and I will stand by the helm. In such a sea, it needs no skill."

"I ought not, my lord, I—"

The youth's eyes suddenly fixed on the sky in hope, and Kurt felt it too, the first effects of a gentle southern breeze. It stirred their hair and their cloaks, touched their faces lightly and ruffled the placid waters.

"*Hya!*" Pan shrieked, and all across the deck men sat up. "The wind, the south wind!"

Men were on their feet, and Kta appeared in the doorway of the cabin and waved his hand in signal to Val, who shouted an order for the men to get moving and set the sail.

In a moment the night-blue sail billowed out full. *Tavi* came to run before the wind. A cheer went up from the crew as they felt it.

"*Ei,* my friends," Kta grinned, "full rations this morning, and permission to indulge,—but moderately. I want no headaches.

That wind will bear *Edrif* along too, so keep a sharp eye on all quarters, you men on watch. You rowers, enjoy yourselves."

The wind continued fair and the battered men of *Tavi* were utterly content to sleep in the sun, to massage heated oil into aching limbs and blistered hands, to lie still and talk, employing their hands as they did so with many small tasks that kept *Tavi* in running order.

Toward evening Kta ordered a course change and *Tavi* bore abruptly northwest, coming in toward the Isles. A ship was on the western horizon at sunset, creating momentary alarm, but the sail soon identified her as a merchant vessel of the house of Ilev, the white bird emblem of that house shining like a thing alive on the black sail before the sun.

The merchantman passed astern and faded into the shadowing east, which did not worry them. Ilev was a friend.

Soon there were visible the evening lights on the shores of a little island. Now the men ran out the oars with a will and bent to them as *Tavi* drew toward that light-jeweled strand: Acturi, home port of Hnes, a powerful Isles-based family of the Indras-descended.

"Gan t'Hnes," said Kta as *Tavi* slipped into the harbor of Acturi, "will not be moved by threats of the Sufaki. We will be safe here for the night."

A bell began to toll on shore, men with torches running to the landing as *Tavi* glided in and ran in her oars.

"*Hya!*" a voice ashore hailed them. "What ship are you?"

"*Tavi,* out of Nephane. Tell Gan t'Hnes that Elas asks his hospitality."

"Make fast, *Tavi,* make fast and come ashore. We are friends here. No need to ask."

"Are you sure of them?" Kurt wondered quietly, as the mooring lines were cast out and made secure. "What if some ship of the Methi made it in first?" He nervously scanned the other ships down the little wharf, sails furled and anonymous in the dark. "Hnes might be forced—"

"No, if Gan t'Hnes will not honor house-friendship, then the sun will rise in the west tomorrow dawn. I have known this man since I was a boy at his feet, and Hnes and Elas have been friends for a thousand years—well, at least for nine hundred, which is as far as Hnes can count."

"And if that was not t'Hnes' word you were just given?"

"Peace, suspicious human, peace. If Acturi had been taken from Hnes' control, the shock would have been felt from shore to shore of the Ome Sin. —*Hya,* Val, run out the gangplank and Kurt and I will go ashore. Stay with the ship and hold the men until I have Gan's leave to bring our crew in."

Gan t'Hnes was a venerable old man and, looking at him, Kurt found reason that Kta should trust him. He was solidly Indras, this patriarch of Acturi's trading empire. His house on the hill was wealthy and proper, the hearthfire tended by lady Na t'Ilev e Ben sh'Kma, wife to the eldest of Gan's three sons, who himself was well into years. Lord Gan was a widower,—the oldest nemet Kurt had seen, and to consider that nemet lived long and very scarcely showed age, he must be ancient.

Of course formalities preceded any discussion of business, all the nemet rituals. There was a young woman, granddaughter to the *chan* of Hnes. She made the tea and served it—and seeing her from the back, her graceful carriage and the lustrous darkness of her hair, Kurt thought of Mim: she even looked a little like her in the face, and when she knelt down and offered him a cup of tea he stared, and felt a pain that brought tears to his eyes.

The girl bowed her head, cheeks flushing at being gazed at by a man, and Kurt took the cup, and looked down and drank his tea, thoughts returning in the quiet and peace of this Indras home that had not touched him since that night in Nephane. It was like coming home, for he had never expected to set foot in a friendly house again; and yet home was Elas, and Mim, and both were gone.

Hnes was a large family, ruled of course by Gan, and by Kma, his eldest, and lady Na; and there were others of the house too, one son being away at sea. There was the aged *chan,* Dek, his two daughters and several grandchildren; Gan's second son Lel and his wife Pym and concubine Tekje h'Hnes; Lel's daughter Imue, a charming child of about twelve, who might be the daughter of either of his two wives: she had

Tekje's Sufak-tilted eyes, but sat beside Pym and treated both her mothers with respectful affection; and there were two small boys, both sons of Lel.

The first round of tea was passed with quiet conversation. The nemet were curious about Kurt, the children actually frightened; but the elders smoothed matters over with courtesy.

Then came the second round, and the ladies left with the children, all but lady Na, the first lady of Hnes, whose opinion was of equal weight with that of the elder men.

"Kta," began the lord of Hnes cautiously, "how long are you out from Nephane?"

"Nigh to fifteen days."

"Then," said the old man, "you were there to be part of the sad tale which has reached us."

"Elas no longer exists in Nephane, my lord, and I am exiled. My parents and the *chan* are dead."

"You are in the house of friends," said Gan t'Hnes. "*Ai,* that I should have lived to see such a day. I loved your father as my great friend, Kta, and I love you as if you were one of my own. Name the ones to blame for this."

"The names are too high to curse, my lord."

"No one is beyond the reach of heaven."

"I would not have all Nephane cursed for my sake. The ones responsible are the Methi Djan and her Sufaki lover Shan t'Tefur u Tlekef. I have sworn undying enmity between Elas and the Chosen of Heaven, and a bloodfeud between Elas and the house of Tefur, but I chose exile. If I had intended war, I could have raised war that night in the streets of Nephane. So might my father, and chose to die rather than that. I honor his self-restraint."

Gan bowed his head in thoughtful sorrow. "A ship came two days ago," he said. "*Dkelis* of Irain in Nephane. Her word was from the Chosen of Heaven herself, that Elas had offended against her and had chosen to remove itself from her sight. —That the—true author of the offense was—forgive me, my guests—a human who did murder against citizens of Nephane while under the guardianship of Elas."

"I killed some of t'Tefur's men," said Kurt, sick at heart. He looked at Kta. "Was that it? Was that what caused it?"

"You know there were other reasons," said Kta grimly. "This

was only her public excuse, a means to pass blame. —My lord Gan, was that the sum of the message?"

"In sum," said Gan, "that Elas is outlawed in all holdings of Nephane; that all citizens must treat you as enemies; that you, Kta, and all with you, are to be killed,—excepting lord Kurt, who must be returned alive and unharmed to the Methi's justice."

"Surely," said Kta, "Hnes will not comply."

"Indeed not. Irain knew that; I doubt even they would execute that order, brought face to face with you."

"What will you, sir? Had you rather we spent the night elsewhere? Say it without offense. I am anxious to cause you no inconvenience."

"Son of my friend," said Gan fiercely, "there are laws older than Nephane, than even the shining city itself, and there is justice higher than what is writ in the Methi's decree. No. Let her study how to enforce that decree. Stay in Acturi. I will make this whole island a fortress against them if they want a fight of it."

"My friend, no, no, that would be a terrible thing for your people. We ask at the most supplies and water, in containers that bear no mark of Hnes. *Tavi* will clear your harbor at dawn. No one saw us come save only Ilev, and they are house-friends to us both. And I do not plan that any should see us go. Elas has fallen. That is grief enough. I would not leave a wake of disaster to my friends where I pass."

"Whatever you need is yours,—harbor, supplies, an escort of galleys if you wish it. But stay, let me persuade you, Kta,—I am not so old I would not fight for my friends. All Acturi's strength is at your command. I do not think that with war against Indresul imminent, the Methi will dare alienate one of her possessions in the Isles."

"I did not think she would dare what she did against Elas, sir, and Shan t'Tefur is likely hard behind us at the moment. We have met him once, and he would act against you without hesitation. I know not what authority the Methi has given him, but even if she would hesitate, as you say, an attack might be an accomplished fact before she heard about it. No, sir."

"It is your decision," said Gan regretfully. "But I think even so, we might hold them."

"Provisions and weapons only. That is all I ask."

"Then see to it, my sons, quickly. Provide *Tavi* with all she needs, and have the hands start loading at once."

The two sons of Hnes rose and bowed their respects all around, then went off quickly to carry out their orders.

"These supplies," said Gan, "are a parting gift from Hnes. There is nothing I can send with you to equal the affection I bear you, Kta, my almost-son. Have you men enough? Some of mine would sail with you."

"I would not risk them."

"Then you are short-handed?"

"I would not risk them."

"Where will you go, Kta?"

"To the Yvorst Ome,—beyond the reach of the Methi and the law."

"Hard lands ring that sea, but Hnes ships come and go there. You will meet them from time to time. Let them carry word between us. *Ai,* what days these are. My sight is longer than that of most men, but I see nothing that gives me comfort now. If I were young, I think I would sail with you, Kta, because I have no courage to see what will happen here."

"No, my lord, I know you. I think were you as young as I, you would sail to Nephane and meet the trouble head-on as my father did. As I would do, but I had Aimu's life to consider, and their souls in my charge."

"Little Aimu. I hesitated to ask. I feared more bad news."

"No, thank heaven. I gave her to a husband, and on his life and honor he swore to me he would protect her."

"What is her name now?" asked lady Na.

"My lady, she is Aimu t'Elas e Nym sh'Bel t'Osanef."

"T'Osanef," murmured Gan, in that tone which said: *Ei, Sufaki,* but with pity.

"They have loved each other from childhood," said Kta. "It was my father's will, and mine."

"Then it was well done," said Gan. "May the light of heaven fall gently on them both." And from an Indras of orthodoxy, it was much. "He is a brave man, this t'Osanef, to be husband to our Aimu now."

"It is true," said Kta, and to the lady Na: "Pray for her, my lady. They have much need of it."

"I shall, and for you, and for all who sail with you," she answered, and included Kurt with a glance of her lovely eyes, to which Kurt bowed in deep reverence.

"Thank you," said Kta. "Your house will be in my thoughts too."

"I wish," said Gan, "that you would change your mind and stay. But perhaps you are right. Perhaps someday things will be different, since the Methi is mateless. Someday it may be possible to return."

"It is possible," said Kta, "if she does not appoint a Sufaki successor. We do not much speak of it, but we fear there will be no return—not for our generation."

Gan's jaw tightened. "Acturi will send ships out tonight, I think."

"Do not fight t'Tefur," Kta pleaded.

"They will sail, I say, and provide at least a warning to *Edrif.*"

"When Djan-methi knows of it—"

"Then she will learn the temper of the Isles," said Gan, "and the Chosen of Heaven will perhaps restrain her ambition with sense."

"*Ai,*" murmured Kta. "I do not want this, Gan."

"This is Hnes' choice. Elas has its own honor to consider. I have mine."

"Friend of my father, these waters are too close to Indresul's. You know not what you could let loose. It is a dangerous act."

"It is," said Gan again, "Hnes' choice."

Kta bowed his head, bound to silence under Gan's roof, but that night he spent long in meditation and lay wakeful on his bed in the room he shared with Kurt.

Kurt watched him, and ventured no question into his unrest. He had enough of his own that evening, beginning to fit together the pieces of what Kta had never explained to him, the probable scene in the Upei as Nym demanded justice for Mim's death, while the Methi had in the actions of Elas' own guest the pretext she needed to destroy Elas.

So Nym had died, and Elas had fallen.

And Djan could claim he had made it all inevitable, his marriage with Mim and his loyalty to Elas being the origin of all her troubles.

—Excepting lord Kurt, who must be returned alive and unharmed to the Methi's justice.

Hanan justice.

The justice of a personal anger, where the charges were nothing she would dare present in the Upei. She would destroy all he loved, but she would not let him go. Being Hanan, she believed in nothing after. She would not grant him quick oblivion.

He lay upon the soft down mattress of Hnes' luxury and stared into the dark, and slept only the hours just before dawn, troubled by dreams he could not clearly remember.

The wind bore fair for the north now, warm from the Tamur Basin. The blue sail drew taut and *Tavi*'s bow lanced through the waves, cutting their burning blue to white foam.

Still Kta looked often astern, and whether his concern was more for Gan t'Hnes or for t'Tefur, Kurt was not sure.

"It is out of our hands," Kurt said finally.

"It is out of our hands," Kta agreed with yet another look aft. There was nothing. He bit at his lip. "*Ei, ei,* at least he will not be with us through the Thiad."

"The Necklace. The Lesser Isles," Kurt knew them by repute, barren crags strung across the Ome Sin's narrowest waters, between Indresul and Nephane and claimed by neither side successfully. They were a maze by fair weather, a killer of ships in storms. "Do we go through it or around?"

"Through if the weather favors us. To Nephane's side—wider waters there—if the seas are rough. I do not treat Indresul's waters with the familiarity the Isles-folk use. Well, well, but past that barrier we are free, my friend, free as the north seas and their miserable ports allow us."

"I have heard," Kurt offered, "that there is some civilization there, some cities of size."

"There are two towns, and those are primitive,—*ei* well, one might be called a city, Haithen. It is a city of wood, of frozen streets. Yvesta the mother of snows never looses those lands. There are no farms, only desolate flats, and impossible mountains, and frozen rivers,—ice masses float in the Yvorst Ome that can crush ships, and there are great sea beasts the like of which do not visit these blue waters. *Ai*, it is nothing like Nephane."

"Are you regretting," Kurt asked softly, "that you have chosen as you have?"

"It is a strange place we go," said Kta, "and yet shame to Elas is worse. I think Haithen may be preferable to the Methi's law. It pains me to say it, but Haithen may be infinitely preferable to the Methi's Nephane. Only when we are passing by the coast of Nephane, I shall think of Aimu, and of Bel, and wish that I had news of them. That is the hardest thing, to realize that there is nothing I can do. Elas is not accustomed to helplessness."

En t'Siran, captain of *Rimaris*, swung onto the deck of the courier ship *Kadese*, beneath the furled red sails. Such was his haste that he did not even sit and take tea with the captain of *Kadese* before he delivered his message; he took the ritual sip of tea standing, and scarcely caught his breath before he passed the cup back to the captain's man and bowed his courtesy to the senior officer.

"T'Siran," said the courier captain, "you signaled urgent news."

"A confrontation," said t'Siran, "between Isles ships and a ship of their own kind."

"Indeed." The captain put his own cup aside, signaled a scribe, who began to write. "What happened? Could you identify any of the houses?"

"Easily on the one side. They bore the moon of Acturi on their sails—Gan t'Hnes' sons, I am well sure of it. The other was a strange sail, dark green with a gold dragon."

"I do not know that emblem," said the captain. "It must be one of those Sufak designs."

"Surely," agreed t'Siran, for the dragon Yr was not one of the lucky symbols for an Indras ship. "It may be a Methi's ship."

"A confrontation, you say. With what result?"

"A long wait. Then dragon-sail turned aside, toward the coast of Sufak."

"And the men of Acturi?"

"Held their position some little time. Then they went back

into the Isles. We drew off quickly. We had no orders to provoke combat with the Isles. That is the sum of my report."

"It is," said the captain of *Kadese,* "a report worth carrying."

"My lord." En t'Siran acknowledged the unusual tribute from a courier captain, bowed his head and, as the captain returned the parting courtesy, left.

The captain of *Kadese* hardly delayed to see *Rimaris* spread sail and take her leave before he shouted an order to his own crew and bade them put about for Indresul.

The thing predicted was beginning. Nephane had come to a point of division. The Methi of Indresul had direct interest in this evidence, which might affect policies up and down the Ome Sin and bring Nephane nearer its day of reckoning.

From now on, *Kadese*'s captain thought to himself, the Methi Ylith would begin to listen to her captains, who urged that there would be no better time than this. Heaven favored it.

"Rowers to the benches," he bade his second, "reliefs at the minimum interval, all available crew."

With four shifts and a hundred and ten oars, the slim *Kadese* was equipped to go the full distance. The wind was fair behind her. Her double red sail was bellied out full, and there was nothing faster on either side of the Ome Sin.

There were scattered clouds, small wisps of white with gray undersides that grew larger in the east as the hours passed. The crew of *Tavi* kept a nervous watch on the skies, dreading the shift of wind that could mean delay in these dangerous waters.

In the west, near at hand, rose the grim jagged spires of the Thiad. The sun declined toward the horizon, threading color into the scant clouds which touched that side of the sky.

The waves splashed and rocked at them as *Tavi* came dangerously close to a rock that only scarcely broke the surface. One barren island was to starboard, a long spine of jagged rocks.

It was the last of the feared islets.

"We are through," exulted Mnek as it fell behind them. "We are for the Yvorst Ome."

Then sail appeared in the dusky east.

Val t'Ran, normally harsh-spoken, did not even swear when it was reported. He put the helm over for the west, cutting dangerously near the fringe rocks of the north Thiad, and sent Pan running to take orders from Kta, who was coming toward the stern as rapidly as Kta ever moved on *Tavi*'s deck.

"To the benches!" Kta was shouting, rousing everyone who had been off duty. Men scrambled before him.

He strode up to the helm and gave Val the order to maintain their present westerly heading.

"Tkel!" he called up to the rigging. "What sail?"

"I cannot tell, my lord," Tkel's voice drifted down from the yard, where the man swung precariously on the footrope. "The distance is too great."

"We shall keep it so," Kta muttered, and eyed mistrustfully the great spires and deadlier rough water which lay to port. "Gently to starboard, Val. Even for good reason, this is too close."

"Aye, sir," said Val, and the ship came a few degrees over.

"They are following," Tkel shouted down after a little time had passed. "They must think we are out of Indresul, my lord."

"The lad is too free with his supposings," Val said between his teeth.

"Nevertheless," said Kta, "that is probably the answer."

"I will join the deck crew," Kurt offered. "Or serve as relief at the benches."

"You are considered of Elas," said Kta. "It makes the men uneasy when you show haste or concern. But if work will relieve your nerves, indulge yourself. Go to the benches."

Kta himself was frightened. It was likely that Kta himself would gladly have taken a hand with the oars, with the rigging, with anything that would have materially sped *Tavi* on her way; Kurt knew the nemet well enough to read it in his eyes, though his face was calm. He burned to do something. They had fenced together: Kurt knew the nemet's impatient nature. The Ancestors, Kta had told him once, were rash men. That was the character of Elas.

In the jolted, moving vision of Kta that Kurt had from the rowers' pit, his own mind numbed by the beat of the oars and the need to breathe, the nemet still stood serenely beside Val at the helm, arms folded, staring out to the horizon.

Then Tkel's shrill voice called down so loudly it rose even over the thunder of the oars.

"Sails off the port bow!"

Tavi altered course. Deck crews ran to the sheets, the oars shuddered a little at the unexpectedly deep bite of the blades, lifted. Chal upon the catwalk called out a faster beat. Breath came harder. Vision blurred.

"They are three sails!" Tkel's voice floated down.

It was tribute to *Tavi*'s discipline that no one broke time to look. Kta looked, and then walked down among the rowers along the main deck so they could see him clearly.

"Well," he said, "we bear due north. Those are ships of Indresul ahead of us. If we can hold our present course and they take interest in the other ship, all will be well. —*Hya*, Chal, ease off the beat. Make it one which will last. We may be at this no little time."

The cadence of the oars took a slower beat. Kta went back to his place at the helm, looking constantly to that threatened horizon. Whatever the Indras ships were doing was something outside the world of the pits: the pace maintained itself, mind lost, no glances at anything but the sweat-drenched back of the man in front, his shoulders, clearing the sweep in back only scarcely, bend and breathe and stretch and pull.

"They are in pursuit," said Sten, whose bench was aftmost port.

The cadence did not falter.

"They are triremes intercepting us," Kta said at last, shouting so all could hear. "We cannot outrun them. Hard starboard. We are going back to Nephane's side."

At least two hundred and ten oars each, double sail.

As *Tavi* bore to starboard, Kurt had his first view of what pursued them, through the oarport: two-masted, a greater and a lesser sail, three banks of oars on a side lifting and falling like the wings of some sea-skimming bird. They seemed to move effortlessly despite their ponderous bulk, gaining with every stroke of their oars, where men would have reliefs from the benches.

Tavi had none. It was impossible to hold this pace long. Vision hazed. Kurt drew air that seemed tainted with blood.

"We must come about," Val cried from the helm. "We must come about, my lord, and surrender."

Kta cast a look back. So, from his vantage point, did Kurt, saw the first of the three Indras triremes pull out to the fore of the others, her gold and white sail taut with the wind. The beat of her oars suddenly doubled, at maximum speed.

"Up the beat," Kta ordered Chal, and Chal shouted over the grate and thunder of the oars, quickening the time to the limit of endurance.

And the wind fell.

The breath of heaven left the sail and had immediate effect on the speed of *Tavi*. A soft groan went up from the crew. They did not slacken the pace.

The leading trireme grew closer, outmatching them in oarage.

"Hold!" Kta shouted hoarsely, and walked to the front of the pits. "Hold! Up oars!"

The rhythm ceased, oars at level, men leaning over them and using their bodies' weight to counter the length of the sweeps, their breathing raucous and cut with hacking coughs.

"Pan! Tkel!" Kta shouted aloft. "Strike sail!"

Now a murmur of dismay came from the men, and the crew hesitated, torn between the habit of obedience and an order they did not want.

"Move!" Kta shouted at them furiously. "Strike sail! You men in the pits, ship oars and get out of there! Plague take it, do not spoil our friendship with mutiny! Get out of there!"

Lun, pit captain, gave a miserable shake of his head, then ran in his oar with abrupt violence, and the others followed suit. Pan and Mnek and Chal and others scrambled to the rigging, and quickly a " 'ware below!" rang out and the sail plummeted, tumbling down with a shrill singing of ropes.

Kurt scrambled from the pit with the others, found the strength to gain his feet and staggered back to join Kta on the quarterdeck.

Kta took the helm himself, put the rudder over hard, depriving *Tavi* of what momentum she had left.

The leading ship veered a little in its course, no longer coming directly at them, and tension ebbed perceptibly among *Tavi*'s men.

Then light flashed a rapid signal from the deck of the rearmost trireme and the lead ship changed course again, near enough now that men could be clearly seen on her lofty deck. The tempo of her oars increased sharply, churning up the water.

"Gods!" Val murmured incredulously. "My lord Kta, they are going to ram!"

"Abandon ship!" Kta shouted. "Val,—go—*go*, man! And you, Kurt—"

There was no time left. The dark bow of the Indras trireme rushed at *Tavi*'s side, the water foaming white around the gleaming bronze of the vessel's double ram. With a grinding shock of wood *Tavi*'s rail and deck splintered and the very ship rose and slid sideways in the water, lifted and pushed into ruin by the towering prow of the trireme.

Kurt flung an arm around the far rail and clung to it, shaken off his feet by the tilting of the deck. With a second tilting toward normal and a grating sound, the trireme began to back water and disengage herself as *Tavi*'s wreckage fell away. Dead were littered across the deck. Men screamed. Blood and water washed over the splintered planking.

"Kurt," Kta screamed at him, "jump!"

Kurt turned and stared helplessly at the nemet, fearing the sea as much as enemy weapons. Behind him the second of the triremes was coming up on the undamaged side of the listing ship, her oars churning up the bloodied waters. Some of the survivors in the water were struck by the blades, trying desperately to cling to them. The gliding hull rode them under.

Kta seized him by the arm and pushed him over the rail. Kurt twisted desperately in midair, hit the water hard and choked, fighting his way to the surface with the desperation of instinct.

His head broke surface and he gasped in air, sinking again as he swallowed water in the chop, his hand groping for anything that might float. A heavy body exploded into the dark water beside him and he managed to get his head above water again as Kta surfaced beside him.

"Go limp," Kta gasped. "I can hold you if you do not struggle."

Kurt obeyed as Kta's arm encircled his neck, went under, and then felt the nemet's hand under his chin lift his face to air again. He breathed, a great gulp of air, lost the surface again. Kta's strong, sure strokes carried them both, but the rough water washed over them. Of a sudden he thought that Kta had lost him, and panicked as Kta let him go: but the nemet shifted his grip and dragged him against a floating section of timber.

Kurt threw both arms over it, coughing and choking for air.

"Hold on!" Kta snapped at him, and Kurt obediently tightened his chilled arms, looking at the nemet across the narrow bit of debris. Wind hit them, the first droplets of rain. Lightning flashed in the murky sky.

Behind them the galley was coming about. Someone on deck was pointing at them.

"Behind you," Kurt said to Kta. "They have us in sight—for something."

Kurt lifted himself from his face on the deck of the trireme, rose to his knees and knelt beside Kta's sodden body. The nemet was still breathing, blood from a head wound washing as a crimson film across the rain-spattered deck. In another moment he began to try to rise, still fighting.

Kurt took him by the arm, cast a look at the Indras officer who stood among the surrounding crew. Receiving no word from him, he lifted Kta so that he could rise to his knees, and Kta wiped the blood from his eyes and leaned over on his hands, coughing.

"On your feet," said the Indras captain.

Kta would not be helped. He shook off Kurt's hand and completed the effort himself, braced his feet and straightened.

"Your name," said the officer.

"Kta t'Elas u Nym."

"T'Elas," the man echoed with a nod of satisfaction. "Aye, I was sure we had a prize. —Put them both in irons. Then put about for Indresul."

Kta gave Kurt a spiritless look, and in truth there was nothing to do but submit. They were taken together into the hold, the trireme having far more room belowdecks than little *Tavi*—and in that darkness and cold they were put into chains and left on the bare planking without so much as a blanket for comfort.

"What now?" Kurt asked, clenching his teeth against the spasms of chill.

"I do not know," said Kta. "But it would surely have been better for us if we had drowned with the rest."

18

Indresul the shining was set deep within a bay, a great and ancient city. Her white, triangle-arched buildings spread well beyond her high walls, permanent and secure. Warships and
merchantmen were moored at her docks. The harbor and the
broad streets that fanned up into the city itself were busy with
traffic. In the high center of the city, at the crest of the hill
around which it was built, rose a second great ring-wall, encircling large buildings of gleaming white stone, an enormous
fortress-temple complex, the Indume, heart and center of Indresul. There would be the temple, the shrine that all Indras-
descended revered as the very hearthfire of the universe.

"The home of my people," said Kta as they stood on the deck
waiting for their guards to take them off. "Our land, which we
call on in all our prayers. I am glad that I have seen it, but I do
not think we will have a long view of it, my friend."

Kurt did not answer him. No word could improve matters.
In the three days they had been chained in the hold, he had had
time to speak with Kta, to talk as they once had talked in Elas,
long, inconsequential talks—sometimes even to laugh, though
the laughter had the taste of ashes. But the one thing Kta had
never said was what was likely to happen to Kurt, only that he
himself would be taken in charge by the house of Elas-in-
Indresul. Kta undoubtedly did suspect and would not say. Perhaps too he knew what would likely become of a human
among these most orthodox of Indras: Kurt did not want to
foreknow it.

* * *

The mournful echo of sealing doors rolled through the vaulted hall, and through the haze of lamps and incense in the triangular hall burned the brighter glare of the holy fire,— the *rhmei* and the *phusmeha* of the Indume-fortress. Kurt paused involuntarily as Kta did, confused by the light and the profusion of faces.

From some doorway hidden by the haze and the light from the hearthfire, there appeared a woman, a shadow in brocade flanked by the more massive figures of armed men.

The guards who had brought them from the trireme moved them forward with the urging of their spear shafts. The woman did not move. Her face was clearer as they drew near her: she was goddesslike, tall, willowy. The shining darkness of her hair was crowned with a headdress that fitted beside her face like the plates of a helm, and shimmered when she moved with the swaying of fine gold chains from the wide wings of it. She was nemet, and of incredible beauty: Ylith t'Erinas ev Tehal, Methi of Indresul.

Her dark eyes turned full on them, and Kta fell on his face before her, full length on the polished stone of the floor. Her gaze did not so much as flicker; this was the obeisance due her. Kurt fell to his knees also, and on his face, and did not look up.

"Nemet," she said, "look at me."

Kta stirred then and sat up, but did not stand.

"Your name," she asked him. Her voice had a peculiar stillness, clear and delicate.

"Methi, I am Kta t'Elas u Nym."

"Elas. Elas of Nephane. How fares your house there, t'Elas?"

"The Methi may have heard. I am the last."

"What, Elas fallen?"

"So Fate and the Methi of Nephane willed it."

"Indeed. —And how is this, that a man of Indras descent is companioned by a human?"

"He is of my house, Methi, and he is my friend."

"You are an offense, t'Elas, an affront to my eyes and to the pure light of heaven. Let t'Elas be given to the examination of the house he has defiled, and let their recommendation be made known to rne."

She clapped her hands: the guards moved, in a clash of metal

and hauled Kta up. Kurt injudiciously flung himself to his
knees, halted suddenly with the point of a spear in his side. Kta
looked down at him with the face of a man who knew his fate
was sealed, and then yielded and went with them.

Kurt flashed a glance at Ylith, anger swelling in his throat.

The staff of the spear across his neck brought him half
stunned to the marble floor, and he expected it to be through his
back in the next instant, but the blow did not come.

"Human." There was no love in that word. "Sit up."

Kurt moved his arms and found purchase against the floor.
He did not move quickly, and one of his guards jerked him up
by the arm and let him go again.

"Do you have a name, human?"

"My name," he answered with deliberate insolence, "is Kurt
Liam t'Morgan u Patrick Edward."

Ylith's eyes traveled over him and fixed last on his face.
"Morgan. This would be your own alien house."

He made no response. Her tone invited none.

"Never have I looked upon a living human," Ylith said softly.
"Indeed,—this seems more intelligent than the Tamurlin, is it
not so, Lhe?"

"I do not believe," said the slender man at her left, "that he is
Tamurlin, Methi."

"He is still of their blood." A frown darkened her eyes. "It is
an outrage against nature. One would take him for nemet but for
that unwholesome coloration,—and until one saw his face. Have
him stand. I would take a closer look at him."

Kurt had both his arms seized, and he was pulled roughly and
abruptly to his feet, his face hot with shame and anger. But if
there was one act that would seal the doom of all Nephane,
friends and enemies alike, it was for the friend of Elas-in-
Nephane to attack this woman. He stubbornly turned his face
away, until the flat of a spear blade against his cheek turned his
head back and he met her eyes.

"Like one of the *inim*-born," the Methi observed. "So one
would imagine them, the children of the upper air,—somewhat
birdlike, the madness of eye, the sharpness of features. But there
is some intelligence there too. Lhe, I would save this human a
little time and study him."

"As the Methi wills it."

"Put him under restraint, and when I find the time I will deal with the matter." Ylith started to turn away, but paused instead for another look, as if the very reality of Kurt was incredible to her. "Keep him in reasonable comfort. He is able to understand, so let him know that he may expect less comfort if he proves troublesome."

Reasonable comfort, as Lhe interpreted it, was austere indeed. Kurt sat against the wall on a straw-filled pallet that was the only thing between him and the bare stones of the floor, and shivered in the draft under the door. There was a rounded circlet of iron around his ankle, secured by a chain to a ringbolt in the stones of the wall, and it was beyond his strength to tear free. There was nowhere to go if he could.

He straightened his leg, dragging the chain along the floor with him, and stretched out face down on the pallet, doubling his chilled arms under him for warmth.

Nothing the Tamurlin had done to him could equal the humiliation of this; the worst beating he had ever taken was no shame at all compared to the look with which Ylith t'Erinas had touched him. They had insisted on washing him, which he would gladly have done, for he was filthy from his confinement in the hold, but they leveled spears at him, forced him to stand against a wall and remove what little clothing he still wore, then scrub himself repeatedly with strong soap. Then they hit him with a bucketful of cold water, and gave him nothing with which to dry his skin. There was a linen breechclout, not even the decency of a *ctan;* that and an iron ring and a cup of water from which to drink: that was the consideration Lhe afforded him.

Hours passed, and the oil lamp on the ledge burned out, leaving only the light that came through the small barred-window from the outer hall. He managed to sleep a little, turning from side to side, warming first his arms and then his back against the mattress.

Then, without warning or explanation, men invaded his cell and forced him from the room under heavy guard, hastening him along the dim halls, the ring on his ankle band a constant, metallic sound at every other step.

Upstairs was their destination, a small room somewhere in the main building, warmed by an ordinary fire in a common hearth. A single pillar supported its level ceiling.

To this they chained his hands, passing the chain behind him around the pillar; then they left him, and he was alone for a great time. It was no hardship: it was warm in this room. He absorbed the heat gratefully and sank down at the base of this pillar, leaning against it and bowing his head, willing even to sleep.

"Human."

He brought his head up, blinking in the dim light. Ylith had come into the room. She sat down upon the ledge beneath the slit of a window and regarded him curiously. She was without the crown now, and her massive braids coiled on either side of her head gave her a strangely fragile face.

"You are one of the human woman's companions," she said, "that she missed killing."

"No," he said, "I came independently."

"You are an *educated* human, as she is."

"As educated as you are, Methi."

Ylith's eyes registered offense, and, it was possible,— amusement. "You are not a civilized human, however, and you are therefore demonstrating your lack of manners."

"My civilization," he said, "is some twelve thousand years old. And I am still looking for evidence of yours in this city."

The Methi laughed outright. "I have never met such answers. You hope to die, I take it. Well, human, look at me. Look up."

He did so.

"It is difficult to accustom myself to your face," she said. "But you do reason. I perceive that. —What is the origin of humans, do you know?"

It was, religiously, a dangerous question. "We are," he said, "children of one of the brothers of the earth, at least as old as the nemet."

"But not light-born," said Ylith, which was to say, unholy

and lawless. "Tell me this, wise human: does Phan light your land too?"

"No. One of Phan's brothers lights our world."

Her brows lifted. "Indeed. *Another* sun?"

He saw the snare of a sudden, realized that the Indras of the shining city were not so liberal and cosmic in their concept of the universe as human-dominated Nephane.

"Phan," she said, "has no equals."

He did not attempt to answer her. She did not rage at him, only kept staring, her face deeply troubled. Not naive, was Ylith of Indresul: she seemed to think deeply, and seemed to find no answer that pleased her. "You seem to me," she said, "precisely what I would expect from Nephane. The Sufaki think such things."

"The *yhia*," he said, venturing dangerously, "is beyond man's grasp, is that not so, Methi? And when man seeks to understand, being man and not god, he seeks within mortal limits, and understands his truth in simple terms and under the guise of familiar words that do not expand his mortal senses beyond his capacity to understand. This is what I have heard. We all—being mortal—deal in models of reality, in oversimplifications."

It was such a thesis as Nym had posed him once over tea, in the peace of the *rhmei* of Elas, when conversation came to serious things, to religion, and humanity. They had argued, and disagreed, and they had been able then to smile and reconcile themselves in reason. The nemet loved debating. Each evening at teatime there was a question posed if there was no business at hand, and they would talk the topic to exhaustion.

"You interest me," said Ylith. "I think I shall hand you over to the priests and let them hear this wonder,—a human that reasons."

"We are," he said, "reasoning beings."

"Are you of the same source as Djan-methi?"

"Of the same kind, not the same politics or beliefs."

"Indeed."

"We have disagreed."

Ylith considered him in some interest. "Tell me, is the color of her hair truly like that of metal?"

"Like copper."

"You were her lover."

Heat flashed to his face. He looked suddenly and resentfully into her eyes. "You are well-informed. Where do you plant your spies?"

"Does the question offend you? Do humans truly possess a sense of modesty?"

"And any other feeling known to the nemet," he returned. "I had *loved* your people. Is this what your philosophy comes to, hating me because I disturb your ideas, because you cannot account for me?"

He would never have said such a thing outside Elas; the nemet themselves were too self-contained, although he could have said it to Kta. He was exhausted; the hour was late. He came close to tears, and felt shamed at his own outburst.

But Ylith tilted her head to one side, a little frown creasing her wide-set brows. "You are certainly unlike the truth I have heard of humans." And after a moment she rose and opened the door, where an elderly man waited,—a white-haired man whose hair flowed to his shoulders, and whose *ctan* and *pel* were gold-bordered white.

The old man made a profound obeisance to Ylith, but he did not kneel: by this it was evident that she knew of his presence there, that they had agreed before hand.

"Priest," she said, "look on this creature and tell me what you see."

The priest straightened and turned his watery eyes on Kurt. "Stand," he urged gently. Kurt gathered his almost paralyzed limbs beneath him and struggled awkwardly to his feet. Of a sudden he hoped; he did not know why this alien priest should inspire that in him, but the voice was soft and the dark eyes like a benediction.

"Priest," urged the Methi.

"Great Methi," answered. the priest, "this is no easy matter. Whether this is a man as we understand the word, I cannot say. But he is not Tamurlin. Let the Methi do as seems just in her own eyes, but it is possible that she is dealing with a feeling and reasoning being, whether or not it is a man."

"Is this creature good or evil, priest?"

"What is man, great Methi?"

"Man," snapped the Methi impatiently, "is the child of Nae. Whose child is he, priest?"

"I do not know, great Methi."

Ylith lowered her eyes then, flicked a glance toward Kurt and down and back again. "Priest, I charge you, debate this matter within the college of priests and return me an answer. Take him with you if it will be needful."

"Methi, I will consult with them, and we will send for him if his presence seems helpful."

"Then you are dismissed," she said, and let the priest go.

Then she left too, and Kurt sank down again against his pillar, confused and mortally tired and embarrassed. He was alone and glad to be alone, so he did not have to be so treated before friends or familiar enemies.

He slumped against his aching joints and tried to will himself to sleep. In sleep the time passed. In sleep he did not need to think.

In sleep sometimes he remembered Mim, and thought himself in Elas, and that the morning bells would never ring.

Doors opened, boomed shut. People stirred around him, shuffling here and there, forcing him back to wakefulness.

The Methi had come back.

This time they brought Kta.

Kta saw him—relief touched his eyes—but he could say nothing. The Methi's presence demanded his attention. Kta came and knelt before her, and went full to his face. His movements were not easy. He appeared to have been hard-used.

And she ignored him, looking above his prostrate form to the tall, stern man who bowed stiffly to his knees and rose again.

"Vel t'Elas," said Ylith, "what has Elas-in-Indresul determined concerning this man Kta?"

Kta's distant kinsman bowed again, straightened. He was of immense dignity, a man reminiscent of Nym. "We deliver him to the Methi for judgment, for life or for death."

"How do you find concerning his dealings with Elas?"

"Let the Methi be gracious: he has kept our law and still honors our Ancestors, except in the offense for which we deliver him up to you: his dealings with this human, and that he is of Nephane."

"Kta t'Elas u Nym," said Ylith.

Kta lifted his face and sat back on his heels.

"Kta t'Elas, your people have chosen an alien to rule them. Why?"

"She was chosen by heaven, Methi, not by men; and it was a fair choosing, by the oracles."

"Confirmed in proper fashion by the Upei and the Families?"

"Yes, Methi."

"Then," she said, looking about at the officers who had come into the room, "heaven has decided to deliver Nephane into our hands once more. —And you, u Nym, who were born Indras,— where is your allegiance now?"

"In my father's land, Ylith-methi, and with my house-friends."

"Do you then reject all allegiance to *this* house of Elas, which was father to your Ancestors?"

"Great Methi," said Kta, and his voice broke, "I reverence you and the home of my Ancestors, but I am bound to Nephane by ties equally strong. I cannot dishonor myself and the Ancestors of Elas by turning against the city that gave me birth. Elas-in-Indresul would not understand me if I did so."

"You equivocate."

"No, Methi. It is my belief."

"What was your mother's name, u Nym? Was she Sufaki or was she Indras?"

"Methi, she was the lady Ptas t'Lei e Met sh'Nym."

"Most honorable, the house of Lei. Then in both lines you are Indras and well descended,—surely of an orthodox house. Yet you choose the company of Sufaki and humans. I find this exceedingly difficult of understanding, Kta t'Elas u Nym."

Kta bowed his head and gave no answer.

"Vel t'Elas," said the Methi, "is this son of your house in any way a follower of the Sufak heresy?"

"Great Methi, Elas finds that he has been educated into the use of alien knowledge and errors, but his upbringing is orthodox."

"Kta t'Elas," said the Methi, "what is the origin of humans?"

"I do not know, Methi."

"Do you say that they are possessed of a soul, and that they are equal to nemet?"

Kta lifted his head. "Yes, Methi," he said firmly, "I believe so."

"Indeed, indeed." Ylith frowned deeply and rose from her place, smoothing the panels of her *chatem*. Then she shot a hard look at the guards. "Lhe,—take these prisoners both to the upper prisons and provide what is needful to their comfort. But confine them separately and allow them no communication with each other. None, Lhe."

"Methi." He acknowledged the order with a bow.

Her eyes lingered distastefully on Kurt. "This," she said, "is nemetlike. It is proper that he be decently clothed. Insofar as he thinks he is nemet, treat him as such."

Light flared.

Kurt blinked and rubbed his eyes as the opening of his door and the intrusion of men with torches brought him out of a sound sleep into panic. Faceless shadows moved in on him.

He threw off the blanket and scrambled up from the cot his new quarters provided him—not to fight, not to fight: it was the worst thing for him and for Kta.

"You must come," said Lhe's voice out of the glare.

Kurt schooled himself to bow in courtesy, instincts otherwise. "Yes, sir," he said, and began to put on his clothing.

When he was done, one guard laid hands on him.

"My lord," he appealed to Lhe, a look of reproach on his face. And Lhe, dignified, elegant Lhe, was the gentleman Kurt suspected; he was too much nemet and too Indras to ignore the rituals of courtesy when they were offered.

"I think that he will come of his own accord," said Lhe to his companions, and they reluctantly let him free.

"Thank you," said Kurt, bowing slightly. "Can you tell me where or why—?"

"No, human," said Lhe. "We do not know, except that you are summoned to the justice hall."

"Do you hold trials at *night?*" Kurt asked, honestly shocked. Even in liberal Nephane, no legal business could be done after Phan's light had left the land.

"You cannot be tried," said Lhe. "You are human."

In some part it did not surprise him, but he had not clearly considered the legalities of his status. Perhaps, he thought, his dismay showed on his face, for Lhe looked uncomfortable, shrugged and made a helpless gesture.

"You must come," Lhe repeated.

Kurt went with them unrestrained, through plain halls and down several turns of stairs, until they came to an enormous pair of bivalve doors and passed through them into a hall of ancient stonework.

The beamed ceiling here was scarcely visible in the light of the solitary torch, which burned in a wall socket. The only furniture was a long tribunal and its chairs.

A ringbolt was in the floor, already provided with chain. Lhe courteously—with immense courtesy—asked him to stand there, and one of the men locked the chain through the ring on his ankle.

He stared up at Lhe, rude, angry, and Lhe avoided his eyes.

"Come," said Lhe to his men. "We are not bidden to remain." And to Kurt: "Human,—you will win far more by humble words than by pride."

He might have meant it in kindness; he might have been laughing. Kurt stared at their retreating backs, shaking all over with rage and fright.

Of a sudden he cried out, kicked at the restraint in a fit of fury, jerked at it again and again, willing, even to break his ankle if it would make them see him, that he was not to be treated like this.

All that he succeeded in doing was in losing his balance, for there was not enough chain to do more than rip the skin around his ankle. He sprawled on the bruising stone and picked himself up, on hands and knees, head hanging.

"Are you satisfied?" asked the Methi.

He spun on one knee toward the voice beyond the torchlight. Softly a door closed unseen, and she came into the circle of light. She wore a robe that was almost a mere *pelan,* gauzy blue, and her dark hair was like a cloud of night, held by a silver circlet around her temples. She stopped at the edge of the tribunal, her short tilted brows lifted in an expression of amusement.

"This is not," she said, "the behavior of an intelligent being."

He gathered himself to sit, nemet-fashion, on feet and ankles, hands palm up in his lap, the most correct posture of a visitor at another's hearth.

"This is not," he answered, "the welcome I was accorded in Nephane, and some of them were my enemies. I am sorry if I have offended you, Methi."

"This is not," she said, "Nephane. And I am not Djan." She sat down in the last of the chairs of the tribunal and faced him so, her long-nailed hands folded before her on the bar. "If you were to strike one of my people,—"

He bowed-slightly. "They have been kind to me. I have no intention of striking anyone."

"*Ai,*" she said, "now you are trying to impress us."

"I am of a house," he answered, hoping that he was not causing Kta worse difficulty by that claim. "I was taught courtesy. I was taught that the honor of that house is best served by courtesy."

"It is," she said, "a fair answer."

It was the first grace she had granted him. He looked up at her with a little relaxing of his defenses. "Why," he asked, "did you call me here?"

"You troubled my dreams," she aid. "I saw fit to trouble yours." And then she frowned thoughtfully. "Do you dream?"

It was not humor, he realized; it was, for a nemet, a religiously reasonable question.

"Yes," he said, and she thought about that for a time.

"The priests cannot tell me what you are," she said finally. "Some urge that you be put to death quite simply; others urge that you be killed by *atia.* Do you know what that means, t'Morgan?"

"No," he said, perceiving it was not threat but question.

"It means," she said, "that they think you have escaped the nether regions and that you should be returned there with such pains and curses as will bind you there. That is a measure of their distress at you. *Atia* has not been done in centuries. Someone would have to research the rites before they could be performed. I think some priests are doing that now. —But Kta t'Elas insists you have a soul, though he could lose his own for that heresy."

"Kta," said Kurt with difficulty through his own fear, "is a gentle and religious man. He—"

"T'Morgan," she said, "you are my concern at the moment, what you are."

"You do not want to know. You will ask until you get the answer that agrees with what you want to hear, that is all."

"You have the look," she said, "of a bird,—a bird of prey. Other humans I have seen had the faces of beasts. I have never seen one alive or clean. Tell me, if you had not that chain, what would you do?"

"I would like to get off my knees," he said. "This floor is cold."

It was rash impudence. It chanced to amuse her. Her laugh held even a little gentleness. "You are appealing. And if you were nemet, I could not tolerate that attitude in you. But what things really pass in your mind? What would you, if you were free?"

He shrugged, stared off into the dark. "I—would ask for Kta's freedom," he said. "And we would leave Indresul and go wherever we could find a harbor."

"You are loyal to him."

"Kta is my friend. I am of Elas."

"You are human. Like Djan, like the Tamurlin."

"No," he said, "like neither."

"Wherein lies the difference?"

"We are of different nations."

"You were her lover, t'Morgan. *Where* do you come from?"

"I do not know."

"Do not know?"

"I am lost. I do not know where I am or where home is."

She considered him, her beautiful face more than usually unhuman with the light falling on it at that angle, like a slightly abstract work of art. "The hearthfire of your kind—assuming you are civilized—lies far distant. It would be terrible to die among strangers, to be buried with rites not your own, with no one to call you by your right name."

Kurt bowed his head, of a sudden seeing another darkened room, Mim lying before the hearthfire of Elas, Mim without her own name for her burying in Nephane: alien words and alien gods, and the helplessness he had felt. He was afraid suddenly with a fear she had put a name to, and he thought of himself dead and being touched by them and committed to burial in the name of gods not his and rites he did not understand. Almost he wished they would throw him in the sea and give him to the fish and to Kalyt's green-haired daughters.

"Have I touched on something painful?" Ylith asked softly. "Did you find the Guardians of Elas did somewhat resent your presence,—or did you imagine that you were nemet?"

"Elas," he said, "was home to me."

"You married there."

He looked up, startled, surprised into reaction.

"Did she consent," she asked, "or was she given?"

"Who—told you of that?"

"Elas-in-Indresul examined Kta t'Elas on the matter. I ask you: did she consent freely?"

"She consented." He put away his anger and assumed humility for Mim's sake, made a bow of request. "Methi, she was one of your own people, born on Indresul's side. Her name was Mim t'Nethim e Sel."

Ylith's brows lifted in dismay. "Have you spoken with Lhe of this?"

"Methi?"

"He is of Nethim. Lhe t'Nethim e Kma, second-son to the lord Kma; and Nethim is of no great friendship to Elas. T'Elas did not mention the house name of the lady Mim."

"He never knew it. Methi, she was buried without her right name. It would be a kindness if you would tell the lord Kma that she is dead, so they could make prayers for her. I do not think they would want to hear that request from me."

"They will ask who is responsible for her death."

"Shan t'Tefur u Tlekef and Djan of Nephane."

"Not Kurt t'Morgan?"

"No." He looked down, unwilling to give way in her sight. The nightmare remembrances he had crowded out of his mind in the daylight were back again, the dark and the fire, and Nym standing before the hearthfire calling upon his Ancestors with Mim dead of his feet. Nym could tell them his grievances in person now. Nym and Ptas—Hef. They had walked and breathed that night and now they had gone to join her. Shadows now, all of them.

"I will speak to Kma t'Nethim and to Lhe," she said.

"Maybe," Kurt said, "you ought to omit to tell them that she married a human."

Ylith was silent a moment. "I think," she said, "that you grieve over her very much. Our law teaches that you have no soul, and that she would have sinned very greatly in consenting to such a union."

"She is dead. Leave it at that."

"If," she continued, relentless in the pursuit of her thought, "*if* I admitted that this was not so,—then it would mean that many wise men have been wrong, that our priests are wrong, that our state has made centuries of error. I would have to admit that in an ordered universe there are creatures which do not fit the order, I should have to admit that this world is not the only one, that Phan is not the only god. I should have to admit things for which men have been condemned to death for heresy. Look up at me, human. Look at me."

He did as she asked, terrified, for he suddenly realized what she was saying. She suspected the truth. There was no hope in argument. It was not politically or religiously expedient to have the truth published.

"You insist," she said, "that there are two universes, mine and yours, and that somehow you have passed into mine. By my rules you are an animal: I reason that even an animal could possess the outward attributes of speech and upright bearing. But in other things you are nemetlike. I dreamed, t'-Morgan. I dreamed, and you were dead in my dream, and I looked upon your face and it troubled me exceedingly. I thought then that you had been alive and that you had loved a nemet, and that therefore you must have a soul. And I woke, and was still troubled—exceedingly."

"Kta," he said, "did nothing other than you have done. He was troubled. He helped me. He ought to be set free."

"You do not understand. He is nemet. The law applies to him. You—can be kept. On him, I must pronounce sentence. Would you choose to die with Kta, rather than enjoy your life in confinement? You could be made comfortable. It would not be that hard a life."

He found surprisingly little difficult about the answer. At the moment he was not even afraid. "I owe Kta," he said. "He never objected to my company, living. And that, among nemet, seems to have been a rare friendship."

Ylith seemed a little surprised. "Well," she said, rising and smoothing her skirts. "I will let you return to your sleep, t'Morgan. I will honor some of your requests. Nethim will give her honor at my request."

"I am grateful for that, at least, Methi."

"Do you want for anything?"

"To speak with Kta," he said, "that most of all."

"That," she said, "will not be permitted."

19

Keys rattled. Kurt stirred out of the torpor of long waiting. Suddenly he realized it was not breakfast. Too many people were in the hall: he heard their moving, the insertion of the key. Another of the moods of Ylith-methi, he reckoned.

Or it was an execution detail, and he was about to learn what had become of Kta.

Lhe led them, Lhe with fatigue-marks under his eyes and his normally impeccable hair disarranged. A *tai,* a short sword, was through his belt.

"Wait down the hall," he said to the others.

They did not want to go. He repeated the order, this time with wildness in his voice, and they almost fled his presence.

No! Kurt started to protest, rising off his cot, but they were gone. Lhe closed the door and stood with his hand clenched on the hilt of the *tai.*

"I am t'Nethim," said Lhe. "My father's business is with Vel t'Elas. Mine is with you. Mim t'Nethim was my cousin."

Kurt recovered his dignity and bowed slightly, ignoring the threat of the fury that trembled in Lhe's nostrils. After such a point, there was little else to do. "I honored her," he said, "very much."

"No," said Lhe. "That you did not."

"Please. Say the rites for her."

"We have said rites, with many prayers for the welfare of her soul. Because of Mim t'Nethim we have spoken well of Elas to our Guardians for the first time in centuries: even in ignorance, they sheltered her. But other things we will not forgive. There is no peace between the Guardians of Nethim and you, human. They do not accept this disgrace."

"Mim thought them in harmony with her choice," said Kurt. "There was peace in Mim. She loved Nethim and she loved Elas."

It did not greatly please Lhe, but it affected him greatly. His lips became a hard line. His brows came as near to meeting as a nemet's might.

"She was consenting?" he asked. "Elas did not command this of her, giving her to you?"

"At first they opposed it, but I asked Mim's consent before I asked Elas. I wished her happy, t'Nethim. If you are not offended to hear it,—I loved her."

A vein beat ceaselessly at Lhe's temple. He was silent a moment, as if gathering the self-control to speak. "We are offended. But it is clear she trusted you, since she gave you her true name in the house of her enemies. She trusted you more than Elas."

"No. She knew I would keep that to myself; but it was not fear of Elas. She honored Elas too much to burden their honor with knowing the name of her house."

"I thank you, that you confessed her true name to the Methi so we could comfort her soul. It is a great deal," he added coldly, "that we *thank* a human."

"I know it is," said Kurt, and bowed, courtesy second nature by now. He lifted his eyes cautiously to Lhe's face; there was no yielding there.

Scurrying footsteps approached the door. With a timid knock, a lesser guardsman cracked the door and awkwardly bowed his apology. "Sir. Sir. The Methi is waiting for this human. Please, sir, she has sent t'Iren to ask about the delay."

"Out," Lhe snapped. The head vanished out of the doorway. Lhe stood for a moment, fingers white on the hilt of the *tai.* Then he gestured abruptly to the door. "Human. You are not mine to deal with. Out."

The summons this time was to the fortress *rhmei,* into a gathering of the lords of Indresul, shadowy figures in the firelit hall of state. Ylith waited beside the hearthfire itself, wearing again the wide-winged crown, a slender form of color and light in the dim hall, her gown the color of flame and the light glancing from the metal around her face.

Kurt went down to his knees and on his face without being forced, despite that a guard held him there with the butt of a spear in his back.

"Let him sit," said Ylith. "He may look at me."

Kurt sat back on his heels, amid a great murmuring of the Indras lords, and he realized to his hurt that they murmured against that permission. He was not fit to meet their Methi as even a humble *chan* might, making a quick and dignified obeisance and rising. He laced his hands in his lap, proper for a man who had been given no courtesy of welcome, and kept his head bowed despite the permission. He did not want to stir their anger. There was nowhere to begin with them, to whom he was an animal; there was no protest and no action that would make any difference to them.

"T'Morgan," Ylith insisted softly.

He would not, even for her. She let him alone after that, and quietly asked someone to fetch Kta.

It did not take long. Kta came of his own volition, as far as the place where Kurt knelt, and there he too went to his knees and bowed his head, but he did not make the full prostration and no one insisted on it. He was at least without the humiliation of the iron band that Kurt still wore on his ankle.

If they were to die, Kurt thought wildly, irrationally, he would ask them to remove it. He did not know why it mattered, but it did: it offended his pride more than the other indignities, to have something locked on his person against which he had no power. He loathed it.

"T'Elas," said the Methi, "you have had a full day to reconsider your decision."

"Great Methi," said Kta in a voice faint but steady, "I have given you the only answer I will ever give."

"For love of Nephane?"

"Yes."

"And for love of the one who destroyed your hearth?"

"No. But for Nephane."

"Kta t'Elas," said the Methi, "I have spoken at length with Vel t'Elas. They would take you to the hearth of your Ancestors, and I would permit that, if you would remember that you are Indras."

He hesitated long over that. Kurt felt the anxiety in him; but he would not offend Kta's dignity by turning to urge him one way or the other.

"I belong to Nephane," said Kta.

"Will you then refuse me, will you *directly refuse me,* t'Elas, knowing the meaning of that refusal?"

"Methi," pleaded Kta, "let me be, let me alone in peace. Do not make me answer you."

"Then you were brought up in reverence of Indras law and the Ind."

"Yes, Methi."

"And you admit that I have the authority to require your obedience? That I can curse you from hearth and from city, from all holy rites, even that of burial? That I have the power to consign your undying soul to perdition to all eternity?"

"Yes," said Kta, and his voice was no more than a whisper in that deathly silence.

"Then, t'Elas,—I am sending you and the human t'Morgan to the priests. Consider, consider well the answers you will give them."

The temple lay across a wide courtyard, still within the walls of the Indume, a cube of white marble, vast beyond all expectation. The very base of its door was as high as the shoulder of a man, and within the triangular *rhmei* of the temple blazed the *phusmeha* of the greatest of all shrines, the hearthfire of all mankind.

Kta stopped at the threshold of the inner shrine, that awful golden light bathing his sweating face and reflecting in his eyes. He had an expression of terror on his face such as Kurt had never seen in him. He faltered and would not go on, and the guards took him by the arms and led him forward into the shrine, where the roar of the fire drowned the sound of their steps.

Kurt started to follow him, in haste. A spearshaft slammed across his belly, doubling him over with a cry of pain, swallowed in the noise.

When he straightened in the hands of the guards, barred from that holy place, he saw Kta at the side of the hearthfire fall to his face on the stone floor. The guards with him bowed and touched hands to lips in reverence, bowed again and withdrew as white-robed priests entered the hall from beyond the fire.

One was the elderly priest who had defended him to the Methi, the only one of all of them in whom Kurt had hope.

He jerked free, cried out to the priest, the shout also swallowed in the roar; Kta had risen and vanished with the priests into the light.

His guards recovered Kurt, snatching him back with violence he was almost beyond feeling.

"The priest," he kept telling them. "That priest, the white-haired one,—I want to speak with him. Can I not speak with him?"

"Observe silence here," one said harshly. "We do not know the priest you mean."

"That priest!" Kurt cried, and jerked loose, threw a man skidding on the polished floor and ran into the *rhmei,* flinging himself facedown so close to the great fire bowl that the heat scorched his skin.

How long he lay there was not certain. He almost fainted, and for a long time everything was red-hazed and the air was too hot to breathe; but he had claimed sanctuary, as Mother Isoi had claimed it first in the Song of the Ind, when Phan came to kill mankind.

White-robed priests stood around him, and finally an aged and blue-veined hand reached down to him, and he looked up into the face he had hoped to find.

He wept, unashamed. "Priest," he said, not knowing how to address the man with honor, "please help us."

"A human," said the priest, "ought not to claim sanctuary. It is not lawful. You are a pollution on these holy stones. Are you of our religion?"

"No, sir," Kurt said.

The old man's lips trembled. It might have been the effect of age, but his watery eyes were frightened.

"We must purify this place," he said, and one of the younger priests said, "Who will go and tell this thing to the Methi?"

"Please," Kurt pleaded, "please give us refuge here."

"He means Kta t'Elas," said one of the others, as if it was a matter of great wonder to them.

"He is house-friend to Elas," said the old man.

"Light of heaven," breathed the younger. "Elas—with *this?*"

"Nethim," said the old man, "is also involved."

"*Ai,*" another murmured.

And together they gathered Kurt up and brought him with them, talking together, their steps beginning to echo now that they were away from the noise of the fire.

Ylith turned slowly, the fine chains of her headdress gently swaying and sparkling against her hair, and the light of the hearthfire of the fortress leaped flickering across her face. With a glance at the priest she settled into her chair and sat leaning back, looking down at Kurt.

"Priest," she said at last, "you have reached some conclusion, surely, after holding them both so long a time."

"Great Methi, the College is divided in its opinion."

"Which is to say it has reached no conclusion, after three days of questioning and deliberation."

"It has reached several conclusions, however—"

"Priest," exclaimed the Methi in irritation, "yea or nay?"

The old priest bowed very low. "Methi, some think that the humans are what we once called the godkings, the children of the great earth-snake Yr and of the wrath of Phan when he was the enemy of mankind, begetting monsters to destroy the world."

"This is an old, old theory, and the godkings were long ago, and capable of mixing blood with man. Has there ever been a mixing of human blood and nemet?"

"None proved, great Methi. But we do not know the origin of the Tamurlin, and he is most evidently of their kind; now you are asking us to resolve, as it were, the Tamurlin question immediately, and we do not have sufficient knowledge to do so, great Methi."

"You have *him.* I sent him to you for you to examine. Does he tell you nothing?"

"What he tells us is unacceptable."

"Does he lie? Surely if he lies, you can trap him."

"We have tried, great Methi, and he will not be moved from what he says. He speaks of another world and another sun. I think he believes these things."

"And do you believe them, priest?"

The old man bowed his head, clenching his aged hands. "Let the Methi be gracious: these matters are difficult or you would not have consulted the College. We wonder this: if he is not nemet, what could be his origin? Our ships have ranged far over all the seas, and never found his like. When humans will to do it, they come to us, bringing machines and forces our knowledge does not understand. If he is not from somewhere within our knowledge, then,—forgive my simplicity—he must still be from somewhere. He calls it another earth. Perhaps it is a failure of language, a misunderstanding,—but where in all the lands we know could have been his home?"

"What if there was another? How would our religion encompass it?"

The priest turned his watery eyes on Kurt, kneeling beside him. "I do not know," he said.

"Give me an answer, priest. I will make you commit yourself. Give me an answer."

"I—had rather believe him mortal than immortal, and I cannot quite accept that he is an animal. Forgive me, great Methi, what may be heresy to wonder,—but Phan was not the eldest born of Ib. There were other beings, whose nature is unclear. Perhaps there were others of Phan's kind. And were there a thousand others, it makes the *yhia* no less true."

"This is heresy, priest."

"It is," confessed the priest. "But I do not know an answer otherwise."

"Priest, when I look at him, I see neither reason nor logic. I question what should not be questioned. If this is Phan's world, and there is another,—then what does this foretell, this—intrusion—of humans into ours? There is power above Phan's, yes; but what can have made it necessary that nature be so upset, so inside-out? Where are these events tending, priest?"

"I do not know. But if it is Fate against which we struggle, then our struggle will ruin us."

"Does not the *yhia* bid us accept things only within the limits of our own natures?"

"It is impossible to do otherwise, Methi."

"And therefore does not nature sometimes command us to resist?"

"It has been so reasoned, Methi, although not all the College is in agreement on that."

"And if we resist fate, we must perish?"

"That is doubtless so, Methi."

"And someday it might be our fate to perish?"

"That is possible, Methi."

She slammed her hand down on the arm of her chair. "I refuse to bow to such a possibility. I refuse to perish, priest, or to lead men to perish. In sum, the College does not know the answer."

"No, Methi, we must admit we do not."

"I have a certain spiritual authority myself."

"You are the viceroy of Phan on earth."

"Will the priests respect that?"

"The priests," said the old man, "are not anxious to have this matter cast back into their hands. They will welcome your intervention in the matter of the origin of humans, Methi."

"It is," she said, "dangerous to the people that such thoughts as these be heard outside this room. You will not repeat the reasoning we have made together. On your life, priest, and on your soul, you will not repeat what I have said to you."

The old priest turned his head and gave Kurt a furtive, troubled look. "Let the Methi be gracious: this being is not deserving of punishment for any wrong."

"He invaded the *Rhmei* of Man."

"He sought sanctuary."

"Did you give it?"

"No," the priest admitted.

"That is well," said Ylith. "You are dismissed, priest."

The old man made a deeper bow and withdrew, backing away. The heavy tread and metal clash of armed men accompanied the opening of the door: and the armed men remained after it was closed. Kurt heard and knew they were there, but he must not turn to look: time was short. He did not want to hasten it.

The Methi still looked down on him, the tiny chains swaying, her dark face soberly thoughtful.

"You create difficulties wherever you go," she said softly.

"Where is Kta, Methi? They would not tell me. Where is he?"

"They returned him to us a day ago."

"Is he—?"

"I have not given sentence." She said it with a shrug, then bent those dark eyes full upon him. "I do not really wish to kill him. He could be valuable to me. He knows it. I could hold him up to the other Indras-descended of Nephane and say: look, we are merciful, we are forgiving, we are your people. Do not fight against us."

Kurt looked up at her, for a moment lost in that dark gaze, believing as many a hearer would believe Ylith t'Erinas: hope rose irrationally in him, on the tone of her gentle voice, her skill to reach for the greatest hopes. And good or evil, he did not know clearly which she was.

She was not like Djan, familiar and human and wielding power like a general. Ylith was a Methi as the office must have been: a goddess-on-earth, doing things for a goddess' reasons and with amoral morality, creating truth.

Rewriting things as they should be.

He felt an awe of her that he had felt of nothing mortal, believed indeed that she could erase the both of them as if they had never been. He had been within the *Rhmei* of Man, had been beside the fire: the skin on his arms was still painful. When Ylith spoke to him he felt the roaring silence of that fire drowning him.

He was fevered. He was fatigued. He saw the signs in himself, and feared instead his own weakness.

"Kta would be valuable to you," he said, "even unwilling." He felt guilty, knowing Kta's stubborn pride. "Elas was the victim of one Methi; it would impress Nephane's families if another Methi showed him mercy."

"You have a certain logic on your side. And what of you? What shall I do with you?"

"I am willing to live," he said.

She smiled that goddess-smile at him, her eyes alone alive. "You existence is a trouble; but if I am rid of you, it will not solve matters. You would still have existed. What should I write at your death? That this day we destroyed a creature which could not possibly exist, and so restored order to the universe?"

"Some," he said, "are urging you to do that."

She leaned back, curling her bejeweled fingers about the carved fishes of the chair arms. "If, on the other hand, we admit you exist, then where do you exist? We have always despised the Sufaki for accepting humans and nemet as one state: herein began the heresies with which they pervert pure religion, heresies which we will not tolerate."

"Will you kill them? That will not change them."

"Heresy may not live. If we believed otherwise, we should deny our own religion."

"They have not crossed the sea to trouble you."

Ylith's hand came down sharply on the chair arm. "You are treading near the brink, human."

Kurt bowed his head.

"You are ignorant," she said. "This is understandable. I know of report that Djan-methi is—highly approachable. I have warned you before. I am not as she is."

"I ask you—to listen. Just for a moment,—to listen."

"First convince me that you are wise in nemet affairs."

He bowed his head once more, unwilling to dispute with her to no advantage.

"What," she said after a moment, "would you have to say that is worth my time? You have my attention, briefly. Speak."

"Methi," he said quietly, "what I would have said, were answers to questions your priests did not know how to ask me. My people are very old now, thousands and thousands of years of mistakes behind us that you do not have to make. But maybe I am wrong, maybe it is—what you call *yhia,* that I have intruded where I have no business to be and you will not listen because you cannot listen. But I could tell you more than you want to hear, I could tell you the future, where your precious little war with Nephane could lead you. I could tell you that my native world does not exist any longer, that Djan's does not,—all for a war grown so large and so long that it ruins whole worlds as yours sinks ships."

"You blaspheme!"

He had begun; she wished him silent. He poured out what he had to say in a rush, though guards ran for him.

"If you kill every last Sufaki you will still find differences to fight over. You will run out of people on this earth before you run out of differences.—Methi, listen to me! You know—if you have any sense you know what I am telling you. You can listen to me or you can do the whole thing over again, and your descendants will be sitting where I am."

Lhe had him, dragged him backward, trying to force him to stand. Ylith was on her feet, beside her chair.

"Be silent!" Lhe hissed at him, his hard fingers clamped into Kurt's arm.

"Take him from here," said Ylith. "Put him with t'Elas. They are both mad. Let them comfort one another in their madness."

"Methi," Kurt cried.

Lhe had help now: they brought him to his feet, forced him from the hall and into the corridor, and there, finally, clear sense returned to him and he ceased to fight them.

"You were so near to life," Lhe said.

"It is all right, t'Nethim," Kurt said. "You will not be cheated."

They went back to the upper prisons. Kurt knew the way, and, when they had come to the proper door, Lhe dismissed the reluctant guards out of earshot. "You are truly mad," he said, fitting the key in the lock. "Both of you. She would give t'Elas honor, which he refuses. He has attempted suicide: we had to prevent him. It was our duty to do this. He was being taken from the temple: he meant to cast himself to the pavement, but we pushed him back, so that he fell instead on the steps. We have provided comforts, which he will not use."

He dared look Lhe in the eyes, saw both anger and trouble there. Lhe t'Nethim was asking something of him: for a moment he was not sure what, and then he thought that the Methi would not be pleased if Kta evaded her justice. Elas had once hazarded its honor and its existence on receiving a prisoner in trust: and had lost. Methi's law. Elas had risked it because of a promise unwittingly false.

Nethim was involved: the priest had said it. The honor of Nethim was in grave danger. Both Elas and the Methi had touched it.

The door opened. Lhe gestured him to go in, and locked the door behind him.

There were two cots within, a table, beneath a high barred window. Kta lay fully clothed, covered with dust and dried blood. They had brought him back the day before; in all that time, they had not cared for him, nor he for himself. Kurt exploded inwardly with fury at all nemet, even with Kta.

"Kta." Kurt bent over him, and saw Kta blink and stare chillingly nothingward. There was vacancy there. Kurt did not ask consent: he went to the table where there was the usual washing bowl and urn. Clean clothes were laid there, and cloths, and a flask of *telise*. Lhe had not lied. It was Kta's choice.

Kurt spread everything on the floor beside Kta's cot, unstopped the *telise* and slipped his arm beneath Kta's head, putting the flask to his lips.

Kta swallowed a little of the potent liquid, choked over it and swallowed again. Kurt stopped the flask and set it aside, then soaked a cloth in water and began to wipe the mingled sweat and blood and dirt off the nemet's face. Kta shivered when the cloth touched his neck; the water was cold.

"Kta," said Kurt, "what happened?"

"Nothing," said the nemet, not even looking at him. "They brought—they brought me back—"

Kurt regarded him sorrowfully. "Listen, friend, I am trying as best I know. But if you need better care, if there are things broken, tell me. They will send for it. I will ask them for it."

"They are only scratches." The threat of outsiders seemed to lend Kta strength. He struggled to rise, leaning on an elbow that was painfully torn. Kurt helped him. The *telise* was having effect, although the sense of well-being would be brief, Kta did not move as if he was seriously hurt. Kurt put a pillow into place at the corner of the wall, and Kta leaned back on it with a grimace and a sigh,—looked down at his badly lacerated knee and shin, flexed the knee experimentally.

"I fell," Kta said.

"So I heard." Kurt refolded the stained cloth and started blotting at the dirt on the injured knee.

It needed some time to clean the day-old injuries, and necessarily it hurt. From time to time Kurt insisted Kta take a sip of *telise,* though it was only toward the end that Kta evidenced any great discomfort. Through it all Kta spoke little. When the injuries were clean and there was nothing more to be done, Kurt sat and looked at him helplessly. In Kta's face the fatigue was evident. It seemed far more than sleeplessness or wounds,—something inward and deadly.

Kurt settled him flat again with a pillow under his head. Considering that he himself had been without sleep the better part of three days, he thought that weariness might be a major part of it: but Kta's eyes were fixed again on infinity.

"Kta."

The nemet did not respond and Kurt shook him. Kta did no more than blink.

"Kta, you heard me and I know it. Stop this and look at me. Who are you punishing? Me?"

There was no response, and Kurt struck Kta's face lightly, then enough that it would sting. Kta's lips trembled and Kurt looked at him in instant remorse, for it was as if he had added the little burden more than the nemet could bear. The threatened collapse terrified him.

Tired beyond endurance, Kurt sank down on his heels and looked at Kta helplessly. He wanted to go over to his own cot and sleep, he could not think any longer, except that Kta wanted to die and that he did not know what to do.

"Kurt." The voice was weak, so distant Kta's lips hardly seemed to move.

"Tell me how to help you."

Kta blinked, turned his head, seeming for the moment to have his mind focused. "Kurt,—my friend, they—"

"What have they done, Kta? What did they do?"

"They want my help and—if I will not,—I lose my life, my soul. She will curse me from the earth,—to the old gods—the—" He choked, shut his eyes and forced a calm over himself that was more like Kta. "I am afraid, my friend, mortally afraid. For all eternity,—But how can I do what she asks?"

"What difference can your help make against Nephane?" Kurt asked. "Man, what pitiful little difference can it make one way or the other? Djan has weapons enough; Ylith has ships enough. Let others settle it. What are you? She has offered you life and your freedom, and that is better than you had of Djan."

"I could not accept Djan-methi's conditions either."

"Is it worth this, Kta? Look at you! Look at you, and tell me it is worth it. Listen, I would not blame you; all Nephane knows how you were treated there. Who in Nephane would blame you if you turned to Indresul?"

"I will not hear your arguments," Kta cried.

"They are sensible." Kurt seized his arm and kept him from turning his face to the wall again. "They are sensible arguments, Kta, and you know it."

"I do not understand reason any longer. The temple and the Methi will condemn my soul for doing what I know is right. Kurt, I could understand dying, but this—this is not justice. How can a reasonable heaven put a man to a choice like this?"

"Just do what they want, Kta. It doesn't cost anyone much, and if you are only alive, you can worry about the right and the wrong of it later."

"I should have died with my ship," the nemet murmured. "That is where I was wrong. Heaven gave me the chance to die—in Nephane, in the camp of the Tamurlin, with *Tavi*. I would have peace and honor then. But there was always you. You are the disruption in my fate. Or its agent. You are always there—to make the difference."

Kurt found his hand trembling as he adjusted the blanket over the raving nemet, trying to soothe him, taking for nothing the words that hurt. "Please," he said. "Rest, Kta."

"Not your fault. It is possible to reason—One must always reason—to know—"

"Be still."

"If," Kta persisted with fevered intensity, "if—I had died in Nephane with my father, then my friends, my crew—would have avenged me. Is that not so?"

"Yes," Kurt conceded, reckoning the temper of men like Val and Tkel and their company. "Yes, they would have killed Shan t'Tefur."

"And that," said Kta, "would have cast Nephane into chaos, and they would have died, and come to join Elas in the shadows.

Now they are dead,—as they would have died—but I am alive. Now I, Elas—"

"Rest. Stop this."

"—Elas was shaped to the ruin of Nephane—to bring down the city in its fall. I am the last of Elas. If I had died before this I would have died innocent of my city's blood. The crime would have been on Djan-methi's hands. Then my soul would have had rest with theirs, whatever became of Nephane. Instead, I lived,—and for that I deserve to be where I am."

"Kta,—hush. Sleep. You have a belly full of *telise* and no food to settle it. It has unbalanced your mind. Please. Rest."

"It is true," said Kta, "I was born to ruin my people. It is just—what they try to make me do—"

"Blame me for it," said Kurt. "I had rather hear that than this sick rambling. Answer me what I am, or admit that you cannot foretell the future."

"It is logical," said Kta, "that human fate brought you here to deal with human fate."

"You are drunk, Kta."

"You came for Djan-methi," said Kta. "You are for her."

Kta's dark eyes closed—rolled back, helplessly. Kurt moved at last, realizing the knot at his belly, the sickly gathering of fear, dread of Guardians and Ancestors and the nemets reasoning.

Kta at last slept. For a long time Kurt stood staring down at him, then went to his own side of the room and lay down upon the cot, not to sleep, not daring to, only to rest his aching back. He feared to leave Kta unwatched, but at some time his eyes grew heavy, and he closed them only for a moment.

He jerked awake, panicked by a sound and simultaneously by the realization that he had slept.

The room was almost in darkness, but the faintest light came from the barred window over the table. Kta was on his feet, naked despite the chill, and had set the water bucket on the table, standing where a channel in the stone floor made a drain beneath the wall, beginning to wash himself.

Kurt looked to the window, amazed to find the light was that of dawn. That Kta had become concerned about his appearance seemed a good sign. Methodically Kta dipped up water and washed, and when he had done what he could by that means, he took the bucket and poured water slowly over himself, letting it complete the task.

Then he returned to his cot and wrapped in the blanket. He leaned against the wall, eyes closed, lips moving silently. Gradually he slipped into the state of meditation and rested unmoving, the morning sun beginning to bring detail to his face. He looked at peace, and remained so for about half an hour.

The day broke full, a shaft of light finding its way through the barred window. Kurt bestirred himself and straightened his clothing that his restless sleeping had twisted in knots.

Kta rose and dressed also, in his own hard-used clothing, refusing the Methi's gifts. He looked in Kurt's direction with a bleak and yet reassuring smile.

"Are you all right?" Kurt asked him.

"Well enough, considering," said Kta. "It comes to me that I said things I would not have said."

"It was the *telise*. I do not take them for intended."

"I honor you," said Kta, "as my brother."

"You know," said Kurt, "that I honor you in the same way."

He thought that Kta had spoken as he did because there were hurrying footsteps in the hall. He made haste to answer, for fear that it would pass unsaid. He wanted above all that Kta understand it.

The steps reached their door. A key turned in the lock.

20

This time it was not Lhe who had charge of them, but another man with strangers around him, that had charge of them and they were taken not to the *rhmei,* but out of the fortress.

When they came into the courtyard and turned not toward the temple again, but toward the outer gate of the Indume complex, Kta cast Kurt a frightened glance that carried an unwilling understanding.

"We are bound for the harbor," he said.

"Those are our orders," said the captain of the detachment, "since the Methi is there and the fleet is sailing. Move on, t'Elas, or will you be taken through the streets in chains?"

Kta's head came up. For the least moment the look of Nym t'Elas flared in his dark eyes. "What is your name?"

The guard looked suddenly regretful of his words. "Speak me no curse, t'Elas. I repeated the Methi's words. She did not think chains necessary."

"No," said Kta, "they are not necessary."

He bowed his head again and matched pace with the guards, Kurt beside him. The nemet was a pitiable figure in the hard, uncompromising light of day, his clothing filthy, his face unshaved—which in the nemet needed a long time to show.

Through the streets, with people stopping to stare at them, Kta looked neither to right nor to left. Knowing his pride, Kurt sensed the misery he felt, his shame in the eyes of these people; and he could not but think that Kta t'Elas would have attracted less comment in his misfortune had he not been laden with the added disgrace of a human companion. Some of the murmured

comments came to Kurt's ears, and he was almost becoming in-
ured to them: how ugly, how covered with hair, how almost-
nemet, and caught with an Indras-descended, more the wonder
—pity the house of Elas-in-Indresul to see one of its foreign
sons in such a state and in such company!

The gangplank of the first trireme at the dock was run out,
rowers and crew scurrying around making checks of equipment.
Spread near its stern was a blue canopy upheld with gold-tipped
poles, beneath which sat Ylith, working over some charts with
Lhe t'Nethim and paying no attention to their approach.

When at last she did see fit to notice them kneeling before
her, she dismissed Lhe back a pace with a gesture and turned
herself to face them. Still she wore the crown of her office, and
she was modestly attired in *chatem* and *pelan* of pale green silk,
slim and delicate in this place of war. Her eyes rested on Kta
without emotion, and Kta bowed down to his face at her feet,
Kurt unwillingly imitating his action.

Ylith snapped her fingers. "It is permitted you both to sit,"
she said, and they straightened together. Ylith looked at them
thoughtfully, most particularly at Kta.

"*Ei,* t'Elas," she said softly, "have you made your decision?
Do you come to ask for clemency?"

"Methi," said Kta, "no."

"Kta," Kurt exclaimed, for he had hoped. "Don't—"

"If," said Ylith, "you seek in your barbaric tongue to advise
the son of Elas against this choice, he would do well to listen
to you."

"Methi," said Kta, "I have considered, and I cannot agree to
what you ask."

Ylith looked down at him with anger gathering in her eyes.
"Do you hope to make a gesture, and then I shall relent afterward and pardon you? Or do they teach such lack of religion
across the Dividing Sea that the consequence is of little weight
with you? Have you so far inclined toward the Sufak heresies
that you are more at home with those dark spirits we do not
name?"

"No, Methi," said Kta, his voice trembling. "Yet we of Elas
were a reverent house, and we do not receive justice from you."

"You say then that I am in error, t'Elas?"

Kta bowed his head, caught hopelessly between yea and nay, between committing blasphemy and admitting to it.

"T'Elas," said Ylith, "is it so overwhelmingly difficult to accept our wishes?"

"I have given the Methi my answer."

"And choose to die accursed." The Methi turned her face toward the open sea, opened her long-fingered hand in that direction. "A cold resting place at best, t'Elas, and cold the arms of Kalyt's daughters. A felon's grave, the sea,—a grave for those no house will claim, for those who have lived their lives so shamefully that there remains no one, not even their own house, to mourn them, to give them rest. Such a fate is for those so impious that they would defy a father or the Upei or dishonor their own kinswomen. But I, t'Elas, I am more than the Upei. If I curse,—I curse your soul not from hearth or from city only, but from all mankind, from among all who are born of this latter race of men. The lower halls of death will have you: Yeknis, those dark places where the shadows live, those unnameable firstborn of Chaos. Do they still teach such things in Nephane, t'Elas?"

"Yes, Methi."

"Chaos is the just fate of a man who will not bow to the will of heaven. Do you say I am not just?"

"Methi," said Kta, "I believe that you are the Chosen of Heaven, and I reverence you and the home of my Ancestors-in-Indresul. Perhaps you are appointed by heaven for the destruction of my people, but if heaven will destroy my soul for refusing to help you, then heaven's decrees are unbelievably harsh. I honor you, Methi. I believe that you, like Fate itself, must somehow be just. So I will do as I think right, and I will not aid you."

Ylith regarded him furiously, then with a snap of her fingers and a gesture brought the guards to take them.

"Unfortunate man," she said. "Blind to necessity and gifted with the stubborn pride of Elas. I have been well-served by that quality in Elas until now, and it goes hard to find fault with that which I have best loved in your house. I truly pity you, Kta t'Elas. Go and consider again whether you have well chosen. There is a moment the gods lend us, to yield before going under. I still offer you life. *That* is heaven's justice. —Tryn, secure them both belowdecks. The son of Elas and his human friend are sailing with us, against Nephane."

The hatch banged open against the deck above and someone in silhouette came down the creaking steps into the hold.

"T'Elas. T'Morgan." It was Lhe t'Nethim, and in a moment the Indras officer had come near enough to them that his features were faintly discernible. "Have you all that you need?" he asked, and sank down on his heels a little beyond the reach of their chains.

Kta turned his face aside. Kurt, feeling somewhat a debt to this man's restraint, made a grudging bow of his head. "We are well enough," Kurt said, which they were, considering.

Lhe pressed his lips together. "I did not come to enjoy this sight. For that both of you—have done kindness to my house, I would give you what I can."

"You have generally done me kindness," said Kurt, yet careful of Kta's sensibilities. "That is enough."

"Elas and Nethim are enemies; that does not change. But human though you are—if Mim could choose you, of her own will you are an exceptional human. And t'Elas," he said in a hard voice, "because you sheltered her, I thank you. We know the tale of her slavery among Tamurlin,—this through Elas-in-Indresul, through the Nethim. It is a bitter tale."

"She was dear to us," said Kta, looking toward him.

Lhe's face was grim. "Did you have her?"

"I did not," said Kta. "She was adopted of the *chan* of Elas. No man of my people treated her as other than an honorable woman, and I gave her at her own will to my friend, who tried with all his heart to treat her well. For Mim's sake, Elas is dead in Nephane. To this extent we defended her. We did not know that she was of Nethim. Because she was Mim, and of our hearth, Elas would have defended her even had she told us."

"She was loved," said Kurt, because he saw the pain in Lhe's eyes, "and had no enemies in Nephane. It was mine who killed her."

"Tell me the manner of it," said Lhe.

Kurt glanced down, unwilling: but Lhe was nemet—some

things would not make sense to him without all the truth. "Enemies of mine stole her," he said, "and they took her; the Methi of Nephane humiliated her. She died at her own hand, Lhe t'Nethim. I blame myself also. If I had been nemet enough to know what she was likely to do,—I would not have let her be alone then."

Lhe's face was like graven stone. "No," he said. "Mim chose well. If you were nemet you would know it. You would have been wrong to stop her. Name the men who did this."

"I cannot," he said. "Mim did not know their names."

"Were they Indras?"

"Sufaki," Kurt admitted. "Men of Shan t'Tefur u Tlekef."

"Then there is bloodfeud between that house and Nethim. May the Guardians of Nethim deal with them as I shall if I find them, and with Djan-methi of Nephane. What is the emblem of Tefur?"

"It is the Great Snake Yr," said Kta. "Gold on green. I wish you well in that bloodfeud, t'Nethim; you will avenge Elas also, when I cannot."

"Obey the Methi," said Lhe.

"No," said Kta. "But Kurt may do as he pleases."

Lhe looked toward Kurt, and Kurt gave him nothing better. Lhe made a gesture of exasperation.

"You must admit," said Lhe, "that the Methi has offered you every chance; and it is a lasting wonder that you are not sleeping tonight at the bottom of the sea."

"Nephane is my city," said Kta. "And as for your war, your work will not be finished until you finish it with me, so stop expecting me to obey your Methi. I will not."

"If you keep on as you are," said Lhe, "I will probably be assigned as your executioner. In spite of the feud between our houses, t'Elas, I shall not like that assignment; but I shall obey her orders."

"For a son of Nethim," said Kta, "you are a fair-minded man with us both. I would not have expected it."

"For a son of Elas," said Lhe, "you are fair-minded yourself. And," he added with a sideways glance at Kurt, "I cannot even fault you the guest of your house. I do not want to kill you. You and this human would haunt me."

"Your priests are not sure," said Kurt, "that I have a soul to do so."

Lhe bit his lip; he had come near heresy. And Kurt's heart went out to Lhe t'Nethim, for it was clear enough that in Lhe's eyes he was more than animal.

"T'Nethim," said Kta, "has the Methi sent you here?"

"No. My advice is from the heart, t'Elas. Yield."

"Tell your Methi I want to speak with her."

"Will you beg pardon of her? That is the only thing she will hear from you."

"Ask her," said Kta. "If she will or will not,—ought that not be her own choice?"

Lhe's eyes were frightened: they locked upon Kta's directly, without the bowing and the courtesy, as if he would drag something out of him. "I will ask her," said Lhe. "I already risk the anger of my father; the anger of the Methi is less quick, but I dread it more. If you go to her, you go with those chains. I will not risk the lives of Nethim on the asking of Elas."

"I consent to that," said Kta.

"Swear that you will do no violence."

"We both swear," said Kta, which as lord of Elas he could say.

"The word of a man about to lose his soul, and of a human who may not have one," declared Lhe in distress. "Light of heaven, I cannot make Nethim responsible for the likes of you."

And he rose up and fled the hold.

Ylith took a chair and settled comfortably before she acknowledged them. She had elected to receive them in her quarters, not on the windy deck. The golden light of swaying lamps shed an exquisite warmth after the cold and stench of between-decks, thick rugs under their chilled bones.

"You may sit," she said, allowing them to straighten off their faces, and she received a cup of tea from a maid and sipped it. There was no cup for them. They were not there under the terms of hospitality, and might not speak until given permission. She finished the cup of tea slowly, looking at them, the ritual of mind-settling before touching a problem of delicacy. At last she returned the cup to the *chan* and faced them.

"T'Elas and t'Morgan. I do not know why I should trouble

myself with you repeatedly when one of my own law-abiding citizens might have a much longer wait for an audience with me. But then, your future is likely to be shorter than theirs. Convince me quickly that you are worth my time."

"Methi," said Kta, "I came to plead for my city."

"Then you are making a useless effort, t'Elas. The time would be better spent if you were to plead for your life."

"Methi, please hear me. You are about to spend a number of lives of your own people. It is not necessary."

"What is? What have you to offer, t'Elas?"

"Reason."

"Reason. You love Nephane. Understandable. But they cast you out, murdered your house; I, on the other hand, would pardon you for your allegiance to them; I would take you as one of my own. Am I behaving as an enemy, Kta t'Elas?"

"You are the enemy of my people."

"Surely," said Ylith softly, "Nephane is cursed with madness, casting out such a man who loves her and honoring those who divide her. I would not need to destroy such a city, but I am forced. I want nothing of the things that happen there—of war, of human ways. I will not let the contagion spread." She lifted her eyes to the *chan* and dismissed the woman, then directed her attention to them again. "You are already at war," she told them. "I only intend to finish it."

"What—war?" asked Kta, though Kurt knew in his own heart then what must have happened and he was sure that Kta did. The Methi's answer was no surprise.

"Civil war," answered Ylith. "The inevitable conflict. Though I am sure our help is less than desired,—we are intervening, on the side of the Indras-descended."

"You do not desire to help the Families," said Kta. "You will treat them as you do us."

"I will treat them as I am trying to treat you. I would welcome you as Indras, Kta t'Elas. I would make Elas-in-Nephane powerful again, as it ought to be, united with Elas-in-Indresul."

"My sister," said Kta, "is married to a Sufaki lord. My friend is a human. Many of the house-friends of Elas-in-Nephane have Sufaki blood. Will you command Elas-in-Indresul to honor our obligations?"

"A Methi," she said, "cannot command within the affairs of a house."

It was the legally correct answer.

"I could," she said, "guarantee you the lives of these people. A Methi may always intervene on the side of life."

"But you cannot command their acceptance."

"No," she said. "I could not do that."

"Nephane," said Kta, "is Indras and Sufaki and human."

"When I am done," said Ylith, "that problem will be resolved."

"Attack them," said Kta, "and they will unite against you."

"What, Sufaki join the Indras?"

"It has happened once before," said Kta, "when you hoped to take us."

"That," said Ylith, "was different. Then the Families were powerful, and wished greater freedom from the mother of cities. Now the Families have their power taken from them which I can offer all that will renounce the Sufak heresy. My honored father Tehal-methi was less mercifully inclined, but I am not my father. I have no wish to kill Indras."

Kta made a brief obeisance. "Methi, turn back these ships then, and I will be your man without reservation."

She set her hands on the arms of her chair and now her eyes went to Kurt and back again. "You do press me too far. You, t'Morgan, were born human, but you rise above that; I can almost love you for your determination—you try so hard to be nemet. But I do not understand the Sufaki, who were born nemet and deny the truth, who devote themselves to despoiling what we name as holy; and least of all"—her voice grew hard—"do I understand Indras-born such as you, t'Elas, who knowingly seek to save a way of life that aims at the destruction of Ind."

"They do not aim at destroying us."

"You will now tell me that the resurgence of old ways in Sufak is a false rumor, that the *jafikn* and the Robes of Color are not now common there, that prayers are not made in the Upei of Nephane that mention the cursed ones and blaspheme our religion. Mor t'Uset ul Orm is witness to these things. He saw one Nym t'Elas rise in the Upei to speak against the t'Tefuri and their blasphemies. Have you less than your father's courage—or do you dishonor his wishes, t'Elas?"

Kurt looked quickly at Kta, knowing how that would affect him, almost ready to hold him if he was about to do something rash; but Kta bowed his head, knuckles white on his laced hands.

"T'Elas?" asked Ylith.

"Trust me," said Kta, lifting his face again, composed, "to know my father's wishes. It is our belief, Methi, and we should not question the wisdom of heaven in settling two peoples on the Ome Sin; and so we do not seek to destroy the Sufaki. I am Indras; I believe that the will of heaven will win despite the action of men; and therefore I live my life quietly in the eyes of my Sufaki neighbors. I will not dishonor my beliefs by contending over them, as if they needed defense."

Ylith's dark eyes flamed with anger for a time, and then grew quiet, even sad. "No," she said, "no, t'Elas."

"Methi." Kta bowed—homage to a different necessity, and straightened, and there was a deep sadness in the air.

"T'Morgan," said the Methi softly, "will you still stay with this man? You are only a poor stranger among us. You are not bound to such as he."

"Can you not see," asked Kurt, "that he wishes greatly to be able to honor you, Methi?" He knew that he shamed Kta by that, but it was Kta's life at stake; and probably now, he realized, he had just thrown his own away too.

Ylith looked, for one of a few times, more woman than goddess, and sad and angry too. "I did not choose this war, this ultimate irrationality. My generals and my admirals urged it, but I was not willing. But I saw the danger growing. The humans return: the Sufaki begin to reassert their ancient ways; the humans encourage this, and encourage it finally to the point when the Families which kept Nephane safely Indras are powerless. I do what must be done. The woman Djan is threat enough to the peace; but she is holding her power by stripping away that of the Indras. And a Sufak Nephane armed with human weapons is a danger which cannot be tolerated."

"It is not all Sufaki who threaten you," Kurt urged. "One man. You are doing all of this for the destruction of one man, who is the real danger there."

"Yes, I know Shan t'Tefur and his late father. —*Ai,* you

would not have heard. Tlekef t'Tefur is dead, killed in the violence."

"How?" asked Kta at once. "Who did so?"

"A certain t'Osanef."

"O gods," Kta breathed. The strength seemed to go out of him. His face went pale. "Which t'Osanef?"

"Han t'Osanef did the killing, but I have no further information. I do not blame you, t'Elas. If a sister of mine were involved, I would worry, I would indeed. Tell me this: why would Sufaki kill Sufaki? A contest for power? A personal feud?"

"A struggle," said Kta, "between those who love Nephane as Osanef does and those who want to bring her down, like t'Tefur. And you are doing excellently for t'Tefur's cause, Methi. If there is no Nephane, which is the likely result of your war, there will be another Chteftikan, and that war you cannot see the end of. There are Sufaki who have learned not to hate Indras; but there will be none left if you pursue this attack."

Ylith joined her hands together and meditated on some thought, then looked up again. "Lhe t'Nethim will return you to the hold," she said. "I am done. I have spared all the time I can afford today, for a man out of touch with reality. You are a brave man, Kta t'Elas; and you, Kurt t'Morgan, you are commendable in your attachment to this gentle madman. *Someone* should stay by him. It does you credit that you do not leave him."

21

"Kurt."

Kurt came awake with Kta shaking him by the shoulder and with the thunder of running feet on the deck overhead. He blinked in confusion. Someone on deck was shouting orders, a battle-ready.

"There is sail in sight," said Kta. "Nephane's fleet."

Kurt rubbed his face, tried to hear any clear words from overhead. "How much chance is there that Nephane can stop this here?"

Kta gave a laugh like a sob. "Gods, if the Methi's report is true, none. If there is civil war in the city, it will have crippled the fleet. Without the Sufaki, the Families could not even get the greater ships out of the harbor. It will be a slaughter up there."

Oars rumbled overhead. In a moment more the shouted order rang out and the oars splashed down in unison. The ship began to gather speed.

"We are going in," Kurt murmured, fighting down panic. A host of images assailed his mind. They could do nothing but ride it out, chained to the ship of the Methi. In space or on *Tavi*'s exposed deck, he had known fear in entering combat, but never such a feeling of helplessness.

"Edge back," Kta advised him, bracing his shoulder against the hull. He took his ankle chain in both hands. "If we ram, the shock could be considerable. Brace yourself and hold the chain. There is no advantage adding broken bones to our misery."

Kurt followed his example, casting a misgiving look at the mass of stored gear in the after part of the hold. If it was not well-secured, impact would send tons of weight down on them, and there was no shielding themselves against that.

The grating thunder of three hundred oars increased in tempo and held at a pace that no man could sustain over a long drive. Now even in the dark hold there was an undeniable sense of speed, with the beat of the oars and the rush of water against the hull.

Kurt braced himself harder against the timbers. What would happen if the trireme itself was rammed and a bronze Nephanite prow splintered in the midships area needed no imagination. He remembered *Tavi*'s ruin and the men ground to death in the collision, and tried not to think how thin was the hull at their shoulders.

The beat stopped, a deafening hush, then the portside oars ran inboard: the ship glided under momentum for an instant.

Wood began to splinter and the ship shuddered and rolled, grating and cracking wood all along her course. Thrown sprawling, Kurt and Kta held as best they could as the repeated shocks vibrated through the ship. Shouting came overhead, over the more distant screaming of men in pain and terror, suddenly overwhelmed by the sound of the oars being run out again.

The relentless cadence recommenced, the trireme recovering her momentum. All-encompassing was the crash and boom of the oars, pierced by the thin shouts of officers. Then the oars lifted clear with a great sucking of water, and held. The silence was so deep that they could hear their own harsh breathing, the give of the oars in their locks, the creak of timbers and the groan of rigging, and the sounds of battle far distant.

"This is the Methi's ship," Kta answered his anxious look. "It has doubtless broken the line and now waits. They will not risk this ship needlessly."

And for a long time they crouched against the hull, staring into the dark, straining for each sound that might tell them what was happening above.

New orders were given, too faintly to be understood. Men ran across the deck in one direction and the other, and still the motion of the ship indicated they were scarcely moving.

Then the hatch crashed open and Lhe t'Nethim came down the steps into the hold, backed by three armed men.

"Do you suddenly need weapons?" asked Kta.

"T'Elas," said Lhe, "you are called to the deck."

Kta gathered himself to his feet, while one of the men bent and unlocked the chain that passed through the ring of the band at his ankle.

"Take me along with him," said Kurt, also on his feet.

"I have no orders about that," said Lhe.

"T'Nethim," Kurt pleaded, and Lhe considered an instant, gnawing his lip. Then he gestured to the man with the keys.

"Your word to do nothing violent," Lhe insisted.

"My word," said Kurt.

"Bring him too," said Lhe.

Kurt followed Kta up the steps into the light of day, so blinded by the unaccustomed glare that he nearly missed his footing on the final step. On the deck the hazy shapes of many men moved around them, and their guards guided them, like blind men toward the stern of the ship.

Ylith sat beneath the blue canopy. There Kurt's sight began to clear. Kta went heavily to his knees, Kurt following his example, finding comfort in him. He began to understand Kta's offering of respect at such a moment: Kta did what he did with grace, paying honor like a gentleman, unmoved by threat or lack of it. His courage was contagious.

"You may sit," said Ylith softly. "T'Elas, if you will look to the starboard side, I believe you may see the reason we have called you."

Kta turned on one knee, and Kurt looked also. A ship was bearing toward them, slowly, relying on only part of its oarage. The black sail bore the white bird of Ilev, and the red immunity streamer floated from its mast.

"As you see," said the Methi, "we have offered the Families of Nephane the chance to talk before being driven under. I have also ordered my fleet to gather up survivors—without regard to nation; even Sufaki, if there be any. Now if your eloquence can persuade them to surrender, you will have won their lives."

"I have agreed to no such thing," Kta protested angrily.

"This is your opportunity, t'Elas. Present them my conditions, make them believe you,—or remain silent and watch these last ships try to stop us."

"What are your conditions?" Kta asked.

"Nephane will again become part of the empire or Nephane will burn. And if your Sufaki can accept being part of the empire,—well, I will deal with that wonder when it presents itself. I have never met a Sufaki, I confess it, as I had never met a human. I should be interested to do so,—on my terms. So persuade them for me, t'Elas, and save their lives."

"Give me your oath they will live," Kta said, and there was a stirring among the Methi's guards, hands laid on weapons.

But Kta remained as he was, humbly kneeling. "Give me your oath," he replied, "in plain words, life and freedom for the men of the fleet if they take terms. I know that with you, Ylithmethi, words are weapons, double edged. But I would believe your given word."

A lifting of the Methi's fingers restrained her men from drawing, and she gazed at Kta with what seemed a curious, even loving, satisfaction.

"They have tried us in battle, t'Elas, and you have tried my patience. Look upon the pitiful wreckage floating out there, and the fact that you are still alive after disputing me with words, and decide for yourself upon which you had rather commit their lives."

"You are taking," said Kta, "what I swore I would not give."

Ylith lowered her eyes and lifted them again, which just failed of arrogance. "You are too reasonable," she said, "to destroy those men for your own pride's sake. You will try to save them."

"Then," said Kta in a still voice, "because the Methi is reasonable—she will allow me to go down to that ship. I can do more there than here, where they would be reluctant to speak with me in your presence."

She considered, nodded finally. "Strike the iron from him. From the human too. —If they kill you, t'Elas, you will be avenged." And, softening that arrogant humor: "In truth, t'Elas, I am trying to avoid killing these men. Persuade them of that, or be guilty of the consequences."

The Ilev longship bore the scars of fire and battle to such an extent it was a wonder she could steer. Broken oars hung in their locks. Her rail was shattered. She looked sadly disreputable as she grappled onto the immaculate trireme of the Methi, small next to that towering ship.

Kta nodded to Kurt as soon as she was made fast, and the two of them descended on a ship's ladder thrown over the trireme's side.

They landed one after the other, barefoot on the planks like common seamen, filthy and unshaved, looking fit company for the men of the battered longship. Shock was on familiar faces all about them: Ian t'Ilev among the foremost, and men of Irain and Isulan.

Kta made a bow, which t'Ilev was slow to return.

"Gods," t'Ilev murmured then. "You keep strange company, Kta."

"*Tavi* went down off the Isles," said Kta. "Kurt and I were picked up, the only survivors that I know of. Since that time we have been detained by the Indras. Are you in command here, Ian?"

"My father is dead. Since that moment, yes."

"May your Guardians receive him kindly," Kta said.

"The Ancestors of many houses have increased considerably today." A muscle jerked slowly in t'Ilev's jaw. He gestured his comrades to clear back a space, for they crowded closely to hear. He set his face in a new hardness. "So do I understand correctly that the Methi of Indresul is anxious to clear us aside and proceed on her way,—and that you are here to urge that on us?"

"I have been told," said Kta, "that Nephane is in civil war and that it cannot possibly resist. Is that true, Ian?"

There was a deathly silence.

"Let the Methi ask her own questions," t'Irain said harshly. "We would have come to her deck."

And there were uglier words from others. Kta looked at them, his face impassive. At that moment he looked much like his father Nym, though his clothing was filthy and his normally ordered hair blew in strings about his face. Tears glittered in his eyes.

"I did not surrender my ship," he said, "though gods know I would have been willing to; a dead crew is a bitter price for a house's pride, and one I would not have paid." His eyes swept the company. "I see no Sufaki among you."

The murmuring grew. "Quiet," said t'Ilev. "All of you. Will

you let the men of Indresul see us quarrel?—Kta, say what she has sent you to say. Then you and t'Morgan may leave, unless you keep asking after things we do not care to share with the Methi of Indresul."

"Ian," said Kta, "we have been friends since we were children. Do as seems right to you. But if I have heard the truth,—if there is civil war in Nephane,—if there is no hope but time in your coming here, then let us try for conditions. That is better than going to the bottom."

"Why is she permitting this? Love of us? Confidence in you? Why does she send you down here?"

"I think," said Kta faintly, "I *think*—and am not sure—that she may offer better conditions than we can obtain from Shan t'Tefur. And I think she is permitting it because talk is cheaper than a fight, even for Indresul. It is worth trying, Ian, or I would not have agreed to come down here."

"We came to gain time. I think you know that. For us— crippled as we are—talk is much cheaper than a battle: but we are still prepared to fight too. Even taking the trouble to finish us can delay her. As for your question about Nephane's condition at the moment—"

The others wished him silent. Ian gave them a hard look. "T'Elas has eyes to see. The Sufaki are not here. They demanded command of the fleet. Some few—may their ancestors receive them kindly—tried to reason with Shan t'Tefur's men. Light of heaven, we had to *steal* the fleet by night, break out of harbor even to go out to defend the city. T'Tefur hopes for our defeat. What do you think the Methi's terms will be?"

There was quiet on the deck. For the moment the men were all listening, spirits and angers failing, all pretense laid aside. They only seemed afraid.

"Ian," said Kta, "I do not know. Tehal-methi was unyielding and bloody; Ylith is—I do not know. What she closes within her hand, I fear she will never release. But she is fair-minded, and she is Indras."

The silence persisted. For a moment there was only the creak of timbers, and the grinding of the longship against the side of the trireme as the sea carried them too close.

"He is right," said Lu t'Isulan.

"You are his house-friend," said a man of Nechis. "Kta sued for your cousin to marry."

"That would not blind me to the truth," said t'Isulan. "I agree with him. I am sick to death of t'Tefur and his threats and his ruffians."

"Aye," said his brother Toj. "Our houses had to be left almost defenseless to get enough men out here to man the fleet. And I am thinking they may be in greater danger at the moment from the Sufaki neighbors than from Indresul's fleet. —*Ei*," he said angrily when others objected to that, "clear your eyes and see, my friends. Isulan sent five men of the main hearth here and fifty from the lesser, and a third are lost. Only the sons of the *chan* are left to hold the door of Isulan against t'Tefur's pirates. I am not anxious to lose the rest of my brothers and cousins in an empty gesture. We will not die of hearing the terms, and if they are honorable, I for one would take them."

Ylith leaned back in her chair and accepted the respects of the small group of defeated men kneeling on her deck. "You may all rise," she said, which was generous under the circumstances. "T'Elas, t'Morgan,—I am glad you have returned safely. —Who heads this delegation?"

T'Ilev bowed slightly. "Ian t'Ilev uv Ulmar," he identified himself. "Lord of Ilev." And there was sadness in that assumption of the title, raw and recent. "I am not eldest, but the fleet chose me for my father's sake."

"Do you ask conditions?" asked Ylith.

"We will hear conditions," said t'Ilev.

"I will be brief," said Ylith. "We intend to enter Nephane, with your consent or without it. I will not leave the woman Djan in authority; I will not deal with her or negotiate with those who represent her. I will have order restored in Nephane and a government installed in which I have confidence. The city will thereafter remain in full and constant communication with the mother of cities. However, I will negotiate the extent of the bond between our cities. Have you any comment, t'Ilev?"

"We are the fleet, not the Upei, and we are not able to negotiate anything but our own actions. But I know the Families will not accept any solution which does not promise us our essential freedoms."

"And neither," Kta interjected unbidden, "will the Sufaki."

Ylith's eyes went to him: behind her, Lhe t'Nethim laid hand uneasily on the hilt of his *ypan*. Ylith's wit and Ylith's power were sufficient to deliver Kta an answer, and Kurt clenched his hands, hoping Kta would not be humiliated before these men. Then of a sudden he saw what game Kta was playing with his life and went cold inside: the Methi too was before witnesses, whose offense now could mean a battle, one ugly and, for the Methi's forces, honorless.

Her lips smiled. She looked him slowly up and down, finally acknowledged him by looking at him directly. "I have studied your city, t'Elas. I have gathered information from most unlikely sources, even you and my human, t'Morgan."

"And what," Kta asked softly, "has the Methi concluded?"

"That a wise person does not contest reality. Sufaki—are a reality. Annihilation of all Sufaki is hardly practical, since they are the population of the entire coast of Sufak. T'Morgan has told me a fable—of human wars. I considered the prospect of dead villages, wasted fields. Somehow this did not seem profitable. *Therefore,* although I do not think the sons of the east will ever be other than trouble to us, I consider that they are less trouble where they are, in Nephane and in their villages, rather than scattered and shooting arrows at my occupation forces. Religiously, I will yield nothing. But I had rather have a city than a ruin, a province than a desolation, and considering that it is your city and your land in question,—you may perhaps agree with me."

"We might," said Ian t'Ilev when she looked aside at him. "If not for that phrase *occupation forces*. The Families rule Nephane."

"*Ai,* no word of Sufaki? Well, but you know the law, t'Ilev. A Methi does not reach within families. The question of precedence would be between your two hearths. How you resolve it is not mine to say. But I cannot foresee that Ilev-in-Indresul would be eager to cross the sea to intervene in the affairs of Ilev-in-Nephane. I do not think occupation would prove necessary."

"Your word on that?" asked Kta.

The Methi gave a curious look to him, a smile of faint irony. Then she opened both palms to the sky. "So let the holy light of heaven regard me: I do not mislead you." She leaned back then, stretched her hands along the arms of her chair, her lovely face suddenly grave and businesslike. "Terms: removal of Djan, the dissolution of the t'Tefuri's party, the death of t'Tefur himself, the allegiance of the Families to Indresul and to me. That is the limit of what I demand."

"And the fleet?" asked Ian t'Ilev.

"You can make Nephane in a day, I think. By this time tomorrow you could reach port. You will have a day further to accomplish what I have named or find us among you by force."

"You mean we are to conquer Nephane for you?" t'Ilev exclaimed. "Gods,—no."

"Peace, control of your own city,—or war. If we enter, we will not be bound by these terms."

"Give us a little time," t'Ilev pleaded. "Let us bear these proposals to the rest of the fleet. We cannot agree alone."

"Do that, t'Ilev. We shall give you a day's start toward Nephane whatever you decide. If you use that day's grace to prepare your city to resist us, we will not negotiate again until we meet in the ruins of your city. We are not twice generous, t'Ilev."

T'Ilev bowed, gathered the three of the crew who had come with him, and the gathered crew of the trireme parted widely to let them pass.

"Methi," said Kta.

"Would you go with them?"

"By your leave, Methi."

"It is permitted. Make them believe you, t'Elas. You have your chance,—one day to make your city exist. I hope you succeed. I shall be sorry if I learn you have failed. Will you go with him, t'Morgan? I shall be sorry to part with you."

"Yes," Kurt said. "By your leave."

"Look," she said. "Look up at me." And when he had done so, he had the feeling that she studied him as a curiosity she might not see again. Her dark eyes held a little of fascinated fear. "You are," she said, "like Djan-methi."

"We are of one kind."

"Bring me Djan," she said. "But not as Methi of Nephane."

And her gesture had dismissed them. They gave back a pace.

But then Lhe t'Nethim bowed at her feet, head to the deck, as one who asked a great favor.

"Methi," he said when she acknowledged him, "let me go with this ship. I have business in Nephane, with t'Tefur."

"You are valuable to me, Lhe," she said in great distress.

"Methi, it is hearth-business, and you must let me go."

"Must? They will kill you before you reach Nephane, and where will your debt be honored then, t'Nethim, and how will I answer your father, that I let his son do this thing?"

"It is family," he said.

The Methi pressed her lips together. "If they kill you," she said, "then we will know how they will regard any pact with us. —T'Elas, be witness. Treat him honorably, however you decide, for his life or for his death. You will answer to me for this."

T'Nethim bowed a final, heartfelt thanks, and sprang up and hurried after them, among the men of Ilev's party who had delayed also to hear what passed.

"Someone *will* cut his throat," t'Ilev hissed at Kta, before they went over the rail. "What is he to you?"

"Mim's cousin."

"Gods! How long have you been of Indresul, Kta?"

"Trust me. If otherwise, let us at least clear this deck. I beg you, Ian."

T'Ilev bit his lip, then made haste to seek the ladder. "Gods help us," he murmured. "Gods help us,—I will keep silent on it. Burden me with nothing else, Kta."

And he disappeared over the side first and quickly descended to the longship, where his anxious crew waited.

The Ilev vessel glided in among the wrecked fleet with the white assembly streamer flying beside the red, and other captains gathered to her deck as quickly as possible: Eta t'Nechis; Pan t'Ranek; Camit t'Ilev, cousin of Ian—others, young men, whose captaincies now told of tragedies at sea or at home.

"Is that it?" shouted Eta t'Nechis when he had heard the terms, and looked at t'Ilev as if other words failed him. "Great gods, t'Ilev, did you decide for all of us? Or have you handed command over to Elas and its company,—to Elas, who ruined us in the first place, with its human guest. And now they bring us an overseas house-friend!"

"Argue it later," said Kta. "Whether you want to fight or negotiate at Nephane, put the fleet about for home now. Every moment we waste will be badly needed."

"We have men still adrift out there!" cried t'Ranek, "men the Indras will not let us reach."

"They are being picked up," said Ian. "That is better than we can do for them. Kta is right. Put about."

"Give the Methi back her man," said t'Nechis, "all three of them,—t'Elas, human and foreigner."

T'Nethim was pale, but he kept his dignity behind the shelter Ian t'Ilev gave the three of them: voices were raised, weapons all but drawn; and finally Ian settled the matter by ordering his ship put about for Nephane with the fleet streamer flying beside the others.

Then they were underway, and the sight of the Methi's fleet dropping astern with no visible evidence of pursuit greatly heartened the men and silenced some of the demands for vengeance.

"What need of them to pursue," asked t'Nechis, "if we do their work for them? Gods, gods, this is wrong!"

And once again there was talk of throat-cutting, of throwing the three of them into the sea with Lhe t'Nethim cut in pieces, until the t'Ilevi together put themselves bodily between the t'Nechisen and Kta t'Elas.

"Stop this," said Ian, and for all that he was a young man and beneath the age of some of the men who quarreled, he put such anger into his voice that there was a silence made, if only a breath of one.

"It is shameful," said Lu t'Isulan with great feeling. "We disgrace ourselves under the eyes of this Indras stranger. Bring tea. It is a long distance to Nephane. If we cannot make a well-thought decision in that length of time, then we deserve our misery. Let us be still and think for a time."

"We will not share fire and drink with a man of Indresul," said t'Nechis. "Put him in irons."

T'Nethim drew himself back with great dignity. "I will go apart from you," he said, the first words they had listened for him to say. "And I will not interfere. I will still be on this ship if you decide for war."

And with a bow of courtesy, he walked away to the bow, a figure of loneliness among so many enemies. His dignity made a silence among them.

"If you will," said Kurt, "I will go there too."

"You are of Elas," said Kta fiercely. "Stand your ground."

There were hard looks at that. It came to Kurt then that Elas had lost a great deal with *Tavi,* not alone a ship, but brave men, staunch friends of Elas. And those who surrounded them now, with the exception of Irain, Ilev and Isulan, were Families which sympathized less with Elas.

And even among those, there were some who hated humans. Such, even, was Ian t'Ilev; it radiated from him, a little shiver of aversion whenever eyes chanced to meet.

Only Lu and Toj t'Isulan, house-friends to Elas, elected to sit by Kta at the sharing of drink: and they sat on Kta's left, Kurt on the right.

Kurt accepted the cup into his fingers gratefully and sipped at the hot sweet liquid. It held its own memories of home and Elas, of sanity and reason—as if there was no power on earth that could change or threaten this little amenity, this odd tribute of the Indras to hearth and civilized order.

Yet everything, their lives and Nephane itself, was as fragile at the moment as the china cup in his fingers.

One round passed in silence. So did most of the second. It was, as the nemet would say, a third-round problem, a matter so disturbing that no one felt calm enough to speak until they had waited through a third series of courtesies and ceremony.

"It is certain," said Ian at last, "that the Methi's word is good so far. We are not pursued. We have to consider that she is indeed a Methi of our own people, and it is unthinkable that she would lie."

"Granted," said t'Nechis. "But then what does the truth leave us?"

"With Nephane standing," said Kta very softly. "And I do love the city, t'Nechis. Even if you hate me, believe that."

"I believe it," said t'Nechis. "Only I suggest that you have perhaps loved honors the Methi promised you—more than is becoming."

"She gave him nothing," said Ian. "And you have my word on that."

"It may be so," conceded t'Nechis, and yet with an uneasy look at Kurt, as if any nemet who consorted with humans was suspect. Kurt lowered his head and stared at a spot on the deck.

"How bad," asked Kta, "have things in Nephane become?"

"T'Elas," said the younger son of Uset-in-Nephane, "we are sorry for the misfortunes of Elas. But that was only the beginning of troubles. In some houses—in Nechis, in Ranek—men are dead: *ypai-sulim* have been drawn. Be careful how you speak to them. Understand the temper of their Guardians."

The Great Weapons, drawn only for killing and never resheathed without it. Kta made a little bow of deference individually to t'Nechis and to t'Ranek, and a gesture with hand to brow that Kurt did not understand: the other men reciprocated. There was silence, and a little easier feeling for that.

"Then," said Kta finally, "there would seem to be question whether there is a city to save. I—have heard a bitter rumor concerning Osanef. Can anyone tell me? Details were sparse."

"It is bad news, Kta," said Ian. "Han t'Osanef killed Tlekef t'Tefur. The house of Osanef was burned by the Tefur partisans, an example to other Sufaki not to remain friendly to us. The vandals struck at night, while the family slept, invaded the house and overthrew the fire to set the house ablaze. The lady Ia, Han's honored wife,—died in the fire."

"And Aimu," Kta broke in. "Bel and my sister?"

"Bel himself was badly beaten; but your lady sister was hurried to safety by the *chan* of Osanef. Both Bel and Aimu are safe, at last report, sheltered in Isulan with your father's sister."

"How did Han die?"

"He chose to die after avenging lady Ia. His funeral was the cause of much bloodletting. —Kta, I am sorry," he added, for Kta's face was pale and he looked suddenly weak.

"This is not all," said Toj t'Isulan. "The whole city is full of such funerals. Han and his lady were not the first or the last to lose their lives to t'Tefur's men."

"He is a madman," T'Nechis said. "He threatened to burn the

fleet—to burn the fleet!—rather than let it sail with Indras captains. They talk of burning Nephane itself and drawing back to their ancestral hills of Chteftikan."

"Aye," said young t'Irain, "and I for my part would gladly have the city in Indresul's hands rather than t'Tefur's."

And that sentiment was approved by a sullen muttering among many of the others. T'Nechis scowled, but even he did not seem to be in total disagreement.

"Sirs," said Kurt, startling everyone. "Sirs, what has Djanmethi done in the situation? Has she—can she do—anything to restore peace in the city?"

"She has the power," said t'Ranek. "She refuses to control t'Tefur. This war is of her creation. She knew *we* would never turn on Indresul, so she puts power in the hands of those who would, those who support her ambition. And that does not respect her office, but neither does she."

"I do not know," said the youngest t'Nechis, "why we answer questions from the Methi's leman."

Kta moved, and if the elder t'Nechis had not imposed his own discipline on his cousin with a sharp gesture, there would have been trouble.

"My apologies," said t'Nechis, words that seemed like gall in his mouth.

"I understand," said Kurt, "that humans have won no love in Nephane or elsewhere. But bear with me. I have a thing to say."

"Say it," said t'Nechis. "We will not deny you that."

"You would do well," he said, "to approach her with a clear request for action and concessions for the Sufaki who are not with t'Tefur."

"You seem to favor her," said t'Ranek, "and to have a great deal of confidence in her. I think we were wrong to sympathize with you for the death of Mim h'Elas."

Kurt threw out a hand to stop Kta, and himself stared at t'Ranek with such coldness that all the nemet grew silent. "My wife," he said, "was as much a victim of you as of Djan-methi, though I swear I tried to feel loyalty to the Families since I was part of Elas. I am human. I was not welcome and you made me know it as you made Djan-methi know it, and the Sufaki before her. If that were not the nature of Nephane, my wife would not be dead."

And before any could object, he sprang up and walked away, to t'Nethim's lonely station at the bow.

Lhe regarded him curiously, then even with pity, which from the enemy was like salt in the wound.

Soon, as Kurt had known, there came someone sent from Kta to try to persuade him back, to persuade him to bow his head and swallow his humanity and his pride and submit in silence.

He heard the footsteps coming behind him, pointedly ignored the approach until he heard the man call his name.

Then he turned and saw that it was t'Ranek himself.

"Kta t'Elas has threatened bloodfeud," said t'Ranek. "Please accept my apologies, t'Morgan. I am no friend of Elas, but I do not want a fight, and I acknowledge that it was not a worthy thing to say."

"Kta would fight over that?"

"It is his honor," said t'Ranek. "He says that you are of Elas. He also," t'Ranek added, with an uneasy glance at Lhe t'Nethim, "has asked t'Nethim to return. He has explained somewhat of the lady Mim h'Elas. Please accept my apology, Kurt t'Morgan."

It was not easy for the man. Kurt gave a stiff bow in acknowledgment, then looked at Lhe t'Nethim. The three of them returned to their places in the circle in utter silence. Kurt took his place beside Kta, t'Ranek with his brother, and Lhe t'Nethim stood nervously in the center until Kta abruptly gestured to him and bade him sit: t'Nethim settled at Kta's feet, thin-lipped and with eyes downcast.

"You have among you," said Kta in that hush, "my brother Kurt, and Lhe t'Nethim, who is under the protection of Elas."

Like the effect of wind over grass, the men in the circle made slight bows.

"I was speaking," Kurt said then, evenly and softly in that stillness. "And I will say one other thing, and then I will not trouble you further. There are weapons in the Afen: if Djan-methi has not used them, it is because Djan-methi has chosen not to use them. Once you have threatened her, you will have to reckon with the possibility that she will use them. You are wrong in some of your suppositions. She could destroy not only

Nephane but Indresul also if she chose. You are hazarding your lives on her forbearance."

The silence persisted. It was no longer one of hate, but of fear. Even Kta looked at him as a stranger.

"I am telling the truth," he said, for Kta.

"T'Morgan," said Ian t'Ilev. "Do you have a suggestion what to do?"

It was quietly, even humbly posed; and to his shame he was helpless to answer it. "I will tell you this," he said, "that if Djan-methi still controls the Afen when Ylith-methi sails into that harbor,—you are much more likely to see those weapons used. And worse,—if Shan t'Tefur should gain possession of them. — She does not want to arm him, or she would have: but she might lose her power to prevent him,—or abdicate it. I should suggest, gentlemen, that you make any peace you must with the Sufaki who will have peace: give them reasonable alternatives, and do all you can to get the Afen out of Djan-methi's hands and out of t'Tefur's."

"The Afen," protested t'Ranek, "has only fallen to treachery, never to attack by nemet. Haichema-tleke is too high, our streets too steep, and the human weapons would make it impossible."

"Our alternative," said Kta, "would seem to be to take the whole fleet and run for the north sea, saving ourselves. And I do not think we are of a mind to do that."

"No," said t'Nechis. "We are not."

"Then we attack the Afen."

22

The smoke over Nephane was visible even from a distance. It rolled up until the west wind caught it and spread it over the city like one of its frequent sea fogs, but blacker and thicker, darkening the morning light and overshadowing the harbor.

The men who stood on *Sidek*'s bow as the Ilev longship put into harbor at the head of the fleet watched the shore in silence. The smoke appeared to come from high up the hill, but no one ventured to surmise what was burning.

At last Kta turned his face from the sight with a gesture of anger. "Kurt," he said, "keep close by me. Gods know what we are going into."

Oars eased *Sidek* in and let her glide, a brave man of Ilev first ashore with the mooring cable. Other ships came into dock in quick succession.

Crowds poured from the gate, gathering on the dockside, all Sufaki, not a few of them in Robes of Color, young and menacing, but there were elders and women with children, clamoring and pleading for news, looking with frightened eyes at the tattered rigging of the ships. Some seamen who had not sailed with their Indras crewmates ran down to the side of them and began to curse and invoke the gods for grief at what had happened to them, seeking news of shipmates.

And swiftly the rumor was running the crowd that the fleet had turned back the Methi, even while Ian t'Ilev and other captains gave quick orders to run out the gangplanks.

The plans and alternate plans had been drilled into the ships' crews in exhortations of captains and family heads and what practice the narrow decks permitted. Now the Indras-descended moved smartly, with such decision and certainty that the Sufaki, confused by the false rumor of victory, gave back.

A young revolutionary charged forward, shrieking hate and trying to inflame the crowd, but Indras discipline held, though he struck one of the t'Nechisen half senseless. And suddenly the rebel gave back and ran, for no one had followed him. The Indras-descended kept swords in sheaths, gently making way for themselves at no greater speed than the bewildered crowd could give them. They did not try to pass the gates: they took their stand on the dock, and t'Isulan, who had the loudest voice in the fleet, held up his arms for silence.

News was what the crowd cried for: now that it was offered, they compelled each other to silence to hear it.

"We have held them a little while," shouted t'Isulan. "We are still in danger. —Where is the Methi to be found? Still in the Afen?"

People attempted to answer in the affirmative, but the replies and the questions drowned one another out. Women began screaming, everyone talking at once.

"Listen," t'Isulan roared above the noise. "Pull back and fortify the wall. Get your women to the houses and barricade the gates to the sea!"

The tumult began anew, and Kta, well to the center of the lines of Indras, seized Kurt by the arm and drew him to the inside as they started to move, t'Nethim staying close by them.

Kurt had his head muffled in his *ctan.* Among so many injured it was not conspicuous, and exposure had darkened his skin almost to the hue of the nemet—he was terrified, nonetheless, that the sight of his human face might bring disaster to the whole plan and put him in the hands of a mob. There had been talk of leaving him on the ship: Kta had argued otherwise.

The Indras-descended began to pass the outer-wall gates, filing peacefully upward toward their homes, toward their own hearths. It was supreme bluff. T'Isulan had hedged the truth with a skill uncommon to that tall, gruff breed that were his Family. It was their hope—to organize the Sufaki to work, and so keep the Sufaki out of the way of the Families.

And at the inner gate, the rebels waited.

There were jeers. Daggers were out. Rocks flew. Two Indras-descended fell, immediately gathered up by their kinsmen. T'Nethim staggered as a rock hit him. Kta hurried him further, half carrying him. The head of the column forced the gate bare-handed, with sheer weight of numbers and recklessness: it was sworn among them that they would not draw weapons, not until a point of extremity.

There was blood on the cobbles as they passed, and smeared on the post of the gate, but the Indras-descended let none of their own fall. They gained the winding Street of the Families, and their final rush panicked the rebels, who scattered before them, disordered and undisciplined.

Then the cause of the smoke became evident. Houses at the rising of the hill were aflame, Sufaki milling in the streets at the scene. Women snatched up screaming children and crowded back, caught between the fires and the rush of fleeing rebels and advancing Indras. A young mother clutched her two children to her and shrank against the side of a house, sobbing in terror as they passed her.

It was the area where the wealthiest Sufak houses joined the Street of the Families, and where the road took the final bend toward the Afen. Two Sufak houses, Rachik and Pamchen, were ablaze, and the blasphemous paint-splashed triangle of Phan gave evidence of the religious bitterness that had brought it on. Trapped Sufaki ran in panic between the roiling smoke of the fire and the sudden charge of the Indras.

"Spread out!" t'Isulan roared, waving his arm to indicate a barrier across the street. "Close off this area and secure it!"

A feathered shaft impacted into the chest of the man next to him; Tis t'Nechis fell with red dyeing his robes. A second and a third shaft sped, one felling an Indras and the other a Sufaki by-stander who happened to be in the line of fire.

"Up there!" Kta shouted, pointing to the rooftop of Dleve. "Get the man, t'Ranek! You men, spread out!—this side, this side, quickly,—"

The Indras moved, their rush to shelter terrifying the Sufaki who chanced to have sought the same protected side: but the In-dras dislodged no one. A terrified boy started to dart out: an Indras seized him, struggling and kicking though he was, and pushed him into the hands of his kin.

"Neighbors!" Kta shouted to the house of Rachik. "We are not here to harm you. Gods, lady shu-t'Rachik, get those children back into the alley! Keep close to the wall."

There were a few grins, for the first lady t'Rachik with her brood was very like a frightened *cachin* with a half dozen of her children about her; other Rachiken were there too, both women and men, and the old father too. They were glad enough to escape the area, and the old man gave a sketchy bow to Kta t'Elas, gratitude. Though his house was burning, his children were safe.

"Shelter near Elas," said Kta. "No Indras will harm you. Put the Pamcheni there too, Gyan t'Rachik."

A cry rang out overhead and a body toppled from the roof to bounce off a porch and onto the stones of the street. The dead Sufaki archer lay with arrows scattered like straws about his corpse.

A girl of Dleve screamed, belatedly, hysterically.

"Throw a defense around this whole section," Kta directed his men. "Ian! Camit!—take the wall-street by Irain and set a guard there. —You Sufaki citizens! get these fires under control: buckets and pikes, quickly! You, t'Hsnet, join t'Ranek, you and all your cousins!"

Men scattered in all directions at his orders, and pushed their way through smoke and frightened Sufaki; but the Sufaki who remained on the street, elders and children, huddled together in pitiful confusion, afraid to move in any direction.

Then from the houses up the street came others of the Indras-descended, and the *chani,* much as had stayed behind to guard the houses when the fleet sailed. Sufaki women screamed at the sight of them, men armed with the deadly *ypai.*

Kta stood free of the wall, taking a chance, for t'Ranek's men were not yet in position to defend the street from archers. He lifted his sword arm aloft in signal to the Indras who were running up, weapons in hand.

"Hold off!" he shouted. "We have things under control. These poor citizens are not to blame. Help us secure the area and put out the fires."

"The Sufaki set them, in Sufak houses," shouted the old *chan* of Irain. "Let the Sufaki put them out!"

"No matter who started them," Kta returned furiously, his face purpling at being fronted by a *chan* of a friendly house. "Help put them out. The fires are burning and they will take our houses too. They must be stopped."

That *chan* seemed suddenly to realize who it was he had challenged, for he came to a sudden halt; and another man shouted:

"Kta t'Elas! *Ei,* t'Elas, t'Elas!"

"Aye," shouted Kta, "still alive, t'Kales! Well met! Give us help here."

"These people," panted t'Kales, reaching him and giving the indication of a bow, "these people deserve no pity. We tried to defend them. They shield t'Tefur's men, even when the fires strike their own houses."

"All Nephane has lost its mind," said Kta, "and there is no time to argue blame. Help us or stand aside. The Indras fleet is a day out of Nephane and we either collect ourselves a people or see Nephane burn."

"Gods," breathed t'Kales. "Then the fleet—"

"Defeated. We must organize the city."

"We cannot do it, Kta. None of these people will listen to reason. We have been beseiged in our own houses."

"Kta!" Kurt exclaimed, for another man was running down the street.

It was Bel t'Osanef. One of the Indras-descended barred his way with drawn *ypan* and nearly ran him through, but t'Osanef avoided it with desperate agility.

"Light of heaven!" Kta cried. "Hold, t'Idur! Let him pass!"

The seaman dropped his point and Bel began running again, reached the place where they stood.

"Kta,—ye gods, Kta!" Bel was close to collapse with his race to get through, and the words choked from him. "I had no hope—"

"You are mad to be on the street," said Kta. "Where is Aimu?"

"Safe. We shelter in Irain. Kta—"

"I have heard, I have heard, my poor friend."

"Then please,—Kta,—these people—these people of mine,

they are innocent of the fires. Whatever—whatever your people say,—they try to make us out responsible—but it is a lie, a—"

"Calm yourself, Bel. Cast no words to the winds. I beg you, take charge of these people and get them to help or get them out of this area. The Indras fleet is coming down on Nephane and we have only a little time to restore order here and prepare ourselves."

"I will try," said Bel, and cast a despairing look at the frightened people milling about, at the dead men in the street. He went to the archer who lay in the center of the cobbled street, knelt down and touched him, then looked up with a negative gesture and a sympathetic expression for someone in the crowd.

There came a young woman—the one who had screamed; she crept forward and knelt down in the street beside the dead man, sobbing and rocking in her misery. Bel spoke to her in words no one else could hear, though there was but for the fire's crackling a strange silence on the street and among the crowd. Then he picked up the dead youth's body himself, and stuggled with it toward the Sufaki side.

"Let us take our dead decently inside," he said. "You men who can,—put the fires out."

"The Indras set them," one of the young women said.

"Udafi Kafurtin," said Bel in a trembling voice, "in the chaos we have made of Nephane, there is really no knowing who started anything. Our only identifiable enemy is whoever will not put them out. —Kta—Kta! Have these men of yours put up their weapons. We have had enough of weapons and threats in this city. My people are not armed, and yours do not need to be."

"Yours shoot from ambush!" shouted one of the Indras.

"Do as he asks!" Kta shouted, and glared about him with such fury that men began to obey him.

Then Kta went and bowed very low before t'Nechis, who had a cousin to mourn, and quietly offered his help, though Kurt winced inwardly and expected temper and hatred from the grieving t'Nechis.

But in extremity t'Nechis was Indras and a gentleman. He bowed in turn, in proper grace. "See to business, Kta t'Elas. The t'Nechisen will take him home. We will be with you as soon as we can send my cousin to his rest."

By noon the fires were out, and the Sufaki who had aided in fighting the blaze scattered to their homes to bar the doors and wait in silence.

Peace returned to the Street of the Families, with armed men of the fleet standing at either end of the street and on rooftops where they commanded a view of all that moved. The scars were visible now, hollow shells of buildings, pavement littered with rubble.

Kurt left Lhe t'Nethim sheltered in the hall of Elas, the Indras grim-faced and subdued to have set foot in a hostile house.

He found Kta standing out on the curb—Kta, like himself, was masked with soot and sweat and the dim red marks of burns from fire fighting.

"They have buried t'Nechis," Kta said hollowly, without looking around. They had been so much together it was possible to feel the other's presence without looking. He knew Kta's face without seeing it, that it was tired and shadow-eyed and drawn with pain.

"Get off the street," Kurt said. "You are a target."

"T'Ranek is on the roof. I do not think there is danger. Fully half of Nephane is in our hands now, thank the gods."

"You have done enough. Go over to Irain. Aimu will be anxious to see you."

"I do not wish to go to Irain," Kta said wearily. "Bel will be there and I do not wish to see him."

"You have to, sooner or later."

"What do I tell him? What do I say to him when he asks me what will happen now? —Forgive me, brother, but I have made a compact with the Indras, and I swore once that was impossible; forgive me, brother, but I have surrendered your home to my foreign cousins;—I am sorry, my brother, but I have sold you into slavery for your own preservation."

"At least," said Kurt grimly, "the Sufaki will have the same chance a human has among Indras; and that is better than dying, Kta, it is infinitely better than dying."

"I hope," said Kta, "that Bel sees it that way. I am afraid for this city—tonight. There has been too little resistance. They are saving something back. And there is a report t'Tefur is in the Afen."

Kurt let the breath hiss slowly between his teeth and glanced uphill, toward the Afen gate.

"If we are fortunate," he said, "Djan will keep control of the weapons."

"You seem to have some peculiar confidence she will not hand him that power."

"She will not do it," Kurt said. "Not willingly. I could be wrong,—but I think I know Djan's mind. She would suffer a great deal before she would let those machines be loosed on nemet."

Kta looked back at him, anger on his face. "She was capable of things you seem to have forgotten. Humanness blinds you, my friend; and I fear you have buried Mim more deeply than earth can put her. I do not understand that. Or perhaps I do."

"Some things," Kurt said, with a sudden and soul-deep coldness, "you still do not know me well enough to say."

And he walked back into Elas, ignoring t'Nethim, retreating into its deep shadows, into the *rhmei,* where the fire was dead, the ashes cold. He knelt there on the rugs as he had done so many evenings, and stared into the dark.

Lhe t'Nethim's quiet step dared the silent *rhmei.* It was a rash and brave act for an orthodox Indras. He bowed himself in respect before the dead firebowl and knelt on the bare floor.

He only waited, as he had waited constantly, attending them in silence.

"What do you want of me?" Kurt asked in vexation.

"I owe you," said Lhe t'Nethim, "for the care of my cousin's soul. I have come because it is right that a kinsman see the hearth she honored. When I have seen her avenged, I will be free again."

It was understandable. Kurt could imagine Kta doing so reckless a thing for Aimu.

Even for him.

He had used rudeness to Kta. Even justified, it pained him. He was glad to hear Kta's familiar step in the entry, like a ghost of things that belonged to Elas, disturbing its sleep.

Kta silently came and knelt down on the rug nearest Kurt.

"I was wrong," said Kurt. "I owe you an accounting."

"No," said Kta gently. "The words flew amiss. You are a

stranger sometimes. I feared—you were remembering—human debts. And you have found no *yhia* since losing Mim. She lies at the heart of everything for you. A man without *yhia* toward such a great loss cannot remember things clearly, cannot reason. He is dangerous to all around him. I fear you. I fear for you. Even you do not know what you are likely to do."

He was silent for a long time. Kurt did not break the silence.

"Let us wash," said Kta at last. "And when I have cleansed my hands of blood I mean to light the hearth of Elas again, and return some feeling of life to these halls. If you dread to go upstairs, use my room, and welcome."

"No," said Kurt, and gathered himself to his feet. "I will go up, Kta. Do not worry for it."

The room that had been his and Mim's looked little different. The stained rug was gone, but all else was the same, the bed, the holy *phusa* before which she had knelt and prayed.

He had thought that being here would be difficult. He could scarcely remember the sound of Mim's voice. That had been the first memory to flee. The one most persistent was that still shape of shadow beneath the glaring hearthfire, Nym's arms uplifted, invoking ruin, waking the vengeance of his gods.

But now his eyes traveled to the dressing table, where still rested the pins and combs that Mim had used, and when he opened the drawer there were the scarves that carried the gentle scent of *aluel*. For the first time in a long time he did remember her in daylight, her gentle touch, the light in her eyes when she laughed, the sound of her voice bidding him good morning, my lord. Tears came to his eyes. He took one of the scarves, light as a dream in his oar-callused hands, and folded it and put it back again. Elas was home for him again, and he could exist here, and think of her and not mourn any longer.

T'Nethim, his peculiar shadow, hovered uncertainly out on the landing. Kurt heard him, looked and bade him come in. The Indras uncertainly trod the fine carpeting, bowed in reverence before the dead *phusa*.

"There are clean clothes," Kurt said to him, flinging wide the closet which held all that had been his. "Take what you need."

He put off his own filthy garments and went into the bath,

washed and shaved with cold water and dressed again in a change of clothing while Lhe t'Nethim did the same for himself. Kurt found himself changed, browner, leaner, ribs crossed by several ridged scars that were still sensitive: those misfortunes were far away, shut out by the friendly walls of this house.

There was only t'Nethim, who followed, silent, to remind him that war hovered about them.

When they had both finished, they went downstairs to the *rhmei* to find Kta.

Kta had relit the holy fire, and the warm light of it leaped up and touched their faces and chased the shadows into the deeper recesses of the high ceiling and the spaces behind the pillars of the hall. Elas was alive again in Nephane.

T'Nethim would not enter here now, but returned to the threshold of Elas, to take his place in the shadows, sword detached and laid before him like a self-appointed sentinel, as in ancient times the *chan* was stationed.

But Kurt went to join Kta in the *rhmei* and listened while Kta lifted hands to the fire and spoke a prayer to the Guardians for their blessing.

"Spirits of my Ancestors," he ended, "of Elas, my fathers, my father, fate had led me here and led me home again. My father, my mother, my friends who wait below, there is no peace yet in Elas. Aid me now to find it. Receive us home again and give us welcome, and also bear the presence of Lhe t'Nethim u Kma, who sits at our gate, a suppliant. Shadow of Mim, one of your own has come. Be at peace."

For a moment he remained still, then let fall his hands and looked back at Kurt. "It is a better feeling," he said quietly. "But still there is a heaviness. I am stifling, Kurt. Do you feel it?"

Kurt shivered involuntarily, and the human part of him insisted it was a cold draft through the halls, blowing the fire's warmth in the other direction.

But all of a sudden he knew what Kta meant of ill feelings. An ancestral enemy sat at their threshold. Unease rippled through the air, disquiet hovered thickly there. T'Nethim existed, t'Nethim waited, in a city where he ought not to have come, in a house that was his enemy.

A piece of the *yhia* out of place, waiting.

Let us bid him go wait in some other house, Kurt almost suggested; but he was embarrassed to do it; and, it was to himself that t'Nethim attached, his own heels the man of Indras dogged.

A pounding came at the front door of Elas. They hurried out, taking weapons left by the doorway of the *rhmei,* and gave a nod of assent to t'Nethim's questioning look. T'Nethim slipped the bar and opened the door.

A man and a woman were there in the light: Aimu, with Bel t'Osanef.

She folded her hands upon her breast and bowed, and Kta bowed deeply to her. When she lifted her face she was crying, tears flooding over her face.

"Aimu," said Kta. "Bel,—welcome."

"Am I truly?" Aimu asked. "My brother, I have waited so long this afternoon, so patiently,—and you would not come to Irain."

"*Ei,* Aimu, Aimu, you were my first thought in coming home—how not, my sister? You are all Kurt and I have left. How can you think I do not care?"

Aimu looked into his face and her hurt became a troubled expression, as if suddenly she read something in Kta that she feared, knowing him. "Dear my brother," she said, "there is no woman in the house. Receive us as your guests and let me make this house home for you again."

"It would be welcome," he said. "It would very welcome, my sister."

She bowed a little and went her way into the women's part of the house. Kta looked back to Bel, hardly able to do otherwise, and the Sufaki's eyes were full sober. They demanded an answer.

"Bel," said Kta, "this house bids you welcome. Whether it is still a welcome you want to accept,—"

"You can tell me that, Kta."

"I am going to finish the quarrel between us and Tefur, Bel." Kta then gave Lhe t'Nethim a direct look, so the Indras knew he was earnestly not wanted; and Lhe retreated down the hall toward the darkness, still not daring the *rhmei.*

"He is a stranger," said Bel. "Is he of the Isles?"

"He is Indras," Kta admitted. "Forget him, Bel. Come into the *rhmei.* We will talk."

"I will talk here," said Bel. "I want to know what you are planning. Revenge on t'Tefur—in that I will gladly join you. I have a debt of blood there too. But why is the street still sealed? What is this silence in Irain? And why have you not come there?"

"Bel, do not press me like this. I will explain."

"You have made some private agreement with the Indras forces. That is the only conclusion that makes sense. I want you to tell me that I am wrong. I want you to account for how you return with the fleet,—for who this stranger is in Elas,—for a great many things, Kta."

"Bel, we were defeated. We have bought time."

"How?"

"Bel,—if you walk out of here now and rouse your people against us, you will be blood-guilty. We lost the battle. The Methi Ylith will not destroy the city if we fulfill her conditions. —Walk out of here if you choose, betray that confidence,—and you will have lives of your people on your conscience."

Bel paused with his hand on the door.

"What would you do to stop me?"

"I would let you go," said Kta. "I would not stop you. But your people will die if they fight, and they will throw away everything we have tried to win for them. Ylith-methi will not destroy the Sufaki, Bel. We would never have agreed to that. I am struggling with her to win your freedom. I think I can,—if the Sufaki themselves do not undo it all."

Bel's eyes were cold, a muscle slowly knotting in his jaw.

"You are surrendering," he said at last. "Did you not tell me once how the Indras-descended would fight to the death before they would let Nephane fall? Are these your promises? Is this the value of your honor?"

"I want this city to live, Bel."

"I know you, my friend. Kta t'Elas took good thought that it was honorable. And when Indras talk of honor, we always lose."

"I understand your bitterness; I do not blame you. But I won you as much as I could win."

"I know," said Bel. "I know it for the truth. If I did not believe it, I would help them collect your head,—Gods, my friend, my kinsman-by-marriage,—of all our enemies, it has to be you to come tell me you have sold us out,—for friendship's sake. Honorably. Because it was fated. *Ai, Kta*—"

"I am sorry, Bel."

Bel laughed shortly, a sound of weeping. "Gods, they killed my house for staying by Elas. My people—I tried to persuade to reason, to the middle course. I argued with great eloquence, *ai,* yes, and most bitter of all, I knew—I knew when I heard the fleet had returned—I knew as sure as instinct what the Indras must have done to come back so soon. It was the reasonable course, was it not, the logical, the expedient, the conservative thing to do? But I did not know until you failed to come to Irain that you had been the one to do it to us."

"T'Osanef," said Kurt, "times change things, even in Indresul. No human would have left Tehal-methi's hands alive. I was freed."

"Have you met with Ylith-methi face to face?"

"Yes," said Kta.

Bel shot him a yet more uneasy look. "Gods, I could almost believe—Did you run straight from here to Indresul? Was t'Tefur right about you?"

"Is that the rumor in the city?"

"A rumor I have denied until now."

"Shan t'Tefur knows where we were," said Kurt. "He tried to sink us in the vicinity of the Isles, but we were captured after that by the Indras, and that is the truth. Kta risked his life for your sake, t'Osanef. You could at least afford him the time to hear all the truth."

Bel considered a moment. "I suppose I can do that," he said. "There is little else I can do, is there?"

"Will you have more tea, gentlemen?" Aimu asked, when the silence lasted overlong among them.

"No," said Bel at last, and gave his cup to her. He looked once more at Kta and Kurt. "Kta,—I am at least able to understand. I am sorry—for the suffering you had."

"You are saying what is in your mind," said Kta, "not what is in your heart."

"I have listened to what you had to say. I do not blame you.

What could you do? You are Indras. You chose the survival of your people and the destruction of mine. Is that so unnatural?"

"I will not let them harm the Sufaki," Kta insisted, while Bel stared at him with that hard-eyed pain which would not admit of tears.

"Would you defy Ylith-methi for us," asked Bel, "as you defied Djan?"

"Yes. You know I would."

"Yes," said Bel, "because Indras are madly honorable. You would die for me. That would satisfy your conscience. But you have already made the choice that matters. Gods, Kta, Kta, I love you as a brother; I understand you, and it hurts, Kta."

"It grieves me too," said Kta, "because I knew that it would hurt you personally. But I am doing what I can to prevent bloodshed among your people. I do not ask your help—only your silence."

"I cannot promise that."

"Bel," Kurt said sharply when t'Osanef made to rise. "Listen to *me*. A people can still hope, so long as they live; even mine, low as they have fallen on this world. You can survive this."

"As slaves again."

"Even so,—Sufaki ways would survive; and if that survives, little by little, you gain. Fight them, spend lives, fall; in the end, the same result: Sufaki ways seep in among the Indras and theirs among you. Bow to good sense. Be patient."

"My people would curse me for a traitor."

"It is too late to do otherwise," said Kurt.

"Are the Families agreed?" Bel asked Kta.

"A vote was taken in the fleet. Enough houses were present to bind the Families to the decision; the Upei's vote would be a formality."

"That is not unusual," said Bel, and suddenly looked at Aimu, who sat listening to everything, pained and silent. "Aimu,—do you have counsel for me?"

"No," she said. "No counsel. Only that you do what you think best. If your honored father were here,—my lord, he surely would have advice for you, being Sufaki, being elder. What could I tell you?"

Bel bowed his head and thought a time, and made a gesture

of deep distress. "It is a fair answer, Aimu," he said at last. "I only hate the choice. Tonight—tonight, when it is possible to move without having my throat cut by one of your men, my brother Kta, I will go to what men of my father's persuasion I can reach. I leave t'Tefur to you. I will not kill Sufaki. I assume you are going to try to take the Afen?"

Kta was slow to answer, and Bel's look was one of bitter humor, as if challenging his trust. "Yes," said Kta.

"Then we go our separate ways this evening. I hope your men will exercise the sense to stay off the harbor-front. Or is it a night attack Indresul plans?"

"If that should happen," said Kta, "you will know that we of the Families have been deceived. I tell you the truth, Bel: I do not anticipate that."

Men came to the door of Elas from time to time as the day sank toward evening,—representatives of the houses, reporting decisions, urging actions. Ian t'Ilev came, to report the street at last under firm control all along the wall of the Afen gate. He brought too the unwelcome news that Res t'Benit had been wounded from ambush at the lower end of the street, grim forecast of trouble to come, when night made the Families' position vulnerable.

"Where did it happen?" asked Kta.

"At Imas," said Ian. It was the house that faced the Sufaki district. "But the assassin ran and we could not follow him into the—"

He stopped cold as he saw Bel standing in the triangular arch of the *rhmei*.

Bel walked forward. "Do you think me the enemy, Ian t'Ilev?"

"T'Osanef." Ian covered his confusion with a courteous bow. "No, I was only surprised to find you here."

"That is strange. Most of my people would not be."

"Bel," Kta reproved him.

"You and I know how things stand," said Bel. "If you will pardon me, I see things are getting down to business and the sun is sinking. I think it is time for me to leave."

"Bel, be careful. Wait until it is securely dark."

"I will be careful," he said, a little warmth returning to his voice. "Kta, take care for Aimu."

"Gods, are you leaving this moment? What am I to tell her?"

"I have said to her what I need to say." Bel delayed a moment more, his hand upon the door, and looked back. "She was your best argument; I remain grateful you did not stoop to that. I will omit to wish you success, Kta. Do not be surprised if some of my people choose to die rather than agree with you. I will not even pray for t'Tefur's death, when it may be the last the world will see of the nation we were. The name, my Indras friends, was Chtelek, not Sufak. But that probably will not matter hereafter."

"Bel," said Kta, "at least arm yourself."

"Against whom? Yours—or mine? Thank you, no, Kta. I will see you at the harbor—or be in it tomorrow morning, whichever fortune brings me."

The heavy door closed behind him, echoing through the empty halls, and Kta looked at Ian with a troubled expression.

"Do you trust him that far?" Ian t'Ilev asked.

"Begin no action against the Sufaki beyond Imas. I insist on that, Ian."

"Is everything still according to original plan?"

"I will be there at nightfall. But one thing you can do: take Aimu with you and put her safely in a defended house. Elas will be no protection to her tonight."

"She will be safe in Ilev. There will be men left to guard it, as many as we can spare: Uset's women will be there too."

"That will ease my mind greatly," said Kta.

Aimu wept at the parting, as she had already been crying and trying not to. Before she did leave the house, she went to the *phusmeha* and cast into the holy fire her silken scarf. It exploded into brief flame, and she held out her hands in prayer. Then she came and put herself in the charge of Ian t'Ilev.

Kurt felt deeply sorry for her and found it hard to think Kta would not make some special farewell, but he bowed to her and she to him with the same formality that had always been between them.

"Heaven guard you, my brother," she said softly.

"The Guardians of Elas watch over thee, my little sister, once of this house."

It was all. Ian opened the door for her and shepherded her out into the street, casting an anxious eye across and up where the guards still stood on the rooftops, a reassuring presence. Kta closed the door again.

"How much longer?" Kurt asked. "It's near dark. Shan t'Tefur undoubtedly has ideas of his own."

"We are about to leave."—T'Nethim appeared silently among the shadows of the further hall. Kta gave a jerk of his head and t'Nethim came forward to join them. "Stay by the threshold," he ordered t'Nethim. "And be still. What I have yet to do does not involve you. I forbid you to invoke your Guardians in this house."

T'Nethim looked uneasy, but bowed and assumed his accustomed place by the door, laying his sword on the floor before him.

Kta with Kurt walked into the firelit *rhmei,* and Kurt realized then the nature of Kta's warning to t'Nethim, for he walked to the left wall of the *rhmei,* where hung the Sword of Elas, Isthain. The *ypan-sul* had hung undisturbed for nine generations, untouched since the expulsion of the humans from Nephane, but for the sometime attention that kept its metal bright and its leather-wrapped hilt in good repair. The *ypai-sulim,* the Great Weapons, were unique to their houses and full of the history of them. Isthain, forged in Indresul when Nephane was still a colony, nearly a thousand years before, had been dedicated in the blood of a Sufaki captive in the barbaric past, carved into battle by eleven men before.

Kta's hand hesitated at taking the age-dark hilt of it, but then he lifted it down, sheath and all, and went to the hearthfire. There he knelt and laid the great Sword on the floor, hands outstretched over it.

"Guardians of Elas," he said, "waken, waken and hear me, all ye spirits who have ever known me or wielded this blade. I, Kta t'Elas u Nym, last of this house, invoke ye; know my presence and that of Kurt Liam t'Morgan u Patrick Edward, friend to this house. Know that at our threshold sits Lhe t'Nethim u Kma. Let your powers shield my friend and myself, and do no harm to him at our door. We take Isthain against Shan t'Tefur u Tlekef, and the cause of it you well know. —And you, Isthain, you shall have t'Tefur's blood or mine. Against t'Tefur direct your anger and against no others. Long have you slept undisturbed, my dread sister, and I know the tribute due you when you are wakened. It will be paid by morning's light, and after that time you will sleep again. Judge me, ye Guardians, and if my cause is just, give me strength. Bring peace again to Elas, by t'Tefur's death or mine."

So saying he took up the sheathed blade and drew it, the holy light running up and down the length of it as it came forth in his hand. Etched in its shining surface was the lightning emblem of the house, seeming to flash to life in the darkness of the *rhmei.* In both hands he lifted the blade to the light and rose, lifted it heavenward and brought it down again, then recovered the sheath and made it fast in his belt.

"It is done," he said to Kurt. "Have a care of me now, though your human soul has its doubts of such powers. Isthain last drank of human life, and she is an evil creature, hard to put to sleep once wakened. She is eldest of the *Sulim* in Nephane, and self-willed."

Kurt nodded and answered nothing. Whatever the temper of the spirit that lived in the metal, he knew the one which lived in Kta t'Elas. Gentle Kta had prepared himself to kill and, in truth, he did not want to stand too near, or to find any friend in Kta's path.

And when they came to the threshold where t'Nethim waited, Lhe t'Nethim bowed his face to the stone floor and let Kta pass the door before he would rise; but when Kurt delayed to close the door of Elas and secure it, t'Nethim gathered himself up and crept out into the gathering dark, the look on his perspiring face that of a man who had indeed been brushed by something that sought his life.

"He has prayed your safety," Kurt ventured to tell him.

"Sometimes," said Lhe t'Nethim, "that is not enough. Go ahead, t'Morgan, but be careful of him. It is the dead of Elas who live in that thing. Mim my cousin—"

He ceased with a shiver, and Kurt put the nemet superstition out of mind with a horror that Mim's name could be entangled in the bloody history of Isthain.

He ran to overtake Kta, and knew that Lhe t'Nethim, at a safe distance, was still behind them.

23

"There" said Ian t'Ilev, nodding at the iron gate of the Afen. "They have several archers stationed inside. We are bound to take a few arrows. You and Kurt must have most care: they will be directly facing you for a few moments."

Kta studied the situation from the vantage point in the door of Irain. It was dark, and there were only ill-defined shapes to be seen, the wall and the Afen a hulking mass. "We cannot help that. Let us go. Now."

Ian t'Ilev bowed shortly, then broke from cover, darting across the street.

In an instant came a heart-stopping shriek, and from the main street poured a force of men bearing torches and weapons: the Indras-descended came in direct attack against the iron gate of the Afen, bearing a ram with them.

White light illuminated the court of the Afen, blinding, and there was an answering Sufak ululation from inside the wall. The blows of the ram began to resound against the iron bars.

Kurt and Kta held a moment, while men from Isulan poured around them. Then Kta broke forth and they followed him to the shadow of the wall. Scaling-poles went up.

The first man took with him the line that would aid their descent on the other side. He gained the top and rolled over, the line jerking taut in the hands of those who secured it on the hitherside.

The next man swarmed up to the top and then it was Kurt's turn. Floodlights swung over to them now, spotting them, arrows beginning to fly in their direction. One hissed over Kurt's

head. He hooked a leg over the wall, flung himself over and slid
for the bottom, stripping skin from his hands on the knotted line.

The man behind him made it, but the next came plummeting
to earth, knocking the other man to the ground. There was no
time to help either. Kta landed on his feet beside him, broke the
securing thong and ripped Isthain from its sheath. Kurt drew his
own *ypan* as they ran, trying to dodge clear of the tracking
floodlight.

The wall of the Afen itself provided them shelter, and there
they regrouped. Of the twenty-four who had begun, at least six
were missing.

T'Nethim was the last into shelter. They were nineteen.

Kta gestured toward the door of the Afen itself, and they
slipped along the wall toward it, the place where the Methi's
guard had taken their stand. Men, they knew those, but there
was no mercy in the arrows which had already taken toll of
them, and none in the plans they had laid. The door must be
forced.

With a crash of iron the wall-gate gave way and the Indras
under Ian t'Ilev surged forward in a frontal assault on the door
to the Afen,—the Sufaki archers, standing and kneeling, firing
as rapidly as they could; and Kta's small force hit the bowmen
from the flank, creating precious seconds of diversion. Isthain
struck without mercy, and Kurt wielded his own blade with less
skill but no less determination.

The swordless archers gave up the bows at such unexpected·
short range and resorted to long daggers, but they had no chance
against the *ypai,* cut down and overrushed. The charge of the Indras carried to the very door, over the bodies of the Methi's
valiant guard, bringing the ram's metal-spiked weight to bear
with slow and shattering force against the bronze-plated wood.

From inside, over all the booming and shouting, came a brief
piercing whine. Kurt knew it, froze inside, caught Kta by the
shoulder and pulled him back, shouting for the others to drop,
but few heard him.

The Afen door dissolved in a sheet of flame and the ram and
the men who wielded it were slag and ashes in the same instant.
The Indras still standing were paralyzed with shock or they
might have fled; and there came the click and whine as the alien

field-piece in the inner hall built up power for the next burst of fire.

Kurt flung himself through the smoking doorway, to the wall inside and out of the line of fire. The gunners swung the barrel about on its tripod to aim at him against the wall, and he dropped, sliding as it moved, the beam passing over his head with a crackle of energy and a breath of heat.

The wall shattered, the support beams turning to ash in that instant; and Kurt scrambled up now with a shout as wild as that of the Indras, several seconds his before the weapon could fire again.

He took the gunner with a sweep of his blade, his ears hurting as the unmanned gun gathered force again, a wild scream of energy. A second man tried to turn it on the Indras who were pouring through the door.

Kurt ran him through, ignoring the man who was thrusting a pike at his own side. The hot edge of metal raked his back and he fell, rolled for protection. The Sufaki above him was aiming the next thrust for his heart. Desperately he parried with his blade crosswise and deflected the point up—the iron head raked his shoulder and grated on the stone floor.

In the next instant the Sufaki went down with Isthain through his ribs, and Kta paused amid the rush to give Kurt his hand and help him up.

"Get back to safety," Kta advised him.

"I am all right,—*No!*" he cried as he saw the Indras preparing to topple the live gun to the flooring. He staggered to the weapon that still hummed with readiness and swung it to where the Indras were pressing forward against the next barred doorway, trying vainly to batter it with shoulders and blades. Behind him the shattered wall and dust and chips of stone sifting down from the ceiling warned how close the area was to collapse. There was need of caution. He controlled the mishandled weapon to a tighter, less powerful beam.

"Have a care," Kta said. "I do not trust that thing."

"Clear your men back," said Kurt, and Kta shouted at them. When they realized what he was about, they scrambled to obey.

The doorway dissolved, the edges of the blasted wood charred and blackened, and Kurt powered down while the Indras surged forward again and opened the ruined doors.

The inner Afen stood open to them now, the lower halls vacant of defenders. For a moment there was silence. There were the stairs leading up to the Methi's apartments, to the human section, which other weapons would guard.

"She has given her weapons to the Sufaki," Kurt said. "There is no knowing what the situation is up there. We have to take the upper level. Help me. We need this weapon."

"Here," said Ben t'Irain, a heavyset man who was housefriend to Elas. He took the thing on his broad shoulder and gestured for one of his cousins to take its base as Kurt kicked the tripod and collapsed it.

"If we meet trouble," Kurt told him, "drop to your knee and hold this end straight toward the target. Leave the rest to me."

"I understand," said the man calmly, which was bravery for a nemet, much as they hated machines. Kurt gave the man a nod of respect and motioned the men to try the stairway.

They went quickly and carefully now, ready for ambush at any turn. Kurt privately feared a mine, but that was something he did not tell them: they had no other way.

The door at the top of the stairs was closed, as Kurt had known it must be; and with Ben to steady the gun, he blasted the wood to cinders, etching the outline of the stone arch on the wall across the hall. The weapon started to gather power again, beginning that sinister whine, and Kurt let it, dangerous as it was to move it when charged: it had to be ready.

They entered the hall leading to the human section of the Afen. There remained only the door of Djan's apartments.

Kurt held up a hand signaling caution, for there must be opposition here as nowhere else.

He waited. Kta caught his eye and looked impatient, out of breath as he was.

With Djan to reckon with, underestimation could be fatal to all of them. "Ben," he said, "this may be worth your life and mine."

"What will you?" Ben t'Irain asked him calmly enough, though he was panting from the exertion of the climb. Kurt nodded toward the door.

T'Irain went with him and took up position, kneeling. Kurt threw the beam dead center, fired.

The door ceased to exist, and in the reeking opening was framed a heap of twisted metal, the shapes of two men in pale silhouette against the cindered wall beyond, where their bodies and the gun they had manned had absorbed the energy.

A movement to the right drew Kurt's attention. There was a burst of light as he turned and Ben t'Irain gasped in pain and collapsed beneath the gun.

T'Tefur. The Sufaki swung the pistol left at Kurt and Kurt dropped, the beam raking the wall where he had been. In that instant two of the Indras rushed the Sufaki leader, one shot down, and Kta, the other one, grazed by the bolt.

Kta vaulted the table between them and Isthain swept in an invisible downstroke that cleaved the Sufaki's skull. The pistol discharged undirected and Kta staggered, raked across the leg as t'Tefur's dying hands caught at him and missed. Then Kta pulled himself erect and leaned on Isthain as he turned and looked back at the others.

Kurt edged over to the whining gun and shut it down, then touched t'Irain's neck to find that there was no heartbeat. T'Tefur's first shot had been true.

He gathered his shaking limbs under him and rose, leaning on the charred doorframe; the heat made him jerk back, and he staggered over to join Kta, past Ian t'Ilev's sprawled body, for he was the other man t'Tefur had shot down before dying.

Kta had not moved. He still stood by t'Tefur, both his hands on Isthain's pommel. Then Kurt bent down and took the gun from Shan t'Tefur's dead fingers, with no sense of triumph in the action, no satisfaction in the name of Mim or the other dead the man had sent before him.

It was a way of life they had killed, the last of a great house. He had died well. The Indras themselves were silent, Kta most of all.

A small silken form burst from cover behind the couch and fled for the open door. T'Ranek stopped her, swept her struggling off her feet and set her down again.

"It is the *chan* of the Methi," said Kta, for it was indeed the girl Pai t'Erefe, Sufaki, Djan's companion. Released, she fell sobbing to her knees, a small, and shaken figure in that gathering of warlike men: but she was also of the Afen, so when she had made the necessary obeisance to her conquerors, she sat back with her little back stiff and her head erect.

"Where is the Methi?" Kta asked her, and Pai set her lips and would not answer. One of the men reached down and gripped her arm cruelly.

"No," Kurt asked of him, and dropped to one knee, fronting Pai. "Pai, Pai, speak quickly. There is a chance she may live if you tell me."

Pai's large eyes reckoned him, inside and out. "Do not harm her," she pleaded.

"Where is she?"

"The temple—" When he rose she sprang to her feet, holding him, compelling his attention. "My lord, t'Tefur wanted her greater weapons. She would not give them. She refused him. My lord Kurt, my lord, do not kill her."

"The *chan* is probably lying," said t'Ranek, "to gain time for the Methi to prepare worse than this welcome."

"I am not lying," Pai sobbed, gripping Kurt's arm shamelessly rather than be ignored. "Lord Kurt, you know her. I am not lying."

"Come on." Kurt took her by the arm and looked at the rest of them, at Kta most particularly, whose face was pale and drawn with the shock of his wound. "Hold here," he told Kta. "I am going to the temple."

"It is suicide," said Kta. "Kurt, you cannot enter there. Even we dare not come after her there, no Indras—"

"Pai is Sufaki and I am human," said Kurt, "and no worse pollution there than Djan herself. Hold the Afen. You have won, if only you do not throw it away now."

"Then take men with you," Kta pleaded with him, and when he ignored the plea: "Kurt, Elas wants you back."

"I will remember it."

He hurried Pai with him, past t'Irain's corpse at the door and down the hall to the inner stairs. He kept one hand on her arm and held the pistol in the other, forcing the *chan* along at a breathless pace.

Pai sobbed, pattering along with small resisting steps, trip-

ping in her skirts on the stairs, though she tried to hold them
with her free hand. He shook her as they came to the landing,
not caring that he hurt.

"If they reach her first," he said, "they will kill her, Pai. As
you love her, move."

And after that, Pai's slippered feet hurried with more sure-
ness, and she had swallowed down her tears, for the brave little
chan had not needed to trip so often. She hurried now under her
own power.

They came into the main hall, through the rest of the Indras,
and men stared, but they did not challenge him; everyone knew
Elas' human. Pai stared about her with fear-mad eyes, but he
hastened her through, beneath the threatening ceiling at the main
gate and to the outside, past the carnage that littered the entrance. Pai gave a startled gasp and stopped. He drew her past
quickly, not much blaming the girl.

The night wind touched them, cold and clean after the stench
of burning flesh in the Afen. Across the floodlit courtyard rose
the dark side of Haichema-tleke, and beneath it the wall and the
small gate that led out into the temple courtyard.

They raced across the lighted area, fearful of some last archer,
and reached the gate out of breath.

"You," Kurt told Pai, "had better be telling the truth."

"I am," said Pai, and her large eyes widened, fixed over his
shoulder. "Lord! Someone comes!"

"Come," he said, and, blasting the lock, shouldered the heavy
gate open. "Hurry."

The temple doors stood ajar, far up the steps past the three triangular pylons. The golden light of Nephane's hearthfire threw
light over all the square and hazed the sky above the roof-
opening.

Kurt drew a deep breath and raced upward, dragging Pai with
him, she stumbling now from exhaustion. He put his arm about
her and half-carried her, for he would not leave her alone to face
whatever pursued them. Behind them he could hear shouting
rise anew from the main gate, renewed resistance—cheers for
victory—he did not pause to know.

Within, the great hearthfire came in view, roaring up from its circular pit to the *gelos,* the aperture in the ceiling, the smoke boiling darkly up toward the black stones.

Kurt kept his grip on Pai and entered cautiously, keeping near the wall, edging his way around it, surveying all the shadowed recesses. The fire's burning drowned his own footsteps and its glare hid whatever might lie directly across it. The first he might know of Djan's presence could be a darting bolt of fire deadlier than the fire that burned for Phan.

"Human."

Pai shrieked even as he whirled, throwing her aside, and he held his finger still on the trigger. The aged priest, the one who had so nearly consigned him to die, stood in a side hall, staff in hand, and behind him appeared other priests.

Kurt backed away uneasily, darted a nervous glance further left, right again toward the fire.

"Kurt," said Djan's voice from the shadows at his far right.

He turned slowly, knowing she would be armed.

She waited, her coppery hair bright in the shadows, bright as the bronze of the helmeted men who waited behind her; and the weapon he had expected was in her hand. She wore her own uniform now, that he had never seen her wear, green that shimmered with synthetic unreality in this time and place.

"I knew," she said, "when you ran, that you would be back."

He cast the gun to the ground, demonstrating both hands empty. "I'll get you out. It's too late to save anything, Djan. Give up. Come with me."

"What, have you forgiven, and has Elas? They sent you here because they won't come here. They fear this place. And Pai, for shame, Pai,—"

"Methi," wailed Pai, who had fallen on her face in misery, "Methi, I am sorry."

"I do not blame you. I have expected him for days." She spoke now in Nechai. "And Shan t'Tefur?"

"He is dead," said Kurt.

There was no grief, only a slight flicker of the eyes. "I could no longer reason with him. He saw things that could not exist, that never had existed. So others found their own solutions, they tell me. They say the Families have gone over to Ylith of Indresul."

"To save their city."

"And will it?"

"I think it has a chance at least."

"I thought," she said, "of making them listen. I had the fire-power to do it—to show them where we came from."

"I am thankful," he said, "that you didn't."

"You made this attack calculating that I wouldn't."

"You know the object lesson would be pointless. And you have too keen a sense of responsibility to get these men killed defending you. I'll help you get out, into the hills. There are people in the villages who would help you. You can make your peace with Ylith-methi later."

She smiled sadly. "With a world between us, how did we manage to do it? Ylith will not let it rest. And neither will Kta t'Elas."

"Let me help you."

Djan moved the gun she had held steadily on him, killed the power with a pressure of her thumb. "Go," she told her two companions. "Take Pai to safety."

"Methi," one protested. It was t'Senife. "We will not leave you with him."

"Go," she said, but when they would not, she simply held out her hand to Kurt and started with him to the door, the white-robed priests melting back before them to clear the way.

Then a shadow rose up before them.

T'Nethim.

A blade flashed. Kurt froze, foreseeing the move of Djan's hand, whipping up the pistol. "Don't!" he cried out to them both.

The *ypan* arced down.

A cry of outrage roared in his ears. He seized t'Nethim's arm, thrown sprawling as the Sufaki guards went for the man. Blades lifted, fell almost simultaneously. T'Nethim sprawled down the steps, over the edge, leaving a dark trail behind him.

Kurt struggled to his knees, saw the awful ruin of Djan's shoulder and knew, though she still breathed, that she was finished. His stomach knotted in panic. He thought that her eyes pitied him.

Then they lost the look of life, the firelight from the doorway flickering across their surface. When he gathered her up against him she was loose, lifeless.

"Let her go," someone ordered.

He ignored the command, though it was in his mind that in the next moment a Sufak dagger could be through his back. He cradled Djan against him, aware of Pai sobbing nearby. He did not shed tears. They were stopped up in him, one with the terror that rested in his belly. He wished they would end it.

A deafening vibration filled the air, moaning deeply with a sighing voice of bronze, the striking of the *Inta,* the notes shaking and chilling the night. It went on and on, time brought to a halt, and Kurt knelt and held her dead weight against his shoulder until at last one of the younger priests came and knelt, holding out his hands in entreaty.

"Human," said the priest, "please, for decency's sake,—let us take her from this holy place."

"Does she pollute your shrine?" he asked, suddenly trembling with outrage. "She could have killed every living thing on the shores of the Ome Sin. She could not even kill one man."

"Human," said t'Senife, half kneeling beside him. "Human, let them have her. They will treat her honorably."

He looked up into the narrow Sufaki eyes and saw grief there. The priests pulled Djan from him gently, and he made the effort to rise, his clothes soaked with her blood. He shook so that he almost fell, and turned dazed eyes upon the temple square, where a line of Indras guards had ranged themselves. Still the *Inta* sounded, numbing the very air and in small groups men came moving slowly toward the shrine.

They were Sufaki.

He was suddenly aware that all around him were Sufaki, save for the distant line of Indras swordsmen who stood screening the approach to the temple.

He looked back, realizing they had taken Djan. She was gone, the last human face of his own universe that he would ever see. He heard Pai crying desolately, and almost absently bent and drew her to her feet, passing her into t'Senife's care.

"Come with me," he bade t'Senife. "Please. The Indras will not attack. I will get you both to safety. There should be no more killing in this place."

T'Senife yielded, nodded to his companion, tired men, both of them, with tired, sorrowful faces.

They came down the long steps. Indras turned, ready to take the three Sufaki, the men and the *chan* Pai, in charge, but Kurt put himself between.

"No," he said. "There is no need. We have lost t'Nethim; they have lost a Methi. She is dead. Let them be."

One was t'Nechis, who heard that news soberly and bowed and prevented his men. "If you look for Kta t'Elas," said t'Nechis, "seek him toward the wall."

"Go your way," Kurt bade the Sufaki, "or stay with me if you will."

"I will stay with you," said t'Senife, "until I know what the Indras plan to do with Nephane." There was cynicism in his voice, but it surely masked a certain fear, and the Methi's guards walked with him as he walked behind the Indras line in search of Kta.

He found Kta among the men of Isulan, with his leg bandaged and with Isthain now secure at his belt. Kta looked up in shock—joy damped by fear. Kurt looked down at his bloody hand and found it trembling and his knees likely to give out.

"Djan is dead," said Kurt.

"Are you all right?" Kta asked.

Kurt nodded, and jerked his head toward the Sufaki. "They were her guards. They deserve honor of that."

Kta considered them, inclined his head in respect. "T'Senife,—help us. Stand by us for a time, so that your people may see that we mean them no harm. We want the fighting stopped."

The rumor was spreading among the people that the Methi was dead. The *Inta* had not ceased to sound. The crowd in the square increased steadily.

"It is Bel t'Osanef," said Toj t'Isulan.

It was in truth Bel, coming slowly through the crowd, pausing to speak a word, exchange a glance with one he knew. Among some his presence evoked hard looks and muttering, but he was not alone. Men came with him, men whose years made the crowd part for them, murmuring in wonder: the elders of the Sufaki.

Kta raised a hand to draw his attention, Kurt beside him,

though it occurred to him what vulnerable targets they both were.

"Kta," Bel said, "Kta, is it true,—the Methi is dead?"

"Yes," said Kta, and to the elders, who expressed their grief in soft murmurings: "That was not planned. I beg you, come into the Afen. I will swear on my life you will be safe."

"I have already sworn on mine," said Bel. "They will hear you. We Sufaki are accustomed to listen, and you Indras to making laws. This time the decision will favor us both, my friend, or we will not listen."

"We could please some in Indresul," said Kta, "by disavowing you. But we will not do that. We will meet Ylith-methi as one city."

"If we can unite to surrender," said one elder, "we can to fight."

Then it came to Kurt, like an incredibly bad dream: the human weapons in the citadel.

He fled, startling Kta, startling the Indras, so that the guard at the gate nearly ran him through before he recognized him in the dark.

But Elas' human had leave to go where he would.

Heart near to bursting, Kurt raced through the battlefield of the court, up the stairs, into the heights of the Afen.

Even those on watch in the Methi's hall did not challenge him until he ordered them sharply from the room and drew his *ypan* and threatened them. They yielded before his wild frenzy, hysterical as he was, and fled out.

"Call t'Elas," a young son of Ilev urged the others. "He can deal with this madman."

Kurt slammed the door and locked it, overturned the table and wrestled it into position against the door, working with both hands now, barring it with yet more furniture. They struck it from the outside, but it was secure. Then they went away.

He sank down, trembling, too weary to move. In time he heard the voice of Kta, of Bel, even Pai pleading with him.

"What are you doing?" Kta cried through the door. "My friend, what do you plan to do?"

But it was a Sufaki's voice, not Bel's, that urged on him the inevitable.

"You hold the weapons that could destroy the Indras fleet, that could free our city. A curse on you if you will not help us!"

But only Kta and Bel did he answer, and then always the same: "Go away. I am staying here."

In time they did go away, and he relaxed somewhat, until he heard a gentle stirring at his barricade.

"Who is there?" he shouted out.

"My lord," said Pai's fearful voice from near the floor. "My lord, you will not use those weapons, will you?"

"No," he said, "I will not."

"They would have forced you. Not Kta. Not Bel. They would not harm you. But some would have forced you. They wanted to attack. Kta persuaded them not to. Please, may I come in?"

"No, Pai. I do not trust even you."

"I will watch here all night, my lord. I will tell you if they come."

"You do not blame me—because I will not do what they want?"

There was a long hesitation. "Djan also would not do what they wished. I honored her. I will watch for you, my lord. Rest. I will not sleep."

He sat down then on the only remaining chair, with his head leaning back, and though he did not intend to, he slept for little periods. Sometimes he would ask Pai whether she slept—but her voice was always there, faithful and calm.

Then came morning, through the glass of the window that overlooked the west. When he went to look out, the sullen light exposed the whole of a great war fleet moving into the harbor.

Ylith's fleet had come.

He waited for a long time after they had docked. There was no sign of fighting. Eventually he sent Pai downstairs to spy out what was happening.

"There are Indras lords in the lower hall," she reported, "strangers. But they have been told you are here. They are trying to decide whether to attack this door or not. My lord, I am afraid."

"Leave the door," he told her. But she did not. He still heard her stirring occasionally outside.

Then he went around the various centers of the section, wrecking machinery, smashing delicate circuits.

"What are you doing?" Pai cried, when she heard the noise.

He did not trouble to answer. He dismantled the power sources as far as he could, the few handweapons he found also, everything. Then he took away the barricade before the door.

She waited outside, her large eyes wide with fear and with wonder,—perhaps no little shock, for he was filthy and bloody and almost staggering with exhaustion.

"They have not threatened you?" he asked.

She bowed her head gravely. "No, lord. They feared to make you angry. They know the power of the weapons."

"Let us go to Elas."

"I am *chan* to Methis," she said. "It is not proper for me to quit my station."

"I am afraid for you with conditions as they are. Visit Elas with me."

She bowed very deeply, straightened and walked beside him.

The shock of seeing him in the lower hall all but paralyzed the men of Indresul, who watched there with a few of the Indras of Nephane. The presence of Nephanites among the occupying forces heartened him somewhat.

"The weapons," he said, "are dismantled beyond my ability to repair them. I am going to Elas if you want to find me."

And to his own surprise they let him pass, and puzzled guards on the Street of the Families did also, for a man of Indresul walked after them, watching them, his presence guarding them.

"No harm must come to you," said that man at last. "This is the order of the Methi Ylith."

There was no Hef to tend the door of Elas. Kurt opened it for himself and with Pai behind him entered its shadows. He stopped at the door of the *rhmei,* for he had not washed from the fighting and he wished to bring no pollution into the peace of that hall.

Kta rose to his feet from the chair of Nym, his face touched with deep relief. By him on lesser chairs sat Bel, Aimu, elders of the Sufaki and a stranger,—Vel t'Elas-in-Indresul.

Kurt bowed, realizing he had interrupted something of great moment, that an Indras of the shining city sat at this hearth.

"I beg your leave," he said. "I have finished at the Afen. No human weapons threaten your peace any longer. Tell your Methi that, Vel t'Elas."

"I had assured Ylith-methi," said Kta, his voice even but full of controlled feeling, "that this would be your choice. Is that Pai t'Erefe with you?"

"She needed a place for a time," he said. "If Elas will accept her as a guest."

"Elas is honored," murmured Kta. "Go wash, and come and sit with us, friend Kurt. We are in the midst of serious business." But before he went upstairs, Kta left his guests and came to him in the hall.

"It was well done," said Kta softly. "My friend, my brother Kurt,—go and wash, and come down to us. We are solving matters. It is a three- and a four-round problem, but the Methi Ylith has vowed to stay in port until it is done. We will talk here; then we will go down to the port to tell her our decisions. There are others of our cousins of Indresul in their several houses at this moment, and each Indras house has taken Sufaki among them, to shelter them at the sanctity of their hearths until this matter is resolved. Not a Sufaki will be harmed, who accepts house-friendship and the peace of our roofs."

"Would they all come?"

"No,—not all, not all. But perhaps the violent ones have fled to their hills, or perhaps they will come down in peace when they see it possible. But on every door of Sufak some Indras Family has set its seal; there will be no plundering. And at every hearth we have taken house-friends. This we did,—while you barricaded yourself behind the Afen door."

Kurt managed a smile. "And that," he said, "was well done too. Am I still welcome here?"

"You are of Elas," Kta exclaimed indignantly. "*Of* this hearth and not simply beside it. Go upstairs."

"I have to find t'Nethim's family," he protested.

"This has been done. —I need you," Kta insisted. "*I* need you. Elas does. When Ylith-methi knows what you have done, and she will, I have no doubt that she will wish to see you, and you cannot go like that, and you cannot go ignorant of the business of your hearth."

He nodded wearily, felt for the stairs.

"Kta," said Bel softly. "See to him if you wish, personally. We will keep peace at your hearth until you return—surely, my lord of Indresul. Perhaps we can even find some things to discuss while you are gone if my lady wife will bring us another round of tea."

Kta considered the two of them, grave old Vel and the young Sufaki of his own age. Then he gave them a bemused slight bow and guided Kurt toward the stairs.

"Come," he said. "You are home, my friend."

HUNTER OF
WORLDS

To my mother, my father,
and to David.

1

Halfway through the second watch the ship put into Kartos Station—the largest thing ever seen in the zone, a gleaming silver agglomeration of vanes cradling an immense saucer body. It was an Orithain craft, with no markings of nationality or identification: the Orithain disdained such conventions.

It nestled in belly-on, larger than the station itself, positioned beside an amaut freighter off Isthe II that was completely dwarfed by its bulk. The umbilical of the tube, the conveyor-connection, went out to it, scarcely long enough to reach, although the Orithain's grapples had drawn herself and the Station into relative proximity.

As soon as that connection was secure, five members of the crew disembarked, four men and a woman. They were kallia, like many of the Station personnel—a race that belonged to Qao V, a tall graceful folk, azure skinned and silver haired; but these had never seen the surface of Aus Qao: each bore on the right wrist the platinum bracelet that marked a nas kame, a servant of the Orithain.

The visitors moved at will through the market, where amaut and kalliran commerce linked the civilized worlds, the *metrosi,* with the Esliph stars. They spoke not at all to each other, but paused together and occasionally designated purchases—lots that depleted whole sections of the market, to be delivered immediately.

The moment the Orithain had entered the zone, the Station office had moved into frantic activity. Station security personnel, both kallia and amaut, were scattered among the regular dock crews in diverse uniforms—not to stop the starlords; that was impossible. They were instead to restrain the Station folk from any unintended offense against them, for the whole of Kartos Station was in jeopardy as long as that silver dreadnaught was anywhere in the zone; an Orithain-lord minutely displeased was a bad enemy for a planet, let alone a manmade bubble like Kartos.

And the commanders of Kartos kept otherwise still, and sent no messages of alarm, either inside or outside the Station. There was a hush everywhere. Those that must move, moved quietly.

Ages ago the Orithain had first contacted the kallia, wrenching the folk of Aus Qao out of feudalism and abruptly into star-spanning civilization. Eight thousand years ago the Orithain had reached out to Kesuat, the home star of the amaut—podgy little gray-skinned farmers, broad-bellied and large-eyed, unlikely starfarers; but amaut were scattered now from Kesuat to the Esliph. The *metrosi* itself was an Orithain creation, modern technology an Orithain gift—but one that came at fearful price, a tyranny unimaginably cruel and irrational.

Then for five hundred years, as inexplicably as they did everything, the Orithain had vanished, even from their home star Kej. Ship-dwellers that they were, they began to voyage outward and elsewhere, and ceased to be seen in the range of kalliran ships or amaut. Some even dared to hope them dead—until seven years ago.

Suddenly Orithain were massing again near Kej. Ship by ship, they were reported coming in, gathering like great birds to the smell of death. The outmost worlds knew it, though the *metrosi* refused to admit it for fact. There was no defense possible: kallia knew this; no weapon would avail against Orithain ships, and the pride that the Orithain took in inventive cruelty was legendary. It was more comfortable not to acknowledge their existence.

But at Kartos, bordering the Esliph, the Orithain made their return to the *metrosi* clear beyond doubt.

At the end of the new-station docks the noi kame separated. Two, one carrying a small gray case, went up toward the Station office. The other three descended toward the old docks, that place notorious as the Blind Market, where berths and facilities were cheap and crowded, where goods were often traded unobserved by the overworked Station authorities: little freighters, small cargoes, often shoddy goods, damaged lots, pirated merchandise. Most of the ships docked here came from the Esliph, bearing raw materials and buying up necessities and a few civilized vices for the poorer, outermost worlds.

The security personnel who maintained their discreet watch were alarmed when the noi kame unexpectedly entered that tangle of small berths, and they were perplexed when the noi kame immediately sought the *Konut,* an ancient freighter from the Esliph fringe. Fat little amaut ran about in its open hold in an agony of panic at their coming, and the captain came waddling up on his short legs, working his wide mouth in an expression of extreme unease.

At the noi kame's order the amaut produced the manifest, which the noi kame scanned as they walked with the captain deep into the hold. Incredibly filthy compartments lined this aisle, a stench of unwashed amaut bodies heavy in the air, for the *Konut* trafficked in indentured labor, ignorant laborers contracted to the purchasing company for the usual ten years on a colonial world in exchange for land there—land, which they desired more than they feared the rigors of the journey. Amaut were at heart farmers and diggers in the earth, and the hope of these forlorn, untidy little folk was a small parcel of land somewhere—anywhere. Most would never achieve it: debt to the company would keep them forever tenant farmers.

And to the rear of the *Konut*'s second hold was a matter which the captain neglected to report to Station customs: a wire enclosure where humans were transported. Kalliran law forbade traffic in human labor: the creatures were wild and illiterate, unable to make any valid contract—the dregs of the stubborn population left behind when the humans abandoned the Esliph stars and retreated to home space. Their ancestors might have been capable of starflight, but these were not even capable of coherent speech. They were sectioned off from the other hold because the amaut would not abide proximity to them: humans were notorious carriers of disease. One of them at the moment lay stiff and unnatural on the wire mesh flooring, dead perhaps from chill, perhaps from something imported from whatever Esliph world had sent him. Another sat staring, eyes dark and mad.

This was the place that interested the noi kame. They stopped, consulted the manifest, conferred with the captain. The one human still stared, crouched up very small as if he sought obscurity; but when the others suddenly rushed to the far corner, shrieking and clawing and climbing over one another in their witless panic, this one sat still, eyes following every movement outside the cage.

When at last the amaut captain turned and pointed at him, that human froze into absolute immobility, resisting the captain's beckoning.

The sweating captain beckoned at the other humans then, spoke one word several times: *chaju*—liquor. Suddenly the humans were listening, faces eager; and when the amaut pointed at the human that crouched at the center of the cage, the others shrieked in excitement and descended on the unfortunate creature, dragging him to the side of the cage despite his struggling and his cries of rage. They pressed him against the mesh until an attendant could administer an injection: his nails raked the attendant, who hit his arm and spat a curse, but already the human was sinking: the curiously alert eyes glazed, and he slumped down to the mesh flooring.

With no further difficulty the attendant entered the cage and dragged the unconscious human out, rewarding the others with a large flask of *chaju* that was instantly the cause of a fight.

The noi kame distastefully ignored these proceedings. They paid the price of the indenture in silver-weight, named a time for delivery, and walked back the way they had come.

The remaining noi kame, a man and a woman, had entered Station control without a glance at the frightened security personnel or a gesture of courtesy toward the Master. They went to the records center, dislodged the technician from his post, and connected the apparatus in the gray case to the machine.

"It will be necessary," said the woman to the Master, who hovered uncertainly in the background, "for this technician to follow our instructions."

The Master nodded to the operator, who resumed his post reluctantly and did as he was told. The Station's records, the log and the personnel files in their entirety, the centuries of accumulated knowledge of Esliph exploration, the patterns of treaties, of lane regulation and zonal government, bled swiftly into the Orithain's ken.

When the process was complete, the apparatus was disconnected, the case was closed, and the noi kame turned as one, facing the Master.

"There is a man on this station named Aiela Lyailleue," said the man. "Deliver his records to us."

The Master made a helpless gesture. "I have no authority to do that," he said.

"We do not operate on your authority," said the nas kame.

The Master gave the order. A section of tape fed out of the machine.

"Dispose of the original record," said the woman, winding the tape about her first finger. "This person Aiela will report to our dock for boarding at 0230 Station Time."

Kallia tended to a look of innocence. Their hair was the same whatever their age, pale and silvery, individual strands as translucent as spun glass. The pale azure of their skin intensified to sapphire in the eyes, which, unlike the eyes of amaut, could look left or right without turning the whole head: it gave them a whole range of communication without words, and made it difficult for them to conceal their feelings. They were an emotional folk—not loud, like amaut, who liked disputes and noisy entertainments, but fond of social gatherings. One kallia proverbially never decided anything: it took at least three to reach a decision on the most trivial of matters. To be otherwise was *ikas*—presumptuous, and a kalliran gentleman was never that.

Security agent Muishiph was amaut, but he had been long enough on Kartos to know the kallia quite well, both the good and the bad in them. He watched the young officer Aiela Lyailleue react to the news—he stood at the door of the kallia's onstation apartment—and expected some outcry of grief or anger at the order. Muishiph had already nerved himself to resist such appeals—even to defend himself; his own long arms could crush the slender limbs of a kallia, although he certainly did not want to do that.

"I?" asked the young officer, and again: "*I?*" as though he still could not believe it. He looked appallingly young to be a ship's captain. The records confirmed it: twenty-six years old, son of Deian of the Lyailleue house, aristocrat. Deian was *parome* of Xolun *arethme,* and the third councilor in the High Council of Aus Qao, a great weight of power and wealth— probably the means by which young Lyailleue had achieved his premature rank. Aiela's hands trembled. He jammed them into the pockets of his short jacket to conceal the fact and shook his head rather blankly.

"But do you have any idea why they singled me out?"

"The Master said he thought you might know," said Muishiph, "but I doubt he wants to be told, in any case."

The young man gazed at him with eyes so distant Muishiph knew he hardly saw him; and then intelligence returned, a troubled sadness. "May I pack?" he asked. "I suppose I may need some things. I hope that I will."

"They did not forbid it." Muishiph thrust his shoulder within the doorframe, for Aiela had begun to lift his hand toward the switch. "But I would not dare leave you unobserved, sir. I am sorry."

Aiela's eyes raked Muishiph up and down with a curiously regretful expression. At least, Muishiph thought uncomfortably, the Master might have sent a kallia to break the news and to be with him; he braced himself for argument. But Aiela backed away and cleared the doorway to let him enter. Muishiph stopped just inside the door, hands locked behind his thighs, swaying; amaut did that when they were ill at ease.

"Please sit down," Aiela invited him, and Muishiph accepted, accepted again when Aiela poured them each a glass of pinkish *marithe*. Muishiph downed it all, and took his handkerchief from his belly-pocket to mop at his face. Amaut perspired a great deal and needed prodigious quantities of liquid. It was the first time Muishiph had been in a kalliran residence, and the warm, dry air was unkind to his sensitive skin, the bright light hurt his eyes. He thrust the handkerchief back into his pocket and watched Aiela. The kallia, his own drink ignored, had taken a battered spaceman's case from the locker and was starting to pack, nervously meticulous.

Muishiph knew the records from the Master, who had sent him. The young kallia captained a small geological survey vessel named *Alitaesa,* just returned from the moons of Pri, far back on the Esliph fringe. That was amaut territory, but some kallia explored there, seeking mining rights with the permission of the great trading *karshatu* that ruled amaut commerce. Amaut, natural burrowers, would work as miners; kallia, strongly industrial, would receive the ore and turn it back again in trade—an arrangement old as the *metrosi.*

But it was a rare kallia who ventured deep into the Esliph. It was a wild place and wide, with a great gulf beyond. Odd things happened there, strange ships came and went, and law was a matter of local option and available firepower. The amaut *karshatu* took care of their own, and brooked no intrusion on *karsh* lanes or *karsh* worlds: the kallia they tolerated, reckoning them harmless, for they were above all law-loving folk, their major vice merely a desire of wealth, not land, but monetary and imaginary. Kallia worshipped order: their universe was ordered in such a way that one could not determine his own worth save in terms of the respect paid him by others—and money was somehow a measure of this, as primogeniture was among amaut in a *karsh.* Muishiph looked on the young man and wondered: as he reckoned kallia, they were shallow folk, never seeking power for its own sake. They had no ambitions: they hated responsibility, feeling that there was something sinister and *ikas* in tampering with destiny. An amaut might dream of having land, of founding a *karsh,* producing offspring in the dozens; but for a kallia the greatest joy seemed to be to retire into a quiet community, giving genteel parties for small gatherings of all the most honorable people, and being a man to whom others resorted for advice and influence—a safe life, and quiet, and never, never involving solitary decisions.

If Aiela Lyailleue was a curiosity to the Orithain, he was no less a puzzle to Muishiph: an untypical kallia, a wealthy *parome's* son who chose the hazardous life of the military, exploring the Esliph's backside. It was the hardest and loneliest command any

officer, amaut or kallia, could have, out where there was no one
to consult and no law to rely on. This was not a kalliran life at all.

Aiela had packed several changes of clothing, everything from
the drawers. "Some things are on my ship," he said. "Surely they
will send my other belongings home to my family."

"Surely," Muishiph agreed, miserable in the lie. When a
karsh outgrew its territory, the next-born were cast out to fend
for themselves. Some founded *karshatu* of their own, some became bondservants to other *karshatu* or sought employment by
the kallia, and some simply died of grief. What amaut literature
there was sang mournfully of the misery of such outcasts, who
were cut off and forgotten quickly by their own kind. The kallia
talked of his house as if it still existed for him. Muishiph rolled
his lips inward and refused to argue with the childish faith.

Aiela gathered his pictures off the desk last of all: an adult-
children group that must be his kin, a young girl with flowers in
her silver hair—*ko shenellis,* the coming-of-age: Muishiph had
heard of the ceremony and recognized it, wondering if the girl
were kinswoman or intended mate. Aiela himself was in the
third picture, a younger Aiela in civilian clothes, standing by a
smiling youth his own age, the crumbling walls of some ancient
kalliran building fluttering with flags in the background. They
were perplexing bits and pieces of a life Muishiph could not
even imagine, things and persons that had given joy to the
kallia, reminders that he once had had roots—things that were
important to him even lost as he was. The pictures were turned,
one by one, face down on the clothing in the case. With them
went a small box of tape cassettes. Aiela closed and locked the
case, turned with a gesture of entreaty.

"Do you suppose," he asked, "that there is time to write a
letter?"

Muishiph doubtfully consulted his watch. "If you do, you
must hurry about it."

Aiela bowed his gratitude, a courtesy Muishiph returned on
reflex; and he waited on his feet while Aiela opened the desk
and sat down, using some of the Station's paper.

After a time Muishiph consulted his watch again and coughed
delicately. Aiela hastened his writing, working feverishly until a
second apologetic cough advised him of Muishiph's impa-

tience. Then he arose and unfastened his collar, drawing over his head a metal seal on a chain: its embossed impression sealed the message—a house crest. Kalliran aristocrats clung to such symbols, prized relics of the feudal culture that had been theirs before the starlords found them.

And before Muishiph realized his intention, Aiela had thrust the seal into the disposal chute. It would end floating in space, disassociated atoms of precious metals. Muishiph gaped in shock; kalliran matters, those seals, but they were ancient, and the destruction of something so old and familial struck Muishiph's heart with a physical sickness.

"Sir," he objected, and met sudden coldness in the kallia's eyes.

"If I had sent it home," said Aiela, "and it had been lost, it would have been a shame on my family; and it is not right to take it as a prisoner either."

"Yes, sir," Muishiph agreed, embarrassed, uneasy at knowing Aiela doubted Kartos' intentions of his property. There was more sense to the kallia than he had reckoned. He became the more perturbed when Aiela thrust the letter into his hands.

"Send it," said Aiela. "Private mails. I know it costs—" He took out his wallet and pressed that too into Muishiph's hand. "There's more than enough. Please. Keep the rest. You'll have earned it."

Muishiph stared from the wallet and the letter to Aiela's anxious face. "Sir, I protest I am an officer of—"

"I know. Break the seal, read it—copy it, I don't care. Only get it to Aus Qao. My family can reward you. I want them to know what happened to me."

Muishiph considered a moment, his mouth working in distress. Then he slipped the letter into his belly-pocket and patted it flat. But he kept only two of the larger bills from the wallet and cast the wallet down on the table.

"Take it all," said Aiela. "Someone else will, that's certain."

"I don't dare, sir," said Muishiph, looking at it a second time regretfully. He put it from his mind once for all with a glance at his watch. "Come, bring your baggage. We have orders to anticipate that deadline. The Station is taking no chances of offending them."

"I am sure they would not." For a moment his odd kalliran eyes fixed painfully on Muishiph, asking something; but Muishiph hurriedly shrugged and showed Aiela out the door, walking beside him as soon as they were in the broad hall. Another security guard, a kallia, met them at the turning: he carried a sheaf of documents and a tape case.

"My records?" Aiela surmised, at which the kalliran guard looked embarrassed.

"Yes, sir," he admitted. "They are being turned over. Everything is."

Aiela kept his eyes forward and did not look at that man after that, nor the man at him.

Muishiph fingered the outline of the letter in his belly-pocket, and carefully extracted his handkerchief and mopped at his face. It was too much to ask. To deceive the lords of *karshatu* and to cross the Qao High Council were both perilous undertakings, but the starlords were an ancient terror and their reach was long and their knowledge thorough beyond belief. The letter burned like guilt against Muishiph's belly. Already he began to imagine his position should anyone guess what he had agreed to do.

And then it occurred to him to wonder if Aiela had told the truth of what it contained.

The Orithain vessel itself was not visible from the dock. There was only the entry tube and its conveyor, disappearing constantly upward as the supplies flooded toward the unseen maw of the ship. Aiela stopped with his escort and set his case beside him on the tiled flooring, the three of them conspicuous in an area where no spectators would dare to be. Aiela shivered; his knees felt loose. He hoped it was not evident to those with him. Courage to cross that small area without faltering: that was all he begged of himself.

He was not, he had assured his family in the letter, expecting to die; execution could be accomplished with far more effect in public. He did not know what had drawn the Orithain's attention to him: he had touched nothing and done nothing that could have accounted for it, to his own knowledge, and what they intended with him he only surmised. He would not return. No one had ever been appropriated by the Orithain and walked out again free; but it would please him if his family would think of him as alive and well. He had saved five thousand lives on Kartos by his compliance with orders: he was well sure of this; there was cause for pride in that fact.

Empty canisters clanged on the dock, the horrid crash rumbling through his senses, dislodging him from his privacy. He looked and saw a frightened amaut crew trying to stop machinery. An amaut had been injured. The minute tragedy occupied him for the moment. None of the bystanders would help. They only stared. Finally the amaut was allowed to lie alone. The others worked feverishly with the lading of canisters, trying to make their deadline. The machinery started again.

His father would understand, between the lines of what he had written. *Parome* Deian was on the High Council, and knew the reports that never went to earthsiders. There was an understanding as old as the kallia's first meeting with the Orithain: their eccentricities were not for comment and their names were not to be uttered; the Orithain homeworld at Kej still lay deserted, legendary cities full of supposed treasure—but *metrosi* ships avoided that star; for nine thousand years the Orithain had been the central fact of *metrosi* civilization, but no research delved into their origins, few books so much as mentioned them save in oblique reference to the Domination, and nothing but legend reported their appearance. But they were remembered. In the independence of space the old tales continued to be told, and legends were amplified now with new horrors of Orithain cruelty. Deian was one of nine men on all Aus Qao who received across his desk all the statistics and the rumors.

And if the statistics preceded his letter, Aiela reflected sorrowfully, his father would receive that cold message first. It would be the final cruelty of so many that had passed between them.

If that were to go first, witnesses would at least say that he had gone with dignity.

At the end, he could give nothing else to his family.

The lefthand ramp had been clear of traffic for several moments. Now it reversed, and one of the noi kame descended. Aiela bent and picked up his case when the man came toward them; and when they met, the kalliran agent gave into the nas

kame's hands the documents and the tape case—the sum of all
records in the zone regarding Aiela and his existence. It was terrible to believe so, but even Qao might follow suit, erasing all
records even to his certificate of birth, forbidding mention of
him even by his family. Fear of the Orithain was that powerful.
Aiela was suddenly bitterly ashamed for his people, for what the
starlords had made them be and do. He began to be angry, when
before he had felt only grief.

"Come," said the nas kame, accepting the sheaf of documents
and the case under his arm. But he looked down in some surprise as the amaut agent suddenly pushed forward, proffering a
letter in his trembling hand.

"His too, lord, his too," said the amaut.

The nas kame took the letter and put it among the documents;
and Aiela looked toward the amaut reproachfully, but the amaut
bowed his head and stood rocking back and forth, refusing to
look up at him.

Aiela turned his face instead toward the nas kame, appalled
that there was no shame there—eyes as kalliran as his that held
no recognition of him and cared nothing for his misery.

The nas kame brought him to the moving ramp and preceded
him up, looking back once casually at the scene below, ignoring
Aiela. Then the belt set them both into the ship's hold.

Aiela's eyes were drawn up by the sheer echoing immensity
of the place. This hold, as was usual with supply holds, was
filled with frames and canisters of goods, row on row, dated,
stamped to be listed in the computer's memory. But it could
have contained an entire ship the size of the one Aiela had lately
commanded—without the frames and the clutter. No doubt there
were other holds that did hold such things as transfer ships and
shuttles available at need. It staggered the mind.

The nas kame took his case from him and handed it to an
amaut, who waddled ahead of them to a counter and had it
stamped and listed and thrust up a conveyor to disappear. Aiela
looked after it with a sinking heart, for among his folded clothing he had put his service pistol—nonlethal, like all he weapons
of the kalliran service. He had debated it; he had done it, terrified in the act and terrified to go defenseless, without it. But
there were no defenses. Standing where he was now, with all

Kartos so small and fragile a place beneath them, he realized it
for a selfish and cowardly thing to do.

"There was a weapon in that," he said to the nas kame.

The nas kame took notice of him directly for the fast time, regarding him with mild surprise. He had just put the documents
and the tape case on the counter to be similarly stamped and
sent up the conveyor. Then he shrugged. "Security will deal
with it," he said, and took Aiela's arm and held his hand on the
counter, compelling him to accept a stamp on the back of his
hand, like the other baggage.

Aiela received it with so deep a confusion that he failed to
protest; but afterward, with the nas kame holding his arm and
guiding him rapidly through the echoing hold, a wave of such
shame and outrage came over him that he was almost shaking.
He should have said something; he should have done something.
He worked his fingers, staring at the purple symbols that rippled
across the bones of his hand, and was only gathering the words
to object to the indignity when the nas kame roughly turned him
and thrust him toward a personnel lift. He went, turned once inside, and expected the nas kame to step in too; but the door slid
shut and he was hurtled elsewhere on his own. The controls resisted his attempt to regain the loading deck.

In an instant the lift came to a cushioned halt and opened on a
cargo area adapted to the reception of live goods; there were a
score or more individual cells and animal pens, some with bare
flooring and some padded on all surfaces. Gray-smocked noi
kame and amaut in green were waiting for him, took charge of
him as he stepped out. One noted the number from his hand
onto a slate, then gestured him to move.

As he walked the aisle of compartments he saw one lighted,
its facing wall transparent; and his flesh crawled at the sight of
the naked pink-brown tangle of limbs that crouched at the rear
of it. It looked moribund, whatever it had been—the Orithain
ranged far: perhaps it was only one of the forgotten humans of
the Esliph; perhaps it was some more dangerous and exotic
specimen from the other end of the galaxy, where no *metrosi*
ship had ever gone. He delayed, looked more closely; a nas
kame pushed him between the shoulders and moved him on, and
by now he was completely overwhelmed, dazed and beyond any

understanding of what to do. He walked. No one spoke to him. He might have been a nonsentient they were handling.

Physicians took him—at least so he reckoned them—kallia and amaut, who ordered him to strip, and examined him until he was exhausted by their thoroughness, the cold, and the endless waiting. He was beyond shame. When at last they thrust his wadded clothing at him and put him into one of the padded cells to wait, he stood there blankly for some few moments before the cold finally urged him to dress.

He shivered convulsively afterward, walking to lean against one and another of the walls. Finally he knelt down on the floor to rest, limbs tucked up for warmth, his muscles still racked with shivers. There was no view, only white walls and a blank, padded door—cold, white light. He heard nothing to tell him what passed outside until the gentle shock of uncoupling threw him off-balance: they were moving, Kartos would be dropping astern at ever-increasing speed.

It was irrevocable.

He was dead, so far as his own species was concerned, so far as anything he had known was concerned. There were no more familiar reference points.

He was only beginning to come to grips with that, when the room vanished.

He was suddenly kneeling on a carpeted floor that still felt strangely like the padded plastics of the cell. The lights were dim, the walls expanded into an immense dark chamber of carven screens and panels of alien design. A woman in black and diaphanous violet stood before him, a woman of the Orithain, of the indigo-skinned iduve race. Her hair was black: it hung like fine silk, thick and even at the level of her shapely jaw. Her brows were dark, her eyes amethyst-hued, without whites, and rimmed with dark along the edge of the lid. Her nose was arched but delicate, her mouth sensuous, frosted with lavender, the whole of her face framed with the absolute darkness of her hair. The draperies hinted at a slim and female body; her complexion, though dusky from the kalliran view, had a lustrous sheen, as though dust of violet glistened there, as if she walked in another light than ordinary mortals, a universe where suns were violet and skies were of shadowy hue.

He rose and, because it was *elethia,* he gave her a proper bow for meeting despite their races: she was female, though she was an enemy. She smiled and gave a nod of her graceful head.

"Be welcome, *m'metane,*" she said.

"Who was it who had me brought here?" he demanded, anger springing out of his voice to cover his fear. "And why did you ask for *me?*"

"*Vaikka,*" she said, and when he did not understand, she shrugged and seemed amused. "*Au, m'metane,* you are ignorant and *anoikhte,* two conditions impossible to maintain aboard *Ashanome.* We carry no passengers. You will be in my service."

"No." The answer burst out of him before he even reckoned the consequences, but she shrugged again and smiled.

"We might return to Kartos," she said. "You might be set off there to advise them of your objections."

"And what then?"

"I would prefer otherwise."

He drew a long breath, let it go again. "I see. So why do you come offering me choices? Noi kame can't make any, can they?"

"I have scanned your records. I find your decision expected. And as for your assumption of noi kame—no: kamethi have considerable initiative; they would be useless otherwise."

"Would you have destroyed Kartos?"

His angry question seemed for the first time to perplex the Orithain, whose gentle manner persisted. "When we threaten, *m'metane,* we do so because of another's weakness, never of our own. It was highly likely that you would choose to come: *elethia* forbids you should refuse. If you would not, surely fear would compel them to bring you. Likewise it is certain that I would have destroyed Kartos had it refused. Any other basis for making the statement would have been highly unreasonable."

"Was it you?" he asked. "Why did you choose me?"

"*Vaikka*—a matter of honor. You are of birth such that your loss will be noticed among kallia: that has a certain incidental value. And I have use for such as you: world-born, but experienced of outer worlds."

He hated her, hated her quiet voice and her evident delight in his misery. "Well," he said, "you'll regret that particular choice."

Her amethyst eyes darkened perceptibly. There was no longer a smile on her face. "*Kutikkase-metane,*" she said. "At the moment you are no more than sentient raw material, and it is useless to attempt rational conversation with you."

And with blinding swiftness the white light of the cell was about him again, yielding white plastic on all sides, narrow walls, white glare. He flinched and covered his eyes, and fell to his knees again in the loneliness of that cubicle.

Then, not for the first time in the recent hour, he thought of self-destruction; but he had no convenient means, and he had still to fear her retaliation against Kartos. He slowly realized how ridiculous he had made himself with his threat against her, and was ashamed. His entire species was powerless against the likes of her, powerless because, like Kartos, like him, they would always find the alternative unthinkably costly.

He came docilely enough when they brought him out into the laboratory, expecting that they would simply lock about his wrist the *idoikkhe,* such as they themselves wore—that ornate platinum band that observers long ago theorized provided the Orithain their means of control over the noi kame.

Such was not the case. They had him dress in a white wrap about his waist and lie down again on the table, after which they forcibly administered a drug that made his senses swim, dispersing his panic to a vague, all-encompassing uneasiness.

He realized by now that becoming nas kame involved more than accepting that piece of jewelry—that he was going under and that he would not wake the same man. In his drugged despair he begged, he invoked deity, he pleaded with them as fellow kallia to consider what they were doing to him.

But they ignored his raving and with an economy of effort, slipped him to a movable table and put him under restraint. From that point his perceptions underwent a rapid deterioration. He was conscious, but he could not tell what he was seeing or hearing, and eventually passed over the brink.

2

The dazed state gave way to consciousness in the same tentative manner. Aiela was aware of the limits of his own body, of a pain localized in the roof of his mouth and behind his eyes. There was a bitter chemical taste and his brow itched. He could not raise his hand to scratch it. The itch spread to his nose and was utter misery. When he grimaced to relieve it, the effort hurt his head.

He slept again, and wakened a second time enough to try to move, remembering the bracelet that ought to be locked about his wrist. There was none. He lifted his hand—free now—and saw the numbers still stamped there, but faded. His head hurt. He touched his temple and felt a thin rough seam. There was the salt of blood in his mouth toward the back of his palate; his throat was raw. He felt along the length of the incision at his temple and panic began to spread through him like ice.

He hated them. He could still hate; but the concentration it took was tiring—even fear was tiring. He wept, great tears rolling from his eyes, and even then he was fading. Drugs, he thought dimly. He shut his eyes.

A raw soreness persisted, not of the body, but of the mind, a perception, a part of him that could not sleep, like an inner eye that had no power to blink. It burned like a white light at the edge of his awareness, an unfocused field of vision where shadows and colors moved undefined. Then he knew what they had done to him, although he did not know the name of it.

"*No!*" he screamed, and screamed again and again until his voice was gone. No one came. His senses slipped from him again.

At the third waking he was stronger, breathing normally, and aware of his surroundings. The sore spot was there; when he worried at it the place grew wider and brighter, but when he forced himself to move and think of other things, the color of the wall, anything at all, it ebbed down to a memory, an imagination of presence. He could control it. Whatever had been done to his brain, he remembered, he knew himself. He tested the place nervously, like probing a sore tooth; it reacted predictably, grew and diminished. It had depth, a void that drew at his senses. He pulled his mind from it, crawled from bed and leaned against a chair, fighting to clear his senses.

The room had the look of a comfortable hotel suite, all in blue tones, the lighted white doorway of a tiled bath at the rear—luxury indeed for a starship. His disreputable serviceman's case rested on the bureau. A bench near the bed had clothing—beige—laid out across it.

His first move was for the case. He leaned on the bureau and opened it. Everything was there but the gun. In its place was a small card: *We regret we cannot permit personal arms without special clearance. It is in storage. For convenience in claiming your property at some later date, please retain this card, 509-3899-345.*

He read it several times, numb to what he felt must be a certain grim humor. He wiped at his blurring vision with his fingers and leaned there, absently beginning to unpack, one-handed at first, then with both. His beloved pictures went there, so, facing the chair which he thought he would prefer. He put things in the drawer, arranged clothing, going through motions familiar to a hundred unfamiliar places, years of small outstations, hardrock worlds—occupying his mind and keeping it from horrid reality. He was alive. He could remember. He could resent his situation. And this place, this room, was known, already measured, momentarily safe: it was *his,* so long as he opened no doors.

When he felt steady on his feet he bathed, dressed in the clothes provided him, paused at the mirror in the bath to look a second time at his reflection, when earlier he had not been able to face it. His silver hair was cropped short; his own face shocked him, marred with the finger-length scar at his temple, but the incision was sealed with plasm and would go away in a few days, traceless. He touched it, wondered, ripped his thoughts back in terror; light flashed in his mind, pain. He stumbled, and came to himself with his face pressed to the cold glass of the mirror and his hands spread on its surface to hold him up.

"Attention please." The silken voice of the intercom startled him, "Attention. Aiela Lyailleue, you are wanted in the *paredre*. Kindly wait for one of the staff to guide you."

He remembered an intercom screen in the main room, and he pushed himself square on his feet and went to it, pressed what he judged was the call button, several times, in increasing anger. A glowing dot raced from one side of the screen to the other, but there was no response.

He struck the plate to open the door, not expecting that to work for him either, but it did; and instead of an ordinary corridor, he faced a concourse as wide as a station dock.

At the far side, stars spun past a wide viewport in the stately procession of the saucer's rotation. Kallia in beige and other colors came and went here, and but for the luxury of that incredible viewport and the alien design of the shining metal pillars that spread ornate flanged arches across the entire overhead, it might have been an immaculately modern port on Aus Qao. Amaut technicians waddled along at their rolling pace, looking prosperous and happy; a young kalliran couple walked hand in hand; children played. A man of the iduve crossed the concourse, eliciting not a ripple of notice among the noi kame—a tall slim man in black, he demanded and received no special homage. Only one amaut struggling along under the weight of several massive coils of hose brought up short and ducked his head apologetically rather than contest right of way.

At the other end of the concourse an abstract artwork of metal over metal, the pieces of which were many times the size of a man, closed off the columned expanse in high walls. At their inner base and on an upper level, corridors led off into distance so great that the inner curvature of the ship played visual havoc with the senses, door after door of what Aiela judged to be other apartments stretching away into brightly lit sameness.

The iduve was coming toward him.

Panic constricted his heart. He looked to one side and the other, finding no other cause for the iduve's interest. And then a resolution wholly reckless settled into him. He turned and began at first simply to walk away; but when he looked back, panic won: he gathered his strength and started to run.

Noi kame stared, shocked at the disorder. He shouldered past and broke into a corridor, not knowing where it led—the ship, vast beyond belief, tempted him to believe he could lose himself, find its inward parts, at least understand the sense of things before they found him again and forced their purposes upon him.

Then the section doors sealed, at either end of the hall.

Noi kame stared at him, dismayed.

"Stand still," one said to him.

Aiela glanced that way: hands took his arms and he twisted out and ran, but they closed and held him. The first man rash enough to come at him from the front flew backward under the impact of his thin-soled boot; but he could not free himself. An amaut took his arms, a grip he could not break, struggle as he would; and then the doors parted and the iduve arrived with a companion, frowning and businesslike. When Aiela attempted to kick at them, that iduve's backhand exploded across his face with force enough to black him out: a hypospray against his arm finished his resistance.

He was not entirely unconscious. He tried to walk because the grip on his arms hurt less when he carried his own weight, but it was some little distance before he even cared where they were taking him. For a dizzying moment they rode a lift, and stepped off into another corridor, and then came into a hall. On the left a screen of translucent blue stone carved in scenes of reeds and birds separated a vast dim hall from this narrower chamber.

Then he remembered this place, this hall like a museum, with its beautiful fretted panels and lacquered ceiling, its cases for display, its ornate and alien furnishings. He had stood here once before from the vantage point of his cell, but this was reality. The carpets he walked gave under his boots, and the woman that awaited them was not projection, but flesh and blood.

"Aiela," she said in her accented voice, "Aiela Lyailleue: I am Chimele, Orithain of *Ashanome*. And such action is hardly an auspicious introduction, nor at all wise. *Takkh-ar-rhei, nasithi.*"

Aiela found himself free—dizzied, bruised, thoroughly dispossessed of the recklessness to chance another chastisement at their hands. He moved a step—the iduve behind him moved him back precisely where he had stood.

She spoke to her people, frowning: they answered. Aiela waited, with such a physical terror mounting in him as he had never felt in any circumstances. He could not even shape it in his thoughts. He felt disconnected, smothered, wished at once to run and feared the least movement.

And now Chimele turned from him and returned with the wide band of an *idoikkhe* open in her indigo fingers—a band of three fingers' width, with a patchwork of many colors of metal on its inner surface, a thread of black weaving through it all. She held it out for him, expecting him to offer his wrist for it, and now, now was the time if ever he would refuse anything again. He could not breathe, and he felt strongly the threat of violence at his back; his battered nerves refused to carry the right impulses. He saw himself raise an arm that seemed part of another body, heard a sharp click as the cold band locked, felt a weight that was more than he had expected as she took her hands away.

A jewel of milk and fire shone on its face. The asymmetry of iduve artistry flashed in metal worth a man's life in the darker places of the Esliph. He stared at it, realizing beyond doubt that he had accepted its limits, that no foreign thing in his skull had compelled the lifting of his arm; there was a weakness in Aiela Lyailleue that he had never found before, a shameful, unmanning terror.

It was as if something essential in him had torn away, left behind in Kartos. He feared. For the first time he knew himself less than other beings. Without dignity he tore at the band, but of the closure no trace remained save a faint diffraction of light—no clasp and no yielding.

"No," she said, "you cannot remove it."

And with a gesture she dismissed the others, so that they stood alone in the hall. He was tempted then to murder, the first time he had ever felt a hate so *ikas*—and then he knew that it was out of fear, female that she was. He gained control of himself with that thought, gathered enough courage to plainly defy her: he spun on his heel to stalk out, to make them use force if they would. That much resolve he still possessed.

The *idoikkhe* stung him, a dart of pain from his fingertips to his ribs. At the next step it hurt; and he paused, measuring the long distance to the door against the pain that lanced in rising pulses up his arm. A greater shock hit him, waves enough to jolt his heart and shorten his breath.

He jerked about and faced her—not to attack: if he had any thought then it was to stand absolutely still, anything, anything to stop it. The pulse vanished as he did what she wanted, and the ache faded slowly.

"Do not fear the *idoikkhe*," said Chimele. "We use it primarily for coded communication, and it will not greatly inconvenience you."

He was shamed; he jerked aside, hurt at once as the *idoikkhe* activated, faced her and felt it fade again.

"I do not often resort to that," said Chimele, who had not yet appeared to do anything. "But there is a fine line between humor and impertinence with us which few *m'metanei* can safely tread. Come, *m'metane-toj,* use your intelligence."

She allowed him time, at least: he recovered his composure and caught his breath, rebuilding the courage it took to anger her.

"So what is the law here?" he asked.

"Do not play the game of *vaikka* with an iduve." He tried to outface her with his anger, but Chimele's whiteless eyes locked on his with an invading directness he did not like. "You are bound to find the wager higher than you are willing to pay. You have not been much harmed, and I have extended you an extraordinary courtesy."

"I don't think so," he said, and knew what to expect for it, knew and waited until his nerves were drawn taut. But Chimele broke from his eyes with a shrug, gestured toward a chair.

"Sit and listen, kameth. Sit and listen. I do not notice your attitude. You are only ignorant. We are using valuable time."

He hesitated, weighed matters; but the change in her manner was as complete as it was abrupt, almost as if she regretted her anger. He still thought of going for the door; then common sense reasserted itself, and he settled on the chair opposite the one she chose.

Pain hit him, excruciating, lancing through his eyes and the back of his skull at once. He bent over, holding his face, unable to breathe. That sensation passed quickly, leaving a throbbing ache behind his eyes.

"Be quiet," she said. "Anger is the worst possible response."

And she brought him a tiny glass of clear liquid. He drank, too shaken to argue, set the empty crystal vessel on the table. He missed the edge with his distorted vision: it toppled off and she imperturbably picked it up off the costly rug and set it securely on the table.

"I am not responsible," she said when he looked hate at her.

There was something at the edge of his mind, the void now full of something dark that reached up at him, and he fought to shut it out, losing the battle as long as he panicked. Then it ceased, firmly, outside his will.

"What was done to me?" he cried. "What was it?"

"The *chiabres*, the implant: I would surmise, though I do not do so from experience, that you reacted on a subconscious level and triggered defenses, contacting what was not prepared to receive you. This *chiabres* of yours has two contacts, mind-links to your asuthi—your companions. One is probably in the process of waking, and I assure you that fighting an asuthe is not profitable."

"I had rather be dead," he said. "I would rather die."

"*Tekasuphre*. Do not try my patience. I called you here precisely to explain matters to you. I have great personal regard for your asuthe. Do I make myself clear?"

"Am I joined to one of you?"

"No," she said, suddenly laughing—a merry, gentle sound, but her teeth were white and sharp. "Nature provided for us in our own fashion, *m'metane*. Kallia and even amaut find *asuthithekkhe* pleasant, but we would not."

And the walls closed about them. Aiela sprang to his feet in alarm, while Chimele arose more gracefully. The light had brightened, and beside them was a bed whereon lay a kalliran woman of great beauty. She stirred in her sleep, silvery head turning on the pillow, one azure hand coming to her breast. There was the faint seam of a new scar at her temple.

"She is Isande," said Chimele. "Your asuthe."

"Is it—usual—that different sexes—"

Chimele shrugged. "We have not found it of concern."

"Was she the one I felt a moment ago?"

"It is not reasonable to ask me to venture an opinion on something I have never experienced. But it seems quite possible."

He looked from Chimele to the sweet-faced being who lay on the bed, the worst of his fears leaving him at once. He felt even an urge to be sorry for Isande, no less than for himself; he wondered if she had consented to this unhappy situation, and was about to ask Chimele that question.

The walls blinked smaller still, and they stood in a room of padded white, a cell. At their left, leaning against the transparent face of the cell, was that same naked pink-brown creature Aiela remembered lying inert in the corner on his entry into the lab. Now it turned in the rapid dawning of terror: one of the humans of the Esliph, beyond doubt, and as stunned as he had been that day—how long ago?—that Chimele had appeared in his cell. The human stumbled back, hit the wall where there was no wall in his illusion, and pressed himself there because there was no further retreat.

"He is *Daniel,*" said Chimele. "We think this is a name. That is all we have been able to obtain from him."

Aiela looked at the hair-matted face in revulsion, heart beating in panic as the human stretched out his hands. The human's dark eyes stared, white around the edges, but when his hands could not grasp them he collapsed into a knot, arms clenched, sobbing with a very manlike sound.

"This," said Chimele, "is your other *asuthe.*"

Aiela had seen it coming. When he looked at Chimele it was without the shock that would have pleased her. He hardened his face against her.

"And you know now," she continued, unmoved, "how it feels to experience the *chiabres* without understanding what it is. This will be of use to you with him."

"I thought," he recalled, "that you had regard for Isande."

"Precisely. *Asuthithekkhe* between species has always failed. I am not willing to risk the honor of *Ashanome* by endangering one of my most valued kamethi. You are presently expendable. Surgery will be performed on this being in two days. You had that interval to learn to handle the *chiabres.* Try to approach the human. Perhaps he will respond to you. Amaut are best able to quiet him, but I do not think he finds pleasure in their company or they in his. Those two species demonstrate a strong mutual aversion."

Aiela nerved himself to take a step toward the being, and another. He went down on one knee and extended his hand.

The creature gave a shuddering sob and scrambled back from any contact, wild eyes locked on his. Of a sudden it sprang for his throat.

The cell vanished, and Aiela had sprung erect in the safety of the Orithain's own shadowed hall. He still trembled, in his mind unconvinced that the hands that had reached for his throat were insubstantial.

"You are dismissed," said Chimele.

The nas kame who escorted him simply abandoned him on the concourse and advised him to ask someone if he lost his way again. There was no mention of any threat, as if they judged a man who wore the *idoikkhe* incapable of any further trouble to anyone.

In effect, he knew, they were right.

He walked away to stand by the immense viewport, watching the stars sweep past, now and again the awesome view of the afterstructure of the ship as the rotation of the saucer carried them under the holding arm, alternate oblivion and rebirth from the dark, rotation after slow rotation, the blaze of *Ashanome's* running lights, the dark beneath, the lights, the star-scattered fabric of infinity, a ceaseless rhythm.

Likely none of the thousands of kallia that came and went on the concourse knew much of Aus Qao. They had been born on the ship, would live their lives, bear their children, and die on the ship. Possibly they were even happy. Children came, their bright faces and shrill voices and the rhymes of the games they played the same as generations before had sung, the same as kalliran children everywhere. They flitted off again, their glad voices trailing away into the echoing immensities of the pillared hall. Aiela kept his face toward the viewport, struggling with the tightness in his throat.

Kartos Station would be about business as usual by now, and its people would have cleansed him from their thoughts and their conscience. Aus Qao would do the same; even his family must pick up the threads of their lives, as they would do if he were dead. His reflection stared back out of starry space, beige-clad, slender, crop-headed—indistinguishable from a thousand others that had been born to serve the ship.

He could not blame Kartos. It was a fact as old as civilization in the *metrosi,* a deep knowledge of helplessness. It was that which had compelled him to take the *idoikkhe.* Kallia were above all peaceful, patiently stubborn, and knew better how to outwait an enemy that how to fight.

To wait.

There was an Order of things, and it was reasonable and productive. For one nas kame to defy the Orithain and die would accomplish nothing. An unproductive action was not a reasonable action, and an unreasonable action was not virtue, was not *kastien.*

Should he have died for nothing?

But all reasonable action on *Ashanome* operated in favor of the Orithain, who understood nothing of *kastien.*

Until the *idoikkhe* had locked upon his wrist, he had been a person of some *elethia.* He had been a man able to walk calmly through Kartos Station under the witness of others. He had even imagined the moment he had just passed, in a hundred different manners. But he had expected oblivion, a canceling of self—a state in which he was innocent.

He had accepted it. He would continue to accept it, every day of his life, and by its weight, that metal now warmed to the temperature of his own body, he would remember what it cost to say no.

He had despised the noi kame. But doubtless their ancestors had resolved the same as he, to live, to wait their chance, which only hid their fear; waiting, they had served the Orithain, and they died, and their children's children knew nothing else.

Something stabbed at him behind his eyes. He caught at his face and reached for the support of the viewport. Waking. Conscious.

Isande.

It stopped. His vision cleared.

But it was coming. He stood still, waiting—impulses to

flight, even to suicide beat along his nerves; but these things were futile, *ikas*. It was possible—he thought blasphemously—that *kastien* demanded this patience of kallia because they were otherwise defenseless.

Slowly, slowly, something touched him, became pressure in that zone of his mind that had been opened. He shut his eyes tightly, feeling more secure as long as outside stimuli were limited. This was a being of his own kind, he reminded himself, a being who surely was in no happier state than himself.

It built in strength.

Different: that was the overwhelming impression, a force that ran over his nerves without his willing it, callous and unfamiliar. It invaded the various centers of his brain, probing one and another with painful rapidity. Light blazed and faded, equilibrium wavered, sounds roared in his ears, hot and cold affected his skin.

Then it invaded his thoughts, his memories, his inmost privacy.

O God! he thought he cried, like a man dying. There was a silence so dark and sudden it was like falling. He was leaning against the viewport, chilled by it. People were staring at him. Some even looked concerned. He straightened and shifted his eyes from the reflection to the stars beyond, to the dark.

"I am Isande." There grew a voice in his mind that had tone without sound, as a man could imagine the sound of his own voice when it was silent. A flawed dim image of the concourse filled his eyes. He saw the viewport at a distance, marked a slender man who seemed tiny against it—all this overlaid upon his own view of space. He recognized the man for himself, and turned, seeing things from two sides at once. Imposed on his own self now was a distant figure he knew for Isande: he felt her exhaustion, her impatience.

"I'll meet you in your quarters," she sent.

Her turning shifted his vision, causing him to stagger off-balance; reflex stopped the image, screened her out. He suddenly realized he had that defense, tried it again—he could not cope with the double vision while either of them was moving. He shut it down, an irregular flutter of on-off. It was hard to will a thing that decisively, that strongly, but it could be done.

And he began to suspect Chimele had been honest when she told him that kamethi found the *chiabres* no terror. It was a power, a compensation for the *idoikkhe,* a door one could fling wide or close at will.

Only what territory lay beyond depended entirely on the conscience of another being—on two asuthi, one of whom might be little removed from madness.

He did not touch her mind again until he had opened the door of his quarters: she was seated in his preferred chair in a relaxed attitude as if she had a perfect right to his things. When he realized she was speculating on the pictures on the bureau she pirated the knowledge of his family from his mind, ripped forth a flood of memories that in his disorganization he could not prevent. He reacted with fury, felt her retreat.

"I'm sorry," she said smoothly, shielding her own thoughts with an expertise his most concentrated effort could not penetrate. She gestured toward the other chair and wished him seated.

"These are my quarters," he said, still standing. "Or do they move you in with me? Do they assume that too?"

Her mind closed utterly when she felt that, and he could not reach her. He had thought her beautiful when he first saw her asleep; but now that her body moved, now that those blue eyes met his, it was with an arrogance that disturbed him even through the turmoil of his other thoughts. There was a mind behind that pretty façade, strong-willed and powerful, and that was not an impression beautiful women usually chose to send him. He was not sure he liked it.

He was less sure he liked her, despite her physical attractions.

"I have my own quarters," she said aloud. "And don't be self-centered. Your choices are limited, and *I* am not one of them."

She ruffled through his thoughts with skill against which he had no defense, and met his temper with contempt. He thrust her out, but the least wavering of his determination let her slip through again; it was a continuing battle. He took the other chair, exhausted, beginning to panic, feeling that he was going to lose everything. He would even have struck her—he would have been shamed by that.

And she received that, and mentally backed off in great haste. "Well," she conceded then, "I am sorry. I am rude. I admit that."

"You resent me." He spoke aloud. He was not comfortable with the *chiabres*. And what she radiated confirmed his impression: she tried to suppress it, succeeded after a moment.

"I wanted what you are assigned to do," she said, "very badly."

"I'll yield you the honor."

Her mind slammed shut, her lips set. But something escaped her barriers, some deep and private grief that touched him and damped his anger.

"Neither you nor I have that choice," she said. "Chimele decides. There is no appeal."

Chimele. He recalled the Orithain's image with hate in his mind, expected sympathy from Isande's, and did not receive it. Other images took shape, sendings from Isande, different feelings: he flinched from them.

For nine thousand years Isande's ancestors had served the Orithain. She took pride in that.

Iduve, she sent, correcting him. *Chimele is the Orithain; the people are iduve.*

The words were toneless this time, but different from his own knowledge. He tried to push them out.

The ship is Ashanome, she continued, ignoring his awkward attempt to cast her back. *WE are Ashanome: five thousand iduve, seven thousand noi kame, and fifteen hundred amaut. The iduve call it a nasul, a clan. The nasul Ashanome is above twelve thousand years old; the ship Ashanome is nine thousand years from her launching, seven thousand years old in this present form. Chimele rules here. That is the law in this world of ours.*

He flung himself to his feet, finding in movement, in any distraction, the power to push back Isande's insistent thoughts. He began to panic: Isande retreated.

"You do not believe," she said aloud, "that you can stop me. You could, if you believed you could."

She *pitied* him. It was a mortification as great as any the iduve had set upon him. He rounded on her with anger ready to pour forth, met a frightened, defensive flutter of her hand, a sealing of her mind he could not penetrate.

"No," she said. "Aiela—no. You will hurt us both."

"I have had enough," he said, "from the iduve—from noi kame in general. They are doing this to me—"

"—to us."

"Why?"

"Sit down. Please."

He leaned a moment against the bureau, stubborn and intractable; but she was prepared to wait. Eventually he yielded and settled on the arm of his chair, knowing well enough that she could perceive the distress that burned along his nerves, that threatened the remnant of his self control.

You fear the iduve, she observed. *Sensible. But they do not hate; they do not love. I am Chimele's friend. But Chimele's language hasn't a single word for any of those things. Don't attribute to them motives they can't have. There is something you must do in Chimele's service: when you have done it, you will be let alone. Not thanked: let alone. That is the way of things.*

"Is it?" he asked bitterly. "Is that all you get from them—to be left alone?"

Memory, swift and involuntary: a dark hall, an iduve face, terror. Thought caught it up, unraveled, explained. *Khasif: Chimele's half-brother. Yes, they feel. But if you are wise, you avoid causing it.* Isande had escaped that hall; Chimele had intervened for her. It haunted her nightmares, that encounter, sent tremors over her whenever she must face that man.

To be let alone: Isande sought that diligently.

And something else had been implicit in that instant's memory, another being's outrage, another man's fear for her—as close and as real as his own.

Another asuthe.

Isande shut that off from him, firmly, grieving. "Reha," she said. "His name was Reha. You could not know me a moment without perceiving him."

"Where is he?"

"Dead." Screening fell, mind unfolding, willfully.

Dark, and cold, and pain: a mind dying and still sending, horrified, wide open. Instruments about him, blinding light. Isande had held to him until there was an end, hurting, refusing to let go until the incredible fact of his own death swallowed him up. Aiela felt it with her, her fierce loyalty, Reha's terror—knew vicariously what it was to die, and sat shivering and sane in his own person afterward.

It was a time before things were solid again, before his fingers found the texture of the chair, his eyes accepted the color of the room, the sober face of Isande. She had given him something so much of herself, so intensely self, that he found his own body strange to him.

Did they kill him? he asked her: He trembled with anger, sharing with her: it was his loss too. But she refused to assign the blame to Chimele. Her enemies were not the iduve of *Ashanome.* His were.

He drew back from her, knowing with fading panic that it was less and less possible for him to dislike her, to find evil in any woman that had loved with such a strength.

It was, perhaps, the impression she meant to project. But the very suspicion embarrassed him, and became quickly impossible. She unfolded further, admitting him to her most treasured privacy, to things that she and Reha had shared once upon a time: her asuthe from childhood, Reha. They had played, conspired, shared their loves and their griefs, their total selves, closer by far than the confusion of kinswomen and kinsmen that had little meaning to a nas kame. For Isande there was only Reha: they had been the same individual compartmentalized into two discrete personalities, and half of it still wakened at night reaching for the other. They had not been lovers. It was something far closer.

Something to which Aiela had been rudely, forcibly admitted.

And he was an outsider, who hated the things she and Reha had loved most deeply. *Bear with me,* she asked of him. *Bear with me. Do not attack me. I have not accepted this entirely, but I will. There is no choice. And you are not unlike him. You are honest, whatever else. You are stubborn. I think he would have liked you. I must begin to.*

"Isande," he began, unaccountably distressed for her. "Could I possibly be worse than the human? And you insist you wanted that."

I could shield myself from that—far more skillfully than you can possibly learn to do to two days. And then I would be rid of him. But you—

Rid? He tried to penetrate her meaning in that, shocked and alarmed at once; and encountered defenses, winced under her rejection, heart speeding, breath tight. She turned off her conscience where the human was concerned. He was nothing to her, this creature. Anger, revenge, Reha—the human was not the object of her intentions: he simply stood in the way, and he was alien—*alien!*—and therefore nothing. Aiela would not draw her into sympathy with that creature. She would not permit it. *NO!* She had died with one asuthe, and she was not willing to die with another.

Why is he here? Aiela insisted. *What do the iduve want with him?*

Her screening went up again, hard. The rebuff was almost physical in its strength.

He was not going to obtain that answer. He had to admit it finally. He rose from his place and walked to the bureau, came back and sprawled into the chair, shaking with anger.

There was something astir among iduve, something which he was well sure Isande knew: something that could well cost him his life, and which she chose to withhold from him. And as long as that was so there would be no peace between them, however close the bond.

In that event she would not win any help from him, nor would the iduve.

No, she urged him. *Do not be stubborn in this.*

"You are Chimele's servant. You say what you have to say. I still have a choice."

Liar, she judged sadly, which stung like a slap, the worse because it was true.

Images of Chimele: ancestry more ancient than civilization among iduve, founded in days of tower-holds and warriors; a companion, a child, playing at draughts, elbows-down upon an *izhkh* carpet, laughing at a *m'metane's* cleverness; Orithain—

—isolate, powerful: *Ashanome's* influence could move full half the *nasuli* of the iduve species to Chimele's bidding—a power so vast there could be no occasion to invoke it.

Sole heir-descendant of a line more than twelve thousand years old. *Vaikka:* revenge; honor; dynasty.

Involving this human, Aiela gleaned on another level.

But that was all Isande gave him, and that by way of making peace with him. She was terrified, to have given him only that much.

"Aiela," she said, "you are involved too, because *he* is, and you were chosen for him. Even iduve die when they stand between an Orithain and necessity. So did Reha."

I thought they didn't kill him.

"Listen to me. I have lived closer to the iduve than most kamethi ever do. If Reha had been asuthe to anyone else but me, he might be alive now, and now you are here, you are Chimele's because of me; and I am warning you, you will need a great deal of good sense to survive that honor."

"And you *love* a being like that." He could not understand. He refused to understand. That in itself was a victory.

"Listen. Chimele doesn't ask that you love her. She couldn't understand it if you did. But she scanned your records and decided you have great *chanokhia,* great—fineness—for a *m'metane.* Being admired by any iduve is dangerous; but an Orithain does not make mistakes. Do you understand me, Aiela?"

Fear and love: noi kame lived by carefully prescribed rules and were never harmed—as long as they remembered their place, as long as they remained faceless and obscure to the iduve. The iduve did not insist they do so. On the contrary the iduve admired greatly a *m'metane* who tried to be more than *m'metane.*

And killed him.

"There is no reason to be afraid on that score," Isande assured him. "They do not harm us. That is the reason of the *idoikkhei.* You will learn what I mean."

His backlash of resentment was so strong she visibly winced. She simply could not understand his reaction, and though he offered her his thoughts on the matter, she drew back and would not take them. Her world was enough for her.

"I have things to teach *you,*" he said, and felt her fear like a wall between them.

"You are welcome to your opinions," she said at last.

"Thank you," he said bitterly enough; but when she opened that wall for a moment he found behind it the sort of gentle being he had seen through Reha's thoughts, terribly, painfully alone.

Dismayed, she slammed her screening shut with a vengeance, assumed a cynical façade and kept her mind taut, more burning than an oath. "And I will maintain my own," she said.

3

Two days could not prepare him, not for this.

He looked on the sleeping human and still, despite the hours he had spent with Isande, observing this being by monitor, a feeling of revulsion went through him. The attendants had done their aesthetic best for the human, but the sheeted form on the bed still looked alien—pale coloring, earth-brown hair trimmed to the skull-fitting style of the noi kame, beard removed. He never shuddered at amaut: they were cheerful, comic fellows, whose peculiarities never mattered because they never competed with kallia; but this   *this*—was bound to his own mind.

And there was no Isande.

He had assumed—they had both assumed in their plans—that she would be with him. He had come to rely on her in a strange fashion that had nothing to do with duty: with her, he knew *Ashanome,* he knew the folk he met, and people deferred to his orders as if Isande had given them. She had been with him, a voice continually in his mind, a presence at his side; at times they had argued; at others they had even found reason to be awed by each other's worlds. With her, he had begun to believe that he could succeed, that he could afterward settle into obscurity among the kamethi and survive.

He had in two days almost forgotten the weight of the bracelet upon his wrist, had absorbed images enough of the iduve that they became for him individual, and less terrible. He knew his way, which iduve to avoid most zealously, and which were reckoned safe and almost gentle. He knew the places open to him, and those forbidden; and if he was a prisoner, at least he owned a fellow-being who cared very much for his comfort—it was her own.

They were two: *Ashanome* was vast: and it was true that kamethi were not troubled by iduve in their daily lives. He saw no cruelty, no evident fear—himself a curiosity among Isande's acquaintances because of his origins: and no one forbade him, whatever he wished to say. But sometimes he saw in others' eyes that they pitied him, as if some mark were on him that they could read.

It was the human.

As this went, he would live or die; and at the last moment, Chimele had recalled Isande, ordering her sedated for her own protection. *I value you,* Chimele had said. *No. The risk is considerable. I do not permit it.*

Isande had protested, furiously; and that in a kameth was great bravery and desperation. But Chimele had not used the *idoikkhe;* she had simply stared at Isande with that terrible fixed expression, until the wretched nas kame had gone, weeping, to surrender herself to the laboratory, there to sleep until it was clear whether he would survive. The iduve would destroy a kameth that was beyond help; she feared to wake to silence, such a silence as Reha had left. She tried to hide this from him, fearing that she would destroy him with her own fear; she feared the human, such that it would have taxed all her courage to have been in his place now—but she would have done it, for her own reasons. She would have stood by him too—that was the nature of Isande: honor impelled her to loyalty. It had touched him beyond anything she could say or do, that she had argued with Chimele for his sake; that she had lost was only expected: it was the law of her world.

"Take no chances," she had wished him as she sank into dark. "Touch the language centers only, until I am with you again. Do not let the iduve urge you otherwise. And do not sympathize with that creature. You trust too much; it's a disease with you. Feelings such as we understand do not reside in all sentient life. The iduve are proof enough of that. And who understands the amaut?"

What do they want of him? he had tried to ask. But she had left him then, and in that place that was hers there was quiet.

Now something else stirred.

He felt it beginning, harshly ordered medical attendants out: they obeyed. He closed the door. There was only the rush of air whispering in the ducts, all other sound muffled.

The darkness spotted across his vision, dimming senses. The human stirred, and light hazed where the dark had been. Then he discovered the restraints and panicked.

Aiela flung up barriers quickly. His heart was pounding against his ribs from the mere touch of that communication. He bent over the human, seized his straining shoulders and held him.

"Be still! Daniel, Daniel—be still."

The human's gasps for breath ebbed down to a series of panting sobs. The dark eyes cleared and focused on his. Because touch was the only safe communication he had, Aiela relaxed his grip and patted the human's shoulder. The human endured it: he reminded Aiela of an animal soothed against its will, a wild thing that would kill, given the chance.

Aiela settled on the edge of the cot, feeling the human flinch. He spoke softly, tried amautish and kalliran words with him without success, and when he at last thought the human calm again, he ventured a mind-touch.

A miasma of undefined feeling came back: pain-panic-confusion. The human whimpered in fright and moved, and Aiela snatched his mind back. His own hands were trembling. It was several moments before the human's breathing rate returned to normal.

He tried talking to him once more, for a long time nothing more than that. The human's eyes continually locked on his, animal and intense; at times emotion went through them visibly—a look of anxiety, of perplexity.

At last the being seemed calmer, closed his eyes for a few moments and seemed to slip away, exhausted. Aiela let him. In a little time more the brown eyes opened again, fixed upon his: the human's face contracted a little in pain—his hand tensed against the restraints. Then he grew quiet again, breathing almost normally; he suffered the situation with a tranquility that tempted Aiela to try mind-touch again, but he refrained, instead left the bedside and returned with a cup of water.

The human lifted his head, trusted himself to Aiela's arm for support while he drained the cup, and then sank back with a shortness of breath that had no connection with the effort. He wanted something. His lips contracted to a white line. He babbled something that had to do with amaut.

He did speak, then. Aiela set the cup down and looked down on him with some relief. "Is there pain?" he asked in the amautish tongue, as nearly as kalliran lips could shape the sounds. There was no evidence of comprehension. He sat down again on the edge.

The human stared at him, still breathing hard. Then a glance flicked down to the restraints, up again, pleading—repeated the gesture. When Aiela did nothing, the human's eyes slid away from him, toward the wall. That was clear enough too.

It was madness to take such a chance. He knew that it was. The human could injure himself and kill him, quite easily.

He grew like Isande, who hated the creature, who would deal with him harshly; like the iduve, who created the *idoikkhei* and maintained matters on their terms, who could see something suffer and remain unmoved.

Better to die than yield to such logic. Better to admit that there was little difference between this wretched creature that at least tried to maintain its dignity, and a kalliran officer who walked about carrying iduve ownership locked upon his wrist.

"Come," he said, loosed one restraint and the others in quick succession, dismissing iduve, dismissing Isande's distress for his sake. *He* chose, *he* chose for himself what he would do, and if he would die it was easier than carrying out iduve orders, terrifying this unhappy being. He lifted the human to sit, steadied him on the edge, found those pale strong hands locked on his arms and the human staring into his face in confusion.

Terror.

Daniel winced, grimaced and clutched at his head, discovered the incision and panicked. He hurled himself up, sprawled on the tiles, and lay there clutching his head and moaning, sobbing words of nonsense.

"Daniel." Aiela caught his own breath, screening heavily: he knew well enough what the human was experiencing, that first horrible realization of the *chiabres,* the knowledge that his very self had been tampered with, that there was something else with him in his skull. Aiela felt pressure at his defenses, a dark force that clawed blindly at the edges of his mind, helpless and monstrous and utterly vulnerable at this moment, like something newborn.

He let the human explore that for himself, measure it, discover at last that it was partially responsive to his will. Aiela sat still, tautly screened, sweat coursing over his ribs; he would not admit it, he would not admit it—it was dangerous, unformed as it was. It moved all about the walls of his mind sensing something, seeking, aggressive and frightened at once. It acquired nightmare shape. Aiela snapped his vision back to *now* and destroyed the image, refusing it admittance, saw the human wince and collapse.

He was not unconscious. Aiela knew it as he knew his own waking. He simply lay still, waiting, waiting—perhaps gathering his abused senses into some kind of order. Perhaps he was wishing to die. Aiela understood such a reaction.

Several times more the ugliness activated itself to prowl the edges of his mind. Each time it fled back, as if it had learned caution.

"Are you all right?" Aiela asked aloud. He used the tone, not the words. He put concern into it. "I will not touch you. Are you all right?"

The human made a sound like a sob, rolled onto an arm, and then, as if he suddenly realized his lack of *elethia* before a man who was still calmly seated and waiting for him, he made several awkward moves and dragged himself to a seated posture, dropped his head onto his arms for a moment, and then gathered himself to try to rise.

Aiela moved to help him. It was a mistake. The human flinched and stumbled into the wall, into the corner, very like the attitude he had maintained in the cell.

"I am sorry." Aiela bowed and retreated back to his seat on the edge of the bed.

The human straightened then, stood upright, released a shaken breath. He reached again for the scar on his temple:

Aiela felt the pressure at once, felt it stop as Daniel pulled his mind back.

"Daniel," he said; and when Daniel looked at him curiously, suspiciously, he turned his head to the side and let Daniel see the scar that faintly showed on his own temple.

Then he opened a contact from his own direction, intending the slightest touch.

Daniel's eyes widened. The ugliness reared up, terrible in its shape. Vision went. He screamed, battered himself against the door, then hurled himself at Aiela, mad with fear. Aiela seized him by the wrists, pressing at his mind, trying to ignore the terror that was feeding back into him. One of them knew how to control the *chiabres:* uncontrolled, it could do unthinkable harm. Aiela fought, losing contact with his own body: sweat poured over him, making his grip slide; his muscles began to shake, so that he could not maintain his hold at all; he knew himself in physical danger, but that inside was worse. He hurled sense after sense into play, seeking what he wanted, reading the result in pain that fed back into him, nightmare shapes.

And suddenly the necessary barrier crashed between them, so painful that he cried out: in instinctive reaction, the human had screened. There was separation. There was self-distinction.

He slowly disengaged himself from the human's grip; the human, capable of attack, did not move, only stared at him, as injured as he. Perhaps the outcry had shocked him. Aiela felt after the human's wrist, gripped it not threateningly, but as a gesture of comfort.

He forced a smile, a nod of satisfaction, and uncertainly Daniel's hand closed—of a sudden the human gave a puzzled look, a half-laugh, half-sob.

He understood.

"Yes," Aiela answered, almost laughed himself from sheer relief. It opened barriers, that sharing.

And he cried out in pain from what force the human sent. He caught at his head, signed that he was hurt.

Daniel tried to stop. The mental pressure came in spurts and silences, flashes of light and floods of emotion. The darkness sorted itself into less horrid form. It was not an attack. The human *wanted;* so long alone, so long helpless to tell—he *wanted.* He wept hysterically and held his hands back, trembling in dread and desire to touch, to lay hold on anyone who offered help.

Barriers tumbled.

Aiela ceased trying to resist. Exhaustion claimed him. Like a man rushing downhill against his will he dared not risk trying to stop; he concentrated only on preserving his balance, threading his way through half-explored contacts, unfamiliar patterns at too great a speed. Contacts multiplied, wove into pattern; sensations began to sort themselves into order, perceptions to arrange themselves into comprehensible form: body-sense, touch, equilibrium, vision—the room writhed out of darkness and took form about them.

Suddenly deeper senses were seeking structure. Aiela surrendered himself to Daniel's frame of reference, where right was human-hued and wrong was different, where morality and normality took shapes he could hardly bear without a shudder. He reached desperately for the speech centers for wider patterns, establishing a contact desperately needed.

"I," he said silently in human speech. "Aiela—I. Stop. Stop. Think slowly. Think of now. Hold back your thoughts to the pace of your words. Think the words, Daniel: my language, yours, no difference."

"What—" the first response attempted. Apart from Aiela's mind the sound had no meaning for the human.

"Go on. You understand me. You can use my language as I use yours. Our symbolizing facility is merged."

"What—" Death was in his mind, gnawing doubt that almost forced them apart. "What is going to happen to me? What are you?"

His communication was a babble of kalliran and human language, amaut mixed in, voiced and thought, echoes upon echoes. He was sending on at least three levels at once and unaware which was dominant. *Home, help, home* kept running beneath everything.

"Be calm," Aiela said. "You're all right. You're not hurt."

"I have—come a long way, a very long way from home. I don't even know where I am or why. I know—" *No, no, not accusation; soft with him, soft, don't make him angry.* "I know that

you are being kind, that I—am being treated well—" Cages
were in his mind; he thought them only out of sight on the other
side of the wall, shrieks and hideous noise and darkness. *At least
he looks human,* the second level ran. *Looks. Looks. Seems.
Isn't. God, help me.* "Aiela, I—understand. I am grateful,
Aiela—"

Daniel tried desperately to screen in his fear. It was a terrible
effort. Under it all, nonverbal, there was fear of a horrible kind,
fear of oblivion, fear of losing his mind altogether; but he would
yield, he would merge, anything, anything but lose this chance.
It was dangerous. It pulled at both of them. Aiela screened
briefly, stopping it.

"I don't know how to help you," Aiela told him gently. "But I
assure you I don't want to harm you. You are safe. Be calm."

*Information—they want—*home came to mind, far distant, a
world of red stone and blue skies. The memory met Aiela's surmise, the burrows of amaut worlds, human laborers, and confused Daniel greatly. *Past or future,* Daniel wondered. *Mine? Is
this mine? Is this what I'm going to?*

Aiela drew back, trying to sort the human thoughts from his
own. Nausea assailed him. The human's terrors began to seem
his, sinister things, alien; and the amaut were at the center of all
the nightmares.

"How did you come here, then?" Aiela asked. "Where did
you come from, if not from the amaut worlds?"

And where is here and what are you? the human responded
inwardly; but in the lightning-sequencing of memory, answers
came, random at first, then deliberate—remembrances of that
little world that had been home: poverty, other humans, anger,
a displaced folk yearning toward a green and beautiful home
that had no resemblance to the red desolation in which they
now lived: an urge toward ships, and voyaging, homecoming
and revenge.

Years reeled backward and forward again: strange suns,
worlds, service in many ships, machinery appallingly primitive,
backbreaking labor—but among humans, human ships, human
ports, scant resources, sordid pleasures. Above all a regret for
that sandy homeland, and finally a homecoming—to a home
dissolved, a farm gone to dust; more port cities, more misery, a

life without ties and without purpose. The thoughts ran aimlessly into places so alien they were madness.

These were not the Esliph worlds. Amaut did not belong there. Human space, then, human worlds, where kalliran and amaut trade had never gone.

Amaut. Daniel's mind seized on the memory with hate. Horrible images of death, bodies twisted, stacked in heaps—prisoners—humans—gathered into camps, half-starved and dying, others hunted, slaughtered horribly and hung up for warnings, the hunters humankind too; but among them moved dark, large-eyed shapes with shambling gait and leering faces—amaut seen through human eyes. Events tumbled one over the other, and Aiela resisted, unknowing what terrible place he was being led next; but Daniel sent, forcefully, no random images now—hate, hate of aliens, of him, who was part of this.

Himself. A city's dark streets, a deserted way, night, fire leaping up against the horizon, strange hulking shapes looming above the crumbling buildings—a game of hunter and hunted, himself the quarry, and those same dread shapes loping ungainly behind him.

Ambush—unconsciousness—death?—smothered and torn by a press of bodies, alien smells, the cutting discomfort of wire mesh under his naked body, echoing crashes of machinery in great vastness, cold and glaring light. Others like himself, humans, frightened, silent for days and nights of cold and misery and sinister amaut moving saucer-eyed beyond the perimeter of the lights—cold and hunger, until in increasing numbers the others ended as stiff corpses on the mesh.

More crashes of machinery, panic, spurts of memory interspersed with nightmare and strangely tranquil dreams of childhood: drugs and pain, now gabbling faces thrust close to his, shaggy, different humans incapable of speech as he knew it, overwhelming stench, dirty-nailed fingers tearing at him.

Aiela jerked back from the contact and bowed his head into his hands, nauseated; but worse seeped in after: cages, transfer to another ship, being herded into yet filthier confinement, the horror of seeing fellow beings reduced to mouthing animals, constant fear and frequent abuse—himself the victim almost always, because he was different, because he could not speak, because he did not react as they did—the cunning humor of the savages, who would wait until he slept and then spring on him, who would goad him into a rage and then press him into a corner of that cage, tormenting him for their amusement until his screams brought the attendants running to break it up.

At last, strangers, kallia; his transfer, drugged, to yet another wakening and another prison. Aiela saw himself and Chimele as alien and shadowy beings invading the cell: Daniel's distorted memory did not even recognize him until he met the answering memory in Aiela's mind.

Enemy. Enemy. Interrogator. Part of him, enemy. The terror boiled into the poor human's brain and created panic, violence echoing and re-echoing in their joined mind, division that went suicidal, multiplying by the second.

Aiela broke contact, sick and trembling with reaction. Daniel was similarly affected, and for a moment neither of them moved.

No matter, no matter, came into Daniel's mind, remembrance of kindness, reception of Aiela's pity for him. *Any conditions, anything.* He realized that Aiela was receiving that thought, and hurt pride screened it in. "I am sorry," he concentrated the words. "I don't hate you. Aiela, help me. I want to go home."

"From what I have seen, Daniel, I much fear there is no home for you to return to."

Am I alone? Am I the only human here?

The thought terrified Daniel; and yet it promised no more of the human cages; held out other images, himself alone forever, victim to strangers—amaut, kallia, aliens muddled together in his mind.

"You are safe," Aiela assured him; and was immediately conscious it was a forgetful lie. In that instant memory escaped its confinement.

They. They—Daniel snatched a thought and an image of the iduve, darkly beautiful, ancient and evil, and all the fear that was bound up in kalliran legend. He associated it with the shadowy figure he had seen in the cell, doubly panicked as Aiela tried to screen. *No! What have you agreed to do for them? Aiela!*

"No." Aiela fought against the currents of tenor. "No. Quiet.

I'm going to have you sedated—*No! Stop that!*—so that your mind can rest. I'm tired. So are you. You will be safe, and I'll come back later when you've rested."

*You're going to report to them—and to lie there—*The human remembered other wakings, strangers' hands on him, his fellow humans' cruel humor. Nausea hit his stomach, fear so deep there was no reasoning. There were amaut on the ship: he dreaded them touching him while he was unconscious.

"You will be moved," Aiela persisted. "You'll wake in a comfortable place next to my rooms, and you'll be free when you wake, completely safe, I promise it. I'll have the amaut stay completely away from you if that will make you feel any better."

Daniel listened, wanting to believe, but he could not. Mercifully the attendant on duty was both kalliran and gentle of manner, and soon the human was settled into bed again, sliding down the mental brink of unconsciousness. He still stretched out his thoughts to Aiela, wanting to trust him, fearing he would wake in some more incredible nightmare.

"I will be close by," Aiela assured him, but he was not sure the human received that, for the contact went dark and numb like Isande's.

He felt strangely amputated then, utterly on his own and—a thing he would never have credited—wishing for the touch of his asuthe, her familiar, kalliran mind, her capacity to make light of his worst fears. If he were severed from the human this moment and never needed touch that mind again, he knew that he would remember to the end of his days that he had for a few moments *been* human.

He had harmed himself. He knew it, desperately wished it undone, and feared not even Isande's experience could help him. She had tried to warn him. In defiance of her advice he had extended himself to the human, reckoning no dangers but the obvious, doing things his own way, with *kastien* toward a hurt and desolate creature.

He had chosen. He could no more bear harm to Isande than he could prefer pain for himself: iduvish as she was, he knew her to the depth of her stubborn heart, knew the *elethia* of her and her loyalty, and she in no wise deserved harm from anyone. Neither did the human. Someone meant to use him, to wring

some use from him, and discard him or destroy him afterward—
be rid of him, Isande had said, even she callous toward him—
and there was in that alien shell a being that had not deserved
either fate.

*It is not reasonable to ask me to venture an opinion on some-
thing I have never experienced,* Chimele had told him at the out-
set. She did not understand kalliran emotion and she had never
felt the *chiabres.* Of a sudden he feared not even Chimele might
have anticipated what she was creating of them, and that she
would deal ruthlessly with the result—a kameth whose loyalty
was half-human.

He was kallia, *kallia!*—and of a sudden he felt his hold on
that claim becoming tenuous. It was not right, what he had
done—even to the human.

Isande, he pleaded, hoping against all knowledge to the contrary for a response from that other, that blessedly kalliran mind.
Isande, Isande.

But his senses perceived only darkness from that quarter.

In the next moment he felt a mild pulse from the *idoikkhe,* the
coded flutter that meant *paredre.*

Chimele was sending for him.

There was the matter of an accounting.

4

Chimele was perturbed. It was evident in her brooding expression and her attitude as she leaned in the corner of her chair; she was not pleased; and she was not alone for this audience: four other iduve were with her, and with that curious sense of *déjà vu* Isande's instruction imparted, Aiela knew them. They were Chimele's *nasithi-katasakke,* her half-brothers and -sister by common-mating.

The woman Chaikhe was youngest: an Artist, a singer of songs; by kalliran standards Chaikhe was too thin to be beautiful, but she was gentle and thoughtful toward the kamcthi. She had also thought of him with interest: Isande had warned him of it; but Chimele had said no, and that ended it. Chaikhe was becoming interested in *katasakke,* in common-mating, the presumable cause of restlessness; but an iduve with that urge would rapidly lose all interest in *m'metanei.*

Beside Chaikhe, eyeing him fixedly, sat her full brother Ashakh, a long-faced man, exceedingly tall and thin. Ashakh was renowned for intelligence and coldness to emotion even among iduve. He was *Ashanome's* Chief Navigator and master of much of the ship's actual operation, from its terrible armament to the computers that were the heart of the ship's machinery and memory. He did not impress one as a man who made mistakes, nor as one to be crossed with impunity. And next to Ashakh, leaning on one arm of the chair, sat Rakhi, the brother that Chimele most regarded. Rakhi was of no great beauty, and for an iduve he was a little plump. Also he had a shameful bent toward *kutikkase*—a taste for physical comfort too great to be honorable among iduve. But he was devoted to Chimele, and he was extraordinarily kind to the noi kame and even to the seldom-noticed amaut, who adored him as their personal patron. Besides, at the heart of this soft, often-smiling fellow was a heart of greater bravery than most suspected.

The third of the brothers was eldest: Khasif, a giant of a man, strikingly handsome, sullen-eyed—older than Chimele, but under her authority. He was of the order of Scientists, a xeno-archaeologist. He had a keen *m'melakhia*—an impelling hunger for new experience—and noi kame made themselves scarce when he was about, for he had killed on two occasions. This was the man Isande so feared, although—she had admitted—she did not think he was consciously cruel. Khasif was impatient and energetic in his solutions, a trait much honored among iduve, as long as it was tempered with refinement, with *chanokhia*. He had the reputation of being a very dangerous man, but in Isande's memory he had never been a petty one.

"How fares Daniel?" asked Chimele. "Why did you ask sedation so early? Who gave you leave for this?"

"We were tiring," said Aiela. "You gave me leave to order what I thought best, and we were tired, we—"

"Aiela-kameth," Chaikhe intervened gently. "Is there progress?"

"Yes."

"Will complete *asuthithekkhe* be possible with this being? Can you reach that state with him, that you can be one with him?"

"I don't—I don't think it is safe. No. I don't want that."

"Is this yours to decide?" Ashakh's tones were like icewater on the silken voice of Chaikhe. "Kameth—you were instructed."

He wanted to tell them. The memory of that contact was still vivid in his mind, such that he still shuddered. But there was no patience in Ashakh's thin-lipped face, neither patience nor mercy nor understanding of weakness. "We are different," he found himself saying, to fill the silence. Ashakh only stared. "Give me time," he said again.

"We are on a schedule," Ashakh said. "This should have been made clear to you."

"Yes, sir."

"Specify the points of difference."

"Ethics, experience. He isn't hostile, not yet. He mistrusts—he mistrusts me, this place, all things alien."

"Is it not your burden to reconcile these differences?"

"Sir." Aiela's hands sweated and he folded his arms, pressing his palms against his sides. He did not like to look Ashakh in the face, but the iduve stared at him unblinkingly. "Sir, we are able to communicate. But he is not gullible, and I'm running out of answers that will satisfy him. That was why I resorted to the sedative. He's beginning to ask questions. I had no more easy answers. What am I supposed to tell him?"

"Aiela." Khasif drew his attention to the left. "What is your personal reaction to the being?"

"I don't know." His mouth was dry. He looked into Khasif's face, that was the substance of Isande's nightmares, perfect and cold. "I try—I try to avoid offending him—"

"What is the ethical pattern, the social structure? Does he recognize kalliran patterns?"

"Close to kallia. But not the same. I can't tell you: not the same at all."

"Be more precise."

"Am I supposed to have learned something in particular?" Aiela burst out, harried and regretting his tone at once. The *idoikkhe* pulsed painlessly, once, twice: he looked from one to the other of them, not knowing who had done it, knowing it for a warning. "I'm sorry, but I don't understand. I was primed to study this man, but no one will tell me just what I was looking for. Now you've taken Isande away from me too. How am I to know what questions to start with?"

His answer caused a little ruffling among the iduve, and merry Rakhi laughed outright and looked sidelong at Chimele. "*Au,* this one has a sting, Chimele." He looked back at Aiela. "And what have you learned, thus ignorant of your purpose, *o m'metane?*"

"That the amaut have intruded into human space, which they swore in a treaty with the *Halliran Idai* they would never do. This man came from human space. They lost most of his shipment because these humans weren't acclimated to the kind of abuse they received. Is that what you want to hear? Until you tell me what you mean to do with him, I'm afraid I can't do much more."

Chimele had not been amused. She frowned and stirred in her chair, placing her hands on its arms. "Can you, Aiela, prepare this human for our own examination by tomorrow?"

"That's impossible. No. And what kind of—?"

"By tomorrow evening."

"If you want something, then make it clear what it is and maybe I can learn it. But he wants answers. He has questions, and I can't keep putting him off, not without creating you an enemy—or do you care?"

"You will have to—put him off, as you express it."

"I'm not going to lie to him, even by omission. What are you going to do with him?"

"I prefer that this human not be admitted to our presence with the promise of anything. Do you understand me, Aiela? If you promise this being anything, it will be the burden of your honor to pay for it; make sure your resources are adequate. I will not consider myself or the *nasul* bound by your ignorant and unauthorized generosity. Go back to your quarters."

"I will not lie to him for you."

"Go back to your quarters. You are not noticed." This time there was no softness at all in her tone, and he knew he dared not dispute with her further. Even Rakhi took the smile from his face and straightened in his chair. Aiela omitted the bow of courtesy, turned on his heel and walked out.

He had ruined matters. When he was stressed his voice rose, and he had let it happen, had lost his case for it. He had felt when he walked in that Chimele was not in a mood for patience; and he realized in hindsight that the *nasithi* had tried to avert disaster: Rakhi, he thought, Rakhi, who had always been kind to Isande, had wished to stop him.

He returned to the kamethi level in utmost dejection, realized the late hour and considered returning to the lab and requesting to have a sedative for himself. His nerves could bear no more. But he had never liked such things, liked less to deal with Ghiavre, the iduve first Surgeon; and it occurred to him that Daniel might wake prematurely and need him. He decided against it.

He went to his quarters and prepared for bed, settled in with notebook and pen and diverted his thoughts to record-keeping on Daniel, then, upon the sudden cold thought that the iduve might not respect the sanctity of his belongings, he tore up everything and threw it into the disposal. The suspicion distressed him. As a kallia he had never thought of such things; he had never needed to suspect such *ikastien* on the part of his superiors.

Daniel had learned such suspicion. It was human.

With that distressing thought he turned out the lights and lay still until his muddled thoughts drifted into sleep.

The *idoikkhe* jolted him, brutally, so that he woke with an outcry and clawed his way up to the nearest chair.

Isande, he had cast, the reflex of two days of dependency; and to his surprised relief there was a response, albeit a muzzy one.

Aiela, she responded, remembered Daniel, instantly tried to learn his health and began to pick up the immediate present: Chimele, summoning him, angry; and Daniel—*What have you done?* she sent back, shivering with fear; but he prodded her toward the moment, thrusting through the gutter of her drug-hazed thoughts.

"This is Chimele's sleep cycle too," he sent. "Does she always exercise her tempers in the middle of the night?"

The *idoikkhe* stung him again, momentarily disrupting their communication. Aiela reached for his clothes and pulled them on, while Isande's thoughts threaded back into his mind. She scanned enough to blame him for matters, and she was distressed enough to let it seep through; but she had the grace to keep that feeling down. Now was important. He was important. He had to take her advice now; he could be hurt, badly.

"Chimele's hours are seldom predictable," she informed him, her outermost thoughts calm and ordered. But what lay under it was a peculiar physical fear that unstrung his nerves.

He looked at the time: it was well past midnight, and Chimele, like Ashakh, did not impress him as one who took the leisure for whimsy. He pulled his sweater over his head, started for the door, but he paused to hurl at Isande the demand that she drop her screening, guide him. He felt her reticence; when it melted, he almost wished otherwise.

Fear came, nightmares of Khasif, chilling and sexual at once. Few things could cause an iduve to act irrationally, but there was one outstanding exception, and iduve when irritated with kamethi were prone to it.

He stopped square in the doorway, blood leaving his face and returning in a hot rush. Her urgency prodded him into motion again, her anger and her terror like ice in his belly. *No,* he insisted again and again. Isande had been terrified once and long ago: she was scarred by the experience and dwelled on it excessively—it embarrassed him, that he had to express that thought: he knew it for truth. He wished her still.

"It happens," Isande insisted, with such firmness that it shook his conviction. "It is *katasukke*—pleasure-mating." And quickly, without preface, apology, or overmuch delicacy, she fed across what she knew or guessed of the iduve's intimate habits— alienness only remotely communicated in *katasukke* with noi kame, a union between iduve in *katasakke* that was fraught with violence and shielded in ritual and secrecy. *Katasukke* was gentler: sensible noi kame were treated with casual indulgence or casual negligence according to the mood of the iduve in question; but cruelty was *e-chanokhia*, highly improper, whatever unknown and violent things they did among themselves. But both *katasakke* and *katasukke* triggered dangerous emotions in the ordinarily dispassionate iduve. *Vaikka* was somehow involved in mating, and it was not uncommon that someone was killed. In Isande's mind any irrationality in the iduve emanated from that one urge: it was the one thing that could undo their common sense, and when it was undone, it was a madness as alien as their normal calm.

He shook off these things, hurried through the corridors while Isande's anxious presence thrust into his mind behaviors and apologies, fawning kameth graces meant to appease Chimele. *Vaikka* with a nas kame had this for an expected result, and if he provoked her further now he would be lucky to escape with his life.

He rejected Isande and her opinions, prideful and offended, and knew that Isande was crying, and frustrated with him and furious. Her anger grew so desperate that he had to screen against her, and bade her leave him alone. He was ashamed enough at this disgraceful situation without having her lodged as resident observer in his mind. He knew her hysterical upon the subject, and even so could not help fearing he was walking into something he did not want to contemplate.

With Isande aware, mind-bound to him.

Leave me alone! he raged at her.

She went; and then he was sorry for the silence.

Chimele was waiting for him, seated in her accustomed chair as a tape unreeled on the wall screen with dizzying rapidity: the day's reports, quite probably. She cut it off, using a manual control instead of the mental ones of which the iduve were capable—a choice, he had learned, which betokened an iduve with mind already occupied.

"You took an unseemly amount of time responding," she said.

"I was asleep." Fear added, shaming him: "I'm sorry."

"You did not expect, then, to be called?"

"No," he said; and doubled over as the *idoikkhe* hit him with overwhelming pain. He was surprised into an outcry, but bit it off and straightened, furious.

"Well, consider it settled, then," she said, "and cheaply so. Be wiser in the future. Return to your quarters."

"All of you are demented," he cried, and it struck, this time enough to gray the senses, and the pain quite washed his mind of everything. When it stopped he was on his face on the floor, and to his horror he felt Isande's hurt presence in him, holding to him, trying to absorb the pain and reason with him to stay down.

"Aiela," said Chimele, "you clearly fail to understand me."

"I don't want—" the *idoikkhe* stung him again, a gentle reproof compared with what had touched him a moment before. It jolted raw nerves and made him cringe physically in dread: the cowardice it instilled made him both ashamed and angry; and there was Isande's anxious intrusion again. The two-sided assault was too much. He clutched his head and begged his asuthe to leave him, even while he stumbled to his feet, unwilling to be treated so.

She can destroy you, Isande sent him hysterically. *She has her honor to think of.* Vaikka, *Aiela,* vaikka!

"Is it Isande?" asked Chimele. "Is it she that troubles you?"

"She's being hurt. She won't go away. Please stop it."

And then he knew that Isande's *idoikkhe* had pained her, once, twice, with increasing severity, and the mournful and loyal presence fled.

"Aiela," said Chimele, "all my life I have dealt gently with my kamethi. Why will you persist in provoking me? Is it ignorance or is it design?"

"It's my nature," he said, which further offended her; but this time she only scowled and regarded him with deep dissatisfaction.

"Your ignorance of us has not been noticed: the nearest equivalent is 'forgiven.' It will be a serious error on your part to assume this will continue without limit."

"I honestly," he insisted, "do not understand you."

"We are not in the habit of patience with *metane-tekasuphre.* Nor do we make evident our discomforts. *Au, m'metane,* I should have the hide from you." There was self-control; and under it there was a rage that made his skin cold: run now, he · thought, and become like the others—no. She would deal with him, explaining matters; he would stand there until she did so.

For a long moment he stood still, expected the touch of the *idoikkhe* for it; she did not move either.

"Aiela," she said then, in a greatly controlled voice, "I was disadvantaged before my *nasithi-katasakke.*" And when he only stared at her, helplessly unenlightened: "For three thousand years *Ashanome* has taken no outsider-*m'metane* aboard," she said. "I have never dealt with the likes of you."

"What am I supposed to say?"

"You disputed with my *nasithi.* Then you turned the same discourtesy on me. Had you no perception?"

"I had cause," he declared in temper too deep-running to reckon of her anger, and his hand went to the *idoikkhe* on reflex. "*This* doesn't turn off my mind or my conscience, and I still want to know what you intend with the man Daniel."

Chimele literally trembled with rage. He had never seen so dangerous a look on any sane and sentient face, but the pain he expected did not come. She stilled her anger with an evident effort.

"*Nas-suphres,*" she said in a tone of cosmic contempt. "You are hopeless, *m'metane.*"

"How so?" he responded. "How so—*ignorant?*"

"Because you provoke me and trust my forbearance. This is the act of a stupid or an ignorant being. And did I truly believe you capable of *vaikka,* you would find yourself woefully outmatched. You are not irreplaceable, *m'metane,* and you are perilously close to extinction at this moment."

"I have no confidence at all in your forbearance, and I well know you mean your threats."

"The clumsiness of your language makes rational conversation impossible. You are nothing, and I could wipe you out with a thought. I should think the reputedly ordered processes of the kalliran mind would dictate caution. I fail to perceive why you attack me."

Mad, he thought in panic, remembering at the same time that she had mental control of the *idoikkhe.* He wanted to leave. He could not think how. "I have not attacked you," he said in a quiet, reasoning voice, as one would talk to the insane. "I know better."

She arose and moved away from him in great vexation, then looked back with some semblance of control restored. "I warned you once, Aiela, do not play at *vaikka* with us. You are incredibly ignorant, but you have a courage which I respect above all *metane*-traits. Do you not understand I must maintain *sorithias*— that I have the dignity of my office to consider?"

"I'm afraid I don't understand."

"*Au,* this is impossible. Perhaps Isande can make it clear."

"*No!* No, let her alone. I want none of her explanations. I have my mind clear enough without need of her rationalizations."

"You are incredible," Chimele exclaimed indignantly, and returned to him, seized both his hands, and made him sit down opposite her, a contact he hated, and she seemed to realize it. "Aiela. Do not press me. I *must* retaliate. We delight to be generous to our kamethi, but we will not have gifts demanded of us. We will not be pressed and not retaliate, we will not be affronted and do nothing. It is physically impossible. Can you not comprehend that?"

Her hands trembled. He felt it and remembered Isande's

warning of iduve violence, the irrational and uncontrollable rages of which these cold beings were capable. But Chimele seemed yet in control, and her amethyst eyes locked with his in deep earnest, so plain a look it was almost like the touch of his asuthi. She let him go.

"I cannot protect you, poor *m'metane,* if you will persist in playing games of anger with us, if you persist in incurring punishment and fighting back when you receive the consequences of your impudence. You do not want to live under our law; you are not capable of it. And if you were wise, you would have left when I told you to go."

"I do not understand," he said. "I simply do not understand."

"Aiela—" Her indigo face showed stress. His hand still rested across his knee as he leaned forward, too tense to move. Now she took it back into hers, her slim fingers moving lightly across the back of it as if she found its color or the texture of his skin something remarkably fascinating. Pride and anger notwithstanding, he sensed nothing insulting in that touch, rather that Chimele drew a certain calm from that contact, that her mood shifted back to reason, and that it would be a perilous move if he jerked his hand away. He sweated with fear, not of iduve science or power—his rational faculty feared that; but something else worked in him, something subconscious that recognized Chimele and shuddered instinctively. He wished himself out that door with many doors between them; but her hand still moved over his, and her violet eyes stared into him.

"If you had been born among the kamethi," said Chimele softly, "you would never have run afoul of me, for no nas kame would ever have provoked me so far. He would have had the sense to run away and wait until I had called him again. You are different, and I have allowed for that—this far. And so that you will understand, ignorant kameth: you were impertinent with others and impertinent exceedingly with me—and being Orithain, I dispense judgments to the *nasithi.* How then shall I descend to publicly chastise a nas kame? They wished to persuade me to be patient; and I chose to be patient, remembering what you are; but then, *au,* after trading words with my *nasithi,* you must ignore my direct order and debate me what disposition I am to make of this human." She drew breath: when she went on it was in a calmer voice. "Rakhi could not reprimand my kameth in my presence; I could not do so in theirs. And there you stood, gambling with five of us in the mistaken confidence that your life was too valuable for me to waste. Were you iduve, I should say that were an extremely hazardous form of *vaikka.* Were you iduve, you would have lost that game. But because you are *m'metane,* you were allowed to do what an iduve would have died for doing."

"And is iduve pride that vulnerable, then?"

"Stop challenging me!"

It was a cry of anguish. Chimele herself looked terrified, reminding him for all the world of an essentially friendly animal being provoked beyond endurance, a creature teased to the point of madness by some child it loved, shivering with taut nerves and repressed instincts. She could not help it, as an animal could not resist a move from its prey.

Vaikka.

He grasped it then—a game that was indeed for iduve only, a name that shielded a most terrifying instinct, one that the iduve themselves must fear, for it tore apart all their careful rationality. The compulsion must indeed be involved in their matings— intricate, unkalliran instinct. It was reasonable that the noi kame feared above all the iduve's affections, feared closeness. A kallia quite literally did not have a nervous system attuned to that kind of contest. A kallia would want to play the game part of the way and then quit before someone was hurt; but there was a point past which the iduve could not quit.

"It is possible," he said carefully, "that I did not use good judgment."

She grew perceptibly calmer at that slight retreat, slowed her breathing, patted his arm with the thoughtless affection one might show a pet, and then drew back her hand as if mindful of his inward shudder. "Surely then," she said, "understanding your nature and ours, you need not stand so straight or stare so insolently when that irrepressible tongue of yours brings you afoul of our tempers."

"I was not educated as kameth."

"I perceive your difficulty. But do not seek to live by our law. You cannot. And it is not reasonable for you to expect us to bear

all the burden of self-restraint. I thrust you into close contact
with us, a contact most kameth-born scarcely know. It cannot be
remedied. I trusted your common sense and forgot kalliran—I
know not whether to say obstinacy or *elethia,* an admirable
trait—but that and our aggressiveness, our *m'melakhia,* is a very
volatile combination."

"I begin to see that."

"Go back to your quarters this night, for your safety's sake. I
will respect your *m'melakhia,* your—protection—of your
human asuthe as much as I can, and I will not remember this
conversation to your hurt. You are wiser than you were. I advise
you to make it apparent to my *nasithi-katasakke* that *vaikka* has
been settled."

"How?"

"By your amended attitude and increased discretion in our
presence."

"I understand," he said, hesitated awkwardly until an impatient gesture made clear his dismissal. Almost he delayed to
thank her, but looking again into her eyes chilled the impulse
into silence: he bowed, turned, felt her eyes on his back the
whole long distance to the door.

The safety of the hall, the sealing of the door behind him,
brought a physical relief. He lowered his eyes and flinched past
an iduve who was passing, secured the lift alone, and was glad
to find the kamethi level, where kallia thronged the concourse—
the alternate day-cycle, whose waking was his night.

He knew the iduve finally.

Predators.

Outsiders had never understood the end of the Domination,
the Sundering of the iduve empire. He began to.

They were hunters from their very origins—a species for
whom all else that moved was prey, for whom others of their
own kind were intolerable. They had hunted the *metrosi* to exhaustion and drifted elsewhere. Now they were back. The enormity of the surmise grew in him like a sickly chill.

The *nasul*—jealously controlling its territory.

Perhaps even the iduve themselves had forgotten what they
were; the pride of ritual and ceremony shielded their instincts,
civilized them, as civilization had dealt with the instincts of

kallia, who had been the natural prey of other hunters in packs, on the plains of prehistoric Aus Qao. Subtle reactions, a tensing of muscles, an interchange of movements, the steadiness of the eyes—these defined hunter and hunted. That was the thing he had looked in the face when he had stared into Chimele's at close range. He had wished to run and had instinctively known better—that if he stayed very, very still, it might pad softly away.

He shivered, the hair rising at the nape of his neck as if she still watched him. When he felt Isande's frightened presence beginning to creep back into his mind, he screened heavily, for he still was shaken, and he was ashamed for her to know the extent of it.

You nearly killed yourself, she accused him. *I warned you, I warned you—*

"Not well enough," he returned. "You have a blind spot. Or you do not understand them."

"I have lived my whole life among them," she retorted, "and I have never seen what you saw tonight—not even from Khasif."

He accepted that for truth. Likely kamethi had been taught never to draw such responses. But he was world-born; he himself had sat by fires at night in the wilds of Lelle, with a ring of light to guard his sleep, and he knew Chimele in all the atavistic fears of his species.

A predator who had assumed civilization.

Who had touched him gently and refrained, despite his best attempt to provoke her—*ignorant,* she had called him, and justly.

"Chimele is iduve," Isande hurled against the warmth of that thought, forcefully, for she hated worse than anything to have her advice ignored. "And you will live longer if you remember that we are only kamethi, and avoid provoking her and avoid attracting her notice to yourself."

This from Isande, Isande who loved Chimele, who willingly served the iduve: who trembled in her heart each time she dealt with Chimele's temper. It was a sorrowful life she had accepted: he let that slip and was sorry, for Isande flared, hot and unshielded.

Am I nothing, she fired at him, *because I was born kameth? My world-born friend, I have been places you have not dreamed*

*of, and seen things you cannot understand. And as it regards the
iduve, my friend, I have lived among them, and what of their
language you know, you lifted from my mind, what of their customs you understand you have learned from me, and what consideration you had from Chimele you have because of me, so do
not lecture me as an expert on the iduve. If you were not so ikas,
you would not have had so dangerous an experience.*

Well, he returned, *I hardly seem to have a monopoly on vanity
or selfishness or arrogance, do I?*

And the resentments that echoed back and forth, too much
truth, sent both personalities reeling apart, hurt.

Isande was first to touch again, grieving. "Aiela," she
pleaded, "Asuthi must not quarrel. Please, Aiela."

"I am vain and arrogant," he admitted, "and I have had almost all the damage my sanity can stand tonight, Isande. I'm
tired. Go away."

Daniel, she remembered, dismay and regret sharp in her; she
remembered other things she had gleaned of his mind, and rif-
fled through all the memory he left unscreened, gathering this
and that with a rising feeling of distress, of outrage. He felt her,
poised to blame him for everything, to accuse him of things the
worse because they were just.

And she did not. He was so tired his legs shook under him,
and he felt himself very lonely, even in her presence: he had dis-
regarded everything she had meant to protect them both, and
now that she had utmost cause to rage against him she pitied
him too much to accuse him. She knew his nature and his inca-
pacity, and she pitied him.

Leave me alone, he wished her. And then furiously: *Leave me
alone, will you?*

She fled.

He undressed, washed, went through all the ritual of preparing for bed, and tried to sleep. It was impossible. Reaction still
had his muscles in knots. When he closed his eyes he saw the
paredre, Chimele—cages.

He arose and walked the floor, tried listening to his old tapes,
that he had brought from Kartos. It was worse than the silence.
He cut off the sound, idly cut in on the monitor that was preset

for Daniel's next-door apartment. The human was still blissfully unconscious.

And the memory returned, how it had felt to live in that envelope of alien flesh. He broke the connection, dizzied and disoriented, wandered back to the bath, drifting as he had a dozen times, to the full-length mirror. It contained all in *Ashanome* that was familiar, that was known.

His image stared back at him, naked of everything but the *idoikkhe* that circled his wrist like some bizarre barbaric ornament. His silver hair was beginning a slow recovery from the surgeons' unimaginative barbering, and he had grown accustomed to the change. His features among kallia were considered proper: straight silver brows, a straight nose with a little flare to the nostrils, a mouth wide enough to show generosity, a chin prominent as with all the Lyailleues. He fingered the high prominence of his cheekbone and the hollow beneath, staring into his own eyes closely in the mirror, wondering how much of the iduve eye was iris. Was it all? And could they see color as kallia could? Humans did. He knew that. He considered the rest of himself, 7.8 *meis* in stature, a little taller than the average, broad-shouldered and slim at the hips, with the slender, well-muscled limbs of an athlete, the flat belly and muscular girdle of a runner, a hard-trained body that had no particular faults. He had never known serious illness, had suffered no wounds, had never known privation that was not his own choice. He was *parome* Deian's only son; if he had had any faults at birth, no money would have been spared to mend them. If he had lacked any in wit, *parome* Deian's money would have purchased every known aid to teach him and improve his mind. When he grew bored, there had instantly been toys and games and hunts and athletics, and when he became a young man, there had been all the loveliest and most proper girls, the most exclusive parties. There were private instructors, the most proper and demanding schools; and there had been family despair when he insisted on pursuing athletics to the detriment of his studies, on risking his life in hunts, on turning down a career in district politics that was calculated to lead to the highest levels of government—a lack of family and filial *giyre* that his father refused to understand ("*Ikas,*" Deian had said, "and ungrateful." "Am I *ikas,*" he had answered, eighteen and all-knowing, "because it is not my pattern to be like you?" "There have been Lyailleues on the High Council for two hundred years, honoring Xolun and this house. My son will not take it on himself to end that tradition.")

Once that year he had thought of hurling his plane (a luxury model) in a pyrotechnic finish at Mount Ryi, in full view of all the fashionable estates and the Xolun zone capitol. The news services would be buzzing with wonder for days: Son of Deian, Suicide; and people would be shaking their heads and making small noises of despair and secretly hating him, thinking if only they had had his advantages they would not have thrown them away. When he was nineteen he had quit school so that his father Deian would disinherit him and his mother and sister would give him up; but he also saw it broke their hearts, and his few passages with the pleasures of the *metrosi's* darker side left him disgusted and embarrassed, for these things were also available in the estates in the shadow of Ryi—without the filth and the fear. In the end he had surrendered and returned home to the respectability planned for him, to learn the business of government.

("Son, it is always necessary to compromise. That's how things are done." "Even when one is right, sir?" "Right—right; you always assume you know exactly where that is, don't you? I'm sure I don't. If you go on like that, no one could ever agree. Compromise. Sometimes you have to yield a little to win a little later on.")

He had tried.

A year later he had sought the anonymity of the service, and even that had proved no refuge secure from Deian's money and influence. Perhaps, he thought, it was his father's way of setting him free; or perhaps Deian still believed he would have come home, older, wiser. He would have come home, sooner or later. He had spent his life pursuing the elusive hope of adequacy, a constant struggle for breath in the rarified atmosphere of his father's ambitions and the *giyre* of his ancient family.

("I would have come home someday," he had written in that final letter. "I have gained the good sense to honor your wisdom and experience, Father, and I have gained enough wisdom of my own to have kept on in my own path. What *giyre* I had of my crew, I earned; and that is important to me. What *giyre* I gave, I chose to give, and that was important too. I honor you, very much; but I would not have left the service.")

It was irony. He closed his hand about the *idoikkhe* and reminded himself what he was worth at the end of all his father's planning and his resisting: a being scantly adequate to serve the iduve, equal to a gracious (if vain) young woman and a battered bit of human freight off an amaut transport. He had lived with the sky overhead to be reached, whether or not he chose to try, and whether or not he had realized it before, he had been an arrogant and a stubborn man. Now he had been shown where the sky stopped, and it was a shattering experience.

He imagined Daniel's image in the glass. The skin went shades of brown and pink, the silver hair turned dark, the eyes shadowed and hunted, his body slight with hunger, crossed with red and purple scars from untreated wounds, feet lacerated by the cruel mesh. His mind held memories of absolute horror, cages, brutality unimagined in the *Halliran Idai*. Even before those, there were memories of hunger, a childhood in a dark, cement-walled house beside a trickling canal, summers of sandstorms that blasted crops, dunes that year by year encroached upon fields, advanced upon the house, threatened the life-giving canal. At some time—Aiela had inherited the memories in bits and snatches—Daniel had left that world for the military, and he had served as a technician of limited skills. He had known a great many primitive human ports, until the life sickened him and he went home again, only to find his father dead, his mother remarried, his brothers gone offworld, the farm buried under dunes.

War. Shipping lanes closed, merchantmen commandeered for military service. Daniel—senior now over inexperienced recruits, wearing the crisp blue of a technician on a decent ship, well fed, with money promised to his account. That had lasted seven days, until two stunning defeats had driven the human forces into retreat and then into rout, and men were required by martial law to seek their home ports and keep order there as the panic spread.

That was the way fortune operated for Daniel. His hands had been emptied every time he had them full; but being Daniel, he would shrug perplexedly, get down on his knees and begin picking up the pieces. He was uneducated, but he had a keen intuition, an intelligence that sucked in information like a vacuum drawing air, omnivorously, taking scrap and debris along with the pure, sorting, analyzing. He had never been anyone, he had never had anything; but he was not going to stop living until he was sure there was nothing to be had. That was Daniel—a man who had always been hungry. *M'melakhia,* Chimele would call it.

And Daniel's desire was the fevered dream of his half-sensible interludes in the cage, when the fields were green and the canal pure and full and orchards bloomed beside a white-walled house. He asked nothing more nor less than that—except the company of others of his kind. He had never deserved to be appropriated to *Ashanome,* swallowed whole by the pride of a Lyailleue and linked to a kalliran woman who had never learned to be kallia, who was more than a little iduve.

Aiela, Isande's thought reproved him, sorrowing.

How long have you been with me? He flushed with anger, for he had been deep in his own concerns and Isande's skill was such that he did not always perceive her touch. It was not the visual sense that embarrassed him: she knew his body as he knew hers, for that was a part of self-concept. It was his mind's privacy that he did not like thus exposed, and he knew at once from the backspill that she had caught rather more than she thought he would like.

"Dear Aiela," her silent voice came echoing. "No, don't screen me out. I am sorry for quarreling. I know I offend you."

"I am sorry," he sent, the merest surface of his thoughts, "for a great many things."

"You are not sure you can handle me," she said. "That troubles you. You are not accustomed to that. You are not half so cruel or fierce as I am, I know it; but you are twice as brave— too much so, sometimes, when that terrible pride of yours is touched."

"I have no pride," he said. "Not since Kartos."

She was amused, which stung. "No. No. It is there; but you have had it bruised—" the amusement faded, regretting his offense, and yet she knew herself right by his very reaction: right, and self-confident. "Chimele—the iduve in general—have touched it. You are just now realizing that this is forever, and it frightens you terribly."

Her words stung, and a feeling wholly *ikas* rose up in him. "I don't need to live on your terms. I will not."

She was silent for a time, sifting matters. "You do not understand *Ashanome*. Tonight you saw the *chanokhia* of Chimele, and I am afraid you have begun to love her. No—no, I know: not in that way. It is something worse. It is *m'melakhia*-love. It is *arastiethe* you want from her—iduve honor; and no *m'metane* can ever have that."

"You can't even think like a kallia, can you?"

"Aiela, Aiela, you are dealing with an iduve. Realize it. You are reacting to her as she *is*. You are thinking *giyre,* but Chimele cannot give you what she cannot even understand. For her there is only *arastiethe,* and the honor of an iduve demands too much of us. It costs too much, Aiela."

"She might be capable of understanding. Isande, she tried—"

"Avoid her!"

Screens dropped. Loneliness, a dead asuthe, years of silence. There was still loneliness, an asuthe who rejected her advice, who blindly, obstinately sought what had killed the other. Was the fault in her? Was it she that killed? She loved Chimele, and gave and gave, and the iduve knew only how to take. Reha had loved Chimele: asuthe to herself, how could he have helped it? He would be alive now, but that he had learned to love Chimele. She would not teach another.

Darkness. Cold. Screens tumbled. Aiela flinched and she snatched the memory away, recovering herself, smothering it as she had learned to do.

You denied, he reminded her gently, *That Ashanome killed him. Was Chimele responsible, after all?*

The screens stayed in place. Only the words came through, carefully controlled. "She was not responsible. Honor is all she can give. To the *nasithi,* that is everything. But what is it worth to a *m'metane?*"

Yet you do love her, Aiela sent, and sad laughter bubbled back.

"Listen—she tried with all her iduvish heart to make me happy. Three times she asked me to take another asuthe. 'He is like you,' she said this time. 'He is intelligent, he is of great *chanokhia* for a *m'metane*. Can you work with this one?' I consented. She risked a great deal to offer me that choice. You would have to know the iduve to realize how difficult that was for her—to try a thing when she has only reason to help her. She does feel—something. I am not sure what. After all these years, I am not sure what. Maybe we *m'metanei* try to read into them what we wish were there. Perhaps that is why we keep giving, when we know better."

"Let me alone," he wished her. "If I'm to make a mistake, then let it be my mistake."

"And when you make it," she said, "we will both pay for it. That is the way this arrangement works, Aiela."

It was truth; he recognized it—resented her being female. It was an unfair obligation. "I am sorry," he said after a moment. "Then it will happen. I will not be held by you."

"I disturb you."

"In several senses."

She snatched a thought half-born from his mind, the suspicion that the iduve knew enough of kalliran emotion to use it, to manipulate it at will. Isande was beautiful: he had eyes to notice that. He kept noticing it, again and again. That she constantly knew it, embarrassed him; he knew that she was not willing to think of him in that way. But, he sent her, if she were in the ungraceful position of having to share a man's inmost thoughts, she might receive things even more direct from time to time. Or had Reha been immune to such things?

The screen closed tightly on those memories, as it always had: the privacy she had shared with Reha was not for him. "He and I began so young we were like one mind; there could never be that between us. Asuthi ought never to share that part of their lives: some illusions have to be maintained. I am not for games, not for your amusement, nor are you for mine, dear friend. There is an end of it. You came too close to that being, you refuse my warnings about the iduve, and I see I can't help you: you resent being advised by a woman. But I can at least exercise the good sense to keep my distance from you when it happens."

Hurt feelings. Bitterly hurt feelings.

"Don't," he said, reaching out to her retreating mind. And

when she lingered, questioning, he searched for something to say. "If you're not going to sleep, stay awhile. It's miserably quiet here."

Softness touched his mind. He had pleased her by asking. Her spirits brightened and amusement rippled from her, to think that he found in her the power to deal with the nightmares that troubled him: human ghosts and iduve went flitting into retreat at her kalliran presence.

"Go to bed," she told him. "You need your rest. I'll stay awhile if it pleases you."

She hovered about his thoughts for a long time thereafter, half-asleep herself at the last and warm in her own bed, lending him the comforting trivia of pleasant memories, the distant voyagings of *Ashanome,* strange worlds and different suns; and she stole from his memories, filching little details of his past and embroidering them with questions until he grew too tired to answer. She, never having walked upon the face of a world, delighted in the memories of wind and rain and sunsets, the scent of green grass after a shower, and the drifting wonder of snow. There were no ill dreams. She held onto his senses and finally, mischievously, she sent him a few drowsy impressions that were less than sisterly.

He fired back indignation. "Games," he reminded her.

Vaikka, she whispered into his consciousness. *And you do not want to tell me to go away, do you?*

He did not, but he screened, and headed himself deliberately toward the darkness of sleep.

5

Isande was there in the morning. Her cheerful presence burst in enthusiastically while Aiela was putting his boots on, and it was as if a door had opened and someone were standing behind him—where there was neither door nor body.

"Must you be so sudden?" he asked her, and her joy plummeted. He was sorry. Isande had never been so vulnerable before. He was concerned about last night and out of sorts about time wasted and a tight schedule with Daniel.

"I would try to help," she offered.

His screens tightened; he knew her opinion of the human, her dislike of the creature. If it were not unlike her, he would have suspected her of wishing to harm Daniel: her feelings were that strong.

What do you expect of me? she asked, offended.

Answers. What do they want with him?

And a strange uneasiness was growing in him now that Daniel was on his mind; Isande's thoughts grew hard to unravel. Daniel was waking; Aiela's own heart began to speed, his breathing grew constricted in sympathetic reaction.

"Calm!" he cast him. "Calm! It's Aiela. It's all right."

Isande—who is Isande?

Daniel perceived her through him. Aiela's impulse was to interrupt that link, protecting both of them; but he sensed no harm from either direction, and he hesitated, suffering a strange double-passage of investigation as they probed each other. Then he received quite an unpleasant impression as the human realized Isande was female: curiosity reached for body-sense, to know.

Violently he snapped that connection, at once prey to the outrage of them both.

"I can fend for myself," Isande voiced to him, seething with offended pride. "He is not of our species, and I'm sure his curiosity means nothing to me."

But Daniel was too angry to voice. He was embarrassed and furious, and for a moment his temper obscured the fact that he was not equal to a quarrel either with Aiela or with his situation.

Aiela fired back his own feelings upon the instant: frustration with the ungovernable Isande, revulsion at having been made the channel for an alien mate's obscene curiosity—male, not man, not fit to touch a kalliran woman.

Barriers went up against him, fell again. Aiela felt the human's despair like a plunge into darkness, a hurt mingled with his own guilt. He was too disoriented to prevent its flow to Isande. Her anguish struck him from the other side, coldly doused as she flung up a screen.

"Aiela! The echo—stop it."

He understood: mind-linked as they were, each brain reacted to the other's emotions. It was a deadly self-accelerating process. His reaction to Daniel's offended masculinity had lowered a screen on an ugliness he had not suspected existed in himself.

"Daniel," he sent, and persisted until the unhappy being acknowledged his presence. It was a terrible flood he received. All screens went, *usuthithekkhe*, mind-link, defense abandoned. The images came so strongly they washed out vision: amaut, cages, dead faces, grief upon grief. Daniel's mind was the last citadel and he hurled it wide open, willing to die, at the end of his resistance.

I am sorry, Aiela hurled into that churning confusion like a voice into a gale. *Daniel! I was hurt too. Stop this. Please. Listen.*

Gradually, gradually, sanity gathered up the pieces again, the broken screens rebuilt themselves into separate silence; and Aiela rested his head in his hands, struggling against a very physical nausea that swelled in his throat. His instincts screamed *wrong,* his hands were cold and sweating at the proximity of a being unutterably twisted, who rejected *giyre* and *kastien,* who loathed the things most kalliran.

Aiela. Daniel reached the smallest tendril of thought toward him. He did not understand, but he would seal the memory behind a screen and not let it out again. Dying was not worse than being alone. Whatever the rules Aiela set, he would conform.

I'm sorry, Aiela replied gently. *But your perceptions of us are not exactly without prejudice; and you were rude with Isande.*

Isande is yours? Daniel snatched at that possibility. It touched something human as well as kalliran. He was anxious to believe he was not hated, that he had only made a mistake.

It was like that, Aiela admitted, embarrassed. He had never expected to have to share such intimate thoughts with the creature. It disturbed him, made him feel unclean; he screened those emotions in, knowing he must dispose of them.

"This arrangement," Daniel said, scanning the situation to the limit Aiela allowed, "with a woman and the two of us—is not the best possible, is it?"

That was sent with wistful humor. The human foresaw for himself a lifetime of being different, of being alone. Aiela was sorry for him then, deeply sorry, for there was in the being an *elethia* worth respect.

"We are at the mercy of the iduve," Aiela said, "who perceive our feelings only at a distance."

"There are so many things I don't understand here that I can hardly keep my thoughts collected. There are moments when I think I'm going to—"

"Please. Keep your questions a little longer. I will find it easier to explain when you have seen a little of the ship. Come, get dressed. Food comes before other things. We'll go out to the mess hall and you can have a look about."

Daniel was afraid. He had caught an impression of the way they would walk, crowds of kalliran strangers; and when Aiela let him know that there would be amaut too, he looked forward to breakfast with no appetite at all.

"Trust me," said Aiela. "If the iduve wished you harm, no place would be safe, and if they wish you none, then you are safe anywhere on this ship. They rule all that happens here."

Daniel acquiesced unhappily to that logic. In a little time they were out on the concourse together, Daniel looking remarkably civilized in his brown clothing—Aiela let that thought slip inadvertently and winced, but Daniel accepted the judgment with wry amusement and little bitterness. He was not a vain man, and the amaut had removed whatever vanity he had had.

It was the mess-hall company he could not abide. As they were eating, two amaut chanced to stand near their table talking, popping and hissing in the odd rhythms of their native tongue. Daniel's hand began to shake in the midst of carrying a bite to his mouth, and he laid the utensil aside a moment and covered the action by reaching for his cup. When Aiela picked up the thought in his mind, the memory of that cage and his voyage, he nearly lost his own appetite.

"These are decent folk," Aiela assured him, silently so the amaut would not realize the exchange.

"See how people look at me when they think I am looking away. I had as soon be an exhibit in a zoo. And I know the amaut. I know them; don't try to tell me otherwise. It doesn't help my confidence in you."

Is the human species then without its bandits, its criminals and deviates?

Aiela caught a disturbing flash of human history as Daniel pondered that question; and with a deliberate effort Daniel put the memory of the freighter from his mind. But he still would not look at the amaut.

Aiela. That was Isande, near them. She queried Aiela, did he mind, and when he extended her the invitation, she came into the mess hall, took a hot drink from the dispenser, and joined them. Through Aiela she reached for Daniel's mind and touched, introducing herself.

Her bright smile (it was a weapon she used consciously) elicited a shy response from Daniel, who was still nervous about Aiela's reactions; but when Aiela had approved, the human opened up and smiled indeed, the first time Aiela had known any moment of unblighted happiness in the being. Isande's presence with them was like a sunshine that drowned all the shadows, an assurance to Daniel that here was a healthy, whole world, a normality he had almost forgotten.

"I," said Daniel aloud, struggling with the unfamiliar sounds of the kalliran language, "I am really very sorry for offending you."

"You are a kind man," said Isande, and patted his hand— Aiela was glad he had his own screens up during that moment. He had foreseen this, and knew Isande well enough to know that she would purposely defy him in some way. Poor Daniel looked quite overcome by her, not knowing what to do then; and Aiela dropped his screen on Isande's contact, letting her know what he thought of her petty *vaikka.*

Stop it, Isande. Be kallia for once. Feel something.

She had not realized about Daniel, not known him so utterly vulnerable and frightened of them. Now she saw him through Aiela's eyes.

"Please," said Daniel, who had not been privy to that small exchange, but was painfully aware of the silence that excluded him. "I am an inconvenience to you both—but save us all embarrassment. Tell me why I have been brought here, why I have been—unwelcomely attached—to you both."

Isande was dismayed and ashamed; but Aiela looked on the human with as much respect at that moment as he had felt for any man.

"Yes," said Aiela, "I think it is time we went aside together, the three of us, and did that."

It would have been merciful, Aiela reflected, if Chimele had elected to talk to the human with as little distraction about him as possible. Instead, when he and his two asuthi entered the *paredre,* there were not only the *nasithi-katasakke,* but what Isande flashed them in dismay was the entire *Melakhis.* The blue screen was thrust back, opening up the audience hall, and nearly fifty iduve were there to observe them. *Kamethi,* Isande sent, *are not normally involved before the Melakhis. Iduve together are dangerous. Their tempers can become violent with no apparent reason. Be very careful, Daniel; be extremely careful and respectful.*

Chimele met them graciously, gave Aiela a nod of particular courtesy. Then she looked full at Daniel, whose heart was beating as if he feared murder.

Be calm, Aiela advised him. *Be calm. Isande and I are here to advise you if you grow confused.*

"Please sit," said Chimele, including them all. She resumed the central chair in the *paredre*—a ceremonial thing, perhaps of great age, ornate with serpents and alien or mythical beasts worked in wood and gold and amber. "Daniel. Do you understand where you are?"

"Yes," he answered. "They have explained to me who you are and that I must be honest with you."

Some of the elder iduve frowned at that; but Chimele heard that naive reply and inclined her head in courtesy. "Indeed. You are well advised to be so. Where is your home, Daniel, and how did you come into the hands of the amaut of *Konut?*"

Suspicion ran through Daniel's mind: attack, plunder—these the agents of it, seeking information. Isande had threshed out the matter with him repeatedly, assuring him of *Ashanome's* indifference to the petty matter of his world. Suddenly Daniel was not believing it. Fight-flight-escape ran through his mind, but he did not move from his chair. Aiela seized his arm to be sure that he did not.

"Pardon," Aiela said to Chimele softly, for he knew her extreme displeasure when Daniel failed to respond. She had shown courtesy to this being before her people; and Daniel for his part looked into those whiteless eyes and met something against which the alienness of the amaut was slight in comparison. They had shown Daniel iduve in his mind; he had even seen Chimele—shadowy and indistinct in his cell; but the living presence of them, the subtle communication of arrogance and their lack of response to emotion, he hated, loathed, feared. *Their pattern is different,* Aiela sent him. *It is affecting you. Don't let it overcome you. Instinct is not always positive for survival when you are offworld. You are the stranger here.*

"*M'metane,*" Chimele said, labored patience in her voice, "*m'metane,* what is the difficulty?"

"I—" Daniel stared a moment into Chimele's violet eyes and tore his glance away, fixing it unfocused on the panel just beyond her shoulder. "I have no way to know that we are not still in human space, or that this is not the upper part of the ship where I was a prisoner. I have seen amaut on my world. I don't know who sent them. Perhaps they brought themselves, but on this ship they take your orders."

There was a great shifting of bodies among the iduve, a dangerous and unpredictable tension; but Chimele leaned her chin on her hand and studied Daniel with heightened interest. Of a sudden she smiled, showing her teeth. "Indeed. I hope you have not seen much similarity between the decks of *Ashanome* and that pestiferous freighter, *m'metane*. Yet your caution I find admirable. Amaut on your world? And where is your world, Daniel? Surely not in the Esliph."

"Why?" Daniel asked, though Isande tried to prevent him. "What exactly do you want to know?"

"*M'metane,* I am informed, perhaps correctly, perhaps not, that your people have been attacked. If this is so, we did not order it. We pursue our own business, and your asuthi will advise you that I am being extraordinarily courteous. Now as you hope for the survival of your species, I advise you not to insult that courtesy by being slow in your answers."

Does she mean that against all humanity—a threat? Daniel asked them, shaken. *Would they declare war? Have they?*

In the name of reason don't try to bargain with her, Aiela flung back. *Iduve don't bluff.*

Daniel folded, sick inside, a simple man out of his depth and fearing both alternatives. He took the one advised and began to tell them the things they wanted to know, his origin on a world named Konig, beyond the Esliph, his life there, his brief service in the military, his world's fall to the amaut. The iduve listened with unnerving patience, even interrupting him to ask more detail of the history of his people, particularly as it regarded the Esliph frontier.

"We never consented, sir," he told Rakhi, who had asked about the human retreat from the Esliph worlds. "Those were our farms, our cities. The amaut drove us out with better weapons and we went back to safe worlds across the Belt."

Rakhi frowned. "Most unfortunate, this human problem," he said to his *nasithi*. "Our departure from the *metrosi* seems to have thrown the amaut and kalliran powers into considerable turmoil. We appear to have served some economic purpose for them. When we withdrew, the amaut seem to have found them-

selves in particular difficulty. They drew back and abandoned
the Esliph. Then the humans discovered it. And, under renewed
population pressures, the amaut return, reclaim the Esliph—it is
altogether logical for them to use force to take land they already
considered theirs, or to use force in meeting competitors. But
m'metane, were there not agreements, accommodations?"

"Only that we were let off with our lives," said Daniel. Of
iduve that questioned him, Rakhi drew the most honest responses; and upon this question, centuries ago as the event was,
Daniel allowed anger to move him. Amaut, iduve, even kallia
blurred into one polity in his image of the forced evacuation of
his people, for the invaders had been faceless beings in ships,
giving orders; and to the human mind, all nonhumans tended to
assume one character. "We were pushed off before we could be
properly evacuated, crowded onto inadequate ships. Some refused to board and commit themselves to that; they stayed to
fight, and I suppose I know what became of them. The ones that
migrated and survived to reach the other side of the Belt were
about twenty out of a hundred. We landed without enough
equipment, hardly with the means to survive the winter. The
worlds were undeveloped, bypassed in our first colonization,
undesirable. We scratched a living out of sand and rock and lost
it to the weather more often than not. Now they've come after
us there."

"Undoubtedly," said Khasif, "as the abandoned humans did
not fit the amaut social pattern, indenture became the amaut's
solution for the humans. Beings that cannot interbreed with
amaut could not exit indenture by normal legal process, so the
humans remain in this status perpetually."

"Yet," objected another of Khasif's order, "one wonders why
the other humans did not eventually seek better territories, if the
worlds in question were so entirely undesirable."

Answer, Isande flashed, for that was a question to Daniel,
stated in the often oblique manner of iduve courtesy. "The Esliph was ours," Daniel replied, "and we always meant to come
and take it back."

"Prha," said Chaikhe to that person, *"vaikka/tomes-melakhia-
sa, ekutikkase."*

"We did not so much want revenge," Daniel responded to the

comment, for he had caught the gist of it through Isande, "as
we wanted justice, our own land back. Now the amaut have
come looking for us, even across the Belt. They're murdering
my people."

"Why?" asked Chimele.

The sudden harshness of her tone panicked the human; his
own murder flashed to mind—the easy, gentle manner of the
others' questions some game they played with him. *No!* Isande
sent him. *Stay absolutely still. Don't move. Answer her.*

"I don't know why. They came—they came. Unprovoked."

"Human ships had not crossed to the Esliph?"

"No," he said quickly, surprised by the accusation. "No."

"How do you know this?"

He did not. He was no one. He had no perfect knowledge of
his people's actions. Aiela sent him an urging to keep still, for
Chimele frowned.

"*M'metane,*" said Chimele, "disputing another's experience is
most difficult. Yet there remains the possibility that the amaut
responded to a human intrusion into Esliph space. They are not
prone to act recklessly where there is an absence of threat to
their own territory, and they are not prone to aggression without
the certainty of profit. When there is either motivation, then they
move most suddenly and decisively. Our acquaintance with the
amaut is long, but I am not satisfied that you know them as well
as you believe. Consider every detail of your acquaintance with
these uncommon amaut, from the beginning. Let Isande have
these thoughts."

He did so, the image of a ship, of amaut faces, another ship, a
city, fire—he flashed backward, seeking the origin, the first inti-
mation of danger to human worlds. Merchant ship, military
ship—vanished, only gaseous clouds to mark their passing.
Ships grounded. Another vessel. Alien. A human war fleet,
drawn from worlds to the interior of human space: this the real
defense of their perimeters, large, ships technologically not far
from par with the *metrosi*. Demolished, traceless. Mindless
panic among human colonies, wild rumors of landings in the
system. A second, local fleet gone, thirty ships at once.

Daniel still sent, but Isande had glanced sharply at Chimele,
and Aiela did not need her interpretation to understand. Amaut

karshatu maintained weapons on their merchantmen, but they were not capable of disposing of whole warfleets: the *karshatu* never combined. In that respect they were as solitary as the iduve.

Amaut, Daniel insisted, and there were amautish ships in his mind, such as he had seen onworld, great hulking transports, hardly capable of fighting: carriers of equipment and indentured personnel; smaller ships, trade ships that plied the high-speed supply runs, taking back the only export these raw new worlds would supply as yet, not to make an empty run on either direction: human cargo, profitably removed from a place where their numbers made them a threat to places where they were a commodity. But these amaut were not fighters either. Daniel, confused, searched into dimmer memories.

Darkness, images on a viewing screen, a silver shape in hazy resolution, last to view almost instantly, pursued in vain. Isande caught at the memory eagerly, drawing more and more detail from Daniel, making him hold the image, concentrate upon it, focus it.

"He has seen an *akites,*" Isande's soft voice translated. "Distant, his ship pursued, lacked speed, lost it. He thinks it was amaut, knows—this was what arrived—disorganized the entire human defense. They resisted—mistook it for several ships, not knowing its speed—perhaps—perhaps more than one, I can't tell—they provoked—they provoked, not knowing what—Daniel, please!"

"Was it yours?" Daniel cried, on his feet, closing screens with abrupt violence. Iduve moved, and Aiela, hardly slower, sprang up to put himself between Daniel and Chimele.

"Sit down," Aiela exclaimed. "Sit down, Daniel."

Contempt came across: it was in Daniel's eyes and burning in his mind. *Theirs. Not your kind either, but you crawl at their feet. You come apart inside when they look at you—I'm sorry—* He felt Aiela's pain, and tears came to his eyes. *What are you doing to us? Not human. Aiela!*

Aiela seized, held to him, shamed by the emotion, shamed to feel when their observers could not. Isande—she, apart, despising, angry. He gained control of himself and forced the dazed

human into a chair, stood over him, his fingers clenched into the
man's shoulder.

Calm, be calm, he kept sending. After a moment Daniel's
muscles relaxed and his mind assumed a quieter level, questioning, terrified.

Why are they asking these things? he kept thinking. *Aiela,
Aiela, help me—tell me the truth if you know it.* And then at the
angry touch of Isande's mind: *Who is Tejef?*

Terror. She flung herself back, screened so violently Daniel
cried out.

And the iduve were utterly still, every eye upon them, the *nasithi* gathered close about Chimele, with such a look of menace
that they seemed to have grown and the room to have shrunk.
Indeed more had come, dark faces frowning with anger, unask-
ing and unasked. Still they came, and the concourse began to be
crowded with them. None spoke. There was only the sound of
steps and the rustling of thousands of bodies.

"Is this aberrance under control?" Chimele wondered quietly,
her eyes on Aiela.

It is not aberrance, he wanted to cry at her. *Can't you perceive it?* But the iduve could not comprehend. He bowed deeply.
"He was alarmed. He perceived a threat to his species."

Chimele considered that. Iduve faces, whose eyes were almost incapable of moving from side to side, had always a direct,
invading stare, communicating little of what processes of
thought. went on behind them, At last she lifted her hand and the
tension in the room ebbed perceptibly.

"This being is capable of a certain *elethia,*" she said. "But he
is not wise to think that *Ashanome* could not deal with his
species more efficiently if their destruction were our purpose.
How long ago, *o m'metane,* did your worlds realize the presence
of such ships?"

"I've lost count," Daniel replied: truth. "A year, perhaps—
maybe a little less. It seems forever."

"Do you reckon in human time?"

"Yes." An impulse rose in him, defiant, suicidal. "Who is
Tejef?"

The effect was like a weapon drawn. But this time Chimele

refused to be provoked. Interest was in her expression, and she held her *nasithi* motionless with a quick lift of her fingers.

"Chimele," said Isande miserably, "he took it from me, when I thought of ships."

"Are you sure it was only then?"

"I am sure," she said, but an iduve from the *Melakhis* stepped into the *paredre* area: a tall woman, handsome, in black as stark and close-fitting as iduve men usually affected.

"Chimele-Orithain," said that one. "I have questions I would ask him."

"Mejakh *sra*-Narach, *sra*-Khasif, you are out of order, though I understand your *m'melakhia* in this matter. *Hold, Mejakh!*" Chimele's voice, soft, snapped like a blow to the face in the stillness, and the woman stopped a second time, facing her.

"This human is not kameth," said Mejakh, "and I consider that he is out of order, Chimele, and probably in possession of more truth than he is telling."

"More than he knows how to tell, perhaps," said Chimele. "But he is mine, o mate of Chaxal. Honor to your *m'melakhia*. It is well known. Have patience. I am aware of you."

"Honor to you," said Khasif softly, drawing that woman to his side. "Honor always, *sra*-of-mine. But do not notice this ignorant being. He is harmless and only ignorant. Be still. Be still."

The room grew quiet again. Chimele looked at last upon Daniel and Aiela. "Estimate a human year in Kej-time. Ashakh, assist them."

It needed some small delay. Daniel inwardly recoiled from Ashakh's close presence, but with quiet, precise questions, the iduve obtained the comparisons he wanted. In a moment more the computer had the data from the *paredre* desk console and began to construct a projection. A considerable portion of the hall went to starry space, where moving colored dots haltingly coincided.

"From the records of Kartos Station," said Ashakh, "we have traced the recent movements of the ships in all zones of the Esliph. This new information seems to be in agreement. See, the movements of amaut commerce, the recent expansion of the lines of this *karsh*"—the image shifted, a wash of red light at the edge of the Esliph nearest human space—"by violent absorption of a minor *karsh* and its lanes; and the sudden shift of commerce here"—another flurry of lights—"indicate a probable direction of origin for that *akites* our instruments indicate over by Telshanu, directly out of human space. Now, if this being Daniel's memory is accurate, the time coincides admirably for the intrusion of that *akites;* again, it falls well into agreement with this person's account."

"In all points?" asked Chimele, and when Ashakh agreed: "Indeed." The image of Esliph space winked into the dim-lighted normalcy of the *paredre.* "Then we are bound for Telshanu. Advise *Chaganokh* to await our coming."

"Chimele!" cried Mejakh. "Chimele, we cannot afford more time. This persistence of yours in—"

"It has thus far preserved *Ashanome* from disaster. You are not noticed, Mejakh. Ashakh, set our course. We are dismissed, my *nasithi.*"

As silently as they had assembled, the *nasul* dispersed, the *Melakhis* and the *nasithi-katasakke* too; and Chimele leaned back in her chair and stared thoughtfully at Daniel.

"Your species," she said, "seems to have begun *vaikka* against one of the *nasuli,* most probably the *vra-nasul Chaganokh.* The amaut are a secondary problem, inconsequential by comparison. If you have been wholly truthful, I may perhaps remove the greater danger from human space. But be advised, *m'metane,* you came near to great harm. You are indeed kameth to *Ashanome,* although not all the *nasithi* seem to acknowledge that fact. Yet for reasons of my own I shall not yet permit you the *idoikkhe*—and you must therefore govern your own behavior most carefully. I shall not again count you ignorant."

"You deny you're responsible for what is happening to Konig?"

"*Tekasuphre.*" Chimele arose and plainly ignored Daniel, looking instead at Isande. "I think it may be well if you make clear to this person and to Aiela my necessities—and theirs."

Isande's quarters, a suite of jewel-like colors and glittering light-panels, had been the place of Daniel's instruction before the interview; it was their refuge after, Isande curled into her favorite chair, Aiela in the other, Daniel sprawled disconsolate on the couch. Their minds touched. It was Daniel they tried to comfort, but he ignored them, solitary and suicidal in his depression. Regarding the impulse to self-destruction, Aiela was not greatly concerned: it was not consistent with the human's other attitudes. Daniel was more likely to turn his destructive urges on someone else, but it would not be his asuthi. That was part of his misery. He had no reachable enemies.

"You have done nothing wrong," said Isande. "You have not hurt your people."

Silence.

Daniel, Aiela sent, *I could not lie to you; you would know it.*

I hate the sight of you, Daniel's subconscious fired out at him; but his upper mind suppressed that behind a confused feeling of shame. "That is not really true," he said aloud, and again, forcefully: "That is not true. I'm sorry."

Aiela cast him a feeling of total sympathy, for proximity still triggered a scream of alarm over his nerves and unsettled his stomach; but the reaction was already becoming less and less. Someday he would shudder no longer, and they would have become one monstrous hybrid, neither kalliran nor human. And now it was Isande who recoiled, having caught that thought. She rejected it in horror.

"I don't blame you," Daniel answered: somehow it did not seem unnatural that he should respond instead, so deeply was he in link with Aiela. He dropped the contact then, grieving, knowing Isande's loathing for him.

"We have not used you," Isande protested.

Daniel touched Aiela's mind again, reading to a depth Aiela did not like. "And haven't we all done a little of that?" Daniel wondered bitterly. "And isn't it only natural, after all?" Was this the beaten, uneducated creature about whose sentience they had wondered? Aiela looked upon him in uncomfortable surmise, all three minds suddenly touching again. From Daniel came a bitter mirth.

You've taught me worlds of things I didn't know. I don't even remember learning most of it; I just touch your minds and I know. And I suppose you could pass for humans if it weren't for

your looks. But what use do they have for me on Ashanome?
Teach me that if you can.

"Our life is a pleasant one," said Isande.

"With the iduve?" Daniel swung his legs off the couch to sit
upright. "They aren't human, they aren't even as human as you
are, and I believe you when you say they don't have feelings
like we do. It agrees with what I saw in there tonight."

"They have feelings," said Isande, letting pass his remark
about the humanity of kallia. "Daniel, Chimele wishes you no
harm."

"Prove it."

She met his challenge with an opening of the mind, from
which he retreated in sudden apprehension. Strange, iduve
things lay beyond that gate. She remained intent upon it even
while she rose and poured them each a glass of *marithe,* pressing it at both of them. She was seated again, and stared at
Daniel.

All right, Daniel sent finally. It was difficult for him, but to
please Aiela, desperate to please someone in this strange place,
he yielded down all his barriers.

Isande sent, with that rough impatience she knew how to use
and Daniel did only by instinct, such a flood of images that for a
time *here* and *now* did not exist. Even Aiela flinched from it,
and then resolved to himself that he would let Isande have her
way, trusting her nature if not her present mood.

There were things incredibly ancient, gleaned of tapes, of
records inaccessible to outsiders. There was Kej IV under its
amber sun, its plains and sullen-hued rivers; tower-holds and
warriors of millennia ago, when each *nasul* had its *dhis,* its nest-
tower, and *ghiaka*-wielding defenders and attackers raged in bat-
tles beyond number—*vaikka-dhis,* nest-raid, when an invading
nasul sought to capture young for its own *dhis,* sought prisoners
of either sex for *katasakke,* though prisoners often suicided.

Red-robed *dhisaisei,* females-with-young, kept the inner
sanctity of the *dhis.* Most females gave birth and ignored their
offspring, but within the *nasul,* there were always certain mater-
nal females of enormous ferocity who claimed all the young,
and guarded and reared them until on a day their *dhisais-*

madness should pass and leave them ready to mate again. Before them even the largest males gave way in terror.

The *dhis* was the heart and soul of the *nasul,* and within it was a society no adult male ever saw again—a society rigid in its ranks and privileges. Highest of rank were the *orithaikhti,* her-children to the Orithain; and lowest in the order, the offspring-without-a-name: no male could claim parentage without the female's confirmation, and should she declare of her offspring: *Taphrek nasiqh*—*"I do not know this child"*—it went nameless to the lowest rank of the *dhis.* Such usually perished, either in the *dhis,* or more cruelly, in adulthood.

It was the object of all conflict, the motive of all existence, the *dhis*—and yet forbidden to all that had once passed its doors, save for the Guardians, for the *dhisaisei,* and for the green-robed *katasathei*—pregnant ones, whose time was near. The *katasathei* were for the rest of the *nasul* the most visible symbol of the adored *dhis:* males full-*sra* to a *katasathe* drove her recent mate and all other males from her presence; females of the *nasul* gave her gifts, and forlorn non-*sra* males would often leave them where she could find them. Her only possible danger came from a female Orithain who also chanced to be *katasathe.* Then it was possible that she could be driven out, forbidden the *dhis* altogether, and her protective *sra* endangered: the ferocity of an Orithain was terrible where it regarded rival offspring, and even other *nasuli* gave way before a *nasul* whose Orithain was *katasathe,* knowing madness ruled there.

That was the ancient way. Then Cheltaris began to rise, city of the many towers, city of paradox. There had never been government or law; *nasuli* clustered, co-existed by means of ritual, stabilized, progressed. It was dimly remembered—Cheltaris: empty now, deserted *nasul* by *nasul* as the *akitomei* launched forth; and what curious logic had convinced the *nasuli* their survival lay starward was something doubtless reasonable to iduve, though to no one else.

Where each *dhis* was, there was home; and yet, shielded as the *dhis* had become within each powerful, star-wandering *akites,* without *vaikka-dhis* and the captures, inbreeding threatened the *nasuli.* So there developed the custom of *akkhres-nasuli,* a union of two *akitomei* for the sharing of *katasakke.*

It was, for the two *nasuli* involved, potentially the most hazardous of all ventures, civilized by oaths, by elaborate ritual, by most strict formalities—and when all else proved vain, by the power and good sense of the two *orithainei.*

Chaxal.

Dead now.

Father to Chimele.

In his time, far the other side of the *metrosi,* by a star called Niloqhatas, there had been *akkhres-nasuli.*

Such a union was rare for *Ashanome;* it was occasioned by something rarer still—a ceremony of *kataberihe.* The Orithain Sogdrieni of *nasul Tashavodh* had chosen Mejakh *sra*-Narach of *Ashanome* to become his heir-mate and bear him a child to inherit *Tashavodh.* The bond between *Tashavodh* and *Ashanome* disturbed the iduve, for these were two of the oldest and most fearsome of the *nasuli* and the exchange they contemplated would make profound changes in status and balance of power among the iduve. Tensions ran abnormally high.

And trouble began with a kameth of *Tashavodh* who chanced to cross the well-known temper of Mejakh *sra*-Narach. She killed him.

Mejakh was already aboard *Tashavodh* in the long purifications before *kataberihe.* But in rage over the matter Sogdrieni burst into her chambers, drove out her own kamethi, and assaulted her. Perhaps when tempers cooled he would have allowed her to begin purifications again, *vaikka* having been settled; but it was a tangled situation: Mejakh was almost certainly now with child, conception being almost infallible with a mating. But he misjudged the *arastiethe* of Mejakh: she killed him and fled the ship.

In confusion, *Ashanome* and *Tashavodh* broke apart, *Tashavodh* stunned by the death of their Orithain, *Ashanome* satisfied that they had come off to the better in the matter of *vaikka.* It was in effect a *vaikka-dhis,* the stealing of young; and to add *chanokhia* to the *vaikka,* in the very hour that Mejakh returned to *Ashanome* she entered *katasakke* with an iduve of nameless birth.

So she violated purification of her own accord this time, and so blotted out the certainty of her child's parentage. With the condemnation—*taphrek nasiqh*—she sent him nameless to the incubators of the *dhis* of *Ashanome*—the dishonored heir of Sogdrieni-Orithain.

Of Mejakh's great *vaikka* she gained such *arastiethe* that she met in *katasakke* with Chaxal-Orithain of *Ashanome*, and of that mating came Khasif, firstborn of *Ashanome*'s present ruling *sra*, but not his heir. Chaxal took for his heir-mate Tusaivre of *Iqhanofre*, who bore him Chimele before she returned to her own *nasul*. Other *katasakke*-mates produced Rakhi, and Ashakh and Chaikhe.

But the nameless child survived within the *dhis*, and when he emerged he chose to be called Tejef.

Isande's mind limned him shadowlike, much resembling Rhasif, his younger half-brother, but a quiet, frightened man despite his physical strength, who suffered wretchedly the violence of Mejakh and the contempt of Chaxal. Only Chimele, who emerged two years later, treated him with honor, for she saw that it vexed Mejakh—and Mejakh still aspired to a *kataberihe* with Chaxal, an heir-mating which threatened Chimele.

Until Chaxal died.

New loyalties sorted themselves out; a younger *sra* came into power with Chimele. There were changes outside the *nasul* too—all relations with the *orith-nasuli*, the great clans, must be redefined by new oaths. There must be two years of ceremony at the least, before the accession of Chimele could be fully accomplished.

Death.

The dark of space.

Reha.

Screens went up. Isande flinched from that. Aiela tore back. *No,* he sent, shielding Daniel. *Don't do that to him.*

Isande reached for her glass of *marithe* and trembled only slightly carrying it to her lips. But what seeped through the screens was ugly, and Daniel would gladly have fled the room, if distance and walls could have separated him from Isande.

"An Orithain cannot assume office fully until all *vaikka* of the previous Orithain is cleared," Isande said in a quiet, precise voice, maintaining her screens. "*Tashavodh*'s Orithain—Kharxanen, full brother to Sogdrieni—had been at great *niseth*—great disadvantage—for twenty years because Chaxal had eluded all his attempts to settle. But now that *Ashanome*'s new Orithain was needing to assume office, settlement became possible. Chimele needed it as badly as Kharxanen.

"So *Tashavodh* and *Ashanome* met. Something had to be yielded on *Ashanome*'s side. Kharxanen demanded Mejakh and Tejef; Chimele refused—Mejakh being *bhan-sra* to her own *nas-katasakke* Khasif, it struck too closely at her own honor. Even *Tashavodh* had to recognize that.

"But she gave them Tejef.

"Tejef was stunned. Of course it was the logical solution; but Chimele had always treated him as if he were one of her own *nasithi,* and he had been devoted to her. Now all those favors were only the preparation of a terrible *vaikka* on him—worse than anything that had ever been done to him, I imagine. When he heard, he went to Chimele alone and unasked. There was a terrible fight.

"Usually the iduve do not intervene in male-female fights, even if someone is being maimed or killed: mating is usually violent, and violating privacy is *e-chanokhia,* very improper. But Chimele is no ordinary woman; all the *sra* of an Orithain have an honorable name, and *taphrek-nasiqh* is applicable only to paternity: the thing Tejef intended would give his offspring the name he lacked; and if he died in the attempt, it would still spite Chimele, robbing her of her accommodation with *Tashavodh.*

"But Chimele's *nasithi-katasakke* broke into the *paredre.* What happened then, only they know, but probably there was no mating—there never was a child. Tejef escaped, and when Mejakh put herself in his way trying to keep him from the lift, he overpowered her and took her down to the flight deck. The *okkitani-as* on duty there knew something terrible was wrong—alarms were sounding, the whole ship on battle alert, for the Orithain was threatened and we sat only a few leagues from *Tashavodh.* But the amaut are not fighters, and they could do little enough to stop an iduve. They simply cowered on the floor until he had gone and then the bravest of them used the intercom to call for help.

"My asuthe Reha was already on his way to the flight deck by the time I reached Chimele in the *paredre.* He seized a second shuttlecraft and followed. A kameth has immunity among iduve,

even on an alien deck, and he thought if he could attach himself
to the situation before *Tashavodh* could actually claim Mejakh,
he could possibly help Chimele recover her and save the *arastiethe* of *Ashanome*.

"But they killed him." Screens held, altogether firm. She
sipped at the *marithe,* furiously barring a human from that privacy of hers; and Daniel earnestly did not want to invade it.
"They swore later they didn't know he was only kameth. It did
not occur to them that a kameth would be so rash. When he
knew he was dying he fired one shot at Tejef, but Tejef was
within their shields already and it had no more effect than if he
had attacked *Tashavodh* with a handgun.

"The iduve—when the stakes are very high—are sensible; it
is illogical to them to do anything that endangers *nasul* survival.
And this was highly dangerous. *Vaikka* had gotten out of hand,
Tashavodh was well satisfied with their acquisition of Mejakh
and Tejef, but in the death of a kameth of *Ashanome,* Chimele
had a serious claim against them. There is a higher authority: the
Orithanhe; and she convoked it for the first time in five hundred
years. It meets only in Cheltaris, and the ships were four years
gathering.

"When the Orithanhe reached its decision, neither Chimele
nor Kharxanen had fully what they had demanded. Mejakh had
been forced into *katasakke* with a kinsman of Kharxanen; and
by the Orithanhe's decision, *Tashavodh's dhis* obtained her unborn child for its incubators and *Ashanome* obtained Mejakh—
no great prize. She has never been quite right since. Chimele
demanded Tejef back; but the Orithanhe instead declared him
out-kindred, outlaw—*e-nasuli.*

"So by those terms, by very ancient custom, Tejef was due his
chance: a Kej year and three days to run. Now *Ashanome* has its
own: two years and six days to hunt him down—or lose rights to
him forever."

"And they have found him?" asked Daniel.

"You—may have found him." Isande paused to pour herself
more *marithe.* She scarcely drank, ordinarily, but her shaken
nerves communicated to such an extent that they all breathed
uneasily and struggled with her to push back the thoughts of
Reha. *Revenge* ran cold and sickly through all her thoughts; and

grief was there too. Aiela tried to reach her on his own, but at
the moment she thought of Reha and did not want even him.

"There is the *vra-nasul Chaganokh,*" said Isande. "Vassal-
clan, a six-hundred-year-old splinter of *Tashavodh,* nearby and
highly suspect. We have sixty-three days left. But you see,
Chimele can't just accuse *Chaganokh* of having aided Tejef with
nothing to support the claim. It's not a matter of law, but of
harachia—seeing. *Chaganokh* will look to see if she has come
merely to secure a small *vaikka* and annoy them, or if she is in
deadly earnest. No Orithain would ever harm them without absolute confidence in being right: *orithainei* do not make mistakes. *Chaganokh* will therefore base its own behavior on what
it sees: by that means they will determine how far *Ashanome* is
prepared to go. If she shows them truth, they will surely bend: it
would be suicide for a poor *vra-nasul* to enter *vaikka* with the
most ancient of all clans—which *Ashanome* is. They will not resist further."

"And what does she mean to show them?"

"You," she said; Aiela instinctively flung the *chiabres*-link
asunder, dismayed by that touch of willful cruelty in Isande: she
enjoyed distressing Daniel. The impulse he sent in her direction
carried anger, and Isande flinched, and felt shame. "We searched
to find you," she said then to Daniel. "Oh, not you particularly,
but it came to Chimele's attention that humans from beyond the
Esliph were turning up—we have followed so many, many leads
in recent months, through the iduve, kallia, even the amaut, in-
vestigating every anomaly. We traced one such shipment toward
Kartos—economical: Chimele knew she would at least find
Kartos' records of value in her search. You were available; and
you have pleased her enormously—hence her extraordinary patience with you. Only hope you haven't misled her."

"I haven't led her at all," Daniel protested. "Amaut were all I
ever saw, the ugly little beasts, and I never heard of iduve in my
life." And hidden in his mind were images of what might become of him if he were given to the iduve of *Chaganokh* for
cross-examination, or if thereafter he had no value to the iduve
at all.

"You are kameth," said Isande. "You will not be discarded.
But I will tell you something: as far as iduve ever bluff, Chimele

is preparing to; and if she is wrong, she will have ruined herself. Three kamethi would hardly be adequate *serach*—funeral gift— for a dynasty as old and honorable as hers. We three would die; so would her *nasithi-katasakke, serach* to the fall of a dynasty. The iduve could destroy worlds of *m'metanei* and not feel as much as they would the passing of Chimele. So be guided by us, by Aiela and by me. If you do in that meeting what you did today—"

Now it was Daniel who screened, shutting off the images from Isande's mind. She ceased.

Do not be hard with him, Aiela asked of her. *There is no need of that, Isande.*

She did not respond for a moment; in her mind was hate, the thought of what she would do and how she would deal with the human if Aiela were not the intermediary, and yet in some part she was ashamed of her anger. Asuthi must not hate; with her own clear sense she knew it, and submitted to the fact that he was appended to them. *If you fail to restrain him,* she sent Aiela, *you will lose him. You have fallen into a trap; I had prepared myself to remain distinct from him, but you are caught, you are merging; and because I regard you, I am caught too. Restrain him. Restrain him. If he angers the iduve, three kamethi are the least expensive loss that will result.*

6

The Orithain of *Chaganokh* was a lonely man in the *paredre* of *Ashanome*. He wore the close-fitting garment common to iduve, but of startling white and complicated by overgarments and robes and a massive silver belt from which hung a *ghiaka*. His name was Minakh, and he was a conspicuous gleam of white and silver among so much indigo and black, with the fair colors of kallia and human an unintentional counterpoint across the room. Chimele faced him, seated, similarly robed and bearing a *ghiaka* with a raptor's head, but her colors were dusky violet.

Tension was electric in the air. Daniel shivered at being thrust so prominently into the midst of them, and Aiela mentally held to him. Contact among the asuthi seemed uncertain, washed out by the miasma of terror and hostilities in the hall, which was filled with thousands of iduve. Bodies went rigid at the presence of Minakh, whiteless eyes dilated to black, breathing quickened. A dozen of the most powerful of *nasul Ashanome* were ranged about Chimele, behind, on either side of her: Khasif, Ashakh—great fearsome men, and two women, Tahjekh and Nophres, who were guardians of the *dhis* and terrible to offend.

Minakh's eyes shifted from this side to that of the gathering. While he was still distant from Chimele he went to his knees and raised both hands. Likewise Chimele lifted her hands to salute him, but she remained seated.

"I am Orithain of the *nasul Chaganokh*," said Minakh. "Increase to the *dhis* of *Ashanome*. We salute you."

"We are *Ashanome*. May your eye be sharp and your reach long. For what grace have you come?"

"We have come to ask the leave of the *orith-nasul Ashanome* to go our way. The field is yours. May your affairs prosper."

"Honor to the *vra-nasul Chaganokh* for its courtesy. We have heard that the zone of Kej is uncommonly pleasant of late. May your affairs prosper there."

Minakh inclined his body gracefully to the carpet at this order, although it must have rankled; and he sat back on his heels, hands at his thighs, elbows outward.

"We rejoice at *Ashanome*'s notice," he said flatly, and again came the concentration of hostilities, scantly concealed.

"Happy are the circumstances when *nasuli* may pass without *vaikka*," said Chimele. "Honor to the wisdom of the Orithanhe which has made this possible."

"Long life to those who respect its decrees."

"Long life indeed, and may we remember this meeting with good pleasure. The *vra-nasul Chaganokh* has voyaged far and accrued honors; at its presence the Esliph shudders, and the untraveled space of the human folk has now been measured."

"The praise of *Ashanome*, hunter of worlds, is praise indeed." Minakh's face was utterly impassive, but his eyes flashed aside to Daniel, dark and terrible.

"Indeed *Chaganokh* is deserving of honor. So great is our admiration for its acquisition of wisdom that we lay at *Chaganokh*'s feet the matter nearest our heart. We search for a man who was once of *Ashanome*. Perhaps this inconsequential person has crossed the affairs of *Chaganokh*. We should not be surprised to learn that he has attempted to shake us from his trail in the uncharted human zones. *Chaganokh*'s recently acquired knowledge of this region seems to us an excellent source of precise knowledge. We are of course in great haste. Our time is slipping from us, and *Chaganokh* in its wisdom will surely accommodate our impatience in this regard."

There was a long and deadly silence. Minakh's eyes rested on Daniel with such hate that it was almost tangible, and every iduve in the room bristled. The silence persisted, broken ominously by a hiss from one of the *dhis*-guardians.

Minakh sweated. His belly heaved with his breathing. At last he prostrated himself and sat back again on his heels, looking dispirited.

"We delight to offer our assistance. This person attached himself to us at a distance. We ceased to notice him shortly after we entered the human zones, near a world known to those creatures as Priamos. Our own affairs occupied us thereafter."

"May your *dhis* ever be safe, o *Chaganokh*. Again let us trouble your gracious assistance. Are the humans wise to think that the amaut are the cause of their unhappy state?"

"When were the *m'metanei* ever wise, o *Ashanome,* hunter of worlds? The amaut are carrion-eaters who seek scraps where we have passed. When has it ever been otherwise?"

"The wisdom of *Chaganokh* is commendable. Prosperity to its affairs and grace to its offspring. Pass, o *Chaganokh*."

Now Minakh arose and backed away, backed entirely out of the *paredre* before he turned. No one of *Ashanome* stirred. No one seemed to breathe until at last the voice of Rakhi from the control station announced Minakh off the ship and the hatch sealed.

"Honor to the discretion of *Chaganokh*," Chimele laughed softly. "Go your ways, my *nasithi*. Ashakh—"

"Chimele."

"Set our course for the human zones as soon as you can make a proper determination from *Chaganokh*'s records. You are clear to put us underway at maximum, priority signal. Secrecy no longer applies. Either I am right, or I am wrong."

Ashakh acknowledged the order with a nod, turned and left. Silently the iduve were dispersing, by ones and by twos, amiable now Minakh's *harachia* was removed; and Chimele leaned back in her chair and looked for the first time at her kamethi.

"And you, poor *m'metanei*—an uncomfortable moment. Did you follow what was said?"

"As far," said Aiela, "as *m'metanei* are wise."

Chimele laughed merrily and rose, a violet splendor in her robes. She put off the *ghiaka* and laid it aside. "The Orithain of *Chaganokh* will not soon forget this day: unhappy puppet. Doubtless *Tashavodh* thrust Tejef off upon him; so he was obliged to try, at least, although his chances were poor from the beginning."

Does she care nothing, Daniel thrust at his asuthi, *for the misery they have caused my people?*

Be still, Isande returned through Aiela. *You do not know Chimele.*

"You look troubled, Daniel."

"Where do my people fit in this?"

"They are not my concern."

She means it kindly, Isande protested against his outrage. *She means no harm to them.*

"What happened to them was your fault," Daniel said to Chimele. "And you owe us at least—"

Aiela saw it coming, caught his human asuthe by the arm to draw him back; but the *idoikkhe* pained him, a lancing hurt all the way to his side, and that arm was useless to him for the moment. He knew that Daniel felt it too, knew the human angered instead of restrained. He seized him with his other hand.

She has been in the presence of an enemy, Isande sent Daniel. *Her nerves are still at raw ends. Be still, be still, o for Aiela's sake, Daniel, be still.*

Daniel's anger flowed over them both, sorrowing at once. "I'm sorry," he told Chimele. "but you had no business to harm him for it."

Chimele gave a slight lift of the brows. "Indeed. But Aiela has a *m'melakhia* for you, *m'metane-toj,* and he chose. Consider that, and consider your asuthi the next time you presume upon my self-restraint. Aiela, I regret it."

The pain had vanished. Aiela bowed, for it was great courtesy that Chimele offered regret: iduve offended her, and received less. Chimele returned him a nod of her head, well pleased.

"Daniel," she said then, "do you know the world of Priamos?"

Hate was in his mind, fear; but so was fear for Aiela. He abandoned his pride. "Yes," he said, "I've been there several times."

"Excellent. You will be provided facilities and assistance. I want maps and names. Is their language yours?"

"It is the same." The impulse was overwhelming. "Why do you want these things? What are you about to do?"

Chimele ignored the question and turned on Aiela a direct and commanding look. "This is your problem," she said. "See to it."

* * *

They had come. Set on a grassy plain a hundred *lioi* from the river settlements, Tejef knew it, facing toward the east where the sun streamed into morning. *Chaganokh* had yielded and *Ashanome* had come.

It had been a long silence, unbearably long. Many times he had thought he would welcome any contact with his own kind, even to die. It was a loneliness no *m'metane* could understand, save one who had been *asuthithekkhe* and separated, a deep and terrible silence of the mind, a stillness where there were no brothers, no *nasithi,* nothing. No iduve could bear that easily, to be separated from *takkhenes,* the constant sense of brother-presence that never ceased, waking and sleeping, the pack-instinct that had been the driving force of his kind since the dawn of the race. From his birth he had it, seldom friendly is its messages, but there, a lodestar about which all life had its direction. It flowed through his consciousness like the blood through his veins, the unity of impulse through which he sensed every mood of his *nasithi,* their presence, their *m'melakhia,* his possession or lack of *arastiethe.*

Now *takkhenes* was back. He felt them, the *Ashanome*-pack, who had given him birth and decreed his death; and he knew that if they grew much closer they could sense him, weak in his own single *takkhenois* though he was. The fine hair at the nape of his neck bristled at that proximity; the life-instinct that had ebbed in him quickened into anger.

They were on the hunt, and he their game this time, he that had hunted with them. He could sort out two of the minds he knew best: Khasif, Ashakh, grim and deadly men. Chimele would not have descended with them to the surface of this wretched world: *Ashanome* would be circling in distant orbit, and Chimele would be scanning the filthy business in progress on its surface, directing the searchers. One day soon they would find him, and *vaikka* would be settled—their victory.

The logical faculty said that he might win something even now by surrendering, cringing at Chimele's feet like a *katasathe.* She would kick him aside and the *nasul* would close on him and maul him senseless, but they would not likely kill him. His life thereafter would be lived from that posture, a constant terror, being forever the recipient of everyone's temper and contempt.

It would gradually take the heart from him: the *takkhenes* would overwhelm all his instinct to fight back and he would exist until he was finally mauled to death by some *nas* in *katasakke,* or starved, or was cast out during *akkhres-nasuli* because the *takkhenes* of neither *nasul* recognized him as theirs. Such were the things that awaited the outcast, and a long shiver of rage ran up the muscles of his belly, for he had his bearings again. *Arastiethe* forbade any yielding. He would end under their hands, literally mauled to death if they could get him within their reach, but they would feel the damage he could do them. Ironically, Tejcf, who until now had lacked the will to be drawn into a confrontation with any of the wretched humans the amaut used for prey on this forsaken world, began to lay plans to work harm on *Ashanome* and to end his life with *chanokhia.*

His resources were few, a miserable and war-torn world where earth-hungry amaut plundered a dying human population, a human species that had gone mad and that now furnished mercenary troops to the brutish amaut for the final pillage of their own world. Such madness, he reflected, would have been understandable had it been a matter of *nasul*-loyalty among these humans, but it was not. They knew no loyalties, committed *arrhei-nasul* at the simple exchange of goods or silver, engaged in *katasakke* and then slaughtered the females, who were pathetic and ineffectual creatures. They gathered no young in this fashion, and indeed slaughtered what young they did find—comprehensible, at least, if there had been *nasithitak* in these human warbands. There were not, and the ultimate result seemed to be suicide for the entire species. Tejef had long since ceased to be amazed by the final madness of this furious people: perhaps this savagery was an instinct no longer positive for survival—it was one that the amaut had certainly turned to their own advantage. Now perhaps there was a way to turn it to the advantage of Tejef *sra*-Sogdrieni, a means to *vaikka* upon *Ashanome,* one that would deserve their respect when they killed him.

The night was warm. A slight breeze blew in through the protective grille of the window and rippled through the drapery behind the bed. The moonlight cast restless shadows of branches on the wall.

One of the dogs began to bark, joined by the others, and the child in the bed stirred, sat upright, eyes wide. She listened a moment, then turned on her knees so that she could lean against the headboard and the sill and look out into the dark. Now the dogs were off at the distance, perhaps chasing some night-wandering bounder through the fields. Their cries echoed among the rocks in which the house was set, secure behind its stone wall and steel gate, with the cliffs towering up on either side.

In Arle's estimation this house was an impenetrable fortress. It had not always needed to be so. The wall and the gate were new, and when she was nine the men had not gone with guns to work the fields, and there had been no guards on the heights. But the world had changed. She was ten now, and thought it settled that she would never again walk to the neighbors' house to play, or even go out the gates to the fields and the orchard without one of her brothers to attend her, rifle over his arm, checking with each of the sentry stations along the way. The family had not been to church in the valley in months, nor valley market, and no one mentioned school starting. This was the way the world had become. And they were fortunate—for there were rumors of burnings downland at the mouth of the Weiss, that very same sleepy river that rolled through their valley and made the crops grow, and made Upweiss the best and richest land on all Priamos.

Arle knew something of the outside, knew that they were from the Esliph, which was very far, and green and beautiful, but she was not sure in her mind whether that were real or not, or only one of the old stories her parents had told her, like faery princesses and heroes. She knew also that they were all once upon a time from a world called Earth, every human that breathed, but it was hard to imagine all the populations of all the worlds she knew of crowded onto one globe. This was too difficult a thought, and she was not sure which stories were about Earth and which were about the Esliph, or whether they were one and the same. She kept it stored up as one of those things she would understand when she was older, which was what her parents answered when her questions ran ahead of her understanding. She was content to let this be, although it seemed that there were many things of late which she was not old enough to know, while her parents talked in secret councils with her grown brothers and with the neighbors and the younger children were sent off to play with guns to guard them.

She was aware of terrible things happening not too far away. Sometimes she heard a thing the adults said and lay awake at night sick at her stomach and wondering if really they were all going to die before she had a chance to grow up and understand it all. But then she would imagine growing up, and that convinced her that the future was still there, all waiting to be experienced; and the grownups understood matters and still planned for next year, for planting crops, hoping for better rains from the mountains, hoping the winds would not come too late in the spring or the hail ruin the grain. These were familiar enemies, and they were forever. These awful gray people that were said to be burning towns and farms and shooting people—she was not sure that they were real. When she was little, her parents had not been able to persuade her not to climb the cliffs, so they had told her about a dog that had gone mad and lived up in those rocks waiting to kill children. It had stalked her nightmares for years and she would rather anything than go up into the dark crevices of those rocks. But now she was ten and knew sensibly that there was no dog, and that it had been all for the good purpose of keeping her from having a bad fall. *That* was the dog in the rocks, her own curiosity; but she was not sure if the downland monsters were not something similar, so that silly children would not ask unanswerable questions.

There had been smoke on the horizon two days ago. All the sentries had reported it, and the children had thronged the big dome rock in the throat of the pass to see it. But then her father had chased them all back into the yard and told them that the strangers would get them if they did not stay where they belonged. So Arle reasoned that it was like the dog, something for them to be afraid of while the grownups understood what it really was and knew how to deal with it. They would take care of matters, and the crops would go in come fall, and be harvested next spring, and life would go on quite normally.

She curled up again in her bed and pulled the sheet up to her chin. It made it feel like bed, and protection. Soon she shut her eyes and drifted back to sleep.

Something boomed, shook the very floor and the bottles on the dresser and lit the branches in red relief on the wall. Arle scrambled for the view at the window, too sleepy and too stunned to have cried out at that overwhelming noise. Men were running everywhere. The gate was down with fire beyond and dark shapes against it, and people ran up and down the hall outside her room. Her oldest brother came bursting in with a flashlight, exclaimed that she should get out of the window and seized her by the wrist, not even waiting for her to get her feet under her. He pulled her with him at a run, taking her, she knew, to the cellar, where the children had always been told to go in an emergency. She began to cry as they hit the outside stairs, for she did not want to go down into that dark place and wait.

Suddenly light broke about them, awful heat and noise, stone chips and powder showering down upon them. Arle sprawled, hurting her hands and ribs and knees upon the steps, crawling back from the source of that light even before her mind had awakened to the fact that something had exploded. Then she saw her brother's face, odd-tilted on the steps, his eyes with the glazed look of a dead animal's. His hand when she took it was loose. Light flashed. Stone showered down again, choking her with dust.

What she did then she only remembered later—tumbling off the side of the steps, landing in the soft earth of the flowerbed, running, lost among the dark shapes that hurtled this way and that.

She found herself crouching in the rubble at the gate, while dark bodies moved against the light a little beyond her. The yard was like that cellar, a horrible dead-end place where one could be trapped. She broke and ran away from the house, trying to go down the pass a little way to that forbidden path up the cliffs, to hide and wait above until she could come back and find her family.

It was dark among the rocks for a moment, the light of the fire cut off by the bending of the road; and then as she rounded the bend toward the narrowing of the cliffs a dark man-shape stood by the dome rock in the very narrowest part of the pass,

outlined against the moon and the downslope of the road toward
the valley fields. Arle saw him too late, tried to scramble aside
into the rocks, but the man seized her, drew her against him with
his arm, and silenced her with a hand that covered her mouth
and nose and threatened to break her neck as well.

He released her when her struggles grew weak, seized the
collar of her thin gown, and raised his other hand to hit her, but
she whimpered and flinched down as small as she could. Instead
he raised her back by both arms and shook her until her head
snapped back. His shadowed face stared into hers in the moonlight. She stood still and suffered him to cup her small face between his rough hands, to smooth her tangled hair, to use his
thumbs to wipe the tears from her cheeks.

"Help us," she said then, thinking this was one of the neigh-
bor men come to aid them. "Please come and help us."

His hands on her shoulders hurt her. He stood there for a moment, while she trembled on the verge of tears, and then he
gripped her arm in one cruel hand and began to walk down the
road away from the house, dragging her with him, making her
legs keep his long strides.

She stumbled on the rocks as they descended from the road to
the orchard and turned her ankle in the soft ground among the
apple and peach trees; and there were thorns and cutting stubble
on the slopes of the irrigation ditch. He strode across the water,
hauling her up the other side by one arm as a careless child
might handle a doll, and waited only an instant to let her gain
her feet before he walked on, dragging her at a near run, until at
last she did stumble and fell to her knees sobbing.

Then he drew her aside, into the shadow of the trees, set her
against the low limb of an aged apple tree, and looked at her,
still holding her by a firm grip on her arm. "Where were you
going?" he asked her.

She did not want to tell him. The scant light there was fil-
tering through the apple leaves showed the outline of boots,
loose trousers, leather harness, clothing such as no farmer
wore, and his lean, hard face was strange to her. But he shook
her and repeated the question, and her lips trembled and clear
sense left her.

"I was going to hide and come back."

"Is there any help you can get to?"

She jerked her head in the direction of the Berney farm, where Rachel Berney lived, and her brother Johann and the Sullivans, who had a daughter her age.

"You mean that house five kilometers west of here?" he asked. "Forget it. Is there anywhere else?"

"I don't know," she said. "I—could hide in the rocks."

He took her hand again, a dry, strong grip that frightened her, for he could crush the bones if he closed down harder. "And where would you go after? There's not going to be anything left back there."

"I want to go home."

"You can't. Think. Think of some place safe I could leave you."

"I don't know any."

"If I left you right here, could you walk down from the heights to the river? Could you walk that far?"

She looked at him in dismay. The river was visible from the heights, far, far down in the valley. When they went, it meant taking the truck and going a long distance down the road. She could not imagine how long it would take to walk it, and it was hot in the daytime—and there were men like him on the roads. She began to cry, not alone for that, for everything, and she cried so hard she was about to be sick. But he shook her roughly and slapped her face. The hurt was already so much inside that she hardly knew the pain, except that she was afraid of them and she was going to be sick at her stomach. Out of fear she swallowed down the tears and the sickness with them.

"You have to think of somewhere I can put you. Stop that sniffing and think."

"I want to go *home*," she cried, at which he looked at her strangely and his grip lessened on her arm. He smoothed her hair and touched her face.

"I know you do. I know. You can't."

"Let me go."

"They're dead back there, can't you understand that? If they catch either one of us now they'll skin us alive. I have to get rid of you."

"I don't know what to do. I don't know. I don't know."

Then she thought he would hit her. She screamed and

flinched back. But instead he put his arms about her, picked her up, hugged her head down into his shoulder, rocking her in his arms as if she had been an infant. "All right," he said. "I'll see what I can do."

Aiela took the corridor to the *paredre,* his mind boiling with frustration and smothered kalliran and human obscenities, and raged at Isande's gentle presence in his thoughts until she let him alone. For fifteen precious days he had monitored Daniel's every movement. The human language began to come more readily than the kalliran: human filth and human images poured constantly through his senses, blurring his own perception of what passed about him, cannibalizing his own life, his own separate thoughts.

Now, confronted by an iduve at the door of the *paredre,* he could scarcely gather enough fluency to explain his presence in any civilized language. The iduve looked at him sharply, for his behavior showed a mental disorder that was suspect, but Chimele had given standing orders and the man relented.

"Aiela?" Chimele arose from her desk across the room, her brows lifted in the iduve approximation of alarm. Aiela bowed very low. Courtesy demanded it, considering the news he bore.

"Daniel has encountered a difficulty," he said.

"Be precise." Chimele took a chair with a mate opposite and gestured him to sit.

"The Upweiss raid," Aiela began hoarsely: Chimele insisted upon the chronological essentials of a thing. He forced his mind into order, screened against the random impulses that fed from Daniel's mind and the anxious sympathy from Isande's. "It went as scheduled. Anderson's unit hit the Mar estate. Daniel hung back—"

"He was not to do so," Chimele said.

"I warned him; I warned him strongly. He knows Anderson's suspicions of him. But Daniel can't do the things these men do. His conscience—his *honor,*" he amended, trying to choose words that had clear meaning for Chimele—"is offended over the killings. He had to kill a man in the last raid."

Chimele made a dismissing move of her hand. "He was attacked."

"I could explain the human ethical—"

"Explain what is at hand."

"There was a child—a girl. It was a crisis. I tried to reason with him. He shut me out and took her away. He is still going, deserting Anderson—and us."

There were no curses in the iduve language. Possibly that contributed to their fierceness. Chimele said nothing.

"I'm trying to reason with him," Aiela said. "He's exhausted—drained. He hasn't slept in twenty hours. He lay awake last night, sick over the prospect of this raid. He's going on little sleep, no water, no food. He can't expect to find water as he's heading, not until the river. They can't make it."

"This is not a rational human response." That was a question. Chimele's voice had an utter calm, not a good sign in an iduve.

"It is a human response, but it is not rational."

Chimele hissed and rose, hands on her hips. "Is it not your duty to anticipate such responses and deal with them?"

"I don't blame him," he said. Then, from his heart: "I'm only afraid I might have done otherwise." And that thought so depressed him he felt tears rise. Chimele looked down on him in incredulity.

"*Au,* by what am I served? Explain. I am patient. Is this a predictable response?"

Aiela could have screamed aloud. The *paredre* faded. He shivered in the cold of a Priamid night, the glory of spiraling ribbons of stars overhead, the fragile sweet warmth of another being in his arms. Tears filled his eyes; his breath caught.

"Aiela," Chimele said. The iduve could not cry; they lacked the reflex. The remembrance of that made him ashamed in her sight.

"The reaction," he said, "is probably instinct. I—have grown so much into him I—cannot tell. I cannot judge what he does any longer. It seems right to me."

"Is it *dhis*-instinct, a response to this child?"

"Something like that," he said, grateful for her attempt at equation. Chimele considered that for a moment, her eyes more perplexed now than angry.

"It is difficult to rely on such unknown quantities. I offer my regret for what you must be feeling, though I am not sure I can comprehend it. Other humans—like Anderson—are immune to this emotion where the young are concerned. Why does Daniel succumb?"

"I don't live inside Anderson. I don't know what goes on in his twisted mind. I only know Daniel—this night—could not have done otherwise."

"Kindly explain to Daniel that we have approximately three days left, his time. That Priamos itself has scarcely that long to live, and that he and the child will be among a million beings perishing if we have to resort to massive attack on this world."

"I've tried. He knows these things, intellectually, but he shuts me out. He refuses to think of that."

"Then we have wasted fifteen valuable days."

"Is that all?"

There was hysteria in his voice; and it elicited from Chimele a curious look, the embarrassment of an observer who had no impulse to what he felt.

"You are exhausted," she judged "You can be sedated for the rest of the world's night. You can do nothing more with this person and I know how long you have worked without true rest."

"No." He assumed a taut control of his voice and slowed his breathing. "I know Daniel. Good sense will come back to him after he has run awhile. That area is swarming with trouble in all forms. He will need me."

"I honor your persistence. Stay in the *paredre*. If you are going to attempt to advise him I should prefer to know how you are faring. If you change your mind about the sedation, tell me; if we are to lose Daniel, your own knowledge of humans becomes twice valuable. I do not want to risk your health. I leave matters in your hands; rest, if you can."

"Thank you." He drew himself to his feet, bowed, and moved away.

"Aiela."

He looked back.

"When you have found an explanation for his behavior, give it to me. I shall be interested."

He bowed once more, struggling between loathing and love for the iduve, and decided for the moment on love. She did try.

She tried with her mind where her heart was inadequate, but she wanted to know.

In the shadows of the *paredre* a comfortable bowl chair, such as the iduve chose when they would relax, provided a retreat. He curled into its deep embrace and leaned his head back upon the edge, slipping again into the mental rhythms of Daniel's body, becoming human, feeling again what he felt.

In the small corner of his mind still himself, Aiela knew the answer. It had been likely from Daniel's first step onto the surface of Priamos.

Years and a world ago, when Aiela was a boy, the staff had brought into the lodge one of the hunting birds that nested in the cliffs of the mountains, wing-broken. He had nursed it, he had been proud of it, thought it his. But the first time it felt the winds of Ryi under its wings, it was gone.

7

Aiela was back. Daniel clamped down a silence against him, shifted the child's slight weight in his arms, and felt her arms tighten reflexively about his neck. Above them a star burned, a blaze of white brighter than any star that had ever shown in Priamid skies. When people saw it they thought *amaut* and shuddered at the presence, aware it was large, but yet having no concept what it was. They might never know. If it swung into tighter orbit it would be the final spectacle in Priamos' skies, that had of late seen so many comings and goings, the baleful red of amaut ships, the winking white of human craft deploying troops, mercenaries serving the amaut. When *Ashanome* came it would be one last great sunset over the world at once, the last option of the iduve in a petty quarrel that threatened the existence of his species, that counted one man or one minor civilization nothing against the games that occupied them.

You know better, Aiela sent him. Simultaneous with the words came rage, concern for them, fear of Chimele. Daniel seized wrathfully upon the latter, which Aiela vehemently denied.

Daniel. Think. You don't know where you're going or what you're going to do with that girl. All right. Defeat. Aiela recognized the loathing Daniel felt for what they had asked him to do. Human as he was, he had been able to cross the face of Priamos unremarked, one of the countless mercenaries that looted and killed in small bands at the amaut's bidding. He was a rough man, was Daniel: he could use that heavy-barreled primitive gun that hung from his belt. His slender frame could endure the marches, the tent-camps, the appallingly primitive conditions under which the human force operated. But he had no heart for this. He had been rackingly sick after the only killing he had done, and Anderson, the mercenary captain, had put him on the notice he would be made an example if he failed in any order. This threat was nothing. If Daniel could ignore the orders of Chimele of *Ashanome*, nothing the brutish Anderson could invent was enough; but Anderson fortunately had not realized that.

I can't help you, Aiela said. *That child cried for home, and you lost all your senses, every other bond. Now I suppose I'm the enemy.*

No, Daniel thought, irritated by Aiela's analysis. *You aren't.* And: *I wish you were*—for it was his humanity that was pained.

Listen to me, Daniel. Accept my advice and let me guide you out of this incredible situation.

The word choice might have been Chimele's. Daniel recognized it. *"Kill the girl." Why don't you just come out with the idea. "Kill her, one life for the many." Say it, Aiela. Isn't that what Chimele wants of me?* He hugged the sleeping child so tightly it wakened her, and she cried out in memory and fought.

"Hush," he told her. "Do you want to walk awhile?"

"I'll try," she said, and he chose a smooth place on the dirt road to set her down, she tugging in nervous modesty at the hem of her tattered gown. Her feet were cut with stubble and bruised with stones. She limped so it hurt to watch her, and held out her hands to balance on the edges of her feet. He swore and reached out to take her up again, but she resisted and looked at him, her elfin face pale in the moonlight.

"No, I can walk. It's just sore at first."

"We're going to cut west when we reach the other road. Maybe we'll find a refugee family—there's got to be somebody left."

"Are you going to leave those men and not go back?"

The question disturbed him. Aiela pressed him with an echo of the same, and Daniel screened. "They'll have my hide if they find me now. Maybe I'll head northwest and pick up with some other band." That for Aiela. *A night's delay, a day at the most. I can manage it. I'll think of something.* "Or maybe I'll go west too. I'll see you safe before I do anything."

A man alone can't make it across that country, Aiela insisted.

*Get rid of her, let her go. No! listen, don't shut me out. I'll help
you. Your terms. Give me information and I'll take your part
with Chimele.*

Daniel swore at him and closed down. Even suggesting harm
to the girl tore at Aiela's heart; but he was afraid. His people had
had awe of the iduve fed into them with their mothers' milk, and
he was not human; Daniel knew the kallia so well, and yet there
were still dark corners, reactions he could not predict, things
that had to do with being kallia and being human. Aiela's people
had no capacity to fight: it was not in the kalliran nature to produce a tyranny, not in a culture where there was no supreme ex-
ecutive, but a hierarchy of councils. One kallia simply lacked
the feeling of adequacy to be either tyrant or rebel. *Giyre* was
supposed to be mutual, and he had no idea how to react when
trust was betrayed. Kallia were easy prey for the iduve: they always yielded to greater authority. In the kalliran mind it just did
not occur that it could be morally wrong, or that the Order in
which they believed did not exist off Aus Qao.

Daniel. The quiet touch was back in his mind, offended, as
angry as Daniel had ever felt him. *The things you do not know
about kallia are considerable. You lack any sense about giyre
yourself, so I suppose it does not occur to you that I have it for
all beings with whom I deal—even for you. I am not human. I do
not lie to my friends, destroy what is useless, or break what is
whole. I can also accept defeat when I meet it. Abandon the
child there. I will get her to safety, I will be responsible, even if I
must come to Priamos myself. Just get out of the area. You've
already created enough trouble for yourself. Don't finish ruining
your cover.*

No, Daniel sent. *One look at that kalliran face of yours and
you would never catch her. Send your ship. But you'll do things
on my terms.*

There was no answer. Daniel looked up again at the star that
was *Ashanome*. A second brilliant light had appeared not far
from it; and a third, unmoving to the eye. They were simply
there, and they had not been.

Aiela, he flung out toward the first star.

But this time Aiela shut him out.

The *paredre* blazed with light. The farthest side of it, bare of furniture, was suddenly occupied by consoles and screens and panels rippling with color. In the midst of it stood Chimele with her *nas-katasakke* Rakhi, and they spoke urgently of the startling appearance of two of the *akitomei.* The image of them hung three-dimensional in the cube of darkness on the table, projection within projection, mirror into mirror.

Suddenly there was only Chimele and the darker reality of the *paredre.* Aiela met her quick glance uneasily, for kamethi were not admitted to control stations.

"Isande has been summoned," said Chimele. "Cast her the details of the situation here. Keep screening against Daniel. Are you strong enough to maintain that barrier?"

"Yes. Are we under attack?"

The thought seemed to surprise Chimele. "Attack? No. The *nasuli* are not prone to such inconsiderate action. This is *harathos,* the Observance. *Tashavodh* has come to see *vaikka* done, and *Mijanothe* is the neutral Observer, who will declare to all the *nasuli* that things were done rightly. This is expected, and unexpected. It might have been omitted. It would have pleased me if it had been."

In his mind, Isande had already started for the door of her apartment, pulled her tousled head through the sweater; the sweater was tugged to rights, her thin-soled boots pattering quickly down the corridor. He fired her what information he could, coherent, condensed, as he had learned to do.

And Daniel? she asked in return. *What has happened to him?*

Her question almost disrupted his screening. He clamped down against it, too incoherent to screen against Daniel and explain about him at once. Isande understood, and he was about to reply again when he was startled by a projection appearing not a pace from him.

Mejakh! He jerked back even as he flashed the warning to Isande. His dealings with the mother of Khasif and Tejef had been blessedly few, but she came into the *paredre* more frequently now that other duties had stripped Chimele of the aid of her *nasithi-katasakke*—for Chaikhe's pursuit of an iduve mate had rendered her *katasathe* and barred her from the *paredre,* Khasif and Ashakh were on Priamos, and poor Rakhi was on watch in the control room trying to manage all the duties of his missing *nasithi* to Chimele's demanding satisfaction. Mejakh accordingly asserted her rank as next closest, of an indirectly related *sra,* for Chimele had no other. Seeing that she had children now adult, she might be forty or more in age, but she had not the apologetic bearing of an aging female. She moved with the insolent grace of a much younger woman, for iduve lived long if they did not die by violence. She was slim and coldly handsome, commanding in her manner, although her attractiveness was spoiled by a rasping voice.

"Chimele," said Mejakh, "I heard."

Chimele might have acknowledged the offered support by some courtesy: iduve were normally full of compliments. All Mejakh received was a stare a presumptuous *nas kame* might have received, and that silence found ominous echo in the failure of Mejakh to lower her eyes. It was not an exchange an outsider would have noted; but Aiela had been long enough among iduve to feel the chill in the air.

"Chimele," Rakhi said by intercom, "projections incoming from *Tashavodh* and *Mijanothe.*"

"Nine and ten clear, Rakhi."

The projections took instant shape, edges blurred together, red background warring against violet. On the left stood a tall, wide-shouldered man, square-faced with frowning brows and a sullen mouth: *Kharxanen,* Isande read him through Aiela's eyes, hate flooding with the name, memories of dead Reha, of Tejef, of Mejakh's dishonor; he was Sogdrieni's full brother, Tejef's presumed uncle. The other visitor was a woman seated in a wooden chair, an iduve so old her hair had silvered and her indigo skin had turned fair—a little woman whose high cheekbones, strong nose, and large, brilliant eyes gave her a look of ferocity and immense dignity. She was robed in black; a chromium staff lay across her lap. Somehow it did not seem incongruous that Chimele paid her deference in this her own ship.

"Thiane," Isande voiced him in a tone of awe. "O be careful not to be noticed, Aiela. This is the president of the Orithanhe."

"Hail *Ashanome,*" said Thiane in a soft voice. "Forgive an old woman her suddenness, but I have too few years left to waste long moments in hailings and well-wishing. There is no *vaikka* between us."

"No," said Chimele, "no, there is not. Thiane, be welcome. And for Thiane's sake, welcome Kharxanen."

"Hail *Ashanome,*" the big man said, bowing stiffly, "Honor to the Orithanhe, whose decrees are to be obeyed. And hail Mejakh, once of *Tashavodh,* less honored."

Mejakh hissed delicately and Kharxanen smiled, directing himself back to Chimele.

"The infant the *sra* of Mejakh prospers," he said. "'The honor of us both has benefited by our agreement. I give you farewell, *Ashanome:* the call was courtesy. Now you know that I am here."

"Hail *Tashavodh,*" Chimele said flatly, while Mejakh also flicked out, vanished with a shriek of rage, leaving Chimele, and Thiane, and Aiela, who stood in the shadows.

"*Au,*" said Thiane, evidently distressed by this display, and Chimele bowed very low.

"I am ashamed," said Chimele.

"So am I," said Thiane.

"You are of course most welcome. We are greatly honored that you have made the *harathos* in person."

"Chimele, Chimele—you and Kharxanen between you can bring three-quarters of the iduve species face to face in anger, and does that not merit my concern?"

"Eldest of us all, I am overwhelmed by the knowledge of our responsibility."

"It would be an incalculable disaster. Should something go amiss here, I could bear the dishonor of it for all time."

"Thiane," said Chimele, "can you believe I would violate the terms? If I had wished *vaikka* with *Tashavodh* to lead to catastrophe, would I have convoked the Orithanhe in the first place?"

"I see only this: that with less than three days remaining, I find you delaying further, I find you with this person Tejef within scan and untouched, and I suspect the presence of *Ashanome* personnel onworld. Am I incorrect, Chimele *sra*-Chaxal?"

"You are quite correct, Thiane."

"Indeed." Her brows drew down fiercely and her old voice shook with the words. "Simple *vaikka* will not do, then; and if you do miscalculate, Chimele, what then?"

"I shall take *vaikka* all the same," she answered, her face taut with restraint. "Even to the destruction of Priamos. The risk I run is to mine alone, and to do so is my choice, Thiane."

"*Au,* you are rash, Chimele. To destroy this world would have sufficed, although it is a faceless *vaikka.* You have committed yourself too far this time. You will lose everything."

"That is mine to judge."

"It is," Thiane conceded, "until it comes to this point: that there be a day remaining, and you have not yet acted upon your necessities. Then I will blame you, that with *Tashavodh* standing by in *harathos,* you would seem deliberately to provoke them to the last, threatening the deadline. There will be no infringement upon that, Chimele, not even in appearance. Any and all of your interference on Priamos will have ceased well ahead of that last instant, so that *Tashavodh* will know that things were rightly done. I have responsibility to the Orithanhe, to see that this ends without further offense; and should offense occur, with great regret, Chimele, with great regret, I should have to declare that you had violated the decrees of the Orithanhe that forbade you *vaikka* upon *Tashavodh* itself. *Ashanome* would be compelled to surrender its Orithain into exile or be cast from the kindred into outlawry. You are without issue, Chimele. I need not tell you that if *Ashanome* loses you, a dynasty more than twelve thousand years old ceases; that *Ashanome* from being first among the kindred becomes nothing. Is *vaikka* upon this man Tejef of such importance to you, that you risk so much?"

"This matter has had *Ashanome* in turmoil from before I left the *dhis,* o Thiane; and if my methods hazard much, bear in mind that our primacy has been challenged. Does not great gain justify such risk?"

Thiane lowered her eyes and inclined her head respectfully. "Hail *Ashanome.* May your *dhis* increase with offspring of your spirit, and may your *sra* continue in honor. You have my admiration, Chimele. I hope that it may be so at our next meeting."

"Honor to *Mijanothe.* May your *dhis* increase forever."

The projection vanished, and Chimele surrounded herself with the control room a brief instant, eyes flashing though her face was calm.

"Rakhi. Summon Ashakh up to *Ashanome* and have him report to me the instant he arrives."

Rakhi was still in the midst of his acknowledgment when Chimele cut him out and stood once more in the *paredre*. Isande, who had waited outside rather than break in upon Thiane, was timidly venturing into the room, and Chimele's sweeping glance included both the kamethi.

"Take over the desk to the rear of the *paredre*. Review the status and positions of every amaut and mercenary unit on Priamos relative to Tejef's estimated location. Daniel must be reassigned."

Had it been any other iduve, even Ashakh, that so ordered him, Aiela would have cried out a reminder that he had been almost a night and a day without sleep, that he could not possibly do anything requiring any wit at all; but it was Chimele and it was for Daniel's sake, and Aiela bowed respectfully and went off to do as he was told.

Isande touched his mind, sympathizing. "I can do most of it," she offered. "Only you sit by me and help a little."

He sat down at the desk and leaned his head against his hands. He thought again of Daniel, the anger, the hate of the being for him over that child. He could not persuade them apart; he had tried, and probably Daniel would not forgive him. Reason insisted, reason insisted: Daniel's company itself was supremely dangerous to the child. They were each safer apart. Priamos was safer for it, he and the child hopeless of survival otherwise; leaving her was a risk, but it was a productive one. It was the reasonable, the orderly thing to do; and the human called him murderer, and shut him out, mind locked obstinately into some human logic that sealed him out and hated. His senses blurred. He shivered in a cool wind, realized the slip too late.

Aiela. Isande's presence drew at him from the other side, worried. He struggled back toward it, felt the physical touch of her hand on his shoulder. The warmth of the *paredre* closed about him again. *Too long in contact,* she sent him. *Aiela, Aiela, think of here. Let go of him, let go.*

"I am all right," he insisted, pushing aside her fear. But she continued to look at him concernedly for a little time more before she accepted his word for it. Then she reached for the computer contact.

The *paredre* door shot open, startling them both, and Mejakh's angry presence stopped Isande's hand in mid-move. The woman was brusque and rude and utterly tangible. Almost Isande called out to Chimele a frightened appeal, but Chimele looked up from her own desk a distance away and fixed Mejakh with a frown.

"You were not called," Chimele said.

Mejakh swept a wide gesture toward Aiela and Isande. "Get them out. I have a thing to say to you, Chimele-Orithain, and it is not for the ears of *m'metanei.*"

"They are aiding me," said Chimele, bending her head to resume her writing. "You are not. You may leave, Mejakh."

"You are offended because I quit the meeting. But you had no answer when Kharxanen baited me. You enjoyed it."

"Your incredible behavior left me little choice." Chimele looked up in extreme displeasure as Mejakh in her argument came to the front of the desk. Chimele laid aside her pen and came up from her chair with a slow, smooth motion. "You are not noticed, Mejakh. Your presence is ignored, your words forgotten. Go."

"*Ashanome* has no honor when it will not defend its own."

Chimele's head went back and her face was cold. "You are not of my *sra,* Mejakh. Once you had honor and Chaxal was compelled to notice you, but in his wisdom he did not take you for *kataberihe.* You are a troublemaker, Mejakh. You threw away your honor when you let yourself be taken into *Tashavodh* by Tejef. There was the beginning of our present troubles; and what it has cost us to recover you to the *nasul* was hardly worth it, o Mejakh, trouble-bringer."

"You would not say so if Khasif were here to hear it."

"For Khasif's sake I have tolerated you. I am done."

Mejakh struggled for breath. Could iduve have wept she might have done so. Instead she struck the desk top with a crash like an explosion. "Bring them all up! Bring up Khasif, yes, and this human *nas kame,* all of them! Wipe clean the surface of this world and be done! It is clear, Orithain, that you have more *m'melakhia* than *sorithias.* It is your own *vaikka* you pursue, a *vaikka* for the insult he did you personally, not for the honor of *Ashanome*."

Chimele came around the side of the desk and Isande's thoughts went white with fear: *Rakhi, get Rakhi in here,* she flashed to Aiela, and reached for the desk intercom; Aiela launched himself toward the two iduve.

His knees went. Unbelievable pain shot up his arm to his chest and he was on his face on the floor, blood in his mouth, hearing Isande's sobs only a few feet away. The pain was a dull throb now, but he could not reach Isande. His limbs could not function; he could not summon the strength to move.

After a dark moment Chimele bent beside him and lifted his head, urging him to move. "Up," she said. "Up, kameth."

He made the effort, hauled himself up by the side of a chair and levered himself into it, searching desperately with his thoughts for Isande. Her contact was active, faint, stunned, but she was all right. He looked about when his vision had cleared and saw her sitting in a chair, head in her hands, and Rakhi standing behind her.

"Both of them seem all right," said Rakhi. "What instructions about Mejakh?"

"She is forbidden the *paredre*," Chimele said, and looked toward her kamethi. "Mejakh willed your death, but I overrode the impulse. It is a sadness; she had *arastiethe* once, but her loss of it at Tejef's hands has disturbed her reason and her sense of *chanokhia*."

"She has had misfortune with her young," said Rakhi. "Against one she seeks *vaikka,* and for his sake she lost her honor. Her third was taken from her by the Orithanhe. Only in Khasif has she honorable *sra,* and he is absent from her. Could it be, Chimele, that she is growing *dhisais?*"

"Make it clear to the *dhis*-guardians that she must not have access there. You are right. She may be conceiving an impulse in that direction, and with no child in the *dhis,* there is no predicting what she may do. Her temper is out of all normal bounds. She has been disturbed ever since the Orithanhe returned her to us without her child, and this long waiting with Priamos in view—*au,* it could happen. Isande, Aiela, I must consider that you are both in mortal danger. Your loss would disturb my plans; that would occur to her, and kamethi have no defense against her."

"If we were armed—" Aiela began.

"*Au,*" Chimele exclaimed, "no, *m'metane,* your attitude is quite understandable, but you hardly appreciate your limitations. You almost died a moment ago, have you not realized that? The *idoikkhei* can kill. *Chanokhia* insists kamethi are exempt from such extreme *vaikka,* but Mejakh's sense of *chanokhia* seems regrettably lacking."

"But a *dhisais,*" Aiela objected, "can be years recovering."

"Yes, and you see the difficulty your attempt to interfere has created. Well, we will untangle the matter somehow, and, I hope, without further *vaikka.*"

"Chimele," said Rakhi, "the kameth has a valid point. Mejakh has proved an embarrassment many times in the matter of Tejef. Barring her from the *paredre* may not prove sufficient restraint."

"Nevertheless," said Chimele, "my decision stands."

"The Orithain cannot make mistakes."

"But even so," Chimele observed, "I prefer to proceed toward infallibility at my own unhurried pace, Rakhi. Have you heard from Ashakh yet?"

"He acknowledged. He has left Priamos by now, and he will be here with all possible speed."

"Good. Go back to your station. Aiela, Isande, if we are to salvage Daniel, you must find him a suitable unit and dispose of that child by some means. I trust you are still keeping your actions shielded from him. His mind is already burdened with too much knowledge. And when I do give you leave to contact him, you may tell him that I am ill pleased."

"I have already made that clear to him."

"She is not his," Chimele objected, still worrying at that thought.

"She attached herself to him for protection. She became his."

"There is no *nasith-tak,* no female, no *katasathe,* no *dhisais.* Is it reasonable that a male would do this, alone?"

"I am sure it is. An iduve would not?"

That was a presumptuous question. Isande reproved his asking, but Chimele lowered her eyes to show decent shame and then looked up at him.

"A female would be moved to do what he has done as if she were *katasathe* and near her time. A male could not, not without the presence of a female with whom he had recently mated. But is not this child-female close to adulthood? Perhaps it is the impulse to *katasakke* that has taken him."

"No," said Aiela, "no, when he thinks of her, it is as a child. That—unworthy thought did cross his mind; he drove it away. He was deeply ashamed."

He wished he had not said that private thing to Chimele. Had he not been so tired he would have withheld it. But it had given her much to ponder. Bewilderment sat in her eyes.

"She is *chanokhia* to him," Aiela said further. "To him she is the whole human race. You and I would not think so, but to him she is infinitely beautiful."

And he rejoined Isande at the desk, where with trembling hands she began to ply the keyboard again and to call forth the geography of Priamos on the viewer, marking it with the sites of occupied areas, receiving reports from the command center, updating the map. There were red zones for amaut occupation, green for human, and the white pinpricks that were iduve: one at Weissmouth in a red zone, that was Khasif; and one in the continental highlands a hundred *lioi* from Daniel, which was Tejef at best reckoning.

When Aiela chanced at last to notice Chimele again she was standing by her desk in the front of the *paredre,* which had expanded to a dizzying perspective of *Ashanome*'s hangar deck, talking urgently with Ashakh.

It was fast coming up dawn in the Weiss valley. The divergent rhythms of ship and planetary daylight systems were not least among the things that had kept Aiela's mind off-balance for fifteen days. He thought surely that Daniel would have been compelled by exhaustion to lie down and sleep. He could not possibly have the strength to go much further. But even wondering about Daniel could let information through the screening. Aiela turned his mind away toward the task at hand, sealing against any further contact.

*　　*　　*

The light was beginning to rise, chasing Priamos' belt of stars from the sky, and by now Daniel's steps wandered. Oftentimes he would stop and stare down the long still-descending road, dazed. Aiela's thoughts were silent in him. He had felt one terrible pain, and then a long silence, so that he had forgotten the importance of his rebellion against Aiela and hurled anxious inquiry at him, whether he were well, what had happened. The silence continued, only an occasional communication of desperation seeping through. It was Chimele's doing, then, *vaikka* against Aiela, thoroughly iduve, but against him, against all Priamos, her retaliation would not be so slight.

In cold daylight Daniel knew what he had done, that a world might die because he had not had the stomach to commit one more murder; but he refused steadfastly to think that far ahead, or to believe that even Chimele could carry out a threat so brutally—that he and the little girl would become only two among a million corpses to litter the surface of a dead world.

His ankle turned. He caught himself and the child's thin arms tightened about his neck. "Please," she said. "Let me try to walk again."

His legs and shoulders and back were almost numb, and the absence of her weight was inexpressible relief. Now that the light had come she looked pitifully naked in her thin yellow gown, very small, very dislocated, walking this wilderness all dressed for bed, as if she were the victim of a nightmare that had failed to go away with the dawn. At times she looked as if she feared him most of all, and he could not blame her for that. That same dawn showed her a disreputable man, face stubbled with beard, a man who carried an ugly black gun and an assassin's gear that must be strange indeed to the eyes of the country child. If her parents had ever warned her of rough men, or men in general—was she old enough to understand such things?—he conformed to every description of what to avoid. He wished that he could assure her he was not to be feared, but he thought that he would stumble hopelessly over any assurances that he might try to give her, and perhaps might frighten her the more.

"What's your name?" she asked him for the first time.

"Daniel Fitzhugh," he said. "I come from Konig."

That was close enough she would have heard of it, and the

mention of familiar places seemed to reassure her. "My name is Arle Mar," she said, and added tremulously: "That was my mother and father's farm."

"How old are you?" He wanted to guide the questioning away from recent memory. "Twelve?"

"Ten." Her nether lip quivered. "I don't want to go this way. Please take me back home."

"You know better than that."

"They might have gotten away." He thought she must have treasured that hope a long time before she brought it out into the daylight. "Maybe they hid like I did and they'll be looking for me to come back."

"No chance. I'm telling you—no."

She wiped back the tears. "Have you got an idea where we should go? We ought to call the Patrol, find a radio at some house—"

"There's no more law on Priamos—no soldiers, no police, nothing. We're all there is—men like me."

She looked as if she were about to be sick, as if finally all of it had caught up with her. Her face was white and she stood still in the middle of the road looking as if she might faint.

"I'll carry you," he offered, about to do so.

"*No!*" If her size had been equal to her anger she would have been fearsome. As it was she simply plumped down in the middle of the road and rested her elbows on her knees and her face in her hands. He did not press her further. He sat down cross-legged not far away and rested, fingers laced on the back of his neck, waiting, allowing her the dignity of gathering her courage again. He wanted to touch her, to hug her and let her cry and make her feel protected. He could not make the move. A human could touch, he thought; but he was no longer wholly human. Perhaps she could feel the strangeness in him; if that were so, he did not want to learn it.

Finally she wiped her eyes a last time, arose stiffly, and delicately lifted the hem of her tattered nightgown to examine her skinned knees.

"It looks sore," he offered. He gathered himself to his feet.

"It's all right." She let fall the hem and gave the choked end of a sob, wiping at her eyes as she surveyed the valley that lay before them in the sun, the gently winding Weiss, the black and burned fields. "All this used to be green," she said.

"Yes," he said, accepting the implied blame.

She looked up at him, squinting against the sun. "Why?" she asked with terrible simplicity. "Why did you need to do that?"

He shrugged. It was beyond his capacity to explain. The truth led worse places than a lie. Instead he offered her his hand. "Come on. We've got a long way to walk."

She ignored his hand and walked ahead of him. The road was soft and sandy with a grassy center, and she kept to the sand; but the sun heated the ground, and by the time they had descended to the Weiss plain the child was walking on the edges of her feet and wincing.

"Come on," he said, picking her up willing or not with a sweep of his arm behind her knees. "Maybe I—"

He stopped, hearing a sound very far away, a droning totally unlike the occasional hum of the insects. Arle heard it too and followed his gaze, scanning the blue-white sky for some sign of an aircraft. It passed, a high gleam of light, then circled at the end of the vast plain and came back.

"All right," he said, keeping his voice casual. *Aiela, Aiela, please hear me.* "That's trouble. If they land, Arle, I want you to dive for the high weeds and get down in that ditch." *Aiela! give me some help!*

"Who are they?" Arle asked.

"Probably friends of mine. Amaut, maybe. Remember, I worked for the other side. I may be picked up as a deserter. You may see some things you won't like." *O heaven, Aiela, Aiela, listen to me!* "I can lie my way out of my own troubles. You, I can't explain. They'll skin me alive if they see you, so do me a favor: take care of your own self, whatever you see happen, and stay absolutely still. You can't do a thing but make matters worse for me, and they have sensors that can find you in a minute if they choose to use them. Once they suspect I'm not alone, you haven't got a chance to hide from them. You understand me? Stay flat to the ground."

It was coming lower. Engines beating, it settled, a great silver elongated disc that was of no human make. A jet noise started as they whined to a landing athwart the road, and the sand kicked

up in a blinding cloud. Under its cover Daniel set Arle down and
trusted her to run, turned his face away and flung up his arms to
shield his eyes from the sand until the engines had died away to
a lazy throb. The ship shone blinding bright in the sun. A darkness broke its surface, a hatch opened and a ramp touched the
ground.

Aiela! Daniel screamed inwardly; and this time there was an
answer, a quick probe, an apology.

Amaut, Daniel answered, and cast him the whole picture in an
eyeblink, the ship, the amaut on the ramp, the humans descending after. *Parker: Anderson's second in command.* Daniel cast in
bursts and snatches, abjectly pleading with his asuthe, forgive
his insubordination, tell Chimele, promise her anything, do
something.

Aiela was doing that; Daniel realized it, was subconsciously
aware of the kallia's fright and Chimele's rage. It cut away at his
courage. He sweated, his hand impelled toward the gun at his
hip, his brain telling it no.

Parker stepped off the end of the ramp, joined by two more of
the ugly, waddling amaut, and by another mercenary, Quinn.

"Far afield, aren't you?" Parker asked of him. It was not
friendliness.

"I got separated last night, didn't have any supplies. I decided
to hike back riverward, maybe pick up with some other unit. I
didn't think I rated that much excitement from the captain." It
was the best and only lie he could think of under the circumstances. Parker did not believe any of it, and spat expressively
into the dust at his feet.

"Search the area," the amaut said to his fellows. "We had a
double reading. There's another one."

Daniel went for his pistol. *No!* Aiela ordered, throwing him
off-time, making the movement clumsy.

The amaut fired first. The shot took his left leg from under
him and pitched him onto his face in the sand. Arle's thin
scream sounded in his ears—the wrist of his right hand was
ground under a booted heel and he lost his gun, had it torn from
his fingers. Aiela, driven back by the pain, was trying to hold
onto him, babbling nonsense. Daniel could only see sideways—

Arle, struggling in the grip of the other human, kicking and cry-ing. He was hurting her.

Daniel lurched for his feet, screamed hoarsely as a streak of fire hit him in the other leg. When he collapsed writhing on the sand Parker set his foot on his wrist and took deliberate aim at his right arm. The shot hit. Aiela left him, every hope of help left him.

Methodically, as if it were some absorbing problem, Parker took aim for the other arm. The amaut stood by in a group, cu-riosity on their broad faces. Arle's shrill scream made Parker's hand jerk.

"No!" Daniel cried to the amaut, and he had spoken the kalli-ran word, broken cover. The shot hit.

But the amaut's interest was pricked. He pulled Parker's arm down; and no loyalty to the ruthless iduve was worth preserving cover all the way to a miserable death. Daniel gathered his breath and poured forth a stream of oaths, native and kalliran, until he saw the mottled face darken in anger. Then he looked the amaut straight in his froggish eyes, conscious of the fear and anger at war there.

"I am in the service of the iduve," he said, and repeated it in the iduve language should the amaut have any doubt of it. "You lay another hand on me or her and there will be cinders where your ship was, and you know it, you gray horror."

"*Hhhunghh.*" It was a grunt no human throat could have made. And then he spoke to Parker and Quinn in human lan-guage. "No. We take thioo thioo." He indicated first Daniel and then Arle. "You, you, walk, report Anderson. Go. Goodbye."

He was turning the two mercenaries out to walk to their camp. Daniel felt a satisfaction for that which warmed even through the pain: *Vaikka?* he thought, wondering if it were human to be pleased at that. A hazy bit of yellow hovered near him, and he felt Arle's small dusty hand on his cheek. The re-membrance of her among the amaut brought a fresh effort from him. He tried to think.

Daniel. Aiela's voice was back, cold, efficient, comforting. *Convince them to take you to Weissmouth. Admit you serve the iduve there; that's all you can do now.* Chimele was furious.

That leaked through, frightening in its implications. The screen went up again.

"That ship overhead," Daniel began, eyeing the amaut, drunk with pain, "there's no place on this world you can hide from that. They have their eye on you this instant."

The other amaut looked up as if they expected to see destruction raining down on them any second; but the captain rolled his thin lips inward, the amaut method of moistening them, like a human licking his lips.

"We are small folk," he said, mouth popping on all the explosive consonants, but he spoke the kalliran language with a fair fluency. "One iduve-lord we know. One only we serve. There is safety for us only in being consistent."

"Listen, you—listen! They'll destroy this world under you. Get me to the port at Weissmouth. That's your chance to live."

"No. And I have finished talking. See to him," he instructed his subordinates as he began to walk toward the ramp, speaking now in the harsh amaut language. "He must live until the lord in the high plains can question him. The female too."

"He had no choice," said Aiela.

Chimele kept her back turned, her arms folded before her. The *idoikkhe* tingled spasmodically. When she faced him again the tingling had stopped and her whiteless eyes stared at him with some degree of calm. Aiela hurt; even now he hurt, muscles of his limbs sensitive with remembered pain, stomach heaving with shock. Curiously the only thing clear in his mind was that he must not be sick: Chimele would be outraged. He had to sit down. He did so uninvited.

"Is he still unconscious?"

Chimele's breathing was rapid again, her lip trembling, not the nether lip as a kalliran reaction would have it: *Attack!* his subconscious read it; but this was Chimele, and she was civilized and to the limit of her capacity she cared for her kamethi. He did not let himself flinch.

"We have a problem," she said by way of understatement, and hissed softly and sank into the chair behind her desk. "Is the pain leaving?"

"Yes." *Isande—Isande!*

His asuthe stood behind him, took his hand, seized upon his mind as well, comforting, interfering between memory and reality. *Be still,* she told him, *be still. I will not let go.*

"Could you not have prevented him talking?" Chimele asked.

"He was beyond reason," Aiela insisted. "He only reacted. He thought he was lost to us."

"And duty. Where was that?"

"He thought of the child, that she would be alone with them. And he believed you would intervene for him if only he could survive long enough."

"The *m'metane* has an extraordinary confidence in his own value."

"It was not a conscious choice."

"Explain."

"Among his kind, life is valued above everything. I know, I know your objections, but grant me for a moment that this is so. It was a confidence so deep he didn't think it, that if he served beings of *arastiethe,* they would consider saving his life and the child's of more value than taking that of Tejef."

"He is demented," Chimele said.

Careful, Isande whispered into his mind. *Soft, be careful.*

"You gave me a human asuthe," Aiela persisted, "and told me to learn his mind. I'm kallia. I believe *kastien* is more important than life—but Daniel served you to the limit of his moral endurance."

"Then he is of no further use," said Chimele. "I shall have to take steps of my own."

His heart lurched. "You'll kill him."

Chimele sat back, lifted her brows at this protest from her kameth, but her hand paused at the console. "Do you care to stay *asuthithekkhe* with him while he is questioned by Tejef? Do not be distressed. It will be sudden; but those who harmed him and interfered with *Ashanome* will wish they had been stillborn."

"If you can intervene to kill him, you can intervene to save him."

"To what purpose?"

Aiela swallowed hard, screened against Isande's interference. He sweated; the *idoikkhe* had taught its lesson. "It is not *chanokhia* to destroy him, any more than it was to use him as you did."

The pain did not come. Chimele stared into the trembling heart of him. "Are you saying that I have erred?"

"Yes."

"To correctly assess his abilities was your burden. To assign him was mine. His misuse has no relevance to the fact that his destruction is proper now. Your misguided *giyre* will cost him needless pain and lessen the *arastiethe* of *Ashanome*. If he comes living into the hands of Tejef he may well ask you why you did not let him die; and every moment we delay, intervention becomes that much more difficult."

"He is kameth. He has that protection. It would not be honorable for Tejef to harm him."

"Tejef is *arrhei-nasuli,* an outcast. It would not be wise to assume he will be observant of *nasul-chanokhia*. He is not so bound, nor am I with him. He may well choose to harm him. We are wasting time."

"Then contact that amaut aircraft and demand Daniel and the child."

"To what purpose?"

The question disarmed him. He snatched at some logic the iduve might recognize. "He is not useless."

"How not? Secrecy is impossible now. Tejef will be alerted to the fact that I have a human nas kame; besides, the amaut in the aircraft would probably refuse my order. Tejef is their lord; they said so quite plainly, and amaut are nothing if not consistent. To demand and to be refused would mean that we had suffered *vaikka,* and I would still have to destroy a kameth of mine, having gained nothing. To risk this to save what I am bound to lose seems a pointless exercise; the odds are too high. I am not sure what you expect of me."

"Bring him back to *Ashanome*. Surely you have the power to do it."

"There is no longer time to consider that alternative. Shall I commit more personnel at Tejef s boundaries? The risk involved is not reasonable."

"No!" Aiela cried as she started to turn from him. He rose from his chair and leaned upon her desk, and Chimele looked up at him with that bland patience swiftly evaporating.

"What are you going to do with Priamos when you've destroyed him?" Aiela asked. "With three days left, what are you going to do? Blast it to cinders?"

"Contrary to myth, such actions are not pleasurable to us. I perceive you have suffered extreme stress in my service and I have extended you a great deal of patience, Aiela; I also realize you are trying to give me the benefit of our knowledge. But there will be a limit to my patience. Does your experience suggest a solution?"

"Call on Tejef to surrender."

Chimele gave a startled laugh. "Perhaps I shall. He would be outraged. But there is no time for a *m'metane's* humor. Give me something workable. Quickly."

"Let me keep working with Daniel. You wanted him within reach of Tejef. Now he is, and whatever else, Tejef has no hold over him with the *idoikkhe*."

"You *m'metanei* are fragile people. I know that you have *giyre* to your asuthe, but to whose advantage is this? Surely not to his."

"Give me something to bargain with. Daniel will fight if he has something to fight for. Let me assure him you'll get the amaut off Priamos and give it back to his people. That's what he wants of you."

Chimele leaned back once more and hissed softly. "Am I at disadvantage, to need to bargain with this insolent creature?"

"He is human. Deal with him as he understands. Is that not reasonable? *Giyre* is nothing to him; he doesn't understand *urasilethe*. Only one thing makes a difference to him: convince him you care what—"

A probing touch found his consciousness and his stomach turned over at foreknowledge of the pain. He tried to screen against it, but his sympathy made him vulnerable.

"Daniel is conscious." Isande spoke, for at the moment he had not yet measured the extent of the pain and his mind was busy with that. "He is hearing the amaut talk. The child Arle is beside him. He is concerned for her."

"Dispense with his concern for her. Tell him you want a report."

Aiela tried. Tears welled in his eyes, an excess of misery and weariness; the pain of the wounds blurred his senses. Daniel was half-conscious, sending nonsense, babble mixed with vague impressions of his surroundings. He was back on the amaut freighter. There was wire all about. *Aiela, Aiela, Aiela,* the single thread of consciousness ran, begging help.

I'm here, he sent furiously. *So is Chimele. Report.*

" 'I,' " Aiela heard and said aloud for Chimele, " 'I'm afraid I have—penetrated Tejef's defenses—in a somewhat different way than she had planned. We're coming down, I think. Stay with me—please, stay with me, if you can stand it. I'll send you what I—what I can learn.' "

"And he will tell Tejef what Tejef asks, and promise him anything. A creature that so values his own life is dangerous." Chimele laced her fingers and stared at the backs of them as if she had forgotten the kamethi or dismissed the problem for another. Then she looked up. "*Vaikka.* Tejef has won a small victory. I have regarded your arguments. Now I cannot intervene without using *Ashanome*'s heavy armament to pierce his defenses—a quick death to Tejef, ruin to Priamos, and damage to my honor. This is a bitterness to me."

"Daniel still has resources left," Aiela insisted. "I can advise him."

"You are not being reasonable. You are fatigued: your limbs shake, your voice is not natural. Your judgment is becoming highly suspect. I have indeed erred to listen to you." Chimele gathered the now-useless position report together and put it aside, pushed a button on the desk console, and frowned. "Ashakh: come to the *paredre* at once. Rakhi: contact Ghiavre is the lab and have him prepare to receive two kamethi for enforced rest."

Rakhi acknowledged instantly, to Aiela's intense dismay. He leaned upon the desk, holding himself up. "No," he said, "no, I am not going to accept this."

Chimele pressed her lips together. "If you were rational, you would recognize that you are exceeding your limit in several regards. Since you are not—"

"Send me down to Priamos, if you're afraid I'll leak information to Daniel. Set me out down there. I'll take my chances with the deadline."

Chimele considered, looked him up and down, estimating.

"Break contact with Daniel," she said. "Shut him out completely."

He did so. The effort it needed was a great one. Daniel screamed into the back of his mind, his distrust of Chimele finding echo in Aiela's own thoughts.

"Very well, you may have your chance," said Chimele. "But you will sleep first, and you will be transported to Priamos under sedation—both of you. Isande is likewise a risk now."

He opened his mouth again to protest: but Isande's strong will otherwise silenced him. She was afraid, but she was willing to do this for him. *No harm will come to us,* she insisted. *Chimele will not permit it. Kallia can hardly operate in secrecy on a human world, so we shall go under* Ashanome's *protection. Besides, you have already pressed her to the limit of her patience.*

He silently acknowledged the force of that argument, and to Chimele he bowed in respect. "Thank you," he said, meaning it.

Chimele waved a hand in dismissal. "I know this kalliran insanity of joy in being disadvantaged. But it would be improper to let you assume I do this solely to give you pleasure. Do not begin to act rashly or carelessly, as if I were freeing you of bond to *Ashanome* or responsibility to me. Be circumspect. Maintain our honor."

"Will we receive orders from you?"

"No." Again her violet nail touched the button, this time forcefully, "Ashakh! Wherever you are, acknowledge and report to the *paredre* at once." She was becoming annoyed; and for Ashakh to be dilatory in a response was not usual.

The door from the corridor opened and Ashakh joined them; he closed the door manually, and looked to have been running.

"There was a problem," he said, when Chimele's expression commanded an explanation. "Mejakh is in an argumentative mood."

"Indeed."

"Rakhi has now made it clear to her that she is also barred from the control center. What was it you wanted of me?"

"Take Aiela and Isande to their quarters and let them collect what they need for their comfort on Priamos. Then escort them to the lab; I will give Ghiavre his instructions while you are at that. Then arrange their transport down to Priamos; and it would not be amiss to provide them arms."

"I have my own weapon," said Aiela, "if I have your leave to collect it from storage."

"Armament can provide you one more effective, I am sure."

"I am kallia. I'm afraid if I had a lethal weapon in my hands I couldn't fire it. Give me my own. Otherwise I can't defend myself as I may need to."

"Your logic is peculiar to your people, I know, but I perceive your reasoning. Take it, then. And as for instruction, kamethi—I provide you none. I am sure your knowledge of Priamos and of Daniel is thorough, and I trust you to remember your responsibility to *Ashanome*. One thing I forbid you: do not go to Khasif and do not expect him to compromise himself to aid you. You are dismissed."

Aiela bowed a final thanks, waited for Isande, and walked as steadily as he could after Ashakh. Isande held his arm. Her mind tried to occupy his, washing it clean of the pain and the weakness. He forbade that furiously, for it hurt her as well.

In his other consciousness he was being handled roughly down a ramp, provided a dizzying view of a daylit sky: he dreaded to think what could happen to Daniel while he was helpless to advise him, and he imagined what Daniel must think, abandoned as he had been without explanation. *We'll be there,* Aiela sent, defying orders; *hold on, we're coming;* but Daniel was fainting. He stumbled, and Isande hauled up against him with all her strength.

"Ashakh!"

The tall iduve stopped abruptly at the corridor intersection a pace ahead of them and roughly shoved them back. Mejakh confronted them, disheveled and with a look of wildness in her eyes.

"They are killing me!" she cried hoarsely and lurched at Ashakh. "O *nas,* they are killing me—"

"Put yourself to order, *nasith,*" said Ashakh coldly, thrusting off her hands. "There are witnesses."

Mejakh's violet eyes rolled aside to Aiela and back again, showing whites at the corners, her lips parted upon her serrate teeth. "What is Chimele up to?" she demanded. "What insanity is she plotting, that she keeps me from controls? Why will no one realize what she is doing to the *nasul? O nas,* do you not see why she has sent Khasif away? She has attacked me; Khasif is gone. And you have opposed her—do you not see? All that dispute her—all that protest against her intentions—die."

"Get back," Ashakh hissed, barring the corridor to her with his arm.

Aiela felt the *idoikkhe* and doubled; but Ashakh's will held that off too, and he shouted at the both of them to run for their lives.

Aiela stumbled aside, Isande's hand in his, Mejakh's harsh voice pursuing them. He saw only closed doors ahead, a monitor panel at the corner such as there was at every turning. He reached it and hit the emergency button.

"Security!" he cried, dispensing with location: the board told them that. "Mejakh—!"

Through Isande's backturned eyes he saw Ashakh recoil in surprise as Mejakh threatened him with a pistol. It burned the wall where Ashakh had been and had he not gone sprawling he would have been a dead man. His control of the *idoikkhei* faltered. Isande's scream was half Aiela's.

The weapon in Mejakh's hand swung left, drawn from Ashakh by the sound. *Down!* Aiela shrieked at Isande and they separated by mutual impulse, low. The smell of scorched plastics and ozone attended the shot that missed them.

Ashakh heaved upward, hit Mejakh with his shoulder, sending her into the back wall of the corridor with a thunderous crash; but she did not fall, and locked in a struggle with him, he seeking to wrest the gun from her hand, she seeking to use it. Aiela scrambled across the intervening distance, Isande's mind wailing terror into his, telling him it was suicide; but Ashakh maintained a tight hold on the *idoikkhei* now so that Mejakh could not send. Aiela seized Mejakh's other arm to keep her from using her hand on Ashakh's throat.

It was like grappling with a machine. Muscles like steel cables dragged irresistibly away from his grip, and when he persisted she struck at him, denting the wall instead and hurting her hand. She swung Ashakh into the way, trying to batter them both against the wall, and Aiela realized to his horror that Isande had thrown herself into the struggle too, trying vainly to distract Mejakh.

Suddenly Mejakh ceased fighting, and so did Ashakh. About them had gathered a number of iduve, male and female, a *dhisais* in her red robes, three *dhis*-guardians in their scarlet-bordered black and bearing their antique *ghiakai*. Mejakh disengaged, backed from them. Ashakh with offended dignity straightened his torn clothing and turned upon her a deliberate stare. It was all that any of them did.

The door of the *paredre* opened at the other end of the corridor and Chimele was with them. Mejakh had been going in that direction. Now she stopped. She seemed almost to shrink in stature. Her movements hesitated in one direction and the other.

Then with a hiss rising to a shriek she whirled upon Ashakh. The *ghiakai* of the *dhis*-guardians whispered from their sheaths, and Aiela seized Isande and pulled her as flat against the wall as they could get, for they were between Mejakh and the others. From the *dhisais* came a strange keening, a moan that stirred the hair at the napes of their necks.

"Mejakh," said Chimele, causing her to turn. For a moment there was absolute silence. Then Mejakh crumpled into a knot of limbs, her two arms locked across her face. She began to sway and to moan as if is pain.

The others started forward. Chimele hissed a strong negative, and they paused.

"You have chosen," said Chimele to Mejakh.

Mejakh twisted her body aside, gathered herself so that her back was to them, and began to retreat. The retreat became a sidling as she passed the others. Then she ran a few paces, bent over, pausing to look back. There was a terrible stillness in the ship, only Mejakh's footsteps hurrying more and more quickly, racing away into distant silence.

The others waited still in great solemnity. Ashakh took Aiela and Isande each by an arm and escorted them back to Chimele.

"Are you injured?" Chimele asked in a cold voice.

"No," said Aiela, finding it difficult to speak in all that silence. He could scarcely hear his own voice. Isande's contact was almost imperceptible.

"Then pass from this hall as quickly as you may. Do you not see the *dhisais?* You are in mortal danger. Keep by Ashakh's side and walk out of here very quietly."

8

It was done at last. From his vantage point behind the glass Tejef watched the human grow still under the anesthetic and trusted him to the workmanlike mercies of the amaut physician—not an auspicious prospect if the wounds were much worse, if there were shattered joints or pieces missing. Then it would need the artistry of an iduve of the Physicians' order. Tejef himself had only a passing acquaintance with the apparatus that equipped his ship's surgery, a patch-and-hope adequacy that had been able to save a few human lives on Priamos. He had not sought them out, of course, but occasionally the *okkitani-as* brought them in, and a few rash humans had actually come begging asylum, desperate and thirsty in the grasslands that surrounded the ship. Most injured that Tejef had treated lived, and acknowledged themselves mortally disadvantaged, and, in the curious custom of their kind, bound themselves earnestly to serve him. He was proud of this. He had gathered twenty-three humans in this way. They were not kamethi in the usual sense, for he had no access to *chiabres* or *idoikkhei;* still he reasoned that their service gave him a certain *arastiethe,* and although it was improper to hold *m'metanei* by no honorable bond of loyalty, but only their own acknowledged disadvantage, that was the way of these beings, and he accepted the offering. He had also a hundred of the amaut attending him as *okkitani-as,* and had others dispersed into every center of amaut authority on Priamos. The amaut knew indeed that there was an iduve among them and they took him into account when they made their plans. In fact, he had directly applied pressure on their high command to give him this surgeon, for it was not proper that he practice publicly what was to him only an amateurish skill. He had been of the order of Science, and although it was his doom to perish world-bound, he still had some pride left in his order, not to soil his hands with work inexpertly done.

As his glance swept the small surgery his attention came again to the small yellow person who had defended the man so bravely. He remembered her hovering on this side and on that of the wounded man as he was borne across the field to the ship, darting one way and the other among the irritated amaut to keep sight of him while they brought him in, actually attacking one—a mottled, thick-necked fellow—who tried to keep her out of the surgery. She had gone for him with her teeth, that being all she had for weapons, and being batted aside, she darted under his reach and ensconced herself on a cabinet top in the corner, defying them all. Tejef had laughed to see it, although he laughed but seldom these days.

Now the wretched little creature sat watching the surgeon work, her face gone a sickly color even for a human. Her hand clutched her rag of a garment to her flat chest; her feet and knees were bloody and incredibly filthy—by no means proper for the surgery. She had not stopped fighting. She fairly bristled each time one of the amaut came near her in his ministrations, and then her eyes would dart again mistrustfully to see what the surgeon was doing with the man.

Tejef opened the door, signed the amaut not to notice him. Her eyes took him in too, seeming to debate whether he needed to be fought also.

"It's all right," he told her, exercising his scant command of her language. She looked at him doubtfully, then unwound her thin legs and came off the countertop, her lips trembling. When he beckoned her she ran to him, and to his dismay she flung her thin dirty arms about him and pressed her damp face against his ribs: he recoiled slightly, ashamed to be so treated before the amaut, who wisely pretended not to notice. The child poured at him a veritable flood of words, much more rapidly than he could comprehend, but she seemed by her actions to expect his protection.

"Much slower," he said. "I can't understand you."

"Will he be all right?" she asked of him. "Please, please help us."

Perhaps, he thought, it was because there was a certain physical similarity between iduve and human: perhaps to her desperate need he looked to be of her kind. He had schooled himself to a certain patience with humans. She was very young and it was doubtless a great shock to her to be hurled out of the security of the *dhis* into this frightening profusion of faces and events. Even young iduve had been known to behave with less *chanokhia*.

"Hush," he said, setting her back and making her straighten her shoulders. "They make him live. You—come with me."

"No. I don't want to."

His hand moved to strike; he would have done so had a youngish iduve been insubordinate. But the shock and incomprehension on her face stopped him, and he quickly disguised the gesture, twice embarrassed before the *okkitani-as*. Instead he seized her arm—carefully, for *m'metanei* were inclined to fragility and she was as insubstantial as a stem of grass. He marched her irresistibly from the infirmary and down the corridor.

A human attendant was just outside the section. The child looked up at the being of her own species in tearful appeal, but she made no attempt to flee to him.

"Call Margaret to the *dhis*," Tejef ordered the man, and continued on his way, slowing his step when he realized how the child was having to hurry to keep up with him.

"Where are we going?" she asked him.

"I will find proper—a proper—place for you. What is your name, *m'metane?*"

"Arle. Please let go my arm. I'll come."

He did so, giving her a little nod of approval. "Arle. I am Tejef. Who is your companion? Is he—a relative?"

"No." She shook her head violently. "But he's my friend. I want him to be all right—please—I don't want him to be alone with them."

"With the amaut? He is safe. *Friend:* I understand this idea. I have learned it."

"What are you?" she asked him plainly. "And what are the amaut and why did they treat Daniel like that?"

The questions were overwhelming. He struggled to think in

her language and abandoned the effort. "I am iduve," he said. "Ask your kind. I don't know enough words." He paused at the entrance of the lift and set his hand on her shoulder, causing her to look up. It was a fine face, an impossibly delicate body. A creature of air and light, he thought in his own language, and rejected it as an expression more appropriate to Chaikhe than to one of his order. As an iduve this little creature would scarcely have survived the *dhis,* where the strength to take meant the right to eat and a *nas* of small stature or nameless birth needed extraordinary wit and will to live. He had survived despite the active persecution of the *dhisaisei* and of Mejakh, and he had done so by a determination out of proportion to his origins. He prized such a trait wherever he found it.

"Are you going to help us?" she asked him.

He took her into the lift and started it moving downward.

"You are mine, you, your friend. You must obey and I must take care for you. You stand straight, have no fear for amaut or human. I take care for you." The door opened and let them out on the level of what had been the *dhis,* sealed and dark until now.

There was Margaret, whom he had not seen in two days. He did not smile at her, being put off by her instant attachment to the child, for she exclaimed aloud and opened her arms to the child, petting her and making much of her with all the protective tenderness of a *dhisais* toward young.

In some measure Tejef was relieved, for he had not been sure how Margaret would react. In another way he was troubled, for her accepting the child made her inappropriate as a mate and made final a parting he still was not sure he wanted. Margaret was the most handsome of the human females, with a glorious mane of fire-colored hair that made her at once the most alien and the most attractive. He had taken her many times in *kata-sukke,* but she troubled him by her insistence on touching him when they were not alone, and in her display of feelings when they were. She had wept when he admitted at last at great disadvantage that he did not understand the emotions of her kind in this regard, and did not know what she expected of him. He had been compelled to dismiss her from the *khara-dhis* after that, troubled by the heat and violence she evoked in him, by the

emotions she expected of him. She certainly could not hold her
own if he forgot himself and treated her as *nas*. He would surely
kill her, and when he came to himself he would regret it bitterly,
for her irritating concern was well-meant, and he had a deep regard for her, almost as if she were indeed one of his own kind.
That was the closest he dared come to what she wanted of him.

"Margaret," he said with great dignity, "she is Arle."

"The poor child." She had her arms about the bedraggled girl
and petted her solicitously. "How did she come here?"

"Ask her. I want to know. She is a child, yes? No?"

"Yes."

He looked upon the pair of them, women that had been his
first mate and this immature being of her own species, and was
deeply disturbed. He knew it was very wrong to have brought
this pale creature to the *dhis* instead of assigning her among the
kamethi, but now that it was done it was good to know that the
dhis held at least one life, and that Margaret, whom he must put
away, had the child he could not give her. It was an honorable
solution for Margaret. It was hard to give her up. Desire still
stirred in him when he looked at her, nor could she understand
why he suddenly rejected her. Hurt pleaded with him out of her
eyes.

"She is yours," he told her. "I give her. You will transfer your
belongings here. She is your responsibility—yes?"

"All right," she said.

He turned away abruptly, not to be troubled more by the
harachia of them. He knew that the door opened and closed,
that the *dhis*, where no male and no nas kame or amaut might
ever go, had been possessed by humans at his own bidding. He
was ashamed of what he had done, but it was done now, and a
strange furtive elation overrode the sense of shame. He had acquired a certain small *vaikka*, not alone in the disadvantaging of
Chimele, but in the acquisition of the *arastiethe* she had decided
to take from him. The *dhis* that had remained dark and desolate
now held light, life, and *takei*—females; his little ship had a
comfort for him now it had lacked before those lights went on
and that door sealed.

The sensible part of him insisted that he had plumbed the
depths of disgrace in letting this happen; but those who decreed

the traditions of honor could not understand the loneliness of an *arrhei-nasuli* and the sweetness there was in knowing he had worth in the sight of his kamethi. It lightened his spirit, and he told himself knowingly a great lie: that he had *arastiethe* and a *takkhenois* adequate to all events. He clutched to himself what he knew was a greater lie: that he might yet outwit *Ashanome* and live. Like a gust of wind he stepped from the lift, grinned cheerfully at some of his startled kamethi and went on to the *paredre*. There were plans to make, resources to inventory.

"My lord." Halph, assistant to the surgeon, came waddling after, operating gown and all. He bobbed his head many times in nervous respect.

"Report, Halph."

"The *chiabres* is indeed present, lord Tejef. The honorable surgeon Dlechish will attempt to remove it if you wish, but removing it intact is beyond his knowledge."

"No," he said, for the human prisoner would be irreparably damaged by amaut probing at the *chiabres* if he allowed it. The human was a danger, but properly used, he could be of advantage. Kameth though he was, Chimele had most likely intended him as a spy or an assassin: against an *arrhei-nasuli* the neutrality of kamethi did not apply, and Chimele was not one to ignore an opportunity; the intricacy of the attempt against him that had failed delighted him. "You have not exposed it, have you?"

"No, no, my lord. We would not presume."

"Of course. You are always very conscientious to consult me. Go back to Dlechish and tell him to leave the *chiabres* alone, and to take special care of the human. Remember that he can understand all that you say. If it can be done safely in his weakened condition, hold him under sedation."

"Yes, sir."

The little amaut went away, and Tejef spied another of the *okkitani-as,* a young female whom her kind honored as extraordinarily attractive. This was not apparent to iduve eyes, but he trusted her for especial discretion and intelligence.

"Toshi, collect your belongings. You are going to perform an errand for me in Weissmouth."

*   *   *

"The kamethi have now been sent to Priamos," said Ashakh. "They will know nothing until they wake onworld. The shuttle crew will deliver them to local authorities for safekeeping."

"I did somewhat regret sending them." Chimele arose, activating as she did so the immense wall-screen that ran ten meters down the wall behind her desk. It lit up with the blue and green of Priamos, a sphere in the far view, with the pallor of its outsized moon—the world's redeeming beauty—to its left. She sighed seeing it, loving as she did the stark contrasts of the depths of space, lightless beauties unseen until a ship's questing beam illuminated them, the dazzling splendors of stars, the uncompromising patterns of dark-light upon stone or machinery. Yet she had a curiosity, a *m'melakhia,* to set foot on this dusty place of unappealing grasslands and deserts, to know what lives *m'metanei* lived or why they chose such a place.

"What manner of people are they?" she asked of Ashakh. "You have seen them close at hand. Would we truly be destroying something unique?"

Ashakh shrugged. "Impossible to estimate what they were. That is a question for Khasif. I am of the order of Navigators."

"You have eyes, Ashakh."

"Then—inexpertly—I should say that it is what one might expect of a civilization in dying: victims and victimizers, pointless destruction, a sort of mass urge to *serach.* They know they have no future. They have no real idea what we are; and they fear the amaut out of all proportion, not knowing how to deal with them.'

"Tejef's *serach* will be great beyond his merits if he causes us to destroy this little world."

"It has already been great beyond his merits," said Ashakh. "*Chaganokh* ruined this small civilization by guiding Tejef among them. It is ironic. If these humans had only known to let them escort Tejef in and depart unopposed, they would not have lost fleets to *Chaganokh,* the amaut would not have been attracted, and they might have had a fleet left to maintain their territories against the amaut if the invasion occurred. Likely then it would have been impossible for us to have traced Tejef before the time expired, and they would not now be in danger from us."

"If the humans are wise, they will learn from this disaster;

they will not fight us again, but let us pass where we will. Still, knowing what I do of Daniel, I wonder if they are that rational."

"They have a certain *elethia*," said Ashakh quietly.

"*Au,* then you have been studying them after all. What have you observed?"

"They are rather like kallia," said Ashakh, "and have no viable *nasul*-bond; consequently they find difficulty settling differences of opinion—rather more than kallia. Humans actually seem to consider divergence of opinion a positive value, but attach negative value to the taking of life. The combination poses interesting ethical problems. They also have a capacity to appreciate *arrhei-akita,* which amaut and kallia do not; and yet they have deep tendency toward permanent bond to person and place—hopelessly at odds with freedom such as we understand the word. Like world-born kallia, they ideally mate-bond for life; they also spend much of their energy in providing for the weaker members of their society, which activity has a very positive value in their culture. Surprisingly, it does not seem to have debilitated them; it seems to provide a *nasul*-substitute, binding them together. Their protective reaction toward weaker beings seems instinctive, extending even to lower life forms; but I am not sure what kind of feeling the *hurachia* of weakness evokes in them. I tend to think this behavior was basic to the civilization, and that what we see now is the work of humans in whom this response has broken down. Their other behavior consequently lacks human rationality."

"In my own experience," Chimele said ruefully, "behavior with this protective reaction also seems highly irrational."

The door opened and there was Rakhi. A little behind him stood Chaikhe, the green robes of a *katasathe* proclaiming her condition to all about her; and when she saw Chimele she folded her hands and bowed her head very low, trembling visibly.

"Chaikhe," said Chimele; and Ashakh, who was of Chaikhe's *sra,* quickly moved between them; Rakhi did the same, facing Ashakh. This was proper: a protection for Chaikhe, a respect for Chimele.

"I am ashamed," said Chaikhe, "to be so when you need me most, I am ashamed."

This was ritual and truth at the same time, for it was proper for a *katasathe* to show shame before an *orithain-tak,* and Chimele had made clear to her a more than casual irritation. ("You are a person of *kutikkase,*" Chimele remembered saying to her: it had bitterly embarrassed the gentle Chaikhe, who prided herself on her *chanokhia,* but it was truly an unfortunate time for the *nas-katasakke* to go off on an emotional bent.)

"Later might have been more appropriate," said Chimele. "But come, Chaikhe. I did not call you here to harm you."

And while Chaikhe still maintained that posture of submission, Chimele came to her and took her by the hands. Then only did Chaikhe straighten and venture to look her in the eyes.

"We are *sra,*" said Chimele to her and to the others, "and we have always been close." With a gesture she offered them to sit and herself assumed a plain chair among them. They looked confused; she did not find that surprising.

"Mejakh has been given a ship," she said softly. "You know that she wanted it so. She had honor once. I debated it much, considering the present situation, but it seemed right to do. She is *e-takkhe* and henceforth *arrhei-nasul.*"

"Hail Mejakh," said Ashakh in a low voice, "for she truly meant to kill you, Chimele, and her *takkhenois* was almost strong enough to try it."

"I perceive your disapproval."

"I am *takkhe.* I agree to your decisions in this matter. At least there is no probability that she will seek union with either *Tashavodh* or *Tejef.*"

"I hope that she will approach *Mijanothe* and that they will see fit to take her. I am relieved to be rid of her, and anxious at once that she may attempt some private *vaikka* on *Tejef.* But to destroy her without Khasif's consent would have provoked difficulty with him and weakened the *nasul.* My alternatives were limited. She made herself *e-takkhe.* What else could I have done?"

Of course there was nothing else. The *nasithi* were both uncomfortable and unhappy, but they put forward no opposition.

"*Mijanothe* and *Tashavodh* have been advised of Mejakh's irresponsible condition," Chimele continued, "and I have warned Khasif. Rakhi, I want her position constantly monitored. Apply what encouragement you may toward her joining *Mijanothe* or departing this star altogether."

"Be assured I shall," said Rakhi.

"We have bitter choices ahead in the matter of Tejef. You know that Daniel has been lost. Against the *arastiethe* of *Ashanome,* Khasif himself has now become expendable."

"Have you something in mind, Chimele," asked Ashakh, frowning, "or are you finally asking advice?"

"I have something in mind, but it is not a pleasant choice. You are all, like Khasif, expendable."

"And shall we die?" asked Rakhi somewhat wryly. "Chimele, I am a lazy fellow, I admit it. I have little *m'melakhia* and the pursuit of *vaikka* is too much excitement for my tastes—"

The *nasithi* smiled gently, for it was high exaggeration, and Rakhi was exceedingly *takkhe.*

"—so, well, but if we are doomed," Rakhi said, "need we be uncomfortable in the process? Perhaps a transfer earthward at the moment of oblivion would suffice. Or if not, perhaps Chimele will honor us with her confidence."

"No," said Chimele, "no, Rakhi, a warning is all you are due at the moment. But"—her face became quite earnest—"I regret it. What I must do, I will do, even to the last of you."

"Then I will go down first," said Ashakh, "because I know that Rakhi would indeed be miserable; and because I do not want Chaikhe to go at all. Omit her from your reckoning, Chimele. She is *katasathe* and carries a life; *Ashanome* has single lives enough for you to spend."

"Inconvenient as this condition is," said Chimele, "still Chaikhe will serve me when I require; but your request to go first I will gladly honor, and I will not treat Chaikhe recklessly."

"It is not my wish," said poor Chaikhe, "but I will give up my child to the *dhis* this day if it will advantage *Ashanome.*"

Chimele leaned over to take the *nasith's* hand and pressed it gently. "Hail Chaikhe, brave Chaikhe. I am not of a disposition ever to become *dhisais.* I shall bear my children for *Ashanome's* sake as I do other things, of *sorithias.* Yet I know how strong must be your *m'melakhia* for the child; you are born for it, your nature yearns for it as mine does toward *Ashanome* itself. I am disadvantaged before the enormity of your gift, and I mean to refuse it. I think you may serve me best as you are."

"The sight of me is not abhorrent to you?"

"Chaikhe," said Chimele with gentle laughter, "you are a great artist and your perception of *chanokhia* is usually unerring; but I find nothing abhorrent in your happiness, nor in your person. Now it is a bittersweet honor I pay you," she added soberly, "but Tejef has always honored you greatly, and so, *katasathe,* once desired of him, you now become a weapon in my hands. How is your heart, Chaikhe? How far can you serve me?"

"Chimele," Ashakh began to protest, but her displeasure silenced him and Chaikhe's rejection of his defense finished the matter. He stretched his long legs out before him and studied the floor in grim silence.

"Once," said Chaikhe, "indeed I was drawn to Tejef, but I am *takkhe* with *Ashanome* and I would see him die by any means at all rather than see him take our *arastiethe* from us."

"Where Chaikhe is," murmured Chimele, "I trust that all *Ashanome*'s affairs will be managed with *chanokhia.*"

9

"**M**y lord nas kame."

Aiela came awake looking into the mottled gray face of an amaut, feeling the cold touch of broad fingertips on his face, and lurched backward with a shudder. There was the yielding surface of a bed under his back. He looked to one side and the other. Isande lay beside him. They were in a plaster-walled room with paned doors open on a balcony and the outside air.

He probed at Daniel's mind and found the contact dark. Fear clawed at him. He attempted to rise, falling on the amaut's arms and still fighting to find the floor with his feet.

"O sir," the amaut pleaded with him, and resorted at last to the strength of his long arms to force him back again. Aiela struggled blindly until the gentle touch of Isande's returning consciousness reminded him that he had another asuthe. She felt his panic, read his fear that Daniel was dead, and thrust a probe past him to the human.

Not dead, her incoherent consciousness judged. *Let go, Aiela.*

He obeyed, trusting her good sense, and blinked sanely up at the amaut.

"Are you all right now, my lord nas kame?"

"Yes," Aiela said. Released, he sat on the edge of the bed holding his head in his hands. "What time is it?"

"Why, about nine of the clock," said the amaut. That was near evening. The amaut used the iduve's ten-hour system, and day began at dawn.

That surprised him. It ought to be dark in Weissmouth, which was far to the east of Daniel and Tejef's ship. Aiela tried to calculate what should have happened, and uneasily asked the date.

"Why, the nineteenth of Dushaph, the hundred and twenty-first of our colony's—"

Aiela's explosive oath made the amaut gulp rapidly and blink his saucer eyes. A day lost, a precious day lost with Chimele's insistence on sedation; and Daniel's mind remained silent in daylight, when the world should be awake.

"And who are you?" Aiela demanded.

The amaut backed a pace and bowed several times in nervous politeness. "I, most honorable sir? I am Kleph son of Kesht son of Griyash son of Kleph son of Oushuph son of Melkuash of *karsh* Melkuash of the colony of the third of Suphrush, earnestly at your service, sir."

"Honored, Kleph son of Kesht," Aiela murmured, trying to stand. He looked about the room of peeling plaster and worn furniture. Kleph in nervous attendance, hands ready should he fall. On Kleph's shoulder was the insignia of high rank: Aiela found it at odds with the amaut's manner, which was more appropriate to a backworld dockhand than a high colonial official. Part of the impression was conveyed by appearance, for Kleph was unhappily ugly even by amaut standards. Gray-green eyes stared up at him under a heavy brow ridge and the brow wrinkled into nothing beneath the dead-gray fringe of hair. Most amauts' hair was straight and neat, cut bowl-fashion; Kleph's flew out here and there in rebel tufts. The average amaut reached at least to the middle of Aiela's chest. Kleph's head came only scantly above Aiela's waist, but his arms had the growth of a larger man's and hung nearly past his knees. As for mottles, the most undesirable feature of amaut complexion, Kleph's face was a patchwork of varishaded gray.

"May I help you, sir?"

"No." Aiela shook off his hands and went out onto the balcony, Kleph hovering still at his elbow.

Weissmouth lay in ruins before them. Almost all the city had been reduced to burned-out shells, from just two streets beyond to the Weiss river, that rolled its green waters through the midst of the city to the salt waters of the landlocked sea. Only this sector preserved the human city as it had been, but there had never been beauty in the red clay brick and the squat square architecture, the concrete-and-glass buildings that crowded so closely on treeless streets. It had a sordid quaintness, alien in its concept, the sole city of an impoverished and failing world. Under amaut care the ravaged land might flourish again: they had skill with the most stubborn ground and their endurance in physical labor could irrigate the land and coax lush growth even upon rocky hillsides, hauling precious water by hand-powered machines as old as civilization in the zones of Kesuat, digging their settlements in under the earth with shovels and baskets where advanced machinery was economically ruinous, breeding until the settlement reached its limit and then launching forth new colonies until the world of Priamos could support no more. Then by instinct or by conscious design the birthrate would decline sharply, and those born in excess would be thrust offworld to find their own way. This was always the pattern.

But, Aiela remembered with a coldness at his belly, in less than two days neither human nor amautish skill would suffice to save the land: there would be only slag and cinders, and the green-flowing Weiss and the salt sea itself would have boiled into steam.

"What do you want here?" Aiela asked of Kleph. "Who sent you?"

Again a profusion of bows. "Lord nas kame, I am *bnesych* Gerlach's Master of Accounts. Also it is my great honor to serve the *bnesych* by communicating with the starlord in the port."

"Khasif, you mean."

Terror shone in the round face. Lips trembled. All at once Aiela realized himself as the object of that terror: found himself the stranger in the outside, and saw Kleph's eyes flinch from his. "Lord—they use no names with us. Please. To the ship in the port of Weissmouth, if that is the one you mean."

"And who assigned you here?"

"*Bnesych* Gerlach, honorable lord. To guard your sleep."

"Well, I give you permission to wait outside."

Kleph looked up and blinked several times, then comprehended the order and bowed and bobbed his way to the door. It closed after, and Aiela imagined the fellow would be close by it outside.

The sun was fast declining to the horizon. Aiela leaned upon the railing with his eyes unfocused on the golding clouds, reaching again for Daniel—not dead, not dead, Isande assured him. So inevitably Daniel would wake and he would be wrenched across dimensionless space to empathy with the human, in whatever condition his body survived. His screening felt increasingly unreliable. Sweat broke out upon him. He perceived himself drawn toward Daniel's private oblivion and fought back; the railing seemed insubstantial.

Isande perceived his trouble. She arose and hurried out to reach him. At her second step from the bed, mind-touch screamed panic. Her hurtling body fell through the door, her hands clutching for the rail. Aiela seized her, straining her stiff body to him. Her eyes stared upward into the sky, her mind hurtling up into the horrifying depth of heaven, a blue-gold chasm that yawned without limit.

He covered her eyes and hugged her face against him, dizzied by the vertigo she felt, the utter terror of sky above that alternately gaped into infinity and constricted into a weight she could not bear. Proud Isande, so capable in the world of *Ashanome:* to lift her head again and confront the sky was an act of bravery that sent her senses reeling.

Nine thousand years of voyaging—and world-sense was no longer in her. "It is one thing to have seen the sky through your eyes," she said, "but I feel it, Aiela, I feel it. Oh, this is wretched. I think I am going to be sick."

He helped her walk inside and sat with her on the bed, holding her until the chill passed from her limbs. She was not sick; pride would not let her be, and with native stubbornness she tore herself free and staggered toward the balcony to do battle with her weakness. He caught her before she could fall, held her with the same gentle force she had lent him so often at need. Her arms were about him and for a brief moment she picked up his steadiness and was content just to breathe.

The feeling of wrongness persisted. Her world had been perceptibly concave, revolving in perceptible cycles, millennium upon millennium. The great convexity of Priamos seemed terrifyingly stationary, defying reason and gravity at once, and science and her senses warred.

"How can I be of use," she cried, "when all my mind can give yours is vertigo? O Aiela, Aiela, it happens to some of us, it happens—but oh, why me? Of all people, why me?"

"Hush." He brought her again to the bed and let her down upon it, propping her with pillows. He sat beside her, her small waist under the bridge of his arm. In deep tenderness he touched her face and wiped her angry tears and let his hand trail to her shoulder, feeling again an old familiar longing for this woman, muted by circumstances and their own distress; but he would hurt with her pain and be glad of her comfort for a reason in which the *chiabres* was only incidental.

My selfishness, he thought bitterly, *my cursed selfishness in bringing you here;* and he felt her mind open as it had never opened, reaching at him, terrified—she would not be put away, would not be forgotten while he chased after human phantoms, would not find him dying and unreachable again.

He sealed against her. It took great effort.

Daniel, she read in tearful fury, jealousy: *Daniel, Daniel, his thoughts, he*—

Human beings: human ethics, human foulness—the experience of an alien being who had known the worst of his own species and of the amaut, things she had known of, but that only he had owned: the attitudes, the habits, the *feeling* of being human. *Asuthithekkhe* with Daniel had been too long, too deep; with all the darknesses left, the secrets—to a devastating degree he *was* human.

"Aiela," she pleaded, put her arms about his neck and touched face to face, one side and the other. Humans showed tenderness for each other differently. Even at such a moment he had to be aware of it, and took her hands from him—too forcefully: he touched his fingers to her cheek, trembling.

A human might have cursed, or struck at something, even at her. Aiela removed himself to the foot of the bed and sat there with his back to her, his hands laced until his azure knuckles paled; and for several moments he strove to gather up the fragments of his *kastien*. To strike was unproductive. To hate was unproductive. To resent Daniel, perfect in his humanity, was disorderly; for Order had drawn firm lines between their species: it was the iduve that had muddled the two of them into one, and the iduve, following their own ethic, were highly orderly.

He felt Isande stir, and foreknew that her slim hand would reach for him; and she, that he would refuse it. *It is not elethia to shut me out,* she sent at him. *No. You think you are going to leave me and do things your own way, but I will follow you, even if my mind is all I can send.*

Stop it. He arose, shut out her thoughts, and went out to the balcony.

Ashanome burned aloft like the earliest star of evening, a star of ill omen for Priamos, ineluctable destruction. A time ago he had been a ship's captain in what now seemed the safety of the Esliph, a *giyre* hardly complicated. Now he was the emissary of the Orithain, holding things the amaut could in no wise know: a day lost, the night advancing, his asuthe crippled, a mission that he could not possibly fulfill. The next noon would see the deadline expire.

Suddenly he doubted Chimele had meant for him to succeed. He was no longer even sure her *arastiethe* would permit her to rescue a pair of lost kamethi before the world turned to cinders. If he defied her and ran through the streets crying the doom to come, it would save no one: the amaut could not evacuate in time. He must witness all of it. Bitterly he lamented that the *idoikkhei* could not send. He would beg, he would implore Chimele to take Isande home at least.

She will not desert us, Isande sent him. But doubt was in it. Chimele did not do things carelessly: it was not negligence that had set them, unconscious and helpless, among amaut. Motives with iduve were always difficult to reckon.

Aiela's pulse quickened with anger that Isande tried to damp, frightened as she always was at defiance of the iduve. But there was one iduve ship at hand, one that would have to leave before the attack. At that remembrance, purpose crystallized in his mind; and Isande clung to the bedpost and radiated terror.

Send me to him? Blast you, no, Aiela! No!

Aiela shut out her objections, returned to the bedside and opened his case, donned a jacket against the cool of evening, and strapped on his service pistol. Isande's rage washed at him, frustrated by his relief at having found help for her.

She sent memories: a younger Khasif seen through the eyes of a frightened kalliran girl, attentions that had gone far beyond what she had ever admitted to anyone—being touched, trapped in a small space with an iduve whose intentions were far more dangerous than *katasukke*. She made him feel these things: it embarrassed them both.

"Chimele forbade us to go to Khasif," she said, foreknowing failure. He would have a *vaikka* to suffer for that: he reckoned that and hoped that he would even have the chance. His mind already drifted away from her, toward the dark of Daniel's consciousness, toward the thing he had come to do.

He is HUMAN! The word shrieked through her thoughts with a naked ugliness from which even Isande recoiled in shame.

You see why I cannot touch you, Aiela said, and hated himself for that unnecessary honesty. She could not help it: something there was that set her inner defenses working when she found Daniel coming close to her, though she strove on the surface to be amiable with him. *Male and alien,* her reactions screamed, and in that order.

Did Khasif do that to you? Aiela wondered, not meaning her to catch it; perhaps it was too accurate—she threw up screens and would not yield them down. Her hands sought his, her mind inaccessible.

"How do you think you can help him?" she asked aloud.

"There are all the resources of Weissmouth. Out of the amaut and the human mercenary forces, there has to be some reasonable chance of finding a way to him."

What she thought of those chances leaked through, dismal and doomsaying. Dutifully she tried to suppress it.

"Khasif favors me," she said. "Greatly. He will listen to me. And I am going to seal myself somewhere I won't compromise his security or Chimele's, so that you can communicate with *Ashanome* through me—instantly, if you need to. Maybe Chimele will tolerate it—and maybe we're lucky it's Khasif: outside the *harachia* of Chimele he can be a very stubborn and independent man; he may decide to help us."

He might be stubborn about other matters: she feared that too, but she would risk that to influence him to Aiela's help. Aiela caught that thought in dismay, almost dissuaded from his plans.

But there was no other way for Isande, no other hope at all. He took her small valise from the bureau and helped her, arm about her waist, toward the door. Her faint hope that mobility would overcome the sensation of falling vanished at once: it was no better at all, and she dreaded above all to be in open spaces, with the sky yawning bottomless overhead.

Aiela expected Kleph outside. To his dismay there were three amaut, bowing and bobbing in courtesy: Kleph had acquired companions. He was surprised to see the gold disc of command on the collar of one, a tall amaut of middling years and considerable girth. That one bowed very deeply indeed.

"Lord and lady," the amaut exclaimed. "*Sushai.*"

"*Sushai-khruuss,*" Aiela responded to the courtesy. "*Bnesych* Gerlach?"

Again the bow, three-leveled. "Most honored, most honored am I indeed by your recognition, lord nas kame. I am Gerlach son of Kor son of Thagrish son of Tophash son of Kor son of Merkush fourteenth generation son of Gomek of *karsh* Gomek." The *bnesych,* governor of the colony, was being brief. In due formality he might have named his ancestors in full. This was the confidence of an immensely important man, for anyone who had been in trade in the *metrosi* knew *karsh* Gomek of Shaphar in the Esliph. They were the largest and wealthiest of the *karshatu* of the colonial worlds. Gomek already controlled the economy of the Esliph, and their intrusion into human space had been no haphazard effort of a few starveling colonials. *Karsh* Gomek had the machinery and the support to make the venture pay, transporting indentured amaut vast distances at small cost to the company, great peril to the desperate travelers, and everlasting misery for the humans docile enough and tough enough to survive the life of laborers for the amaut. This place could be made a viable base of further explorations in search of richer prizes. Daniel's kind were indeed in danger, if struggle with the iduve had weakened them or thrown them into disorder. As long as the human culture had within it the potential for another and another Priamos, with humans selling each other out, the amaut, who did not fight, could keep spreading.

"And this," added the *bnesych,* bending a long-fingered hand at the young amaut female that stood at his elbow, "this is my aide Toshi."

"Toshi daughter of Igrush son of Toshiph son of Shuuk of *karsh* Shuuk." A person of middling stature, Toshi was as fair as Kleph was ugly—not by kalliran standards, surely, but palest gray. Her flat-chested figure was also flat-bellied and her carriage was graceful, but her pedigree was modest indeed, and Aiela surmised uncharitably what had recommended the young lady to the great *bnesych*.

Are you satisfied with your allies? Isande's xenophobia pricked at him, she restless within the circle of his arm. In her vision they were pathetic little creatures, ineffectual little waifs of dubious morality.

Mind your manners, Aiela fired back. *I need the* bnesych's *good will.*

Don't trouble yourself. Kick an amaut and he will bow and thank you for the honor of your attention. You are nas kame. You do not ask in the outside world: you order.

"You may serve us," said Aiela, ignoring her, "by providing us transportation to the port."

"Ai, my lord," murmured *bnesych* Gerlach, "but the noi kame said you were to remain here. Are the accommodations perhaps not to your liking? They are humanish foul, yes, for which we must humbly beg your pardon, but you have been among us so short a time—we have gathered workmen who will repair and suit quarters to your most exacting order. Anything we may do for you, we should be most honored."

"Your courtesy does you credit." The kalliran phrase fell quite naturally from Aiela's lips, irritating Isande. The *arastiethe* of *Ashanome* had been damaged; Chimele would have bristled had she heard it. "But you see," Aiela continued over her objections, "I shall be staying. My companion will not. And I still require a means to go to the port, and I am in a hurry."

Bnesych Gerlach opened and shut his mouth unhappily, rolled his lips in, and bowed. Then he began to give orders, hustled Toshi and Kleph off, while he clung close to Aiela and Isande, managing amazingly enough to scurry along with them and bow and talk at the same time, assuring them effusively of his cooperation, his wish to be properly remembered to the great lords, his delight at the honor of their presence under his roof, which he would memorialize with a stone of memory in his *karsh* nest on Shaphar.

Isande, ill and dizzied, fretted miserably at his attendance, but bowing to Aiela's wishes she did not bid the creature begone. When they descended in the antiquated cable lift, she lost all her combative urges and simply leaned against Aiela, cursing the nine thousand years of noi kame which had produced a being such as herself.

On ground level they found themselves in an immense foyer with glass doors opening onto a street busy with amaut pedestrians. A hovercraft obscured the view, dusting all and sundry, and settled to an awkward halt outside their building.

"Your car," said the *bnesych* as Toshi and Kleph rejoined them. "Is it not, Toshi?"

"Indeed so," said Toshi, bowing.

"Please escort our honorable visitors, Kleph."

Now Kleph began the series of bows, curtailed as Aiela impatiently paid a nod of courtesy to the *bnesych,* to Toshi, and helped his ailing asuthe toward the door. Kleph hurried ahead to open the door for them, pried the valise from Aiela's fingers, rushed ahead to the door of the hovercraft, and had the steps down for them in short order, scrambling in after they settled in the tight passenger space.

"To which ship?"

Aiela stared at him. "Which?"

"A second landed at noon today," Kleph explained, moistening his lips. "I had thought perhaps it—in my presumption— forgive me, most honorable lord nas kame. To the original ship, then? Of course I did not mean to meddle, oh, most assuredly not, most honorable noi kame. I am not in the habit of prying."

Ashakh must have returned, Isande sent, which worried her, for Ashakh was an unknown quantity in their plans.

"The original ship," said Aiela, and Kleph extracted his handkerchief and mopped at his face. Occupying the cab of the hovercraft with two nervous amaut at close quarters, one could notice a slight petroleum scent. The cleanliness of *Ashanome* and its filtered air rendered them unaccustomed to such things. The scents of amaut and wet earth, decaying matter, wet masonry, and the river—even Aiela noticed these things more than casually, and for Isande they were loathsome.

The little hovercraft proceeded on its way, a humming thunder kicking up sand in a cloud that often obscured their vision. It was getting on toward dark, that hour the amaut most loved for social occasions. Sun-hating, they stayed indoors and underground during the brightest hour and sought the pleasant coolness of the evening to stroll above-ground. *Habishu* were opening, and from them would be coming the merry notes of *geshe* and *rekeb;* their tables were set out of doors, disturbed by the passage of the hovercraft. Irritated *habishaapu* would be forced to wipe the tables again, and amaut on the streets turned their backs on the dust-raising hovercraft and shielded their faces. Such things were not designed for the streets, but then, streets and cities were a novelty to the amaut. It went against their ethic to spoil land surface with structures.

The hovercraft crossed the river in a cloud of spray and came up dripping on an earthen ramp, a bridge accessible but with some of its supports in doubtful condition. The fighting had badly damaged this sector. Hollow, jagged-rimmed shells reared ugliness against a heaven that had now gone dull. They followed a street marked with ropes and flags, at times riding one edge up and over rubble that spilled from shattered buildings.

The port was ahead, the base ship brightly lighted, rising huge and silver and beautiful among the amaut craft, a second ship, a sleek probe-transport, its smaller double. One thought of some monstrous nest, amaut vessels like gray, dry chrysalides, with the bright iduve craft shining among them like something new-hatched.

The hovercraft veered toward the larger, the original ship, but the amaut driver halted the vehicle well away from it. Human attendants came running to lower the hovercraft's ramp, crowding about.

Isande misliked being set down among such creatures. She had accustomed herself to Daniel's face; indeed there were times when she could forget how different it was. These were ugly, and they had an unwashed human stench. Even Aiela disliked the look of them, and helped Isande down himself, protecting her from their hands. He stepped to the concrete and looked at the two ships that shone before them under the floodlights, still a goodly walk distant. But Isande felt steadier: the dimming of the sun had brought out the first stars, and those familiar, friendly lights brought sanity to the horror of color that was the day sky.

I think I can walk, she said, and wistfully: *if it were only a question of moving at night, I could probably—*

No. No. You're safer with him. Come, we'll never get these amaut closer to those ships. Besides, arastiethe *won't permit* Khasif *to argue with us with them to witness it. If we want that ship to open to us, we had better be alone.*

You are learning the iduve, Isande agreed. *But he will take us inside before he asks why. Then—*

The *idoikkhei* burned, jolted, whited out their minds. When Aiela knew that he was still alive and that Isande was, he found himself fallen partially on her, his head aching from an impact with the pavement, his right arm completely paralyzed to the shoulder. He touched Isande's face with his left hand, cold and sick as he saw a line of blood between her lips; and this was the iduve's doing, a punishment for their presumption. He hated. *Ikas* as it was to hate, he did so with a strength that made Isande cringe in terror.

"They will kill you," she cried. And then the *idoikkhei* began to pulse again.

It was different, not pain, but an irregular surge of energy that made one anticipate pain, and it had its own variety of torment.

Two minds, Aiela realized suddenly, remembering the sensation: *two opposing minds,* and his anger became bewilderment. Isande tried to rise with his help, found she could not, and then through her vision came a view of the other ship, hatch opening, a tall slim figure in black descending.

An iduve, onworld, among outsiders.

Even Tejef had maintained his privacy; that a *nasul* so exposed itself was unthinkable. Even in the midst of their private terror it occurred to the asuthi simultaneously that Priamos might die for seeing what it was seeing, an iduve among them. Had it happened on Kartos there would have been panic and mass suicides.

Mejakh! Isande recognized the person, and her thoughts became a babble of terror. The iduve was coming toward them. The *idoikkhei* were beginning to cause pain as Mejakh's nearness overcame Khasif's interference.

Aiela hauled Isande to her feet and tried to run with her. The pain became too much. They stumbled again, trying to rise.

The hatch of the base ship opened and another iduve descended, careless of witnesses. Aiela forgot to struggle, transfixed by the sight. It was incredible how fast the iduve could move when they chose to run. Khasif crossed the intervening space and came to an abrupt halt still yards distant from Mejakh.

Sound exploded about them all, light: the ground heaved and a wall of air flung Aiela down, dust and cement chips showering about him as he tried to shield Isande. Choking black smoke confounded itself with the darkness: lights on the field had gone out. Amaut poured this way and that, gabbling alarm, human shapes among them. Powerful lights from off the field were sweeping the clouds of smoke, more obscuring than aiding.

Isande! he cried; but his effort to reach her mind plunged him into darkness and pitched him off balance: he felt her body loose, slack-limbed. His hand came away wet from hers, and he wiped the moisture on his jacket, sick with panic.

Hands seized him, hauled him up, attempted to restrain him: humans. He fired and dropped at least one, blind in the dark and smoke.

But when he was free again and sought Isande, he could not find her. Where she should have been there was no one, the pavement littered with stone and powder.

And close at hand an airship thundered upward, its twin lights glaring barefully through the roiling smoke.

Don't let it go, Aiela implored the silent form of the base ship; but both his asuthi were dark and helpless, and the base ship made no effort to intervene. Weaponsfire laced the dark. More shadows, human-tall, raced toward him. Of the hovercraft there was no sign at all. It had deserted them.

A projectile kicked up the pavement near him. The chips stung his leg.

He ran, falling often, until the pounding in his skull and the pain in his side made him seek the shelter of the ruins and wait the strength to run again.

10

Tejef came infrequently to the outside of his ship. Considering the proximity of *Ashanome* he did not think it wise to put too great a distance between himself and controls at any moment. But the burden this aircraft brought was a special one. First off the ramp was Gordon, a thin, wiry human with part of two fingers missing. He was not a handsome being, but he had been even less so when he arrived. He was senior among the kamethi, and of authority second only to Margaret.

"Toshi has a report to give," Gordon said, gesturing toward the little amaut who was supervising the unloading of three stretchers. "She can tell it better than I can. We took casualties: Brown, Ling, Stavros, all unrecovered."

"Dead, you say. Dead."

"Yes."

"A sadness," Tejef said. The three had been devoted and earnest in their service. But his attention was for the three being unloaded.

"A male and female of your kind," said Gordon. "And another—something different. Toshi says she's kallia."

The litters neared them, and Khasif was the first: Tejef looked into the face that was so nearly the mirror image of his own, felt the impact of *takkhenes* as Khasif's eyes partially opened. They must have poured considerable amounts of drug into his veins. It would have been the only way to transport him, else he would seize control of the aircraft and wreck them all. Even now the force of him was very tangible.

"Mainlevel compartment twelve is proof against him," Tejef

told the bearers. "Put a reliable guard there to warn the humans clear of that area. I think you understand the danger of confronting him once the drug has worn off."

"Yes, sir. We will be careful."

And there was Isande. The kallia and he were of old acquaintance. He was glad to see that she was breathing, for she was of great *chanokhia*.

"She must go to the lab," he told the amaut. "Dlechish will see to her."

And the third one was shrouded in a blanket, darkish blood seeping through it. So the humans treated the dead, concealing them.

This would be the female of his kind. He reached for the blanket, unknowing and uneasy. Chimele it would not be: the Orithain of *Ashanome* would not die by such a sorry mischance, or so shamefully. But for others, for gentle Chaikhe, for fierce old Nophres or Tahjekh, he would feel a certain regret.

The ruined face that stared back at him struck him with a *harachia* that drained the blood from his face and wrung from him a hiss of dismay. Mejakh. Quickly he let fall the blanket.

"Are there rites you do, sir?" asked Gordon.

"How you say?" Tejef asked, not knowing the word.

"Ceremonies. Burial. What do you do with the dead?"

She was *sra* of his. It was not *chanokhia* to let her be bundled into the disintegration chamber by the hands of *m'metanei*. He must dispose of her, he. He conceded Mejakh that final *vulkka* upon him, to force him to do her that honor. There was no other iduve able to do so.

"I see to her. Put her down. Put down!"

He had raised his voice, *e-chanokhia,* disgracing himself before the shocked faces of the *m'metanei*. He walked away from the litter to take himself from the *harachia* of the situation, to compose himself.

"Sir." Toshi came up at his elbow and bowed many times, so that he was forewarned he might not have reason to be pleased with her. "Have I done wrong or right?"

"How was this done?"

"I urged the authorities in Weissmouth to remember their loyalty to you, my lord, and they heard me, although it needed utmost persuasion. There were delays and delays: transportation must be arranged; human mercenaries must be engaged; it must not be done in the headquarters itself. All was prepared. We aimed only for the kamethi, who were accessible; but when the great ships opened and presented us such a chance—my lord, your orders did direct us to seize any opportunity against such personnel—"

"It was most properly done," said Tejef, and Toshi gave a sigh of utmost relief and bowed almost double, long hands folded on her breast.

"But sir—the other nas kame—I confess fault: we lost him in the dark. Our agents are scouring Weissmouth for him at this moment. We felt pressed to lift off before the great lords your enemies could resolve to stop us. I think it was our good fortune we escaped even so."

"Few things are random where Chimele is concerned. This kallia that escaped: his name?"

"Aiela."

"Aiela." Tejef searched his memory and found no such name. "Go back to Weissmouth and make good your omission, Toshi. You acted wisely. If you had waited, you would surely have been taken. Now see if you can manage this thing more discreetly."

"Yes, sir." Toshi gave a deep breath of relief and bowed, then backed a pace and turned, hurried off shouting orders at the crew of her aircraft. Tejef dismissed the matter into her capable hands.

There was still the unpleasant necessity of Mejakh. Harshly he ordered the kamethi to stand aside, and he knelt and gathered the shattered body into his arms.

Tejef washed meticulously and changed his clothes before he entered the *paredre* again. The remembrance of Mejakh's face, the knowledge of Khasif a prisoner in the room down the corridor, worked at his nerves and his temper with the corrosive effect of *takkhenes* out of agreement. It grew stronger. Khasif must be coming out from under the effect of the drug.

Tejef mind-touched the projection apparatus where he stood and connected it to the unit in Khasif's cell.

The *nasith* was a sorry sight. He had gained his feet, and he was dusty and bruised and bleeding, but he attempted a show of hostility.

Tejef was amazed to find that he did have the advantage of his proud *iq-sra*. Perhaps it was the drug still dulling Khasif's mind, or perhaps it was the knowledge that Mejakh was dead and that he had fallen to *m'metanei* and amaut. Undoubtedly Khasif had already attempted the door with his mind, and found its mechanism proof against an iduve's peculiar kind of tampering—the lock primitive and manual. Now Khasif simply withdrew to the farthest corner, stumbled awkwardly into the wall he could not see in his vision of the *paredre*. He leaned there as if it were difficult to hold his feet.

"I have sent Mejakh hence," Tejef said softly, "but she had nothing for *serach* but what she wore and the blanket they wrapped her in, and I vented the residue world-bound. Hail Mejakh, who was *sra* to us both."

Khasif ought to have reacted to that pretty *vaikka*. He did not move. Tejef felt his own strength coursing along his nerves, felt Khasif's weakness and his fear.

"You could be free," Tejef assured him, "if you declared yourself *arrhei-nasul* and made submission to me. I would take it."

Khasif made a small sound of anger. That was all. It was a beaten sound.

"Sir." Gordon's voice sounded beyond the walls of Khasif's room, and Tejef ceased the projection and stood in the *paredre* once more, facing Gordon and the man Daniel.

"Let him go," said Tejef. "The restraint is not necessary."

Gordon released his prisoner, who showed a disheveled appearance that had no reasonable connection with his having been aroused from sleep. There was blood on his mouth. The human wiped at it at his first opportunity, but he seemed indisposed to quarrel with an iduve. Tejef dismissed Gordon with a nod.

"I assume you are in contact with your asuthe," said Tejef.

"Is Isande on this ship?" the human demanded, and Tejef would have corrected his belligerence instantly had the man worn the *idoikkhe*. He did not, and risked a chastisement of more damaging nature if his insolence persisted.

"Isande is here; but I would surmise that the man who asked that question is named Aiela."

"I thought *arastiethe* forbade guesswork."

"Hardly an unreasonable assumption. And I am not wrong, am I? It was Aiela who asked."

"Yes," Daniel admitted.

"Tell this Aiela that should he wish to surrender himself, I will appoint him the place and the person."

"Arle—the little girl." Daniel ignored the barb to make that broken-voiced plea. "Where is she? Is she alive?"

Vaikka was practically meaningless against such a vulnerable creature as this, one so lacking in pride. Tejef had allowed himself to be vexed; now he dismissed his anger in disgust, made a gesture of inconsequence. He dealt with humans—it was all that could be expected.

"Chimele sent you to Priamos with asuthi to guide you, but without the *idoikkhe*—without its danger and its protection. Was it in order to kill me—to draw near to me, and to seem only human?"

"Yes," said Daniel, so plainly that Tejef laughed in surprise and pleasure. And at once the human's face changed, anger flaring; unprepared for the creature's maniacal lunge, Tejef slapped the human in startled reaction—open-handed, not to kill. The blow was still hard enough to put the fragile being to the floor, and Tejef waited patiently until the human began to stir, and bent and seized his arm, dragging him to his feet.

"Probably you are recently kameth, for I cannot believe that Chimele would have chosen a stupid being to serve her. I could have broken your neck, *m'metane*. I simply did not choose to."

And he let the human go, steadying him a moment until he had his balance; the *m'metane* seemed more defensive now than hostile; he stumbled backward and nearly tripped over a chair.

"I should prefer to reason with you," said Tejef.

"If *that's* your aim, try reasoning with Chimele. Haven't you sense enough to know you're going to get yourself killed?"

"Then it is important," said Tejef, "to do so properly, is it not? What does your asuthe say to that?"

Daniel told him, plainly; and Tejef laughed.

"Please," Daniel pleaded. "Where is Arle? Is she all right?"

"Yes. Quite safe."

"Please let me see her."

"No," said Tejef; but he knew his anger on the subject was, in human terms, irrational. The child herself incessantly begged for this meeting, and, child of the *dhis* as she was, she was human, only human, and knew Daniel for *nas*—a friend, as she put it. It was not the same as if she had been iduve young, and it was well for him to remember it.

Then it occurred to him that a human according to his peculiar ethic would feel a certain obligation for the favor: *niseth-kame,* paradoxical as the term was.

"Arle is not from *Ashanome,*" Daniel persisted. "She is no possible harm to you."

Tejef reasoned away his disgust, reminding himself that sometimes it was necessary to deal with *m'metanei* as *m'metanei,* expecting no *arastiethe* in them.

"I shall take you where she is," said Tejef.

Margaret answered the call to the door of the *dhis,* but Arle was not far behind her, and Tejef was quite unprepared for the child's wild shout and her plunge out the door into Daniel's arms. The man embraced her tightly, asking over and over again was she well, until she had lost her breath and he set her back. But then the child turned to Tejef and wanted to embrace him too. He stiffened at the thought, but as he recoiled she remembered her manners and refrained, hands still open as if she did not know what else to do with them.

"You see," Tejef told her. "Daniel walks; he is well. Be not so uncontrolled, Arle."

She dried her face dutifully and crept back to the shelter of Daniel's arm: the touch between them frayed at Tejef's sensibilities.

"He hasn't hurt you—he hasn't touched you?" Daniel insisted to know, and when Arle protested that she had been treated very well indeed, Daniel seemed both confused and relieved. He caressed the side of her face with the edge of his hand and gave a slight nod of courtesy to Margaret and to Tejef. "Thank you," he said in the kalliran tongue. "But when your time is up and Chimele attacks—what is your kindness to her worth?"

"For my own kamethi," Tejef admitted, "I have great regret. But I shall not regret having a few of Chimele's for *serach*."

"There's no sense in all these people dying. Where is the *arastiethe* in that? Give up."

"Hopelessly irrational, *m'metane. Arastiethe* is to possess and not to yield. I am iduve. Express me that thought of yours in my own language, if you can."

That set the human back, for of course it was a contradiction and could not be translated to mean the same thing. "But," Daniel persisted, "you iduve claim to be the most intelligent of species—and can't you and Chimele resolve a quarrel short of this?"

"Yet your species fights wars," said Tejef, "and mine does not. I have a great *m'melakhia* for your kind, human, I truly do. I do not willingly harm you, and if I were able, I would spend time among your worlds learning what you are. But you know my people, however lately you are kameth and asuthe. I think you know enough to understand. There is *vaikka* involved; and to yield is to die; morally and physically, it is to die. One cannot survive without *arastiethe*."

"And what *arastiethe* have you," Daniel cried, "if you are unable to save even your own kamethi, that trust you?"

"They are *mine*," Tejef answered, lost in Daniel's tangled logic.

"Because you have taken advantage of them, because you hold the truth from them—because they trust you're going to protect them."

"Daniel!" Arle cried, alarmed by the shouting if not the knowledge of what he had said. That was what saved him, for she thrust herself between, and her high, thin voice chilled the air.

Tejef turned away abruptly, painfully aware of the illogicalities at war in him. His pulse raced, the skin at the base of his scalp tightened, his respiration quickened. He knew that he must remove himself from the *harachia* of these beings before he lost his dignity entirely. Khasif's *takkhenois* and the *harachia* of Mejakh's corpse had upset him: the nearness of other iduve reminded him of reality, of forgotten *chanokhia*. He had set humans in the *dhis;* and now he had lost control of them. The child should not have come out. He himself had brought a strange male to them, reckoning human *chanokhia* different: but he had erred. He had been disadvantaged, had affronted the honor of Margaret, who was almost *nas,* and this child he had given to her he had allowed to be seen—to be touched—by this *m'metane-toj.* All his careful manipulation of humans lost its important in the face of simple decency. *Harachia* tore at his senses, almost as if they three, human: male, female, and child, possessed a *takkhenes* united against him—when *m'metanei* could possess no such thing. *He* was the one who had given them power against him. Perverted, the kalliran language expressed it: his own had not even the concept to lend shape to his fears about himself.

"Tejef." Margaret's light steps came up behind him; her hand caught his arm. "Tejef? What's wrong? What did he say?"

"Go back!" he cried at her, realizing with a tightening of his stomach she had abandoned Arle and the open *dhis* to Daniel. "Go!"

"What's wrong?" she asked insistently. "Tejef—"

He had wanted this female, still wanted her; and her contaminating touch brought a swell of rage into his throat. What else she said he did not hear, and only half realized the reflexive sweep of his arm, her shriek of terror abruptly silenced. It shocked the anger out of him, that cry: he was already turning, saw her hit the wall and the wall bow before she slid down, and the child screamed like an echo of Margaret. He fell to his knees beside her, touched her face and tried to ease the limbs that were twisted and broken, strained by the way she was lying.

Daniel grasped his shoulder to jerk him back, and Tejef hit him with a violence that meant to kill: but the human was quick and only the side of his arm connected, casting him sprawling across the polished floor. He rolled and scrambled up to the attack.

"No!" Arle wailed, stopping him, wisely stopping him; and Tejef turned his attention back to Margaret.

She was conscious, and sobbed in pain as he tried to ease her legs straight; and Tejef jerked back his hands, wiping them on his thighs, desiring to turn and kill the human for witnessing this, for causing it. But Arle was between them, and when Margaret began to cry Daniel moved the child aside and knelt down disregarding Tejef, comforting Margaret in her own language with far more fluency than Tejef could use.

Tejef seized Daniel's wrist when he ventured to touch her, but the human only stared at him as if he realized the aberrance of an iduve who could not rule his own temper.

The amaut must be called. Tejef arose and did so, and in a mercifully little time they had Margaret bundled neatly onto a stretcher and on her way to Dlechish and the surgery. Tejef watched, wanting to accompany them, ill content to wait and not to know; but he would not be further shamed before the amaut, and he would not go.

He felt Arle's light fingers on his hand and looked down into her earnest face.

"Can I please go with her, sir?"

"No," said Tejef; and her small features contracted into tears. He cast a look over her head, appealing to Daniel. "What is your custom?" he asked in desperation. "What is right?"

Daniel came then, hugged Arle to him and quieted her sobs, saying all the proper and fluent human things that comforted her. "Perhaps," he said to her insistence, "perhaps they'll let you come up and sit with her later, when she's able to know you're there. But she'll be asleep in a moment. Now go on, go on back into your apartments and wash your face. Come on, come on now, stop the tears."

She hugged him tightly a moment, and then ran away inside, into the echoing hall of the *dhis* where neither of them could follow.

"I will honor your promises to her," Tejef told Daniel with great restraint. "Now go up to surgery. I want someone with her who can translate for the amaut. Dlechish does not have great fluency in human speech."

"And what happens," Daniel asked, "when you lose your temper with Arle the way you just did with her?"

Tejef drew a quick breath, choking down his anger. "I had no wish to harm my kamethi."

Daniel only stared at him, thinking, or perhaps receiving something from his asuthe. Then he nodded slowly. "You care for them," he observed, as if this were a highly significant thing.

"*M'melakhia* does not apply. They *are* mine already." He did not know why he felt compelled to argue with a *m'metane*, except that the human had puzzled him with that word. He felt suddenly the gulf of language, and wished anew that he understood *metane* behavior. *Arastiethe* would not let him ask.

"Call *Ashanome*," Daniel said softly. "Surrender. The kamethi do not have to die."

Tejef felt a chill, for the human's persistent suggestion quite lost its humor; he meant it seriously. It was human to do such a thing, to give up one's own *arastiethe* and become nothing. The inverted logic that permitted such thinking seemed for the moment frighteningly real.

"Did I ask your advice?" Tejef replied. "Go up to surgery."

"She might take it kindly if you came. That is our *arastiethe,* knowing someone cares. We also tend to die when we are denied it."

Tejef pondered that, for it explained much, and posed more questions. Was that *caring,* he wondered; and did it always demand that one yield *arastiethe* by demonstrating concern? But if human honor were measured by gathering concern to one's self, then it was by seeking and accepting favors: the perversity of the idea turned reason itself inside out. In that realization the cleanliness of death at the hands of *Ashanome* seemed almost an attractive prospect. His own honor was not safe in the hands of humans; and perhaps he wounded his own kamethi—and Margaret—in the same way.

"Will you come up?" Daniel asked.

"Go," Tejef ordered. "Put yourself in the hands of one of the kamethi and he will escort you there at your asking."

"Yes, sir." Daniel bowed with quiet courtesy and walked away to the lift. It was kalliran, Tejef realized belatedly, and was warmed by the fact that Daniel had chosen to pay him that respect, for humans did not generally use that custom. It filled him with regret for the clean spaciousness of *Ashanome,* for familiar folk of honorable habits and predictable nature.

The lift ascended, and Tejef turned away toward the door of the *dhis,* troubled by the *harachia* of the place where Margaret had lain, a dent in the metal paneling where her fragile body had hit. She had often disadvantaged him, held him from *vaikka* against humans and amaut, shamed him by her attentions. It was not the deference of a kameth but the tenacious *m'melakhia* of a *nasith-tak*—but of course there was no *takkhenes,* no oneness in it; and it depended not at all on him. She simply chose to belong to him and him to belong to her, and the solitary determination of her had an *arastiethe* about it which made him suspect that he was the recipient of a *vaikka* he could only dimly comprehend.

He was bitterly ashamed of the grief his perverted emotion had brought her in all things, for in one private part of his thoughts he knew absolutely what he had done, saw through his own pretenses, and began now to suspect that he had hurt her in ways no iduve could comprehend. For the first time he felt the full helplessness of himself among a people who could not pay him the *arastiethe* his heart needed, and he felt fouled and grieved at the offering they did give him. The contradictions were madness; they gathered about him like a great darkness, in which nothing was understandable.

"Sir?" Arle was in the doorway again, looking up at him with great concern (*arastiethe? Vaikka?*) in her kallia-like eyes. "Sir, where's Daniel?"

"Gone. Up. With Margaret. With Dlechish. He can talk for her. She has great avoidance for amaut: I think all humans have this. But Dlechish—he cares for her; and Daniel will stay with her." It was one of the longest explanations in the human language he had attempted with anyone but Margaret or Gordon. He saw the anger in the child's eyes soften and yield to tears, and he did not know whether that was a good sign or ill. Humans wept for so many causes.

"Is she going to die?"

"Maybe."

The honest answer seemed to startle the child; yet he did not know why. Plainly the injuries were serious. Perhaps it was his tone. The tears broke.

"Why did you have to hit her?" she cried.

He frowned helplessly. He could not have spoken that aloud had he been fluent. And out of the plenitude of contradictions that made up humans, the child reached for him.

He recoiled, and she laced her fingers together as if the compulsion to touch were overwhelming. She gulped down the tears. "She loves you," she said. "She said you would never want to hurt anybody."

"I don't understand," he protested; but he thought that some gesture of courtesy was appropriate to her distress. Because it was what Margaret would have done, he reached out to her and touched her gently. "Go back to the *dhis*."

"I'm afraid in there," she said. The tears began again, and stopped abruptly as Tejef seized her by the arms and made her straighten. He cuffed her ever so lightly, as a *dhisais* would a favored but misbehaving child.

"This is not proper—being afraid. Stand straight. You are *nas*." And he let her go very suddenly when he realized the phrase he had thoughtlessly echoed. He was ashamed. But the child did as he told her, and composed herself as he had done for old Nophres.

"May I please go up and stay with Margaret too, sir?"

"Later. I promise this." The prospect did not please him, having her outside the *dhis,* but the illusions must cease, for both their sakes: the child was human, and there was no one left in the *dhis* to care for her. The time was fast running out, and it was not right that the child should be alone in this great place to die. She should be near adults, who would show her *chanokhia* in their own example.

"Are you going there now?" Arle asked.

"Yes," he conceded. He looked back at her standing there, fingers still clenched together. "Come," he said then, holding out his hand. "Come, now. With me."

Most of the lights in the *paredre* of *Ashanome* were out save the ones above the desk, but Chimele knew well the shadowy figure that opened the hall door, a smallish and somewhat heavy iduve who crossed the carpets on silent feet. She straightened and lifted her chin from her hand to gaze on Rakhi's plump, earnest face.

"You were to sleep," he chided. "Chimele, you must sleep."

"I shall. I wanted to know how you fared. Sit, Rakhi. How is Chaikhe?"

"Well enough, and bound for Weissmouth. We considered,

and decided it would be best to pursue this adjustment long-distance."

"But is the *asuthithekkhe* bearable, Rakhi?"

The *nasith* gave a weak grin and massaged his freshly scarred temple. "Chaikhe bids your affairs prosper, Chimele-Orithain. She is very much with me at this moment."

"I bid hers prosper, most earnestly. But now you must close down that contact. We two must talk a moment. Can you do so?"

"I am learning," he replied, and leaned back with a sigh. "Done. Done. *Au,* Chimele, this is a fearsome closeness. It is embarrassing."

"O my Rakhi," said Chimele in distress, "Khasif is gone. Now I have sent Ashakh in his place, and to risk you and Chaikhe at once—"

"Why, it is a light thing," he said. "Do not mere *m'metanei* adjust to this? Is our intelligence not equal to it? Is our self-control not more than theirs?"

She smiled dutifully at his spirit. It was not as easy as Rakhi said, and she did not miss the trembling of his hands, the pain in his eyes; and for Chaikhe, *katasathe,* such proximity to a half-*sra* male must be torment indeed. But of the three remaining *nasithi-katasakke* this pairing had seemed best, for Ashakh's essentially solitary nature would have made *asuthithekkhe* more painful still.

"Chaikhe is really bearing up rather well," said Rakhi, "but I fear I shall have Ashakh to deal with when he sees her on Priamos and knows that I have—in a manner—touched her. I really do not see how we will keep this from him if he is still to direct Weissmouth operations. He will sense something amiss a decad of *lioi* distant."

"Well, you must advise Chaikhe to avoid *harachia.* Ashakh must remain ignorant of this arrangement, for I fear he could complicate matters beyond redemption. And do not you fail me, Rakhi. I have been confounded by one *dhisais* male human, and if you develop any symptoms I insist you warn me immediately."

Rakhi laughed outright, although he flushed dark with embarrassment. "Truly, Chimele, *asuthithekkhe* is not so impossible for iduve as it was always supposed to be. Chaikhe and I—we maintain a discreet distance in our minds. We leave one another's emotions alone, and I suppose it has helped that I am a very lazy fellow and that Chaikhe's *m'melakhia* is directed toward her songs and the child she carries."

"Rakhi, Rakhi, you are always deprecating yourself, and that is a *metane* trait."

"But it is true," Rakhi exclaimed. "Quite true. I have a very profound theory about it. Chaikhe and I would be at each other's throats otherwise. Could you imagine the result of an *asuthithekkhe* between Ashakh and myself? I shudder at the thought. His *arastiethe* would devour me. But the direction of *m'melakhia* is the essential thing. Chaikhe and I have no *m'melakhia* toward each other. In truth," he added upon a thought, "the *m'metanei* misinformed us, for they said strong *m'melakhia* one for the other is essential. I shall make a detailed record of this experience. I think it is unique."

"I shall find it of great interest," Chimele assured him. "But it would be a great bitterness to me if harm comes to you or to her."

"The novelty of the experience is exhilarating, but it is a great strain. I wonder if the *m'metanei* predict correctly when they say that the strain grows less in time. Perhaps the converse will occur for iduve there too. I surely hope not."

"As do I, *nasith*. Will you go rest now?"

"I will, yes."

"Only do this: advise Chaikhe that Ashakh will be within Weissmouth itself, and she must remain in isolation and wait for my orders. I am summoning up all ships save the two that will remain in port. Mejakh has cost us. I fear the cost may run higher still."

"Ashakh?"

She ignored the question. "May your sleep be secure, o *nas*."

"Honor be yours, Chimele."

She watched him go, heard the door close, and rested her forehead once more on her hands, restoring her composure. Rakhi was the last, the last of all her brave *nasithi,* and it was lonely knowing that others had the direction of *Ashanome,* that for the first time in nine thousand years the controls were not even under the nominal management of one of her *sra.* She bore the guilt for that. Of the fierceness of her own *arastiethe,* she had postponed bearing the necessary heir until it was too late for the long ceremonies of *kataberihe,* and *vaikka* had taken heavy toll of those about her. Mejakh was gone, her *sra* on the point of extinction: Khasif and Tejef together. Tamnakh's *sra* was in imminent danger: Ashakh and Chaikhe and the unborn child in her; and if Rakhi *sra*-Khuretekh suffered madness and died, then the *orith-sra* of *Ashanome* came down to her alone.

She felt a keen sense of *m'melakhia* for Tejef, for the adversary he had been, a deep and fierce appreciation. He had run them a fine chase indeed, off the edge of the charts and into *likatis* and *tomes* unknown to iduve. And *Ashanome*'s victory would be bitter indeed to *Tashavodh,* dangerously bitter.

Perhaps to ease the sting of it a *nas-katasakke* of Kharxanen could be requested for *kataberihe,* for *Tashavodh*'s *m'melakhia* to gain *sra* within the *orith-sra* of *Ashanome* was of long standing. Chaxal her predecessor had refused it, and Chimele bristled at the thought: she would bear the heir *Ashanome* needed, perhaps two for safety's sake, as rapidly as her health could bear. Then she could declare dissatisfaction with her mate and send him packing to his own *nasul* in dishonor; that would not be a proper *vaikka*—the Orithanhe forbade—but it would be pleasant.

But defeat—at the hands of Tejef and *Tashavodh*—to see him welcomed in triumph—was unthinkable. She would not bear it.

And there was that growing fear. *Ashanome* had been set back, and this was not an accustomed thing. It had been a hard decision, to sacrifice Khasif. In accepting risk, iduve disliked the irrational, a situation with too many variables. Were there any choice, common sense would dictate withdrawal; but there was no choice, and Tejef would surely seize upon the smallest weakness, the least hesitation: he was unorthodox and rash himself, *e-chanokhia*—but such qualities sometimes made for unpleasant surprises for his adversaries. Occasionally Isande could win at games of reason; the human Daniel had confounded skillfully laid plans by doing what no iduve would have done; and Qao-born Aiela managed to have his own way of an Orithain much more often than was proper. The fact was that *m'metanei* often bypassed the safe course. At times they did bluff, opposing themselves empty-handed to forces they ill understood, everything in the balance. This was not courage in the iduve sense, to whom acting as if one had what one did not smacked of falsity and unreason, which indicated a certain bent toward insanity. For the Orithain of *Ashanome* to bluff was indeed impossible: *arastiethe* and *sorithias* forbade.

But reversing the proposition, to allow another to assume he had what he did not, that was *chanokhia,* a *vaikka* with humor indeed, if it worked. It it did not—the loss must be reckoned proportional to the failure of gain.

Her eyes strayed to the clock. As another figure turned over, the last hour of the night had begun. Soon the morning hour would begin the last day of Tejef's life, or of her own.

"Chimele," said the voice from control: Raxomeqh, fourth of the Navigators. "Projection from *Mijanothe*."

Predictable, if not predicted, Chimele sighed wearily and rose. "Accepted," she said, and saw herself and her desk suddenly surrounded by the *paredre* of *Mijanothe*. She bowed respectfully before aged Thiane.

"Hail Thiane, venerable and honored among us."

"Hail *Ashanome*," said Thiane, leaning upon her staff, her eyes full of fire. "But do I hail you reckless or simply forgetful?"

"I am aware of the time, eldest of us all."

"And I trust memory also has not failed you."

"I am aware of your displeasure, reverend Thiane. So am I aware that the Orithanhe has given me this one more day, so despite your expressed wish, you have no power to order me otherwise."

Thiane's staff thudded against the carpeting. "You are risking somewhat more than my displeasure, Chimele. Destroy Priamos!"

"I have kamethi and *nasithi* who must be evacuated. I estimate that as possible within the limit prescribed by the Orithanhe. I will comply with the terms of the original and proper decree at all deliberate speed."

"There is no time for equivocation. Standing off to moonward is *Tashavodh*, if you have forgotten. I have restrained Kharxanen with difficulty from seeking a meeting with you at this moment."

"I honor you for your wisdom, Thiane."

"Destroy Priamos."

"I will pursue my own course to the limit of the allotted time. Priamos will be destroyed or Tejef will be in our hands."

"If," said Thiane, "if you do this so that it seems *vaikka* upon *Tashavodh,* then, *Ashanome,* run far, for I will either outlaw you, Chimele, and see you hunted to Tejef's fate, or I will see the *nasul Ashanome* itself hunted from star to star to all time. This I will do."

"Neither will you do, Thiane, for if I am declared exile, I will seek out *Tashavodh* and kill Kharxanen and as many of his *sra* as I can reach when they take me aboard. I am sure he will oblige me."

"Simplest of all to hear me and destroy Priamos. I am of many years and much travel, Chimele. I have seen the treasures of many worlds, and I know the value of life. But Priamos itself is not unique, not the sole repository of this species nor essential to the continuance of human culture. Our reports indicate even the human authorities abandoned it as unworthy of great risk in its defense. Need I remind you how far a conflict between *Tashavodh* and *Ashanome* could spread, through how many star systems and at what hazard to our own species and life in general?"

"It is not solely in consideration of life on Priamos that I delay. It is my *arastiethe* at stake. I have begun a *vaikka* and I will finish it on my own terms."

"Your *m'melakhia* is beyond limit. If your *arastiethe* can support such ambition, well; and if not, you will perish miserably, and your dynasty will perish with you. *Ashanome* will become a whisper among the *nasuli,* a breath, a nothing."

"I have told you my choice."

"And I have told you mine. Hail *Ashanome.* I give you honor now. When next we meet, it may well be otherwise."

"Hail *Mijanothe,*" said Chimele, and sank into her chair as the projection flicked out.

For a moment she remained so. Then with a steady voice she contacted Raxomeqh.

"Transmission to Weissmouth base two," she directed, and the *paredre* of the lesser ship in Weissmouth came into being about her. Ashakh greeted her with a polite nod.

"Chaikhe is landing," said Chimele, "but I forbid you to wait to meet her or to seek any contact with her."

"Am I to know the reason?"

"In this matter, no. What is Aiela's status?"

"Indeterminate. The amaut are searching street by street with considerable commotion. I have awaited your orders in this matter."

"Arm yourself, locate Aiela, and go to him. Follow his advice."

"Indeed," Ashakh looked offended, as well he might. His *arastiethe* had grown troublesome in its intensity in the *nasul:* it had suffered considerably in her service already. She chose not to react to his recalcitrance now and his expression became instead bewildered.

"For this there is clear reason," she told him. "Aiela's thinking will not be predictable to an iduve, and yet there is *chanokhia* in that person. In what things honor permits, seek and follow this kameth's advice."

"I have never failed you in an order, Chimele-Orithain, even at disadvantage. But I protest Chaikhe's being—"

She ignored him. "Can you sense whether Khasif or Mejakh is alive?"

"Regarding Mejakh, I—feel otherwise. Regarding Khasif, I think so; but I sense also a great wrongness. I am annoyed that I cannot be more specific. Something is amiss, either with Tejef or with Khasif. I cannot be sure with them."

"They are both violent men. Their *takkhenes* is always perturbing. It will be strange to think of Mejakh as dead. She was always a great force in the *nasul.*"

"Have you regret?"

"No," said Chimele. "But for Khasif, great regret. Hail Ashakh. May your eye be keen and your mind ours."

"Hail Chimele. May the *nasul* live."

He had given her, she knew as the projection went out, the salutation of one who might not return. A kameth would think it ill-omened. The iduve were not fatalists.

11

Isande came awake slowly, aware of aching limbs and the general disorientation caused by drugs in her system. Upon reflex she felt for Aiela, and knew at once that she did not lie upon the concrete at the port. She was concerned to know if she had all her limbs, for it had been a terrible explosion.

Isande. Aiela's thoughts burst into hers with an outpouring of joy. Pain came, cold, darkness, and the chill of earth, but above all relief. He read her confusion and fired multilevel into her mind that she must be aboard Tejef's ship, and that amaut treachery and human help had put her there. A shell had exploded near them. He was whole. Was she? And the others?

Under Aiela's barrage of questions and information she brought her blurred vision to focus and acknowledged that indeed she did seem to be aboard a ship. Khasif and Mejakh—she did not know. *No. Mejakh—dead, dead—*a nightmare memory of the inside of an aircraft, Mejakh's corpse a torn and bloody thing, the explosion nearest her.

Are you all right? Aiela persisted, trying to feel what she felt.

I believe so. She was numb. There was plasmic restruct on her right hand. The flesh was dark there. And hard upon that assessment came the realization that she, like Daniel, like Tejef, was trapped on the surface of Priamos. Aiela could be lifted offworld. She could not. Aiela would live. At least she had that to comfort her.

No! and with Aiela's furious denial came a vision of sky with a horizon of jagged masonry, the cold cloudy light of stars overhead. He hurt, pain from cracking his head on the pavement, bruises and cuts beyond counting from clambering through the ruins to escape—*Escape what? The ship inaccessible?* Isande began to panic indeed; and he pleaded with her to stop, for her fear came to him, and he was so overwhelmingly tired.

Another presence filtered through his mind—Daniel. Although his thoughts reached to Weissmouth and back, he stood in a room not far away. A pale child—Arle, her image never before so clear—slept under sedation: he worried for her. And in that room was a woman whose name was Margarct, a poor, broken thing kept alive with tubings and life support. A dark man sat beside the woman, talking to her softly, and this was Tejef.

Rage burned through Isande, rejected instantly by Daniel: *Murderer!* she thought; but Daniel returned: *At least this one cares for his people, and that is more than Chimele can do.*

Blind! Isande cried at him, but Daniel would not believe it.

Chimele would be a target I would regret less.

And that disloyalty so upset Isande that she threw herself off the bed and staggered across the little room to try the door, cursing at the human the while in such thoughts as she did not use when her mind was whole.

I cannot reason with Daniel, said Aiela; *but he knows the choice this world has and he will remember it when he must. Humans are like that.*

Kill him, Isande raged at Daniel. *You have the chance now: kill him, kill him, kill him!*

Daniel foreknew defeat, weaponless as he was; and Isande grew more reasoning then and was sorry, for Daniel was as frightened as she and nearly as helpless. Yet Aiela was right: when the time came he would make one well-calculated effort. It was the reasonable thing to do, and that, he had learned of the iduve—to weigh things. But he resented it: Chimele had more power to choose alternatives than Tejef, and stubbornly refused to negotiate anything.

Iduve do not negotiate when they are winning or when they are losing. Isande flared back, hating that selective human blindness of his, that persistence in reckoning everyone as human; *and that Tejef you honor so has already killed millions by his actions; by iduve reckoning, his was the action that began this. He knew what would happen when he sheltered here among humans.*

Tejef has given us our lives, Daniel returned, with that reverence upon the word *life* that a kallia would spend upon *giyre*. Tejef was fighting for his own life, and that struck a response from the human at a primal level. Still Daniel would kill him. The contradictions so shocked Isande that she withdrew from that tangle of human logic and fiercely agreed that it would certainly be his proper *giyre* to his asuthi and *Ashanome* to do so.

The thought that echoed back almost wept. *For Arle's life, for this woman Margaret's, for yours, for Aiela's, I will try to kill him. I am afraid that I will kill him for my own—I am ashamed of that. And it is futile anyway.*

You are not going to die, Aiela cast at them both, and the stars lurched in his vision and loose brick rattled underfoot as he hurled himself to his feet. *I am going to do something. I don't know what, but I'm going to try, if I can only get back to the civilized part of town.*

Through his memory she read that he had been trying to do that for most of the night, and that he had been driven to earth by human searchers armed with lights, hovercraft thundering about the ruined streets, occasional shots streaking the dark. He was exhausted. His knees were torn from falling and felt unsure of his own weight. If called upon to run again he simply could not do it.

Try the ship, she pleaded with him. *Chimele will want you back. Aiela, please—as long as you can hold open any communication between Daniel and myself*—the revulsion crept through even at such a moment—*we are a threat to Tejef.*

Forget it. I can't reach the port. They're between me and there right now. But even if I do get help, all I want is an airship and a few of the okkitani-as. *I'm going to come after you.*

Simplest of all for me to tell Tejef where you are, she sent indignantly, *and I'm sure he'd send a ship especially to transport you here. Oh, you are mad, Aiela!*

One of Tejef's ships is an option I'm prepared to take if all else fails. That was the cold stubbornness that was always his, world-born kallia, ignorant and smugly self-righteous; but she recognized a touch of humanity in it too, and blamed Daniel.

Aiela did not cut off that thought in time: it flowed to his asuthe. *No,* said Daniel, *I'm afraid that trait must be kalliran, because I've already told him he's insane. I can't really blame him. He loves you. But I suppose you know that.*

Daniel was not welcome in their privacy. She said so and then was sorry, for the human simply withdrew in sadness. In his way he loved her too, he sent, retreating, probably because he saw her with Aiela's eyes, and Aiela's was not capable of real malice, only of blindness.

Oh, blast you, she cried at the human, and hated herself.

Stop it, Aiela sent them both. *You're hurting me and you know it. Behave yourselves or I'll shut you both out. And it's lonely without you.*

"Your asuthi," asked Tejef, coming through Daniel's contact. He had risen from Margaret's side, for she slept again, and now the iduve looked on Daniel with a calculating frown. "Does that look of concentration mean you are receiving?"

"Aiela comes and goes in my mind," said Daniel. *Idiot,* Aiela sent him: *Don't be clever with him.*

"And I think that if Isande were conscious, you might know that too. Is she conscious, Daniel? She ought to be."

"Yes, sir," Daniel replied, feeling like a traitor. But Isande controlled the panic she felt and urged him to yield any truth he must: Daniel's freedom and Tejef's confidence that he would raise no hand to resist him were important. Iduve were unaccustomed to regard *m'metanei* as a threat; they were simply appropriated where found, and used.

Through Daniel's eyes she saw Tejef leave the infirmary, his back receding down the corridor; she felt Daniel's alarm, wishing the amaut were not watching him. Potential weapons surrounded him in the infirmary, but a human against an amaut's strength was helpless. He dared go as far as the hall, closed the infirmary door behind him, watching Tejef.

Then came the audible give of the door lock and seal. Isande backed dizzily from the door, knocking into a table as she did so. Tejef was with her: his *harachia* filled the little room, an indigo shadow over all her hazed vision. The force of him impressed a sense of helplessness she felt even more than Aiela's frantic pleading in her mind.

"Isande," said Tejef, and touched her. She cringed from his hand. His tone was friendly, as when last they had spoken, before Reha's death. Tejef had always been the most unassuming of iduve, a gentle one, who had never harmed any kameth— save only Reha. Perhaps it did not even occur to him that a kameth could carry an anger so long. She hated him, not least of all for his not realizing he was hated.

"Are you in contact with your asuthi?" he asked her. "Which is yours? Daniel? Aiela?"

Admit the truth, Aiela sent. *Admit to anything he asks.* And when she still resisted: *I'm staying with you, and if you make him resort to the* idoikkhe, *I'll feel it too.*

"Only to Aiela," she replied.

"This kameth is not familiar to me."

"I will not help you find him."

A slight smile jerked at his mouth. "Your attitude is understandable. Probably I shall not have to ask you."

"Where is Khasif?" Aiela prompted that question. She asked it.

The room winked out, and they were projected into the room that held Khasif. The iduve was abed, half-clothed. A distraught look touched his face; he sprang from his bed and retreated. It frightened Isande, that this man she had feared so many years looked so vulnerable. She shuddered as Tejef took her hand in his, grinning at his half-brother the while.

"*Au, nasith sra-Mejakh,*" said Tejef, "the *m'metane-tak* did inquire after you. I remember your feeling for her: Chimele forbade you, but any other *nas* has come near her at his peril, so she has been left quite alone in the matter of *katasukke.* I commend your taste, *nasith.* She is of great *chanokhia.*"

Knowing Khasif's temper, Isande trembled; but the tall iduve simply bowed his head and turned away, sinking down on the edge of his cot. Pity touched her for Khasif: she would never have expected it in herself—but this man was hurt for her sake.

The room shrank again to the dimensions of Isande's own quarters, and she wrenched herself from Tejef a loose grip with a cry of rage. Aiela fought to tell her something: she would not hear. She only saw Tejef laughing at her, and in that moment she was willing to kill or to die. She seized the metal table by its legs and swung at him, spilling its contents.

The metal numbed her hands with the force of the blow she had struck, and Tejef staggered back in surprise and flung up an arm to shield his face. She swung it again with a force reckless of strained arms and metal-scored hands, but this time he ripped the wreckage aside and sprang at her.

The impact literally jolted her senseless, and when she could see and breathe again she was on the floor under Tejef's crushing weight. He gathered himself back, jerked her up with him. She screamed, and he bent both her arms behind her and drew her against him with such force that she felt her spine would be crushed. Her feet were almost off the floor and she dared not struggle. His heart pounded, the hard muscles of his belly jerked in his breathing, his lips snarled to show his teeth, a weapon the iduve did not scorn to use in quarrels among themselves. His eyes dilated all the way to black, and they had a dangerous madness in them now. She cried out, recognizing it.

The rubble gave, repaying recklessness, and Aiela went down the full length of the slide, stripping skin from his hands as he tried to stop himself, going down in a clatter of brick that could have roused the whole street had it been occupied. He hit bottom in choking dust, coughed and stumbled to his feet again, able to take himself only as far as the shattered steps before his knees gave under him. In his other consciousness he lurched along a hallway—Isande's contact so heavily screened by shame he could not read it: guards at the door—Daniel crashed into them with a savagery unsuspected in the human, battered them left and right and hit the door switch, unlocking it, struggling to guard it for that vital instant as the recovering guards sought to tear him away.

"Khasif!" Daniel pleaded.

One of the guards tore his hand down and hit the close switch, and Daniel interposed his own body in the doorway. Aiela flinched and screamed, anticipating the crushing of bones and the severing of flesh—but the door jammed, reversed under Khasif's mind-touch. The big iduve exploded through the door and the human guards scrambled up to stop him—madness. One of them hit the wall, the echo booming up and down the corridor, the other went down under a single blow, bones broken; and

Daniel flung himself out of Khasif's way, shouting at him Isande's danger, the third door down.

Khasif reached it, Daniel running after, Aiela urging him to get Isande out of the way—clenching his sweating hands, trying to penetrate Isande's screening to warn her.

She gave way: Tejef's face blurred in double vision over Daniel's sight of the door. Khasif's ominous tall form outlined in insane face and back overlay, receding and advancing at once. Isande cried out in pain as Khasif tore her from Tejef and hurled her out the door into Daniel's arms: Daniel's face superimposed over Khasif's back, and then nothing, for Isande buried her face against the being that had lately been so loathsome to her, and clung to him; and Daniel, shaken, held to her with the same drowning desperation.

Metal crashed, and little by little Khasif was giving ground, until he was battling only to hold Tejef within the room.

Ship's controls! Aiela screamed at his asuthi.

They tried. Section doors prevented them, and amaut guards and humans converged from all sides, forcing them into retreat. Khasif stood as helpless as they under the threat of a dozen weapons.

Tejef occupied the hallway, a dark smear of blood on his temple. He gave curt orders to the armed humans to hold the *nasith* for him at the end of the hall. Aiela shuddered as he found that look resting next on Isande and on Daniel.

"Go to your quarters," Tejef said very quietly. But when Daniel started to obey, too, Tejef tilted his head back and looked at him from eyes that had gone to mere slits. "No," he said, "not you."

Aiela, Isande appealed, *Aiela, help him, oh help him!* For she knew what Daniel had done for her.

Do as Tejef tells you, said Aiela. *Daniel—give in, whatever happens: no temper. No resistance. They react to resistance. They lose interest otherwise.*

"Sir," said Daniel in a voice that needed no dissembling to carry a tremor, "sir—I acted not against you. For Isande, for her. Please."

The iduve stared at him for a long cold moment. Then he let go a hissing breath. "Get out of my sight. Go to your quarters, and stay there or I will kill you."

Go! Aiela hurled at Daniel: *Bow your head and don't look him in the eyes! Go!* And blessedly the human ignored his own instincts, took the advice, and edged away carefully. *He's all right, he's all right,* Aiela said then to Isande, who collapsed in the wreckage of her quarters, crying. He probed gently to know if she were much hurt.

No, she flung back. *No.* Fear leaked through, shame, the ultimate certainty of defeat. *Go away, go away,* she kept thinking, *o go away, reach the ship and leave. I learned to survive after losing Reha. It's your turn. We've lost whatever chance we had because of me, because I started it, I did, I did, nothing gained.*

It's all right, came Daniel's unbidden intervention. He shook all over, he was so afraid, alone in his quarters. It was a terrible thing for a man of his kind to yield down screens at such a moment: but along with the fear another process was taking place: he was gathering his mental forces to replot another attack. Of a sudden this humanish stubbornness, so different from kalliran methodical process, came to Isande as a thing of *elethia.* She wept, knowing his blind determination; and she appealed to Aiela to reason with him.

Luck, said Aiela, *is what humans wish each other when they are in that frame of mind. I do not believe in luck: kastien forbids. But trust him, Isande. You're going to be all right.*

And that was a hope as irrational as Daniel's, and as little honest. He did not want to tear his mind away, but the triple flood of thoughts distorted his perceptions and tore at his emotions. At last he had to let them both go, for he, like Daniel, was determined to try; and he knew what they would both say to that.

He had come at last near the streets of the occupied quarter. The sounds and smells of a *habish* told him so, and guided him down the alley. It lacked some few hours until daylight, but by now even most of the night-loving amaut had given up and gone home. The place was quiet.

Thus, at the most one other street lay between him and the safety of headquarters, but far more effort would be needed to thread the maze of Weissmouth's alleys, with their turnings often running into the impassable rubble of a ruined building. Aiela had no stomach for recklessness at this stage; but neither had he much more strength to spend on needless effort. He tried the handle of the *habish's* alley door, jerked it open, and walked through, to the startled outcries of the few drunken patrons remaining.

He closed the front door after him and found to his dismay that it was not the headquarters street after all: but at least it was clear and in the right section of town. He knew his way from here. The headquarters lay uphill and he set out in that direction, walking rapidly, hating the spots of light thrown by the occasional streetlamps.

A dark cross-street presented itself. He took it, hurrying yet faster. Footsteps sounded behind him, silent men, running. He gasped for air and gathered himself to run too, racing for what he hoped was the security of the main thoroughfare.

He rounded the corner and had sight of the bulk of the headquarters budding to his left, but those behind him were closing. He jerked out his gun as he ran, almost dropping it, whirled to fire.

A hurtling body threw him skidding to the pavement. Human bodies wrestled with him, beat the gun from his hand and pounded his head against the pavement until he was half-conscious. Then the several of them hauled him up and forced him to the side of the street where the shadows were thick.

He went where they made him go, not attempting further resistance until his head should clear. They held him by both arms and for half a block he walked unsteadily, loose-jointed. They were going toward the headquarters.

Then they headed him for a dark stairs into the basement door of some shop.

He had hoped in spite of everything that they were mercenaries in the employ of the amaut authorities that had muddled their instructions or simply seized the opportunity to vent their hate on an alien of any species at all. He could not blame them for that. But this put a grimmer face on matters.

He lunged forward, spilling them all, fought his way out of the tangle at the bottom of the steps, kneed in the belly the man quickest to try to hold him. Other hands caught at him: he hit another man in the throat and scrambled up the stairs running for his life, expecting a shot between the shoulders at any moment.

The headquarters steps were ahead. For that awful moment he was under the floodlights that illumined the front of the building, and rattling and pounding at the glass doors.

An amaut sentry waddled into the foyer and blinked at him, then hastened to open. Aiela pushed his way past, cleared the exposed position of the doors, leaned against the wall to catch his breath, staggered left again toward *bnesych* Gerlach's darkened office door, blazoned with the symbols of *karsh* Gomek authority.

"Most honorable sir," the sentry protested, scurrying along at his side, "the *bnesych* will be called." He searched among his keys for that of the office and opened it. "Please sit down, sir. I will make the call myself."

Aiela sank down gratefully upon the soft-cushioned low bench in the outer office while the sentry used the secretary's phone to call the *bnesych*. He shook in reaction, and shivered in the lack of heating.

"Sir," said the sentry, "the *bnesych* has expressed his profound joy at your safe return. He is on his way. He begs your patience."

Aiela thrust himself to his feet and leaned upon the desk, took the receiver and pushed the call button. The operator's amaut-language response rasped in his ear.

"Get me contact with the iduve ship in the port," he ordered in that language, and when the operator protested in alarm: "I am nas kame and I am asking you to contact my ship or answer to them."

Again the operator protested a lack of clearance, and Aiela swore in frustration, paused open-mouthed as an amaut appeared in the doorway and bowed three times in respect. It was Toshi.

"Lord Aiela," said the young woman, bowing again. "Thank you, Aphash. Resume your post. May I offer you help, most honorable lord nas kame?"

"Put me in contact with my ship. The operator refuses to recognize me."

Toshi bowed, her long hands folded at her breast. "Our profound apologies. But this is not a secure contact. Please come with me to my own duty station next door and I will be honored to authorize the port operator to make that contact for you with no delay. Also I will provide you an excellent flask of *marithe*. You seem in need of it."

Her procedures seemed improbable and he stood still, not liking any of it; but Toshi kept her hands placidly folded and her gray-green eyes utterly innocent. Of a sudden he welcomed the excuse to get past her and into the lighted lobby; but if he should move violently she would likely prove only a very startled young woman. He took a firmer grip on his nerves.

"I should be honored," he said, and she bowed herself aside to let him precede her. She indicated the left-hand corridor as he paused in the lobby, and he could see that the second office was open with the light on. It seemed then credible, and he yielded to the offering motion of her hand and walked on with her, she waddling half a pace behind.

It was a communications station. He breathed a sigh of relief and returned the bow of the technician who arose from his post to greet them.

And a hard object in Toshi's hand bore into his side. He did not need her whispered threat to stand still. The technician unhurriedly produced a length of wire from his coveralls and waddled around behind him, drawing his wrists back.

Aiela made no resistance, enduring in bitter silence, for if Toshi were willing to use that gun, he would be forever useless to his asuthi. He was surely going to join Isande and Daniel, and all that he could do now was take care that he arrived in condition to be of use to them. It was by no means necessary to Tejef that he survive.

They faced him about and took him out the door, down a stairs and to a side exit. Toshi produced a key and unlocked it, locked it again behind them when they stood on the steps of some dark side of the building.

Fire erupted out of the dark. The technician fell, bubbling in agony. Toshi crumpled with a whimper and scuttled off the steps against the building, while Aiela flung himself off, fell, struggled to his feet and sprinted in blind desperation for the lights of the main street.

Faster steps sounded behind him and a blow in the back threw him down, helpless to save himself. His shoulder hit the pavement as he twisted to shield his head, and humans surrounded him, hauled him up, and dragged him away with them. Aiela knew one of them by his cropped hair: they were the same men.

They took him far down the side street away from the lights and pulled him into an alley. Here Aiela balked, but a knee doubled him over, repaying a debt, and they forced him down into the basement of a darkened building. When they came to the bottom of the steps, he began to struggle, using knee and shoulders where he could; and all it won him was to be beaten down and kicked.

A dim light swung in the damp-breathing dark, a globe-lamp at the wrist of an amaut, casting hideous leaping shadows about them. Aiela heaved to gain his feet and scrambled for the stairs, but they kicked him down again. He saw the amaut thrust papers into the hands of one of the humans, snatching the stolen kalliran pistol from the man's belt before he expected it and putting it into his own capacious pocket.

"Ffife ppasss," the amaut said in human speech. "All ffree, all run country, go goodbpye."

"How do we know what they say what you promised?" one made bold to ask.

"Go goodbpye," the amaut repeated. "Go upplandss, ffree, no more amautss, goodbpye."

The humans debated no longer, but fled, and the amaut went up and closed the street door after them, waddling down the steps holding up his wrist to cast a light that included Aiela upon the floor.

It was Kleph, his ugly face more than usually sinister in the dim lighting. Cold air and damp breathed out from some dark hole beyond the light, an amaut burrow, tunnels of earth that would twist and meet many times beneath the surface of Weissmouth. Aiela had not been aware that this maze yet existed, but it was expected. He knew too that one hapless kallia could be slain and buried in this earthen maze, forever lost from sight and knowledge save for the *idoikkhe* on his wrist, and amaut ingenuity could solve that as well.

"What are you after?" Aiela asked him. "Are you here to cover your high command's mistakes?"

"Most honorable sir, I am devastated. You were given into my hands to protect."

Aiela let go a small breath of relief, for the fellow did not reasonably need to deceive him; but it was still in his mind that Kleph had access to humans such as had attacked them at the port, and had just evidenced it. The little fellow waddled over and freed him, put his arm about him, helping him and compelling him at once as they sought the depths of the tunnel. Shadows rippled insanely over the rudimentary plaster of the interior, the beginnings of masonry.

"Kleph," Aiela protested, "Kleph, I have to find a way to contact my ship."

"Impossible, sir, altogether impossible."

The squat little amaut forced him around a corner despite his resistance; and there Aiela wrenched free and sought to run, striking the plaster wall in the dark, turning and running again, following the rough wall with his hands.

He did not come to the entrance when he expected it, and after a moment he knew that he was utterly, hopelessly lost. He sank down on the earthen floor gasping for breath, and leaned his shoulders against the chill wall, perceiving the bobbing glow of Kleph's lamp coming nearer. In a moment more Kleph's ugly face materialized at close quarters around the corner, and he made a bubbling sound of irritation as he squatted down opposite.

"Most honorable sir," said Kleph, rocking back on his heels and clasping his arms about his knees in a position the amaut found quite comfortable. "There is a word in our language: *shakhshoph*. It means the hiding-face. And, my poor lord, you have gotten quite a lot of *shakhshoph* since you arrived in our settlement. One is always that way with outsiders: it is only decency. Sometimes too it hides a lie. Pay no attention to words with my people. Watch carefully a man who will not face you squarely and beware most of all a man who is too polite."

"Like yourself."

Kleph managed a bow, a rocking forward and back. "Indeed, most honorable sir, but I am fortunately your most humble servant. Anyone in the colony will tell you of Kleph. I am a man of most insignificant birth; I am backworld and my manners want polish. I have come from the misfortune of my origin to an apprentice clerkship with the great *karsh* Gomek, to ship's accountant, to my present most honored position. My lord must understand then that I am very reluctant to defy the orders of *bnesych* Gerlach. But we observe a simple rule, to choose a loyalty and stay by it. It is the single wisdom of our law. *Bnesych* Gerlach gave my service to the ship in the port, and as you serve the lord of that ship, I am interested in saving your life."

"You—chose a remarkable way of demonstrating it."

"They have injured you." Kleph's odd-feeling hand most unwelcomely patted Aiela's neck and shoulder. "*Ai,* most honorable sir, had I the opportunity I would have shot the lot of them—but they will take the passes and disappear far into the uplands. If one wishes to corrupt, one simply must pay his debts like a gentleman. They are filthy animals, these humans, but they are not stupid: a few corpses discovered could make them all flee my employ in the future. But for the passes to get them clear of our lines, they will gladly do anything and suffer anything and seek my service gladly."

"Like those that fired a shell among us at the port?"

Kleph lifted a hand in protest. "My lord, surely you have realized that was not my doing. But I am Master of Accounts, and so I know when men are moved and ships fly; and I have human servants, so I know when these things happen and do not get entered properly in the records. Therefore I am in danger. There are only two men on this world besides myself who can bypass the records: one is under-*bnesych* Yasht, and the other is *bnesych* Gerlach."

"Who hired it done?"

"One or the other of them. No *shakhshoph.* It is what I told you: one chooses a loyalty and remains constant; it is the only way we know to survive—as for instance my own lords know where my loyalty in this matter must logically lie, and so I shall need to stay out of sight until the crisis is resolved: a cup of poisoned wine, some such thing—it is only reasonable to eliminate those men known to serve the opposition. I am highly expendable; I am not of this *karsh,* and therefore I was given to the lord in the port. I also was meant to be eliminated at the port; and now it is essential that we both be silenced."

"Why?" Aiela had lost his power to be shocked. His mind simply could not grasp the turns of amaut logic.

"Why, my lord nas kame, if the population of this colony realizes the *bnesych* serves the other lord, it would split the colony into two factions, with most bloody result. We are not a fighting people, no, but one protects his own nest, after all—and the *bnesych* has many folk in this venture who are not of *karsh* Gomek: out-*karsh* folk, exiles, such as myself. Such loyalties can be lost quickly. There is always natural resentment toward a large *karsh* when it mismanages. And if it no longer appears the action at the port was on human initiative, it would be most, most distressing in some quarters." He pressed his broad-tipped fingers to Aiela's brow, where there was a swelling raised. "Ai, sir, I am sorry for your unhappy state, and I did try to find you before you wandered into a trap, but you were most elusive. When I knew you had entered the headquarters and when I saw the northside lights out, I acted and disposed my human agents at once, or you would be in the other lord's hands before dawn."

"Get me to the ship at the port," Aiela said, "or get me a means to contact them, or there are going to be people hurt."

"Sir?" asked Kleph, his squat face much distressed. He gulped several times in amaut sorrow. "O sir, and must the great lords blame those who are guiltless? See, here am I, out-*karsh,* helping you. Surely then your masters will understand that not all of us in this colony are to blame. Surely they will realize how faithfully we serve them."

It was impossible to tell Kleph that the iduve did not understand the custom of service and reward, or that harm and help were one and the same to them. Aiela made up his mind to a half-truth. "I will speak for you," he said, "maybe—if you help me."

"Sir, what you ask is impossible just now, if you only under—"

"It had better not be impossible," Aiela said.

Kleph rocked back and forth uncomfortably. "The port— these tunnels are not complete, nor shored properly all the way, and your—*hhhunhh*—size will not make the passage easy. But at this hour, honest folk will be abed, and no human mercenary would be down here; they fear such places."

"Then take me to the port." Aiela gathered his stiffening legs under him, straightening as much as he could in this low-ceilinged chamber. Kleph scrambled up with much more agility and Aiela snatched at his collar, for it occurred to him Kleph could run away and leave him to die in these tunnels, lost in a dark maze of windings and pitfalls. He knew of a certainty that he could not best the creature in a fight or hold him if he were determined, but he intended to make it clear Kleph would have to harm him to avoid obeying him.

"You recovered my gun," Aiela said. "Give it back."

Kleph did not like it. He bubbled and boomed in his throat and twisted about unhappily, but he extracted the weapon from his belly-pocket and surrendered it. Aiela holstered it without letting go Kleph's collar, and then pushed at the little fellow to start him moving. They came to tunnel after tunnel and Kleph chose his way without hesitation.

Light burst suddenly like a sun exploding, heat hit their faces, and the stench of ozone mingled with the flood of outside air. A shadow of manlike shape dropped from above into their red-hazed vision, and Aiela hauled back on Kleph to flee. But the pain of the *idoikkhe* paralyzed his arm and he collapsed to his knees, while beside him on his face Kleph groveled and gibbered in terror, his saucer eyes surely agony, for the amaut could scarcely bear noon daylight, let alone this.

"Aiela," said a chill, familiar voice, and the *idoikkhe's* touch was gentle now, a mere signature: *Ashakh.*

Aiela expelled his breath in one quick sob of relief and picked himself up to face the iduve, who stood amid the rubble of the tunnel and in the beam of light from the street above.

What of the amaut? asked the pulses of the *idoikkhe. Will you be rid of him?*

"No," Aiela said quickly.

A response in which I find no wisdom, Ashakh replied. But he put the small hand weapon back in his belt and looked down on the amaut, coming closer. "Get up."

Kleph obeyed, crouching low and bowing and bobbing in extreme agitation. The light at his wrist swung wildly, throwing hideous shadows, leaping up and down the rough walls. Ashakh was a darkness, dusky of complexion and clad in black, but his eyes cast an uncanny mirror-light of dim rose hue, damped when he moved his head.

This person was aiding you? Ashakh asked.

"If Kleph is right, *bnesych* Gerlach was behind what happened at the port, and Kleph risked a great deal helping me."

"Indeed," mused Ashakh aloud. "Do you believe this?"

"I have reason to."

As you have reason for letting this amaut live? I fail to understand the purpose of it.

"Kleph knows Weissmouth," said Aiela, "and he will be willing to help us. Please," he added, sweating, for the look on Ashakh's grim face betokened a man in a hurry, and the iduve understood nothing of gratitude. He misliked being advocate for Kleph, but it was better than allowing the little fellow to be killed.

Chimele values your judgment; I do not agree with it.

But Ashakh said no more of killing Kleph, and Aiela understood the implication: it was on his shoulders, and *vaikka* was his to pay if his judgment proved wrong.

"Yes, sir," said Aiela. "What shall we do?"

"Have you a suggestion?"

"Get a ship and get the others out of Tejef's hands."

Ashakh frowned. "And have you a means to accomplish this?"

"No, sir."

"Well, we shall go to the port, and this person will guide us." Ashakh fixed the trembling amaut with a direct stare and Kleph scurried to get past him and take the lead. The tall iduve must bend to follow as they pursued their way through the winding passages.

"Do they know—does the Orithain know," Aiela asked, "what happened?"

We had a full account from Tesyel, who commands the base ship. And then in un-Ashakh fashion, the iduve volunteered further conversation. *Chimele sent me to find you. I was puzzled at first by the direction of the signal, but remembering the amaut's subterranean habits I resolved the matter—not without giving any persons trying to track us a sure indication of the direction of our flight. We had best make all possible haste. And I still mislike this small furtive person, Aiela-kameth.*

"I can only decide as a kallia, sir."

Honor to your self-perception. What are your reasons for mistrusting Gerlach?

12

The touch of Rakhi's mind came softly, most softly. It had hurt before, and Chaikhe accepted it cautiously, her nape hairs bristling at the male presence. She fought to subdue the rage that beat along her veins, and she felt Rakhi himself struggling against a very natural revulsion, for *chanokhia* forbade intimacy with a *katasathe*. She was for gift-giving and for honor, not for touching.

And there was his own distinctive *harachia*, a humorous, subdued presence. His *arastiethe* suffered terribly at close range, much more than hers did, for although folk judged Rakhi scandalously careless of his reputation, he was not really a person of *kutikkase* and his sense of *chanokhia* was keen in some regards. He cared most intensely what others thought of him, and found even the disapproval of a nas kame painful; but where others bristled and had recourse to the *idoikkhei* or engaged in petty *vaikka*, Rakhi laughed and turned inward. It was the shield of a nature as solitary in its own way as Ashakh's, and of a man of surprising intelligence. Even Chimele scarcely understood how much Rakhi dreaded to be known, how much he loathed to be touched and to touch; but Chaikhe felt these things, and kept her distance.

"*Nasith*," Rakhi voiced. He used this means, although other communication was swifter and carried sensory images as well; but this let him keep the essence of himself in reserve. "*Nasith*, Chimele is with me. She asks your state of health."

"I am quite well, *nasith-toj*."

"She advises you that Ashakh is presently attempting to recover the kameth Aiela. He has not communicated with you?"

"*Nasith,* I certainly would not have thought of violating Chimele's direct order in this regard. No, nor would I accept it if he contacted me."

But you are iq-*sra through both lines,* he thought, *and Ashakh does as Ashakh pleases when he likes his orders as little as he likes the one that separated you. We shall have him to deal with sooner or later.* "Contact *bnesych* Gerlach and re-establish communications with the amaut authorities. Under no circumstance admit humans within your security. They do not know us, and they have a great *m'melakhia,* tempered with very little judgment of reality, as witness their actions against Khasif and Mejakh. They also have a certain tendency toward *arrhei-akita,* which makes *vaikka* upon the few no guarantee that the example will deter others. Many of their actions arise from logical processes based on biological facts we do not yet understand, or else from their ignorance of us. Remember Khasif and use appropriate discretion."

"I will bear this in mind."

"*Ashanome* has suffered *vaikka* at the hands of someone in Weissmouth in the matter of Khasif. Chimele puts the entire business into your capable hands, *nasith-tak.* Whatever the fate of Priamos as a whole, this *vaikka* must be paid. Look to it, for we have been disadvantaged under the witness of both *Mijanothe* and *Tashavodh.*"

"Does Chimele not suggest a means?" inquired Chaikhe, proud and anxious at once, for the *arastiethe* of *Ashanome* was a great burden to bear alone.

Chimele's *harachia* came over Rakhi's senses, a rather uncertain contact at the distance he preserved: her *takkhenois* was full of disturbance, so that Chaikhe shivered. "Tell Chaikhe that Weissmouth is hers, and what she does with those beings is hers to determine, but I forbid her to risk her loss to us without consulting me."

"Tell Chimele I will handle the matter on those terms," she said, uncomforted. Chimele's disturbance lingered, upsetting her composure and making her stomach tight.

Chaikhe. Rakhi let Chimele's image fade. "Dawn is beginning in Weissmouth. I urge you make all possible haste."

"I shall. Leave me now. I shall begin at once."

He broke contact, but he was back before she had crossed the deck to the command console. *Chaikhe, understand: I must—*

His trouble set her teeth on edge and backlashed to such an extent that he hastily withdrew the feeler. She took firm grip on her rational faculty and invited his return.

Chaikhe, I—must stay. I do not lack chanokhia, *I protest I am not sensitive to your distress. I dislike this proximity. It grates, it hurts—*"I must remain in contact. Chimele's order, *nasith*. She judges it necessary." *But Chimele does not suffer, she does not feel this.*

Chaikhe shuddered as he did. The consciousness of the child within her sent a quick pulse of fury over her, an impulse to kill: and that impulse directed at Rakhi distressed her greatly. Something powerful stirred in her blood. Chemistry beyond her control was already beginning subtle changes in her; her temper almost ruled her. Her *takkhenois* was devastating. Her own power frightened her. *Is it this, to be* katasathe?

"Chaikhe," Rakhi's thought reached her, faint and timid, "Chaikhe, honor to you, *nasith-tak,* but I must do as I am told. Chimele—"

"I perceive, I perceive, I perceive." For a moment the faculty of reasonable response left her, and she was a prey to the anger; but then there was the cold clarity of Rakhi's thought in her mind. Au, *Chaikhe, Chaikhe, what is happening?*

And Chaikhe looked down at the green robes that were the honor of a *katasathe* and felt a moment of panic, a wish to shed these and the child at once and to be Chaikhe again. The violence growing in her mind went against everything she had always honored; and it was the child's doing.

Yet the thought of yielding up the child before the time shocked her. She could not. The process would complete itself inexorably and the madness, the honorable madness, would fasten itself upon her, a possession over which logic had no power.

Dhisais!

Long moments later Rakhi felt again toward her mind, fear at first, and then that characteristic humor that was Rakhi. "O *nasith-tak,* being *katasathe* is a situation of ultimate frustration to a male. If I should also become *dhisais,* I know not what I shall do with myself. Will they let me in the *dhis,* do you think?" *Or shall I die, nasith-tak? I should rather that, than to lose my mind.*

In another male his language would have been unbearably offensive to her condition—for to be *katasathe* was to hold a *m'melakhia* so private and so possessive that proximity to others as equals was unbearable. Had she been aboard *Ashanome*, she would have resigned her other activities and settled into a period of waiting, accepting gifts of the *nasul,* protection of Ashakh, increasingly occupied with her own thoughts. But in a strange way Rakhi did share with her, and could not really share or threaten; and she felt his disadvantage as her own. Their *urusti-ethe* had become almost one, and Rakhi had a right to such frankness.

We have begun to merge, he thought suddenly. *Au, Chaikhe, Chaikhe-nasith, what will become of me?*

Go away. Chimele's orders notwithstanding, go, now! Give me my privacy for a moment. Something is happening to me. I fear—I fear—

She is ill, she perceived Rakhi telling Chimele in great alarm, sweating, for he felt it too.

"'No,'" came Chimele's answer, and in her mind she could see Chimele's brooding face sketched by the tone of the answer. "'No, no illness. What was put into Chaikhe's veins while she slept was no more than nature would have sent soon enough. My profound regret, Chaikhe.'"

You are driving me to this state! she realized suddenly, with a flood of anger that hurt Rakhi no less; she felt the tremor that ran through him and his shame at having unwittingly participated. Then bitter laughter rose in her. *Honor to Chimele* sra-*Chaxal. Vaikka, vaikka, o Chimele, shadow-worker. From all others I knew how to defend myself; but those that come between Chimele and necessity must suffer for it. Honor to you indeed,* nasith.

"I knew nothing of it," Rakhi protested. "I did not, Chaikhe."

We are both disadvantaged, nasith-toj. *But when did one ever deal with Chimele and profit from it? Go. Go away.*

He fled in great discomfort, and Chaikhe sank down at the control console, her indigo fingers clenched together until the knuckles turned pale. Then with an abrupt act of will she forced her mind to business and fired an impulse to Tesyel, nas kame in charge of the base ship. *Tesyel,* she sent him, *have Neya escort the* bnesych *Gerlach to me immediately, giving him no opportunity for delay. If he be sleeping or naked as the day he was born, still give him no time to turn aside. If there are others with him, bring them. If they resist, destroy them. Use whatever of the* okkitani-as *you need in this.*

A light flashed on the board, Tesyel's signaled acknowledgment. Chaikhe noted it as a matter expected and put the wide scan from the base ship on her own screens.

Something flashed there, coming hard, at the far limit of the screen. She exerted herself to fire, almost a negligent gesture, for she meant to seal Weissmouth against all aircraft until Ashakh was heard from, and had it been Ashakh, she was sure she would have been advised.

The incoming ship brushed off the fire and varied nothing from its course, far outstripping amaut capabilities in its speed and defenses. It was huge, just inside the limits for intra-atmosphere operation.

The recognition occupied less than a second in Chaikhe's mind, as long as it took to flash a warning to Tesyel aboard the base command ship.

Tejef! her mind cried at Rakhi, shamefully hysterical, and rage and the wish to kill washed over her to the depths of her belly. Her ship blasted out a futile barrage at the incoming vessel, which showed every evidence of intending a landing: stalemate. Greater expense of energy could wipe out Weissmouth and the surrounding valley and still not penetrate the other's defenses.

Calm! Rakhi insisted. *Calm! Think as Chaikhe, not as a* dhisais. *O nasith-tak, if ever you needed your wits it is now. Conserve power, conserve, waste nothing and do not let him harm our people in the city. You are the citadel of our power on Priamos. If you fall, it is over. Do not add yourself to Tejef for* serach.

Power fluctuated wildly. In mental symbiosis with the ship's mechanisms, Chaikhe felt it like a wound and shuddered. *We are attacked. And Tesyel cannot control the base ship like an iduve.* But while the attack continued, her mind centered on one delicate task, an electronic surgery that altered contacts and began to unite her little ship with Tesyel's larger one, putting systems into communication so that she could draw upon the greater weapons of the base ship and command the computer that regulated its defensive systems. This would hold as long as her ship retained power to send command impulses. When that faded, she would lose command of the base ship. When that happened, Tejef would hold Priamos alone.

A half-day remained. When the sun stood at zenith over Weissmouth, the deadline would have expired; and Tejef's ship could force her to exhaust her power reserves well before that time, pounding at her defenses, forcing her to extend the power of her ship simply to survive.

13

"They are down," said Aiela. His mind wrenched from his asuthi and became again aware of Ashakh's face looking into his in the dim light of Kleph's wrist-glove, a witchfire flicker of color in the eyes of the iduve. Insanely he thought of being pent in a close space with a great carnivore, felt his heart laboring at the mere touch of the iduve's sinewy hand on his shoulder. Iduve weighed more than they looked. They were hard muscle, explosive power with little long-distance endurance. Even the touch of them felt different. Aiela tried not to flinch and concentrated anew on what his asuthi were sending now—awareness of engine shutdown, their own frustration and helplessness, locked as they were within their own quarters.

I was not secured until we lifted, Daniel sent him, bitter with self-accusation. *I waited, I waited, hoped for a better chance. But now that door is sealed and locked.*

And that communication flowed to the tunnels of Weissmouth through Aiela's lips, a hoarse whisper.

"Is Khasif possibly conscious?" Ashakh asked.

" 'No,' " Daniel responded. " 'At least I doubt it.' "

"It agrees with my own perception. But free him, if you should find the chance. Bend all your efforts to free him."

" 'I understand,' " sent Isande. " 'Where are you?' "

"Do not ask," Ashakh sent sharply and used Aiela's *idoikkhe* enough to sting. Aiela pulled back from the contact, for he was weary enough to betray things he would not have sent knowingly. His asuthi sent him a final appeal, private: *Get off this world; if you have the option, take it to get out of here.* And

Isande sent him something very warm and very sad at once, which he treasured.

"What are they saying?" Ashakh asked, pressing his shoulder again; but the iduve might have broken the arm at that moment and Aiela would still have returned the same blank refusal to say. His mind was filled with two others and his eyes were blinded with diffused light.

Get out, Daniel sent him, pushing through his faltering screens, and Isande did the same, willing him to go, warning him of Ashakh and of trusting the amaut. They left a great emptiness behind them.

"*M'metane.*" Ashakh's grip hurt, but he did not use the *idoikkhe* this time. "What is wrong?"

"They—cannot help. They don't know what to do."

The iduve's brows were drawn into a frown, his thin face set in an anger foreign to his harsh but disciplined person. "I sense his presence, whether he senses mine or not—and Chaikhe— Chaikhe—"

Something troubled Ashakh. His eyes were almost wild, so that Kleph shrank from him and Aiela stayed very still, fearing the iduve might strike at any sudden move. But the iduve rested kneeling, as if he were listening for a voice that no other could hear, like a man hearing the inner voice of an asuthe. His eyes stared into space, his lips parted as if he would cry out, but with an apparent effort he shook off the thing that touched him.

"There is a wrongness," he exclaimed, "a fear—one of my *nasithi* is afraid, and I do not know which. Perhaps it is Tejef. We were once of the same *nasul* and we were *takkhe.* Perhaps it is his dying I feel."

And it was indicative of his confusion that he spoke such things aloud, within the hearing of a *m'metane* and an outsider. In another moment he looked aware, and his face took on its accustomed hardness.

"You are empaths," Aiela realized, and said it without thinking.

"No—not—quite that, *m'metane.* But I feel the *takkhenes* of two minds from the port—Chaikhe—Tejef—I cannot sort them out. If she and he are diverting a great portion of their attention to managing ships' systems, it could account for the oddness— but it is wrong, *m'metane,* it is wrong. And from Khasif, I receive nothing—at least I surmise that his mind is the silent one." He had spoken in his native tongue, conceding this to Aiela, but not to Kleph, who huddled in terror against the wall, and now he turned a burning look on the amaut.

"We are still going to the port," he said to Kleph, "and you are involved in our affairs to an extent no outsider may be. From now on you are *okkitan-as* to *Ashanome,* the *nasul* of which we two are part."

"Ai, sir, great lord," wailed Kleph, making that gulping deep in his throat which was amautish weeping. "I am nothing, I am no one, I am utterly insignificant. Please let this poor person go. I will show you the port, oh, most gladly, sir, most gladly, serving you. But I am a clerk, no fighter, and I am not accustomed to weapons and I do not wish to be *okkitan-as* and travel forever."

Ashakh said nothing, nor glowered nor threatened; there was only a quiet thoughtfulness in his eyes, a wondering doubtless when would be the most rationally proper time to dispose of Kleph. Aiela moved quickly to interpose his calming *harachia* and to warn Kleph with a painful grip of his fingers that he was going too far.

"Kleph is indeed a clerk," Aiela confirmed, "and wished to become a farmer, quite likely; his mind is unprepared for the idea of service to a *nasul*. But he is also sensible and resourceful, and he would be an asset."

"He has a choice. I have a homing sense adequate to return us to the port even in these tunnels, but it would be a convenience if this person showed us the quickest way."

"Yes, sir." Kleph seemed to catch the implication of the alternative, for his pale saucer eyes grew very wide. "I shall do that."

And the little fellow turned upon hands and feet and scrambled up to go, they following; and ever and again Aiela could detect small thudding sounds which were sobs from the amaut's resonant throat. It was well for Kleph that the iduve allowed his species liberties in accordance with their (from the kalliran view) amoral nature. But quite probably Ashakh no more understood the workings of Kleph's mind than he did that of a serpent. The drives and needs that animated this little fellow could scarcely be translated into iduve language, and it would probably be Ashakh's choice to destroy him if the perplexity grew great enough to overpower advantage. The iduve were essentially a cautious people.

As for Kleph, Aiela thought, Ashakh might have bought him body and soul if he had offered him ten *lioi* of land; but it was too late for that now.

Suddenly Kleph thrust his light within the belly-pocket of his coveralls and Ashakh made a move for him that threw Aiela against the earthen wall, bruised; the little fellow hissed like a steam leak in the grip of the iduve, the wrong sound to make with an angry starlord; but he tried to gabble out words amid his hissing sounds of pain, and Aiela groped in the dark to try to stop the iduve from killing the creature.

"Stop, ai, stop," wailed Kleph, when Ashakh let up enough that he could speak. He restored a bit of light from his pocket: his face was contorted with anguish. "No trick, sir, no trick— please, we are coming to an inhabited section. O be still, sirs, please."

"Are there no other paths?" asked Ashakh.

"No, lord, not if my lord wishes to go to the port. Only a short distance through. All are sleeping. We post no guards. No humans dare come down. They hate the deeps."

Ashakh looked at Aiela for an answer, putting the burden of judging Kleph on his shoulders, treating him as *nas;* and he would be treated as *nas* if he erred, Aiela realized with a sinking feeling; but refusing would lower him forever in this iduve's sight. Suddenly he comprehended *arastiethe,* the compulsion to take, and not to yield: *giyre* in truth did not apply with Ashakh: one did not abdicate responsibility to the next highest—one assumed, and assumed to the limit of one's ability, and paid for errors dearly. *Arastiethe* was in one's self, and had great cost.

"I'll deal with Kleph, sir," said Aiela, "either for good or for ill, I'll deal with him, and he had better know it."

"I do not mean to lead you astray," Kleph protested again in a whisper, and he pointed and doused the wan light. There appeared in the distance a faint, almost illusory glow.

Aiela kept a firm hold on Kleph's arm while they went, and now they trod on stone, and a masonry ceiling arched overhead high enough that Ashakh might straighten without fear for his head. They came to a place where light came from dim globes mounted along the ceiling—a path that broadened into a hall, and rimmed a descending trail that wound down and down past amaut residences, side-by-side dwellings cut into the stone of the city's foundations. A chill damp breathed out from that pit, a musty scent of water. Aiela imagined that did he find a pebble to dislodge on the rim of that place, it would fall a great way and then—as it reached the level of the river and the water table—it would splash. They were still on the heights of Weissmouth, where the tunnels could reach to great depth. In amaut reckoning, it was a fine residential area, a pleasant place of cool dark and damp. And a sound from Kleph now would bring thousands of startled sleepers awake. It occurred to Aiela that Kleph's strength would easily suffice to hurl him to his death in the pit, were it not fear of an armed starlord behind him.

They passed on to a closer tunnel, still one where they had headroom, and where lights glowed at the intersection of all the lesser tunnels, so that they had no need of Kleph's little globe.

And around a corner came a startled party of amaut, who carried picks upon their shoulders and light-globes on their wrists, and who scattered shrieking and hissing in terror when they saw what was among them. In a moment all the tunnels were re-sounding with alarm, mad echoes pealing up and down the depths, and Aiela looked back at Ashakh, who was grimly returning his weapon to his belt.

"They would not understand nor would it stop the alarm," said Ashakh. He turned on Kleph a look that withered. "Redeem your error. Get us to safety."

Kleph was willing. He seized Aiela's arm to make him hurry, but shrank from contact with Ashakh, whom he urged with gestures, and took them off into one of the side corridors. The light-globe glowed into new life, their only source of illumination now, Kleph leading them where they knew not, further and further, until Aiela refused to follow more and backed the little fellow into a wall. Kleph gave a shrieking hiss and tried to vanish into another passage, but Ashakh brought his struggling to an end by his fingers laid on Kleph's broad chest and a look that would freeze water.

"Where do you intend to take us?" Aiela demanded, seeing

that Ashakh waited his intent with the creature. "I feel us going down and down."

"Necessary, necessary, o lord nas kame. We are near the river, descending—listen! Hear the pumps working?"

It was true. In an interval of deep silence there was a faint pulsing, like a giant's heartbeat within the maze. When they did not move, nowhere was there another sound but that. The alarm and the shouting had long since died away. Wherever they were, it seemed unlikely that this was a main corridor.

"Is there no quicker way?" Aiela asked.

"But the great lord said to take you to safety, and I have been doing that. See, there is no alarm."

"Be silent," said Aiela, "and stop pretending you have forgotten what we want. Whatever your personal preference, we had better come out near the port, and quickly."

Kleph's ugly face contorted in the swaying light, making his grimace worse than usual. He bubbled in his throat and edged past them without looking either of them in the eyes, retracing his steps to a tunnel they had bypassed. It angled faintly upward.

"O great lords," Kleph mourned in audible undertone, "your enemies are so great and so many, and I am not a fighter, my lords, I could not hurt anyone. Please remember that."

Ashakh hit him—no cuff, but a blow that hurled the little fellow stunned into the turning wall of the corridor; and Kleph cowered there on his knees and covered his head, shrilling a warble of alarm, a thin, sickly note. Aiela seized the amaut's shoulder, frightened by the violence, no less frightening when he looked back at Ashakh. The iduve leaned against the stone wall, clinging by his fingers to the surface. His rose-reflecting eyes were half-lidded and pale, showing no pupil at all.

A scramble of gravel beside him warned Aiela. He spun about and whipped out his gun. Kleph froze in the act of rising.

"If you douse that light," Aiela warned him, "I can still stop you before you get to the exit. I've stood between you and Ashakh until now. Don't press my generosity any further."

"Keep him away," Kleph bubbled in his own language. "Keep him away."

Aiela glanced at Ashakh, feeling his own skin crawl as he looked on that cold, mindless face: Ashakh, most brilliant of the

nasithi, cerebral master of *Ashanome's* computers and director
of her course—bereft of reason. Kallia though he was, he felt
takkhenes, the awareness of the internal force of that man, a life-
force let loose with them into that narrow darkness, at enmity
with all that was not *nas.*

A slow pulse began from the *idoikkhe,* panic multiplying in
Aiela's brain as the pulse matched the pounding of his own
heart; his asuthi knew, tried to hold to him. He thrust them away,
his knees in contact with the ground, the gravel burning his
hands, his paralyzed right hand losing its grip on the gun. Kleph
was beside him, gray-green eyes wide, his hand reaching for the
abandoned gun.

The pain ceased. Aiela struck left-handed at the amaut and
Kleph cowered back against the wall, protesting he had only
meant to help.

Aiela, Aiela, his asuthi sent, wondering whether he was all
right. But he ignored them and lurched to his feet, for Ashakh
still hung against the wall, his face stricken; and Aiela sensed
somehow that he was not the origin of the pain, rather that
Ashakh had saved him from it. He seized the iduve, felt that
lean, heavy body shudder and almost collapse. Ashakh gripped
his arms in return, holding until it shut the blood from his hands,
and all the while the whiteless eyes were inward and blank.

"Chaikhe," he murmured, "Chaikhe, *nasith-tak, prha-
Ashanome-ta-e-takkhe, au,* Chaikhe—Aiela, Aiela-*kameth*—"

"Here. I am here."

"A being—whose feel is *Ashanome,* but a stranger, a stranger
to me—*he,* he, reaching—hypothesis: Tejef, Tejef one-and-not-
one, Khasif—Chaikhe—Chaikhe, operating machinery, extended, mindless life-force—*e-takkhe, e-takkhe, e-takkhe!*"

Stop him! Isande cried in agony. *Stop him! He is deranged, he
can die—*

He—needing something? Daniel wondered. He hated Ashakh
to the depth of all that was human. Tejef had a little compassion.
Ashakh was as remorseless as *Ashanome's* machines. In a per-
verse way it pleased Daniel to see him suffer something.

Daniel, what is the matter with you? Isande exclaimed in
horror.

Aiela broke them asunder, for their quarreling was like to

drive him mad. Isande's presence remained on the one side, stunned, fearing Daniel; and Daniel's on the other, hating the iduve of *Ashanome,* hating dying. That was at the center of it—hating dying, hating being sent to it by beings like Ashakh and Chimele, who loved nothing and feared nothing and needed no one.

"Ashakh." Aiela thrust that yielding body hard against the wall and the impact seemed to reach the iduve; but moments passed before the gazed look left his eyes and he seemed to know himself again. Then he looked embarrassed and brushed off Aiela's hands and straightened his clothing.

"*Niseth,*" he said, avoiding Aiela's eyes. "I am disadvantaged before you."

"No, sir," said Aiela. "You saved my life, I think."

Ashakh inclined his head in appreciation of that courtesy and felt of the weapon at his belt, looking thoughtfully at the amaut. It could not comfort Ashakh in the least that an outsider had witnessed his collapse, and if Kleph could have known it, he was very close to dying in that moment. But Kleph instinctively did the right thing in crouching down very small and appearing not at all to joy in the situation.

"You are correct," said Ashakh to Aiela. "You were in danger, but it was side effect, a scattering of impulses. I feel—even yet—a disconnection, a disharmony without resolution. Tejef turned his mind to us and he is stronger than ever I felt him. He is—almost an outsider, not—outsider in the sense of *e-nasuli* but *e-iduve.* I cannot sort the minds out; they—he—Chaikhe— are involved with the machines—their impulses—hard to untan gle. The strangeness burns—it confuses—"

"Perhaps," said Aiela, ignoring Daniel's silent indignation, "perhaps he has been too long among humans."

Ashakh frowned. "You are *m'metane,* and you are not expected to go further in this. Tejef is a formidable man, and whatever Chimele's orders, you are free of bond to me. It is not reasonable to waste you where there is no cause, and I doubt I shall have to face Chimele's anger for disobeying her. Could you really aid me in some way, it would be different, but Tejef's arrival in the city has altered the situation. She did not anticipate this when she instructed you."

"My asuthi are aboard that ship."

"*Au,* kameth, what do you expect to do? I shall be hard put to defend myself, and I can hardly hold him from you forever. Should I fall in the attempt, as I doubtless will, there you will stand with *that* upon your wrist and that ridiculous weapon of yours, quite helpless. In the first place you will hinder me, and in the second event, you will die for nothing."

Aiela rested his hand on the offending pistol and looked up at the iduve with a hard set to his jaw. "My people are not killers," he said, "but it doesn't mean we can't fend for ourselves."

Ashakh hissed in contempt. "*Au.* Kallia have had the luxury to be so sparing of life ever since we came and brought order to your worlds. But Tejef will bend every effort to destroy me. If he succeeds, you are disarmed. I would cheerfully give you this weapon of mine instead, but see, there is no external control, and you can neither calibrate nor fire it. No, Chimele gave her orders, and I assume she is casting me away as she did Khasif. She forbade me to seek out Chaikhe, but you are under no such bond. I do not require you for *serach,* though it would do me honor; and I should prefer to have you providing Chaikhe contact with your asuthi aboard Tejef's ship."

Listen to him, Isande urged, joy and relief flooding over her. But her happiness died when she met his determined resistance.

"No, sir," said Aiela. "I'm going with you."

He half expected a touch of the *idoikkhe* for his impudence, but Ashakh merely frowned.

"*Tekasuphre,*" the iduve judged. "Chimele said you were prone to unpredictable action."

"But I am going," Aiela said, "unless you stop me."

Ashakh broke into a sudden grin, a thing more terrible than his frown. "A *vaikka-dhis,* then, kameth. We will do what we can do, and he will notice us before Chimele burns this wretched world to cinders."

"Ai, sir!" wailed Kleph, and applied his hands to his mouth in dismay at his own outburst.

In the next moment he had doused the light and attempted flight. Aiela snatched at him and seized only cloth, but Ashakh's arm stopped the amaut short, restoring light that flashed wildly about the tunnel with the flailing of Kleph's arms, and he had the being by the throat, close to crushing it, had Aiela not intervened. Ashakh simply dropped the little wretch, and Kleph tucked himself up in a ball and moaned and rocked in misery.

"Up," Aiela ordered him, hauling on his collar, and the amaut obediently rose, but would not look him in the face, making little hisses and thuds in his throat.

"This person is untouchable," said Ashakh; and in his language the word was *e-takkhe,* out of *takkhenes.* No closer word to enemy existed in the iduve vocabulary, and the killing impulse burned in Ashakh's normally placid eyes.

"I have a bond on him," Aiela said.

"Be sure," Ashakh replied, no more than that: iduve manners frowned on idle dispute as well as on interference with another's considered decisions.

What do you think you are? Isande cried, slipping through his screening. *Aiela, what do you think you're doing?*

He shut her out with a mental wince. *Not fair, not fair,* her retreating consciousness insisted. *Aiela, listen!*

He seized poor Kleph by the arm and shook at the heavy little fellow. "Kleph: now do you believe I meant what I said? Does it offend your precious sensibilities, all this fine world gone to cinders? If you have any other plans for it, then get us to the port. Maybe we can stop it. Do you understand me this time?"

"Yes," said Kleph, and for the first time since Ashakh's arrival the saucer eyes met his squarely. "Yes, sir."

Kleph edged past him to take the lead. His low brow furrowed into a multiplication of wrinkles so that his eyes were fringed by his colorless hair. His thin lips rolled in and out rapidly. How much he honestly could understand, Aiela was not sure. Almost he wished the little amaut would contrive to escape as soon as they made the port.

Aiela, Isande sent, *what are you doing? Why are you screening?*

Aiela shut her out entirely. Pity was dangerous. Let it begin and screens tumbled one after the other. He had to become for a little time as cold as the iduve, able to kill.

His mind fled back to the safe and orderly civilization of Aus Qao, where crime was usually a matter of personal disorder, where theft was a thing done by offworlders and the clever rich,

and where murder was an act of aberration that destined one for
restructuring. No kalliran officer had fired a lethal weapon on
Aus Qao in five thousand years.

He was not sure that he could. Ashakh could do so without
even perceiving the problem: he only reacted to the urgings of
takkhenes, of the two of them the more innocent. A kallia must
somehow, Aiela thought, summon up the violence of hate before
he could act.

He could not kill. The growing realization panicked him.
Conscience insisted that he tell his iduve companion of this
weakness in himself before it cost Ashakh his life. Something—
arastiethe or fear, he knew not which—kept him silent. *Giyre*
was impossible with this being: did he try to explain, Ashakh
would send him away. All that he could do was to expend everything, conscience and *kastien* as well, and stay beside the iduve
as far as his efforts could carry him.

14

Rakhi sweated. Great beads of perspiration rolled down the sides of his face, and the serenity of the *paredre* of *Ashanome* flashed in and out with the nervous flicker of a half-hearted mind-touch at the projection apparatus. But it was not projection. Between pulses the air was close and stank of burning; he occupied a woman's body, felt the urge to *takkenes* with the life within it, a strangeness of yearning where there was yet neither movement nor fully mind—only the most primitive sort of life, but selfed, and precious. Rage surged coldly over his nerves: lights dimmed, lights flashed, screens flared and went dark. He dared do nothing but ride it out, joined, aware, occasionally guiding Chaikhe's tired mind when she faltered in reaction. His body had limbs of vast size, his mind extended into a hundred circuits; he felt with her as her mind touched and manipulated contacts, shunted power from one system to another with a coordination as smooth as that of a living body.

And he perceived the hammering of Tejef's weapons against the ship/body, the flow of energies on the shields, a debilitating drainage of power that required a great effort to balance defense between weakness and waste and destruction to the city. It began to be evident: Tejef's ship, a small *akites,* had Chaikhe's power supply from two lesser ships at a disadvantage. Chaikhe could, by skill and efficient management, prolong the struggle, but she was incapable of offensive action. Tejef could not down her shields, for probe and transfer ships such as Chaikhe commanded were heavily shielded, but their combined weaponry, while adequate to level a city, had no effect against an *akites.*

The chronometer continued its relentless progress, ticking off the moments as *Ashanome*-time proceeded toward main-dark, and Kej, light-years away, had fled the ambered sea of Thiphrel: shadow flooded the coastal plain to the east of Mount Im, advancing toward ancient Cheltaris. Priamos-time, on the inner track, went more slowly, but had less time to run. Nine hours had passed since midnight. When three more had gone, Priamos would blaze like a novaed star and die.

Life-support/cooling had shut down entirely save for the control room. Lights were out everywhere but the panel even there. In the base ship Tesyel and the remaining crew huddled on the bridge, five degrees cooler than Chaikhe's command center. The amaut with Tesyel suffered cruelly in the heat, mopping dry skin with moistened cloths, lying still, listless. Communications were almost out. Only the sensors that maintained the field and the shields were still fully operative.

The attack slacked off. It did so at irregular intervals, and Chaikhe allowed the automatic cutback to the secondary shields. But groundscan was picking up movement in what had been a dead zone; Chaikhe mentally reached for the image and the dark silhouette of an iduve appeared on the screen—no human, that lean quick shadow. *Takkhenes* reached and confirmed it: she saw the image hesitate at the touch, felt the ferocity that was Ashakh.

Chimele's orders! Rakhi sent. *Break, break contact, now!* And Chimele in the *paredre* was on her feet, her face dark with anger. Chaikhe flinched from the wrath Rakhi transmitted; but her attack reflexes had reacted before Rakhi's cooler counsel prevailed, shunted power to the attack and expended heavily against Tejef's shields.

Think! Rakhi sent. *Nothing can live amid those energies. Hold back before you kill Ashakh.*

She cut back suddenly—return fire damaged systems. She began to replot. But in another part of her mind she knew Ashakh still alive, about to die if she kept her shields extended as she must. *Warn him, warn him,* she thought. *Does he expect me to lower defenses for him and die? What is he doing?*

Calm! Rakhi insisted, and winced from the fury of her mind, *m'melakhia* for Ashakh is deadly conflict with that for the child in her, fury washing out reason. *Kill!* The impulse surged through her being, but Rakhi's singleminded negative imposed control and she extended her mind to watch Ashakh's progress.

More of the witless humans were creeping out from cover, as if the lesson of scores of human and amaut dead were not enough to teach them the peril of the field about the embattled ships; and like the stubborn creatures they were they moved out, stalking Ashakh and his two companions.

Aiela, Chaikhe recognized the azure-skinned being that moved beside Ashakh, but the small person with them, an amaut—

Tesyel, she sent by the *idoikkhe: Have you dispatched any* okkitan-as *to Weissmouth?*

"Negative," came the nas kame's voice. "We had no time. I scan that one, but I do not know him."

A Priamid amaut. Ashakh's witlessness appalled her, his lack of *m'melakhia* for *Ashanome* in taking on such a servant sent waves of heat to her face. *Ashakh!* she hurled an impact of mind at him that he had no means to receive, but perhaps *takkhenes* itself carried her anger. Ashakh hesitated, looked full toward the ship.

—And arched his back and fell, trying even in the motion to bring his weapon to bear. Chaikhe gave a shrill hiss of rage, seeing the humans that had done it, a shot from beyond him. Ashakh fired: a hundred *ehsim* of port landscape became a hemisphere of light and a handful of humans and an amaut aircraft were not there when it imploded into darkness, nor again when normal light returned, Tejef's shields tightened and flared at the rippling of that energy, sucked outward toward Ashakh. Chaikhe reacted instantly, aware of the distant figures of the nas kame and the amaut trying to drag Ashakh back out of the exposed area. She hit at Tejef's shields, and as her searching mind found no consciousness in Ashakh a rage grew in her, a determination to destroy everything, to force *Ashanome* to wipe out *akites* and port and population entire. If her *sra* was to die, it deserved that for *serach,* she and Ashakh and her child.

"No!" Rakhi shouted into her mind. "Chimele forbids! Chimele forbids, Chaikhe!"

She gave a moan, a keening of rage, and desisted. But another impulse seized her, a fierceness to *vaikka* upon the power against whom she and Ashakh struggled, be it Chimele, be it Tejef.

Chaikhe! Rakhi cried. Through his mind Chimele radiated terrible anger. But Chaikhe wrapped herself in the chill of her own *arastiethe,* suddenly diverted power from the shields to communications, playing mental havoc with the circuitry of the ship until she patched into amaut communications citywide. The whole process took a few blinks of an eye. The frightened chatter of amaut voices came back to her.

Be sure what you do, Rakhi advised her, Chimele's order; but Chimele's *takkhenois* lost some of its fierceness and flowed into alignment, feeding her will, supporting her now that her mind was clear.

"Open citywide address channels," Chaikhe ordered, and received the acknowledgment of the terrified amaut in command of their communications.

"I am the emissary of the Orithain," Chaikhe began softly, the phrase that had heralded the terror of iduve decrees since the dawn of civilization in the *metrosi.* "Hail Priamos. We pose you now alternatives. If this rebel iduve is not ours before midday, we shall destroy as much of Weissmouth and of Priamos as is necessary to take or destroy him; if this colony seems to side with him, we shall eliminate it. Evacuation is logistically impossible and the use of this field is extremely hazardous. I counsel you against it. I have said."

She ceased, and listened in satisfaction as amaut communications went chaotic with incoming and outgoing calls, amaut asking orders, officers reacting in harried outbursts of emotion, sometimes a human's different voice calling in, incomprehensible and distraught.

The panic had begun. It would run through the city, into the tunnels, and into every command station in the amaut colony. *Vaikka,* Chaikhe told herself with satisfaction. *They are sure we are among them now.* And the knowledge that these pathetic beings scattered before her attack filled her with a shuddering desire to pursue the *vaikka* further; but other duties called. Tejef. Tejef was the objective.

Attack resumed, ineffectual *vaikka* from Tejef for the damage done him among the amaut who trusted him for protection.

Aiela had taken Ashakh beyond the range of weapons fire, and there was the grateful feel of returning consciousness from Ashakh. Her heart swelled with gladness.

No! cried Rakhi. "Chimele will not permit contact, Chaikhe."

The attack increased. Systems faltered. There was no time to dispute.

The spate of fire was a brief one; the glow about the iduve ships dimmed and the humans dared come from cover again. Aiela saw them moving far across the field and fired his own pistol to put a temporary stop to it. The humans were not yet aware that the weapon could not kill. He feared they would not be long in learning, about as long as it took for the first that he had fired on to recover; and as for the iduve weapon, that black thing like an elongate egg, there was indeed no way to operate it save by mind-touch.

"Let us go back, please, let us go back," Kleph pleaded. "Let us get off this awful field, into the safe dark, o please, sir."

A small projectile exploded not far away, and Kleph winced into a tighter crouch, almost a single ball of knees and arms, moaning.

It was indeed too close. Aiela seized Ashakh's limp arm and snapped at Kleph in order to take the other. It was the first order Kleph had obeyed with any enthusiasm, and they hurried, pulling the iduve back into the cover of the basement from which they had emerged onto the field. There they had only the light of Kleph's lamp and what came from the open door; and the very foundations shook with the pounding of fire out on the field. The wailing of sirens went on and on.

Ashakh stirred at last. He had been conscious from time to time, but only barely so. The shot that had struck him in the back would have likely been a mortal wound had he been kallia; but Ashakh's heart, which beat to right center of his chest, had kept a strong rhythm. This time when he opened his eyes they were clear and aware.

"A human weapon?" Ashakh asked.

"Yes, sir."

"*Niseth,*" murmured the proud iduve for the second time. "*Au, kameth, Tejefu-prha-idoikkhe—*"

"He has not used it."

That much puzzled Ashakh. Aiela could see the perplexity go through his eyes. Then he struggled to get his hands under him, Aiela's protests notwithstanding. "Either Tejef is too busy to divert his attention to you or Chaikhe has been taking care of you, kameth. I think the latter. This would be a serious error on his part."

"Chaikhe gave him something to worry about," said Aiela. "It was over the loudspeakers all over the field. She advised Priamos what it could expect—I don't doubt it went to the city too. The field emptied quickly after that announcement, except for a determined few. We saw one aircraft try to take off."

"It hit the shields," burst out Kleph, his saucer eyes wide. "O great lord, it went in a puff of fire."

"*Tekasuphre,*" judged Ashakh. He struggled to sit upright, and it was probable that he was in great pain, although he gave no demonstration of it. He suffered in silence while Aiela made a bandage of Kleph's folded handkerchief and attempted to wedge it into position within Ashakh's belt. There was surprisingly little bleeding, but the iduve's normally hot skin was cold to the touch, and the iduve seemed distracted, mentally elsewhere. So much of the iduve's life was mind: Aiela wondered now if mind were not being diverted toward other purposes, sustaining body.

"Sir," he said, "Ashakh—you have to have help, and we don't know what to do. How bad is it?"

It was badly asked: Aiela realized it at once, for Ashakh's face clouded and the *idoikkhe* tingled, the barest prickling. *Arastiethe* forbade—and yet Ashakh forebore temper.

"I meant," Aiela amended gently, "that I can't tell what it hit, or how to deal with it. In a kallia, it would be serious. I have no knowledge of iduve anatomy."

"It is painful," Ashakh conceded, "and my concentration is necessarily impaired. I regret, kameth, but I advise you to seek Chaikhe at your earliest opportunity. I remind you I predicted this."

"I have long since found it is futile to expect explanations between iduve and kallia to make sense," said Aiela, all the while his asuthi heard and pleaded with him to take Ashakh's offer. "My interests lie with my asuthi and with you, and once with Chaikhe I can't do much for either."

Ashakh frowned. "You are kameth, not *nas*."

Aiela shrugged. It was not productive to become involved in an argument with an iduve. Silence was the one thing they could not fight. He simply did not go, and looked up toward Kleph, who, ignored, had begun to creep toward the dark of the tunnel opening.

"Stay where you are," Aiela warned him.

"Ai, sir," said Kleph, "I did not—" And suddenly the amaut's mouth made one quick open and shut and he scrambled backward, while Ashakh reached wildly for the weapon that was no longer in his belt but in Aiela's, rescued from the outside pavement.

Toshi and Gerlach and two humans were in the tunnel opening, weapons leveled.

Fire! Daniel screamed at Aiela; and Isande sent a negative.

Aiela, cursing his own lack of foresight, simply gathered himself up in leisurely dignity, dropped Ashakh's weapon and his own from his belt, and bent again to assist Ashakh, who was determined to get to his feet. Kleph shrugged and dusted himself off busily as if his presence there were the most natural thing in the world.

"Sir," exclaimed Kleph to Gerlach, "I am relieved. May I assist you with these persons?"

Never had Aiela seen an amaut truly overcome with anger, but Gerlach fairly snarled at Kleph, a spitting sound; and Kleph scampered back out of his reach, forgetting to bow on the retreat, his face twisted in a grimace of fright and rage.

"Kleph double-heart, Kleph glib of speech," exclaimed Gerlach, "you are to blame for this disaster." He seemed likely to rush at Kleph in his fury; but then he fell silent and seemed for the first time to realize the enormity of his situation, for Ashakh drew himself up to his slim towering height, folded his arms placidly, and looked down at their diminutive captor.

"*Prha,* kameth?" Ashakh asked of Aiela. *Arastiethe* forbade he should take direct account of the likes of Gerlach and Toshi.

"Gerlach knows well enough," said Aiela, "that *karsh* Gomek would pay dearly should he kill you, sir; they would pay with every Gomek ship in the Esliph and the *metrosi*. If he were wise at all, he would leave iduve business to the iduve."

"We want Priamos," Gerlach protested, "Priamos with its fields undamaged."

"That will not be," said Aiela, "unless you stand aside."

"If my lords will yield gracefully, I shall see that this matter is indeed settled by iduve, by the lord-on-Priamos."

"You have chosen the wrong loyalty," said Aiela.

"We had only one knowable choice," said Gerlach. "We know that the lord-on-Priamos wants this world intact and the lord-above-Priamos wants to destroy us. Perhaps our choice was wrong; but it is made. We know what the lord-above-Priamos will do to us if we lose the lord-on-Priamos to protect us. We are little people. We shelter in what shade is offered us, and only the lord-on-Priamos casts a shadow on this world."

Aiela thought that was for Ashakh to answer; but the iduve simply stared at the little fellow, and of course it was unproductive to argue. *Elethia* insisted upon silence where no proof would convince; and Gerlach was left to sweat in the interval, faced with the necessity of moving a starlord who was not in a mood to reason.

"Guard them," he said suddenly to Toshi. "I have other matters to attend." And he scurried up the steps to daylight, not without a snarl at Kleph. "Shoot this one on the least excuse," he told Toshi, looking back. Then he was gone.

"What good do you get from this?" Aiela asked then in human speech, addressing himself to the mercenaries with Toshi. "What's your gain, except a burned world?"

"We know you," said the dark-faced one. "You and your companions cost us three good friends the last trip into this city."

"But what," asked Aiela, "do you have to gain from Tejef?"

The man shrugged, a lift of one shoulder, as humans did. "We aren't going to listen to you."

How do I reason with that? Aiela asked of Daniel.

Forget it, Daniel sent. *Tejef's kamethi chose to be with him. They have giyre.*

Believe this, sent Daniel. *They'll kill you where you stand. If Ashakh drops, that little devil of an amaut will send them for your throat, and you'll have no more mercy out of them than from her.*

Aiela looked uneasily at Ashakh, who with great dignity had withdrawn to the brick wall and leaned there in the corner, arms folded, one foot resting on a bit of pipe. The iduve merely stared at the humans and at Toshi, looking capable of going for their throats, but a moment ago he had been in a state of complete collapse, and Aiela had the uncomfortable feeling that *arastiethe* alone was keeping the man on his feet, pure iduve arrogance. It would not hold him there forever.

Something was mightily amiss in the ship. Amaut bustled up and down the corridor, and the lights had been dimming periodically. Arle watched from the security of the glass-fronted infirmary and saw the hurrying outside become frantic. The lights dimmed again. She scurried back to the banks of instruments at Margaret's bedside and wondered anxiously whether they varied because the power was going out or because there was something wrong with Margaret.

She slept so long.

("You stay, watch," Tejef had told her personally, setting her at this post and making her secure before the sickening lunge the ship had made aloft and down again; and Dlechish, the awful little amaut surgeon, had been there through that, making sure all went well with Margaret.)

Dlechish was gone now, Arle had had the infirmary to herself ever since this insanity with the lights had begun, and she was glad at least not to have to share the room with amaut.

But Margaret was so pale, and breathed with such difficulty. When the instruments faltered, Arle would clench her hands on the edge of her hard seat and hold her own breath until the lines resumed their regular pattern. Of the machines themselves she understood nothing but that these lines were Margaret's life, and when they ceased, Margaret's existence would have ceased also.

The lights dimmed again and flickered lower. Margaret stirred in her sleep, tossing, struggling to move against the restraints and the frames and the tubing. When Arle attempted to hold her still, Margaret tried the harder to rid herself of the encumbrances, and began to work her hand free. Arle pleaded. Margaret's movements were out of delirium and nightmare. She began to cry out in her pain.

"Tejef!" Arle cried at the intercom. And when no answer came she went out and tried to find someone, one of the guards, anyone at all. She began to run, hard-breathing, to one and another of the compartments off the infirmary, trying to find at least one of the amaut attendants.

The fourth door yielded an amaut who gibbered at her and thrust an ugly black gun at her. She screamed in fright, and her eyes widened as she saw the dark man who lay inside the room, unconscious or dead, in the embrace of restraints and strange instruments.

She tried to dart under the amaut's reach. He seized her arm in one strong amautish hand and twisted it cruelly. Of a sudden he let her go.

She kicked him and fled, and met a black-clad man chest-on. She looked up and was only realizing it was Tejef when his hand cracked across her face.

It threw her down, hurt her jaw, and made her deaf for a moment; but dazed and hurt as she was she knew that he had slapped, not hit, and that the tempers which gripped him would pass. She gave a desperate sob of effort, scrambled to her feet, and raced for the infirmary, for Margaret, and safety.

He had followed her, coming around the corner not long after she had shut and locked the door; and to her horror she saw the door open despite the lock, without his touching it. She fled back to Margaret's bedside and sank down there hard-breathing. She sought to ignore him by way of defense, and did not look at him.

"You're not hurt?" Tejef demanded of her. Arle shook her head. One did not talk to Tejef when he was angry. Margaret had advised her so. She was sick with fear.

"I say stay with Margaret, *m'metane-tak*. Am I mistaking meaning—*stay?*"

"Margaret got worse. And I thought it was you in there. I'm sorry, sir."

"I?" Tejef seemed greatly surprised, even upset, and fingered gently the hot place his blow had left on her cheek. "You are a child, Arle. A child must obey."

"Yes, sir."

"*Niseth.* I regret the blow."

She looked up at him, perceiving that he was indeed sorry. And she knew that it embarrassed him terribly to admit that he was wrong. That was to be a man—not being wrong. Her father had been like that.

"Tejef," said Margaret. Her eyes had opened. "Tejef, where are we?"

"Still on Priamos." As if it were a very difficult thing he offered his hand to her reaching fingers.

"I thought I felt us move."

"Yes."

The confusion seemed to overwhelm her. She moaned a tiny sound and clenched her fingers the more tightly upon his; but he disengaged himself gently and quietly went about preparing Margaret's medicines himself. The lights dimmed. Things shook in his hands.

"Sir?" Arle exclaimed, half-rising.

The lights came on again and he continued his work. He returned to Margaret's side, ignoring Arle's questions of lights and machines, administered another injection and waited for it to take effect.

"Tejef," Margaret pleaded sleepily.

His lips tightened and he kept his eyes fixed upon the machines for a moment; but then he bent down and let her lips brush his cheek. Gently he returned the gesture, straightened, hissed very softly, and walked out, his long strides echoing down the hall.

When Arle looked at Margaret again, she was quiet, and slept.

"Priamos-time," said Rakhi, "one hour remains."

Then let me use it unhindered, Chaikhe retorted, not caring to voice or to screen. Rakhi's periodic reminders of the time disrupted her concentration and lessened her efficiency. She had her own internal clock; cross-checking with Rakhi's was a nuisance.

Exhaustion is lowering your efficiency, dimming your perceptions, and rendering you most difficult, Chaikhe. His mind seemed a little strained also. Chimele hovered near him like a foreboding of ruin to come. *I know you are tired and short of temper. So am I. It is senseless to work against me.*

Go away. Chaikhe flung herself back from the console, abandoning manual and mental controls. It was rashness. Tejef's attacks were fewer during the last half-hour, but no less fierce. Tejef also knew the time. He was surely saving what he could for some last-moment effort.

"Do you think this man who has run us so long a chase will be predictable at the last?" Rakhi restrained his impatience; he fought against the vagaries of her hormone-heightened temper with a precise, orderly process quite foreign to his own tastes, but he could use it when he chose.

Rakhi, thought Chaikhe distractedly, *there is a bit of Chaxal in your blood after all. You sound like Ashakh, or Chimele.*

Sit down, he ordered rudely, *and remember that Tejef has* arastiethe *enough to choose his own moment. What chance has he of outlasting us, with* Ashanome *overhead? He knows that he must die, but he will try to make the terms not to our liking. This is not the moment for tempers,* nasith-tak.

She flared for a moment, but acknowledged reason when she heard it, and scanned the instruments for him, feeding him knowledge of fading power levels, blown systems. *I have done as much for this little ship as reasonably possible,* she told him, *and being of the order of Artists, I consider I have exceeded expectations.*

"Quite true, *nasith-tak.*"

And at this point even Ashakh could not keep this ship functioning, she continued bitterly. *Chimele knew my power on this world and she knew Tejef's, and she drew back one ship that we might have had down here. She might have made me capable of attack, not only of defense. Am I only bait,* nasith? *Was I only a lure, and did she deceive me with half-truths as she did Khasif and Ashakh?*

"'Impertinence!'" Chimele judged, when Rakhi conveyed that to her; and the impact of her anger was unsettling.

Did you deceive me?

"'Your question was not heard and your attitude was not perceived, *nasith.* However I use you, I will not be challenged. Follow my orders.'"

Tell her my shields are failing.

"'Continue in my orders.'"

Hail Chimele, she said bitterly, but Rakhi did not translate the bitterness. *Tell me I am honored by her difficulty with me. But of course I am going to comply. Honor to* Ashanome, *and to the last of us. Walk warily, Rakhi. May the* nasul *live.*

Rakhi stopped translating. *A* katasthe *ought to show more respect for one who can destroy her or exile her forever. Be sensible. The Orithain's honor is* Ashanome's. *Are you* takkhe? *Au, Chaikhe, are you?*

I am dhisais! she raged at him. *I am* akita! *Not even Chimele has power over me.* And Rakhi fled for a moment, struggling with the impulses of his own body. His blood raced faster, his borrowed fierceness tore at his nerves, tormented by Chimele's *harachia.*

"We shall both be fit for the red robes," came Rakhi's slight mind-touch, his wonted humor a timorous thing now, and soft. "Chaikhe, do not press me further, do not."

About the ship the shields flared once more under attack, shimmering in and out of the visible spectrum as they died, an eerie aurora effect in the late morning sun. Chaikhe shuddered, feeling the dying of the ship, wild impulses in *serach* and to death at war with the life in her.

Think! Rakhi's male sanity urged.

Tesyel: her mind reached for the *idoikkhe* of the kameth of the base ship, a last message. *I shall leave you power enough to safeguard yourself and get offworld. I do not require you for* serach. *A world will be quite enough. See to your own survival.*

"Are you hurt?" His kalliran voice came through with anxious stress. Tesyel was a good man, but he had his people's tendency to become personally involved in others' crises. Perhaps in the labyrinthine kalliran ethic he conceived that he had suffered some sort of *niseth* in being shown inadequate to ward off the misfortune of *Ashanome,* m'metane though he was. In some situations a kallia had a fierce *m'melakhia* of responsibility.

I am not injured, said Chaikhe, *and you are without further responsibility, kameth. You have shown great* elethia *in my service. Now I return you to the* nasul. *Do nothing without directly consulting* Ashanome.

"I am honored to have served you," murmured the kameth sadly. His voice was almost lost in static. "But if I—"

The static drowned him out. In the next moment the shields collapsed. The control room went black for a few seconds. Chaikhe sought desperately to restructure the failed mechanisms, bypassing safety devices.

The attack resumed. Overheated metal stank. Light went out and dimly returned. A whining of almost harmonic sound pulsed through the ship's structure. Power was dying altogether.

Chaikhe mind-touched the doors through to the airlock, desperately seeking air. Reserve batteries were fading too, and she fought to reach the door in the dark and the roiling smoke, choking. She fell.

Long before she knew anything else she was aware of Rakhi's frantic pleading, trying with his own will to animate her exhausted body.

And then she knew another thing, that someone trod the inner corridor of the ship, and *m'melakhia* drove her to her feet, graceless and stumbling as she sought a weapon in the dark.

"Chimele forbids," Rakhi told her, and that stunned her into angry indecision.

Forbids? What is she about to do?

Her senses reeled. Her eyes poured water, stung by the smoke, and she hurled herself blindly down the corridor.

A squat amaut shadow stood outlined against the smoke-filled light from the airlock. Chaikhe had never felt real menace in a non-iduve before: this being radiated it, a cold sickly *m'melakhia* that came over her crisis-heightened sensitivity. It was repugnant. She had received from kalliran minds before, particularly in *katasukke;* it was a talent suspect and embarrassedly hidden, *e-chanokhia.* Kallia held a cleanly muddle of stresses and inhibitions, cramped but intensely orderly. This creature was venomous.

"My lady," it said with a bow, "*Bnesych* Gerlach at your service, my lady."

Chaikhe felt the almost-*takkhenes* of the child in her. Her lips quivered. Her vision blurred at the edges and became preternaturally clear upon Gerlach's vulnerable self. She could crack his brute neck so easy, so satisfyingly. He would know it was coming; his terror would be delightful.

No! Rakhi cried. *Chaikhe, rule yourself. Control. Calm.*

M'melakhia focused briefly upon her *asuthe*, sweet and satisfying, full of the scent of blood.

I am you, he protested, horrified. *It is not reasonable.*

He suffered; their *arastiethe* was one, and to live they each must yield. The situation defied reason.

Leave me, she pleaded, aware of Gerlach's eyes on her, a shame that Chimele's orders left her powerless to remedy.

He lacked the control to break away. Their joined *arastiethe* made him fear her fear, suffer shame with her, dread injury to the child, feel its *takkhenois* within his own body—things rationally impossible.

Is this what m'metanei *mean by* m'melakhia *one for the other?* Rakhi wondered out of the chaos of his own thoughts. Au, *I am drowning, I am suffocating, Chaikhe, and I am too weary to let go. If he touches you, I think I shall be ill.*

Gerlach was beside her. Fire had leapt up in the corridor, control room systems too damaged to prevent it, smoke choking them as the ship deteriorated further. Gerlach seized her arm and drew her on. The collapse of systems with which her mind was in contact dazed and confused her.

Let go, Rakhi urged her, *let go, let go.*

Her mind went inward, self-seeking, dead to the outside. She saw the *paredre* of *Ashanome* briefly; and then Rakhi performed the same inwardness and that vision went. She knew her limbs had lost their strength. She knew Gerlach's coarse broad hands taking her, a loss of breath as she was slung across his shoulder. For a moment she was in complete withdrawal; then the pain of his jolting last step to the pavement jarred her free again.

Kill him! Rakhi's voice in her mind was a shuddering echo and re-echo, down vast corridors of distance. Chimele's strong nails bit into his/her shoulder, reminding them of calm. Other minds began to gather: Raxomeqh's cold brilliance, Achiqh, Najadh, Tahjekh, like tiny points of light in a vast darkness. But Chaikhe concentrated deliberately on the horror of Gerlach, his oiliness, the grotesqueries of his waddling gait and panting wheezes for breath, learning what *m'metanei* called hate, a disunity beyond *e-takkhe,* a desire beyond *vaikka-nasul,* a lust beyond reason.

Dhisais, dhisais, Rakhi reminded her, Chimele's incomprehensible orders twisted through his hearing and his mind. *Be
Chaikhe yet for a little time more. Restraint!*

She had never been so treated in her life. Not even in the
fierceness of *katasakke* had she been compelled to be touched
against her will. Did *m'metanei* suffer such self-lessening in being
kameth, in taking part in *katasukke?* The thought appalled her.

Stop it, Rakhi shuddered. *Au, Chaikhe, this is obscene.*

Male, he, it, this—dhisais, dhisais, akita, *I—kill him. My
honor, mine, male, mate, male,* e-takkhe, *I—*

Rakhi's fists slammed into the desk top, pain, pain, shattered
plastics, bleeding, his wrists lacerated. The physical shock shuddered through Chaikhe's body. She felt the wounds on her own
wrists, the flow of the warm blood over her hands, tension
ebbing.

We, he kept repeating into her mind, *we, together, we.*

For the last few moments, Ashakh had not moved. Aiela
stared at him tensely, wondering how much longer the iduve
could manage to stand. He rested still with his back against the
corner, his arms folded tightly across his chest, eyes closed; and
whether the bleeding had started again the cellar was too dark to
show. From time to time his eyes would still open and glimmer
roseate fire in the light of Toshi's wrist-globe. The little amaut
never varied the angle of the gun she trained upon the both of
them. Aiela began to fear that it would come soon, that Ashakh's
growing weakness would end the stalemate and render them
both helpless.

Dive for an exit, Daniel advised him. *The second Ashakh
falls, they'll see only him. Dive for any way out you can take.
Isande, Isande, you reason with him.*

Peace, Aiela pleaded. He had another thing in mind, an attack
before necessity came upon them. Toshi had one hand bandaged, thanks, no doubt, to Kleph's hirelings outside the headquarters; and if Kleph, who huddled near Ashakh, had the will
to fight, Kleph could handle Toshi—the only one of them now
who had the strength for that. Aiela began instead to size up the
two humans, wondering what chance he would have against the
two of them.

Precious little, Daniel estimated. *You've no instinct for it. Get yourself out of there. Get to Chaikhe. If you can't send any more, Isande and I are cut apart, as good as dead too. We have nothing left without you.*

Isande had no words: what she sent was yet more unfairly effective, and it took the heart from him. He hesitated.

Ashakh's eyes opened slightly. "You still have the option," he told Toshi, "to cast down your weapons and rescue yourselves."

Toshi gave a nervous bubbling of laughter, to which the humans did not respond, not understanding.

"He said get out of here," said Aiela, and the men looked at Ashakh as if they thought of laughing and then changed their minds. Iduve humor was something outsiders would not recognize, nor appreciate when they saw it in action. Ashakh was indulging in a bit of *vaikka,* he realized in chill fear, absolutely straight-faced and far from bluffing; likely as his own death was at the moment, *arastiethe* forbade any unseemly behavior.

One human fled. Toshi did not let herself be distracted.

The cellar went to eye-wrenching light and dark and rumbled in collapse. Aiela and Kleph clenched themselves into a unified ball, seeking protection from the cascading cement and brick, and for a moment Aiela gave himself up to die, uncertain how much weight of concrete there was above. A large piece of it crashed into his head, bruising his protecting fingers, and at that he thought of Ashakh and scrambled the few feet to try to protect him.

In the next breath it was over, and Aiela found daylight flooding in through a gap where the door had been, and the side of the room where Toshi and the human had been was a solid mound of rubble.

A dusty and bloodied Ashakh dragged himself to his feet and leaned unsteadily on the edge of the basement steps. *"Niseth,"* he proclaimed. "The effect considerably exceeded calculations."

And upon that he nearly fainted, and would have fallen, but Kleph and Aiela held him on his feet and helped him up to daylight, where the air was free of dust.

"What was it, great lord?" Kleph bubbled nervously. "What happened?"

"Aiela," said Ashakh, catching his breath, "Aiela, go down, see if you can locate our weapons."

Aiela hurried, searching amid the grisly rubble, pulling brick aside and fearing further collapse. He knew by now what Ashakh had done, delicately mind-touching the weapon he had so casually dropped, and negating a considerable portion of the cellar.

His own gun lay accessible. When he found Ashakh's, it looked unscathed too, and he brought it up into the daylight and put it into the iduve's hand.

"Damaged," Ashakh judged regretfully. His indigo face had acquired a certain grayish cast, and his hand seemed to have difficulty returning the weapon to his belt.

"Chaikhe," he said, and could tell them little more than that. He shook off Kleph's hand with a violence that left the little amaut nursing a sore wrist, and stumbled forward, unreasoning, heedless of their protests. There was nothing before them but open ground, the wide expanse of the port, Chaikhe's ship with its ramp down and the base ship beyond: closest was Tejef's ship, hatch opened, and a smallish figure toiling toward its ramp.

"Come back," Kleph cried after Ashakh. "O great lord, come back, come back, let this small person help you."

But Aiela hesitated only a moment: mad as the iduve was, that ramp was indeed down and access was possible. There would not be another chance, not with the sun inching its way toward zenith. He ran to catch up, and Kleph, with a squeal of dismay, suddenly began to run too, seizing the iduve's other arm as Aiela sought to keep him from wasting his strength in haste.

Ashakh struck at Aiela, half-hearted, his violet eyes dilated and wild; but when he realized that Aiela meant only to keep him on his feet, he cooperated and leaned on him.

And after a few *meis* more, it was clear that Ashakh could summon no more strength: *arastiethe* insisted, but the iduve's slender body was failing him. His knees buckled, and only Kleph's strength saved him from a headlong collapse.

"We must get off this field," cried Kleph in panic. "O lord nas kame, let us take him to the other ship and beg them to let us in."

Ashakh pushed away from the amaut. His effort carried him a few steps to a fall from which he could not rise.

"Let us go," cried Kleph.

Self-preservation insisted go. The base ship would lift off before *Ashanome* struck. Daniel and Isande insisted so; but before them was Ashakh's objective, and an open hatch that was the best chance and the last one.

"Get him to the greater ship," Aiela shouted at Kleph, and began to run. "He can mind-touch the lock for you, get you in—move!"

He thought then that he had saved Ashakh's life at least, for Kleph would not abandon him, thinking Ashakh his key to safety; and the bandy-legged fellow had the strength to manage that muscle-heavy body across the wide field.

Aiela, Aiela, mourned Isande, *oh, no, Aiela.*

He ran, ignoring her, mentally calculating a triangle of distance to that open hatch for himself and for the amaut that struggled along with his burden. He might make it. His side was splitting and his brain was pounding from the effort, but he might possibly make it before one instant's notice from the iduve master of that ship could kill him.

Distract Tejef, he ordered his asuthi. *Do anything you can to get free. I'm going to need all the help possible. Keep his mind from me.*

Daniel cast about for a weapon, seized up a chair from its transit braces, and slammed it into monitor panel, door, walls, shouting like a madman and trying to do the maximum damage possible.

Only let one of the human staff respond to it, Daniel kept hoping. He meant to kill. The ease with which he slipped into that frame of mind affected Aiela and Isande with a certain queasiness, and stirred something primitive and shameful.

Isande began to pry at the switchplate, seeking some weakness that could trigger even the most minor alarm, but Aiela could not advise her. He could no longer think of anything but the amaut that was now striving to run under his burden.

Then his vision resolved what Ashakh's *takkhenois* had told him from a much greater distance.

That bundle of green was a woman, indigo-skinned and robed as a *katasathe*.

Aiela had his gun in hand: though it was not designed to kill, firing on a pregnant woman gave him pause—the shock and the fall together might kill her.

And the amaut whirled suddenly in midstep, and his hand that was under Chaikhe's body held a weapon that was indeed lethal.

Aiela fired, reflexes quicker than choice, tumbling both amaut and iduve woman into a heap, unconscious.

There was no stopping to aid Chaikhe. He ran, holding his side, stumbled onto the glidewalk of the extended ramp, daring not activate it for fear of advising Tejef of his presence. He raced up it, the hatchway looming above. It came to him that if it started to close, it could well cut him in half.

It stayed open. He almost fell onto the level surface of the airlock, ran into the corridor, his boots echoing down the emptiness.

Then the *idoikkhe's* pain began, slowly pulsing, unnerving in its gradual increase. Coordination failed him and he fell, reaching for his gun, trying to brace his fingers to hold that essential weapon, expecting, hoping for Tejef's appearance, if only, if only the iduve would once make the mistake of overconfidence.

Leave me, go! he cried at his asuthi, who tried to interfere between him and the pain.

Something was breaking. The light-dimming had ceased for a time, but now a steady crashing had begun down the hall, a thunderous booming that penetrated even Margaret's drugged sleep. She grew more and more restless, and Arle's soothing hand could not quiet her.

Someone cried out, thin and distant, and when Arle opened the infirmary door she could hear it more plainly.

It was Daniel's voice, Daniel as she had heard him cry out once before in the hands of the amaut, and such crashing as Margaret's body had made when Tejef struck her. That flashed into her mind, Margaret broken by a single unintended blow.

She cried out and began to run, hurrying down the hall to that corner room, the source of the blows and the shouting. Her knees felt undone as she reached it; almost she had not the courage to touch that switch and free it, but she did, and sprawled back with a shriek as a chair hurtled down on her.

The wreckage crashed down beside her on the floor; and then Daniel was kneeling, gathering her up and caressing her bruised head with anxious fingers, stilling her sobs by crushing her against him. He pulled her up with him in the next breath and ran, hitting another door-switch to open it.

A woman met them, of a kind that Arle had never seen, a woman whose skin was like a summer sky and whose hair was light through thistledown; and no less startling was the possessive caress she gave, assuming Arle into her affections like some unsuspected kin, taking her by the arm and compelling her attention.

"Khasif," she said, "Arle—a man like Tejef, an iduve—have you seen him? Do you know where he is?"

Her command of human language was flawless. That alone startled Arle, who had found few of the strangers capable of any human words at all; and her assumption of acquaintance utterly robbed her of her power of thought.

"Arle," Daniel pleaded with her.

Arle pointed. "There," she said. "The middle door in the lab. Daniel!" she cried, for they left her at a run. She went a few paces to follow them, and then did not know what to do.

The kameth no longer resisted. Tejef saw the fingers of his left hand jerk spasmodically at the pistol, but the kallia no longer had the strength to complete the action. Tejef kicked the weapon spinning down the corridor, applied his foot to the kameth's shoulder, and heaved him over onto his back.

Life still remained in him and the *harachia* of that force worked at his nerves; but there was little enough point in killing one who could not feel, nor in committing the *e-chanokhia* of destroying a kameth. The eyelids jerked a little but Tejef much doubted there was consciousness. He abandoned him there and went down the corridor to the airlock. It lacked a little of noon. Chimele had cast her final throw. He felt greatly satisfied by the realization that she had failed any personal *vaikka* upon him, even though she would not fail to destroy him; and then he felt empty, for a moment only empty, the minds about him suddenly stilled, *takkhenes* almost gone, the air full of a hush that settled about his heart.

Then came a touch, faint and bewildered, a thing waking, female and sensitive.

Chaikhe.

He willed the monitor into life and saw the field, four forms, three of which moved—a squat amaut dragging Ashakh's limp body in undignified fashion. Ashakh too tall a man for such a small amaut to handle; and Gerlach lying very still by the ramp, and a mound of green stirring toward consciousness, feebly trying to rise.

Katasathe. The *harachia* of the green robes and the realization that he had fired on her, once *nas,* hit his stomach like a blow. The sight of her tangled with Gerlach's squat body— beautiful Chaikhe tumbled in the dust of the pavement—was a painful one. Such a prisoner as she, was a great honor to a *nasul,* a prize for *katasakke* or *kataberihe* to an Orithain, the life within her for the *dhis* of her captors, great *vaikka,* if that *nasul* could bend her to its will.

So long alone, always mateless; the illusions of kamethi melted into what they were—*e-chanokhia,* emptiness.

She arose, lifted her face: *takkhenes* reached and touched, an impact that slammed unease into his belly. She seemed to know he watched. Anger grew in her, a fierceness that overwhelmed.

He must kill her. Obscene as the idea was, he must kill her. He faltered, hesitated between the hatch control and the weaponry, and knew that the indecision itself was a sickness.

Her mind-touch seized the lock control, held it, felt toward other mechanisms. Uncertain then, he gave backward, realizing she would board the ship—*dhisais, e-takkhe* with him. He could not let it happen. In cold sanity he knew it was a risk to face her, but he could not reach her with the weapons now. She was ascending the ramp in firm control of the mechanisms. He gathered himself to wrest that control from her.

Takkhenes reached out for him, a fierceness of *we* incredibly strong, as if a multiplicity of minds turned on him—not Chaikhe's alone, not Ashakh's, whose mind was silent. It was as if thousands of minds bore upon him at once, focused through the lens of Chaikhe's, like the *takkhenes-nasul* of all *Ashanome,* willing his death, declaring him *e-takkhe,* anomaly, ugliness, and alone, cosmically alone.

It acquired a new source, a muddled echo that had the essence of Khasif about it, leftward, same-level. Tejef realized that presence, felt it grow, and desperately reached his mind toward intervening door locks, knowing he must hold them.

They activated, opening, one after the other. Khasif was nearer, fully alert now, a fierceness and anger that yet lacked the force that Chaikhe sent.

Death took root in him, cold and certain, and the rage that he felt at Chimele was all that held it from him. He could not decide—Khasif or Chaikhe—he could not find strength to face either, caught between.

And Chimele, knowing: he felt it.

He turned, flight in his mind, to seize manual control of the ship and tear her aloft, self-destroying, taking the *e-takkhei* with him to oblivion.

"Nasith."

Chaikhe's image occupied the screens now at her own will. Her dark and lovely face stared down at him. Doors refused to open to his mind: he operated them manually and ran.

A lock sprang open before he touched it. Khasif was there, the kamethi Isande and Daniel with him—and with a reaction quicker than reason Tejef went for Khasif, Khasif yet weak from his long inactivity and his wounds—Tejef's *takkhenois* gathered strength from that realization. The kamethi themselves attempted interference, dragging at them from behind.

He spun, swung wildly to clear them from him, and saw Isande's face, in his mind Margaret, her look; that it was which kept the strength from his blow.

And a shout of anger beyond, from her asuthe the kallia, who had stumbled after, gun in hand. Tejef's eyes widened, foreknowing.

Aiela fired, left-handed, saw Isande and the iduve hit the floor at once. He tried to reach her, but it was all he could do to lean against the wall and hold himself on his feet. Daniel was first to her side, gathered her up and held her, assuring him over and over again that she was alive. Above them both stood

Khasif, whose sharp glance away from Isande warned Aiela
even as a soft step sounded behind him.

Chaikhe.

The very act of breathing grew difficult, concentration impossible. The gun tumbled from Aiela's fingers and crashed against
the flooring, sounding distant.

"She is *dhisais,*" said Khasif. "And it was not wise for you to
have interfered among iduve, kamethi. You have interfered in
vaikka."

Run, Daniel thought desperately; burdened with Isande's
weight, he tensed his muscles to try.

No! Aiela protested. He leaned against the wall, shut his eyes
to remove the contact of Chaikhe's; and hearing her move, he
dared to look again.

She had turned, and walked back in the direction of controls.

Doors closed between them, and Khasif at last stirred from
where he stood, looking down at Tejef with a long soft hiss.

The ship's engines stirred to life.

"We are about to lift," said Khasif softly, "and Tejef will give
account of himself before Chimele; perhaps that is the greater
vaikka. But it was not wise, kameth."

"Ashakh," Aiela exclaimed, remembering, hardly recognizing
his own voice. "Ashakh—is still out there."

"I am instructing Teysel on the base ship to take him up to
Ashanome. For Priamos there is no longer need of haste. For us,
there is. See to yourselves, kamethi."

15

The *melakhis* was in session, and the entire body of the *nasul* with them, in the great hall beyond the *paredre*. The *paredre* projected itself and a hundred Chimele's, reflection into reflection, down the long central aisle of the hall, and thousands of iduve gathered, a sea of indigo faces, same projections, some not. There were no whisperings, for the sympathic iduve when assembled used other than words. *Takkhenes* gathered thick in the room, a heaviness of the air, a possession, a power that made it difficult even to draw breath, let alone to speak. Words seemed out of place; hearing came as through some vast gulf of distance.

And for a handful of *m'metanei* summoned into the heart of the *nasul,* the silence was overwhelming. Hundreds, thousands of iduve faces were the walls of the *paredre;* and Chimele and Khasif were in the center of it. Another pair of figures materialized among those that lined the hall, Ashakh's slim dark form and the shorter, stouter one of Rakhi—solid, both of them, who silently joined the company in the center. Ashakh's presence surprised Aiela. The base ship had hardly more than made itself secure in the hangar deck, and here was the *nasith,* stiff with his injuries, but immaculately clean, bearing little resemblance to the dusty, bloody being that had exited the collapse of the basement. He joined Chimele, and received a nod of great respect from her, as did Rakhi.

Then Chimele looked toward the kamethi and beckoned. They moved carefully in that closeness of iduve, and Daniel kept a tight grip on Arle's shoulder. Chimele greeted them courteously, but only Aiela and Isande responded to it: Daniel kept staring at her with ill-concealed anger. It rose in a surge of panic when he saw her take a black case and open it. The platinum band of an *idoikkhe* gleamed within.

No! was in Daniel's mind, frightening his asuthi. But they were by him, and Arle was there; and Daniel was prisoner of more than the iduve. He took it upon his wrist with that same helpless panic that Aiela had once felt, and was bitterly ashamed.

Is this what takkhenes *does to* m'metanei? Aiela wondered to himself. Daniel hated *Ashanome;* indeed, he had not feared Tejef half so much as he feared Chimele. But he yielded, and Aiela himself could not imagine the degree of courage it would take for one *m'metane* to have defied the *nasul.*

Outsiders both of you, Isande judged sadly. *Oh, I am glad I never had to wrestle with your doubts. You are simply afraid of the iduve. Can't you accept that? We are weaker than they. What does it take to make you content?*

Chimele had grown interested in Arle now, and gazed upon the child's face with that look Aiela knew and Daniel most hated, that bird-of-prey concentration that cast a spell over the recipient. Arle was drawn into that stillness and seemed more hypnotized than afraid.

"This is the child that was so important to you, Daniel-kameth, so important that your asuthi could not restrain you?"

Daniel's heart thudded and seemed to stop as he realized that *vaikka* need not involve the real offender, that reward and punishment had no human virtue with the starlords. He would have said something if he could have gathered the words; as it was, he met Chimele's eyes and fell into that amethyst gaze, that chill calm without pity as *m'metanei* knew it. Perhaps Chimele was laughing. None of the kamethi could detect it in her. Perhaps it was a *vaikka* in itself, a demonstration of power.

"She has a certain *chanokhia,*" said Chimele. "Arrangements will be made for her proper care."

"I can manage that," said Daniel. It was the most restrained thing he could manage to say.

And suddenly the center of the *paredre* itself gave way to a projection, red and violet, *Tashavodh* and *Mijanothe,* Kharxanen and Thiane.

"Hail *Ashanome,*" said Thiane. "Are you satisfied?"

Chimele arose and inclined her head in reverence to the eldest of all iduve. "You are punctual, o Thiane, long-living."

"It is the hour, o *Ashanome,* hunter of worlds, and Priamos still exists. We have seen ships rejoining you. I ask again: are you satisfied?"

"You have then noted, o Thiane, that all of our interference on the world of Priamos has ceased ahead of the time, and that all equipment and personnel have been evacuated."

Thiane frowned, nettled by this mild *vaikka.* "There is only one being whose whereabouts matters, o *Ashanome.*"

"Then see." Chimele looked to her left and extended her hand. Another projection took shape, a man in dark clothing, seated. His eyes widened as he realized where he was: he arose and Arle began an outcry, stopped by Isande's fierce grip on her arm.

"This person," said Chimele softly, "was once of *Ashanome.* We have him among us again, and we are capable of settling our own internal matters. We give you honor, *Mijanothe,* for the propriety you constantly observed in *harathos.* And, o Kharxanen of *Tashavodh,* be advised that *Ashanome* will be ranging these zones for some time. In the interests of the ban on *vaikka* which the Orithanhe set upon us both, it seems to us that it would be proper for the *nasul Tashavodh* to seek some other field. We are in prior occupation of this space, and it is not proper for two *orith-nasuli* to share so close quarters without the decency of *akkhres-nasuli* and its binding oaths."

There was a silence. Kharxanen's heavy face settled into yet a deeper frown; but he inclined himself in a stiff bow. "Hail *Ashanome.* We part without *vaikka.* These zones are without interest to us; we delight that *Ashanome* is pleased to possess them. It seems to us an excellent means of disentangling our affairs. I give you farewell, Chimele."

And without further courtesy, his image winked out.

It seemed, though one could not be certain, that a smile touched the face of Thiane, a smile which was no longer present as she turned to stare at the being who stood in the shaft of pale light. Then she inclined her head in respect to Chimele.

"Honor is yours, *Ashanome*," declared Thiane. She set both hands on her staff and looked about her at all the assembly, the confident attitude of a great power among the iduve. Chimele resumed her chair, easy and comfortable in the gesture, undisturbed by the *harachia* of Thiane.

And Thiane turned last to the image of Tejef in its shaft of light, and he bowed his head. All threat, all strength was gone from him; he looked far less imposing than Thiane.

"He is near," said Chimele softly. "He is not held from joining us in the *paredre:* it has not been necessary to restrain him. Perhaps to honor you he would come to your summons."

"Tejef," said aged Thiane, looking full at him, and he glanced up. A low murmuring came from the *nasul,* the first sound and an ugly one. Suddenly Tejef tore himself from the area of the projection and vanished.

He was not long in coming, tangible amid the multitude of projections that lined the *paredre.* Isande's mind went cold and fearful even to look upon him, but he passed her without giving her notice, though her fair complexion made her most obvious in the gathering. He stopped before Chimele and Thiane, and gave Thiane a bow of courtesy, lifting his eyes again to Thiane, as if the action were painful.

"Tejef," said Thiane, "if you have a message for *Tashavodh,* I will bear it."

"No, eldest of us all," answered Tejef softly, and bowed again at this exceptional courtesy from Thiane.

"Was it properly done?" asked Thiane.

Tejef's eyes went to Aiela; but perhaps to blame a *m'metane* was too great a shame. There was no anger, only recognition; he did not answer Thiane.

"You have seen," said Chimele to Thiane. "*Harathos* is satisfied. And hereafter he is *Ashanome*'s and it is the business of the *nasul* what we do."

"Hail *Ashanome,* ancient and *akita.* May we always meet in such a mind as we part now."

"Hail *Mijanothe,* far-seeing. May your seekings be satisfied and your prosperity endless. And hail Thiane, whose honor and *chanokhia* will be remembered in *Ashanome.*"

"As that of Chimele among us," murmured Thiane, greatly

pleased, and flicked out so quickly that her echoes were still dying.

Then it broke, the anger of *Ashanome,* a murmuring against Tejef that sent him to the center of the *paredre,* looking about at them and trying to show defiance when they crowded him. Two *dhis*-guardians, Tahjekh and Nophres, drew their *ghiakai* and rested them point-down on the priceless carpets, crossed, barring his way to Chimele.

An iduve hand caught Aiela's arm and the *idoikkhei* stung the three of them simultaneously. "Out," said Ashakh. "This is no place for *m'metanei.*"

Isande took a step to obey, but stopped, for Daniel was not coming, and Aiela stayed, terrified for what Daniel was likely to do.

Get the child out of here, Aiela appealed to him. But there was chaos already in the hall, iduve bodies intruding into the projection area, seeming to invade the *paredre,* real and unreal mingling in kaleidoscope combination. Tejef shrank back, less and less space for him. Someone dealt him a heavy blow; bodies were between and the kamethi could not see.

"Hold!" Khasif's voice roared, bringing order; and Chimele arose and the iduve melted back from her. An uneasy silence settled.

"Tejef," said Chimele.

He attempted to give a hiss of defiance. It was so subdued that it sounded far otherwise.

"There is a human female who claims to be your mate," said Chimele. "She will have treatment for her injuries. It was remiss of you to neglect that—but of course, your abilities were limited. The amaut who sheltered in your protection have realized their error and are leaving Priamos in all possible haste. Your *okkitan-as* Gerlach perished in the lifting of your ship: Chaikhe found no particular reason to clear him from beside the vessel. And as for *karsh* Gomek in general, I do not yet know whether we will choose to notice the inconvenience these beings have occasioned us. It is even possible the *nasul* would choose not to notice your offenses, Tejef, if you were wise, if you made submission."

The oppressive feeling in the air grew stronger. Tejef stood among them, sides heaving, sweat pouring down his indigo face.

He shook his face to clear the sweat from his eyes and seemed likely to faint, a creature sadly fallen from the whole and terrible man who had faced them onworld. *To yield,* Daniel had heard from him once, *is to die; morally and physically, it is to die;* and if ever a man looked apt to die from such a cause, this one did, torn apart within.

Tejef's wild shout of anger drowned all the rising murmur of the *nasul.* Iduve scattered from his first blows, voices shrieked and hissed. Isande snatched Arle and hugged the human child's face against her breast, trying to shut out the awful sight and sound, for the *ghiakai* of the guardians faced Tejef now, points level. When he would try to break free of the circle they would crowd him; and by now he was dazed and bleeding. With a shout he flung himself for Chimele; but there were the guardians and there was Khasif, and Khasif's blow struck him to the floor.

Daniel thrust his way into the circle, jerked at the shoulder of a young iduve to push his way past before the youth realized what had happened—and cried out in pain, collapsing under the discipline of the *idoikkhe.*

Pain backwashed: Aiela forced his own way through the breach, trying to aid his stricken asuthe, cried out Chimele's name and felt the impact of all that attention suddenly upon himself.

"*M'metanei,*" said Chimele, "this is not a place for you. You are not noticed." She lifted her hand and the iduve parted like grass before the wind, opening the way to the door. When Daniel opened his mouth to protest the dismissal: "Aiela," she said most quietly. It was a last warning. He knew the tone of it.

Daniel rose, turned his face to Tejef, appealing to him; he wanted to speak, wanted desperately, but Daniel's courage was the kind that could act: he had no eloquence, and words always came out badly. In pity, Aiela said it. Daniel would not yield otherwise.

"We interfered. I did. We are sorry."

And to Aiela's dismay the iduve gave back all about them, and they were alone in the center with Tejef—and Daniel moved closer to Isande, who clenched Arle's hand tightly in hers, and gazed fearfully as Tejef gained his feet.

"Kamethi," said Chimele, "I have not heard, I have not noticed this behavior. You are dismissed. Go away."

"He had honor among his kamethi," said Aiela, echoing what was in Daniel's heart. It was important Tejef know that before they left. The *idoikkhe* touched, began and ceased. Isande radiated panic, she with the child, wanting to run, foreseeing Daniel's death before their eyes—Aiela's with him. It was her unhappiness to have asuthi as stubborn as herself—her pride, too. They were both mad, her asuthi, but she had accepted that already.

And Chimele looked upon the three of them: a kallia's eyes might have varied, shown some emotion. Hers scarcely could, no more than they could shed tears. But Aiela pitied her: if he had disadvantaged her once before her *nasithi* alone and merited her anger, he could only surmise what he did to her now with the entire *Metakhis* and *nasul* to witness.

"Chimele-Orithain," he said in a tone of great respect, "we have obeyed all your orders. If a kameth can ask anything of you—"

A tall shadow joined them—Ashakh, who folded his arms and gave a nod in curt deference to Chimele.

"This kameth," said Ashakh, "is about to encounter trouble with which he cannot deal. He is a peculiar being, this *m'metane*, a little rash with us, and without any sense of *takkhenes* to feel his way over most deadly ground; but his *chanokhia* appeals to me. I oppose his disrespect, but I am not willing to see harm come to him or to his asuthi—one of whom is, after all, human as well as outsider, and even more ignorant of propriety than this one. I have borne with much, Chimele. I have suffered and my *sra* has suffered for the sake of *Ashanome*. But this kameth and his asuthi are of worth to the *nasul*. Here I say no, Chimele."

"Ashakh," said Chimele in a terrible voice, "it has not been the matter of the kamethi alone in which you have said no."

"I do not oppose you, Chimele."

"I perceive otherwise. I perceive that you are not *takkhe* with us in the matter of Tejef, that someone lends him support."

"Then you perceive amiss. My *m'melakhia* has always been

for the well-being of *Ashanome*. We have been able to compose our differences before, *nasith-tak*."

"And they have been many," said Chimele, "and too frequent. No!" she said sharply as Tejef moved. He came no closer, for there were the *dhis*-guardians between, and Khasif and Ashakh moved to shield her as reflexively as they always had. The closeness was heavy in the air again: oppressive, hostile, and then a curiously perturbing fierceness. Chimele glanced at Rakhi in alarm.

"You do not belong here," she said, but her anger seemed smothered by fright, and it was not clear to whom she spoke.

Tejef moved nearer, as near as the *ghiakai* would permit. "Chimele-Orithain. You cast me out; but Mejakh's *takkhenois* is gone and the touch of the *nasul* is easier for that, Chimele *sra*-Chaxal. I have always had *m'melakhia* for this *nasul,* and not alone for the *nasul*. I was *nas,* Chimele."

Chimele's breath was an audible hiss. "And your life in the *nasul* was always on scant tolerance and we have hunted you back again. Your *m'melakhia* is *e-takkhe—e-takkhe* and unspeakably offensive to me."

A fierce grin came to Tejef's face. He seemed to grow, and set hands on knees as he fell to kneel on the carpets. His gesture of submission was itself insolence; slowly he inclined his body toward the floor and as slowly straightened.

Arle cried out, a tiny sound, piercing the intolerable heaviness in the air. Isande hugged her tightly, silencing her, for Ashakh sent a staccato message to the three *idoikkhei* simultaneously: *Do not move!*

"Go!" Chimele exploded. "If you survive in the *nasul,* I will perhaps not seek to kill you. But there is *vaikka* you have yet to pay, o Tejef no-one's-getting."

"My *sra,*" answered Tejef with cold deliberation, "will have honor." But he backed carefully from her when he had risen.

"You are dismissed," Chimele said, and her angry glance swept the hall, so that Tejef had no more than cleared the door before others began to disperse in haste, projections to wink out in great numbers, the concourse clearing backwards as the iduve departed into that part of the ship that was theirs.

"Stay," she said to the *nasithi-katasakke* when they would as gladly have withdrawn; and she ignored them when they had frozen into waiting, and bent a fierce frown on Aiela. The *idoikkhe* sent a signal that made him wince.

M'metane, *it is your doing that I bear this disadvantage. It is your doing, that gave this being* arastiethe *to defy me, to draw aid from others. Your ignorance has begun what you cannot begin to comprehend. You have disadvantaged me, divided the* nasul, *and some of us may die for it. What are you willing to pay for that,* m'metane *that I honored, what* vaikka *can you perceive that would be adequate?*

He stared at her, pain washing upward from the *idoikkhe,* and was stricken to realize that not only might he lose his life, he might in truth deserve it. He had Isande's misery to his account; now he had Chimele's as well.

And in the disadvantaging of an Orithain, he had threatened the existence of *Ashanome* itself.

"I did what was in me to do," he protested.

Ashakh saved him. He realized that when the pain cleared and he heard Isande and Daniel's faint, terrified presences in his mind, and felt the iduve's viselike grip holding on his feet.

"Chimele," said Ashakh, "that was not disrespect in him: it was very plain kalliran logic. And perhaps there is merit in his reasoning: after all, you found *chanokhia* in him, and chose him, so his decisions are, in a manner of speaking, yours. Perhaps when one deals with outsiders, outsider-logic prevails, and events occur which would not occur in an iduve system."

"I perceive your *m'melakhia* for these beings, Ashakh, and I am astounded. I find it altogether excessive."

The tall iduve glanced aside, embarrassed. "I comprehend the *chanokhia* that Tejef found in these beings, both human and kallia."

"You were responsible for swinging the *takkhenes* of *Ashanome* toward Tejef—your *vaikka* for Chaikhe."

Again he had looked toward her, and now bowed his head slightly. "Chaikhe is *dhisais*—as Rakhi can tell you: beyond *vaikka* and no longer appropriate for my protection. I understand what you did, since you did not spare Rakhi, for whom you have most regard, and I admire the strength and *chanokhia* of your action, o Chimele. You disadvantaged me repeatedly in your maneuvering, but it was in the interests of *Ashanome*."

"Is it in our interests—what you have done?"

"Chimele," said Rakhi softly, and such a look went between them that it seemed more than Rakhi might have spoken to her in that word, for Chimele seemed much disquieted.

"Khasif," said Chimele suddenly, "can you be *takkhe* with this matter as it is?"

Khasif bowed. "I have brought you Tejef; and that *vaikka* is enough. He is *sra* to me, Chimele, as you are. Do not ask me questions."

"Chaikhe—" Chimele said.

"Orithain," said Rakhi, "she has followed your orders amazingly well: but remember that she was scarcely out of the *dhis* when she acquired Tejef's interest."

Her lips tightened. "Indeed," she said, and after a moment: "Aiela, the *harachia* of yourself and your asuthi is a disturbance for the moment. You did serve me and I rejoice in the honor of your efforts. You are dismissed, but you still owe me a *vaikka* for your presumption today."

He owed her at least the same risk he had taken for Tejef, to restore what he had stolen from her, though every instinct screamed *run!* "Chimele," he said, "we honor you—from the heart, we honor you."

Chimele looked full into his eyes. "*M'metane,*" she said, "I have a *m'melakhia* for the peculiarity that is Aiela Lyailleue. Curiosity impels me to inquire further and to refrain from dealing with you as you have so well deserved. You are the only *m'metane* I have seen who has not feared to be *m'metane* among us. You are *Ashanome*'s greatest living curiosity—and so you are free with us, and you are getting into the perilous habit of taking liberties with *Ashanome.* The contagion has spread to your asuthi, I do perceive. In moderation, it has been of service to me."

"I am honored by your interest, Chimele."

Her attention fumed then to Ashakh. By some impulse that passed between them, Ashakh bowed very low, hands upon his thighs, and remained in that posture until Chimele's agitation had passed. He seemed to receive that too, for he straightened without looking up before, and slowly lifted his face.

"Chimele, I protest I am *takkhe*."

"I perceive your approval of these outrageous beings."

"And I," said Ashakh, "feel your disapproval of me. I am disadvantaged, Chimele, for I do honor you. If you insist, I shall go *arrhei-nasul,* for my *m'melakhia* is not adequate to challenge you, certainly not at the peril of the dynasty itself. You are essential and I am not. Only permit me to take these kamethi with me. *Arastiethe* forbids I should abandon them."

Chimele met his eyes a moment, then fumed aside and reached for Aiela's arm. Her incredibly strong fingers numbed his hand, but it was not an act of anger.

"When we deal with *m'metanei*," she wondered softly, "are we bound by the *kastien* you observe? I protest we are *akita, m'metane.*"

"I do not understand," Aiela said.

"We are *takkhe*," she said to Ashakh then, and walked away into the inner recesses of the *paredre*.

One did not often see the *nasithi-katasakke* on the kamethi level; and the presence of Rakhi caused a mild stir—only mild, for even the kamethi knew the eccentricity of this iduve. So it was not a great shock for Aiela and Isande to find the *nasith* greeting them in passing. Beside them the great viewport showed starry space, no longer the sphere of Priamos. *Ashanome* was free and running again.

"Sir," the kamethi acknowledged his courtesy, bowing at once.

"And that third person?"

"'I am here,'" said Daniel through Aiela's lips. *Trouble, Aiela? What does a* nas *want with us at this hour?*

Be calm. If Chimele meant harm, she would do that harm for herself, with no intermediary. Aiela compelled his asuthi to silence and kept his eyes on Rakhi's so the *nasith* should not know that communication flickered back and forth: this three-way communication bemused one to a point that it was hard not to appear to drift.

"Is the *asuthithekkhe* pleasant?" Rakhi wondered, with the nearest thing to wistfulness they had ever heard in an iduve.

"It has its difficulties," Aiela answered, ignoring the feedback from his asuthi. "But I would not choose otherwise."

"The silence," said Rakhi, "is awesome—without. For us the experience is not altogether pleasant. But being severed—makes a great silence."

Aiela understood then, and pitied him. It was safe to pity Rakhi, whose *m'melakhia* was not so fierce. "Is Chaikhe well, sir?"

"She is content. She is inward now—altogether. *Dhisaisei* grow more and more that way. I have felt it." Rakhi silenced himself with an embarrassed glance toward the viewport. The body of *Ashanome* passed under the holding arm. For a moment all was dark. Their reflections, pale kallia and dusky iduve, stared back out of the viewport. "There is a small amaut who mentioned you with honor. His name is Kleph. Ashakh bade me say so: *arastiethe* forbids the first of Navigators should carry messages. This person was greatly joyed by the sight of the gardens of *Ashanome*. Ashakh procured him this assignment. *Arastiethe* forbade—"

"—that Ashakh should admit to gratitude."

Rakhi frowned, even he a little nettled to be thus interrupted by a *m'metane*. "It was not *chanokhia* for this amaut to have delivered Ashakh in a helpless condition aboard the base ship. This being could not appreciate *vaikka* in any reasonable sense, save to be disadvantaged in this way. Has Ashakh erred?"

"No," said Aiela, "and Ashakh knows he has not."

The ghost of a smile touched the *nasith's* face, and Aiela frowned, suspecting he himself had just been the victim of a bit of iduve humor, straightfaced in delivery. Perhaps, he thought, the iduve had puzzled out the ways of *m'metanei* more than the iduve chose to admit. Yet not even this most gentle of iduve was to be provoked: one had to remember that they *studied* gratitude, could perhaps practice it for humor's sake. Whether anything then stirred the cold of their dark hearts was worthy of debate.

Let be with him, Isande advised. *Even Rakhi has his limits.*

"*M'metanei,*" said Rakhi, "I should advise that you go soft of step and well-nigh invisible about the *paredre* for the next few days. Should Chimele summon you, as she will, be most agreeable."

"Why, sir?" asked Isande, which was evidently the desired question.

"Because Chimele has determined a *vaikka* upon *Tashavodh* that the Orithanhe and its ban cannot deny her." The iduve grinned despite himself. "Kharxanen's *m'melakhia* for a bond with the dynasty of *Ashanome* is of long standing—indeed, the origin of all these matters. It will go frustrated. The Orithanhe itself has compelled Kharxanen and Tejef to deny they are *sra* to each other; so Kharxanen cannot claim any bond at all when Chimele chooses Tejef for the *kataberihe* of *Ashanome*. Purifications will begin. One child will there be; and then this *nas* Tejef will have a ship and as many of the *okkitani-as* and kamethi as Chimele chooses to send with him."

"She is creating a *vra-nasul?*" asked Isande, amazed. "After all the grief he has caused?" Resentment flared in her, stifled by Daniel's gladness; and Aiela fended one from the other.

"They are *takkhe,*" said Rakhi. "*M'metane,* I know your minds somewhat. You have long memories for anger. But we are not a spiteful folk; we fight no wars. Chimele has taken *vaikka,* for his *sra* as a *vra-nasul* will serve *Ashanome* forever; but the *sra* she will take from him under her own name as her heir will forever be greater than the dynasty he will found. *Vra nasul* in mating can put no bond on *orith-nasul.* So Tejef will make submission and both will keep their honor. It is a reasonable solution—one of your own working, *m'metanei.* So I advise you keep secret that small *vaikka* of yours lest Chimele be compelled to notice it. She is amused by your *chanokhia:* she has struggled greatly to attain that attitude—for if you know us, you know that we are frequently of a loss to determine any rationality for your behavior. We make an effort. We have acquired the wisdom to observe and wait upon what we do not understand: it is an antidote for the discord of impulses which govern our various species. I recommend the practice to you too, kamethi."

And with a nod of his head he went his way, mounted into the lift, and vanished from sight.

Aiela, came Isande's thought, *Chimele sent him.*

We have been honored, he replied, and expected argument from Daniel.

But Daniel's consciousness when it returned to them dismissed all thoughts but his own for the moment, for he had suddenly recognized across the concourse a human child and a red-haired woman.

He began, quickly, to thread his way through the traffic; his asuthi in this moment gave him his privacy.

Glossary of Foreign Terms

I

THE KALLIRAN LANGUAGE: like human speech in its division of noun and verb concepts. There is, however, a fossilized Ethical from the time of the Orithain Domination. Although the Ethical corresponds to the Verb of Orithain speech, it has been made an Adjective in the kalliran language.

arethme   (ah-RETH-may) city-deme of kalliran political structure: on the home world, equal to a city and all its land and trade rights; in the colonies, often equal to a hemisphere or an entire world, with its attendant rights.

ehs, pl. *ehsim*   (ACE) cubed measurement approximately 10 inches.

elethia   (el-eh-THEE-ya) honor, gentility, sensitivity to proper behavior; faithfulness to duty.

Esliph   (EHS-lif) the Seven Stars: a heavily planeted region lying between the *metrosi* and human space.

giyre   (GIU-rey) recognition of one's proper place in the cosmic Order of things; also, one's proper duty toward another. It is ideally mutual.

Halliran Idai	(hah-lee-HRAN ee-DYE) the Free Union, the political structure of the *metrosi,* the capital of which is Aus Qao, the fifth of Qao.
ikas	(EE-kas) disregarding of *giyre* and *kastien*: presumptuous.
kallia	(KAL-lee-ah) man, woman; men, women.
kamesule	(kah-MAY-soo-leh) to associate with the iduve; to be servile of manner.
kastien	(KAHS-tee-yen) being oneself; virtue, wisdom; observing harmony with others and the universe by perfect centering in one's *giyre* toward all persons and things.
marithe	(mah-REE-theh) a pale-pink wine.
men, pl. *meis*	(MEN, MACE) a linear measurement of approximately 10 inches.
metrosi	(MAY-tro-see) the Civilized Worlds, those within the original area of kalliran-amaut colonization.
Orithain	(o-rih-THAIN) mistakenly used as generic term for the iduve.
parome	(PAHR-ohm) governor of an *arethme*.
Qao	(KRUA-o) the Sun; home star of the kalliran species.

II

THE IDUVE LANGUAGE: differs from both kalliran and human speech to such a degree that translation cannot be made literally if it is to be understandable. Paraphrase is the best that can be done.

First, there is no clear distinction between the concepts of noun and verb, between solid and action. Reality consists instead of the situational combination of Tangibles and Ethicals; but an Ethical may be converted to a Tangible and vice versa. Most ideas are grammatically complete in two words: an Ethical is affixed to the Tangible. Meanings may be altered or augmented by Prefix, Infix, or Suffix upon either Ethical or Tangible. The nature of these added particles may be: Negative, Intensive, Honorific, Hypothetical, Interrogative, Imperative, Directional, Futuritive or Historical, Relational or Descriptive.

Second: the language has only scant designation of gender. It is impossible to distinguish sex save by adding the male Honorific *-toj* or the female Honorific *-tak* to the word in question. Concepts which would seem to make gender distinction inevitable (man, woman, mother, father, brother, sister, husband, wife) exist only as artificial constructs in the iduve language.

In the pronunciations given below, an asterisk (*) indicates a guttural sibilant produced by -kk or -kh-: a throat-sounded hiss resembling a soft *kh*.

akites, akitomei	(ah-kee-TEHS) a Voyaging Ship.
akitomekkhe	(ah-kee-toh-MEK*-heh) worldbound; having bond to person or place outside the *nasul*.
akkhres-nasuli	(AK*-hress-NAH-su-lee) joining of two *akitomei* for the purpose of *katasakke* among the members of both clans.
anoikhte	(ah-noik*-TEH) bondless; not "free" (*akita*) but "loose," and therefore fair game for *m'melakhia, q.v.* Manlings (*m'metanei*) cannot enjoy *arrhei-akita;* by their very terrestrial natures they are *akitomekkhe* and therefore limited in their sensitivities.
arastiethe	(ah-rahs-tee-AY-theh) honor; the power and burden of being iduve, of being of a particular *nasul,* or simply

of being oneself. Honor is the obligation to use power, even against personal preference, to maintain moral and physical integrity. *M'metanei* naturally possess no *arastiethe,* but to describe admirable traits in *m'metanei,* the iduve have adopted the kalliran word *elethia.*

arrhei-akita — (AH-hrrey-ah-kee-TAH) being free; an ethical necessity for the happiness and *arastiethe* of the *nasul;* especially, the free range of their ship.

arrhei-nasul — (AH-hrrey-nah-SOOL) leaving clan, usually for *kataberihe* with another's Orithain. Doing so for any other reason is to invite violence from the receiving clan. Not the same as *arrhei-nasuli* (AH-hrrey-nah-su-LEE), which is exile from all the Kindred, equal to a death sentence.

Ashanome — (ah-SHAH-no-may)

asuthe, asuthi — (ah-SOOTH, ah-su-THEE). lit.: companion. A person linked to another by *chiabres.*

asuthithekkhe — (ah-su-thi-THEK*-heh) mental linkage.

Chaganokh — (cHag-ah-NOKH*)

chanokhia — (cHan-ok*-HEE-ah) artistry; (2) as an Ethical: the practice of virtue, the studied avoidance of crudity, and a searching after elegance and originality.

chiabres — (cHee-AH-bress) internal device for communication.

dhis (d*eesss) lit.: nest. A communal embryonics laboratory and nursery for the *nasul*. Children leave at maturity.

dhisais, dhisaisei (d*EE-sice) female driven to temporary madness by biological changes at childbirth; may last years.

e- (ay) negative prefix: not, un-.

ghiaka, ghiakai (zhee-AH-kah) curved sword, now ceremonial.

harachia (ha-rak*-HEE-yah) lit.: presence, seeing. Visual impact of a person, thing, or situation which elicits an irrational emotional response.

idoikkhe, idoikkhei (ih-DOYK*-heh) from *idois*, jewel. The bracelet of a nas kame, patterned with the heraldry of the *nasul*, and capable of transmitting sensory impulses.

iduve (ih-DOOVh) man, woman, mankind.

Iqhanofre (ik-HAH-no-fray)

izhkh (izsk*) mountainous region of Kej IV famed for its geometric art.

kameth, kamethi (KAH-met') Honorific of nas kame.

kataberihe (kah-tah-beh-REE-heh) mating of an Orithain to produce *orithaikhti*, heir-children. Only children of such a mating may inherit the title; it goes to the eldest regardless of sex. The bond of *kataberihe* forbids the woman in the pair from *katasakke* for ten months after announcing her intention; the male suffers a ritual abstinence for twenty days. This is for the sake of establishing paternity, and for mental

	preparation, as *kataberihe-* mates are usually from another *nasul.*
katasathe	(kah-ta-SATH) pregnant
katasakke	(kah-ta-SAK*h) mating-for-children, requiring a three-month abstinence should the woman desire to change mates. It is also counted improper for the male to have more than one current mate. Each *katasakke* mating will almost certainly result in a child; such a high rate of conception was once advantageous to species survival. Extreme longevity and limited space on the *akitomei* have made it otherwise, giving rise to the custom of *katasukke.*
katasukke	(kah-ta-SOOK*h) mating-for-pleasure, done with *m'metanei,* and not (for aesthetic reasons) with amaut. This cannot result in offspring, and neither the purification period of *kataberihe* nor that of *katasakke* forbids *katasukke.*
Kej	(Kezh) the Sun; home star of the iduve.
-kkh-	relational infix, from *kame,* bond, bind. Binding or obligation: necessity.
kutikkase	(ku-tih-KAH-seh) lit.: things. Earthly necessities, food, bodily comforts, all arts save the pursuit or use of intangibles. Opposite of *chanokhia.*
lis, lioi	(lihss, LEE-oi) 1,000 paces, approximately ¾ mile.
Melakhis	(meh-lakh-HEESS) from *m'melakhia;* the Council of Acquisition, composed of the Orithain, his/her *sra,* and one member from each of the elder or major *sri* of the *nasul.* The *Melakhis*

assists the Orithain in decisions of major importance and technical complexity.

Mijanothe	(mee-jah-NOTHe)
m'melakhia	(meh-meh-lak*-HEE-ya) desire of acquisition; sometimes used to approximate *m'metane* concept of "love"; sometimes translated "ferocity." A basic and constant activity of the iduve, necessary for *arastiethe.* (2) *m.-tomes:* the acquisition of prestige or spatial lordship, needful as operating room for the dignity and freedom of the *nasul.* (3) *m.-likatis:* acquisition of knowledge, most honorable of activities.
m'metane, m'metanei	(meh-MEH-tah-nay) manling: a being which approximately conforms to iduve appearance: kallia and humans.
nasithi	(nah-sih-THEE) Honorific plural of *nas,* a member of the *nasul.*
nas kame, noi kame	(nahs KAH-may, noi KAH-may) bond-child; a *m'metane* in service to the *nasul.*
okkitan-as, okkitani-as	(OK*-hee-tahn-AHSS) lit.: helper. Amaut in service to the *nasul.*
Orithanhe	(oh-rih-THAHN-heh) council of all available *orithainei* of *orith-nasuli,* at least twenty for a quorum. It meets on the home world. Due to the iduve predilection toward *arrhei-akita,* it is almost never convoked.
paredre	(pahr-ED-hre) ceremonial center of authority of an *akites;* the hall of the Orithain.

prha   (prah) particle meaning "hypothesis" or "one supposes."

serach   (SEH-rak*) funeral display; a destruction of *kutikkase* in proportion to the *arastiethe* of the dead.

sorithias   (so-rih-THEE-ahss) from *orithois*, mastery. The obligation of an Orithain to the *nasul*.

sra   (ssrah) bloodkin (ship) (2) *bhan-sra:* vertical (parent-child). (3) *iq-sra:* lateral (brother-sister; half-brother and half-sister).

-tak   female Honorific suffix.

takkhe   (tak*h) having *takkhenois* in agreement.

takkhenes   (TAKH*-he-nayss) group-consciousness of the *nasul,* by which decisions are made and justice determined.

Tashavodh   (tah-sha-VOD*h)

tekasuphre   (tek-ah-SU-frey) stupidity, irrationality, nonsense.

-toj   (tozh) male Honorific suffix.

vaikka   (VAI-k*hah) or (vai-K*HAH!) a demonstration of *arastiethe;* could roughly be translated as "revenge" if not that *vaikka* is often taken in advance of actual injury, to offset *niseth* (disadvantage). *Vaikka* need not involve damage, for *arastiethe* can be demonstrated by help as well as harm. It is, however, a fighting or predatory instinct basic to the iduve psychology.

vaikka-chanokhia   an art form peculiarly iduve, practiced generally upon other iduve, as *m'metanei* have limited appreciation of *chanokhia*. True *vaikka-chanokhia* is such that the recipient cannot possibly reciprocate.

vra-nasul   (vrah-nah-SOOL) subject-clan; formed when an elder clan splits because of size or disunity.

III

THE AMAUT LANGUAGE: similar to kalliran speech in structure, with many kalliran words appropriated into the language, and showing much tendency to imitate the elaborate politeness styles of the iduve. The alphabet is native, but literature as such dates from first contact with the iduve.

amaut   (ah-MAUT) man, woman; people.

bnesych   (b'NAY-sikK) director; *karsh-* head at colony's foundation.

chaju   (CHAH-ju) a musky, potent liquor.

geshe   (GESSH-eh) a stringed instrument.

habish   (hah-BEESH) all-night bar and sidewalk cafe, featuring music, singing, dancing, and *chaju*.

habishaap   (hah-beesh-APPPH) keeper of a *habish*.

karsh, karshatu   (kahrssh) basic family unit of the amaut, taking its name from the founder, either male or female, who acquired land and began the family line. Without land there is no *karsh* save the one of ancestry. Possessing land entitles one to found a *karsh* of a size commensurate with the productive capacity of the land.

Kesuat	(KEZ-wat) the Sun; home star of the amaut.
rekeb	(REK-ebp) a sistrum-like musical instrument.
shakhshoph	(sshak-SHOPPH) lit.: hiding-face. Politeness to hide true feelings from outsiders.
sushai	(ssu-SHAI) from *sus*, Shade. A word of greeting.

CJ Cherryh
Classic Series in New Omnibus Editions

THE DREAMING TREE
Contains the complete duology *The Dreamstone* and *The Tree of Swords and Jewels*. 0-88677-782-8

THE FADED SUN TRILOGY
Contains the complete novels *Kesrith*, *Shon'jir*, and *Kutath*. 0-88677-836-0

THE MORGAINE SAGA
Contains the complete novels *Gate of Ivrel*, *Well of Shiuan*, and *Fires of Azeroth*. 0-88677-877-8

THE CHANUR SAGA
Contains the complete novels *The Pride of Chanur*, *Chanur's Venture* and *The Kif Strike Back*.
  0-88677-930-8

ALTERNATE REALITIES
Contains the complete novels *Port Eterntiy*, *Voyager in Night*, and *Wave Without a Shore* 0-88677-946-4

AT THE EDGE OF SPACE
Contains the complete novels *Brothers of Earth* and *Hunter of Worlds*. 0-7564-0160-7

To Order Call: 1-800-788-6262

CJ Cherryh
EXPLORER

"Serious space opera at its very best by one of the leading SF writers in the field today." —*Publishers Weekly*

The *Foreigner* novels introduced readers to the epic story of a lost human colony struggling to survive on the hostile world of the alien atevi. In this final installment to the second sequence of the series, diplomat Bren Cameron, trapped in a distant star system, faces a potentially bellicose alien ship, and must try to prevent interspecies war, when the secretive Pilot's Guild won't even cooperate with their own ship.

Be sure to read the first five books in this action-packed series:

Julie E. Czerneda

THE TRADE PACT UNIVERSE

"Space adventure mixes with romance...a heck of a lot of fun." —*Locus*

Sira holds the answer to the survival of her species, the Clan, within the multi-species Trade Pact. But it will take a Human's courage to show her the way.

A THOUSAND WORDS FOR STRANGER
0- 88677-769-0

TIES OF POWER
0-88677-850-6

TO TRADE THE STARS
0-7564-0075-9

To Order Call: 1-800-788-6262